Mel Bay's
COMPLETE BOOK OF
BASS CHORDS

By Dana Roth

Preface

A thorough knowledge of chords is essential to every bass player in creating bass lines and solos. This book is designed as a reference guide with over 1200 different chord positions based on 36 chords. There are extensive fingerboard diagrams to the 24th fret, chord formulas and symbols. This system of study enables the bassist to easily become familiar with the various chord forms, arpeggios and applications. The appendix presents 21 additional chords for further reference. Sight reading is not necessary to understand this material, as bass tablature is provided along with standard musical notation.

CONTENTS

Intervals

Intervals consist of only two notes and are considered to be incomplete chords. They are identified by their position on the diatonic major scale and are named according to the distance between the letter names which form it. For example, C to A is a *sixth* because it spans six notes; CDEFGA. There are various forms of intervals and they are recognized as the basis of all chords.

Intervals In C Major Scale

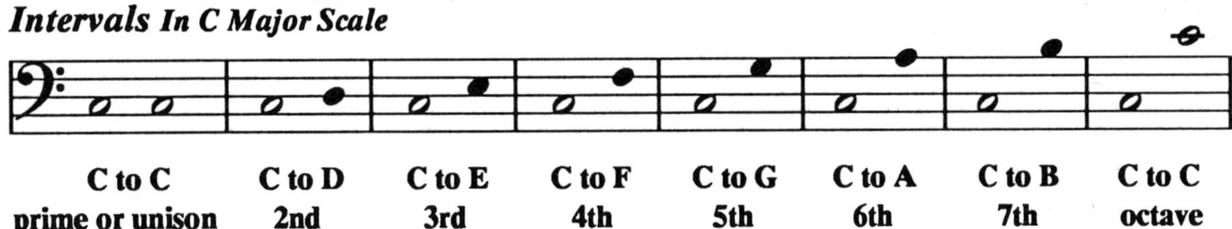

When the notes of an interval are played one after the other it is a *"melodic interval,"* when they are played together it is a *"harmonic interval."*

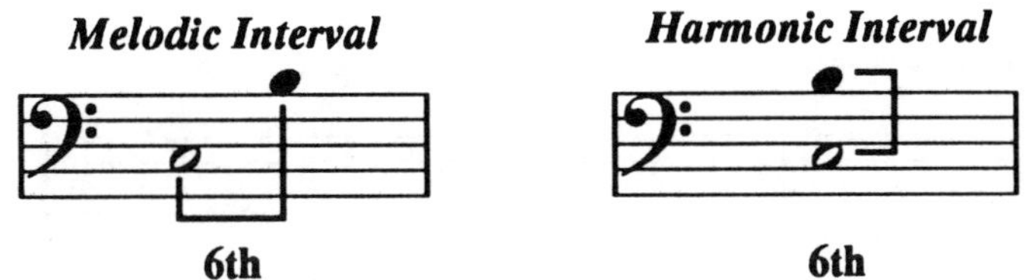

Intervals have a sound quality of *perfect, major, minor, augmented,* or *diminished.* Interval quality is determined by the relation of the upper note to the diatonic major scale, constructed on the lower note.

Perfect intervals (P): The upper note of the interval is a *(prime) unison, fourth, fifth,* or *octave* and is within the diatonic major scale, built on the lower note.

Perfect Intervals In C Major

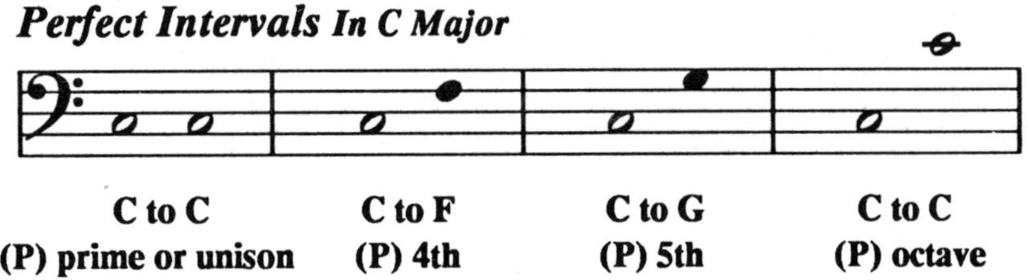

Major intervals (M): The upper note of the interval is a *second, third, sixth,* or *seventh* and is within the diatonic major scale, built on the lower note.

Major Intervals In C Major

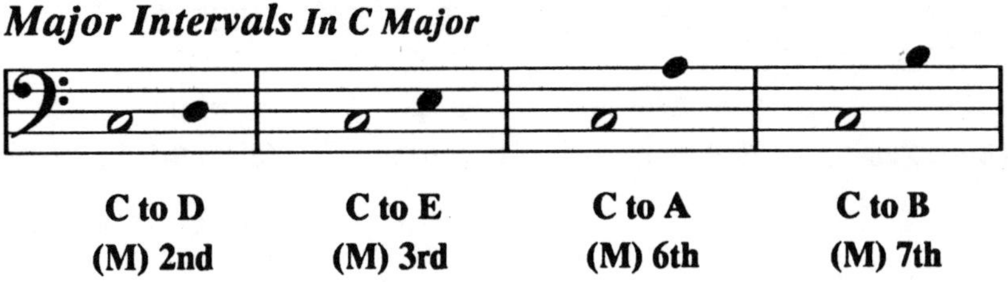

Minor intervals (m): The upper note of the *major* interval is lowered a semi-tone, built on the lower note.

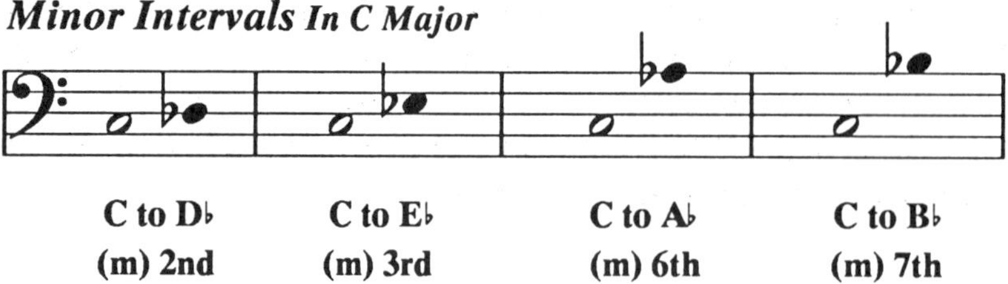

Augmented intervals (Aug): The upper note of the "*major*" or "*perfect*" interval is raised a semi-tone, built on the lower note.

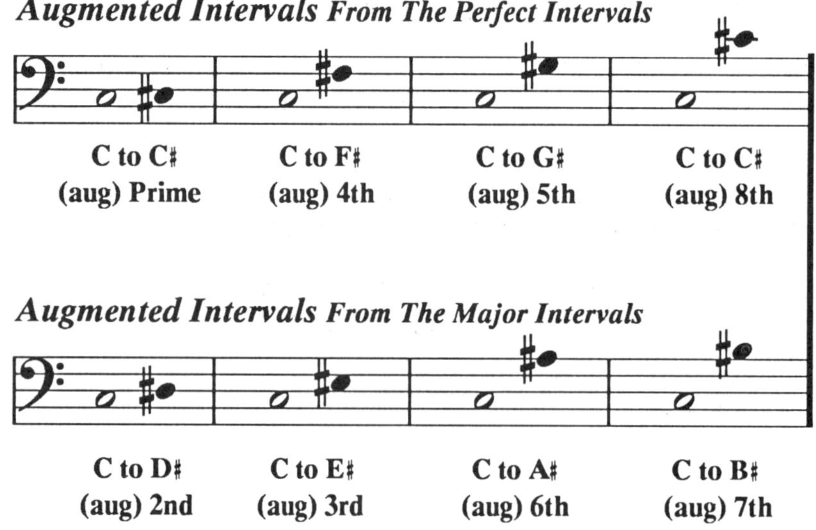

Diminished intervals (Dim): The upper note of the "*minor*" or "*perfect*" interval is lowered a semi-tone, built on the lower note.

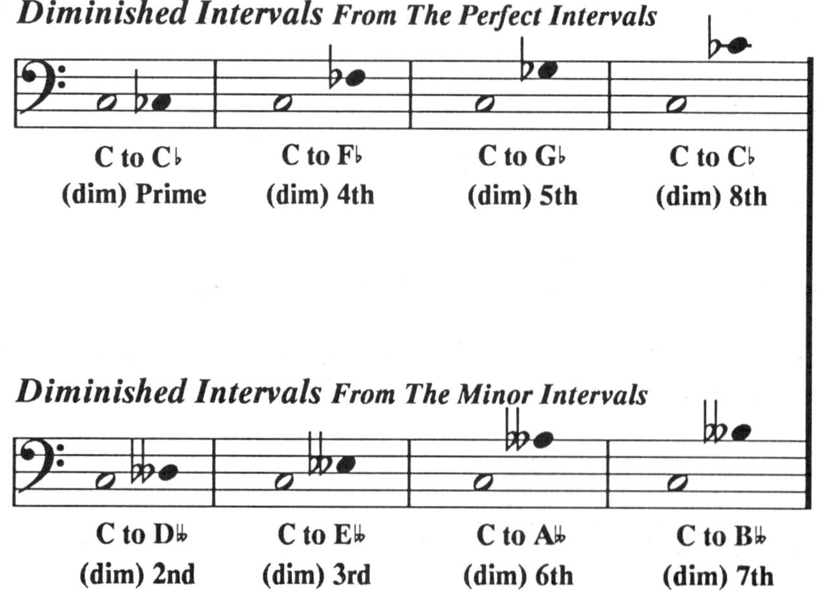

Compound intervals: Intervals exceed the extent of the octave, for example as in the *major ninth* (octave + major second.)

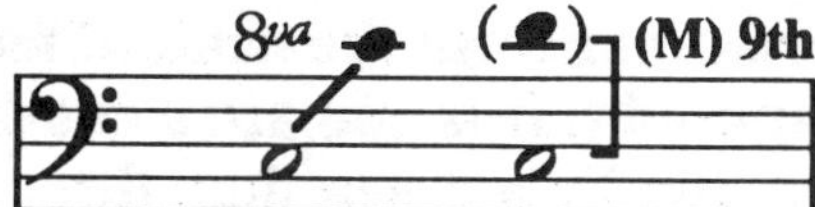

Tritone intervals: The *diminished fifth* and *augmented fourth* are tritone intervals. They each span six semi-tones and have a dissonance sound quality.

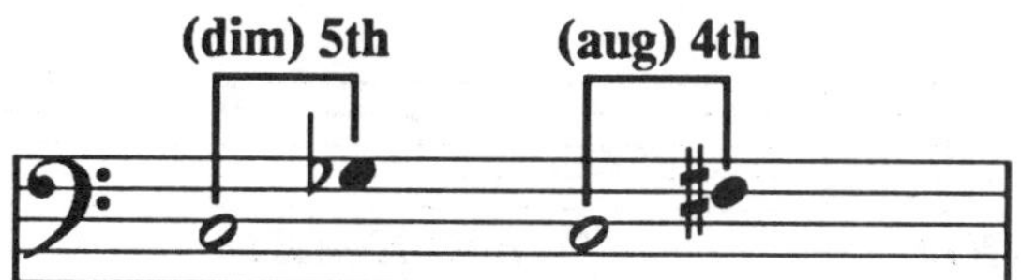

Interval inversions: A note of the interval is inverted, (the higher note is lowered an octave,) or vice versa. The inversion is always 9 and the quality is reversed, except for the perfect intervals which stay perfect. For example, The inversion of a *"perfect fifth"* would be a *"perfect fourth;"* a *"major second"* would be a *"minor seventh;"* a *"diminished sixth"* would be an *"augmented third,"* etc.

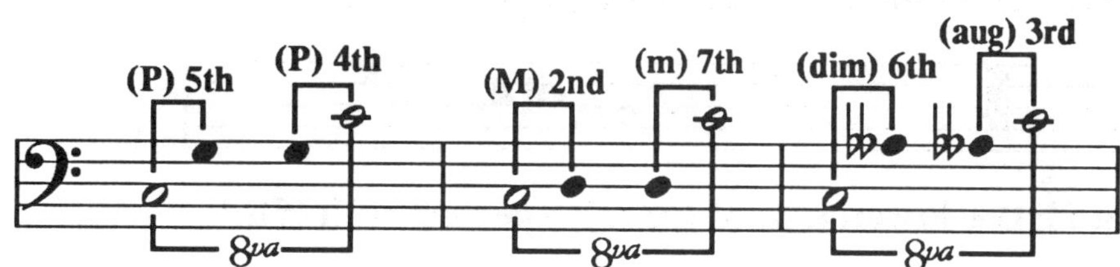

CHART ON INTERVALS

(1) Pitch In Key Of C **(2)** Name **(3)** Distance **(4)** Numerical System **(5)** Intervals From C **(6)** Degree

①	②	③	④	⑤	⑥
C	Unison	zero	I (1st)	C to C	Tonic
D♭	Minor Second	1 semi-tone	ii (♭2nd)	C to D♭	Supertonic
D	Major Second	2 semi-tones	II (2nd)	C to D	Supertonic
E♭	Minor Third	3 semi-tones	iii (♭3rd)	C to E♭	Mediant
E	Major Third	4 semi-tones	III (3rd)	C to E	Mediant
F	Perfect Fourth	5 semi-tones	IV (4th)	C to F	Sub-dominant
F♯	Augmented Fourth	6 semi-tones	IV+(♯4th)	C to F♯	Tritone
G♭	Diminished Fifth	6 semi-tones	V°(♭5th)	C to G♭	Tritone
G	Perfect Fifth	7 semi-tones	V (5th)	C to G	Dominant
G♯	Augmented Fifth	8 semi-tones	V+(♯5th)	C to G♯	Sub-mediant
A♭	Minor Sixth	8 semi-tones	vi (♭6th)	C to A♭	Sub-mediant
A	Major Sixth	9 semi-tones	VI (6th)	C to A	Sub-mediant
B♭♭	Diminished Seventh	9 semi-tones	vii°(♭♭7th)	C to B♭♭	Sub-mediant
B♭	Minor Seventh	10 semi-tones	vii (♭7th)	C to B♭	Sub-tonic
B	Major Seventh	11 semi-tones	VII (7th)	C to B	Leading Note
C	Octave	12 semi-tones	I (1st)	C to C	Tonic

Chords

Chords and their association to each other form the basis of harmony. Most chords
are created on a system of superimposed thirds and are a combination of two or more
different notes played together, but usually not less than three. All chords originate from
the diatonic major scale and are placed on the staff in a vertical position. They are called
"block chords." The notes of a chord can also be played consecutively, rather than
simultaneously, and are called *"broken chords"* or *"arpeggiated chords."*

Triads are three-note chords and are formed by a combination of intervals. They
contain the *first, third* and the *fifth* degree of the diatonic major scale. The lowest note
of a triad is the *"root"* or *"tonic"* note. The note just above the root is the *"third"* and is
the third above the root. The last note is the *"fifth"* of the triad and is a fifth above the
root. There are four basic triads:

Major (M): Root (1st) + unaltered third (3rd) + perfect fifth (5th)

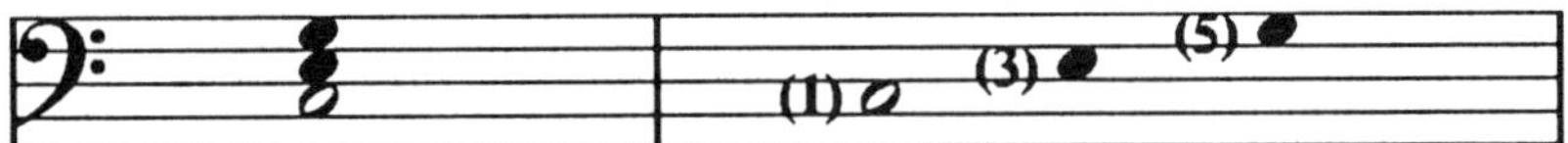

Minor (m): Root (1st) + lowered third (♭3rd) + perfect fifth (5th)

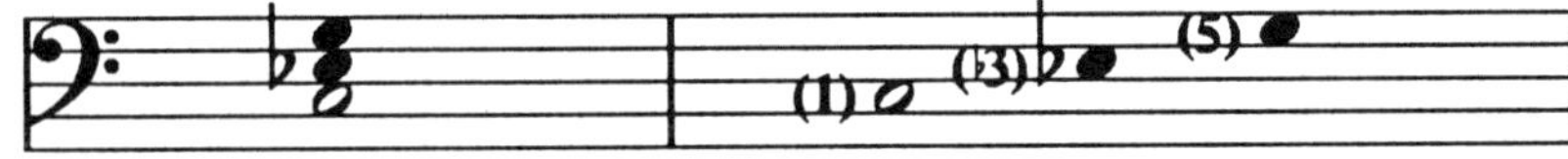

Augmented (+): Root (1st) + unaltered third (3rd) + raised fifth (♯5th)

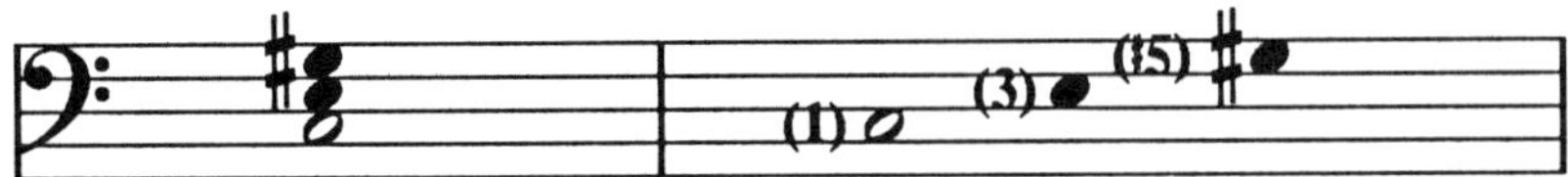

Diminished (○): Root (1st) + lowered third (♭3rd) + lowered fifth (♭5th)

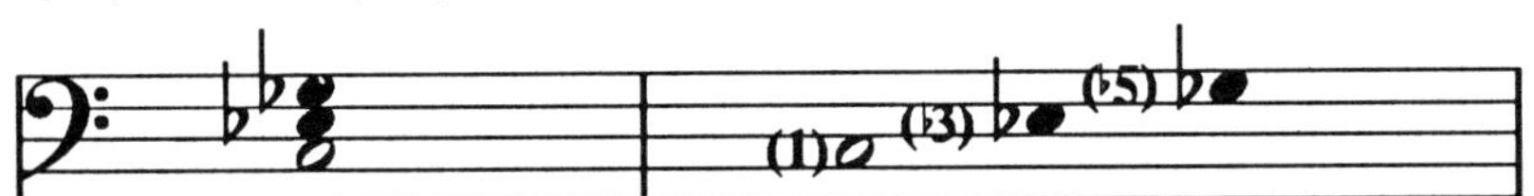

Triad inversions: The *third* or *fifth* degree of any triad is inverted to the lowest note.
The notes of the triad still have the same key-center and tonality, no matter how it is
inverted, and the name of the triad stays the same. The *"first inversion"* occurs when
the third degree of the triad is inverted to the lowest note. The *"second inversion"*
occurs when the fifth degree of the triad is inverted to the lowest note.

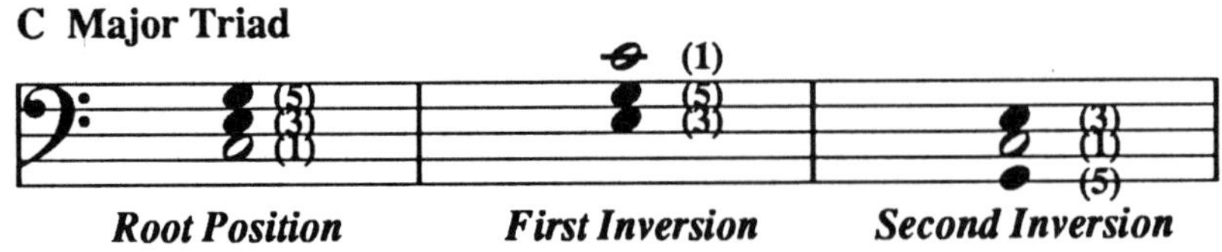

**Chords with four or more notes are called *higher numbered chords* or *extended chords*
and are labeled in accordance with the highest interval, constructed in root position.**

Chord Construction

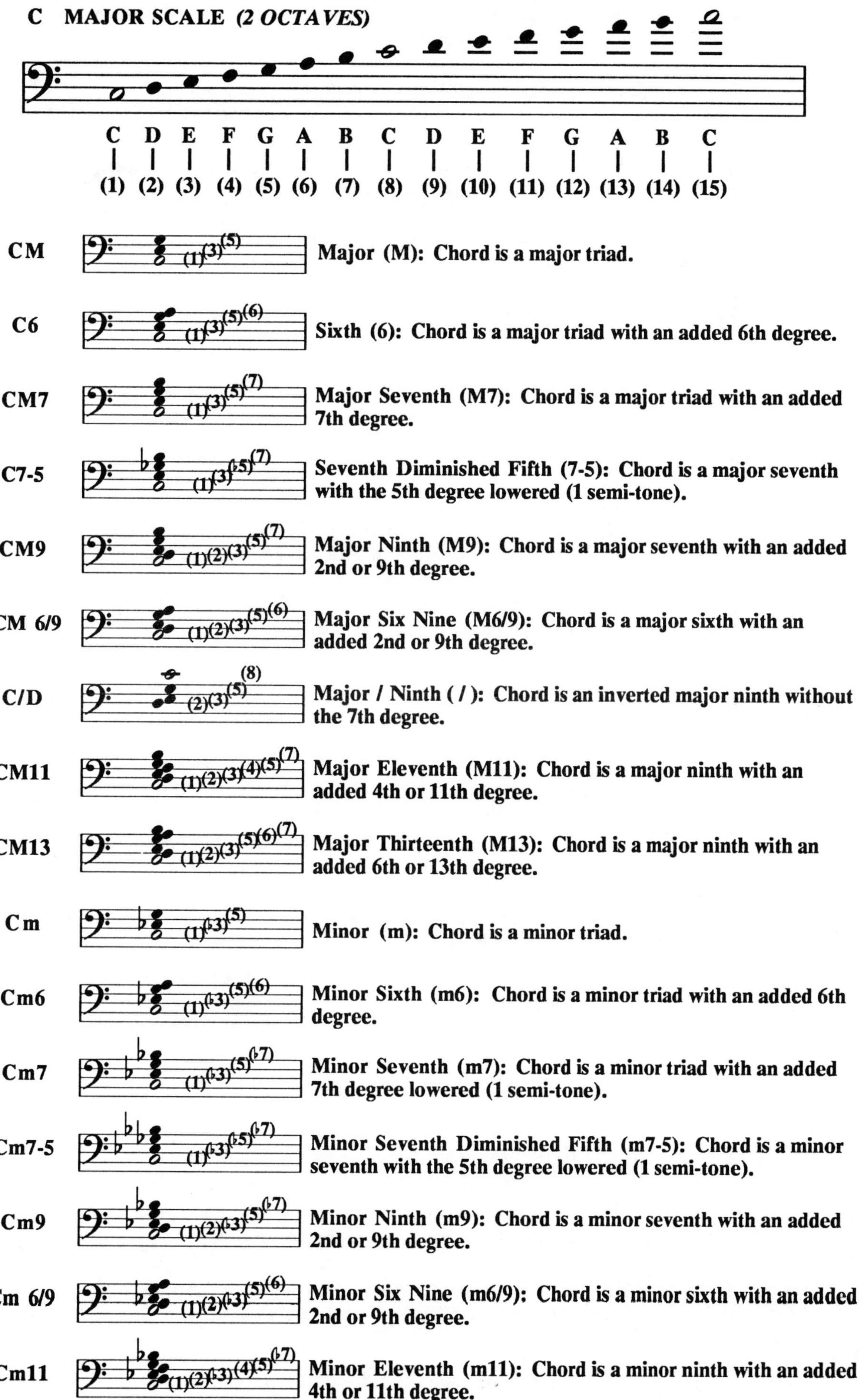

CM — Major (M): Chord is a major triad.

C6 — Sixth (6): Chord is a major triad with an added 6th degree.

CM7 — Major Seventh (M7): Chord is a major triad with an added 7th degree.

C7-5 — Seventh Diminished Fifth (7-5): Chord is a major seventh with the 5th degree lowered (1 semi-tone).

CM9 — Major Ninth (M9): Chord is a major seventh with an added 2nd or 9th degree.

CM 6/9 — Major Six Nine (M6/9): Chord is a major sixth with an added 2nd or 9th degree.

C/D — Major / Ninth (/): Chord is an inverted major ninth without the 7th degree.

CM11 — Major Eleventh (M11): Chord is a major ninth with an added 4th or 11th degree.

CM13 — Major Thirteenth (M13): Chord is a major ninth with an added 6th or 13th degree.

Cm — Minor (m): Chord is a minor triad.

Cm6 — Minor Sixth (m6): Chord is a minor triad with an added 6th degree.

Cm7 — Minor Seventh (m7): Chord is a minor triad with an added 7th degree lowered (1 semi-tone).

Cm7-5 — Minor Seventh Diminished Fifth (m7-5): Chord is a minor seventh with the 5th degree lowered (1 semi-tone).

Cm9 — Minor Ninth (m9): Chord is a minor seventh with an added 2nd or 9th degree.

Cm 6/9 — Minor Six Nine (m6/9): Chord is a minor sixth with an added 2nd or 9th degree.

Cm11 — Minor Eleventh (m11): Chord is a minor ninth with an added 4th or 11th degree.

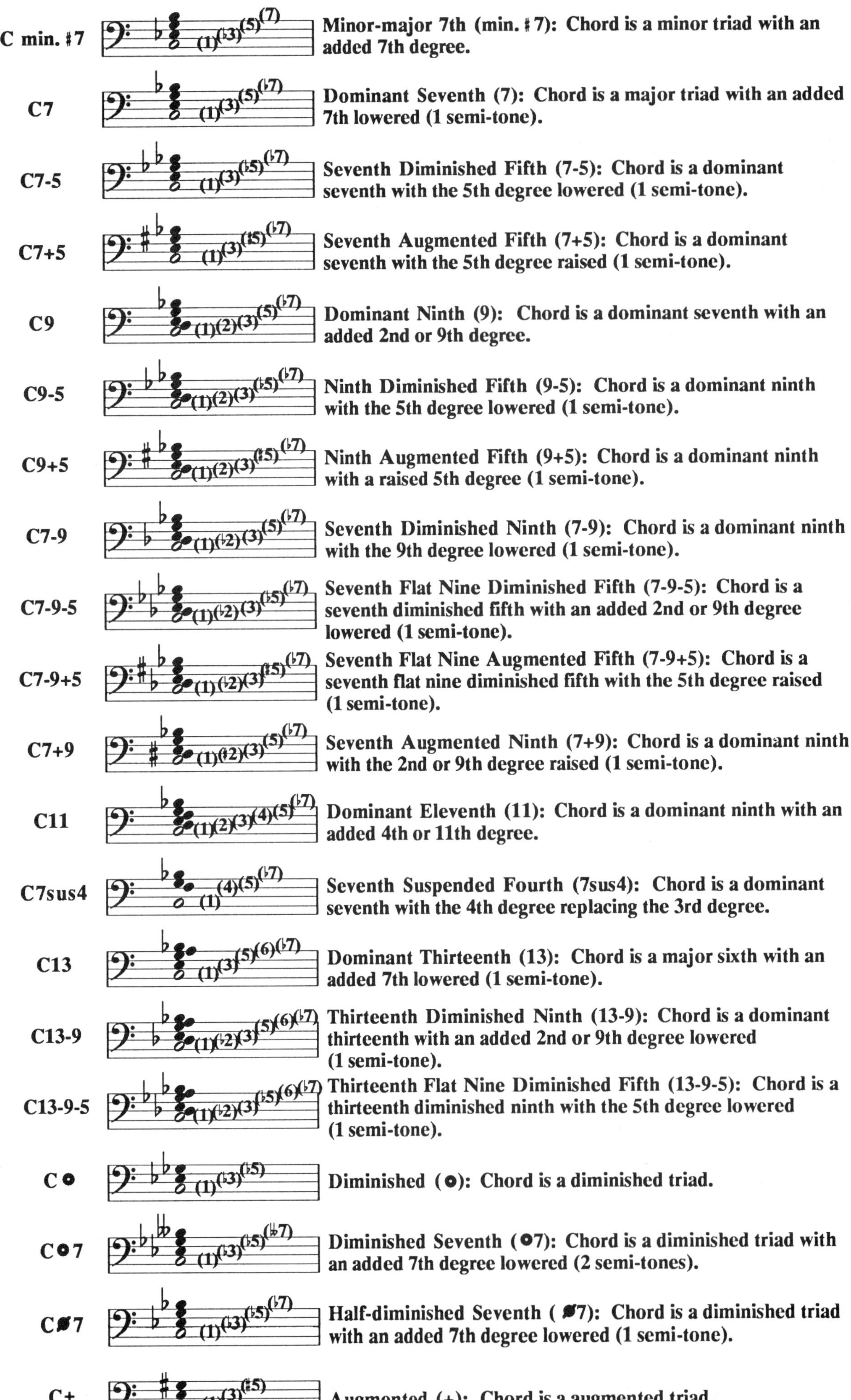

C min. ♯7 — Minor-major 7th (min. ♯7): Chord is a minor triad with an added 7th degree.

C7 — Dominant Seventh (7): Chord is a major triad with an added 7th lowered (1 semi-tone).

C7-5 — Seventh Diminished Fifth (7-5): Chord is a dominant seventh with the 5th degree lowered (1 semi-tone).

C7+5 — Seventh Augmented Fifth (7+5): Chord is a dominant seventh with the 5th degree raised (1 semi-tone).

C9 — Dominant Ninth (9): Chord is a dominant seventh with an added 2nd or 9th degree.

C9-5 — Ninth Diminished Fifth (9-5): Chord is a dominant ninth with the 5th degree lowered (1 semi-tone).

C9+5 — Ninth Augmented Fifth (9+5): Chord is a dominant ninth with a raised 5th degree (1 semi-tone).

C7-9 — Seventh Diminished Ninth (7-9): Chord is a dominant ninth with the 9th degree lowered (1 semi-tone).

C7-9-5 — Seventh Flat Nine Diminished Fifth (7-9-5): Chord is a seventh diminished fifth with an added 2nd or 9th degree lowered (1 semi-tone).

C7-9+5 — Seventh Flat Nine Augmented Fifth (7-9+5): Chord is a seventh flat nine diminished fifth with the 5th degree raised (1 semi-tone).

C7+9 — Seventh Augmented Ninth (7+9): Chord is a dominant ninth with the 2nd or 9th degree raised (1 semi-tone).

C11 — Dominant Eleventh (11): Chord is a dominant ninth with an added 4th or 11th degree.

C7sus4 — Seventh Suspended Fourth (7sus4): Chord is a dominant seventh with the 4th degree replacing the 3rd degree.

C13 — Dominant Thirteenth (13): Chord is a major sixth with an added 7th lowered (1 semi-tone).

C13-9 — Thirteenth Diminished Ninth (13-9): Chord is a dominant thirteenth with an added 2nd or 9th degree lowered (1 semi-tone).

C13-9-5 — Thirteenth Flat Nine Diminished Fifth (13-9-5): Chord is a thirteenth diminished ninth with the 5th degree lowered (1 semi-tone).

C ⊙ — Diminished (⊙): Chord is a diminished triad.

C ⊙7 — Diminished Seventh (⊙7): Chord is a diminished triad with an added 7th degree lowered (2 semi-tones).

C ⦰7 — Half-diminished Seventh (⦰7): Chord is a diminished triad with an added 7th degree lowered (1 semi-tone).

C+ — Augmented (+): Chord is a augmented triad.

C MAJOR

FORMULA - (C) Root (E) 3rd (G) 5th

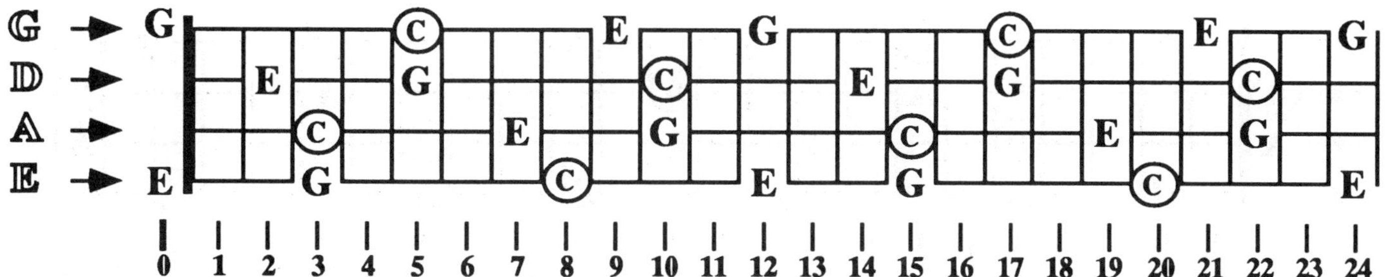

Positions

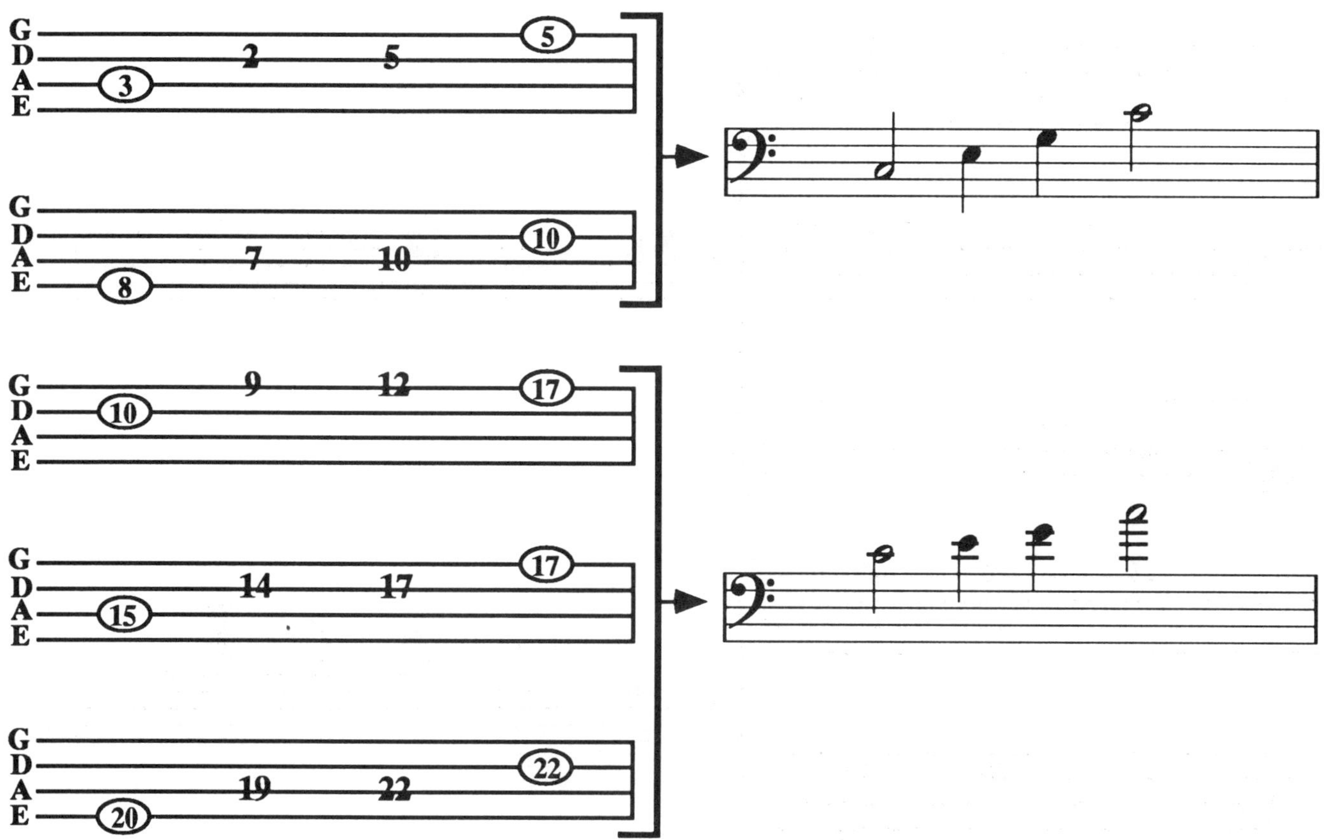

Riff

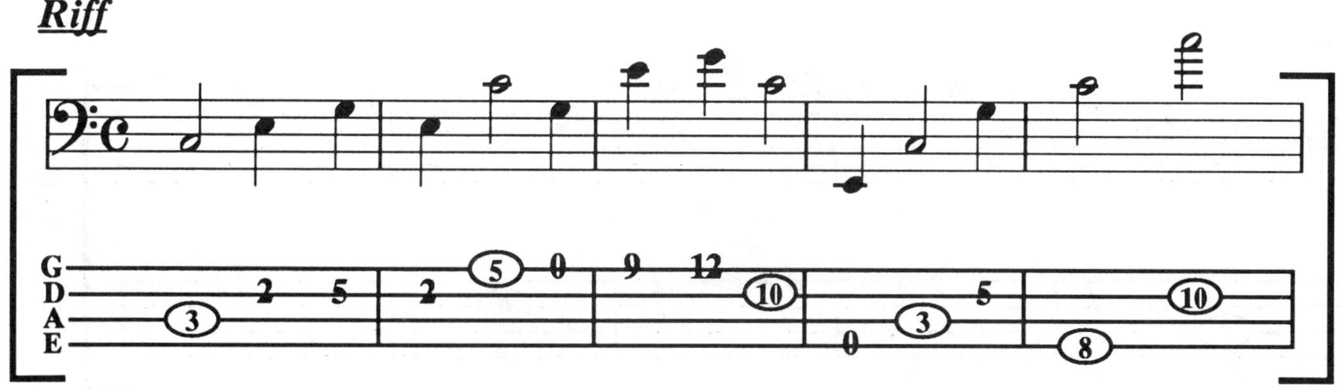

D MAJOR
FORMULA - (D) Root (F♯) 3rd (A) 5th

D△

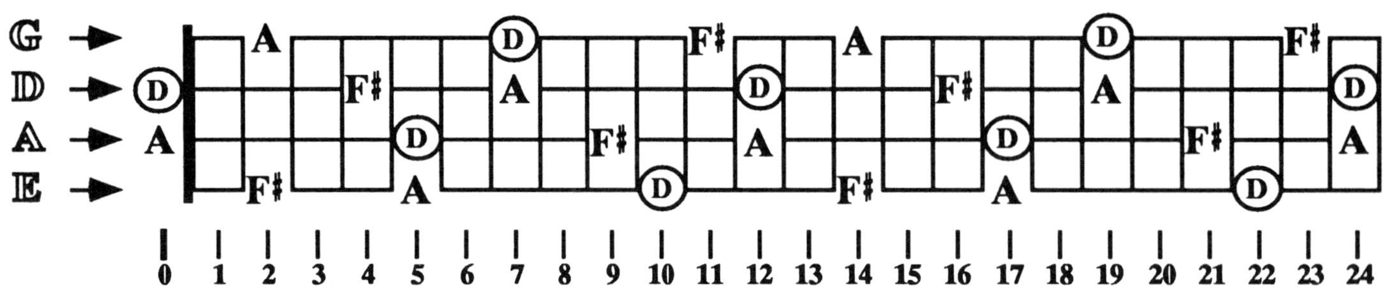

Positions

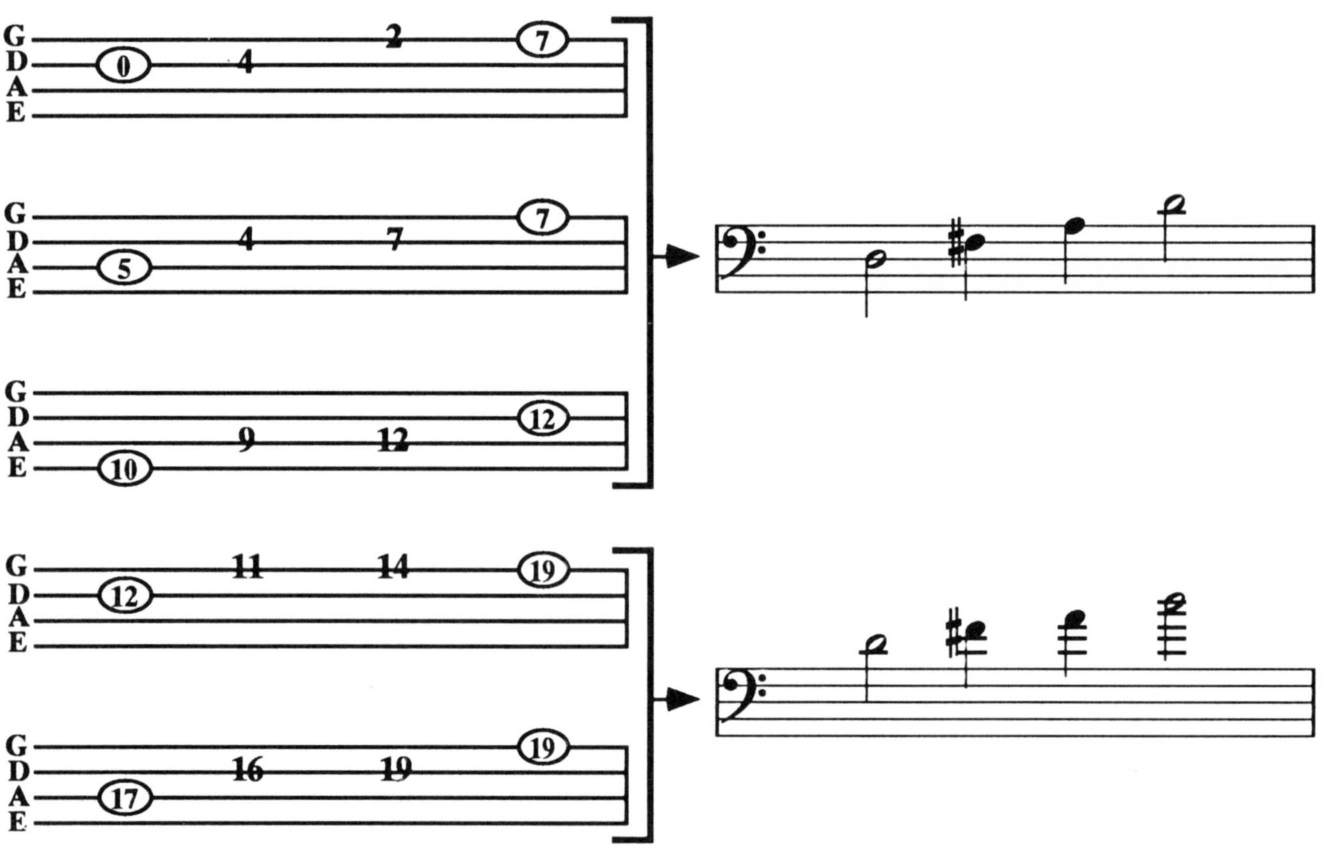

Riff

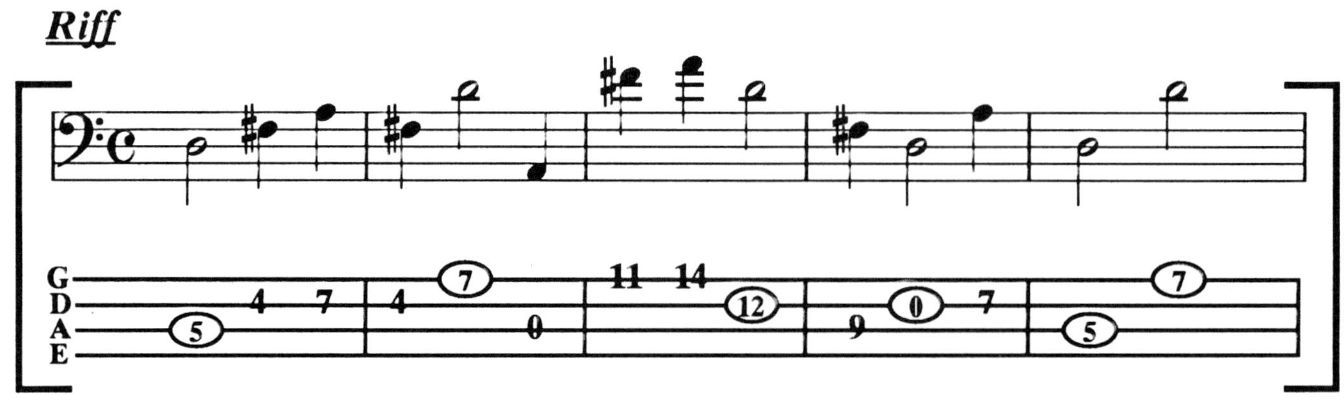

E MAJOR

FORMULA - (E) Root (G♯) 3rd (B) 5th

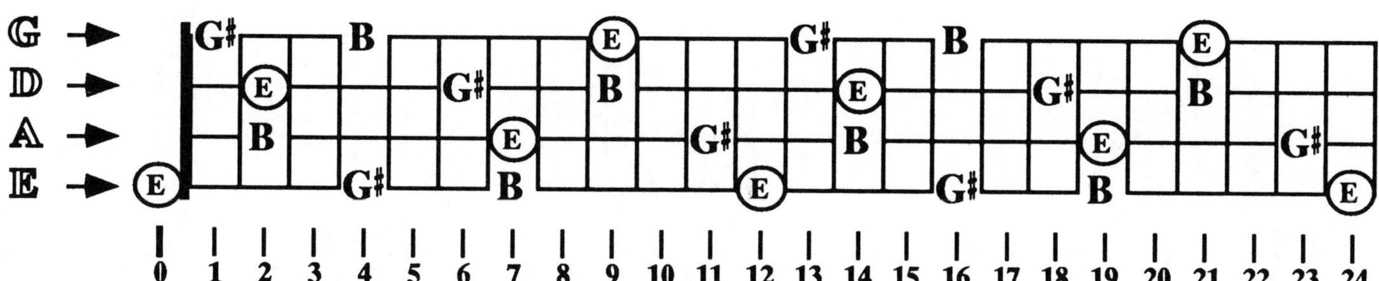

Positions

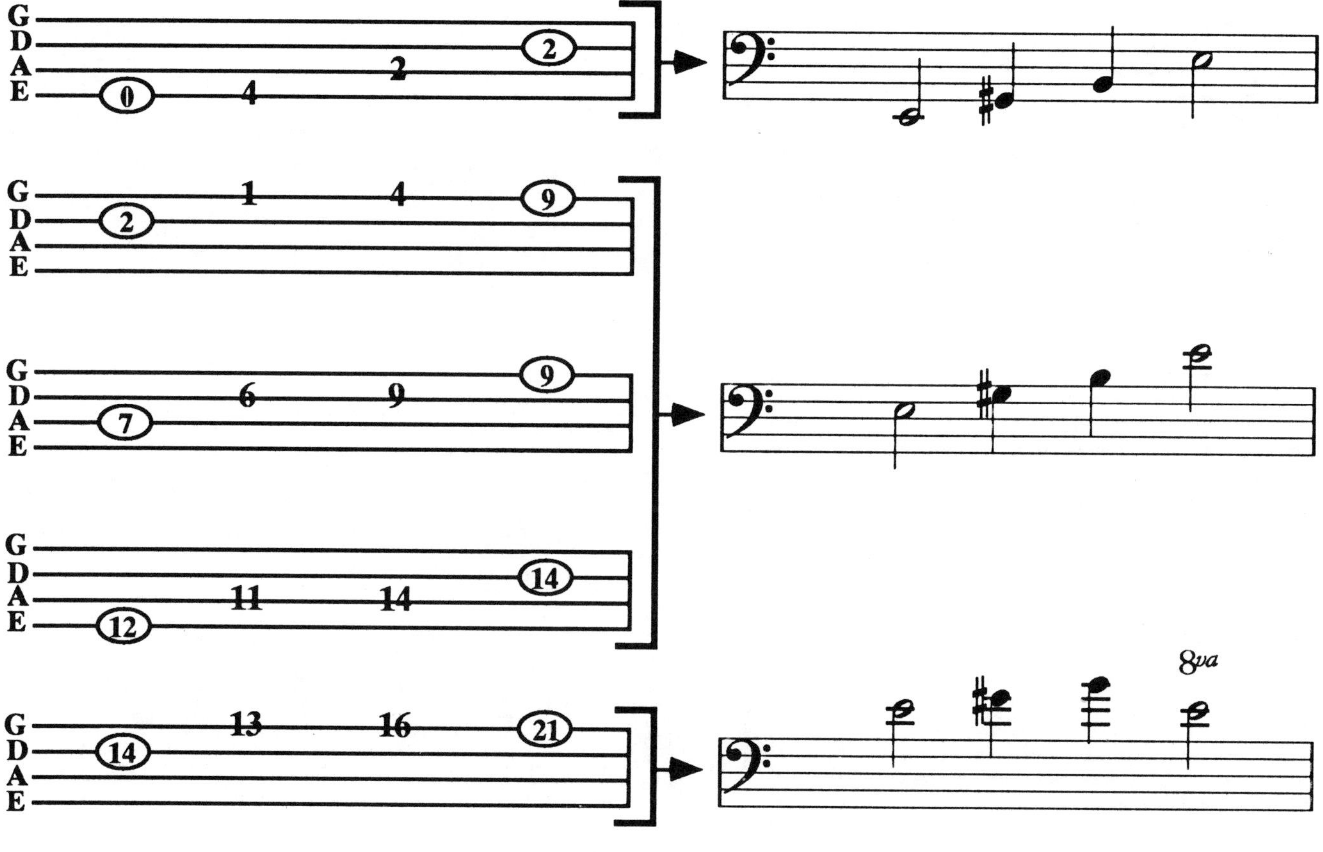

Riff

F MAJOR

FORMULA - (F) Root (A) 3rd (C) 5th

F△

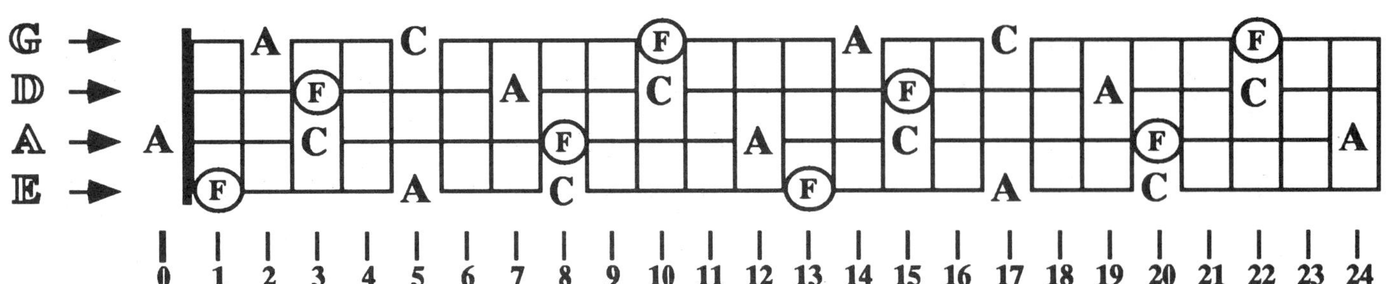

Positions

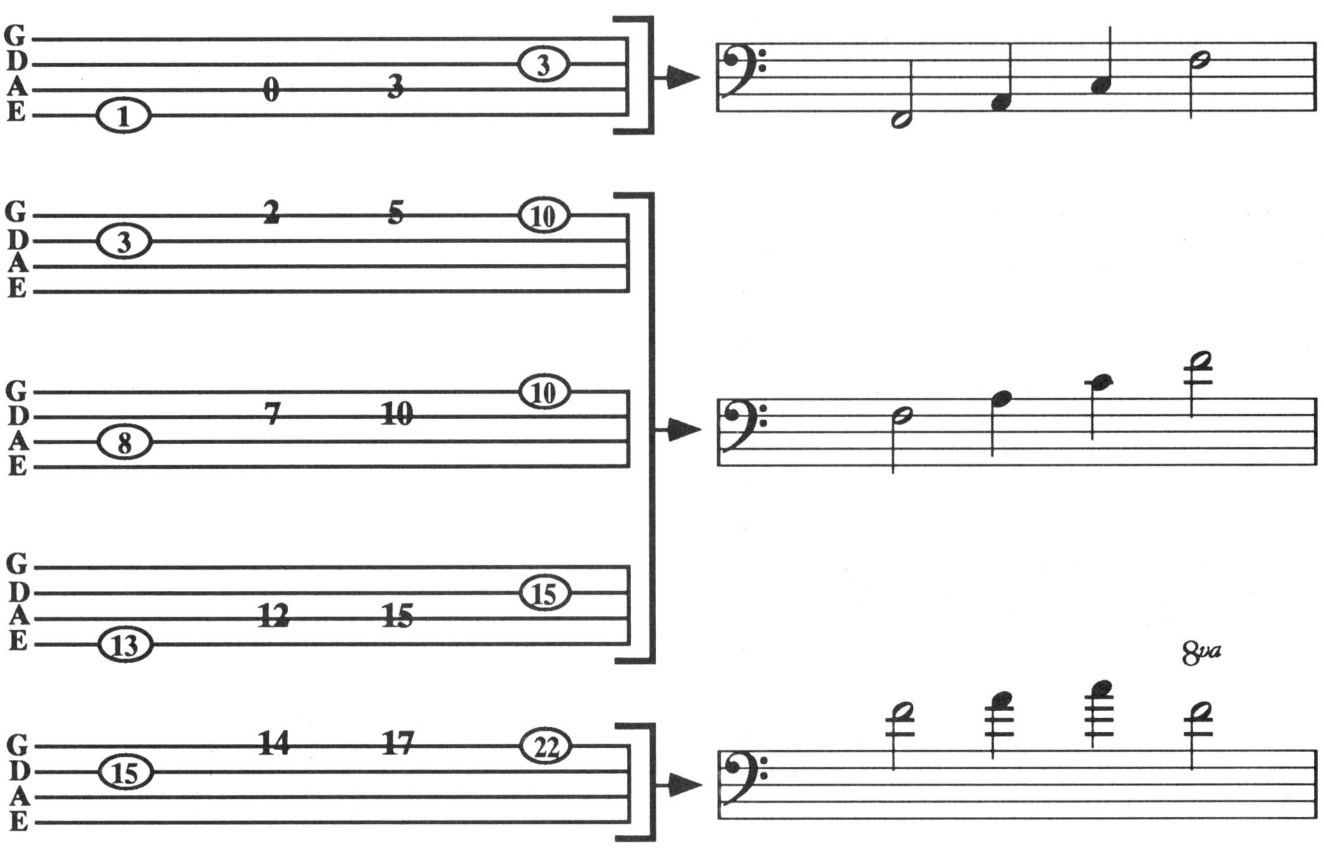

Riff

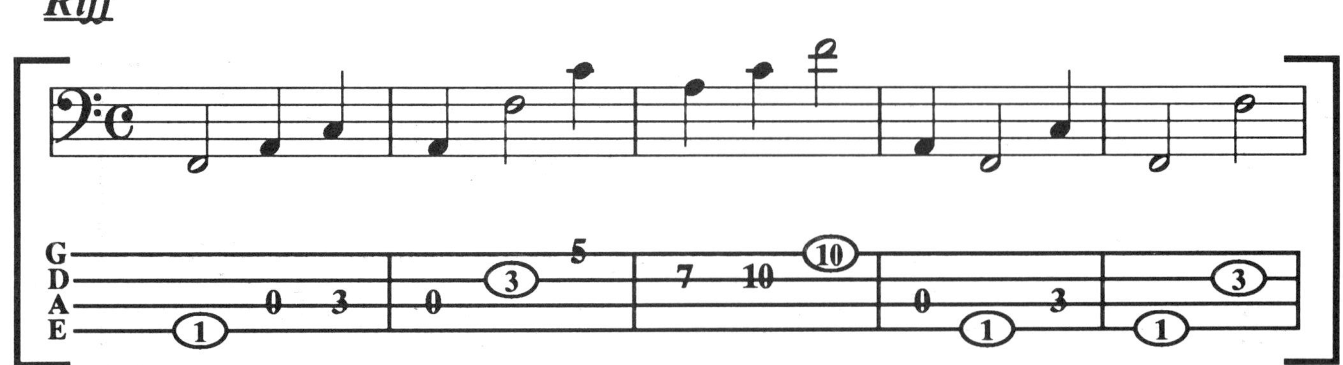

G MAJOR

FORMULA - (G) Root (B) 3rd (D) 5th

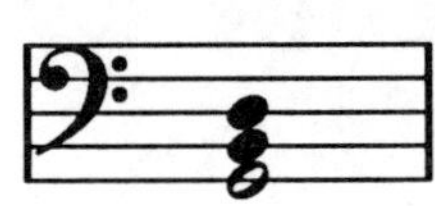

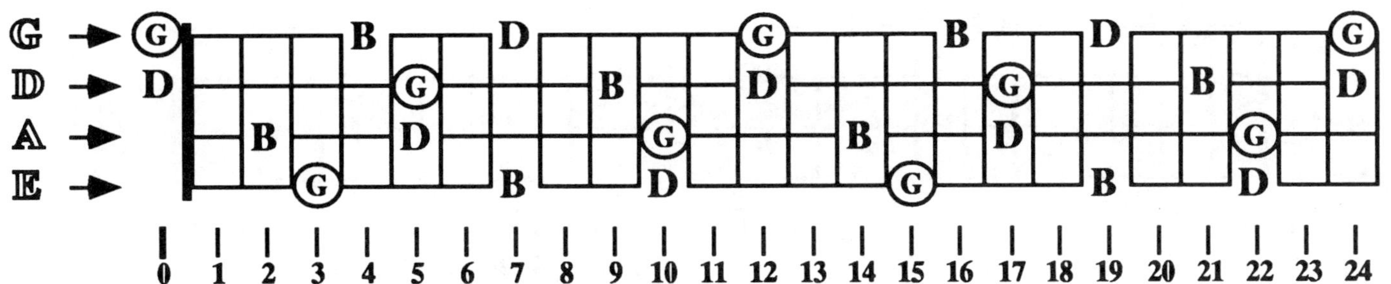

Positions

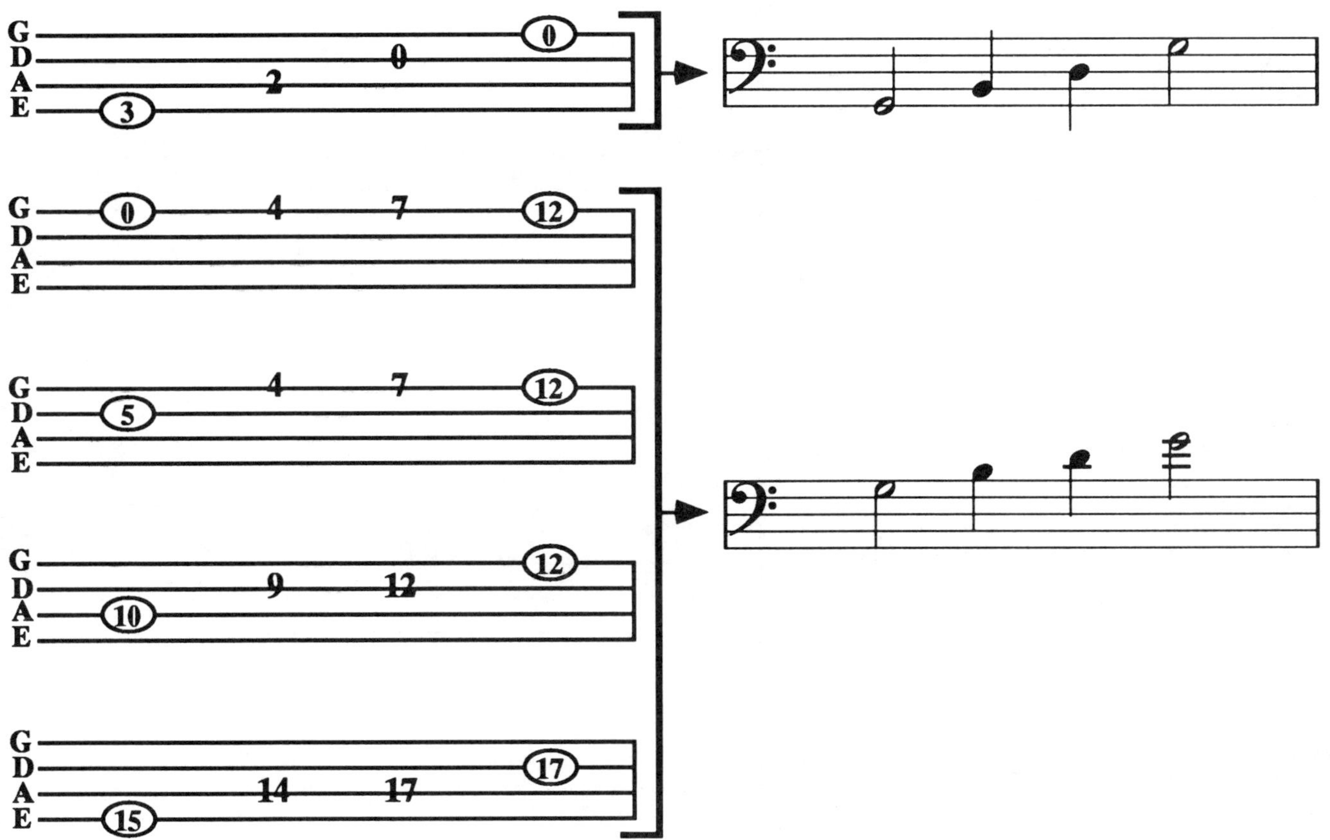

Riff

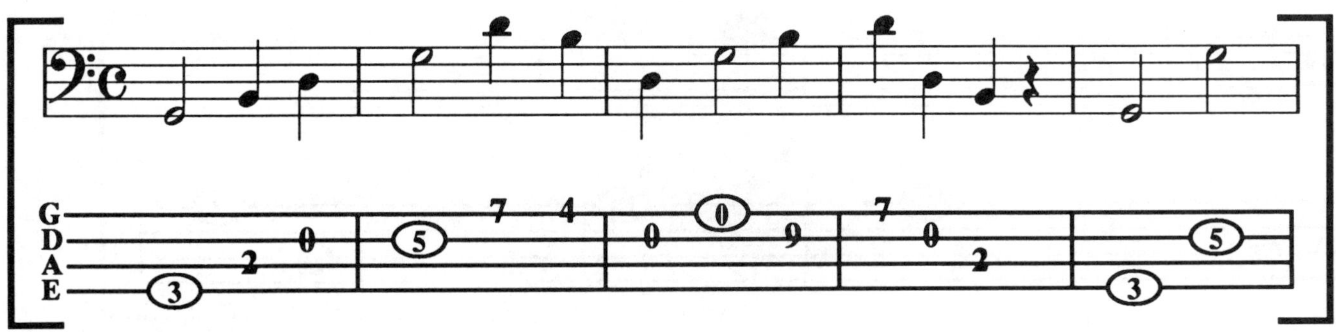

A MAJOR
FORMULA - (A) Root (C♯) 3rd (E) 5th

A△

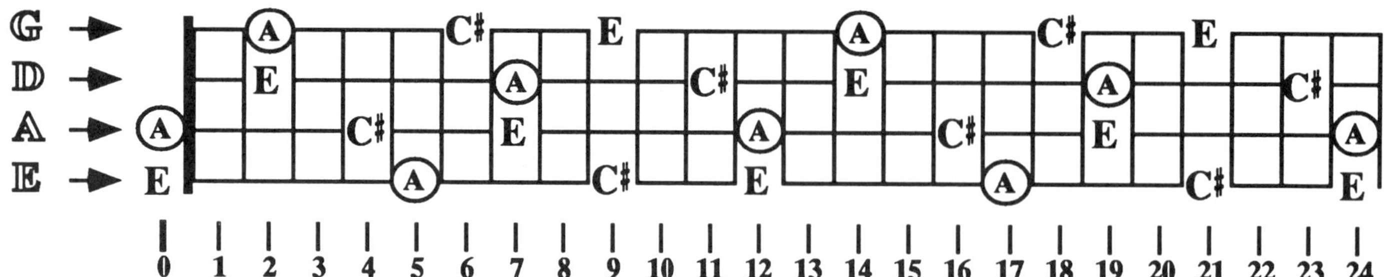

Positions

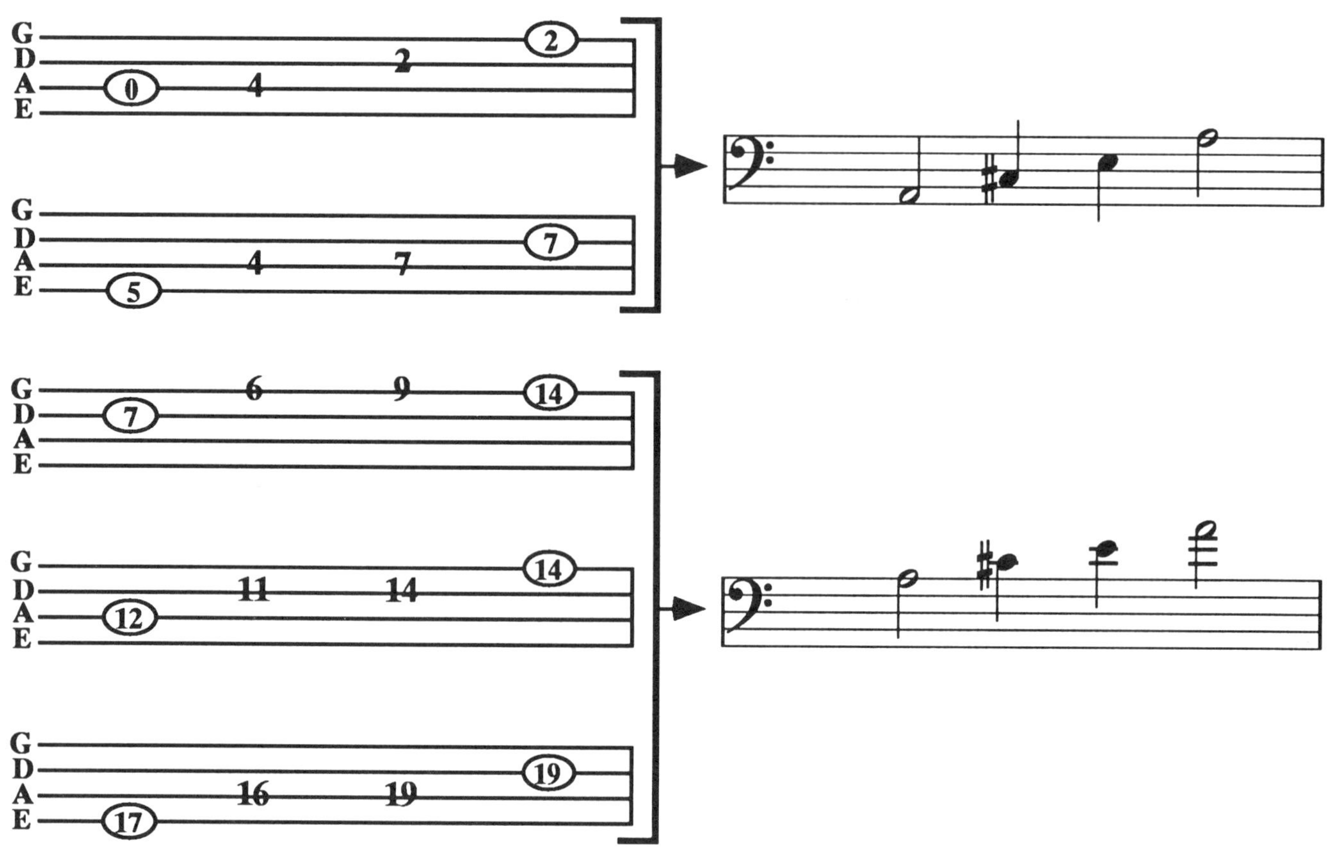

Riff

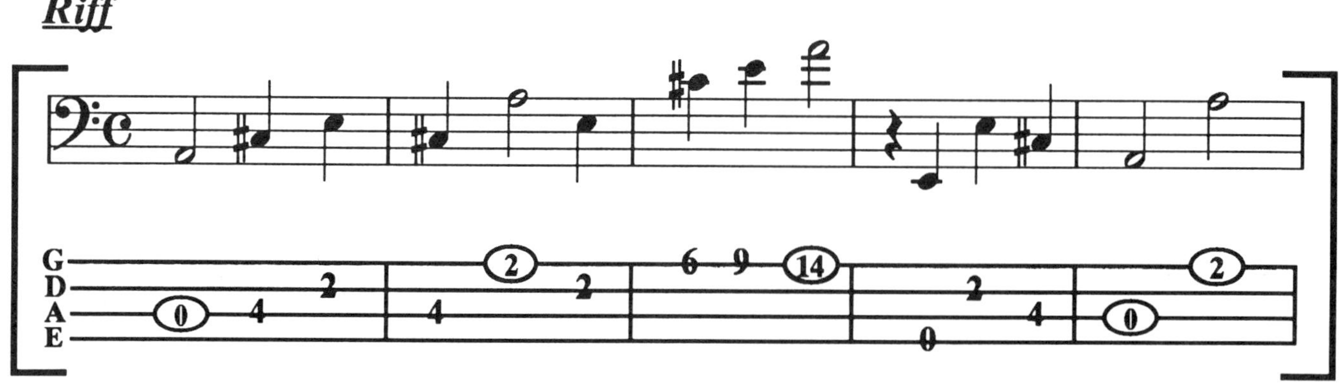

B MAJOR

FORMULA - (B) Root (D♯) 3rd (F♯) 5th

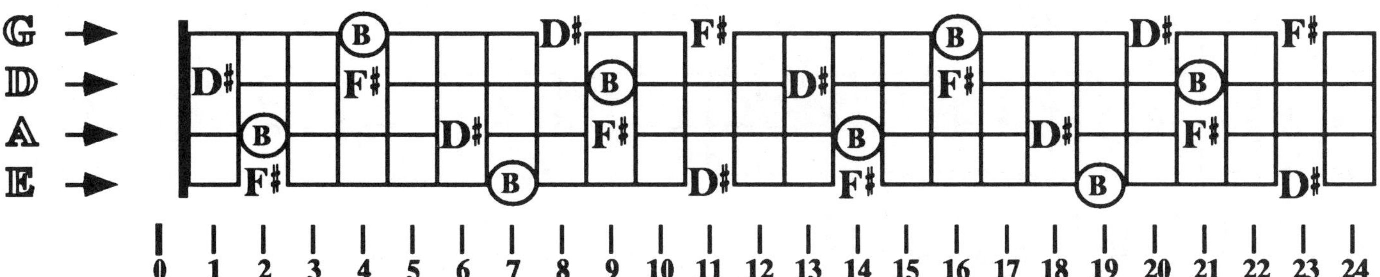

Positions

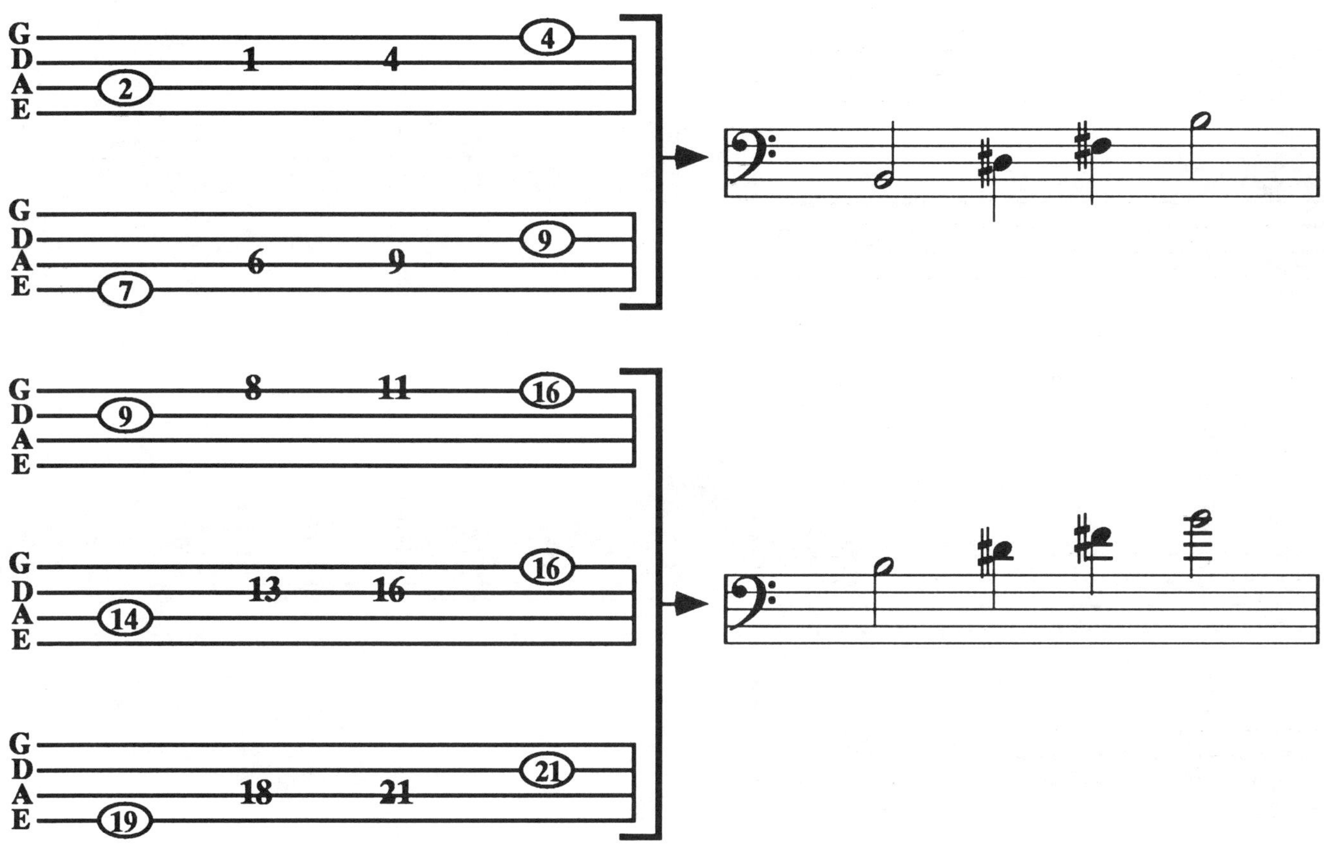

Riff

C SIXTH

FORMULA - (C) Root (E) 3rd (G) 5th (A) 6th

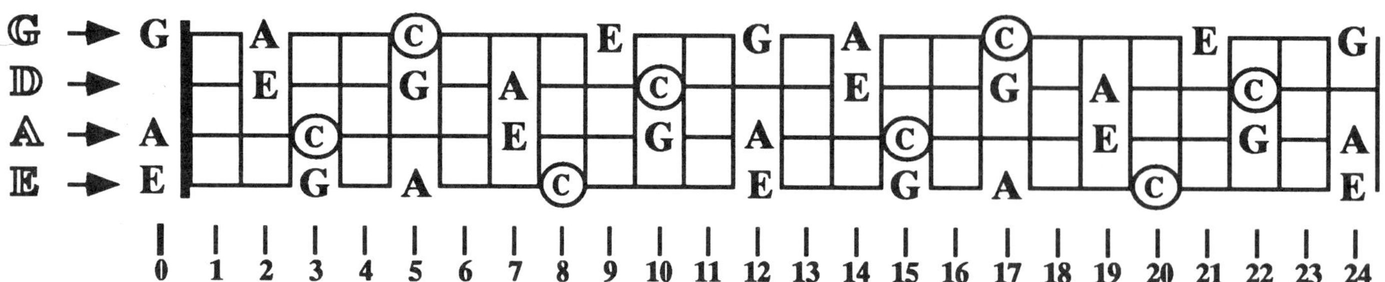

Positions

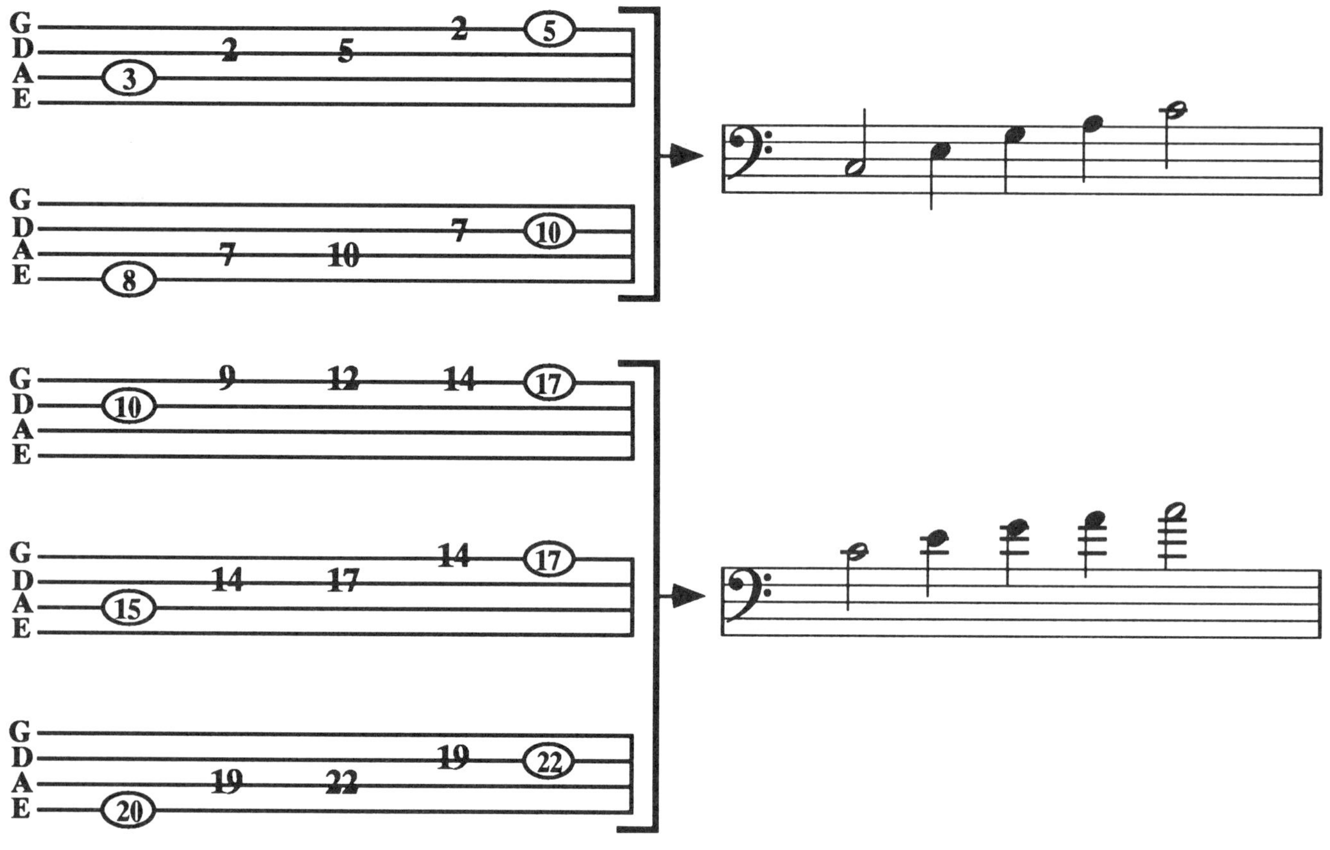

Riff

D SIXTH

FORMULA - (D) Root (F♯) 3rd (A) 5th (B) 6th

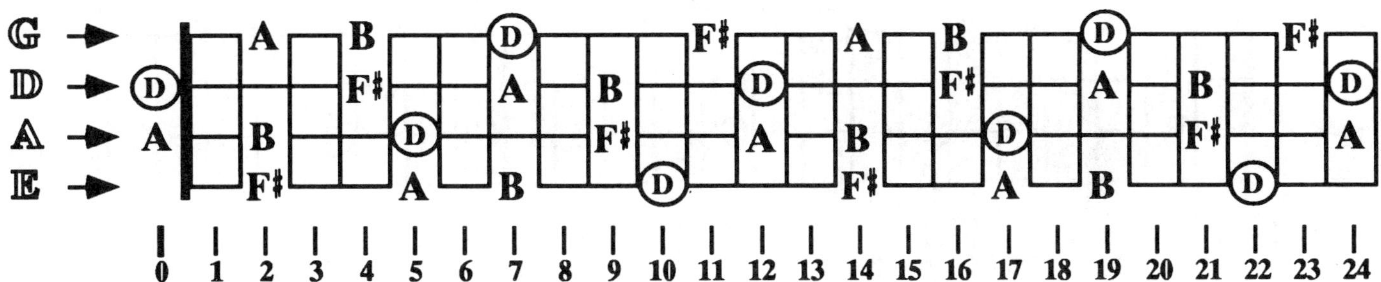

Positions

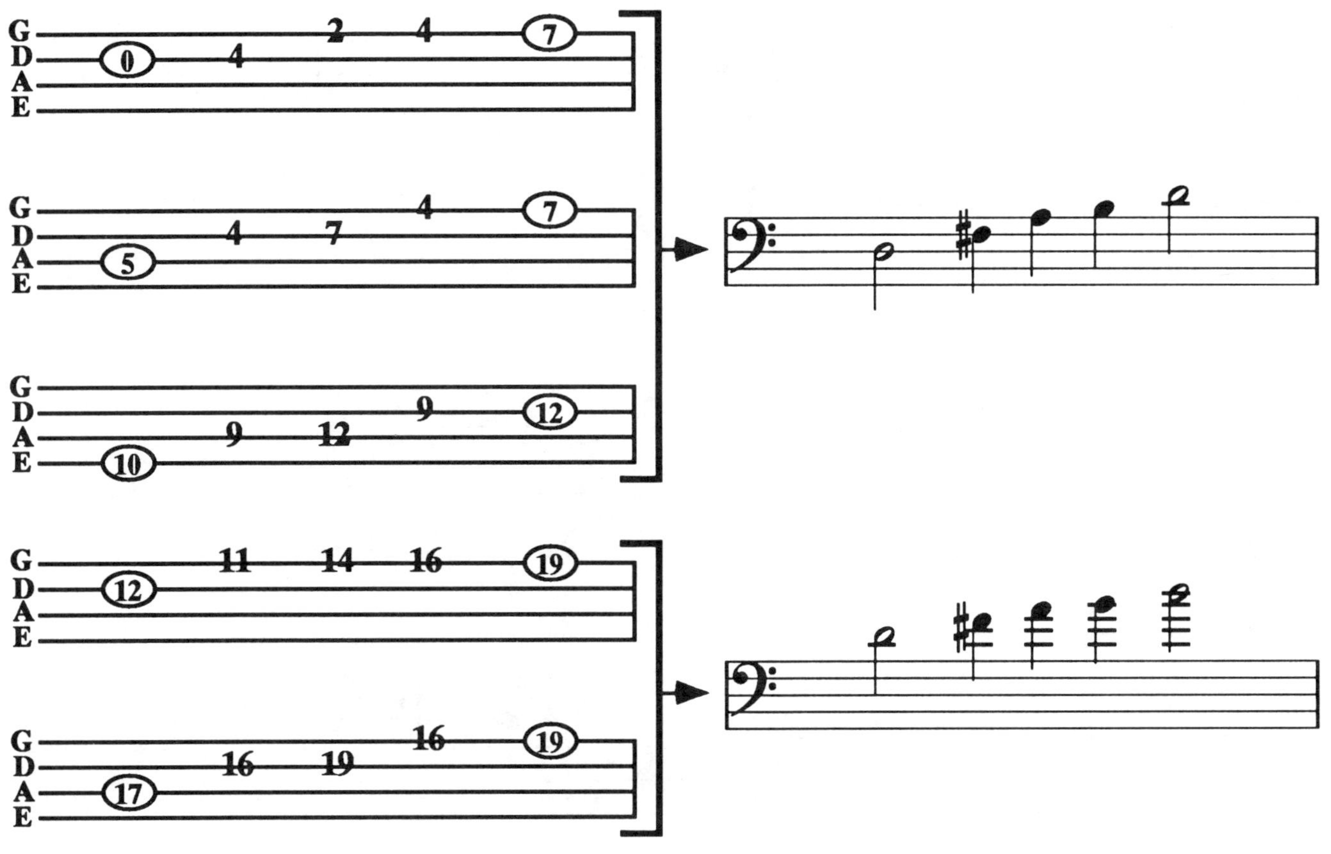

Riff

E SIXTH

FORMULA - (E) Root (G♯) 3rd (B) 5th (C♯) 6th

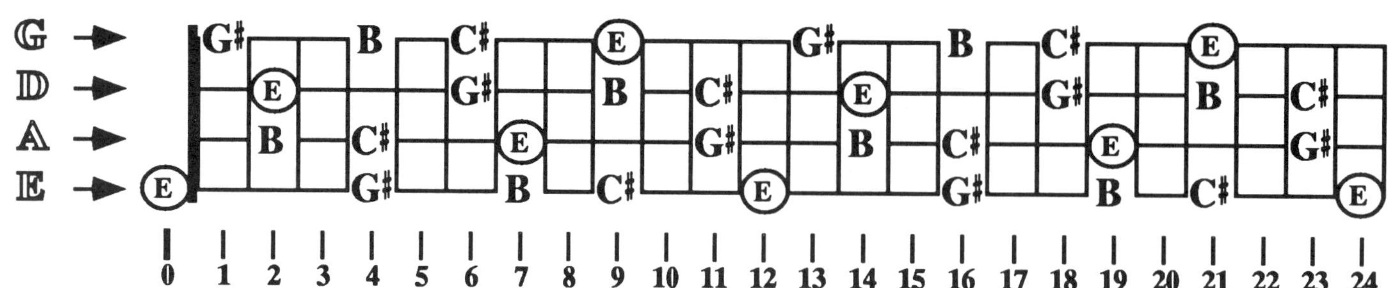

Positions

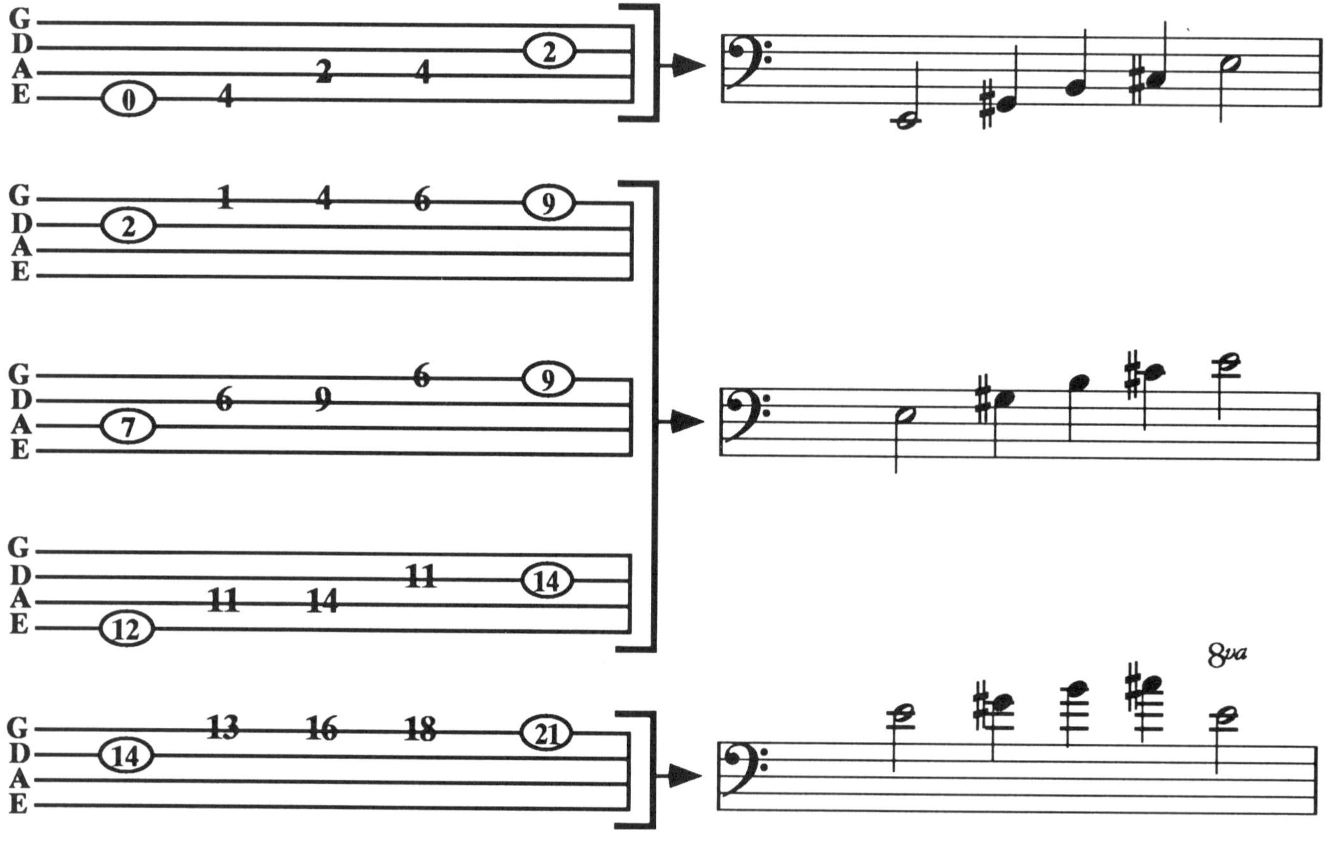

Riff

F SIXTH

FORMULA - (F) Root (A) 3rd (C) 5th (D) 6th

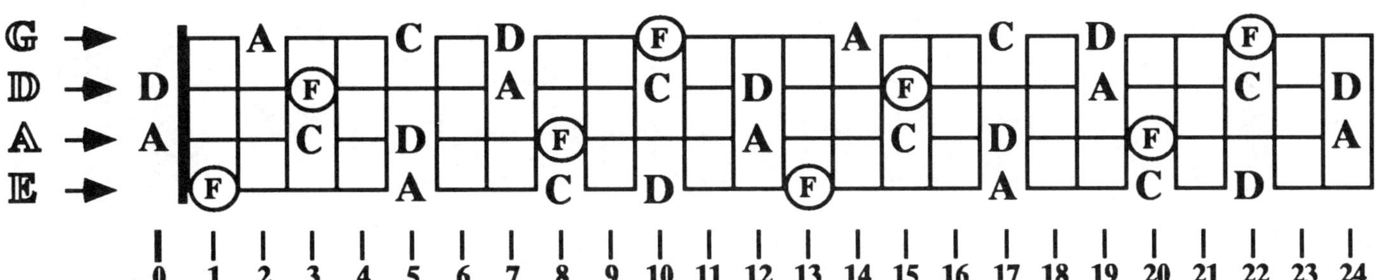

Positions

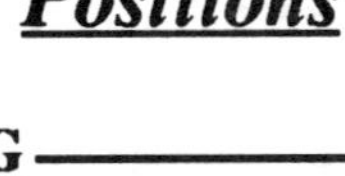

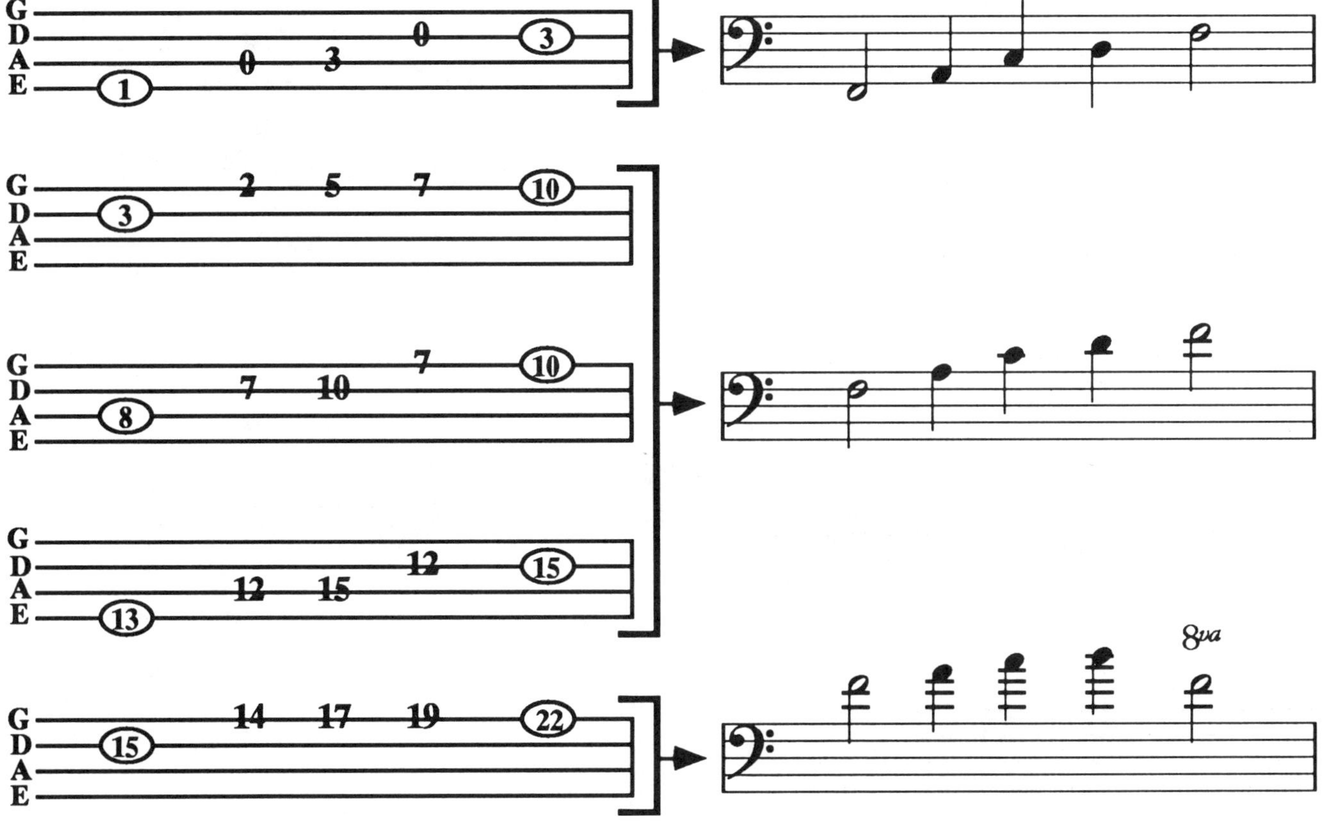

Riff

G SIXTH

FORMULA - (G) Root (B) 3rd (D) 5th (E) 6th

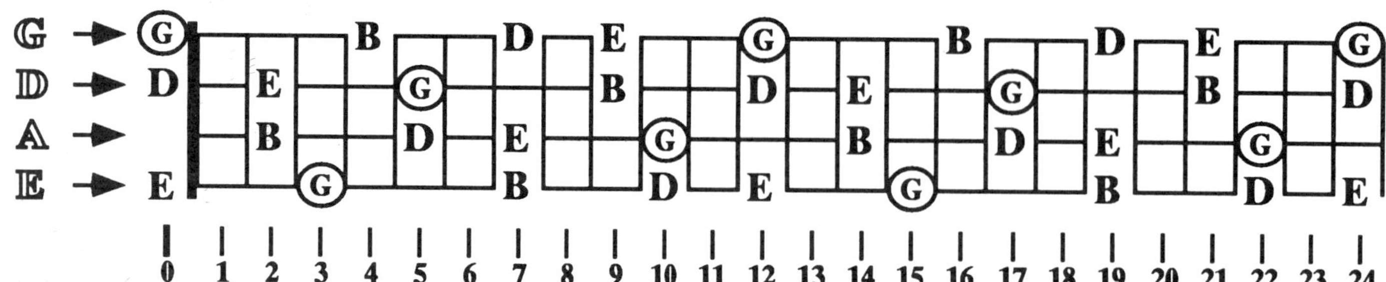

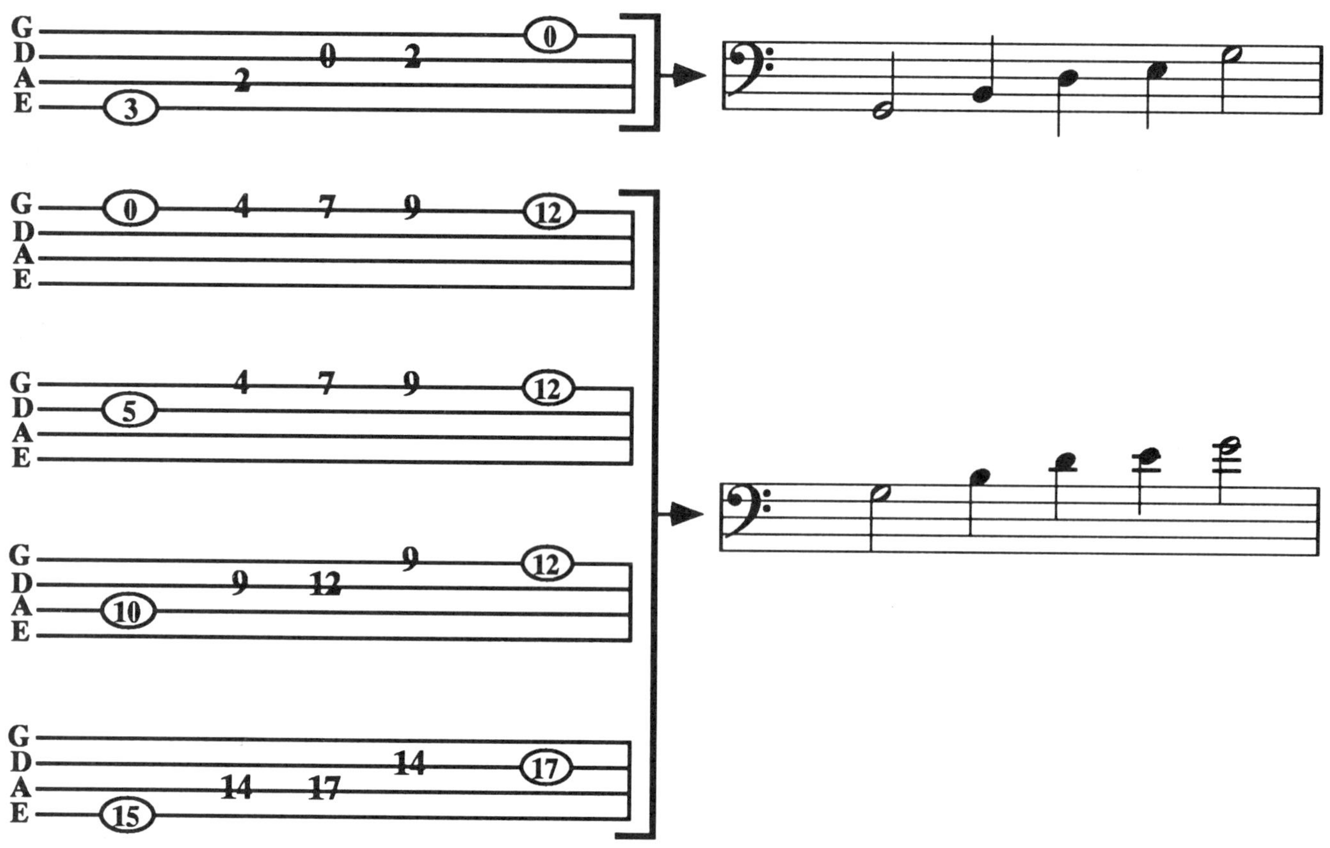

Positions

Riff

A   SIXTH
FORMULA - (A) Root (C♯) 3rd (E) 5th (F♯) 6th

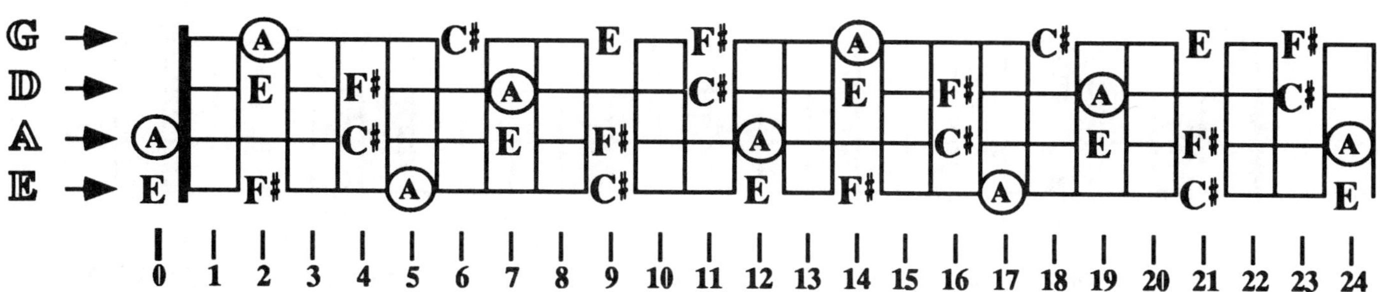

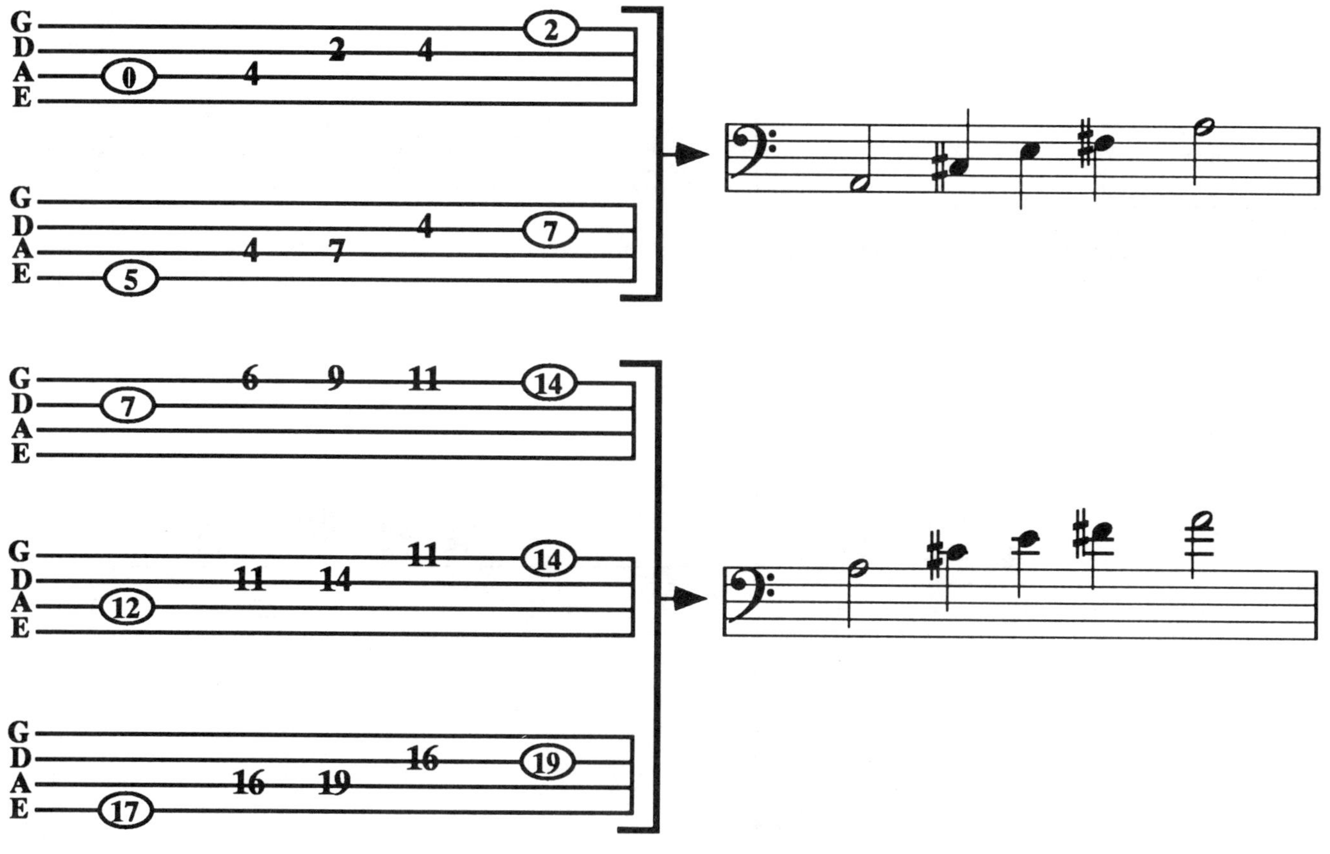

Positions

Riff

B SIXTH

FORMULA - (B) Root (D♯) 3rd (F♯) 5th (G♯) 6th

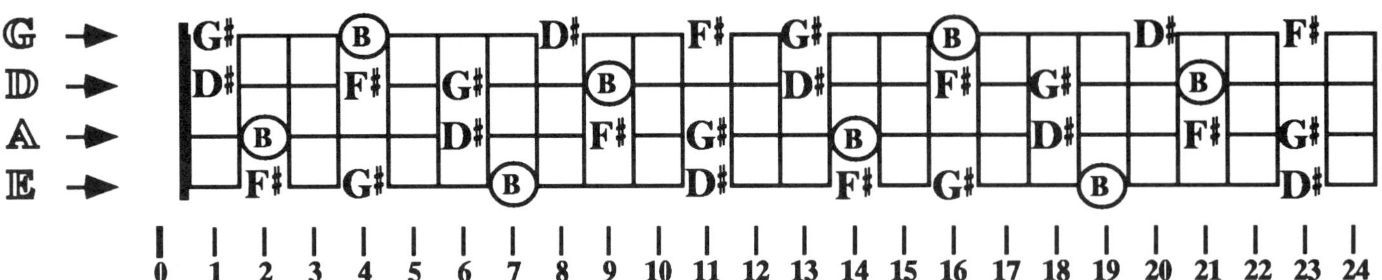

Positions

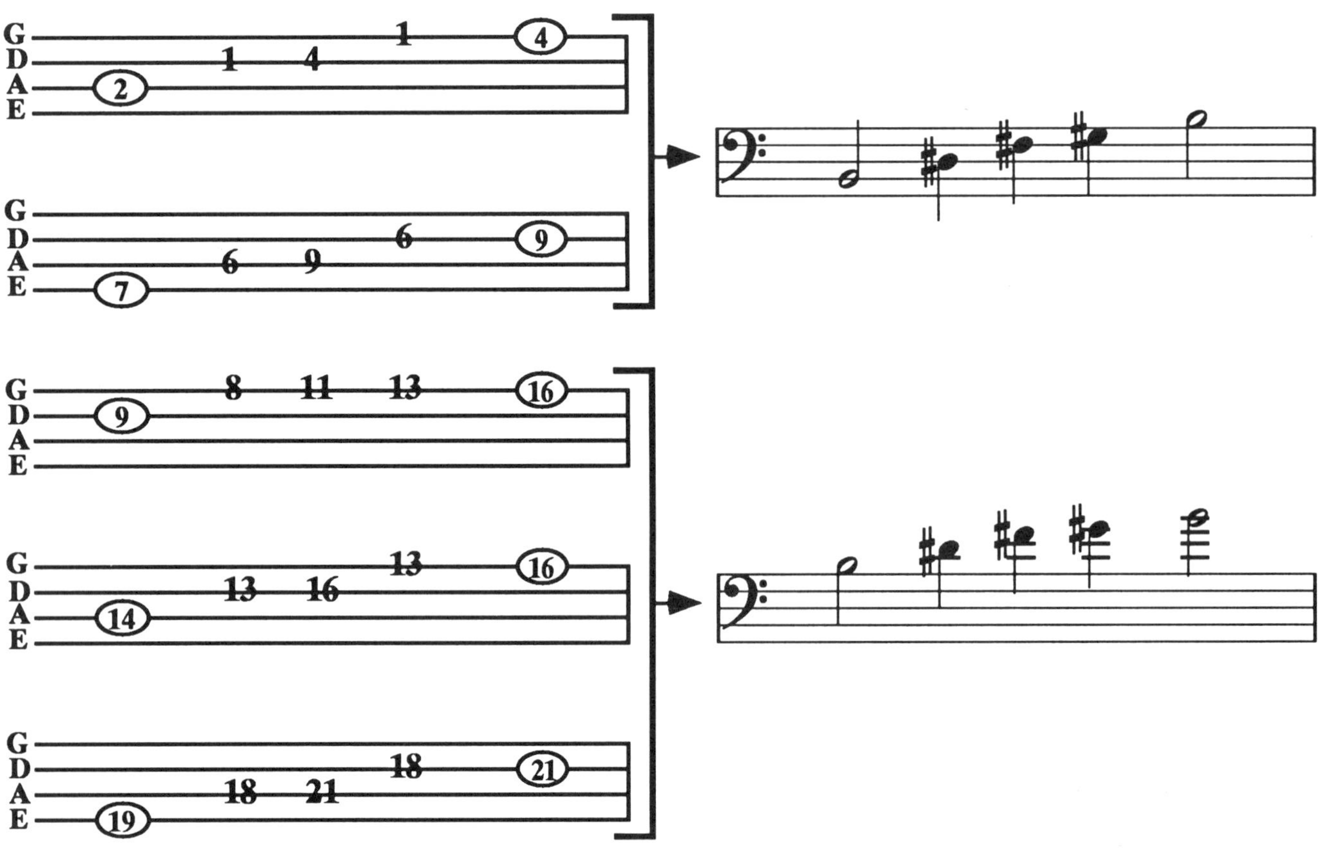

Riff

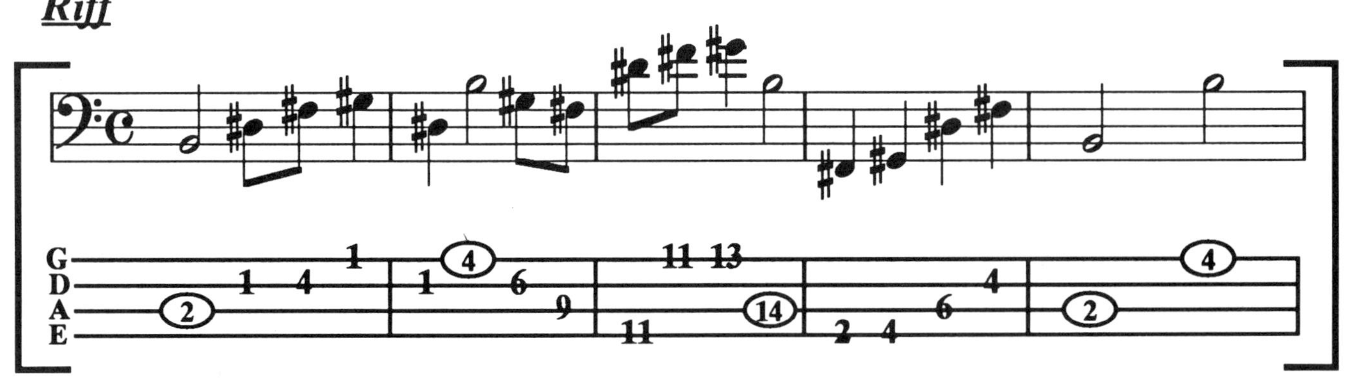

C MAJOR 7TH

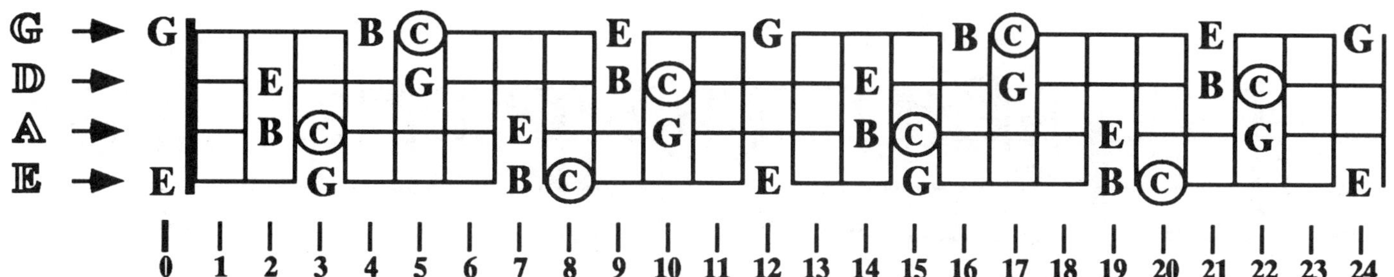

FORMULA - (C) Root (E) 3rd (G) 5th (B) 7th

Positions

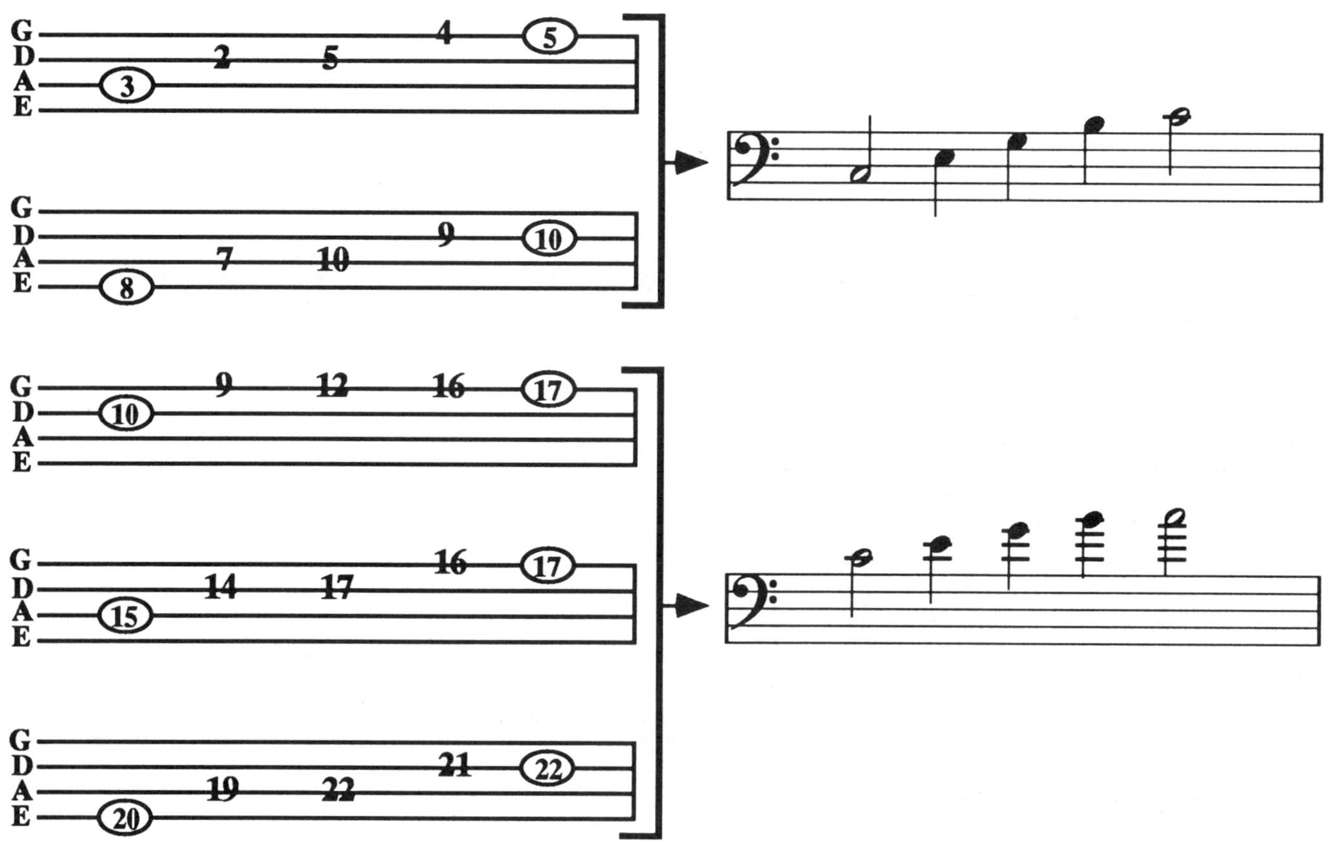

Riff

D MAJOR 7TH

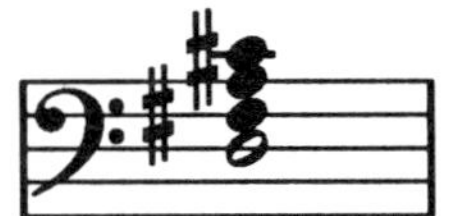

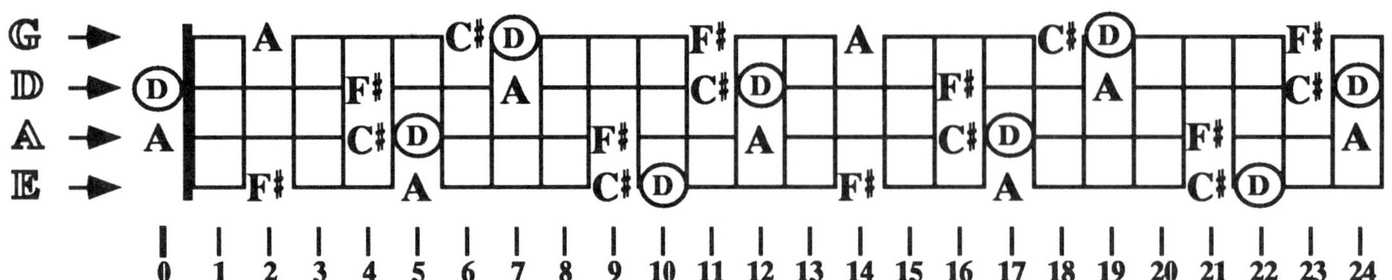

Positions

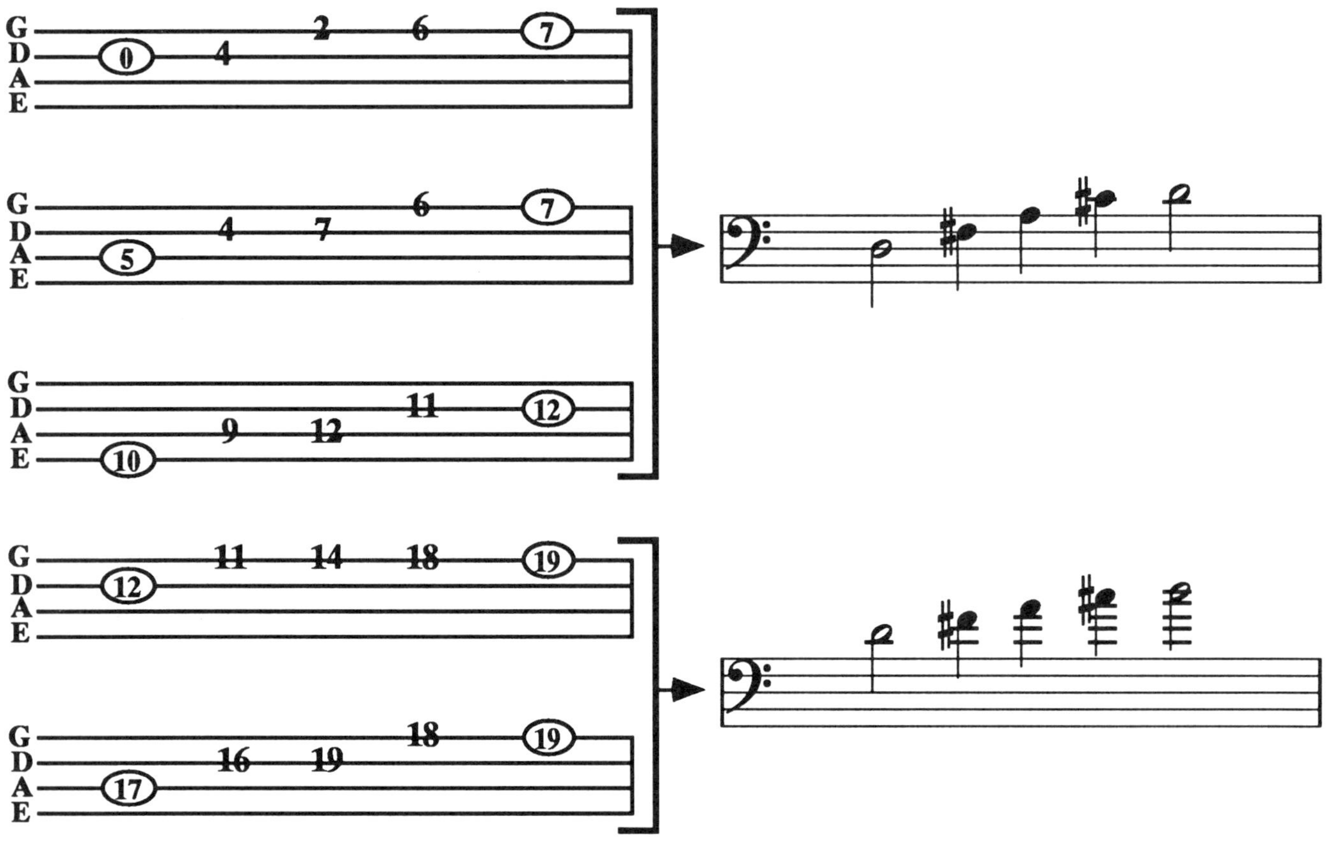

Riff

E MAJOR 7TH

FORMULA - (E) Root (G♯) 3rd (B) 5th (D♯) 7th

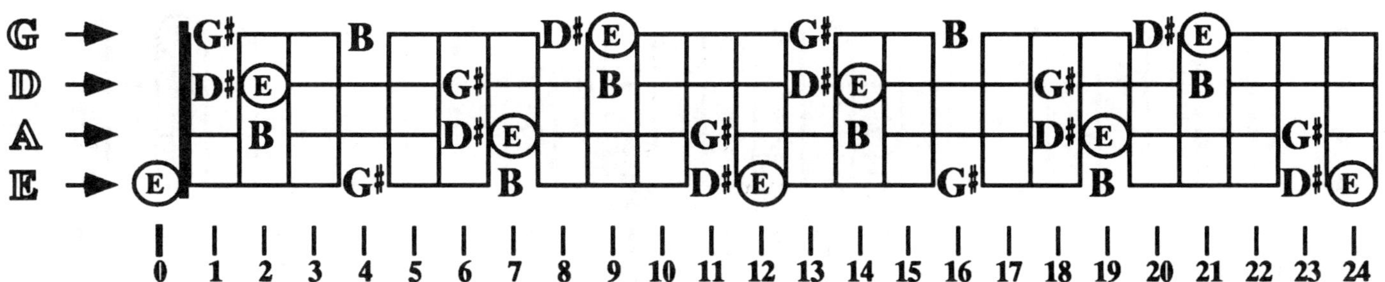

Positions

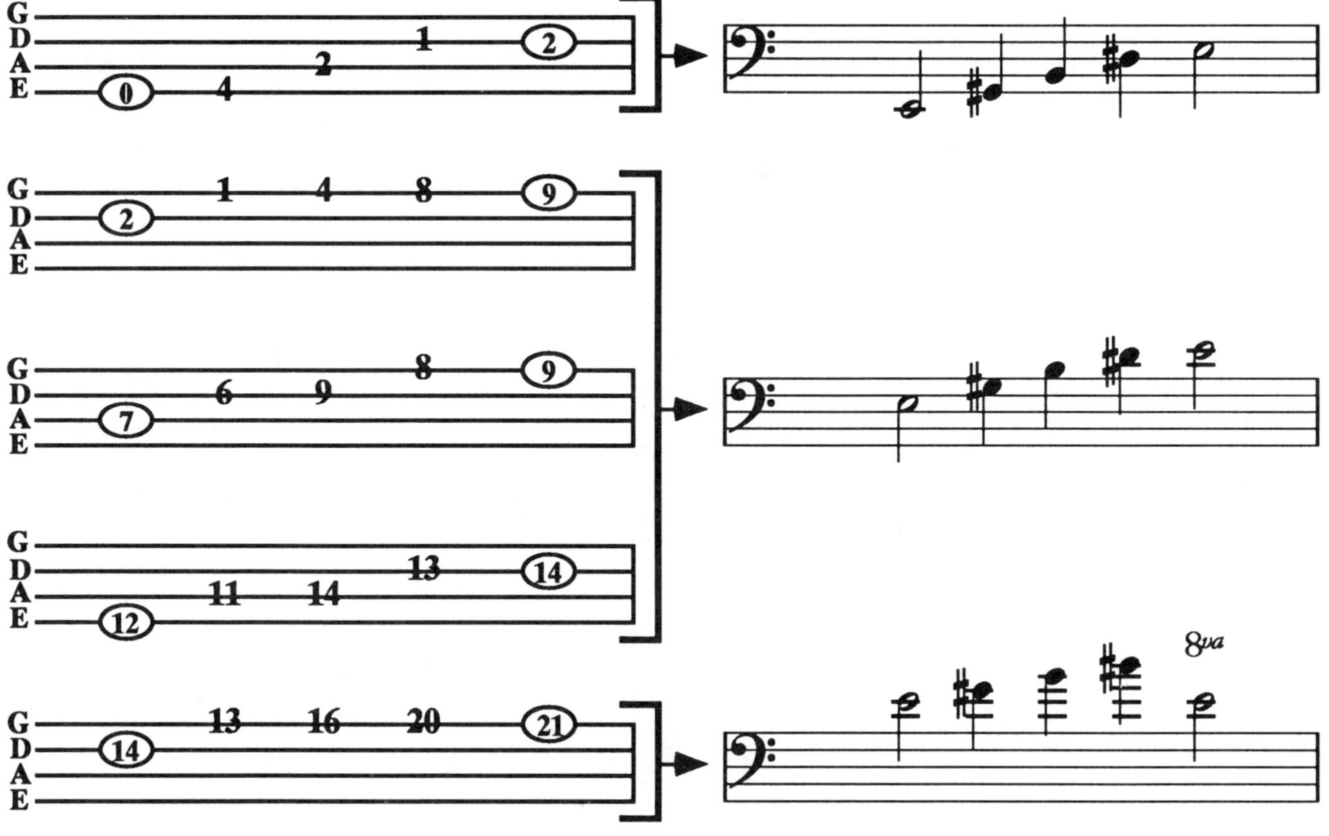

Riff

F MAJOR 7TH

FORMULA - (F) Root (A) 3rd (C) 5th (E) 7th

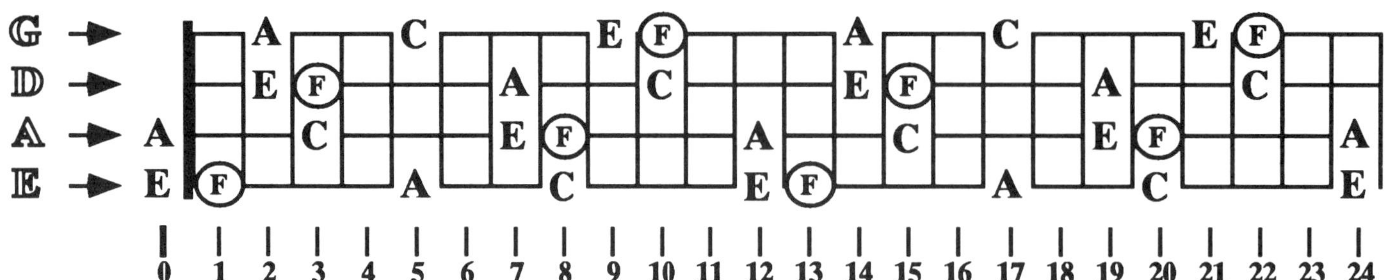

Positions

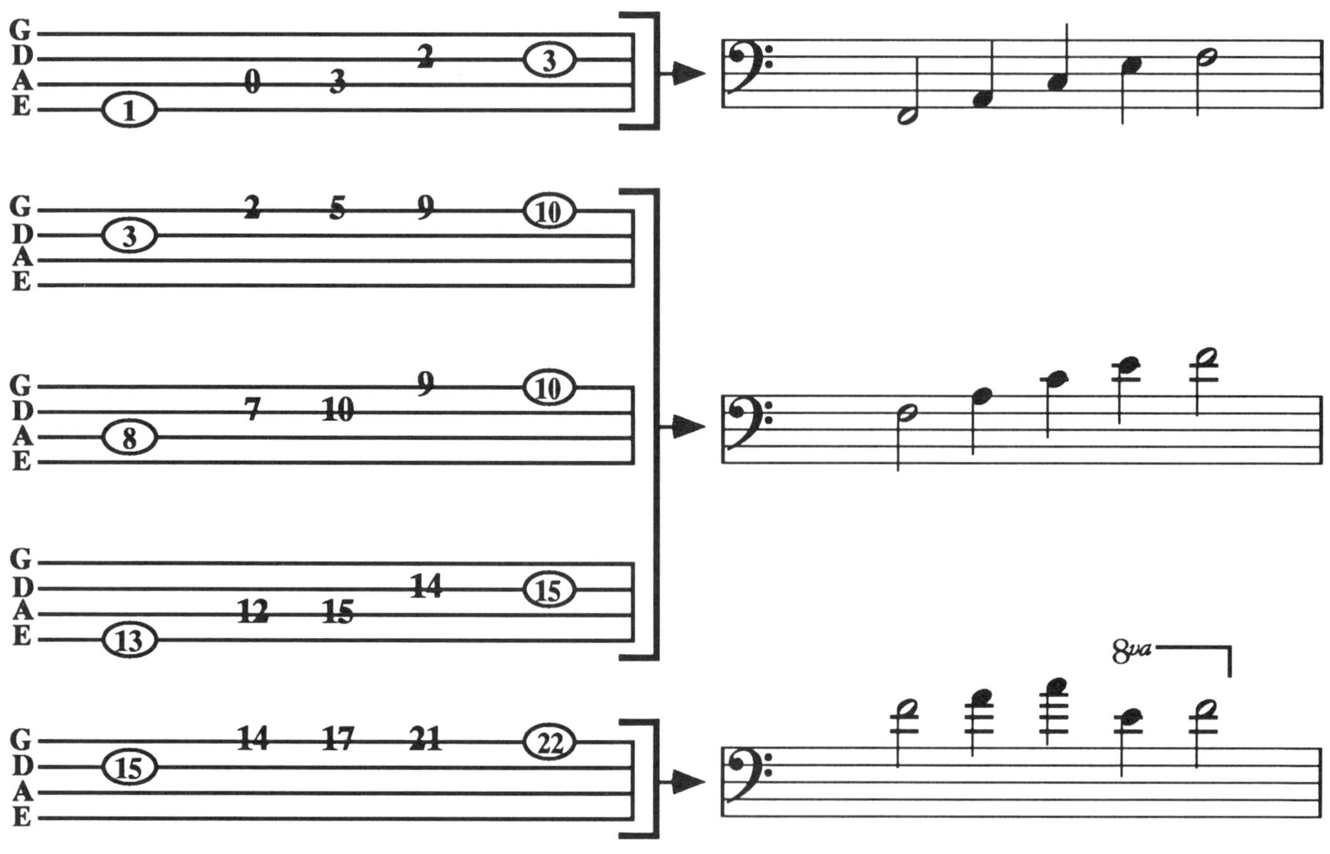

Riff

G MAJOR 7TH
FORMULA - (G) Root (B) 3rd (D) 5th (F♯) 7th

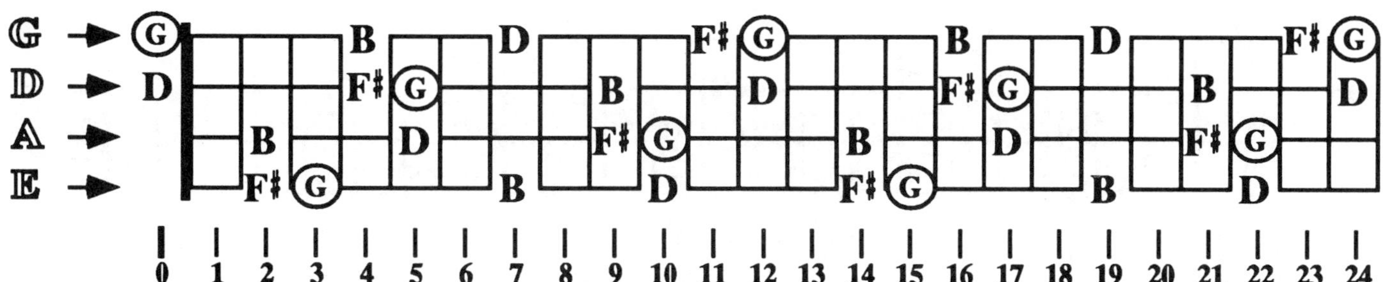

Positions

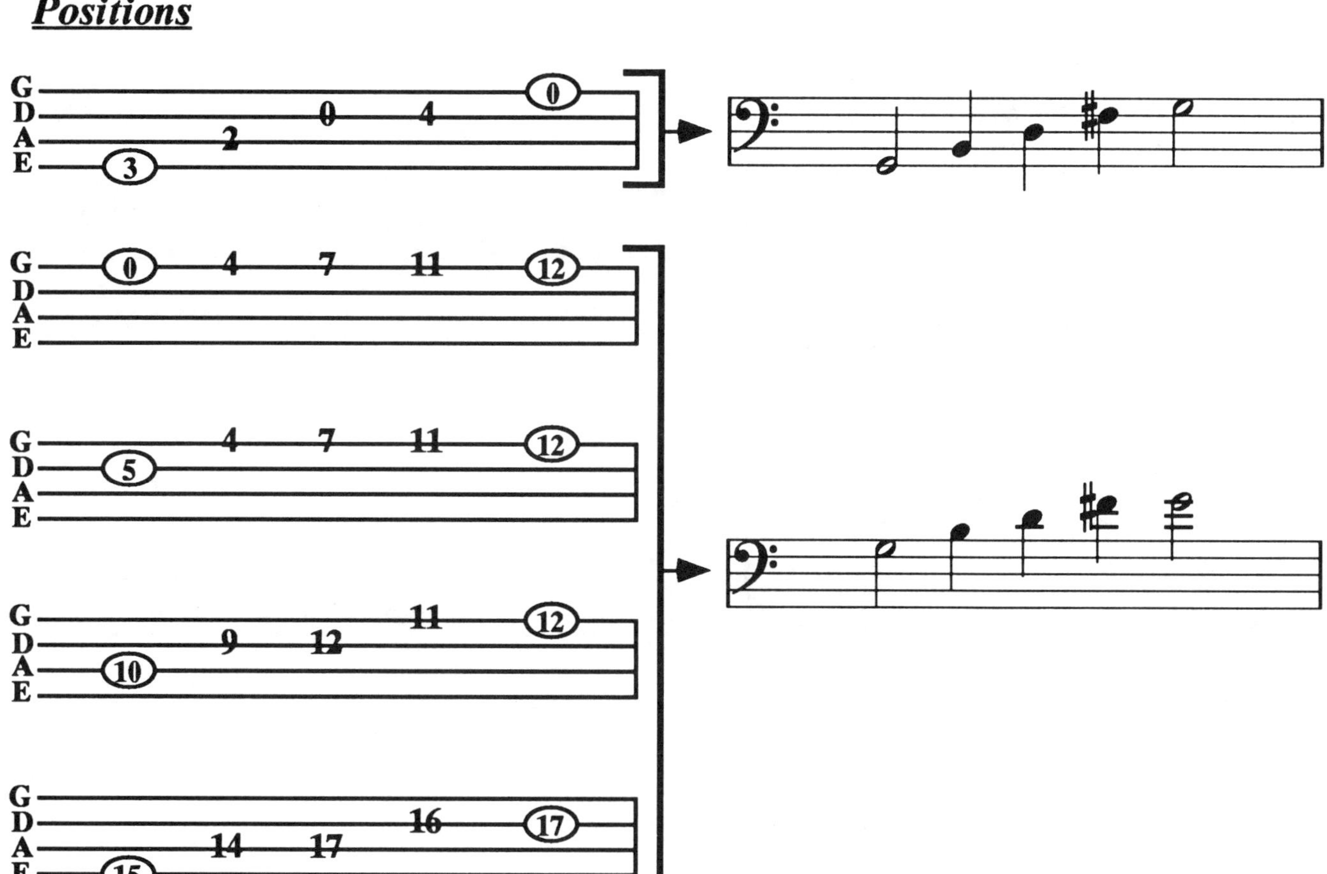

Riff

A MAJOR 7TH

FORMULA - (A) Root (C♯) 3rd (E) 5th (G♯) 7th

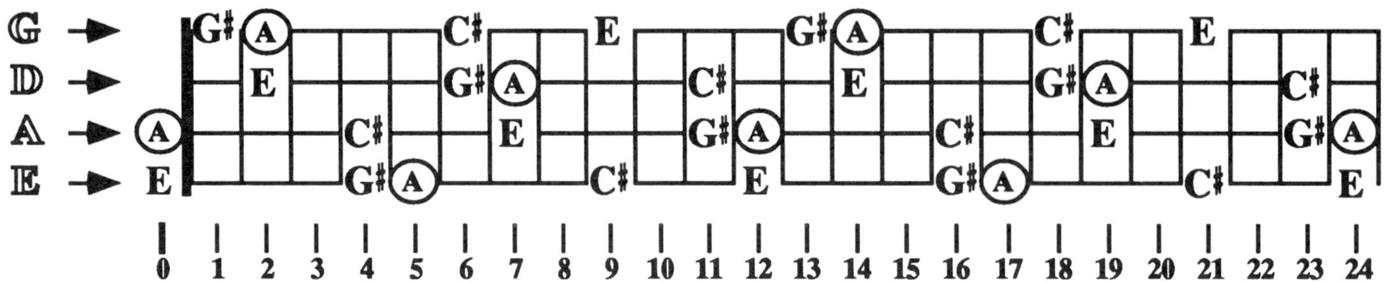

Positions

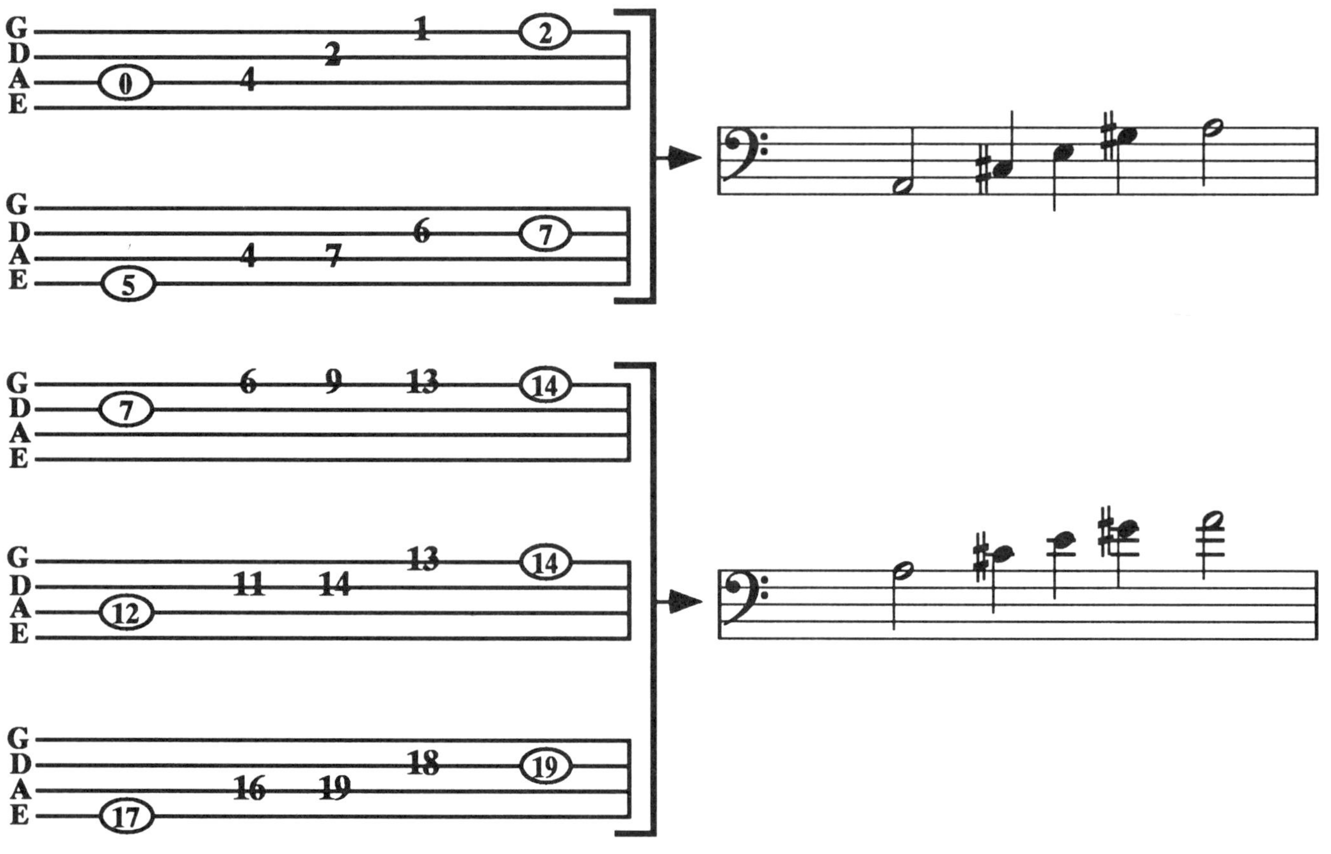

Riff

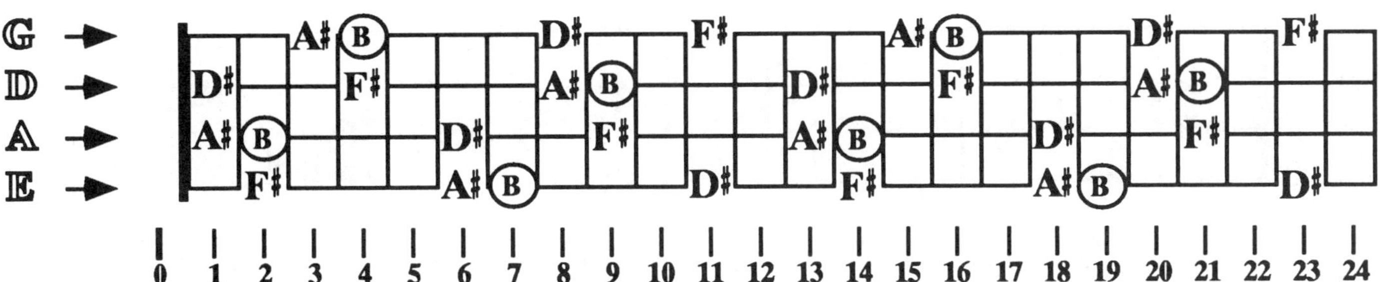

B MAJOR 7TH

FORMULA - (B) Root (D♯) 3rd (F♯) 5th (A♯) 7th

Positions

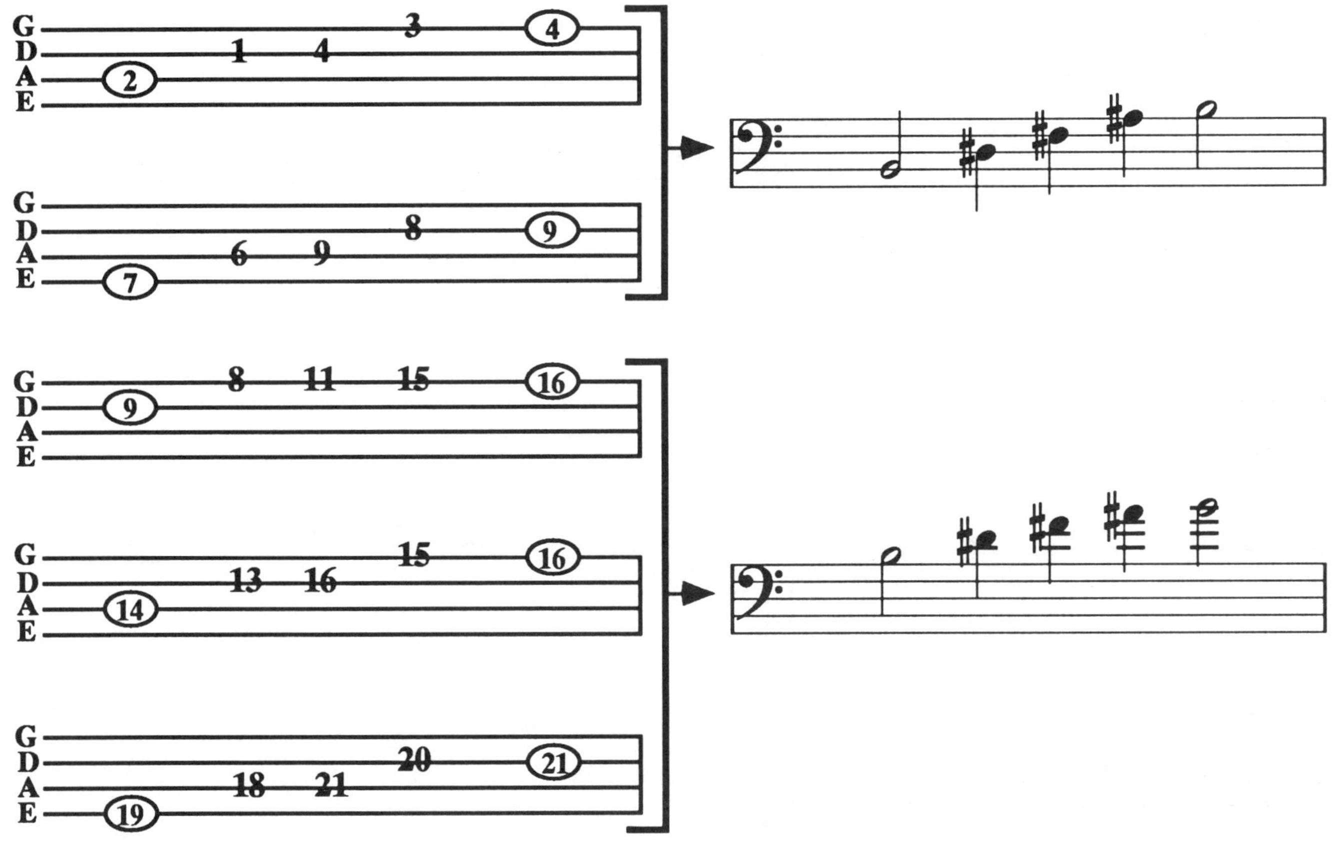

Riff

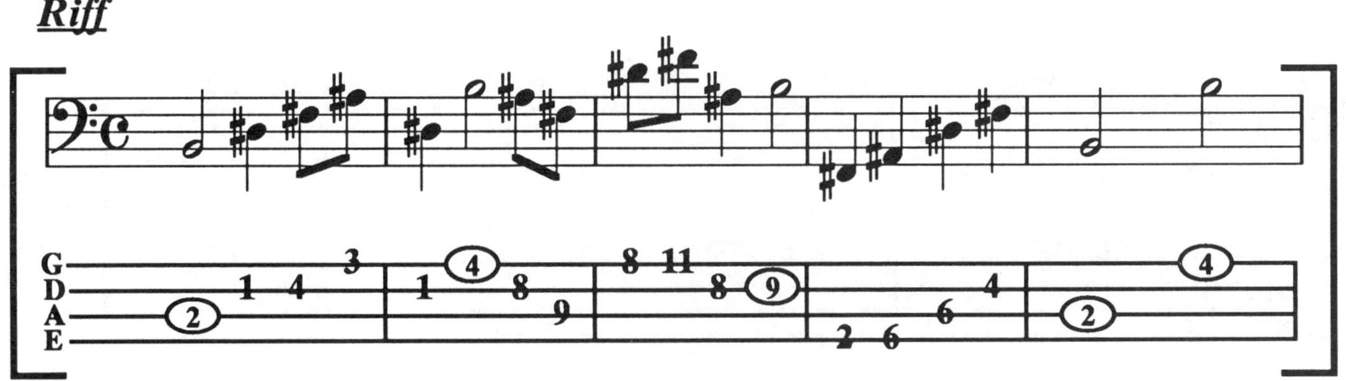

C MAJOR 7TH ♭5TH

FORMULA - (C) Root (E) 3rd (G♭) ♭5th (B) 7th

C Maj. 7-5

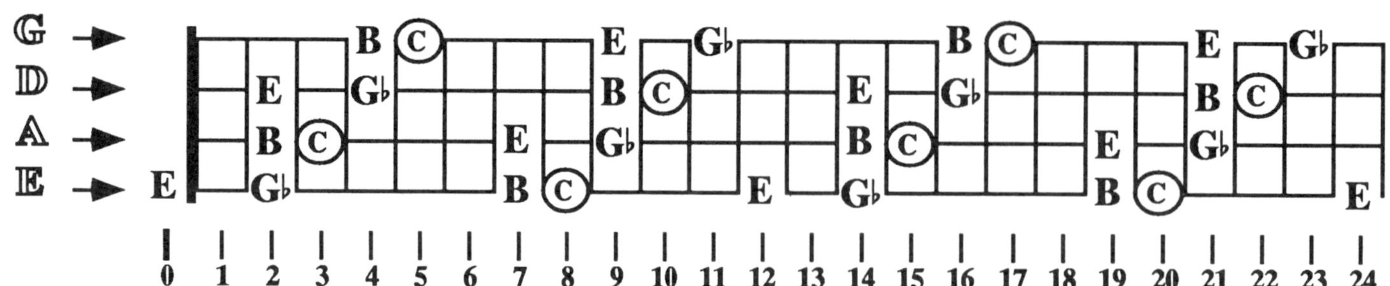

Positions

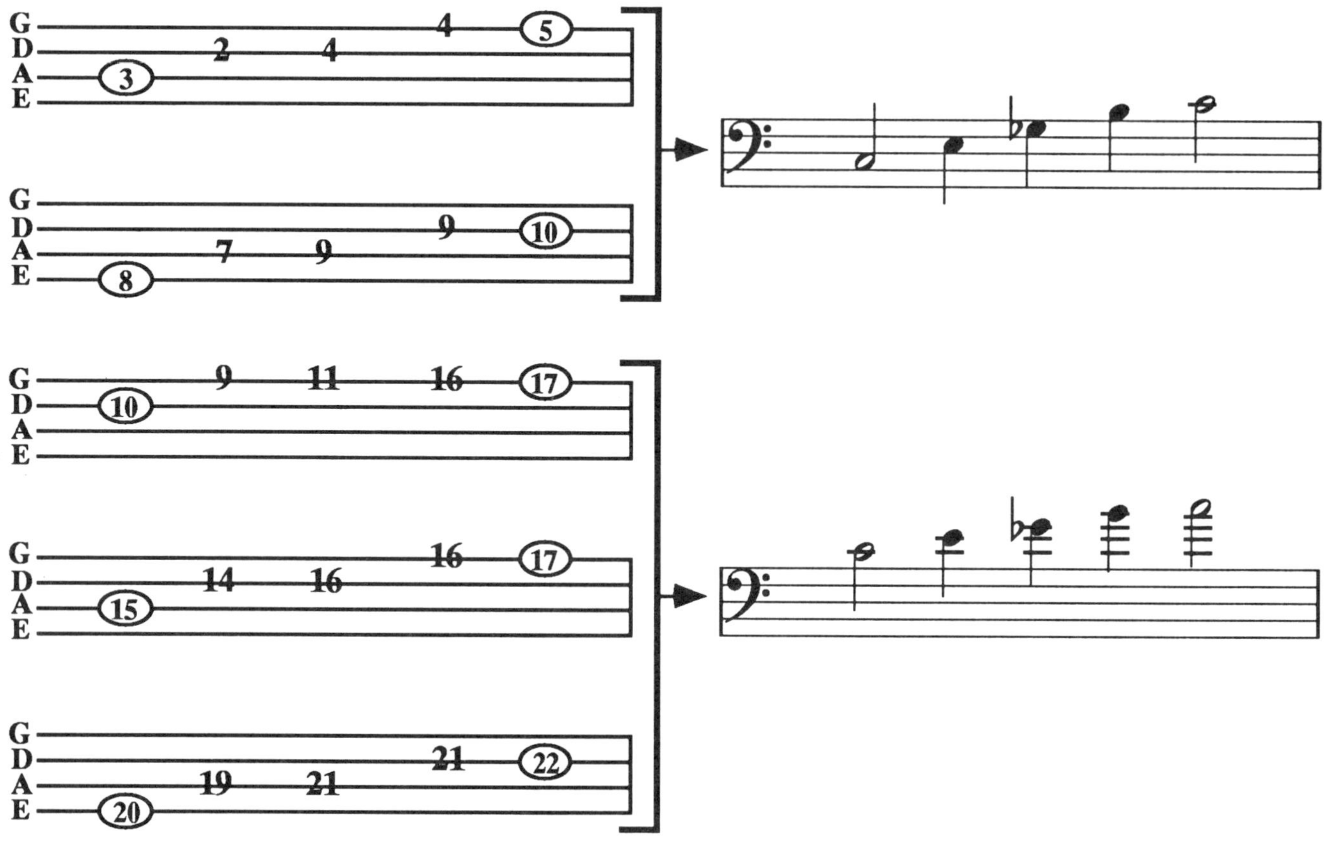

Riff

D MAJOR 7TH ♭5TH

D Maj. 7-5

FORMULA - (D) Root (F♯) 3rd (A♭) ♭5th (C♯) 7th

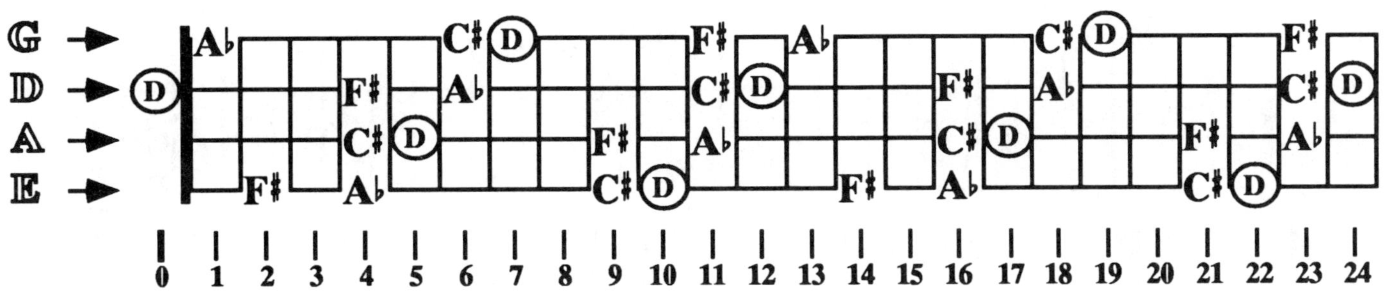

Positions

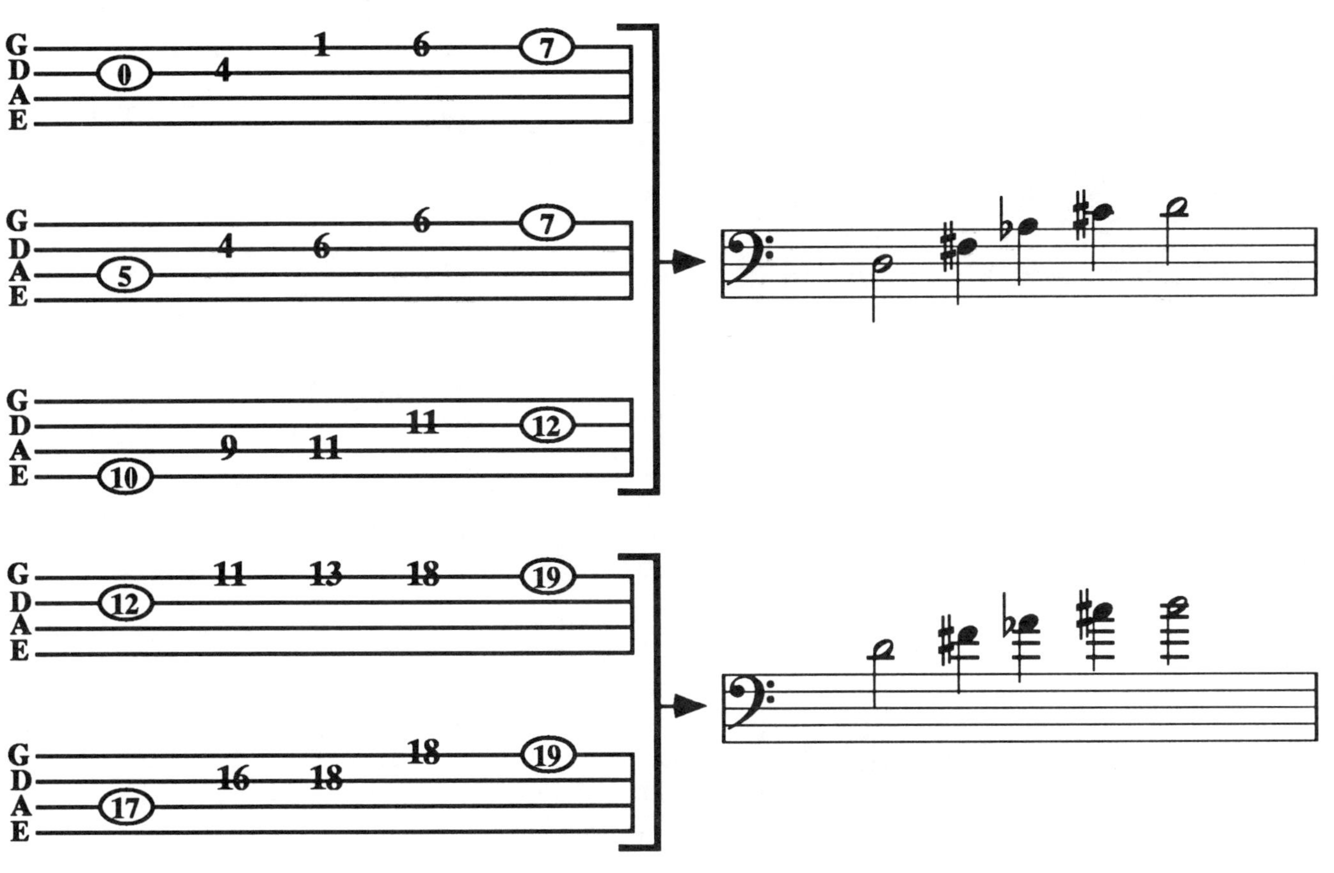

Riff

E MAJOR 7TH ♭5TH

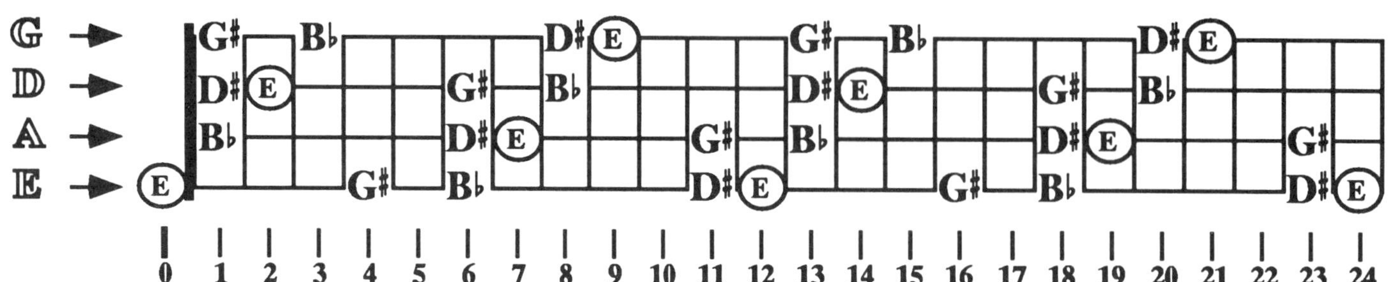

FORMULA - (E) Root (G♯) 3rd (B♭) ♭5th (D♯) 7th

E Maj. 7-5

Positions

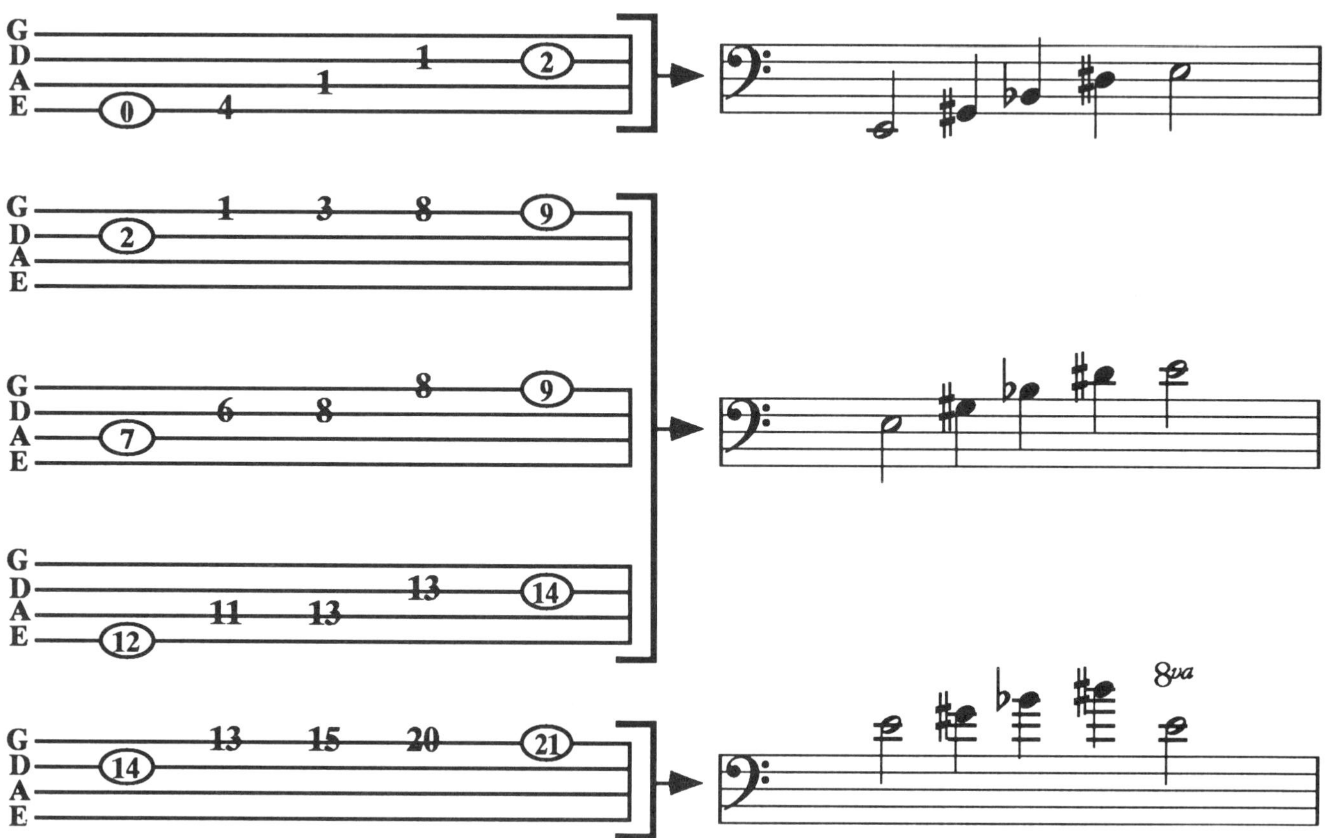

Riff

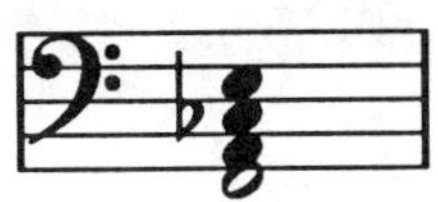

F MAJOR 7TH ♭5TH

FORMULA - (F) Root (A) 3rd (C♭) ♭5th (E) 7th

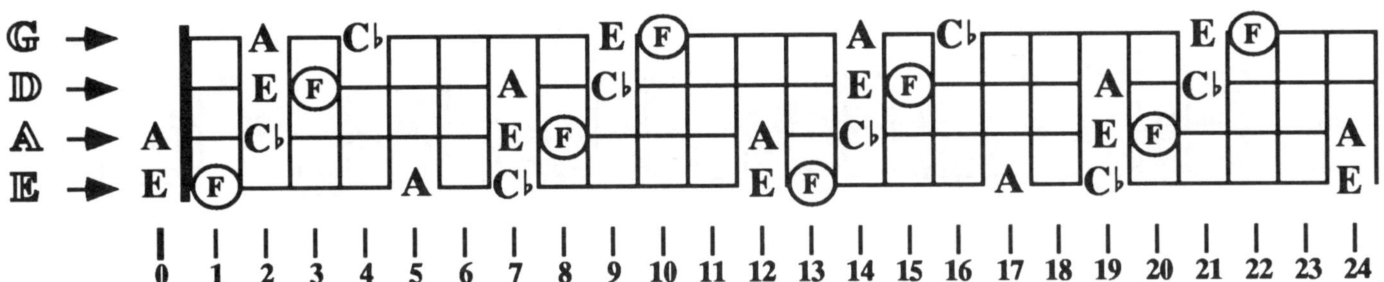

Positions

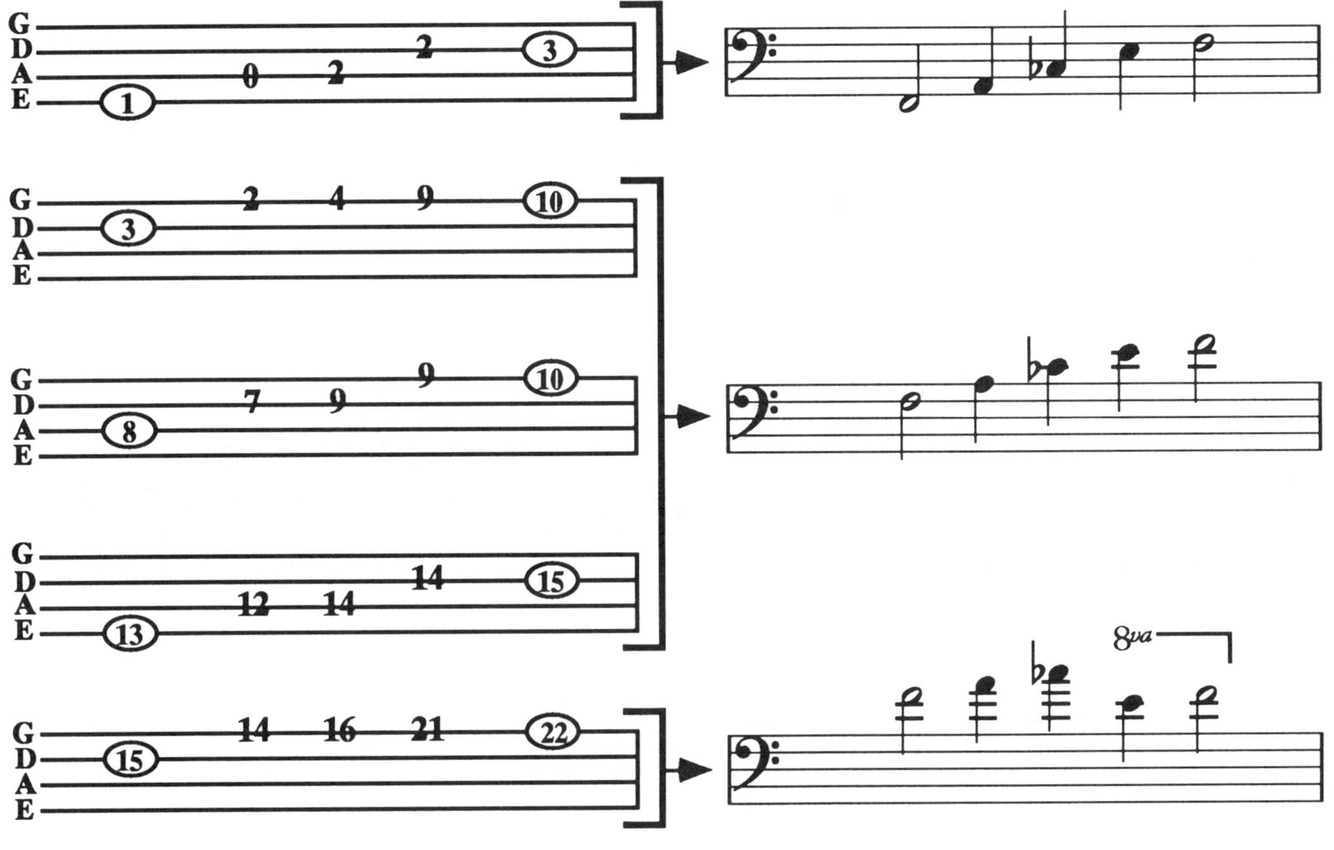

Riff

G MAJOR 7TH ♭5TH

FORMULA - (G) Root (B) 3rd (D♭) ♭5th (F♯) 7th

G Maj. 7-5

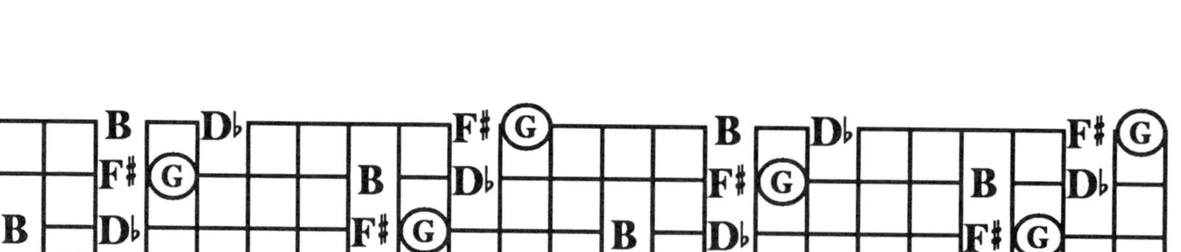

Positions

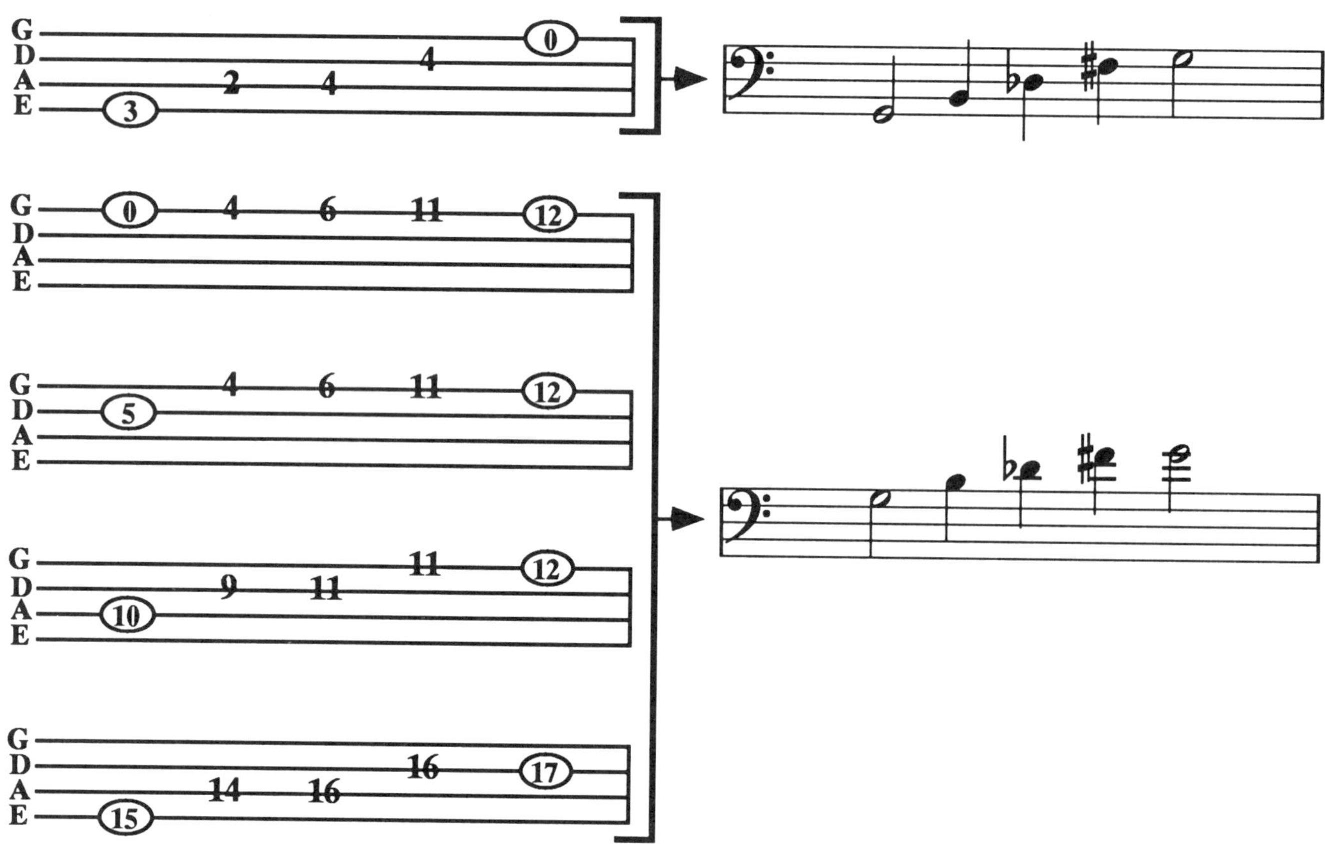

Riff

A MAJOR 7TH ♭5TH

FORMULA - (A) Root (C♯) 3rd (E♭) ♭5th (G♯) 7th

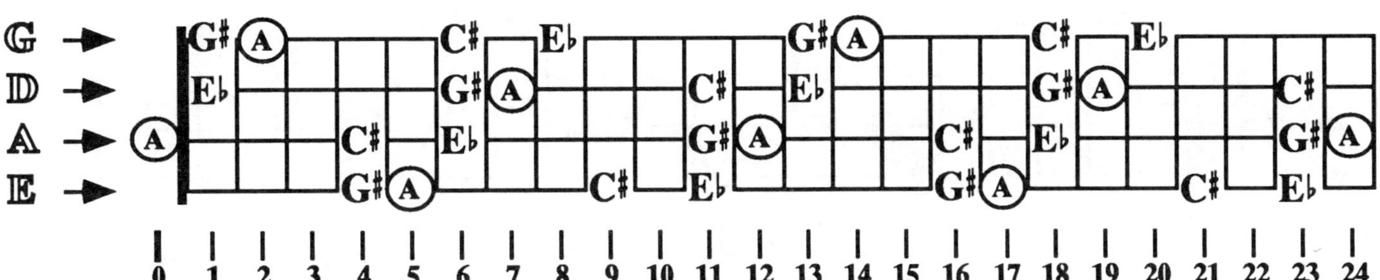

Positions

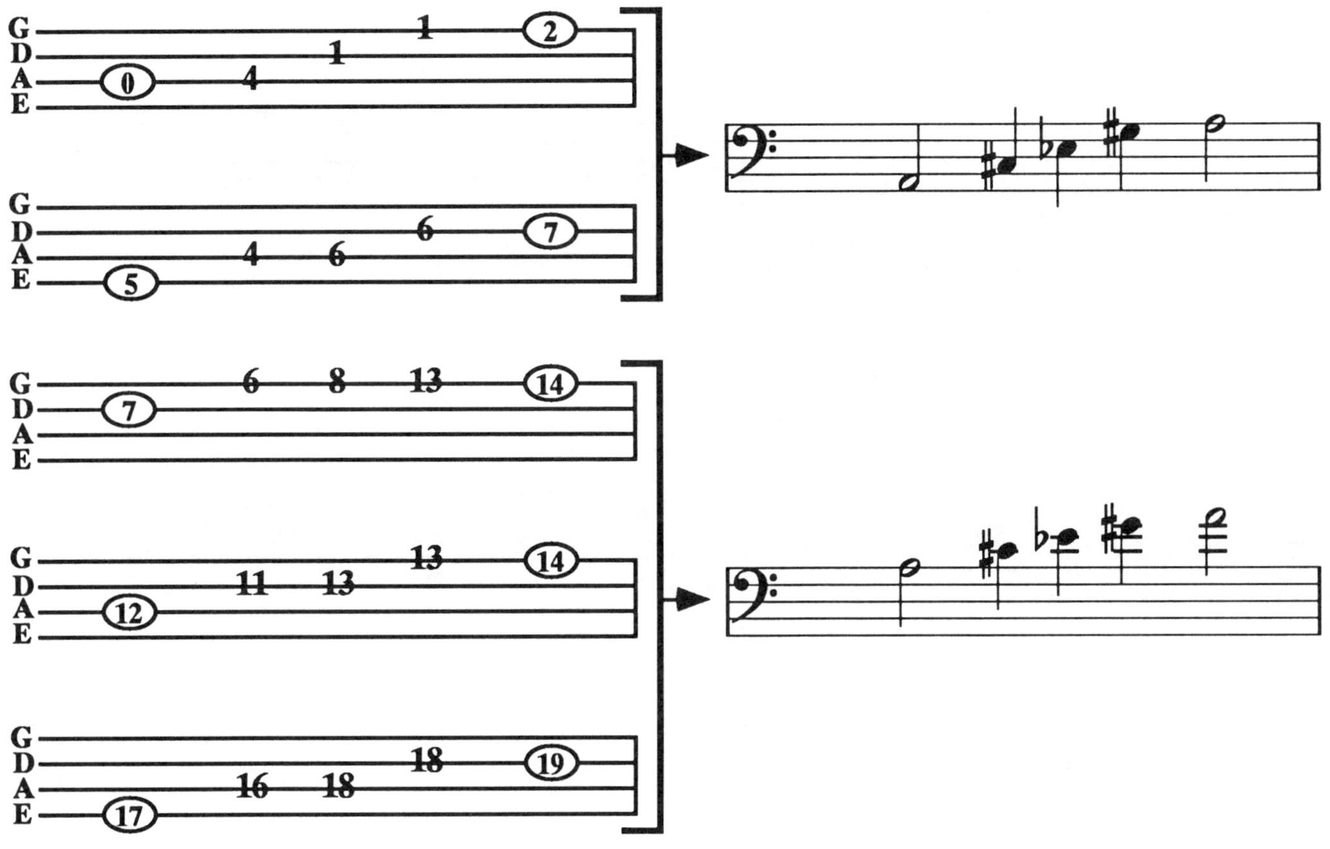

Riff

27

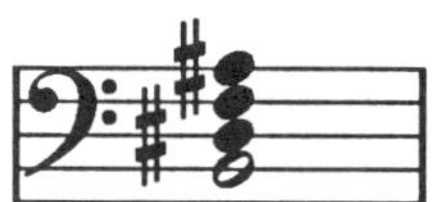

B MAJOR 7TH ♭5TH

FORMULA - (B) Root (D♯) 3rd (F) ♭5th (A♯) 7th

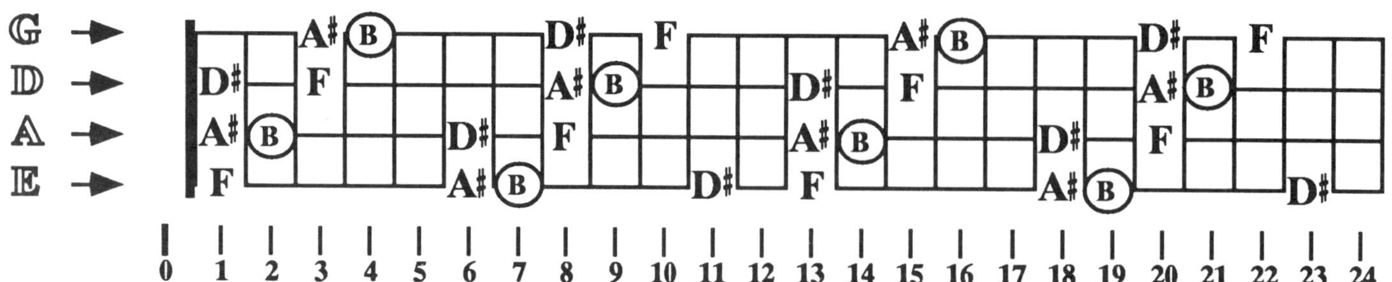

Positions

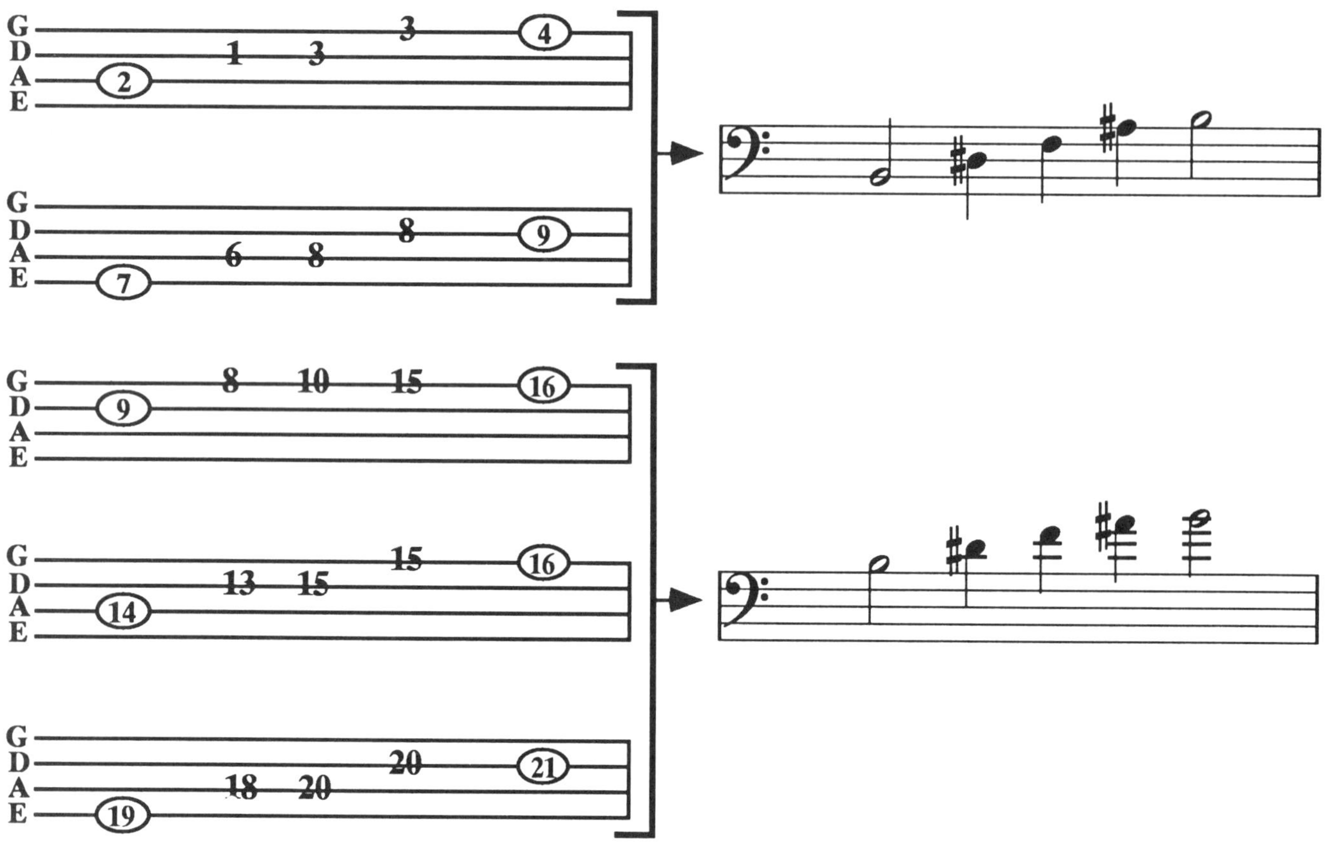

Riff

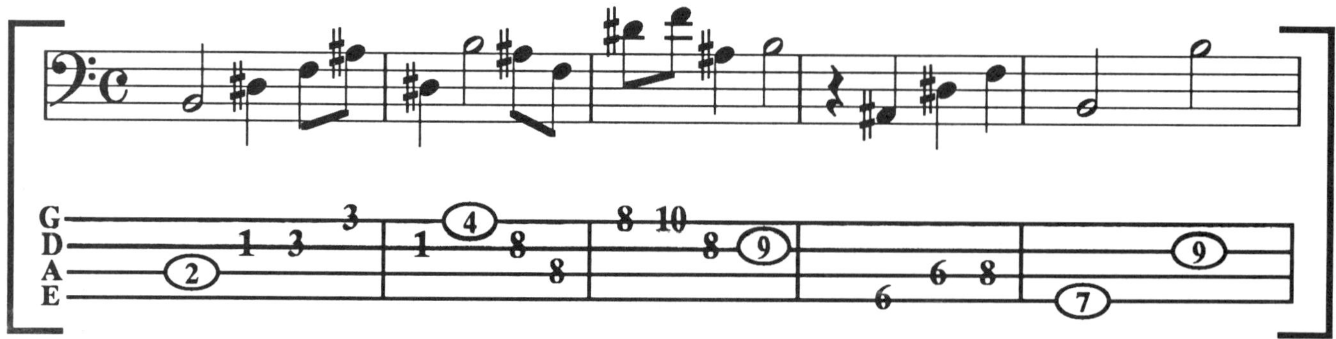

C MAJOR 9TH

FORMULA - (C) Root (E) 3rd (G) 5th (B) 7th (D) 9th

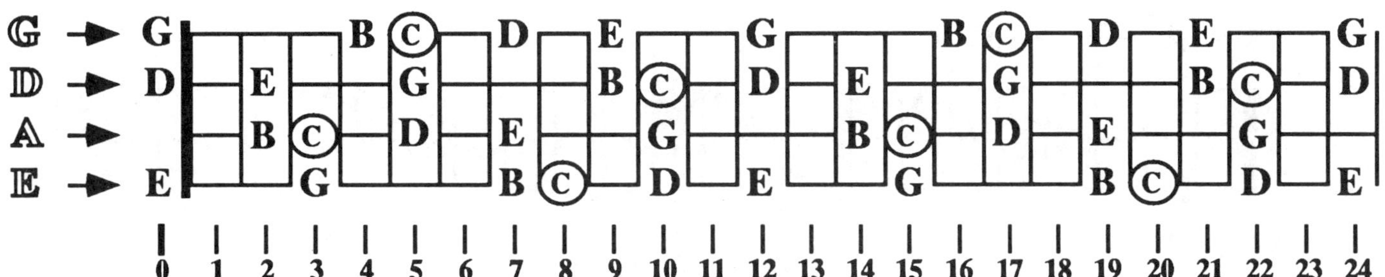

Positions

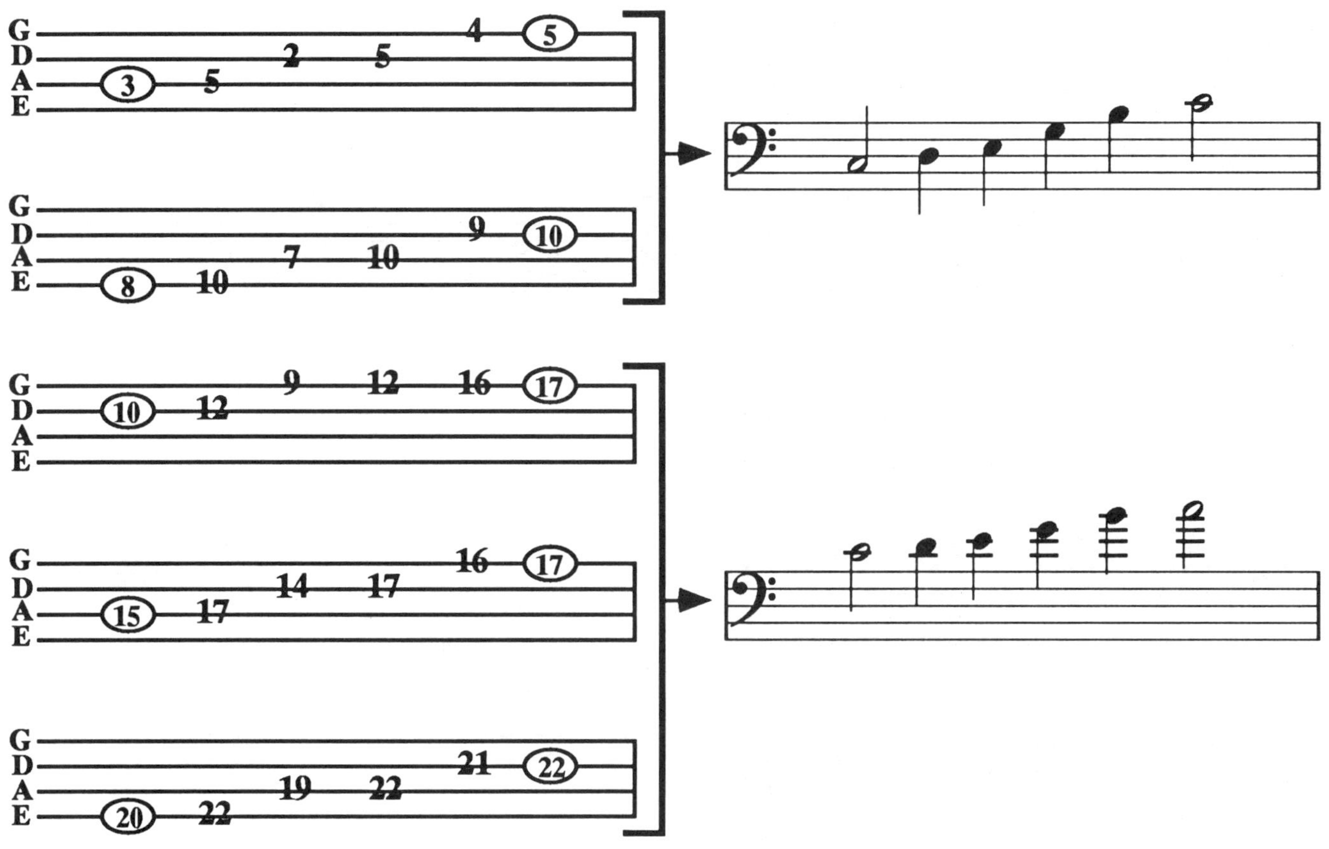

Riff

D MAJOR 9TH

D Maj. 9

FORMULA - (D) Root (F♯) 3rd (A) 5th (C♯) 7th (E) 9th

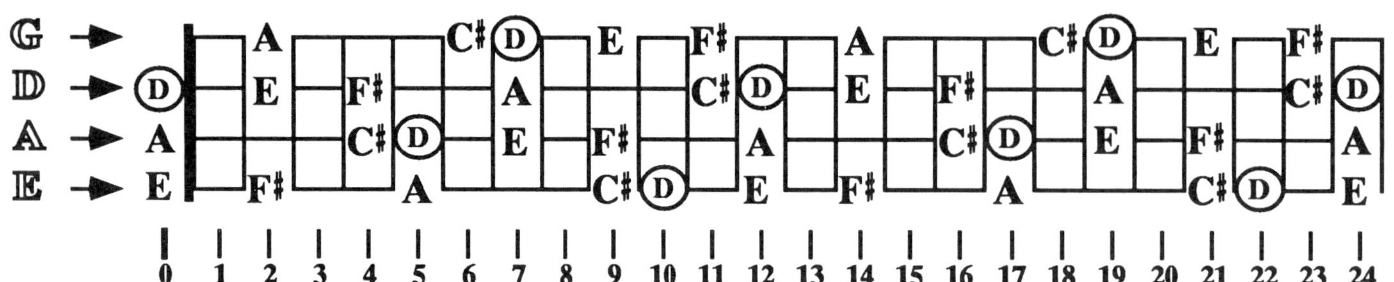

Positions

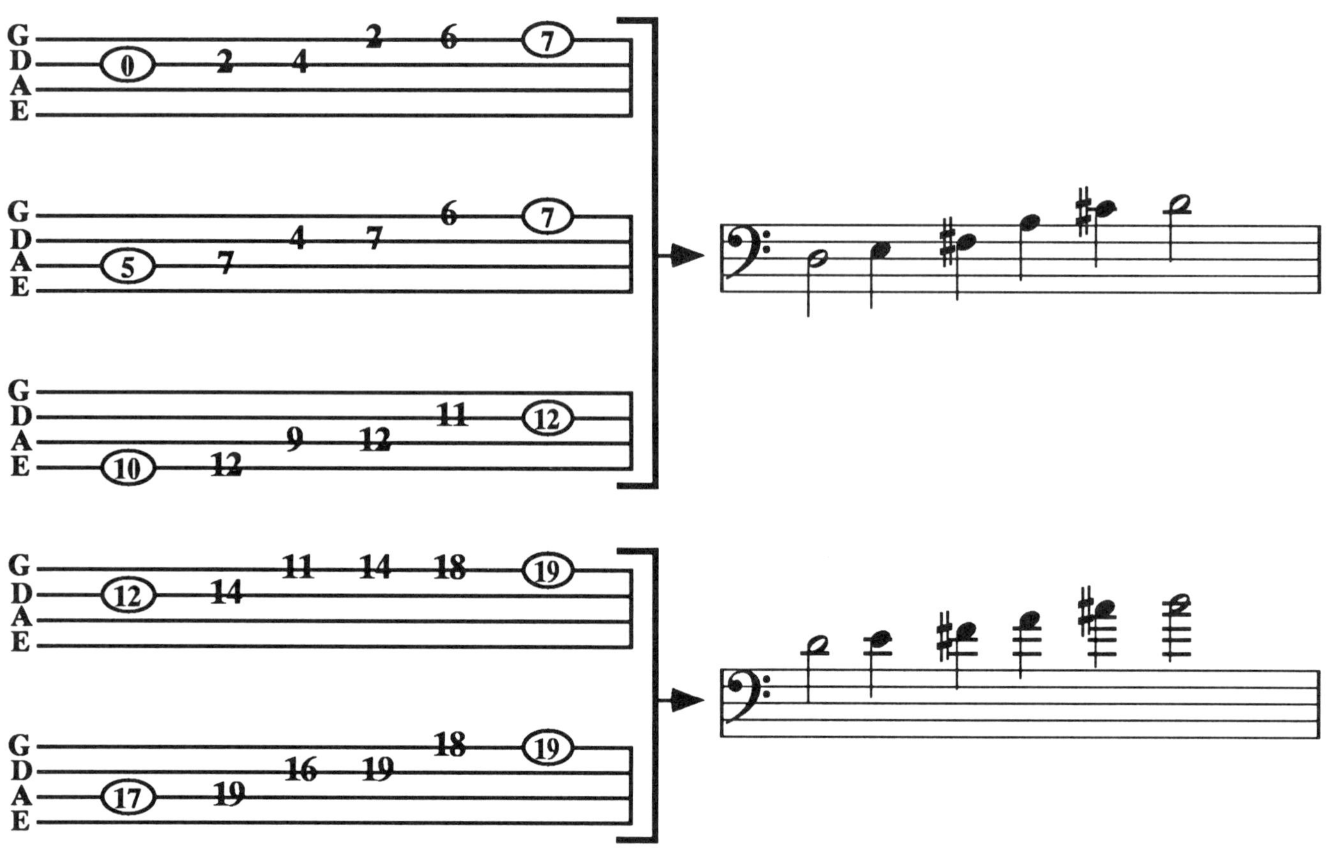

Riff

E MAJOR 9TH

FORMULA - (E) Root (G♯) 3rd (B) 5th (D♯) 7th (F♯) 9th

E Maj. 9

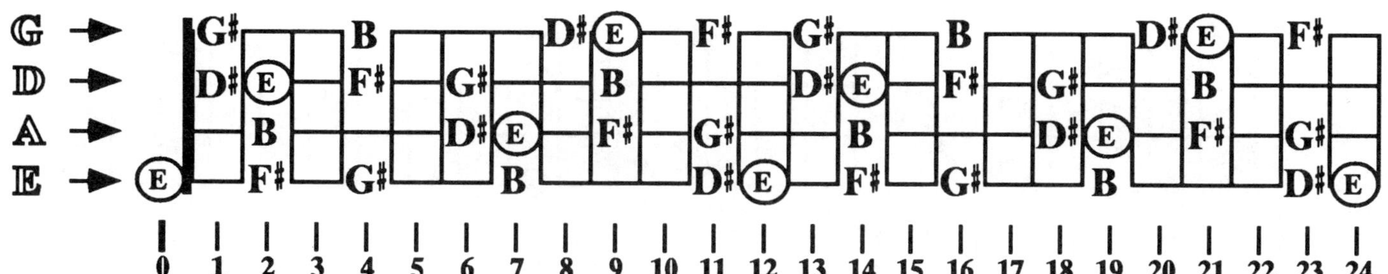

Positions

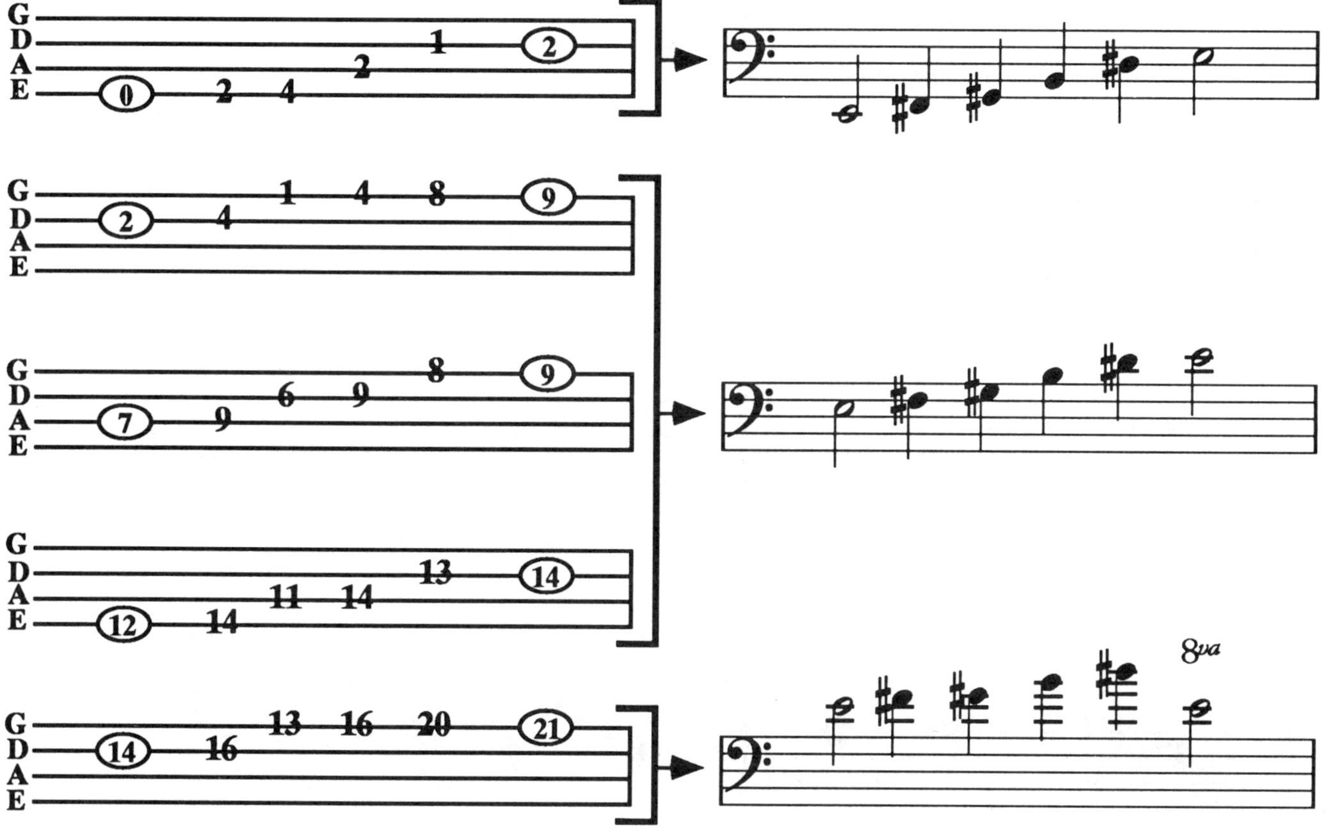

Riff

F MAJOR 9TH

FORMULA - (F) Root (A) 3rd (C) 5th (E) 7th (G) 9th

F Maj. 9

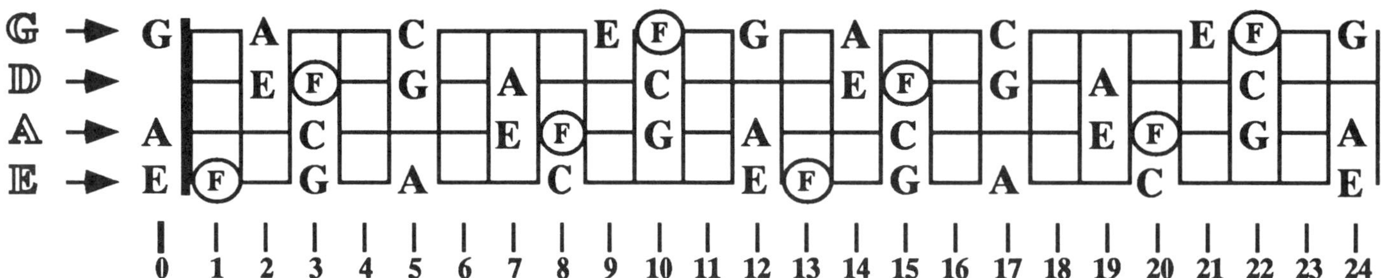

Positions

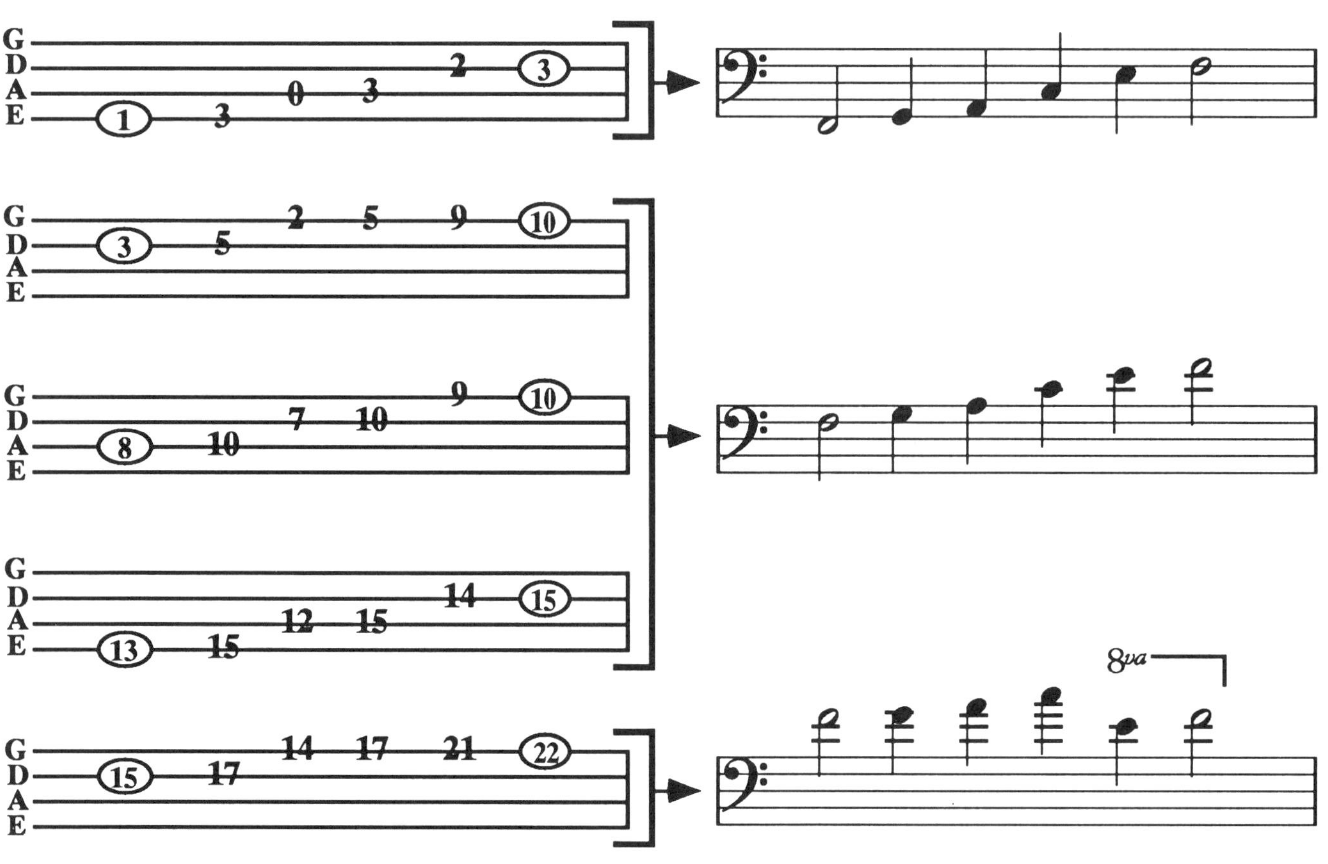

Riff

G MAJOR 9TH

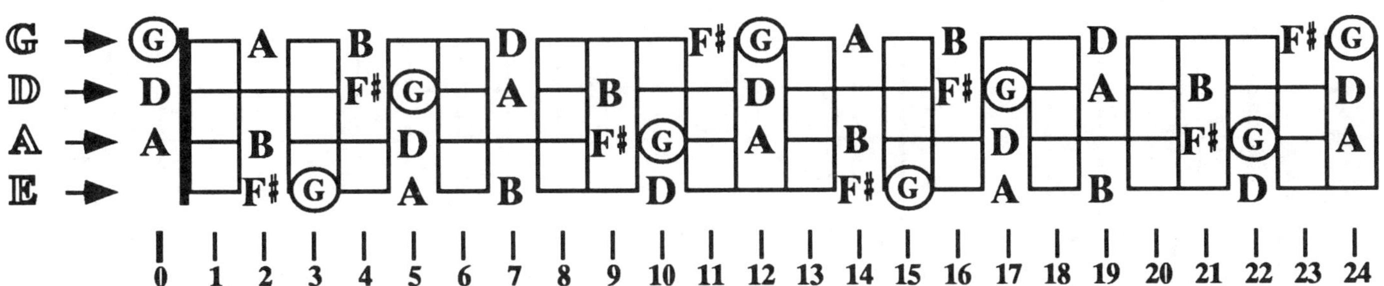

Positions

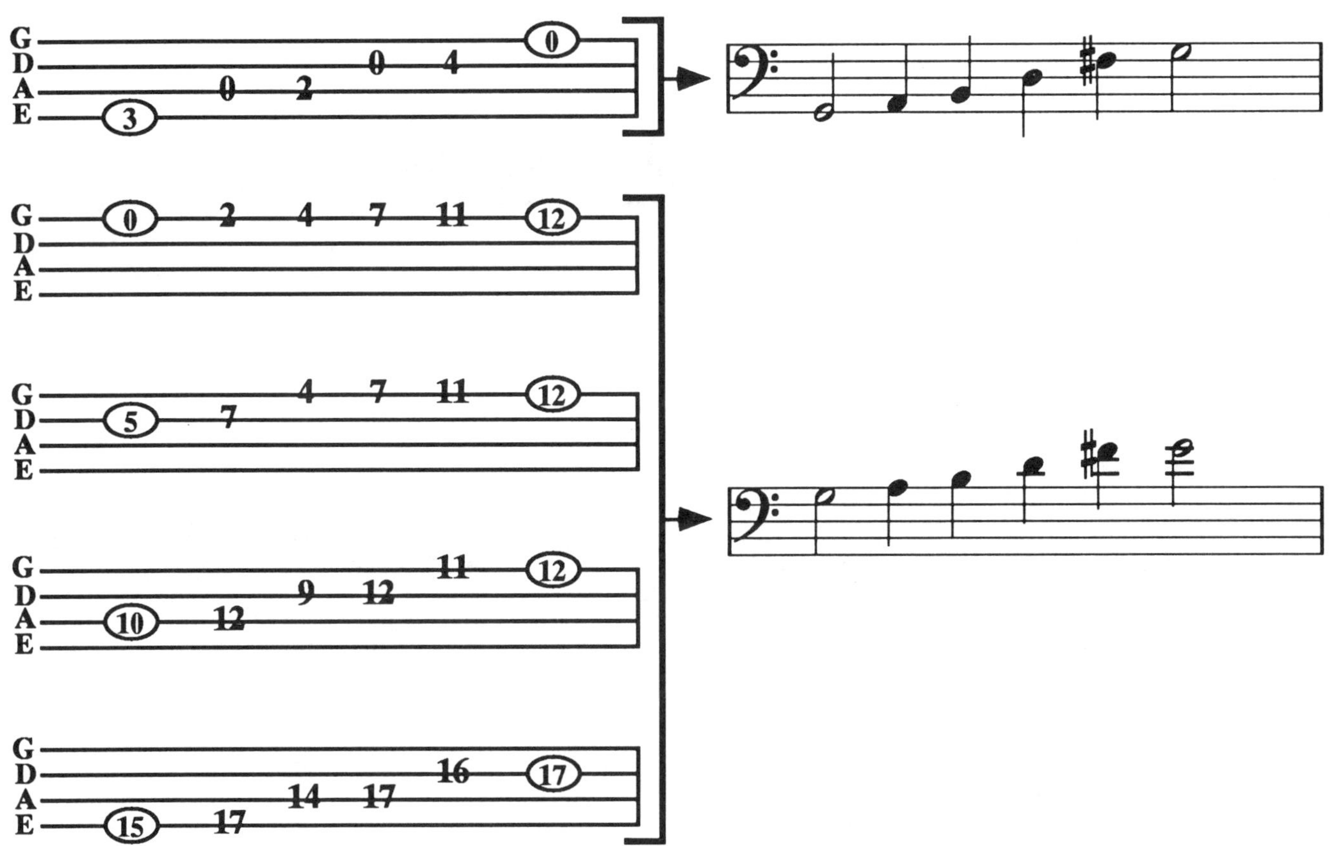

Riff

A MAJOR 9TH

FORMULA - (A) Root (C♯) 3rd (E) 5th (G♯) 7th (B) 9th

A Maj. 9

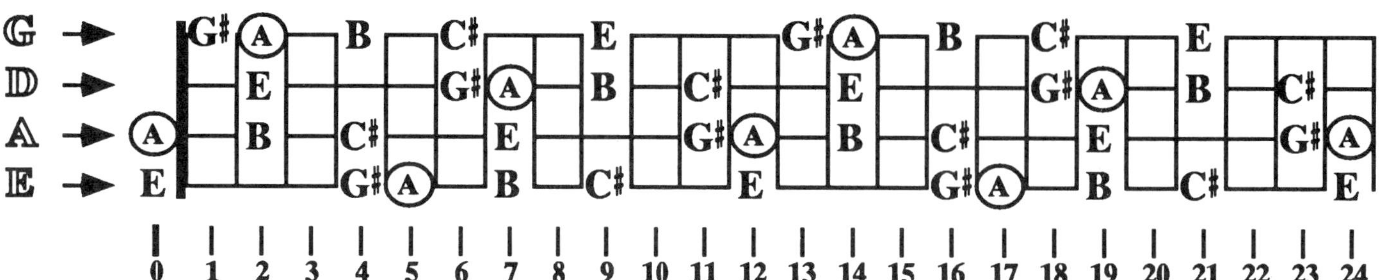

Positions

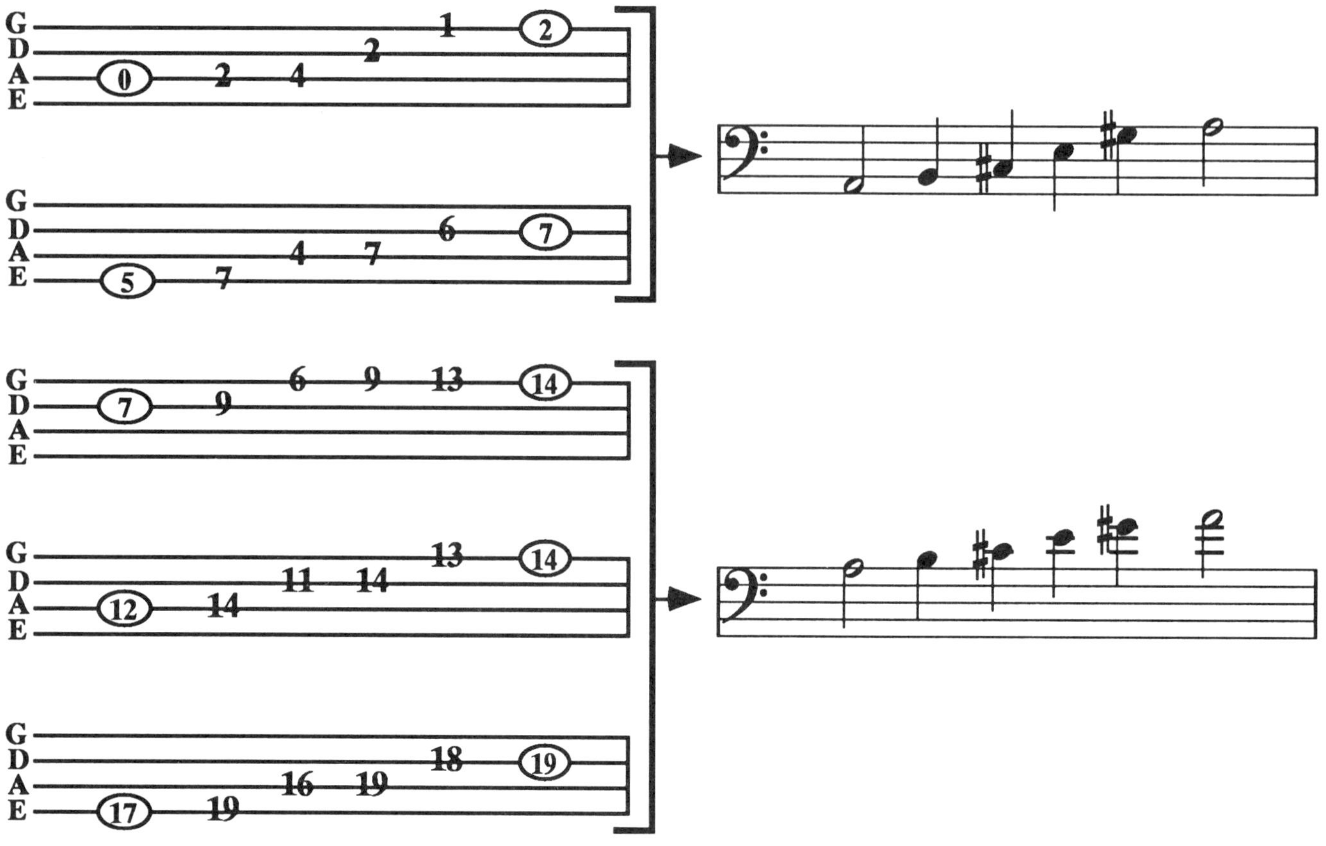

Riff

B MAJOR 9TH

FORMULA - (B) Root (D♯) 3rd (F♯) 5th (A♯) 7th (C♯) 9th

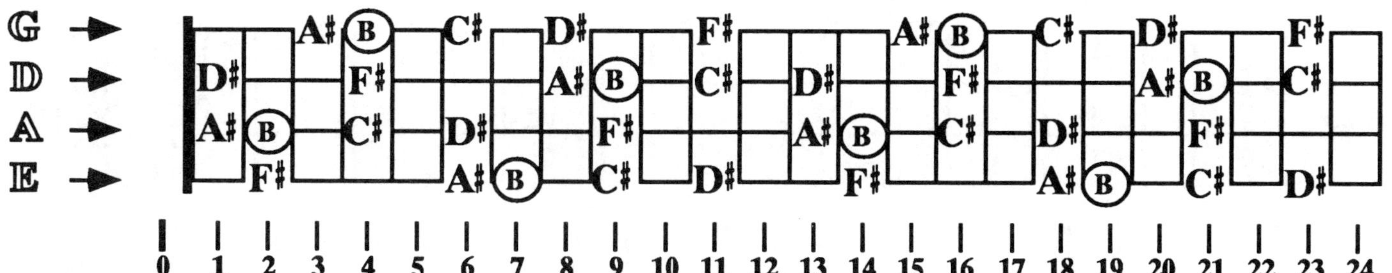

Positions

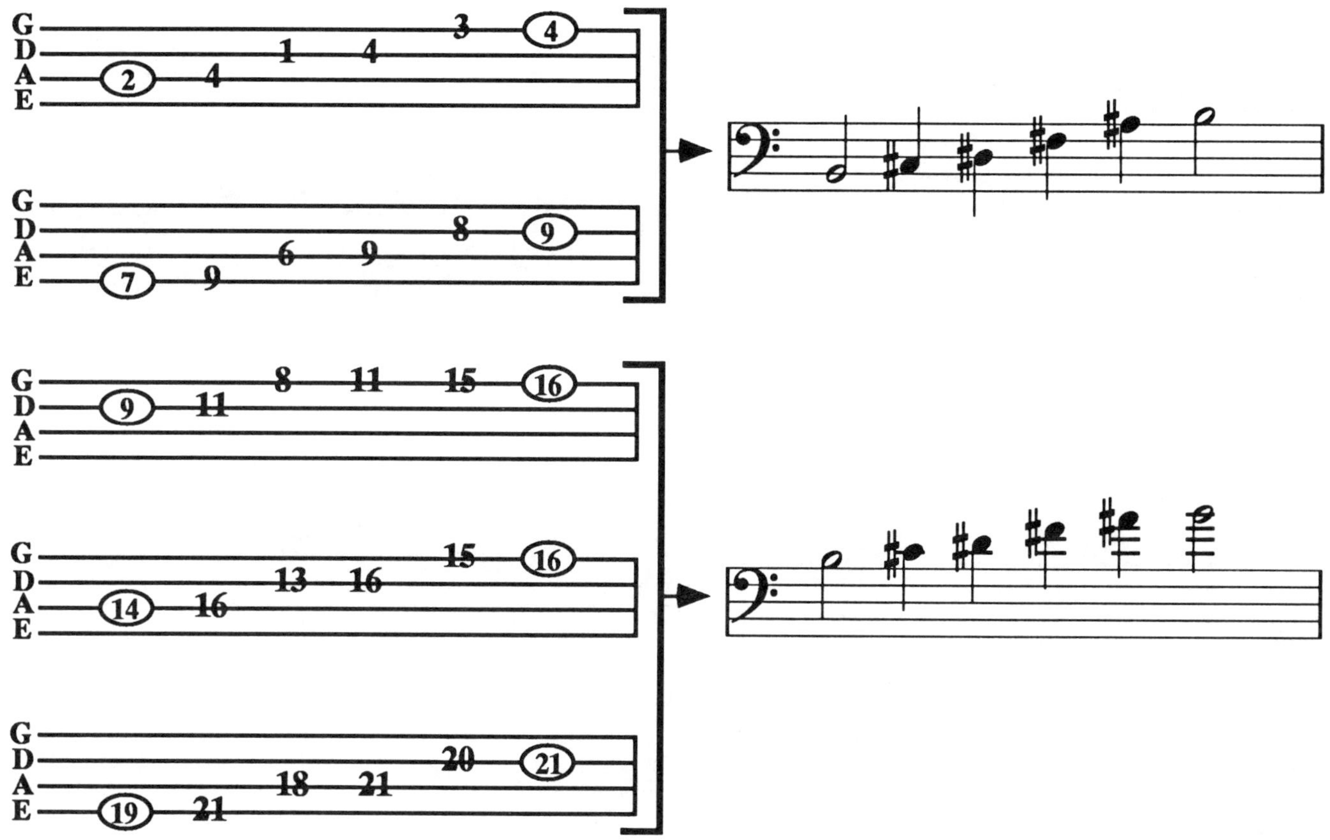

Riff

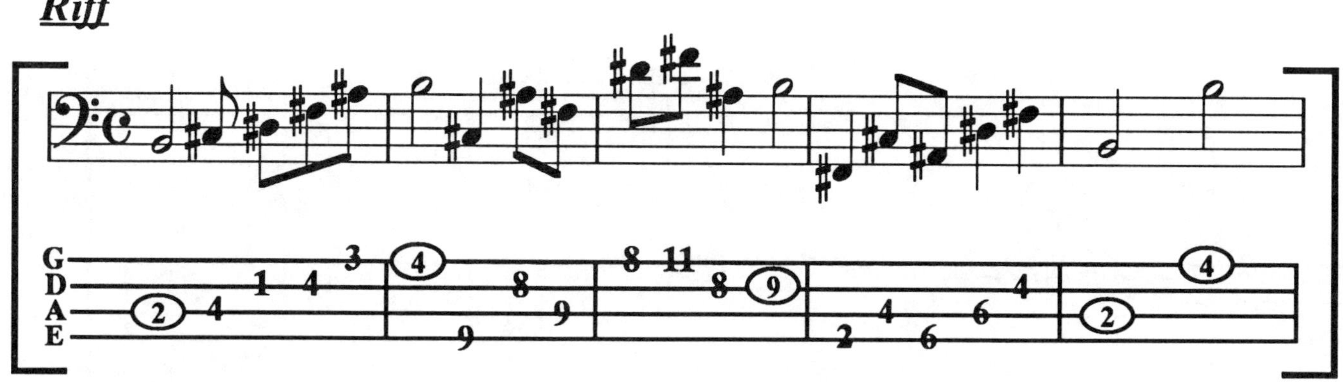

C   MAJOR 6TH-9TH

C Maj. 6/9

FORMULA - (C) Root (E) 3rd (G) 5th (A) 6th (D) 9th

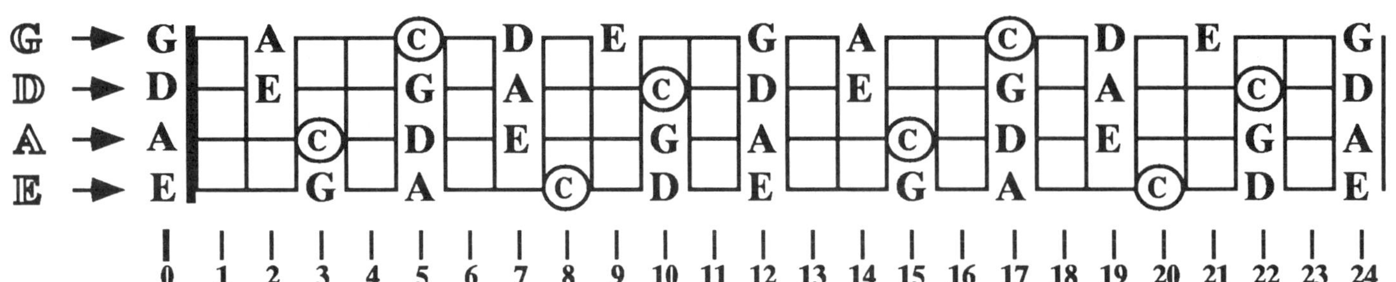

Positions

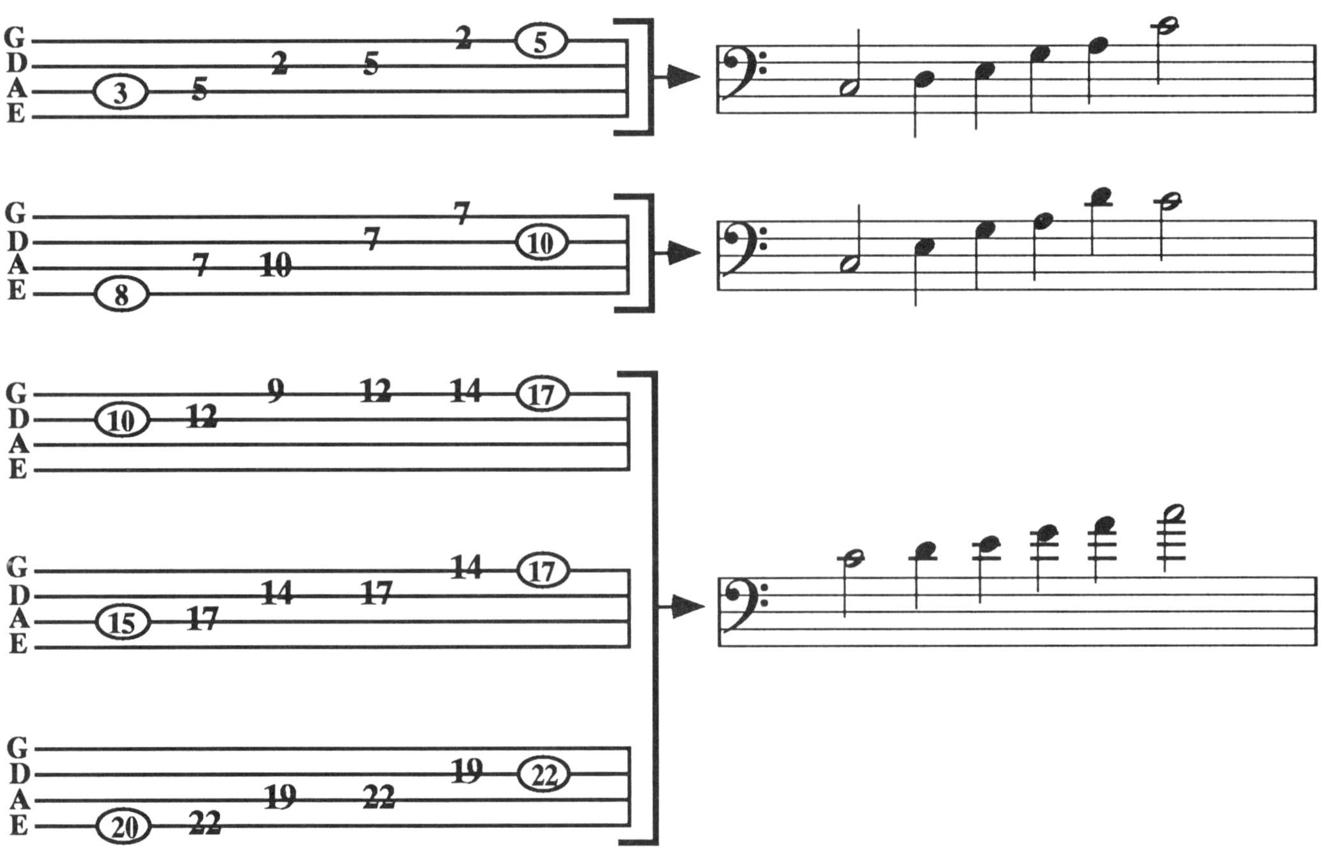

Riff

D MAJOR 6TH-9TH

FORMULA - (D) Root (F♯) 3rd (A) 5th (B) 6th (E) 9th

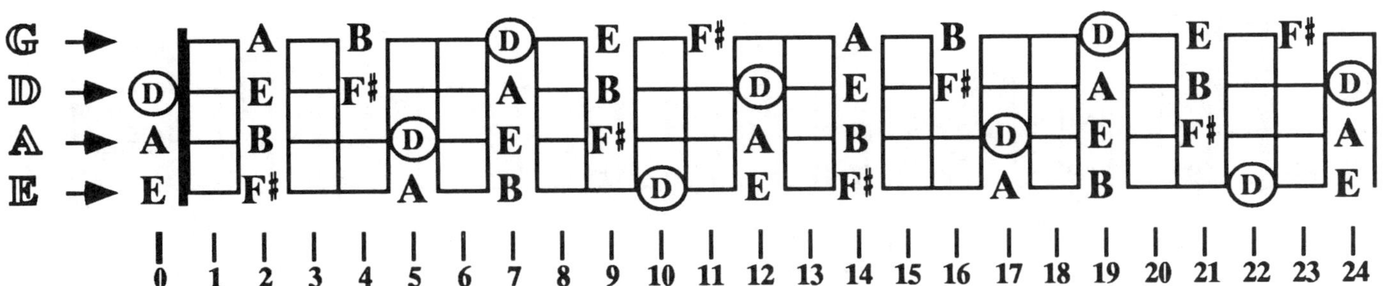

Positions

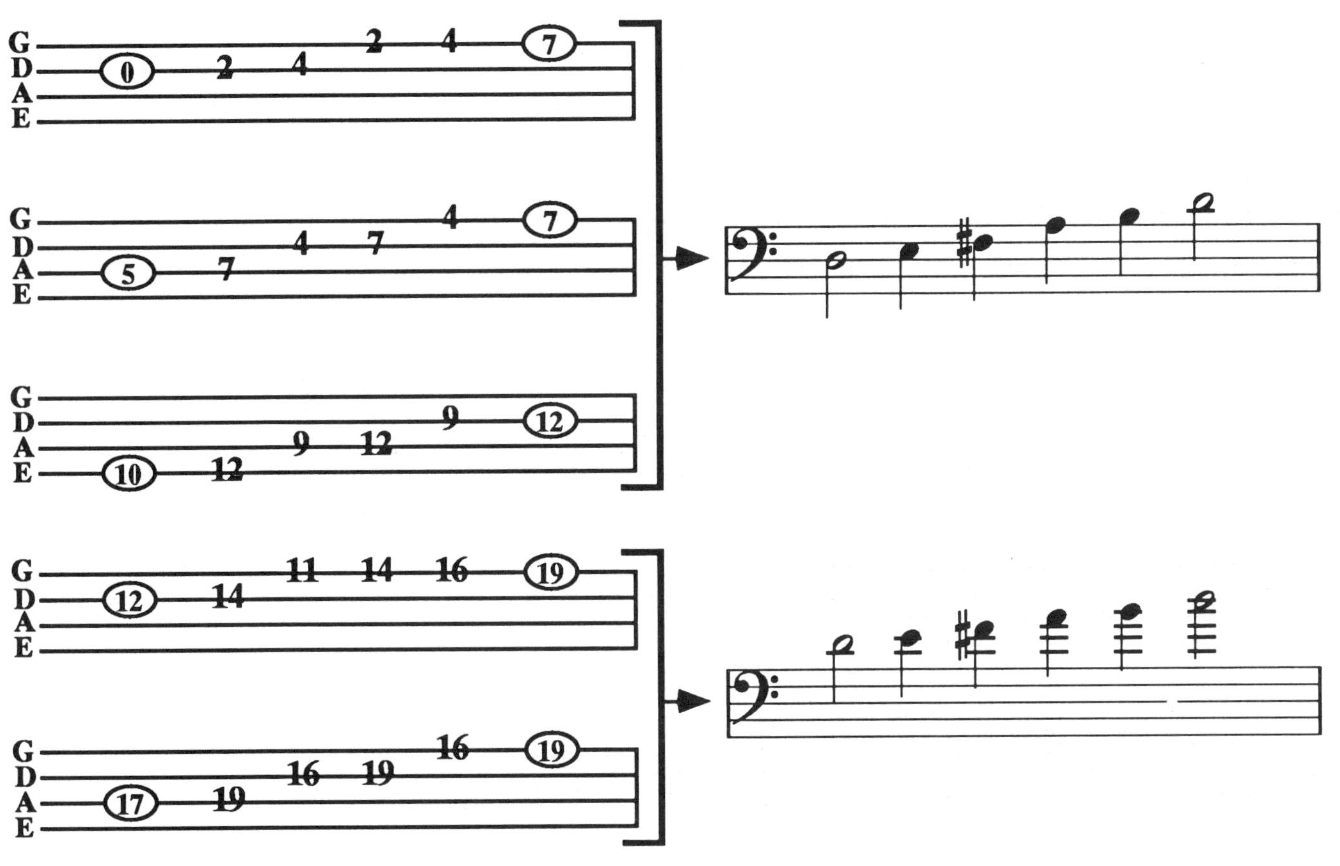

Riff

E MAJOR 6TH-9TH

FORMULA - (E) Root (G♯) 3rd (B) 5th (C♯) 6th (F♯) 9th

E Maj. 6/9

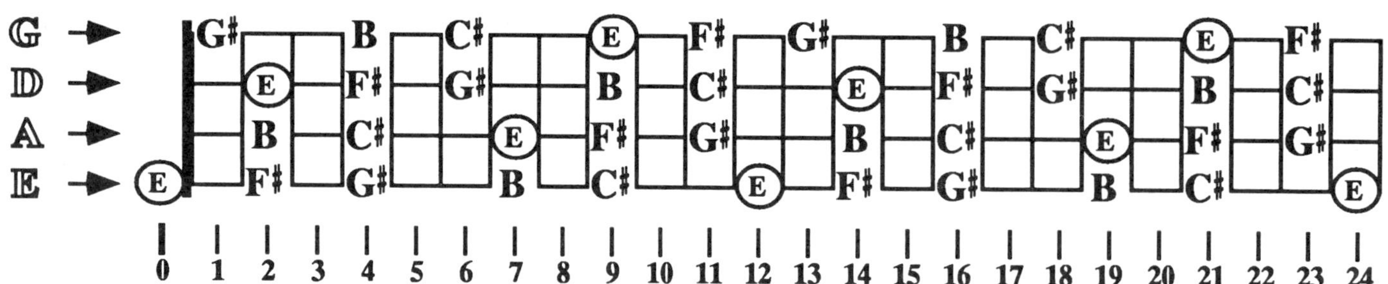

Positions

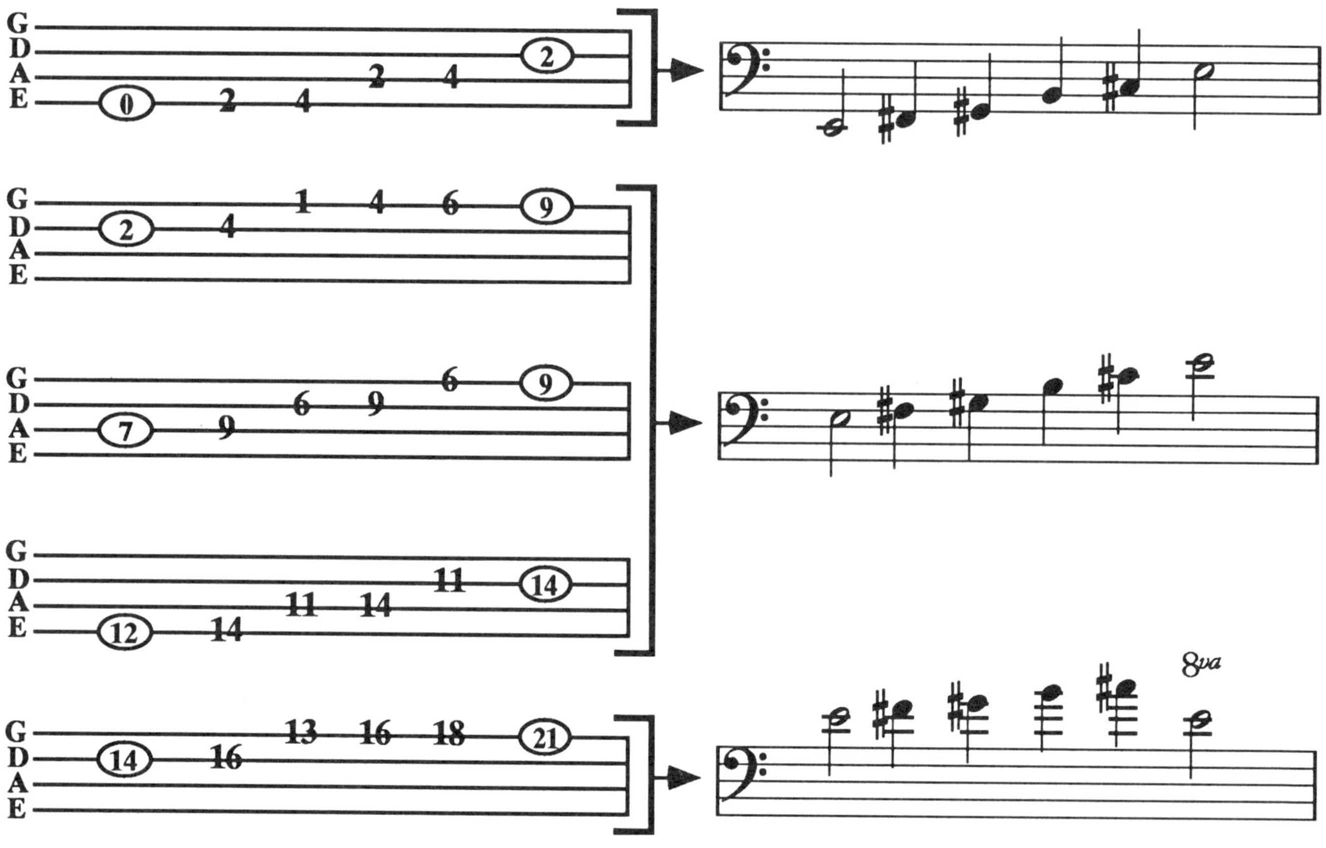

Riff

F MAJOR 6TH-9TH

F Maj. 6/9

FORMULA - (F) Root (A) 3rd (C) 5th (D) 6th (G) 9th

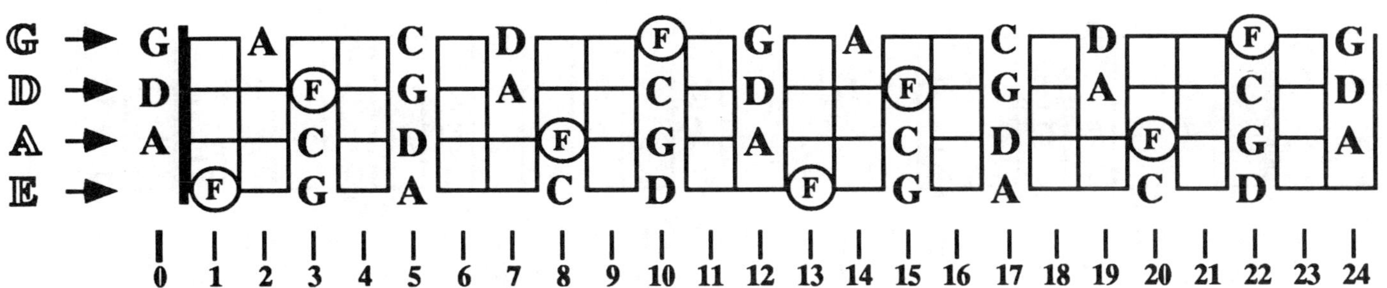

Positions

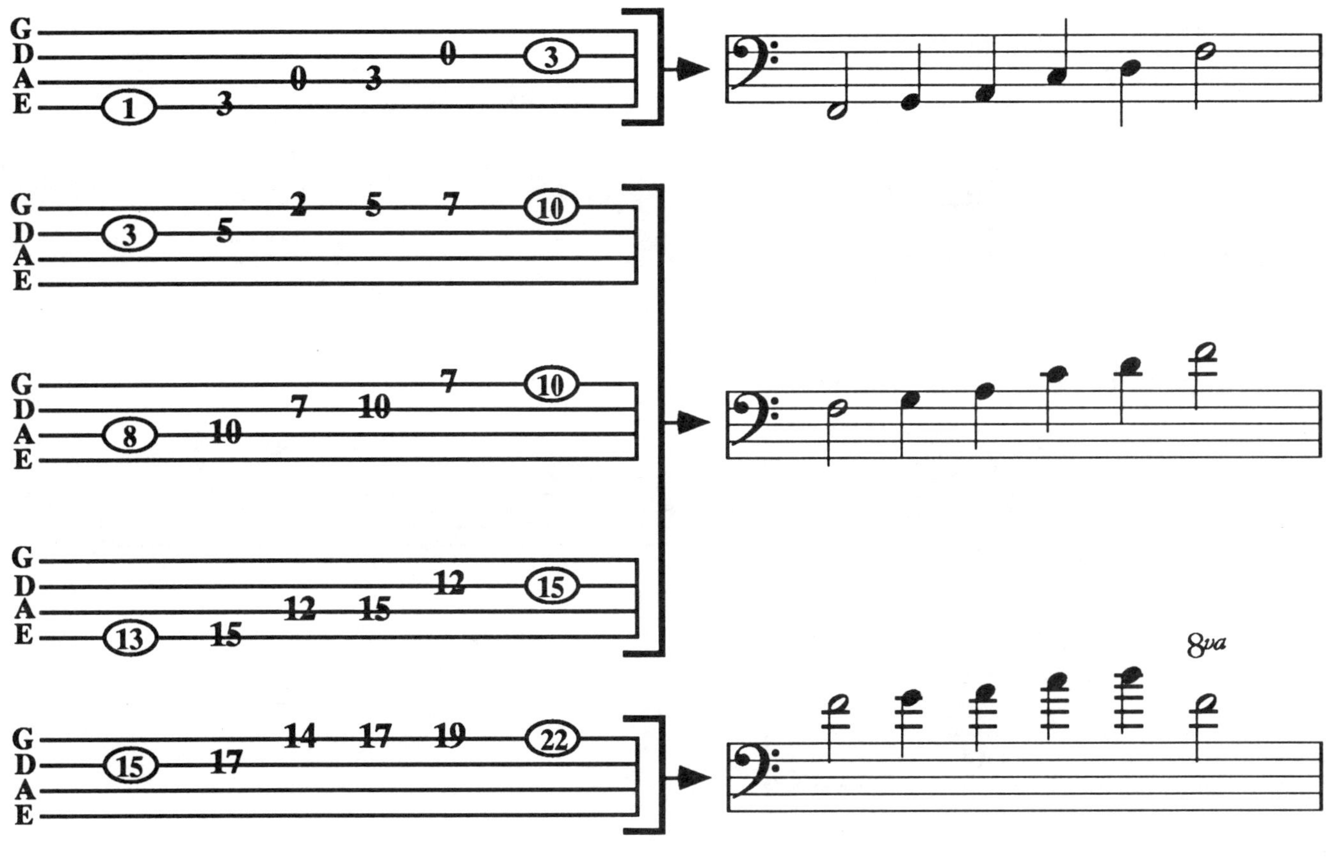

Riff

G MAJOR 6TH-9TH

FORMULA - (G) Root (B) 3rd (D) 5th (E) 6th (A) 9th

G Maj. 6/9

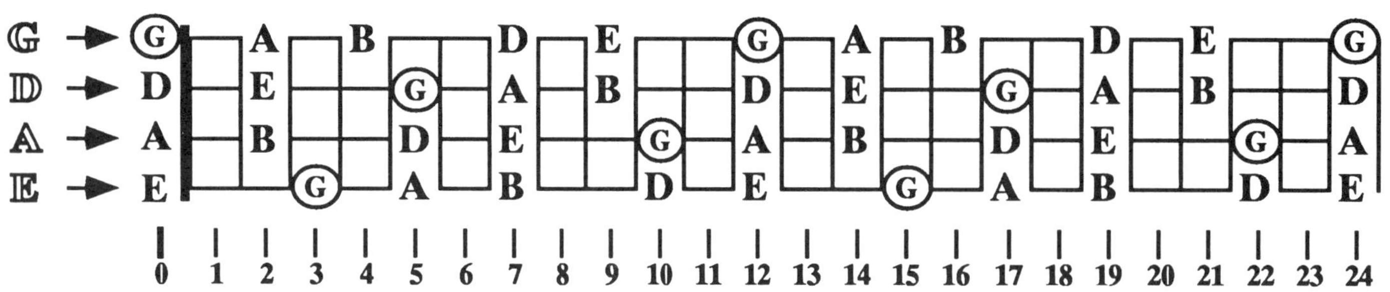

Positions

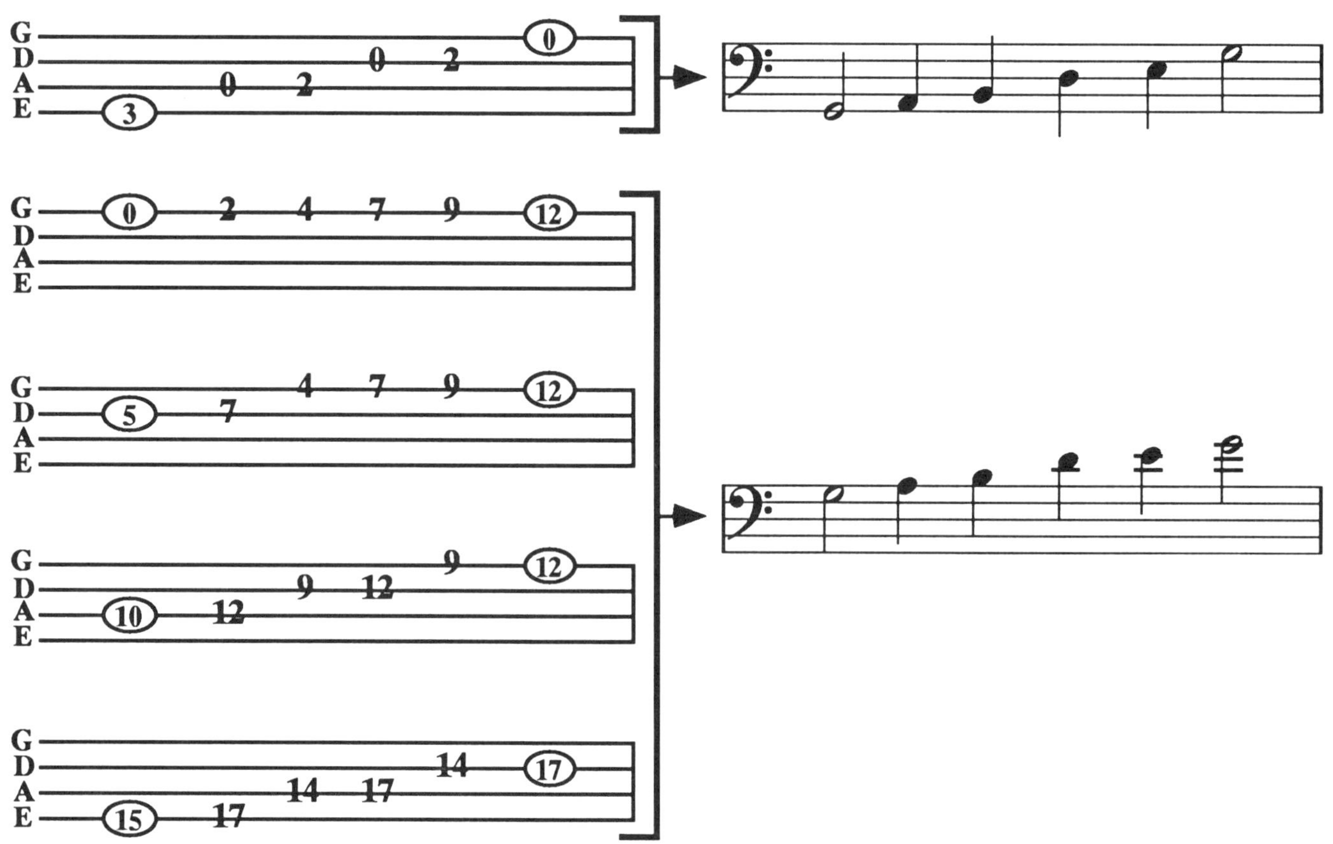

Riff

A MAJOR 6TH-9TH

FORMULA - (A) Root (C♯) 3rd (E) 5th (F♯) 6th (B) 9th

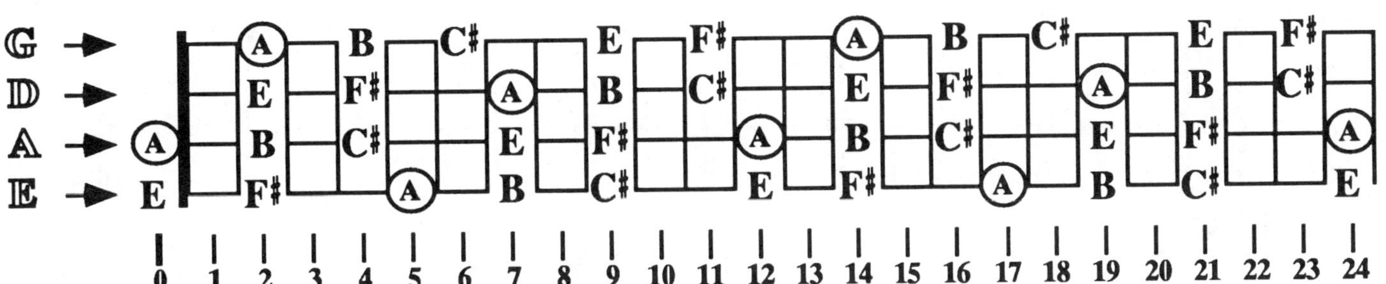

Positions

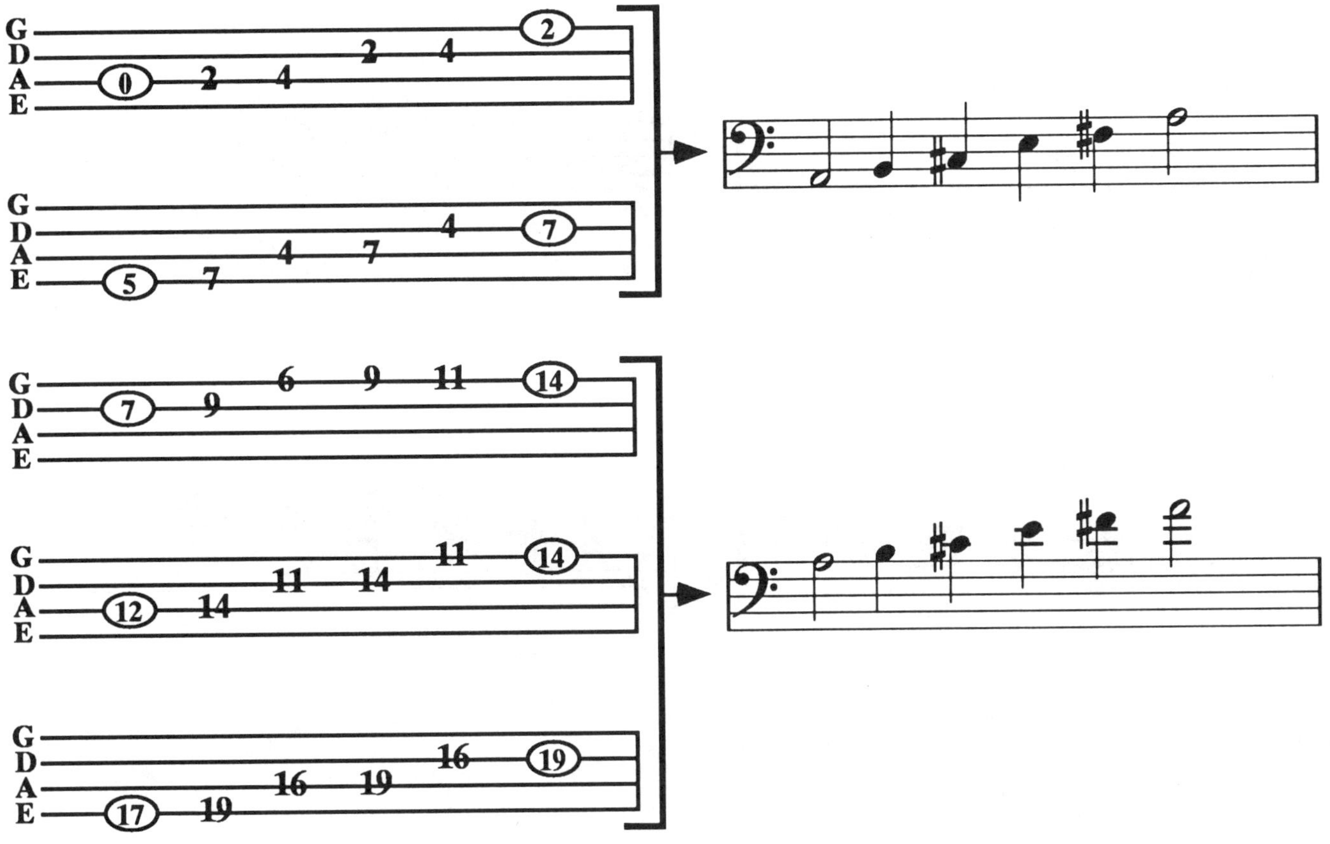

Riff

B MAJOR 6TH-9TH

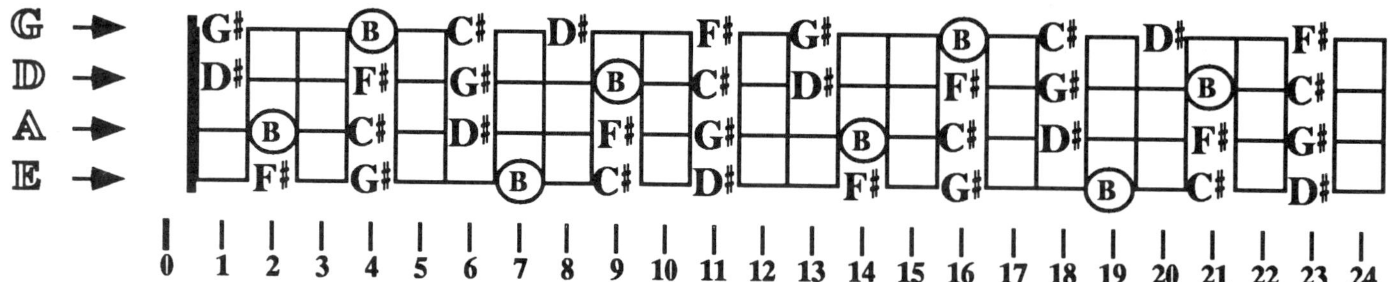

Positions

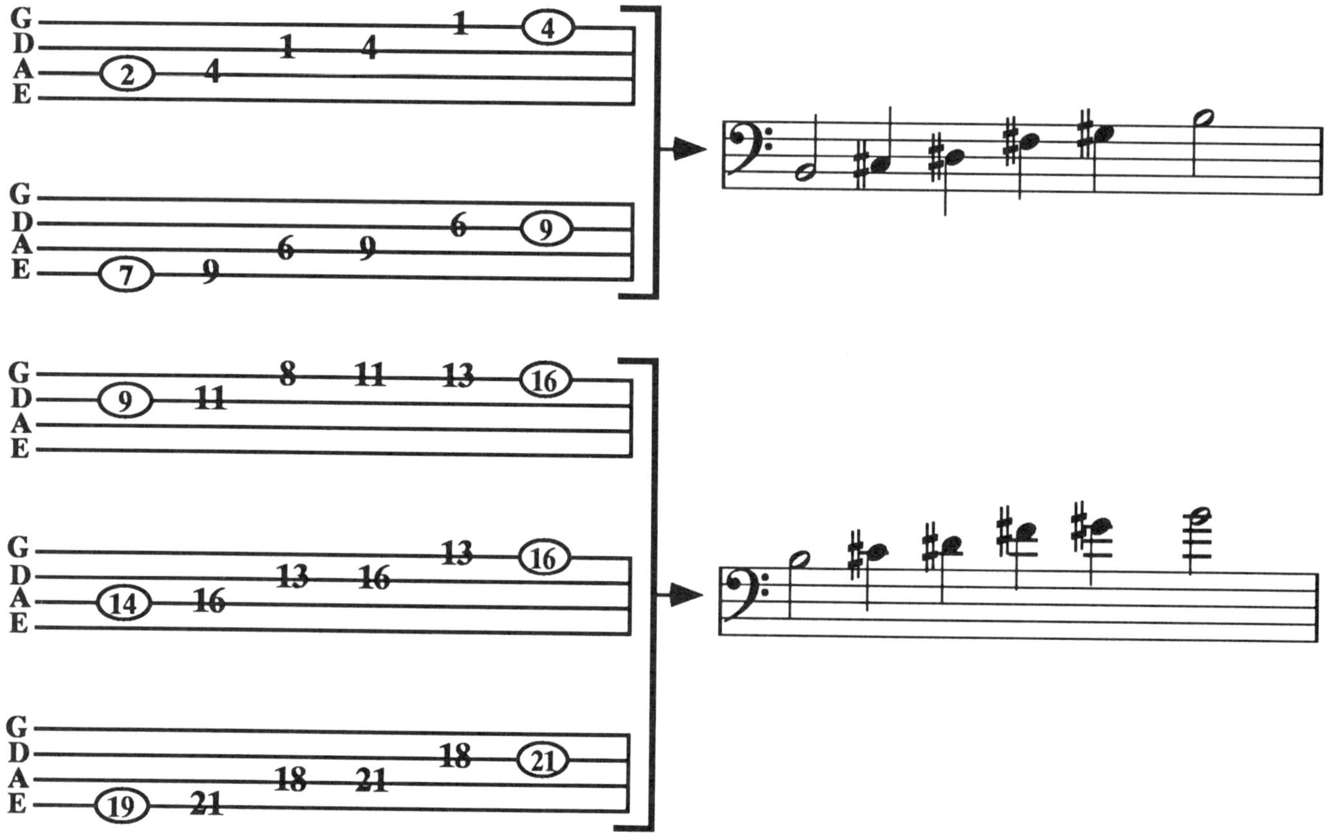

Riff

42

C MAJOR / 9TH

FORMULA - (D) 9th (E) 3rd (G) 5th (C) Root

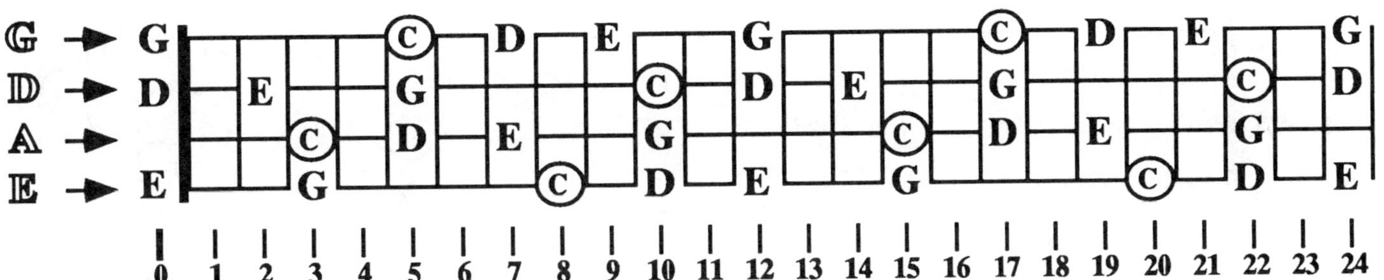

Positions

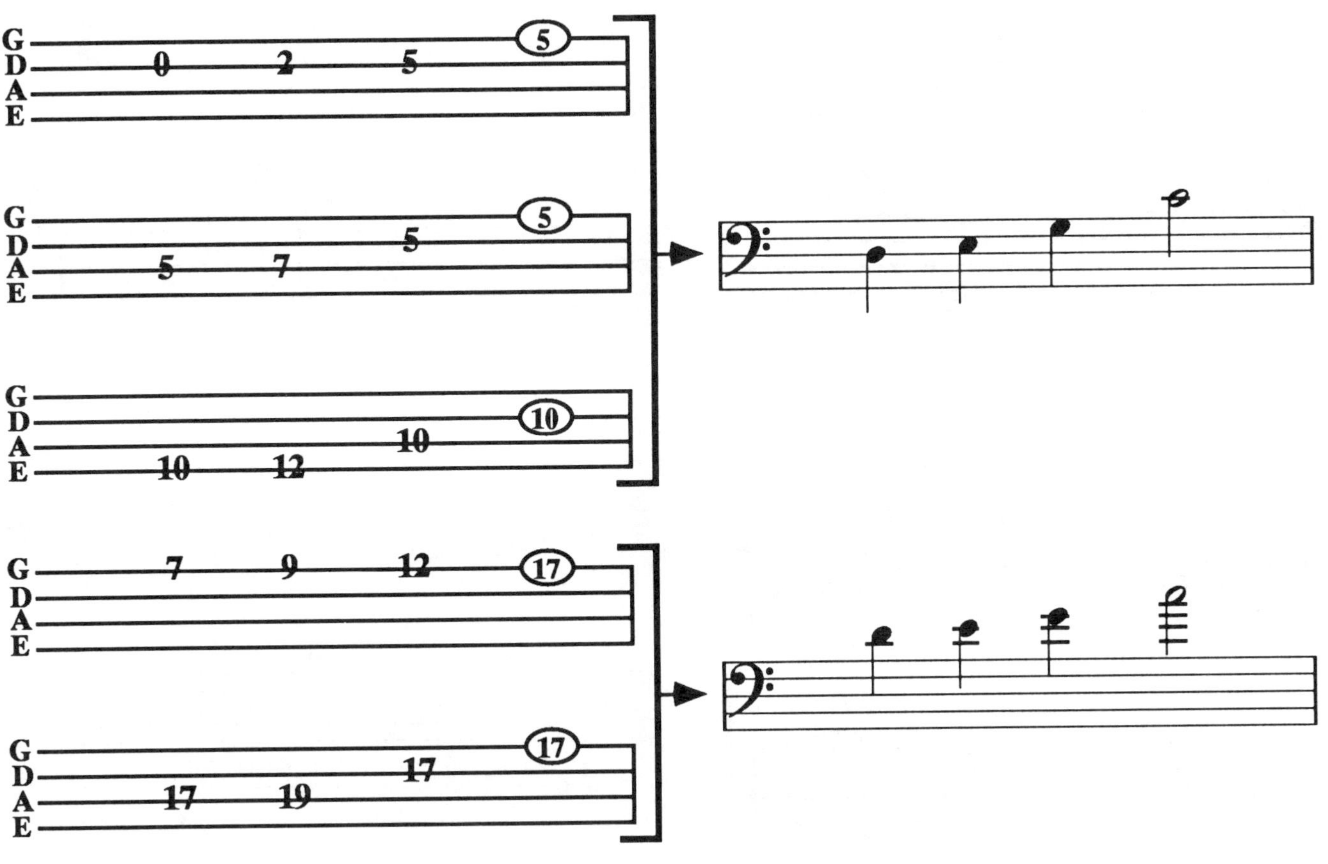

Riff

D MAJOR / 9TH

FORMULA - (E) 9th (F♯) 3rd (A) 5th (D) Root

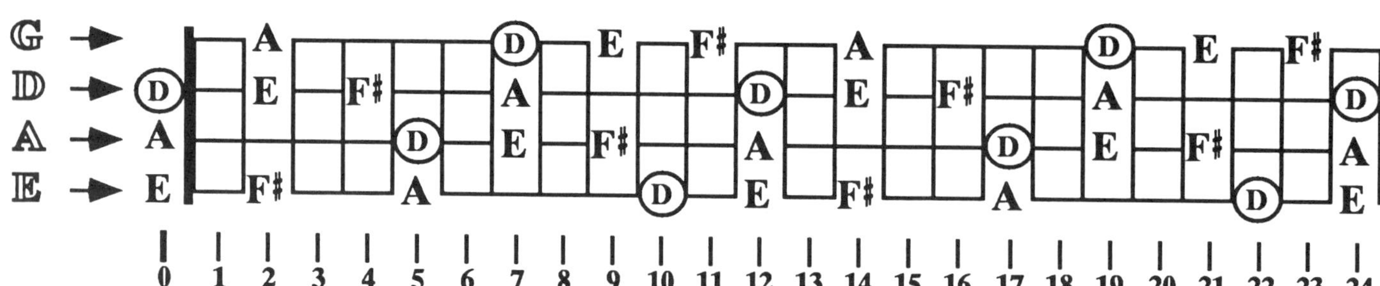

Positions

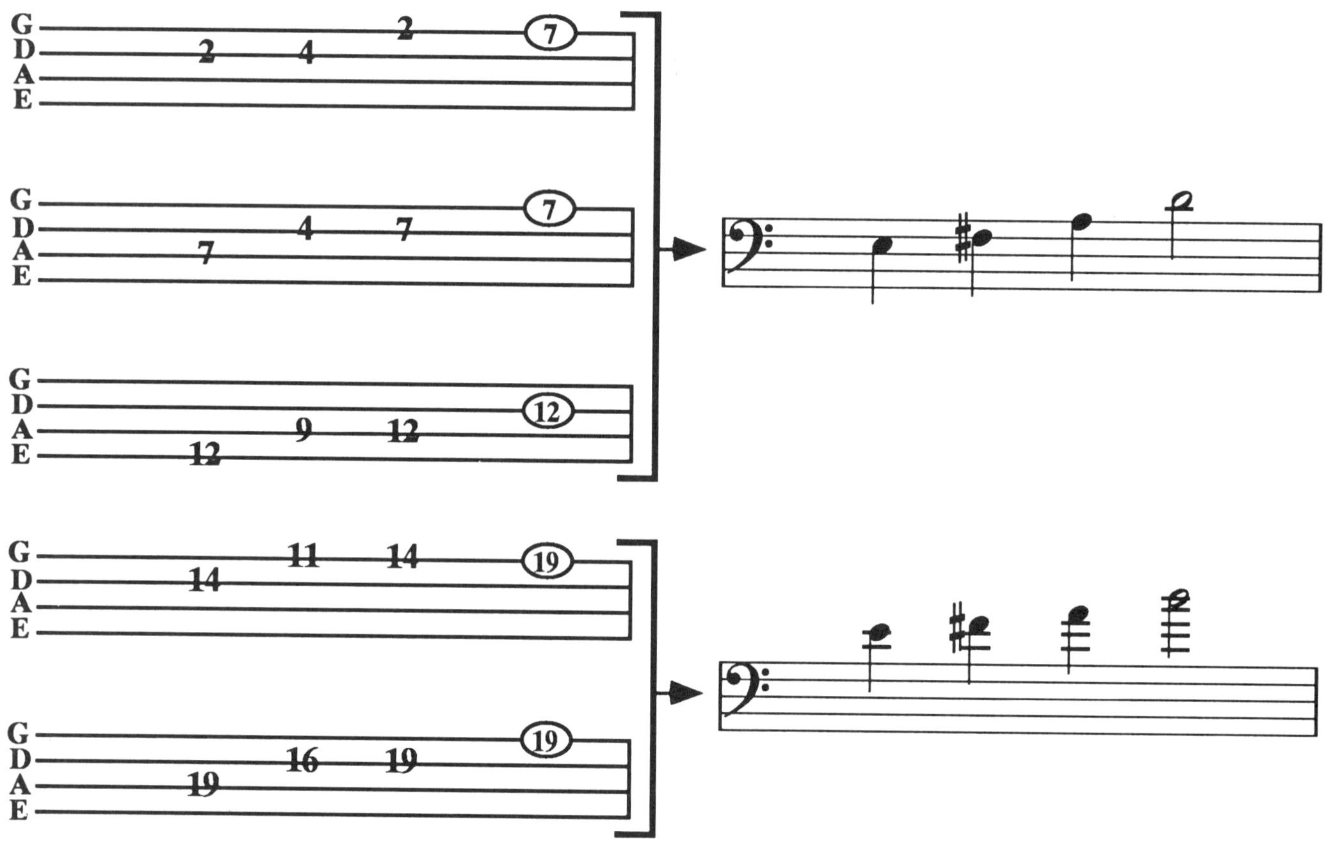

Riff

E MAJOR / 9TH

FORMULA - (F♯) 9th (G♯) 3rd (B) 5th (E) Root

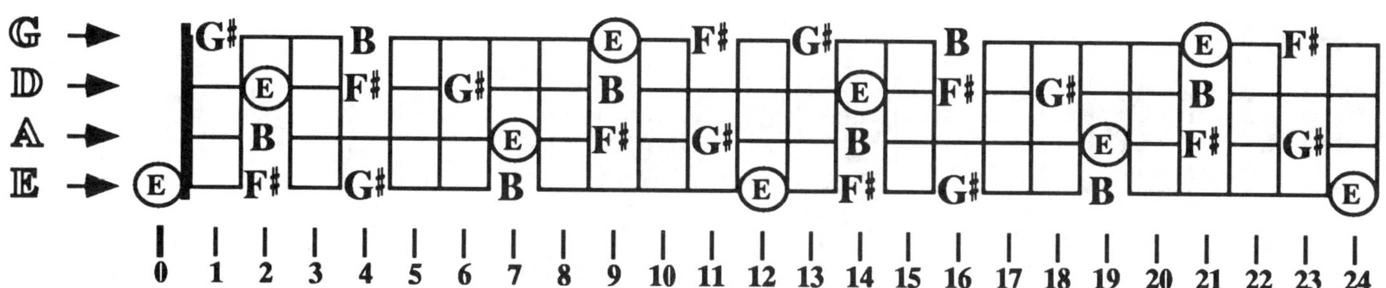

Positions

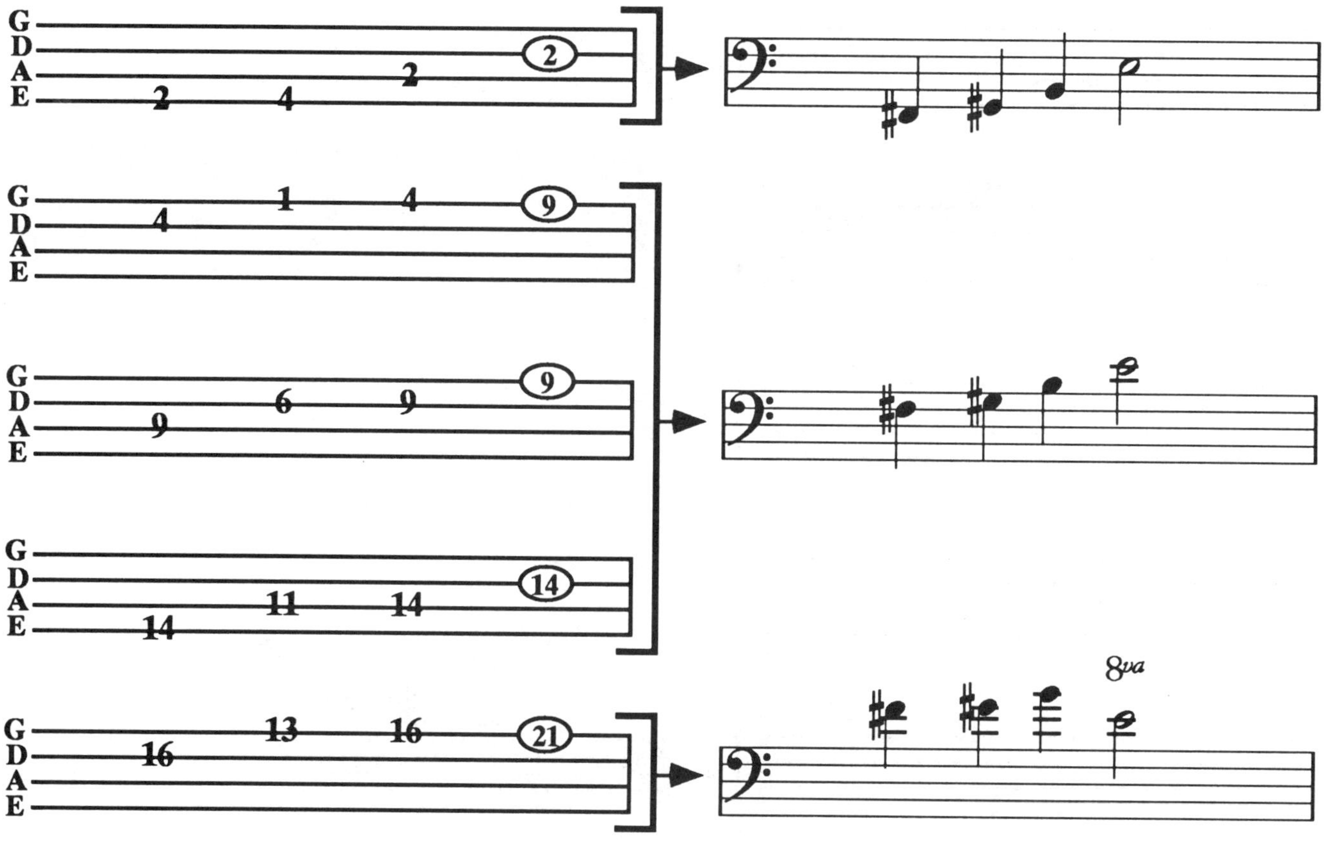

Riff

F MAJOR / 9TH

FORMULA - (G) 9th (A) 3rd (C) 5th (F) Root

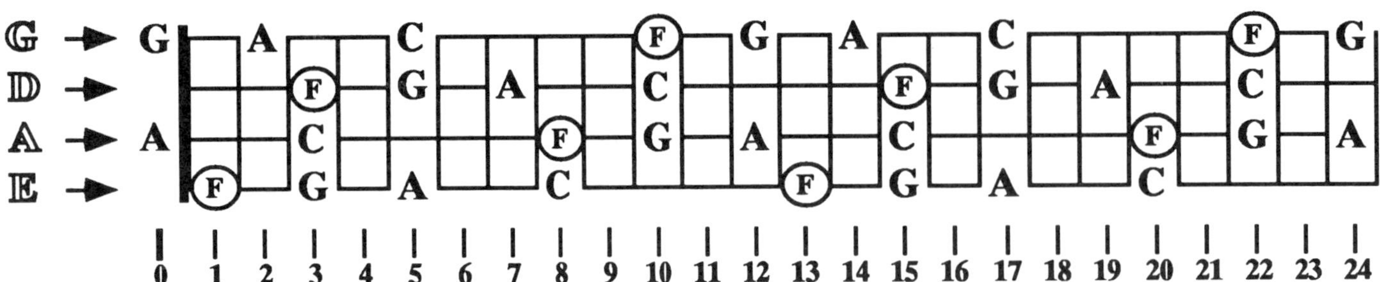

Positions

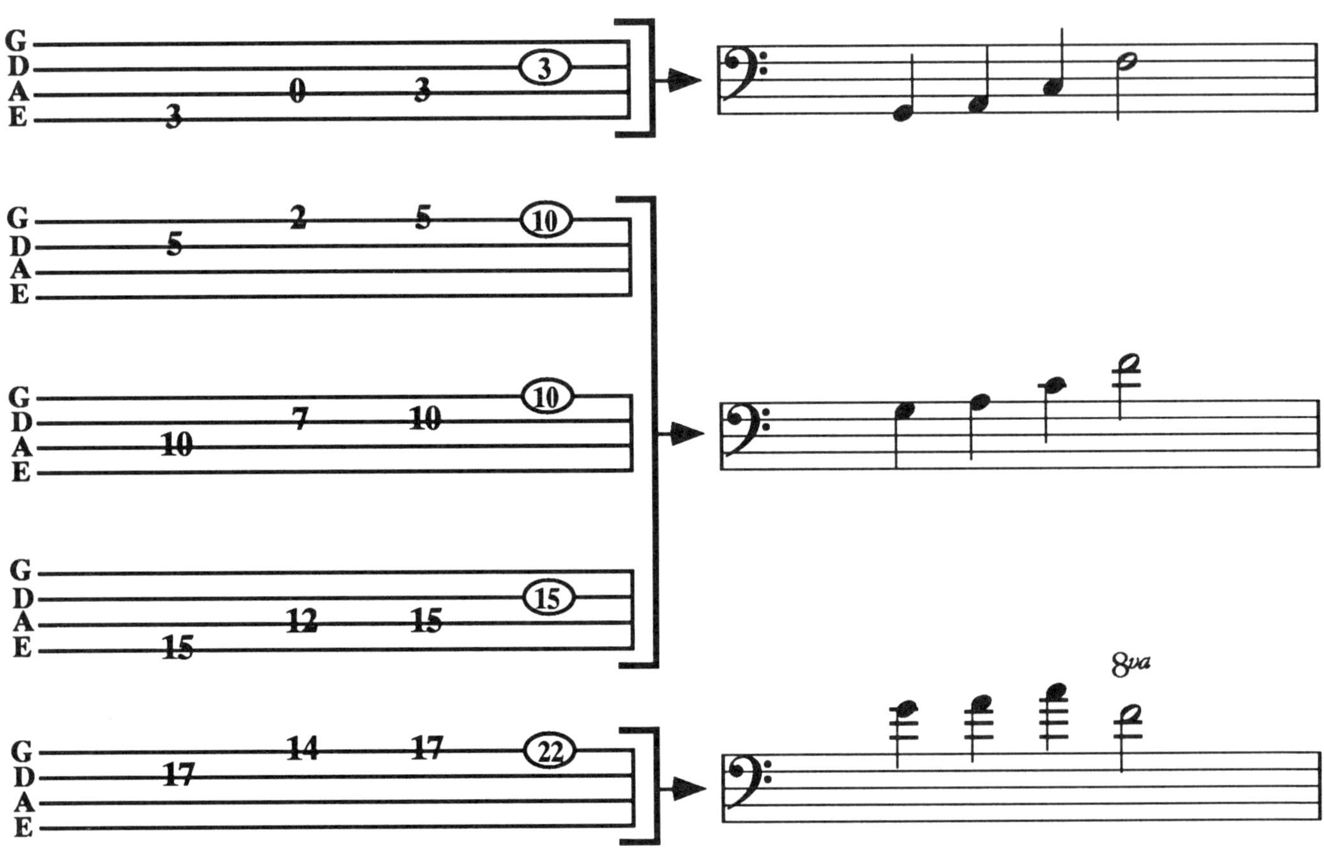

Riff

G MAJOR / 9TH

FORMULA - (A) 9th (B) 3rd (D) 5th (G) Root

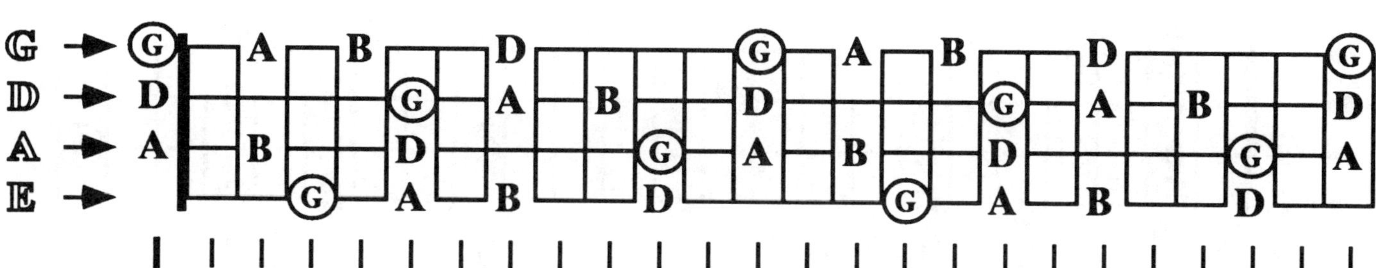

Positions

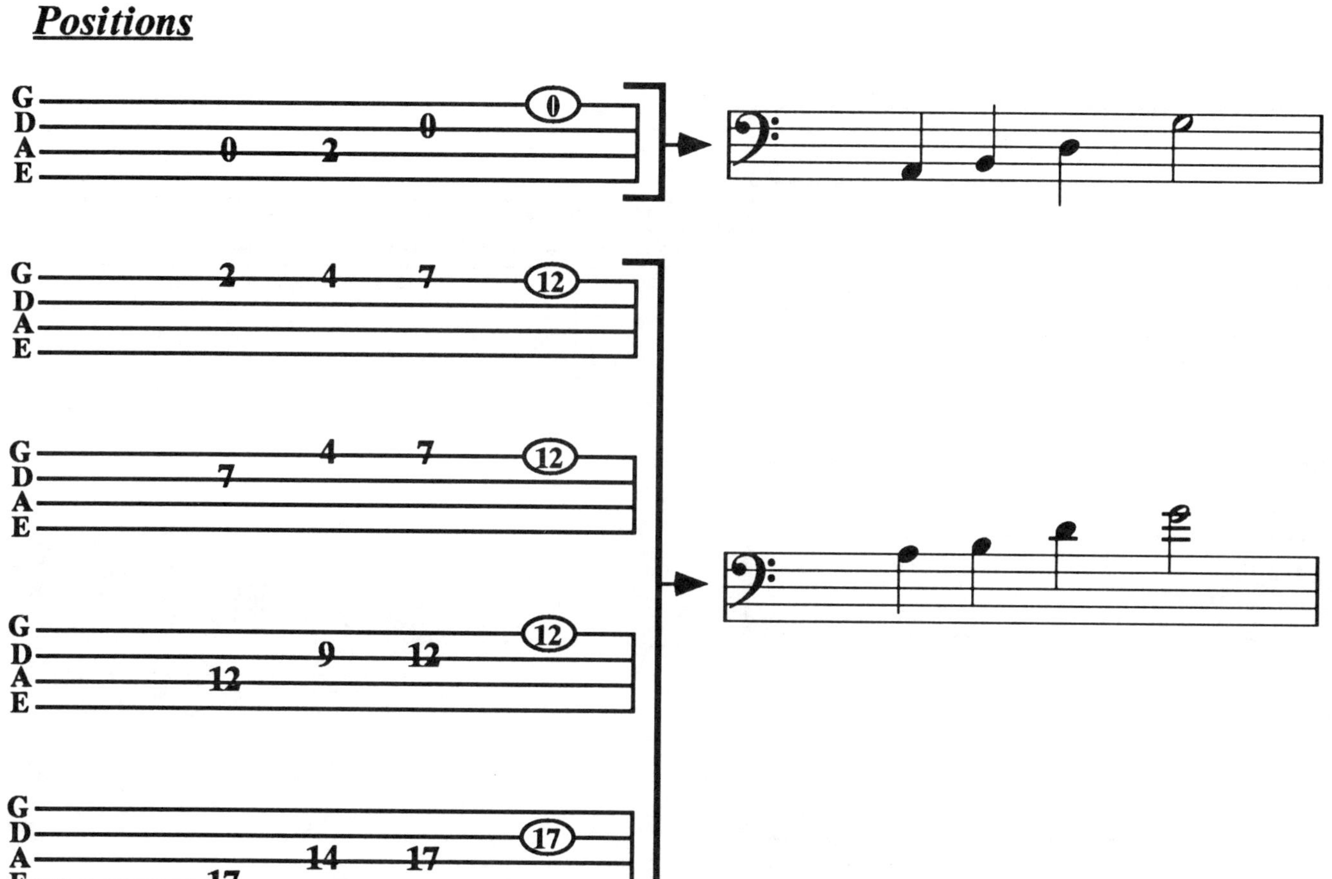

Riff

A MAJOR / 9TH

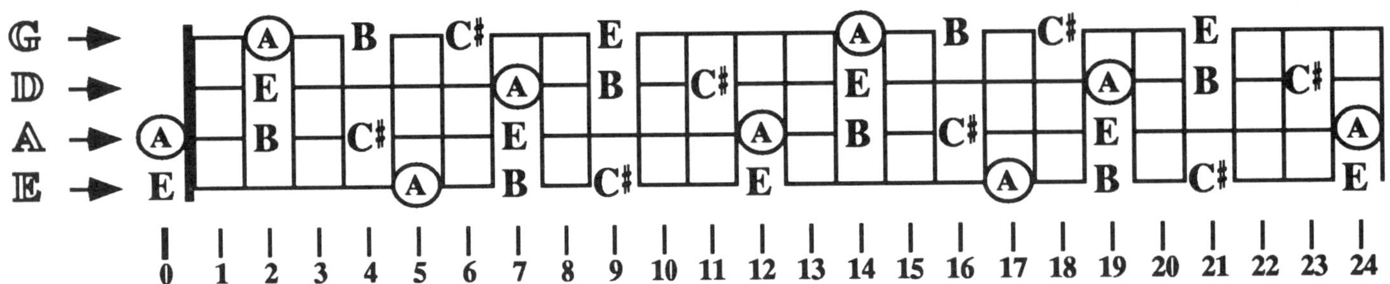

Positions

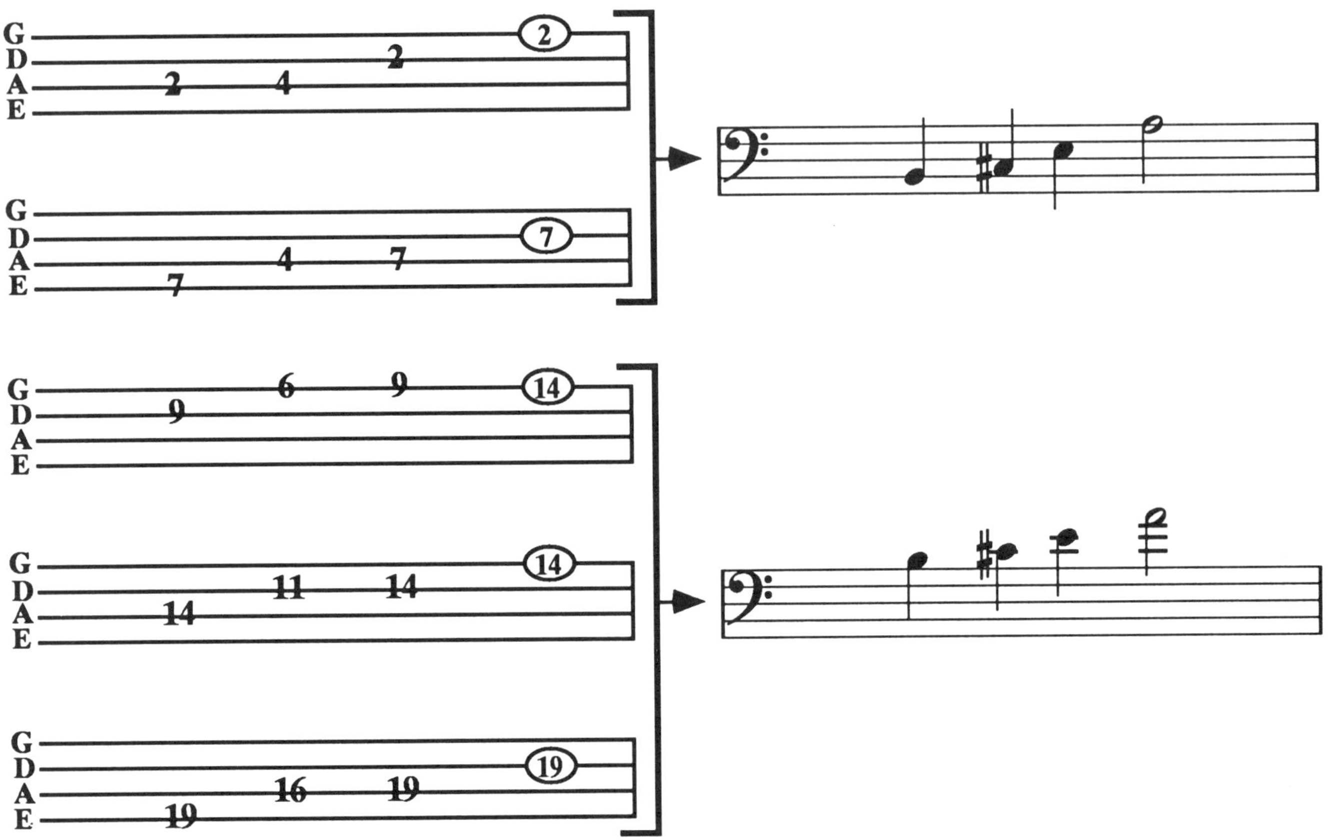

Riff

B MAJOR / 9TH

FORMULA - (C#) 9th (D#) 3rd (F#) 5th (B) Root

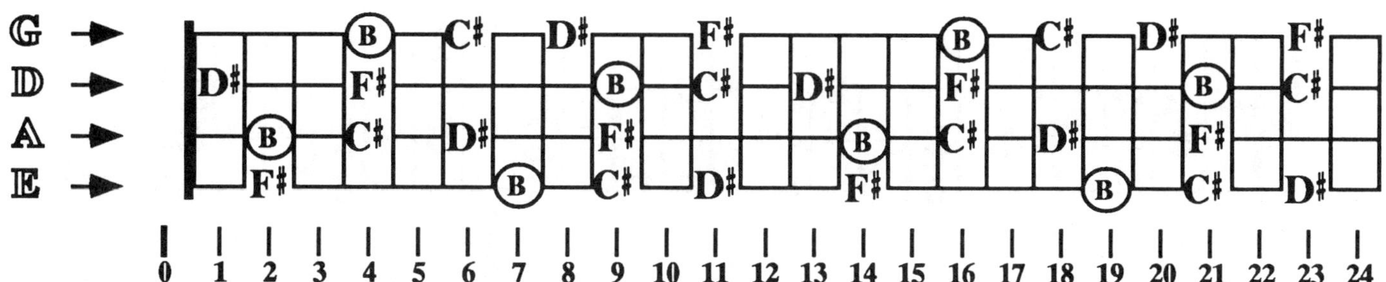

Positions

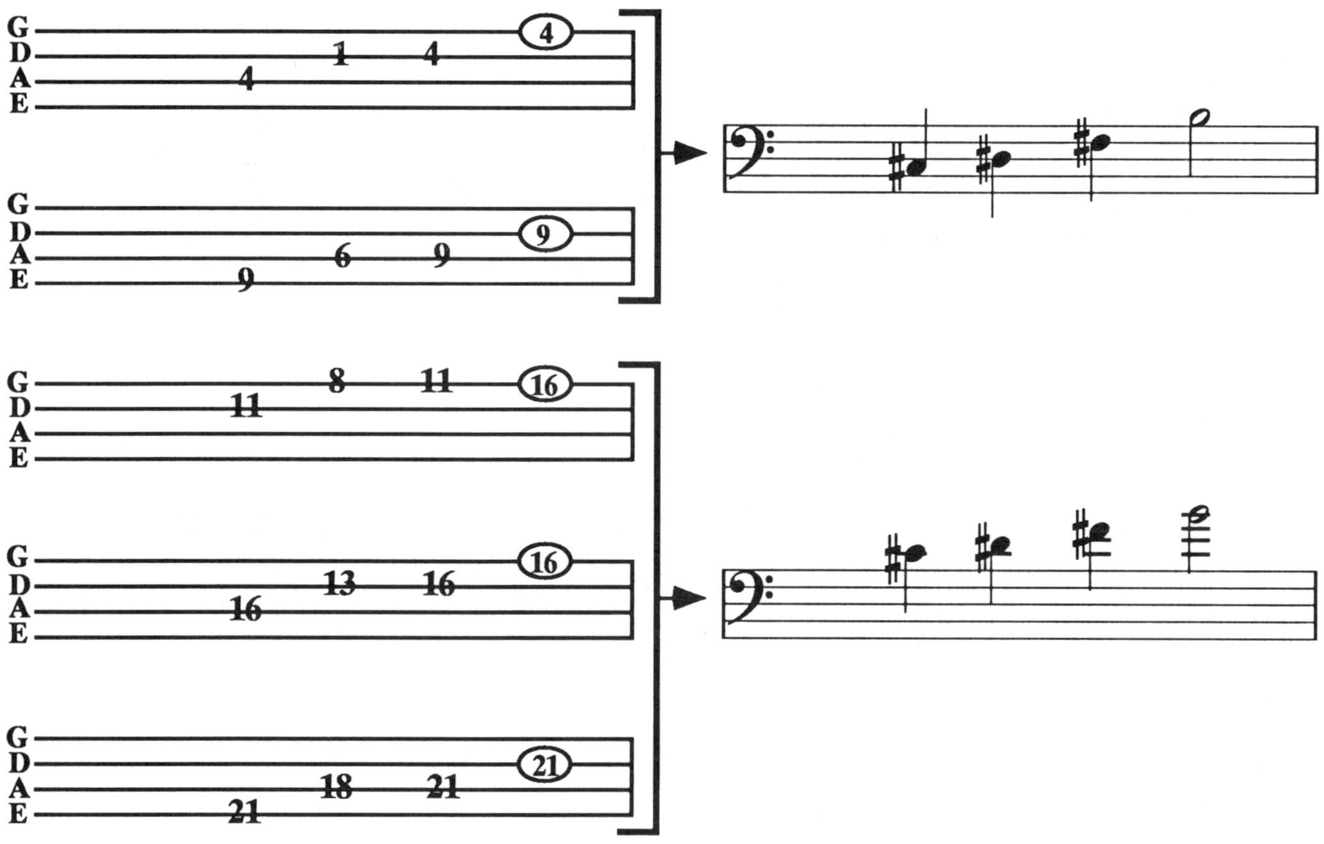

Riff

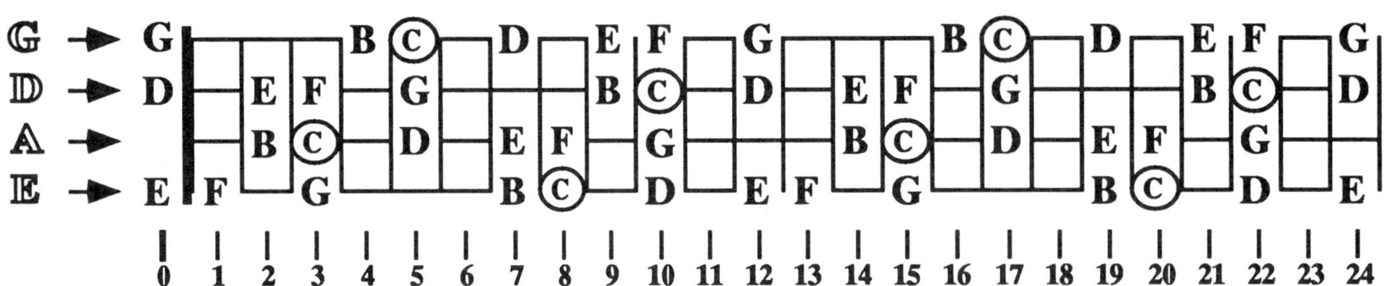

Positions

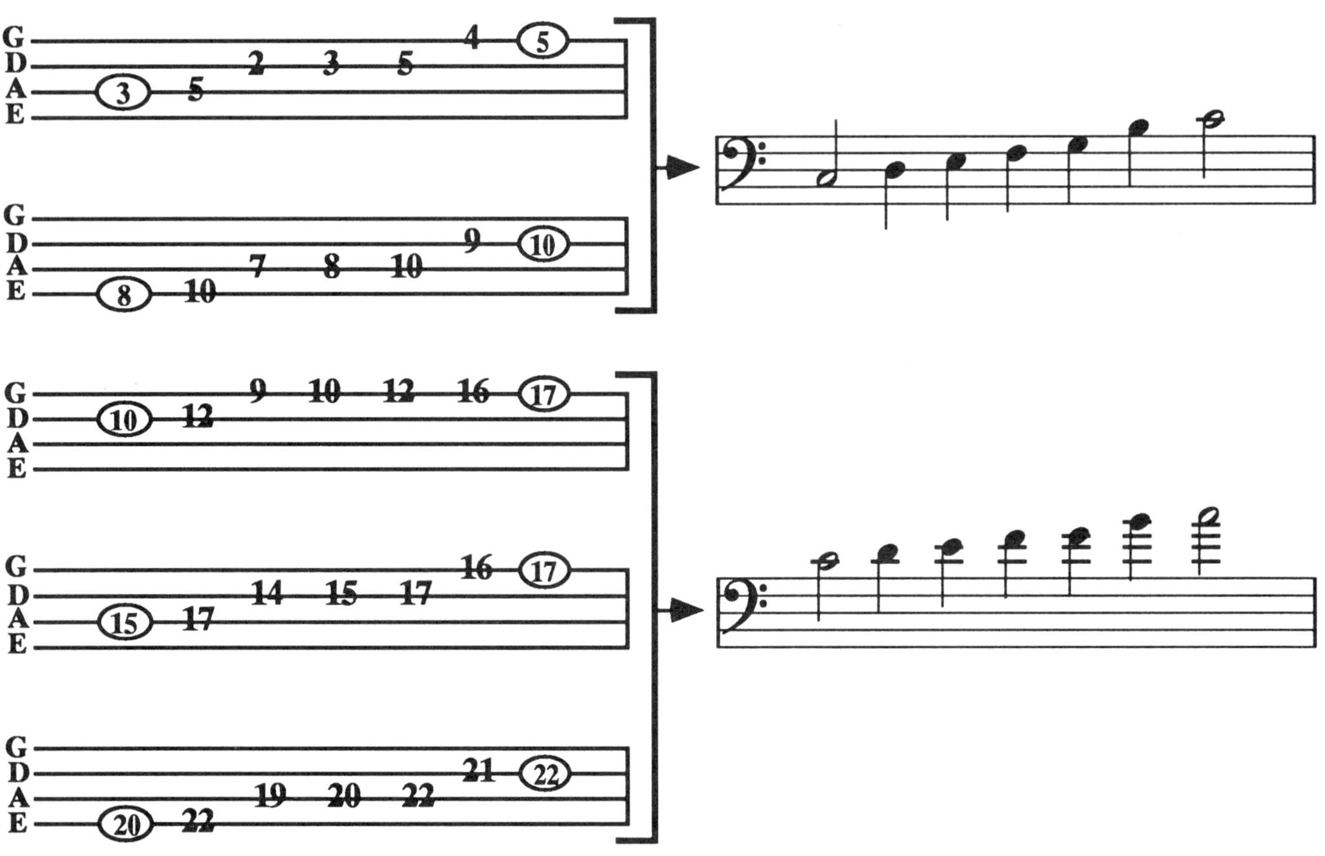

Riff

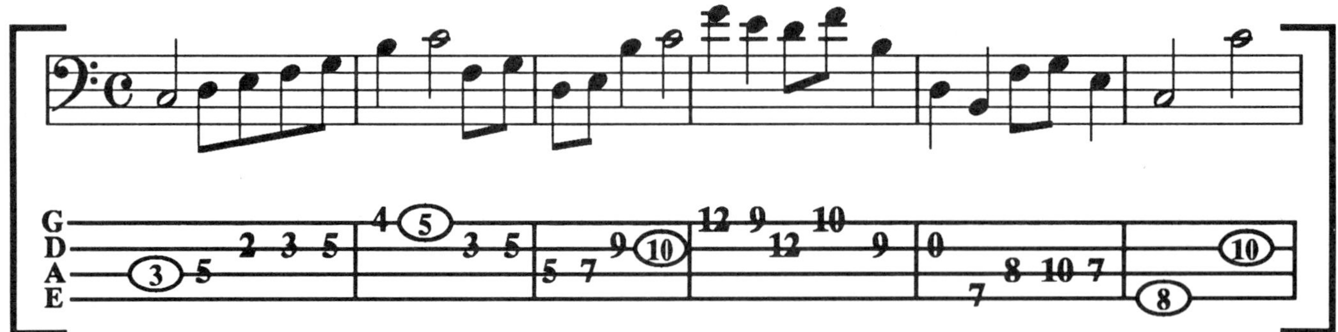

D MAJOR 11TH

**FORMULA - (D) Root (F♯) 3rd (A) 5th
(C♯) 7th (E) 9th (G) 11th**

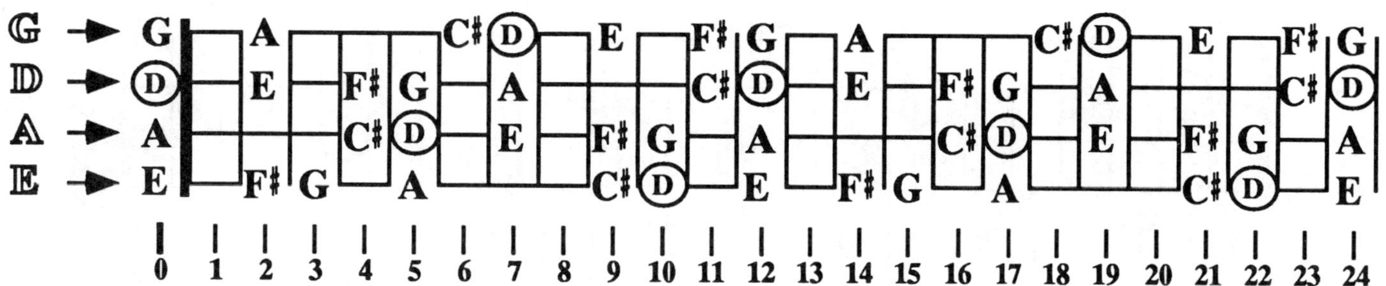

Positions

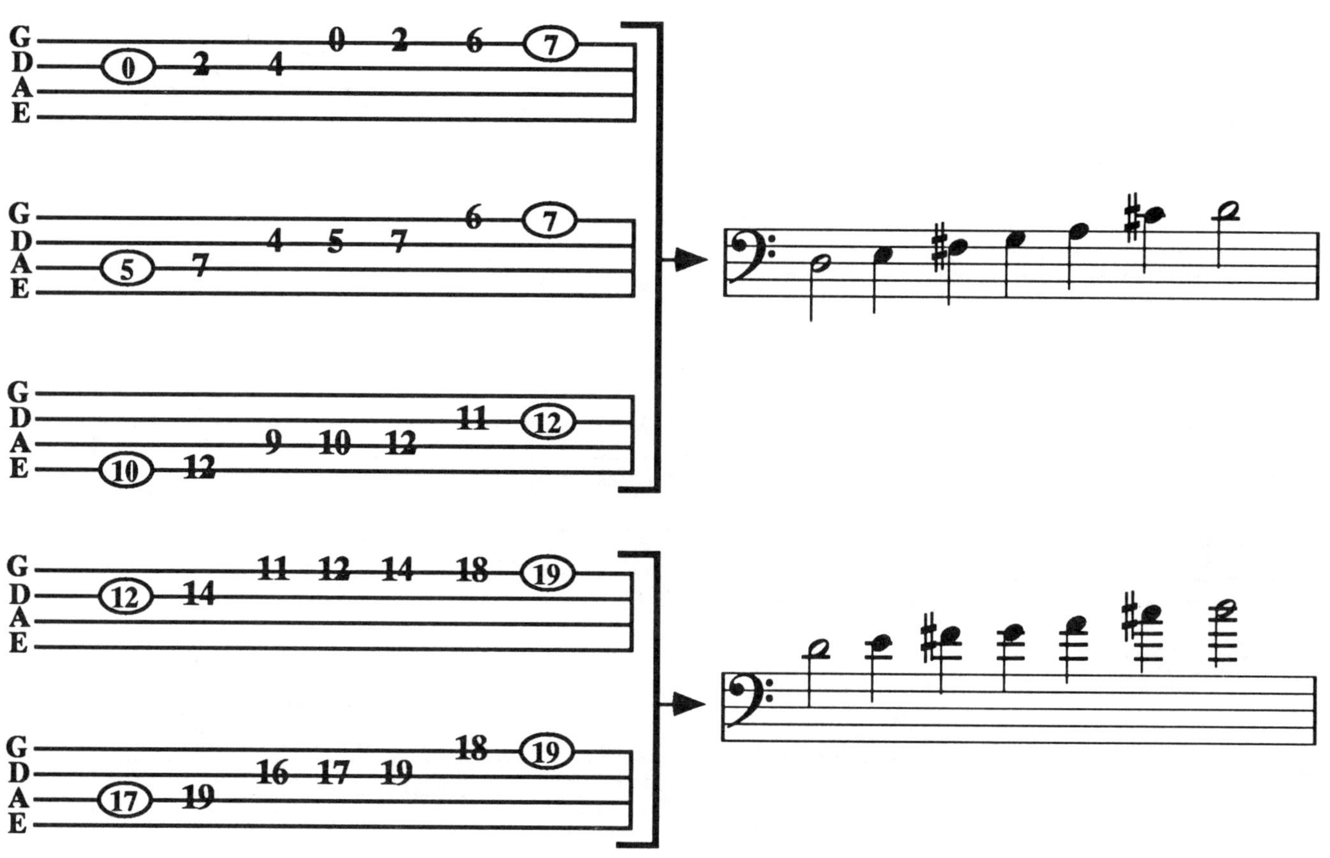

Riff

E MAJOR 11TH

FORMULA - (E) Root (G♯) 3rd (B) 5th
(D♯) 7th (F♯) 9th (A) 11th

E Maj. 11

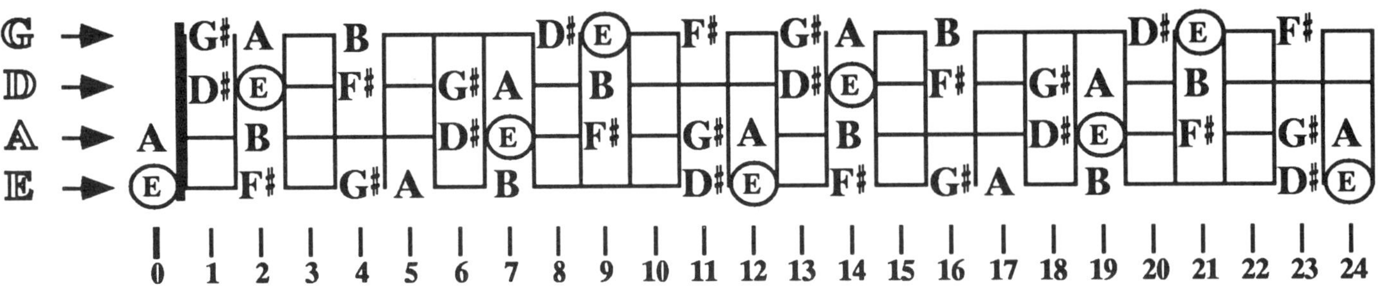

Positions

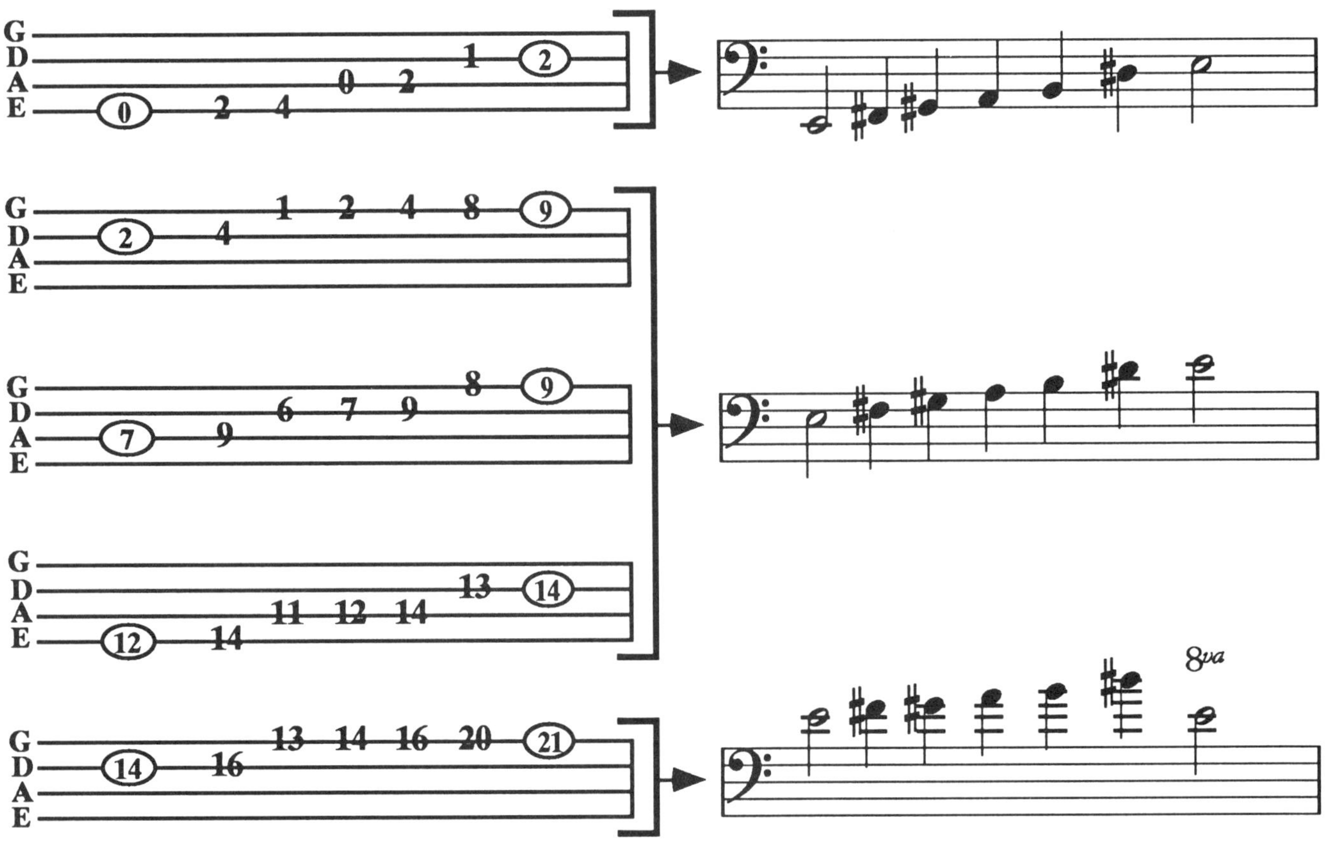

Riff

F MAJOR 11TH

**FORMULA - (F) Root (A) 3rd (C) 5th
(E) 7th (G) 9th (B♭) 11th**

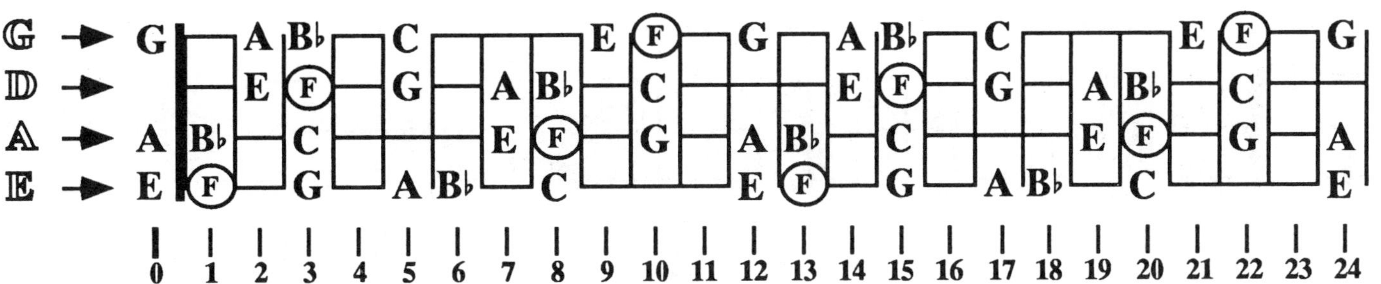

Positions

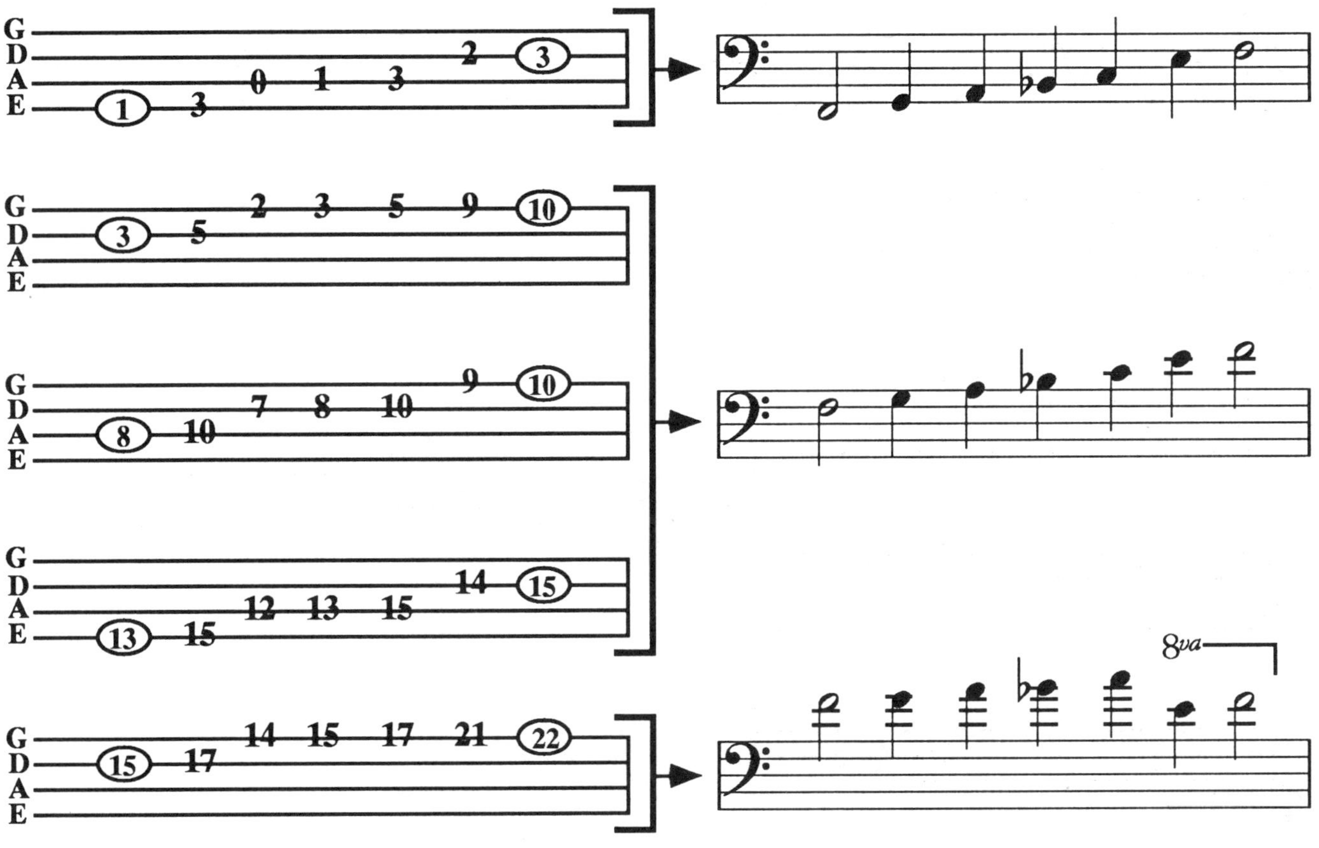

Riff

G   MAJOR 11TH
FORMULA - (G) Root (B) 3rd (D) 5th
(F♯) 7th (A) 9th (C) 11th

G Maj. 11

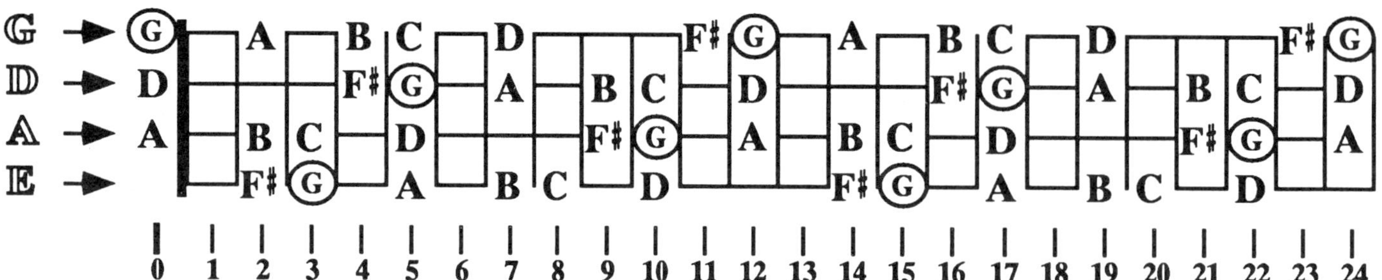

Positions

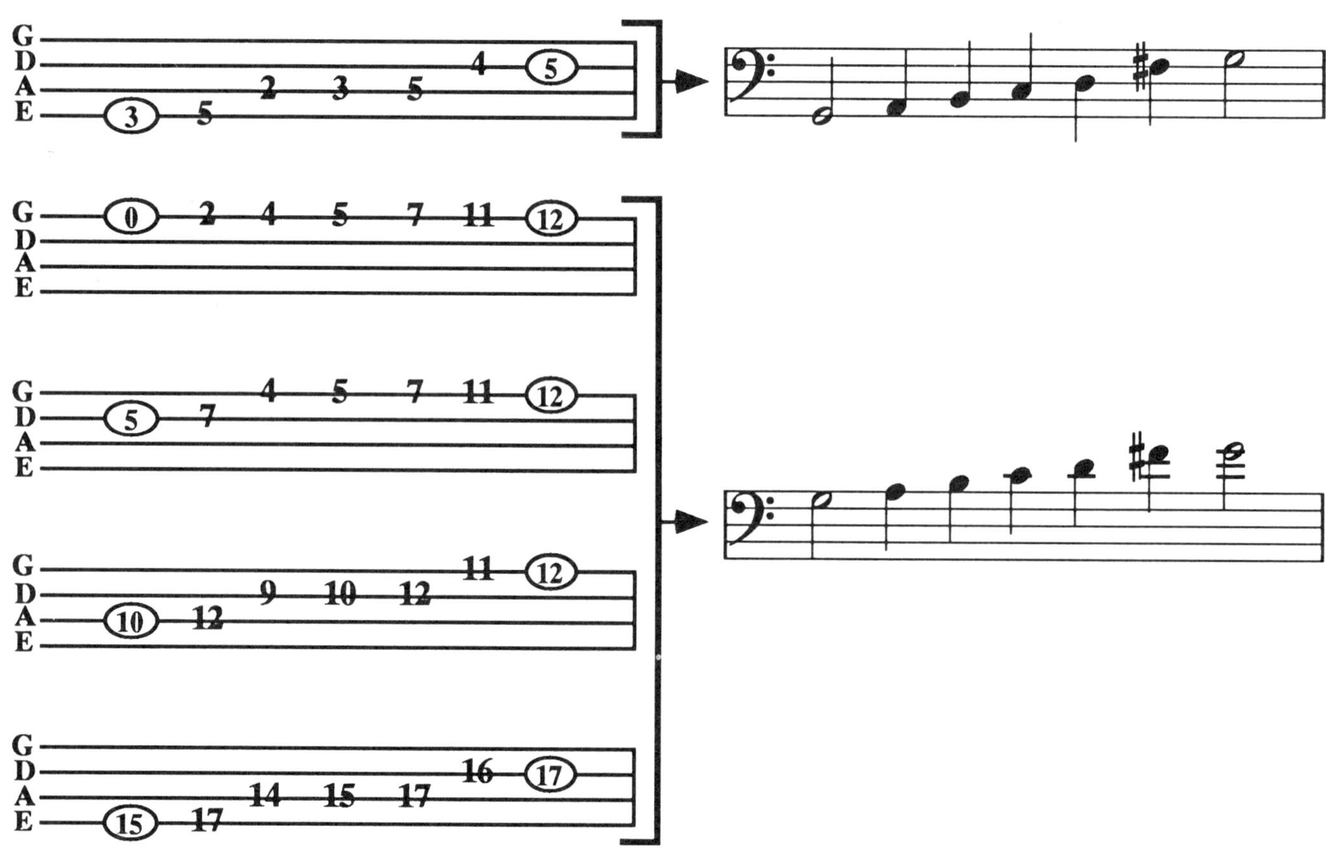

Riff

A MAJOR 11TH

FORMULA - (A) Root (C♯) 3rd (E) 5th (G♯) 7th (B) 9th (D) 11th

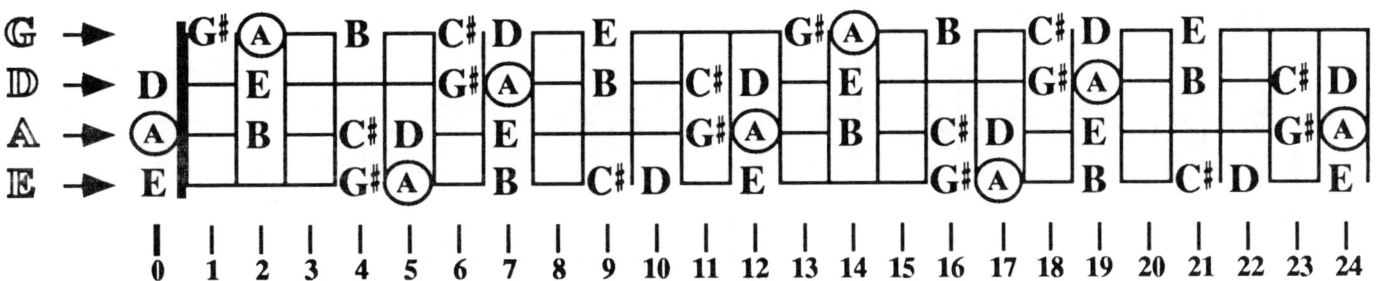

Positions

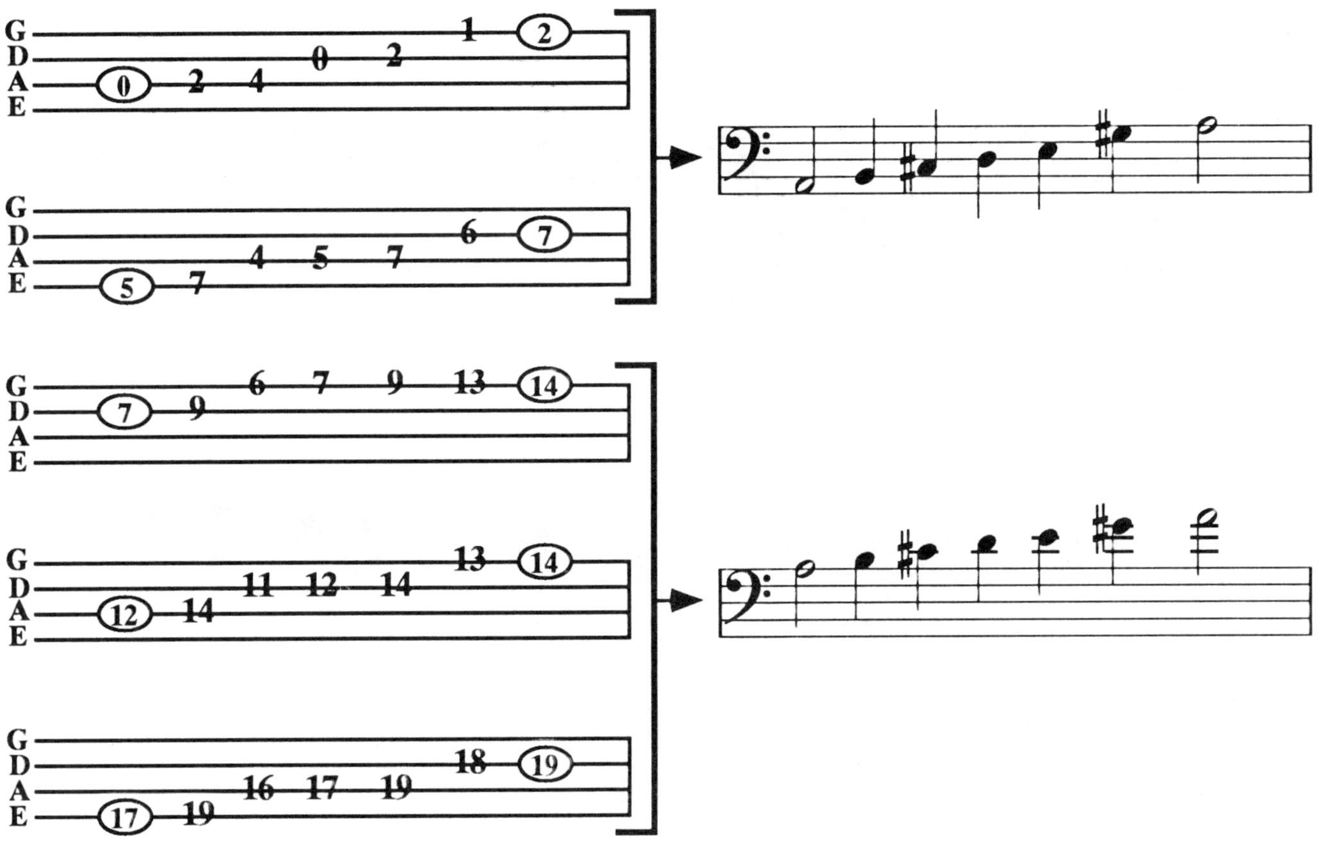

Riff

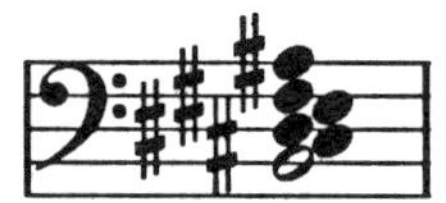

B MAJOR 11TH

**FORMULA - (B) Root (D♯) 3rd (F♯) 5th
(A♯) 7th (C♯) 9th (E) 11th**

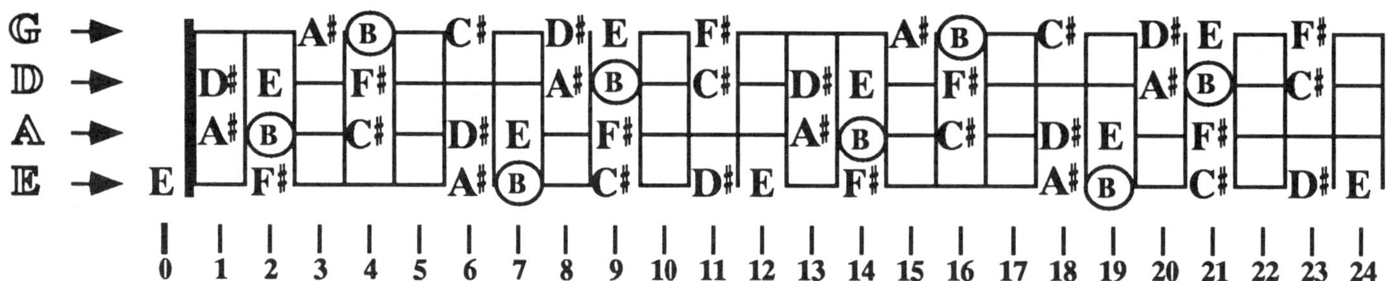

Positions

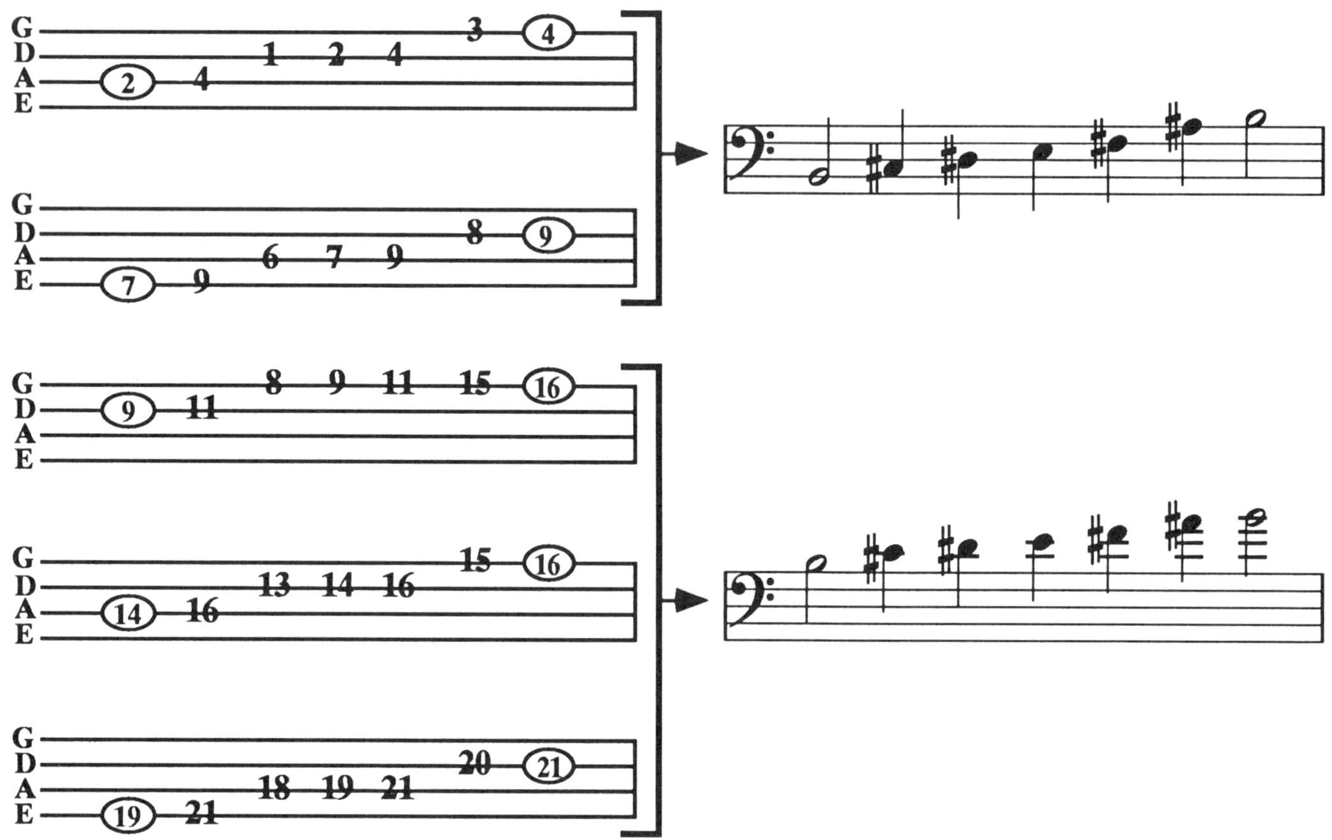

Riff

C MAJOR 13TH

FORMULA - (C) Root (E) 3rd (G) 5th (A) 13th (B) 7th

C Maj. 13

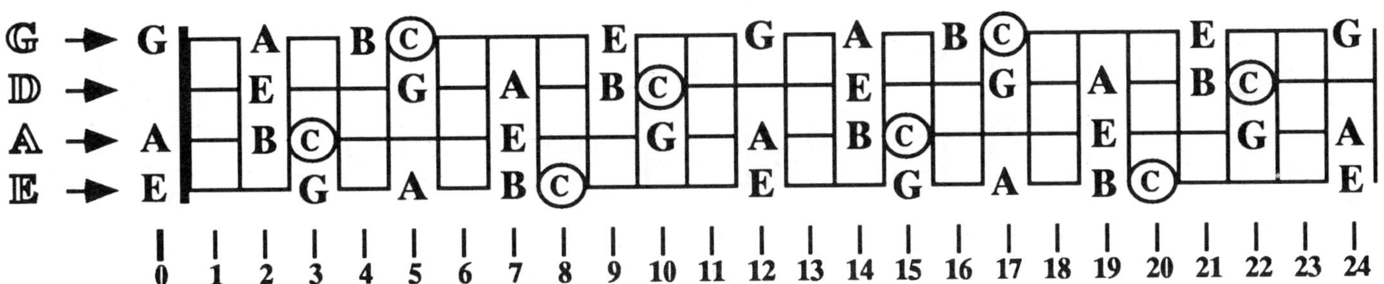

Positions

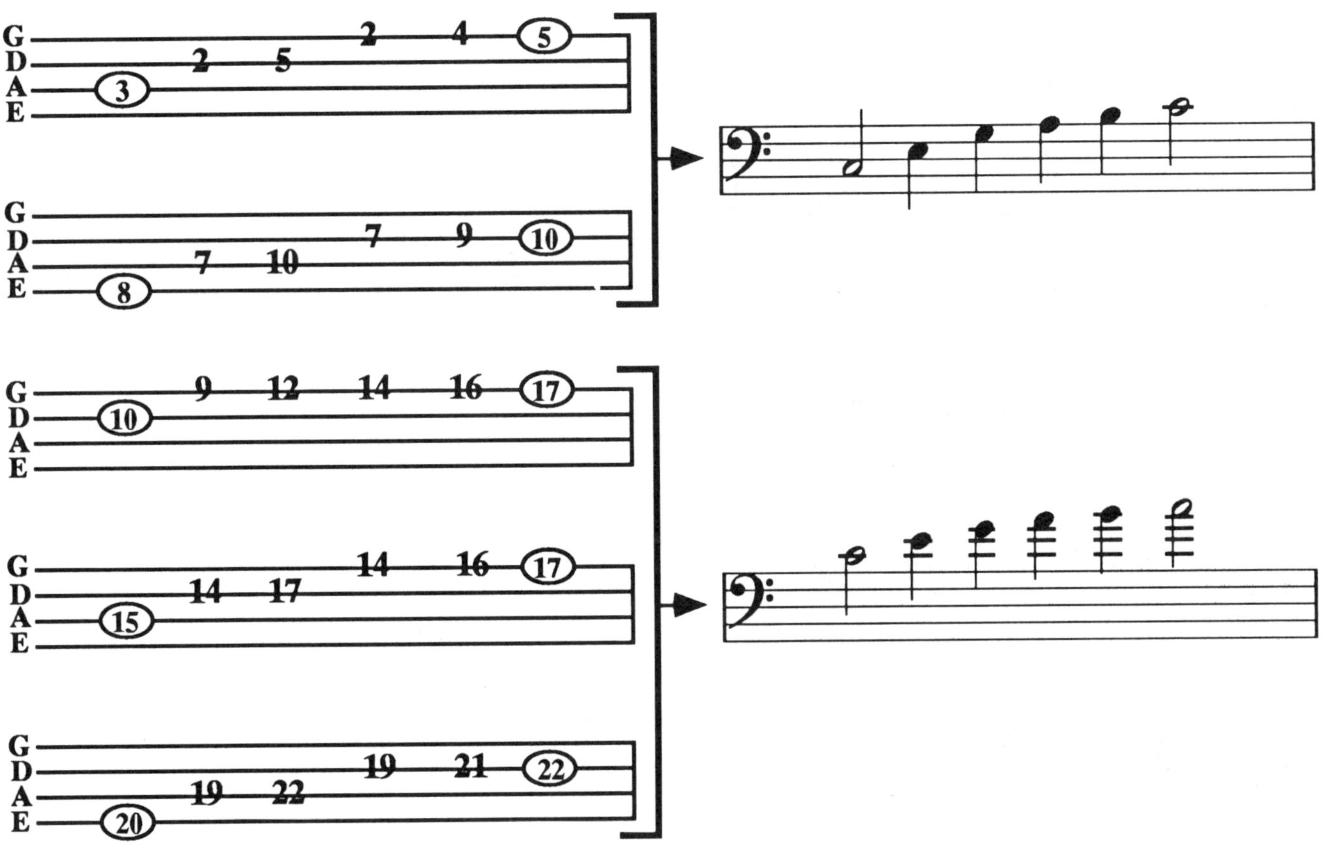

Riff

D MAJOR 13TH

FORMULA - (D) Root (F♯) 3rd (A) 5th (B)13th (C♯) 7th

D Maj. 13

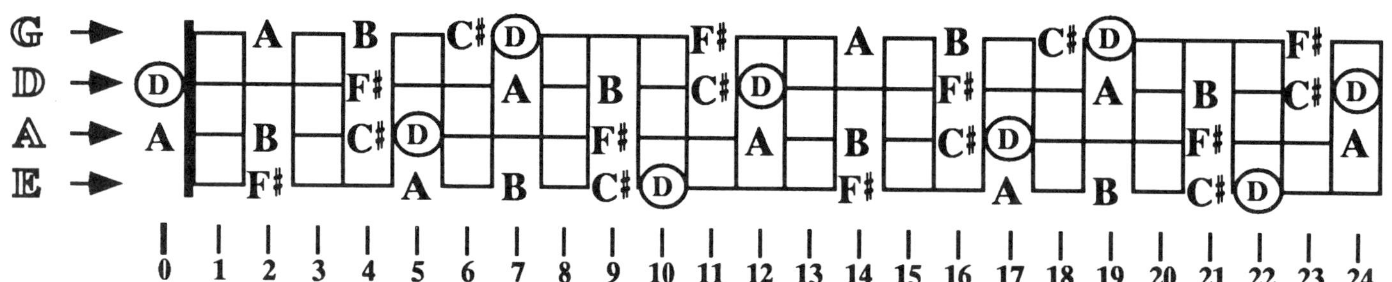

Positions

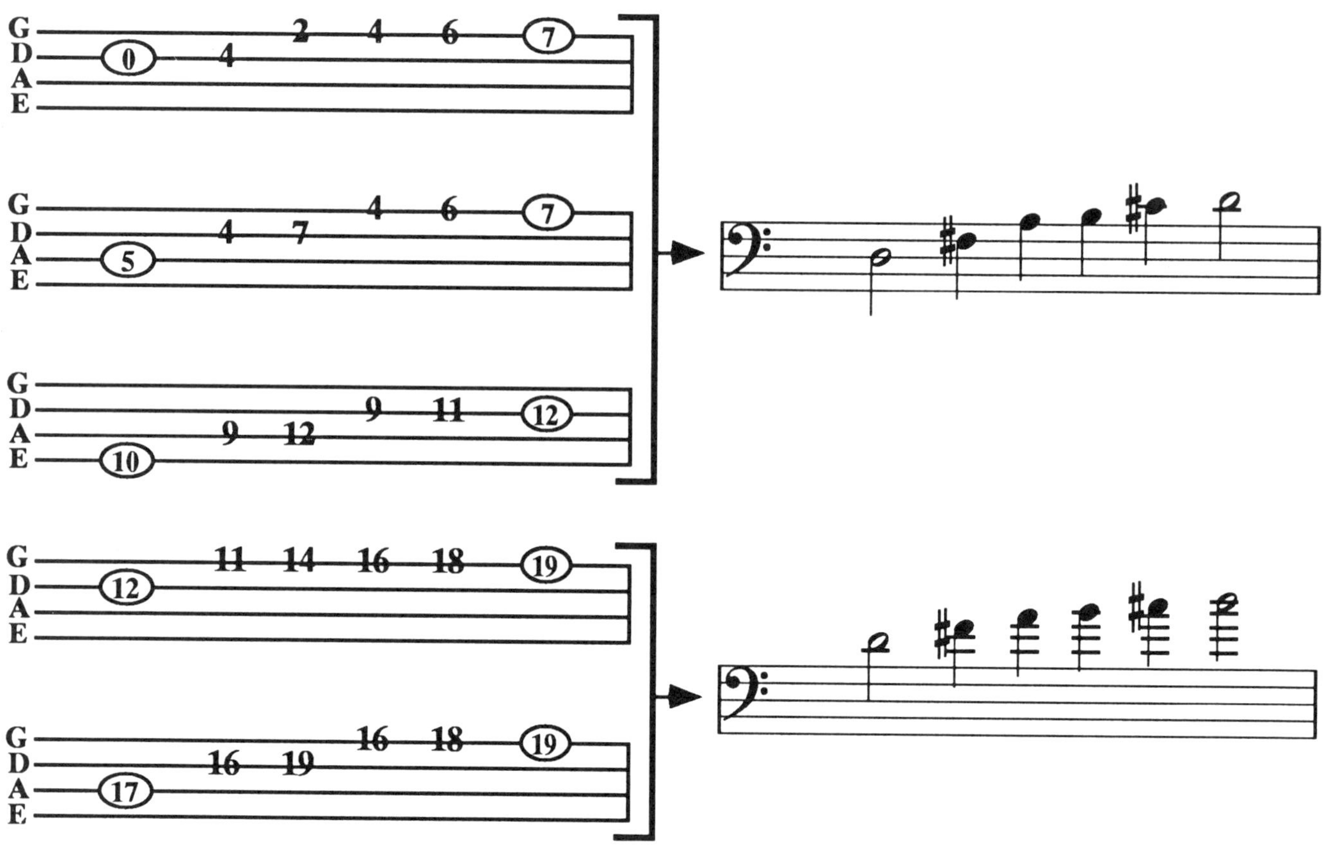

Riff

E MAJOR 13TH

FORMULA - (E) Root (G♯) 3rd (B) 5th (C♯) 13th (D♯) 7th

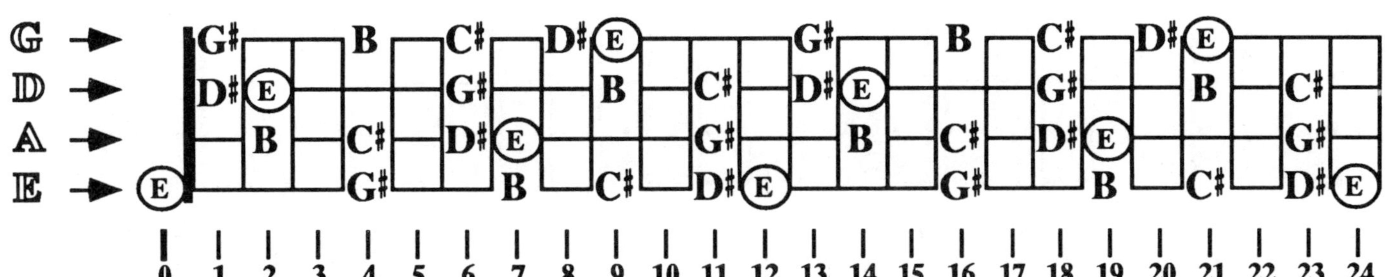

Positions

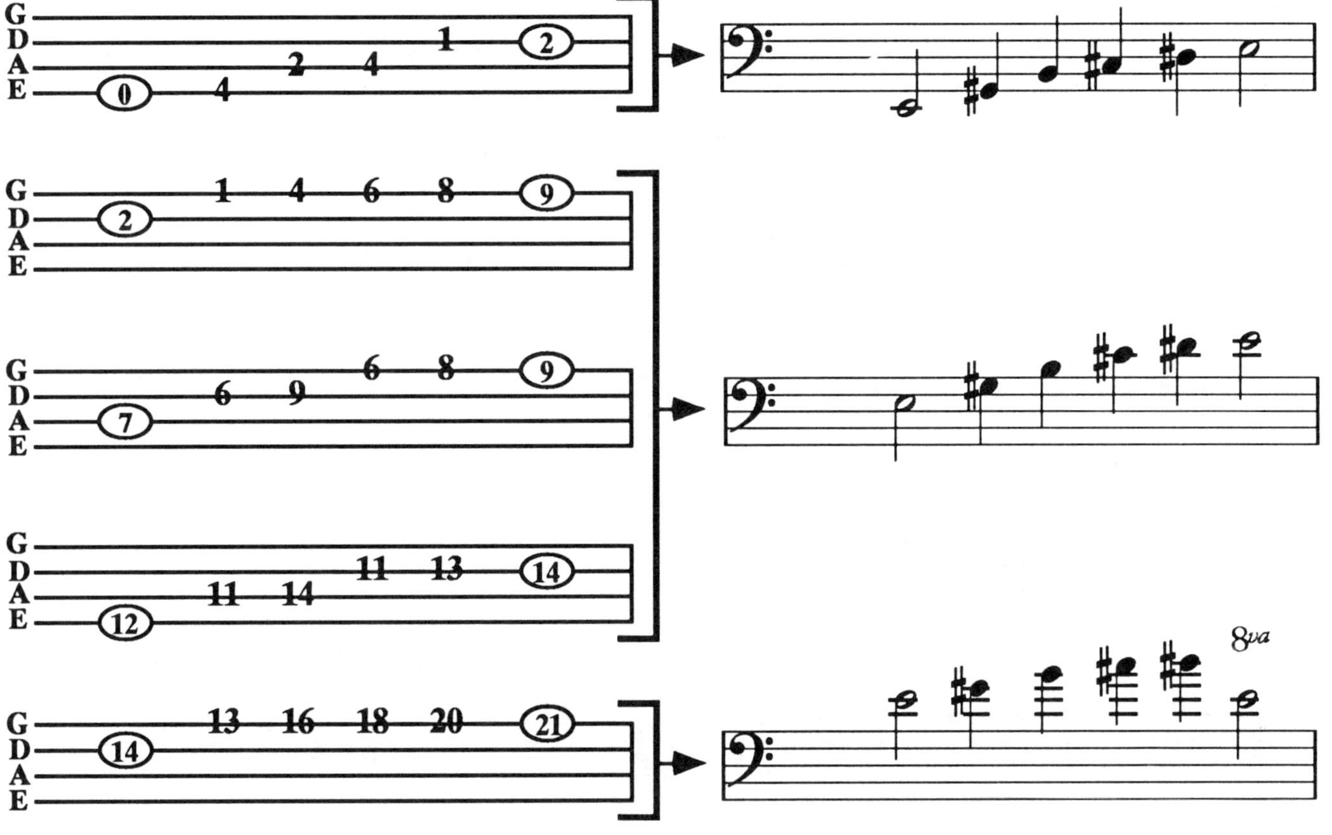

Riff

F MAJOR 13TH

FORMULA - (F) Root (A) 3rd (C) 5th (D) 13th (E) 7th

F Maj. 13

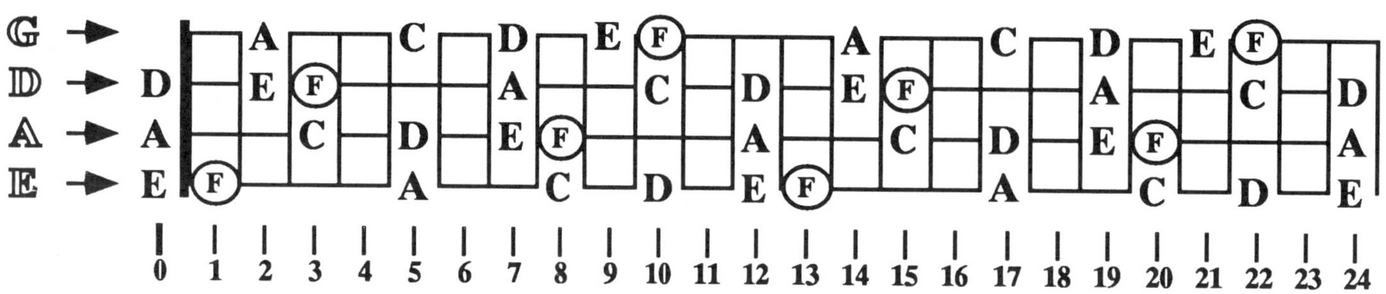

Positions

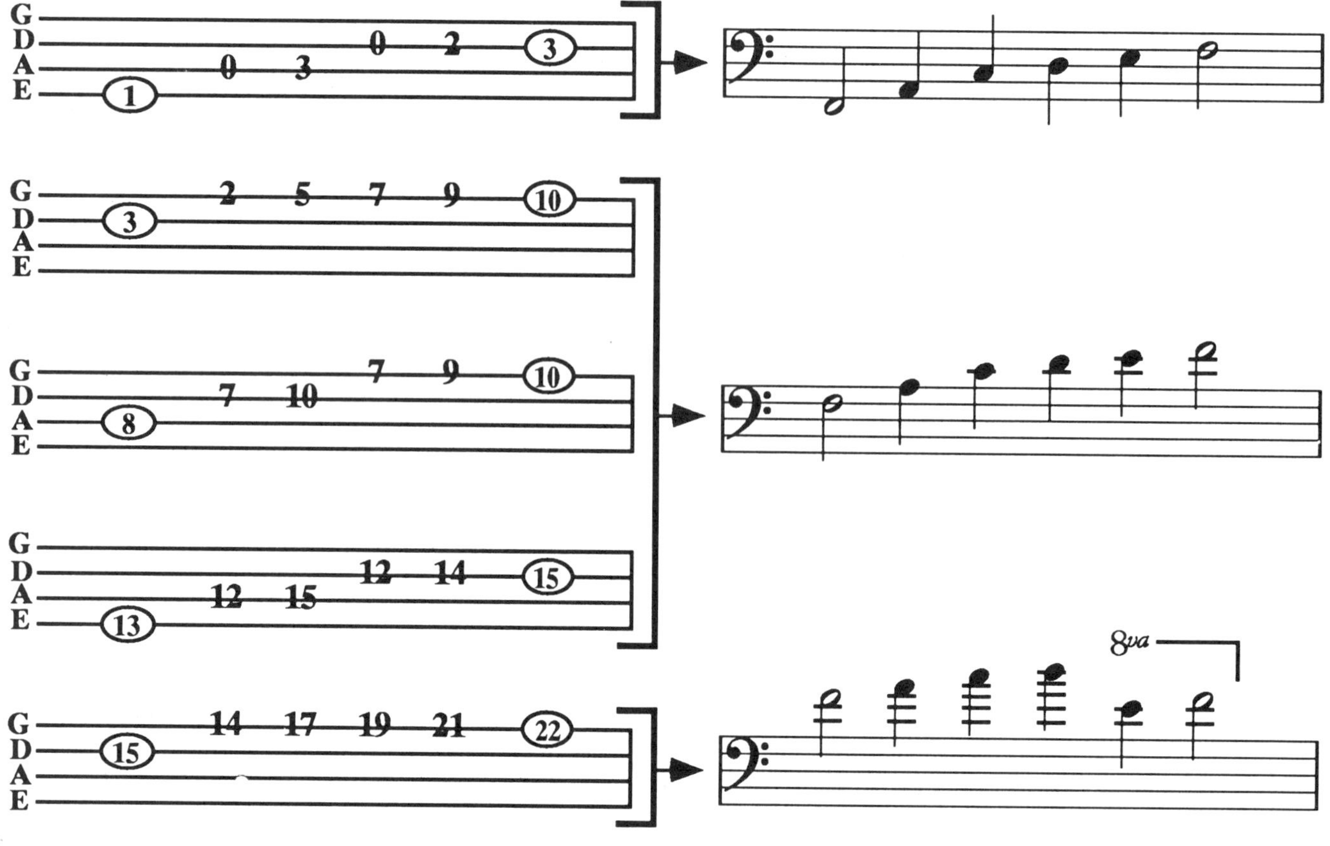

Riff

G MAJOR 13TH

FORMULA - (G) Root (B) 3rd (D) 5th (E) 13th (F♯) 7th

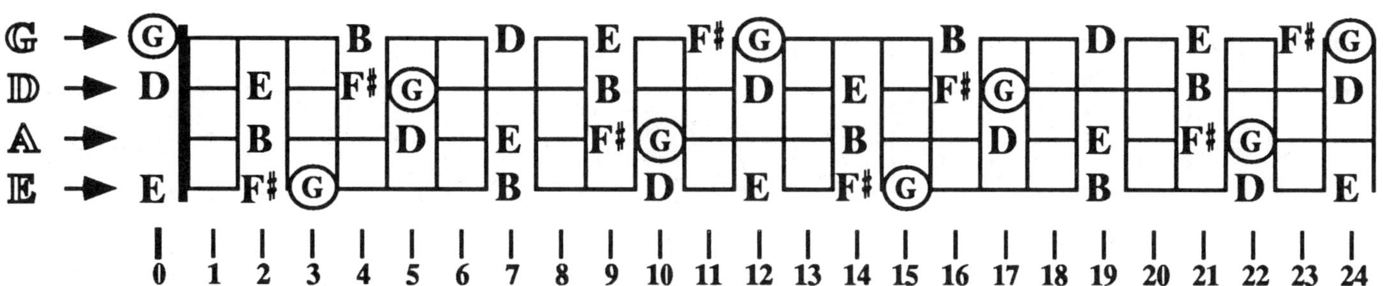

Positions

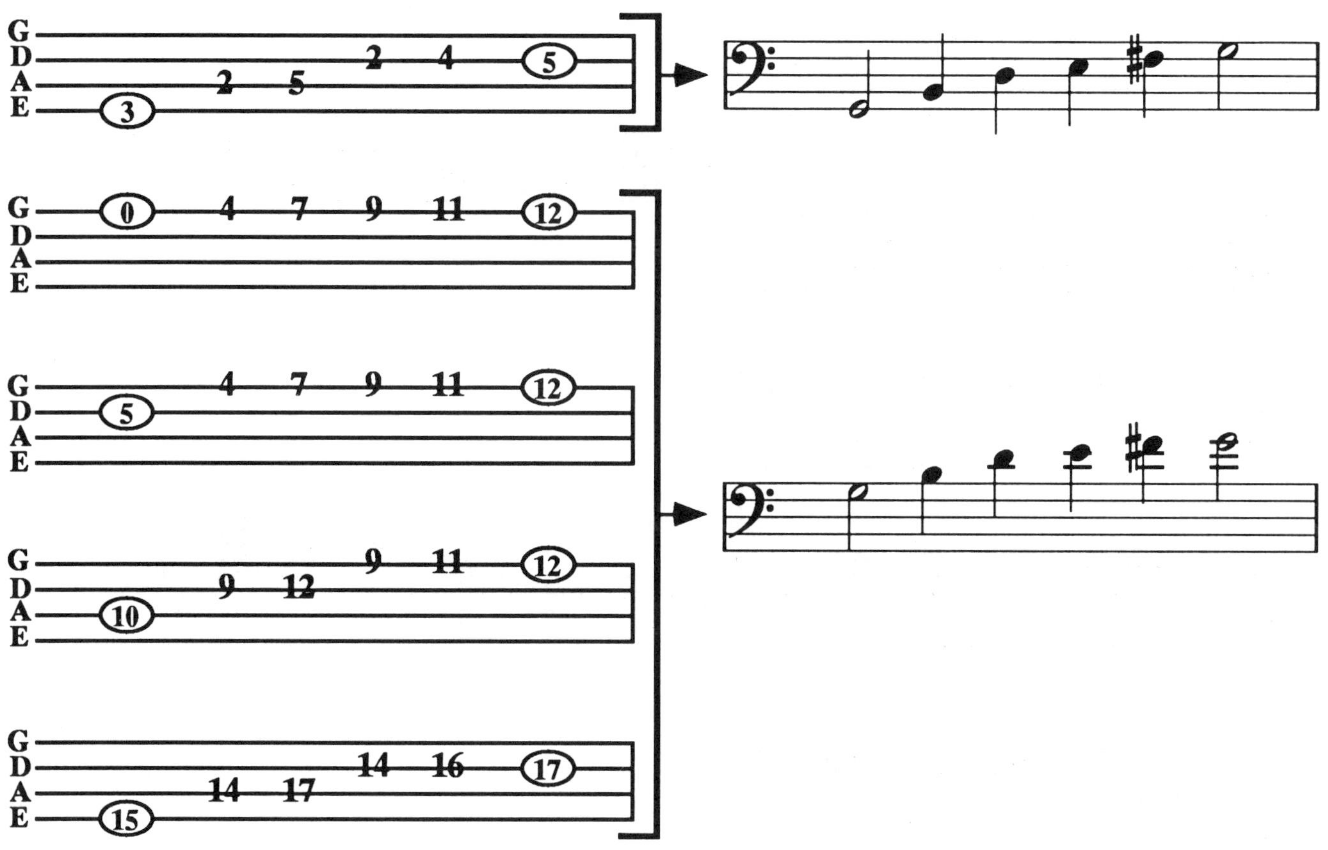

Riff

A MAJOR 13TH

A Maj. 13

FORMULA - (A) Root (C♯) 3rd (E) 5th (F♯)13th (G♯) 9th

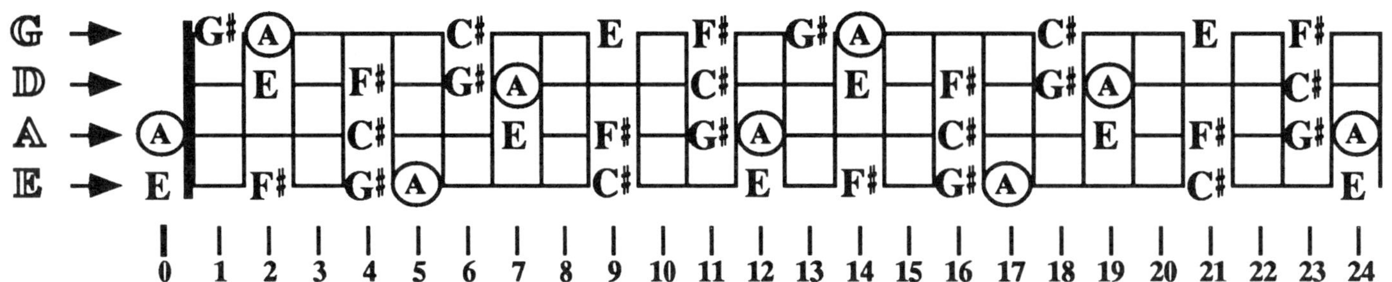

Positions

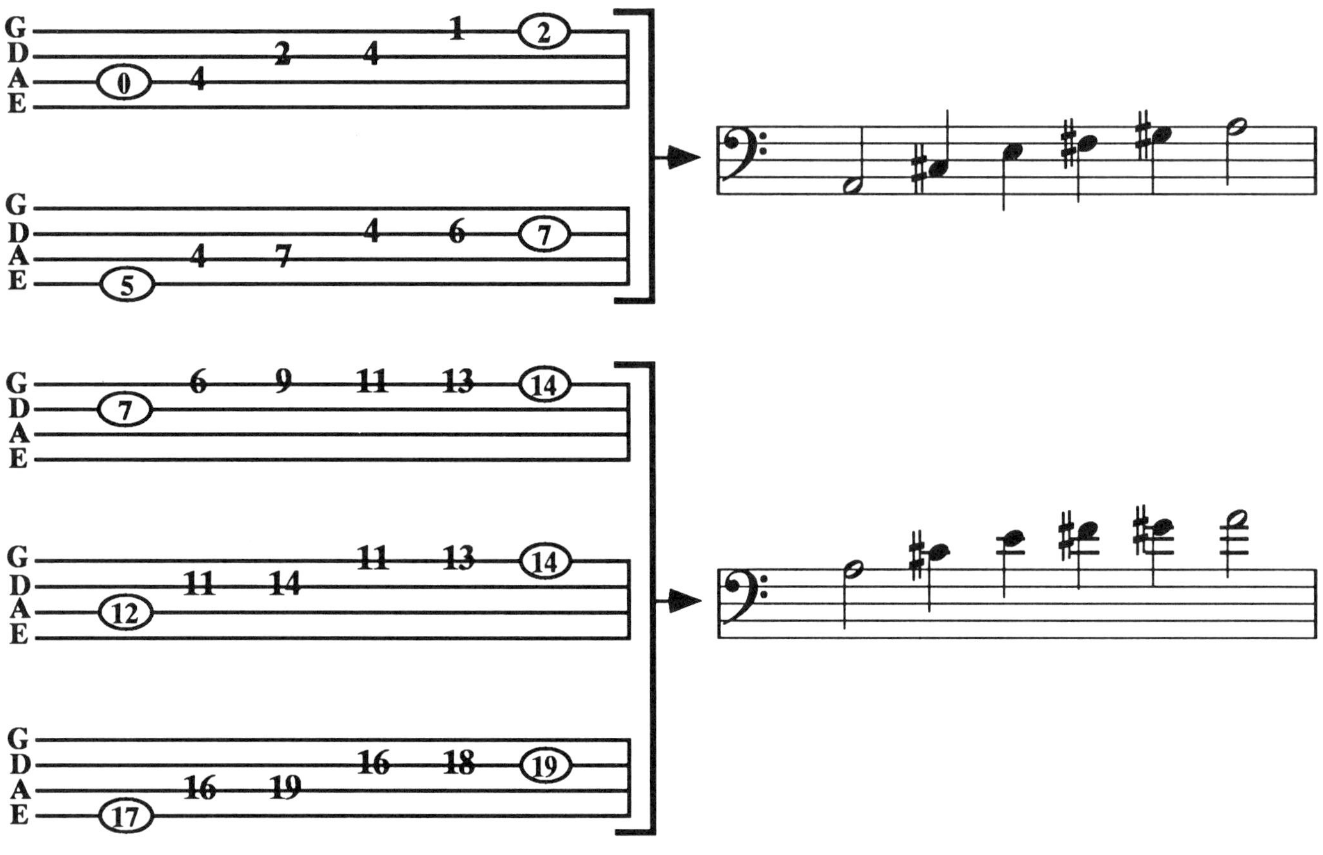

Riff

B MAJOR 13TH

B Maj. 13

FORMULA - (B) Root (D♯) 3rd (F♯) 5th (G♯) 13th (A♯) 7th

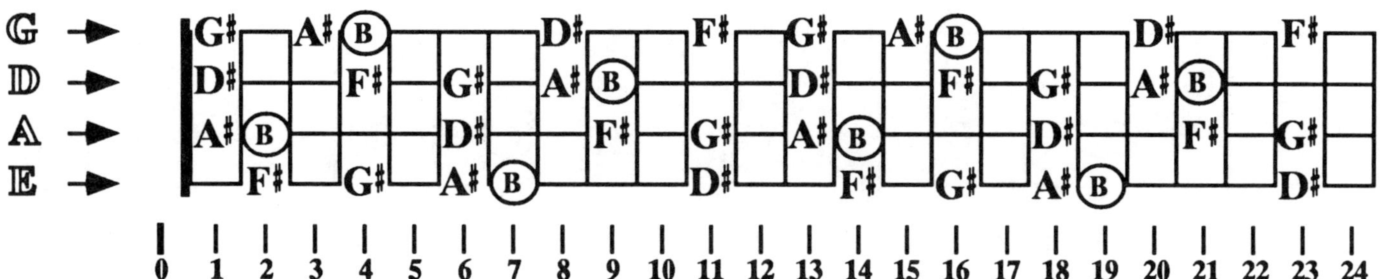

Positions

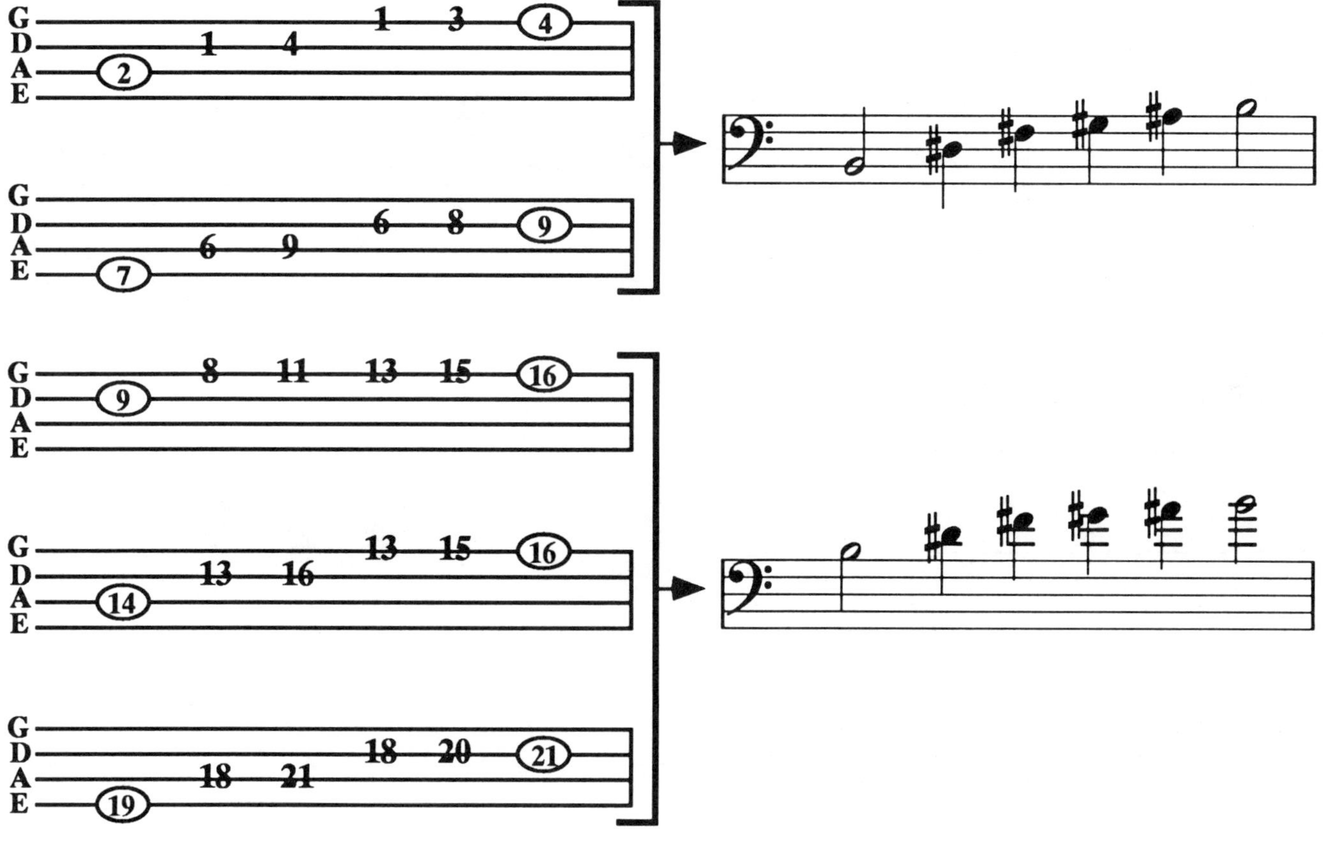

Riff

C MINOR

FORMULA - (C) Root (E♭) ♭3rd (G) 5th

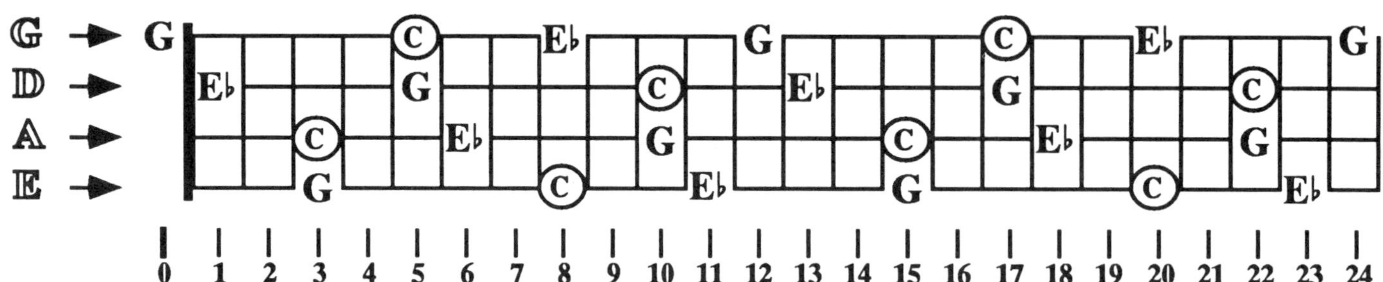

Positions

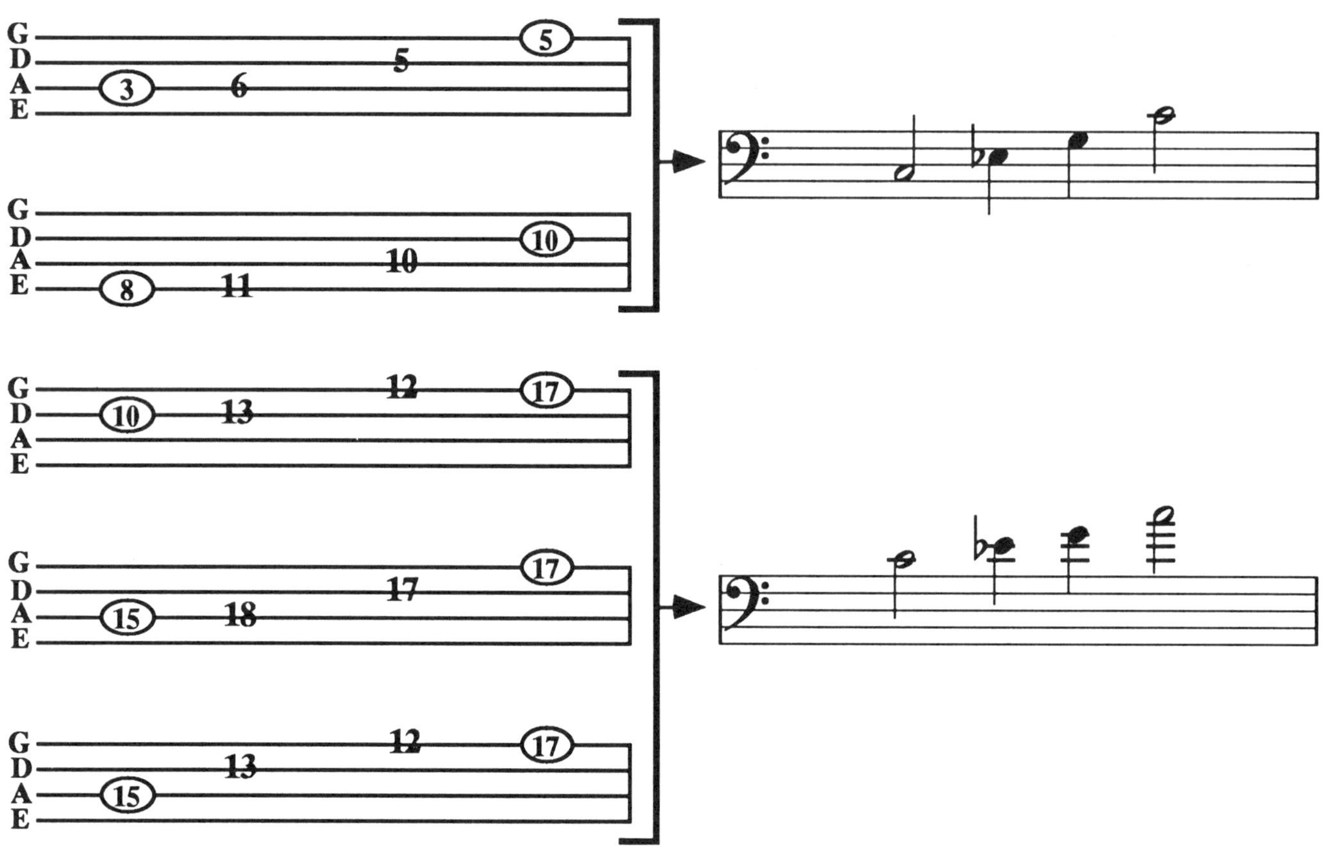

Riff

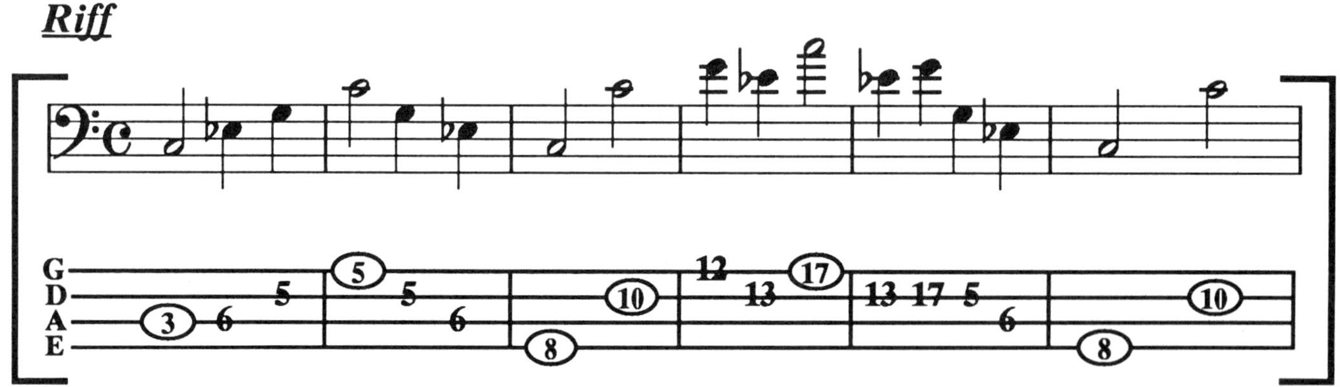

D MINOR

FORMULA - (D) Root (F) ♭3rd (A) 5th

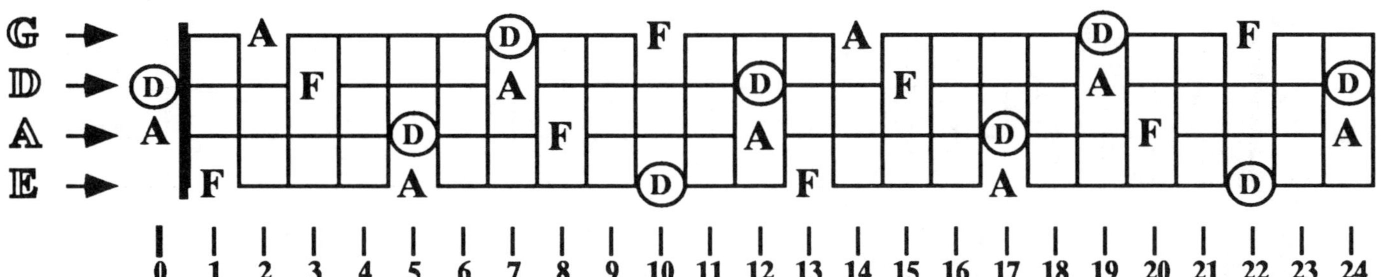

Positions

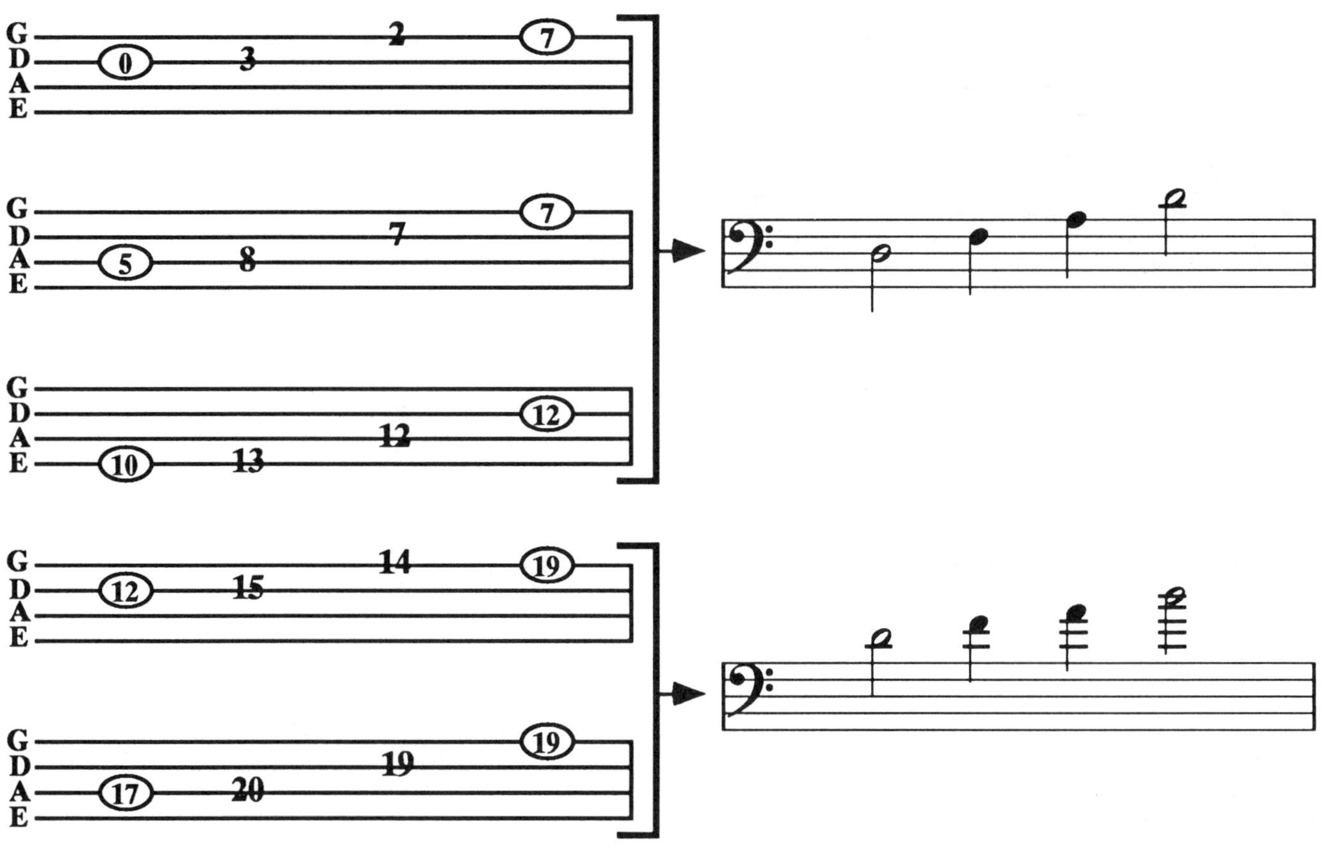

Riff

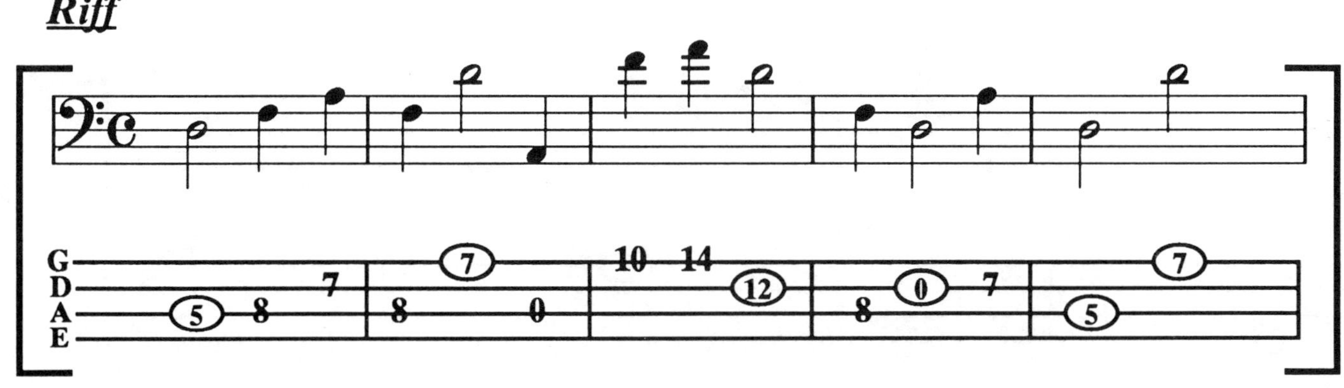

E MINOR

FORMULA - (E) Root (G) ♭3rd (B) 5th

Em

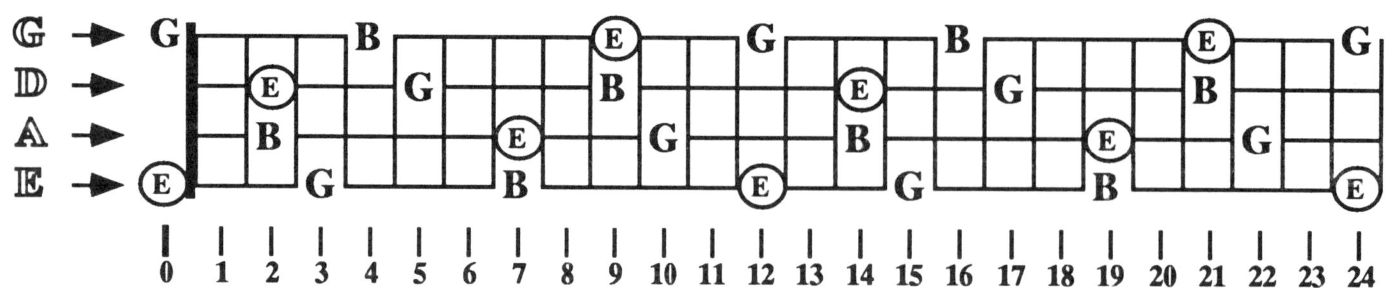

Positions

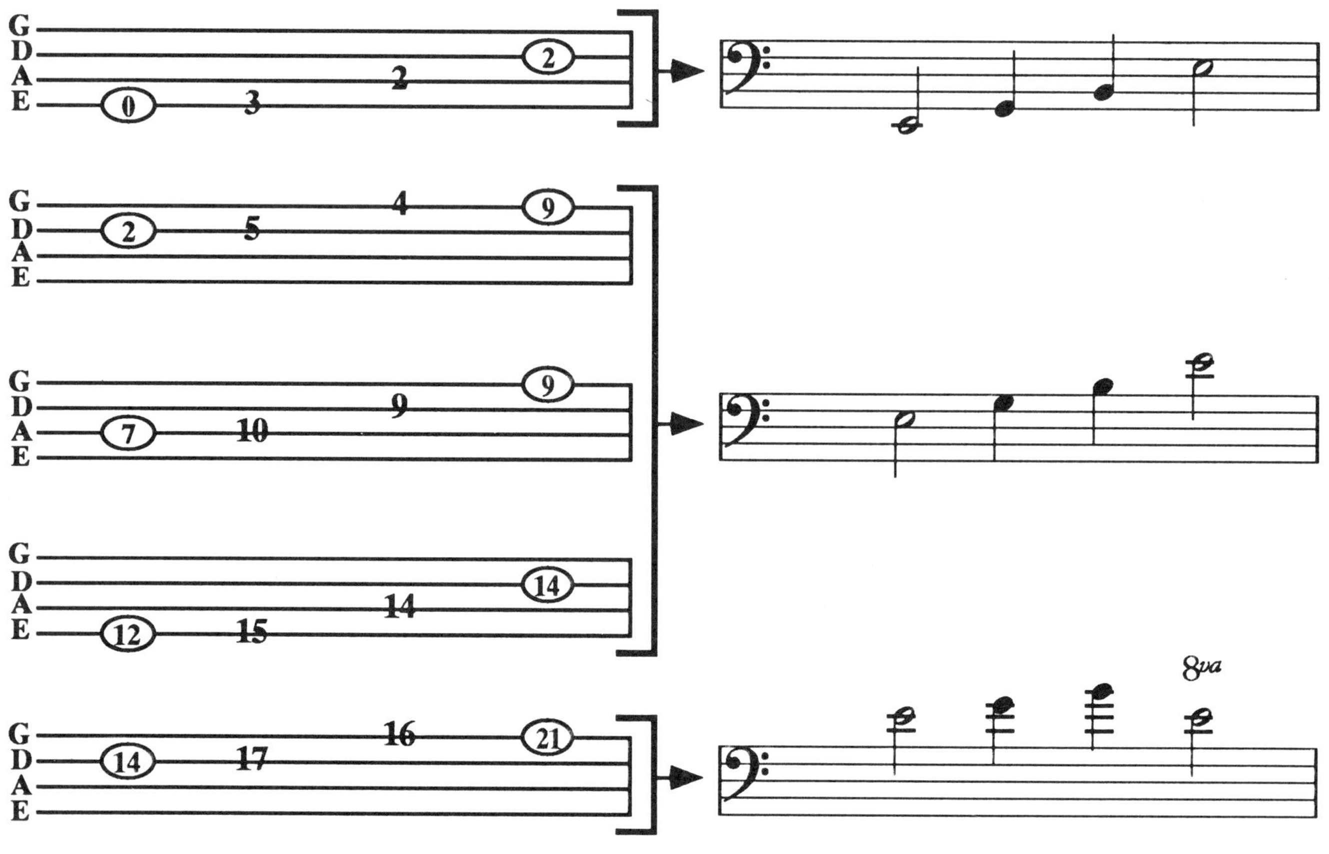

Riff

F MINOR

Fm

FORMULA - (F) Root (A♭) ♭3rd (C) 5th

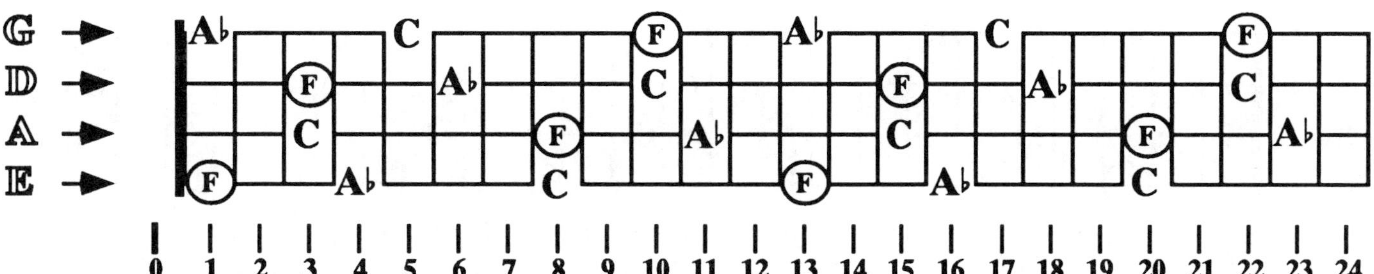

Positions

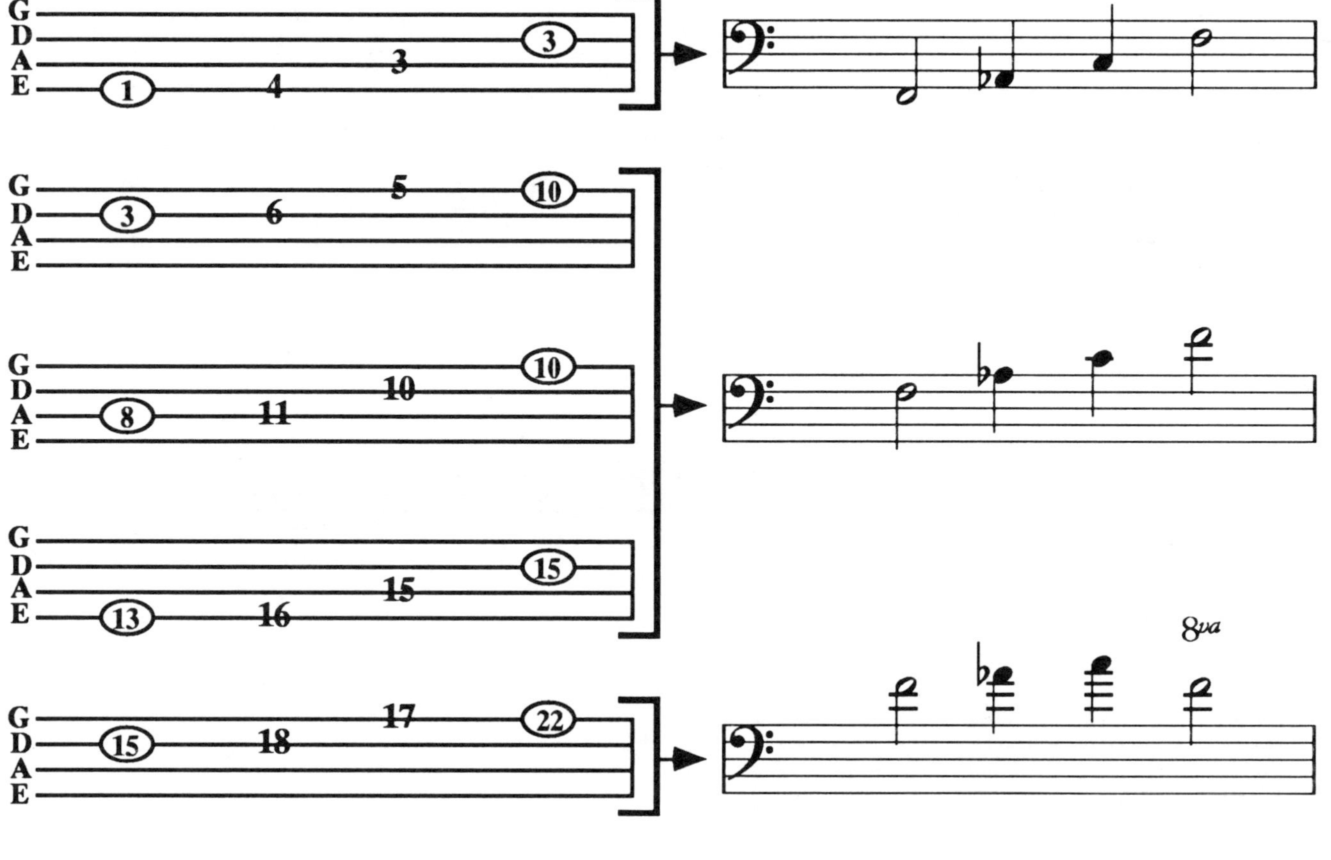

Riff

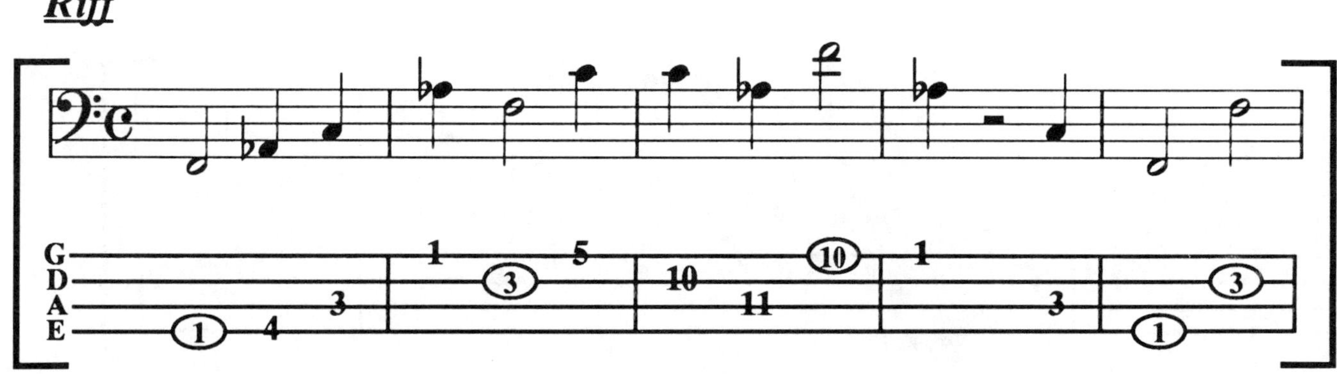

G MINOR

FORMULA - (G) Root (B♭) ♭3rd (D) 5th

Gm

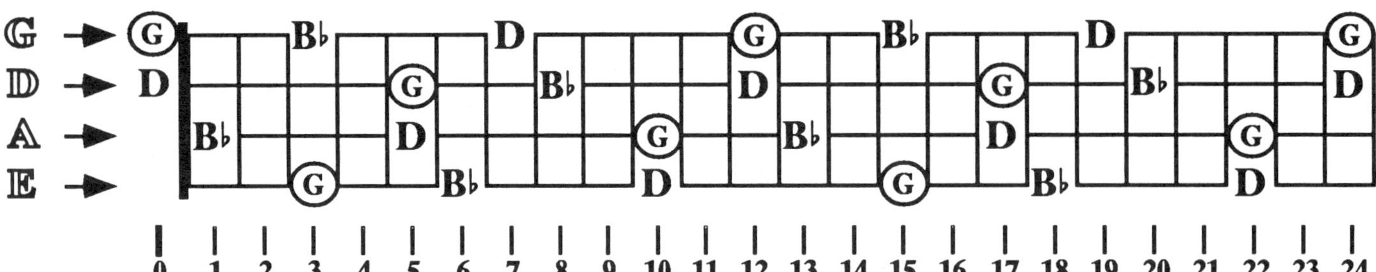

Positions

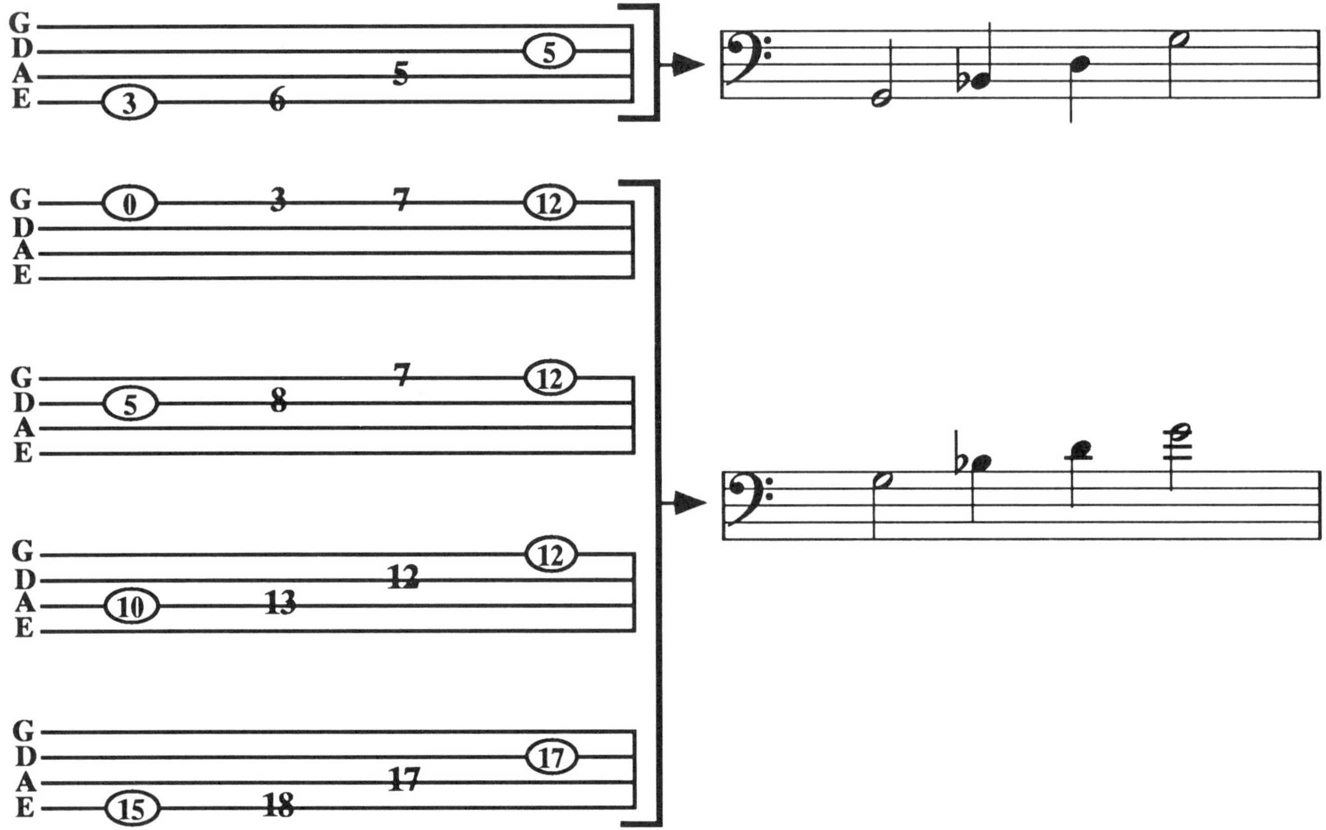

Riff

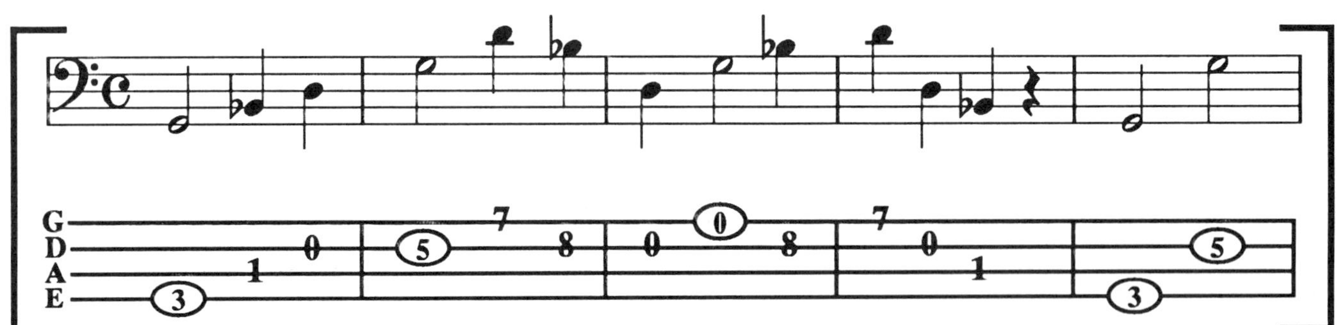

A MINOR

FORMULA - (A) Root (C) ♭3rd (E) 5th

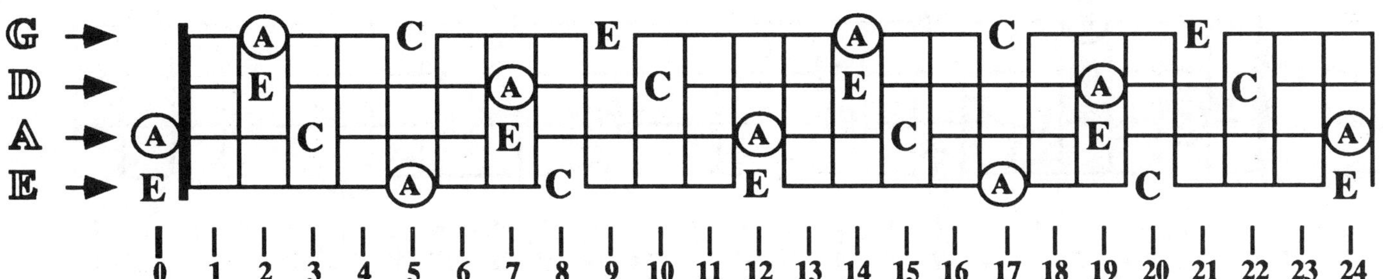

Positions

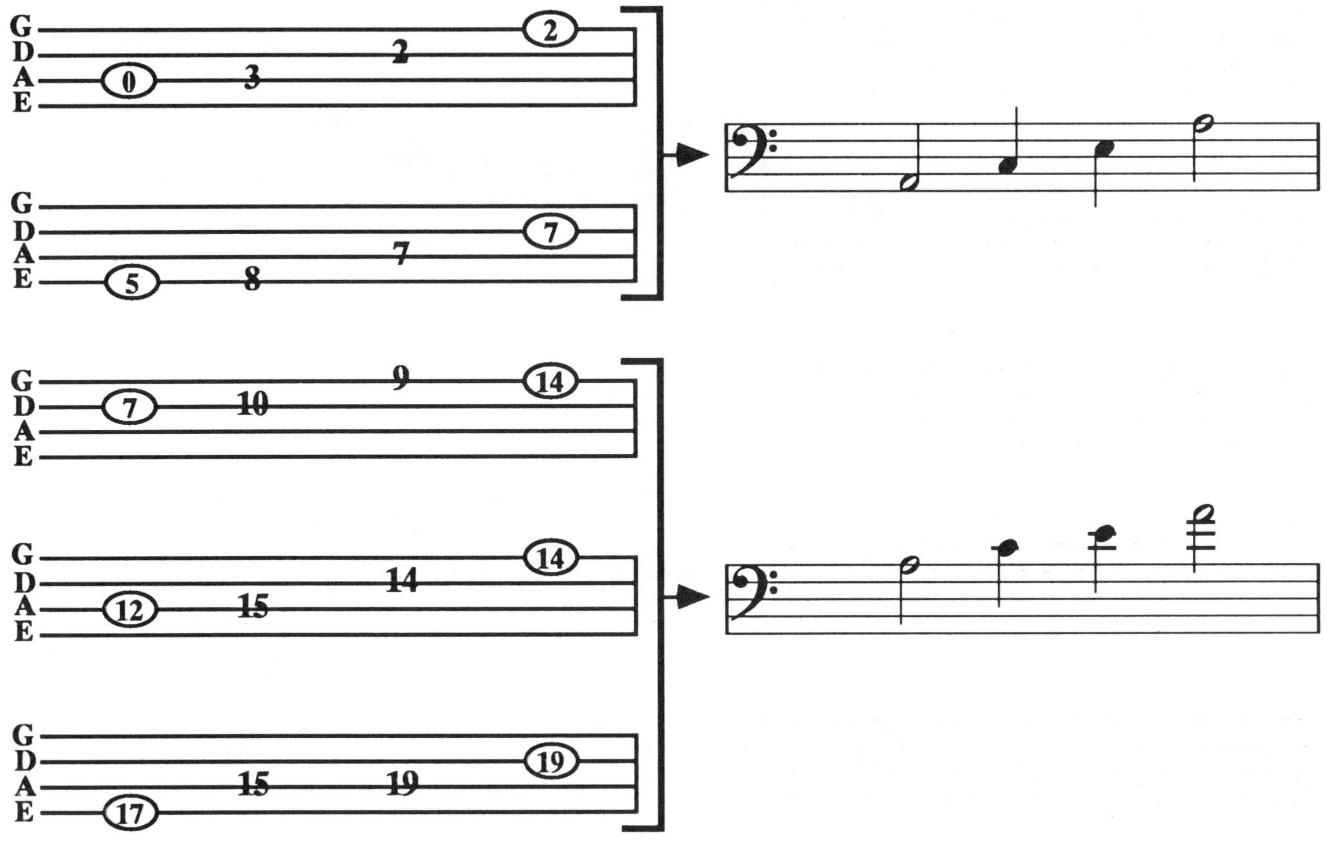

Riff

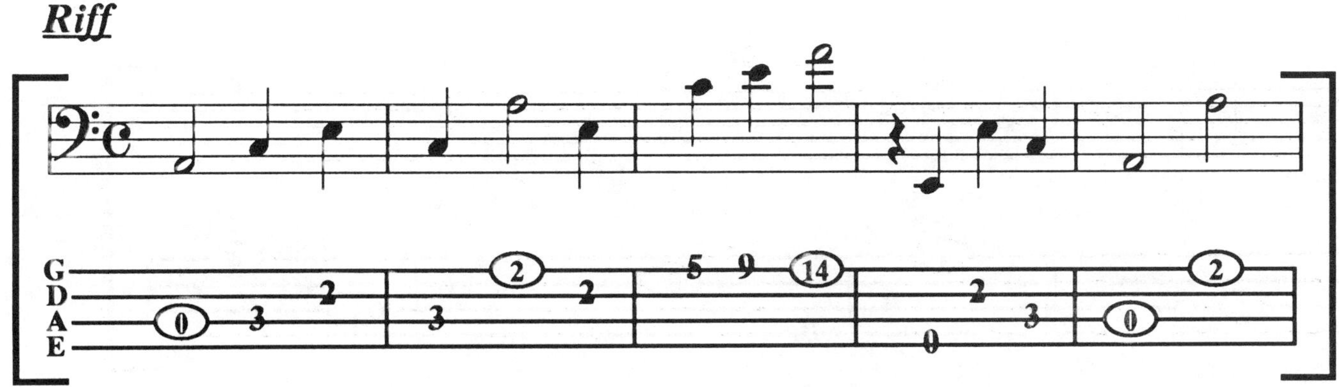

Bm

B MINOR
FORMULA - (B) Root (D) ♭3rd (F♯) 5th

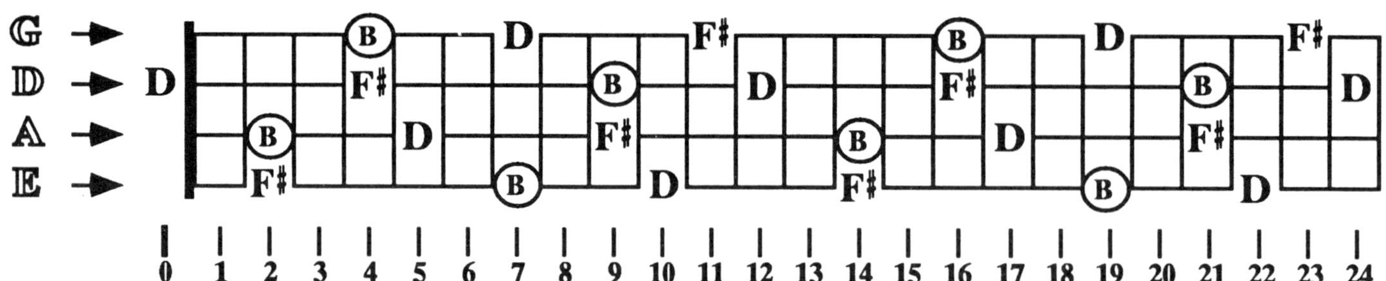

Positions

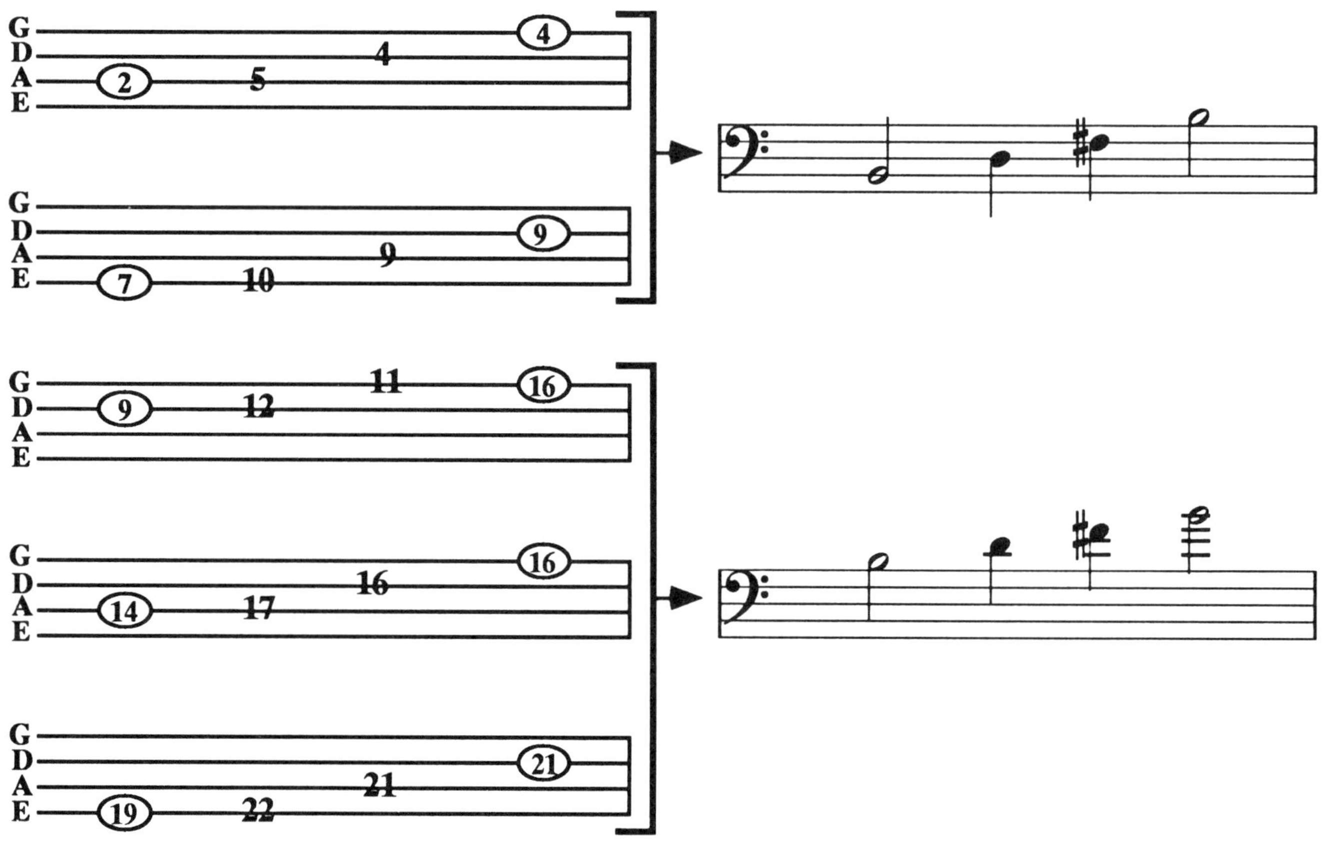

Riff

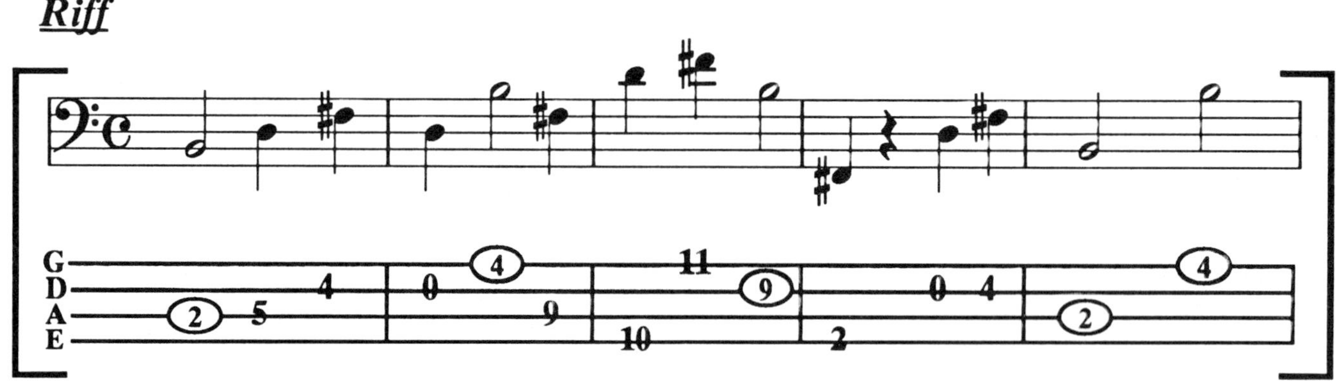

C MINOR 6TH

Cm6

FORMULA - (C) Root (E♭) ♭3rd (G) 5th (A) 6th

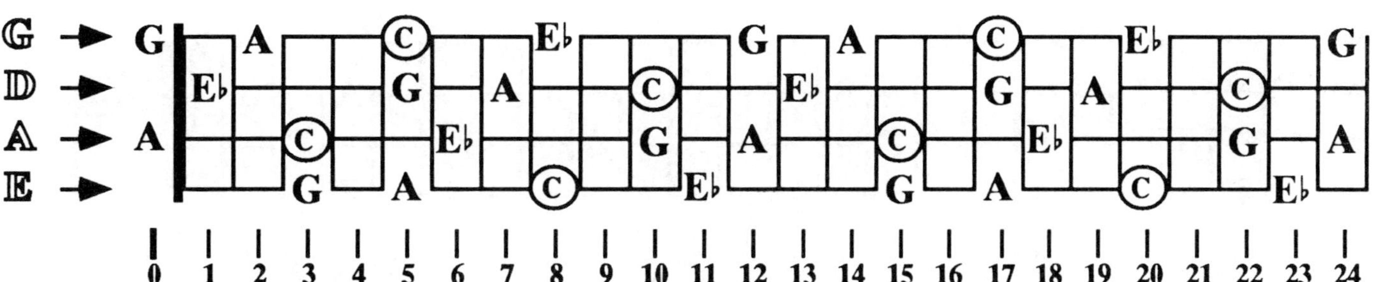

Positions

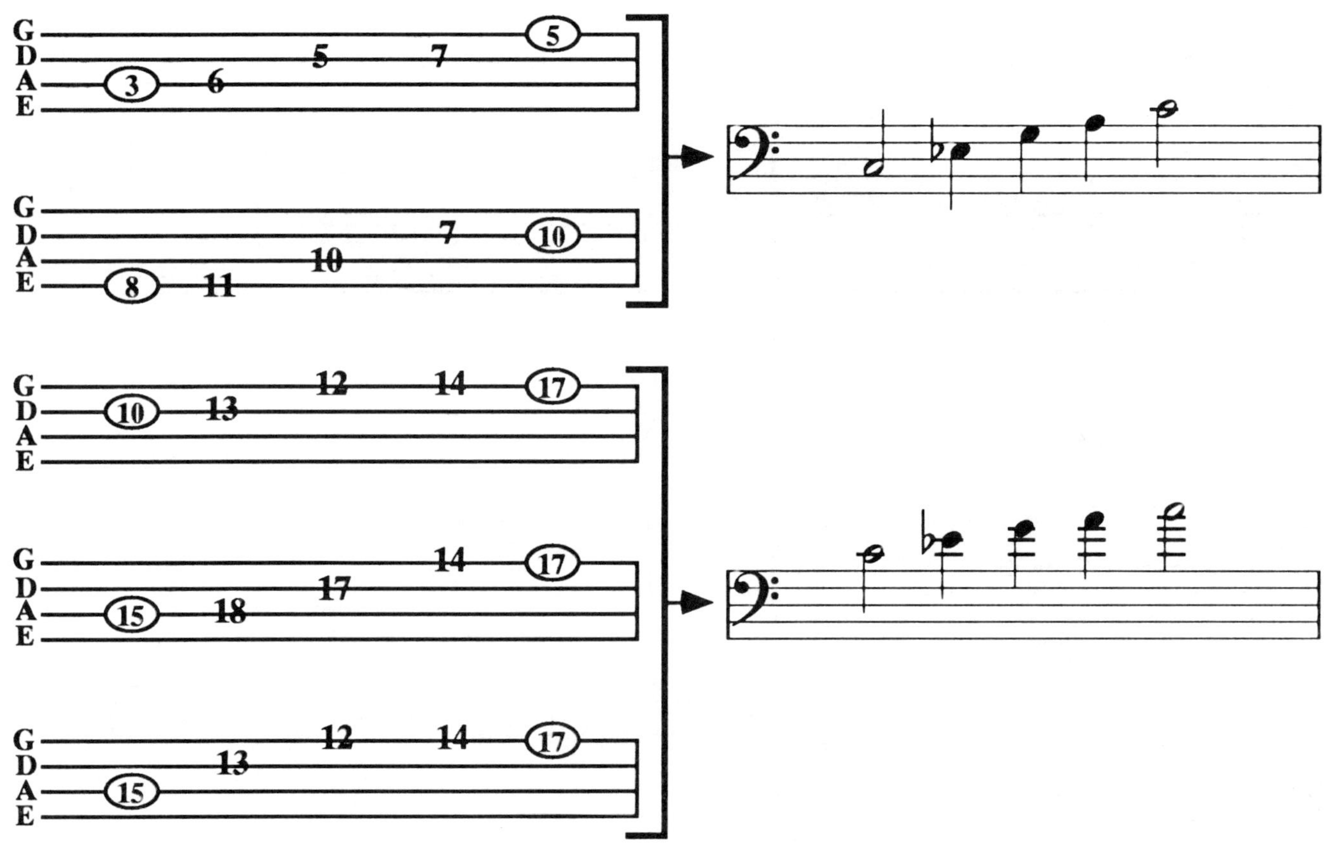

Riff

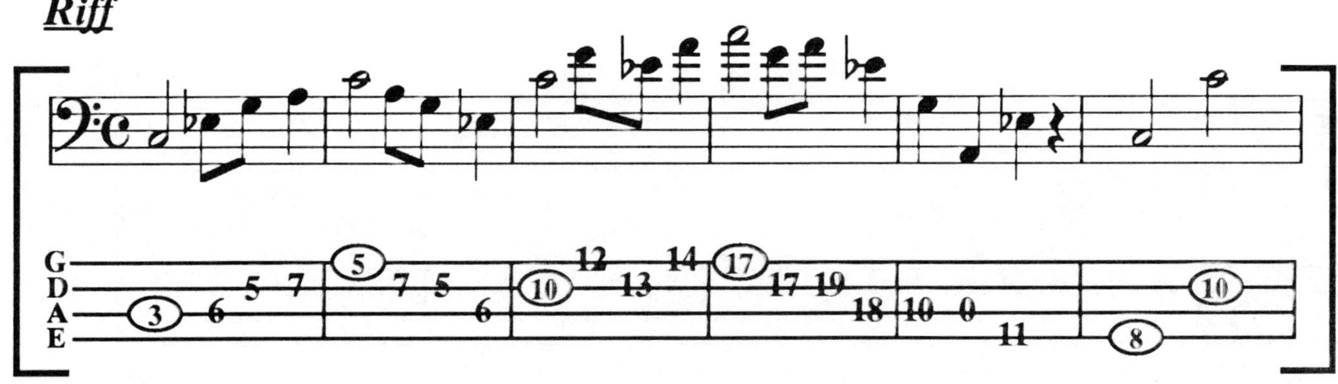

D MINOR 6TH

FORMULA - (D) Root (F) ♭3rd (A) 5th (B) 6th

Dm6

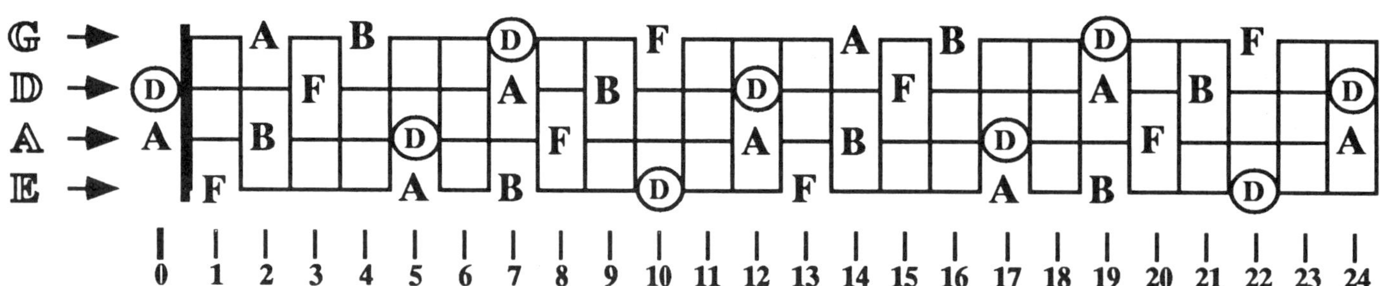

Positions

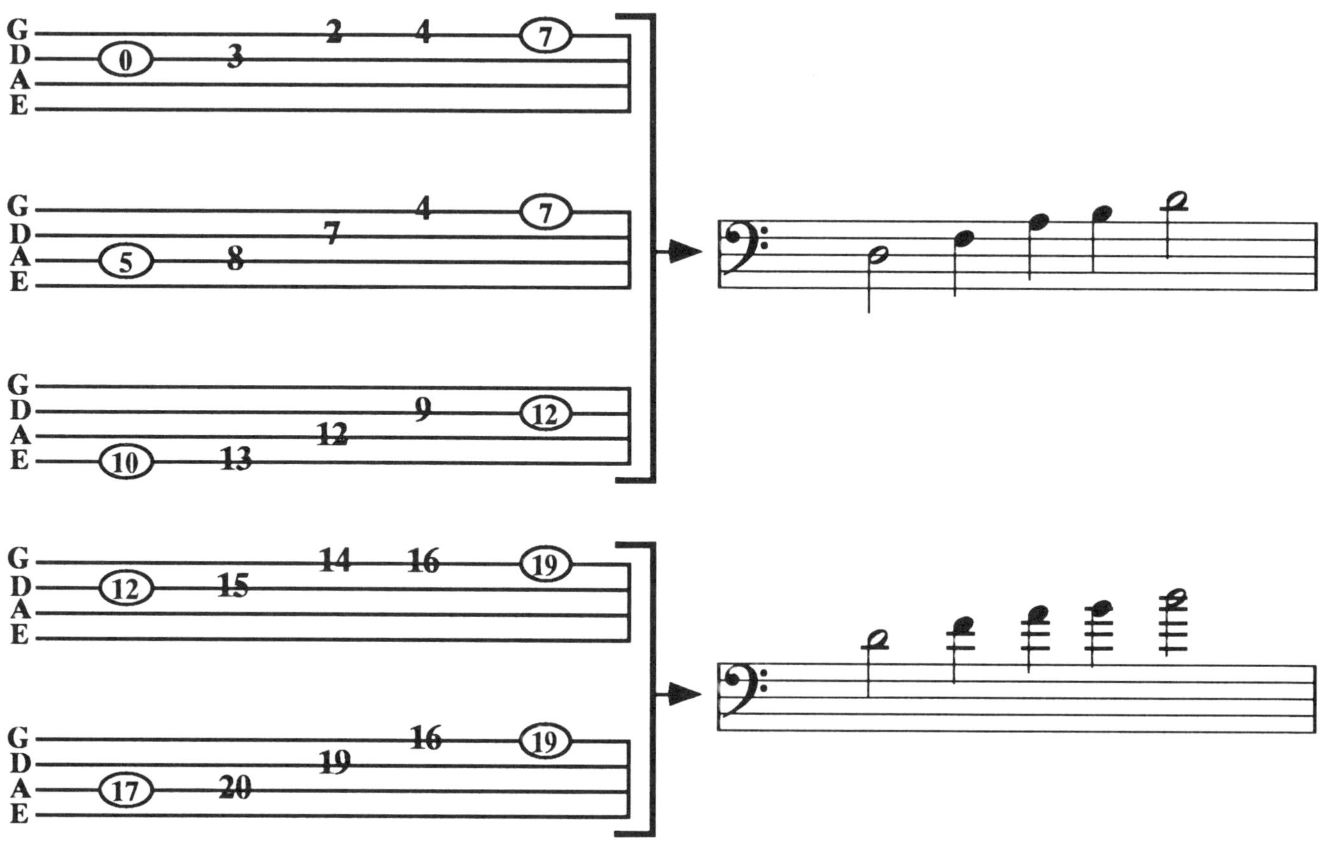

Riff

E MINOR 6TH

FORMULA - (E) Root (G) ♭3rd (B) 5th (C♯) 6th

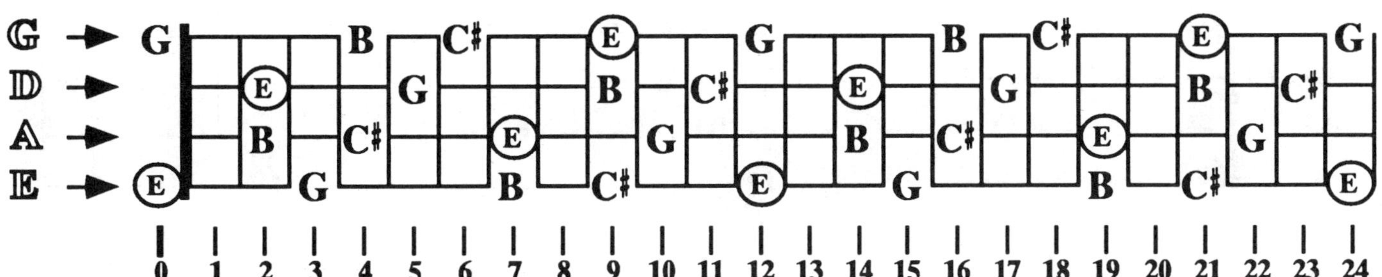

Positions

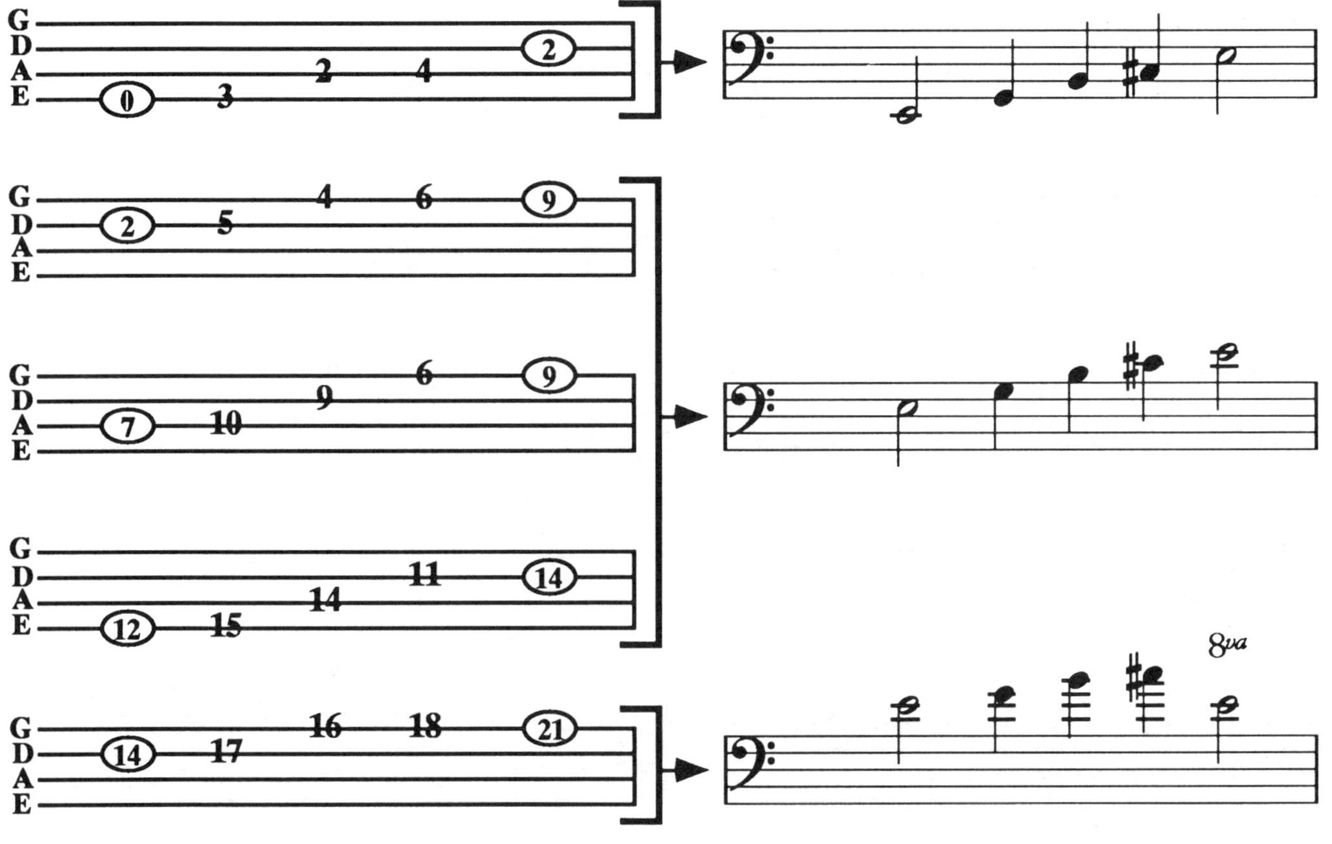

Riff

F MINOR 6TH

FORMULA - (F) Root (A♭) ♭3rd (C) 5th (D) 6th

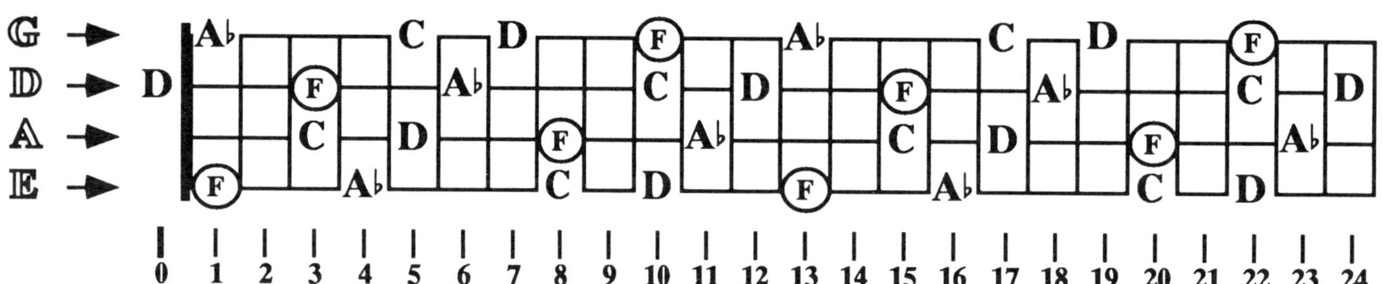

Positions

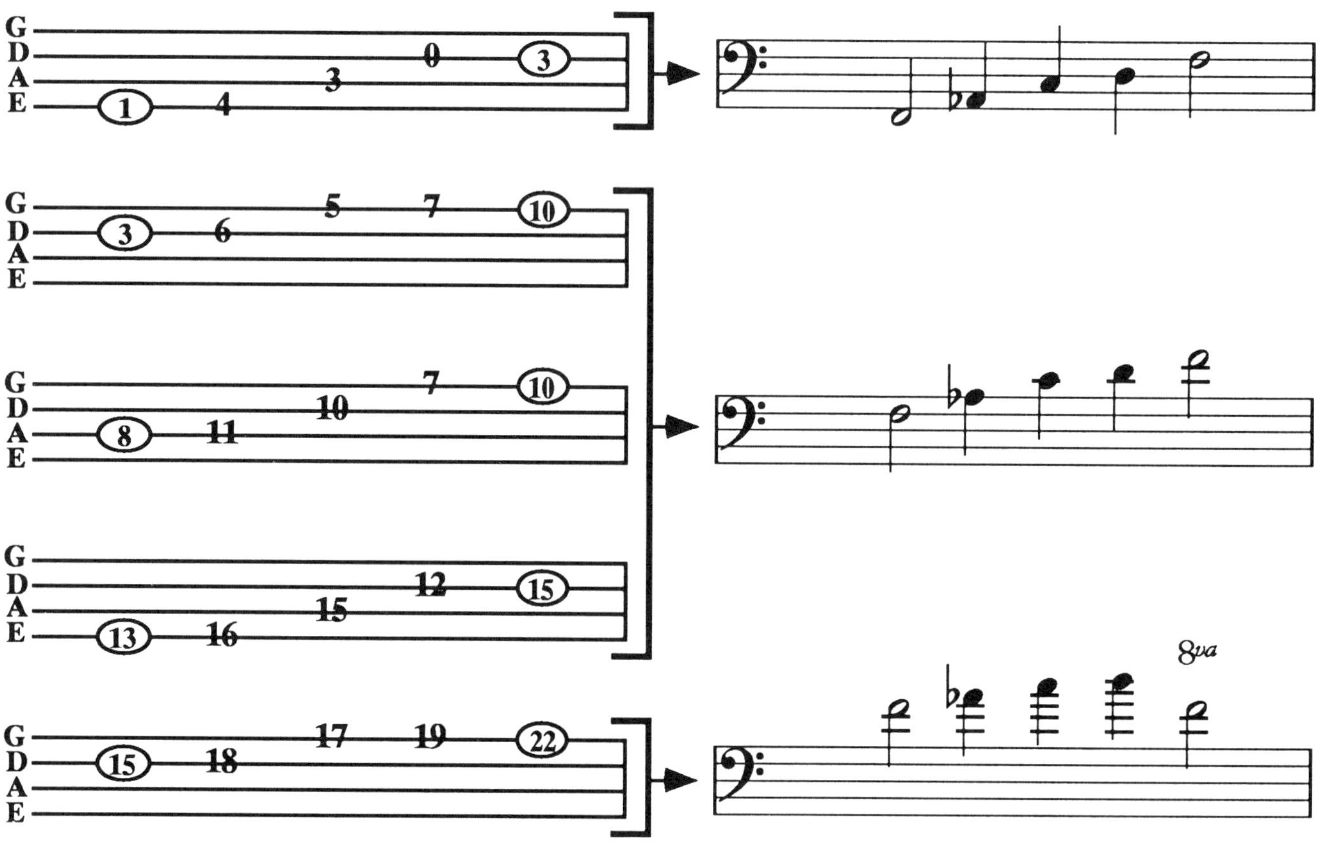

Riff

G MINOR 6TH

Gm6

FORMULA - (G) Root (B♭) ♭3rd (D) 5th (E) 6th

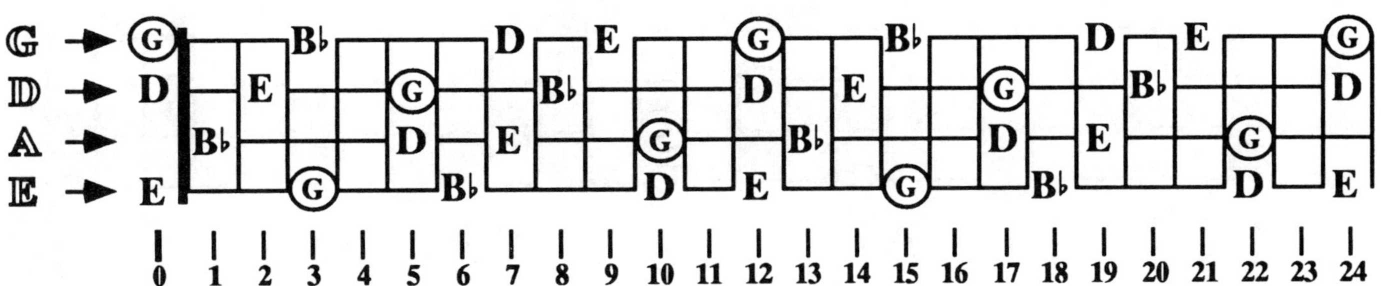

Positions

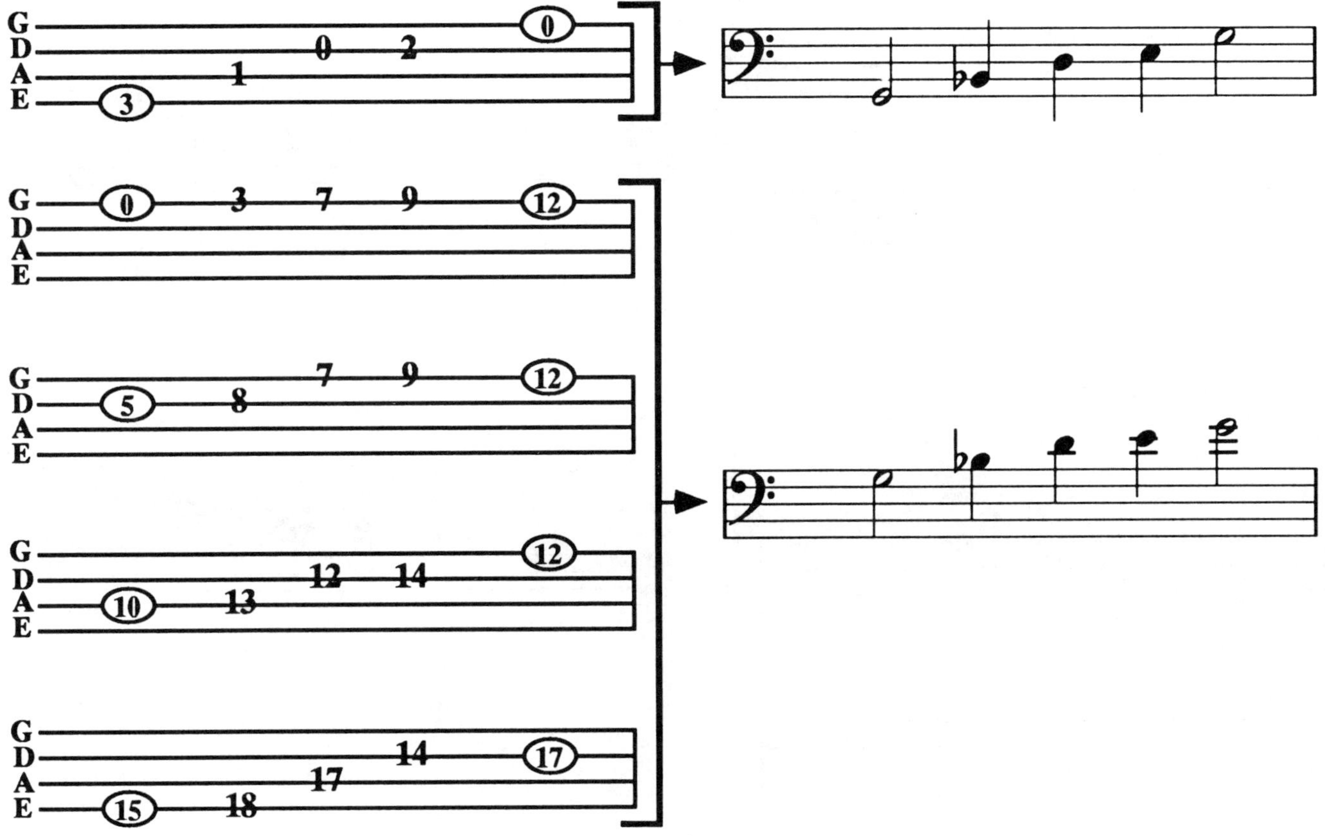

Riff

A MINOR 6TH

FORMULA - (A) Root (C) ♭3rd (E) 5th (F♯) 6th

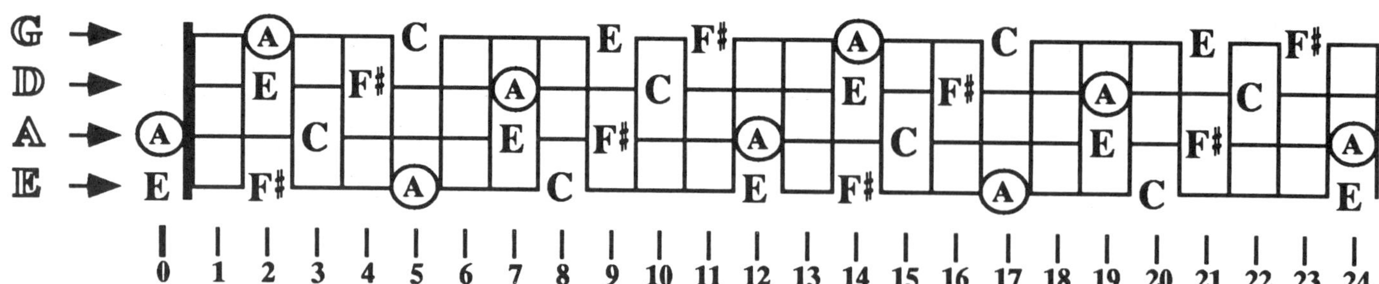

Positions

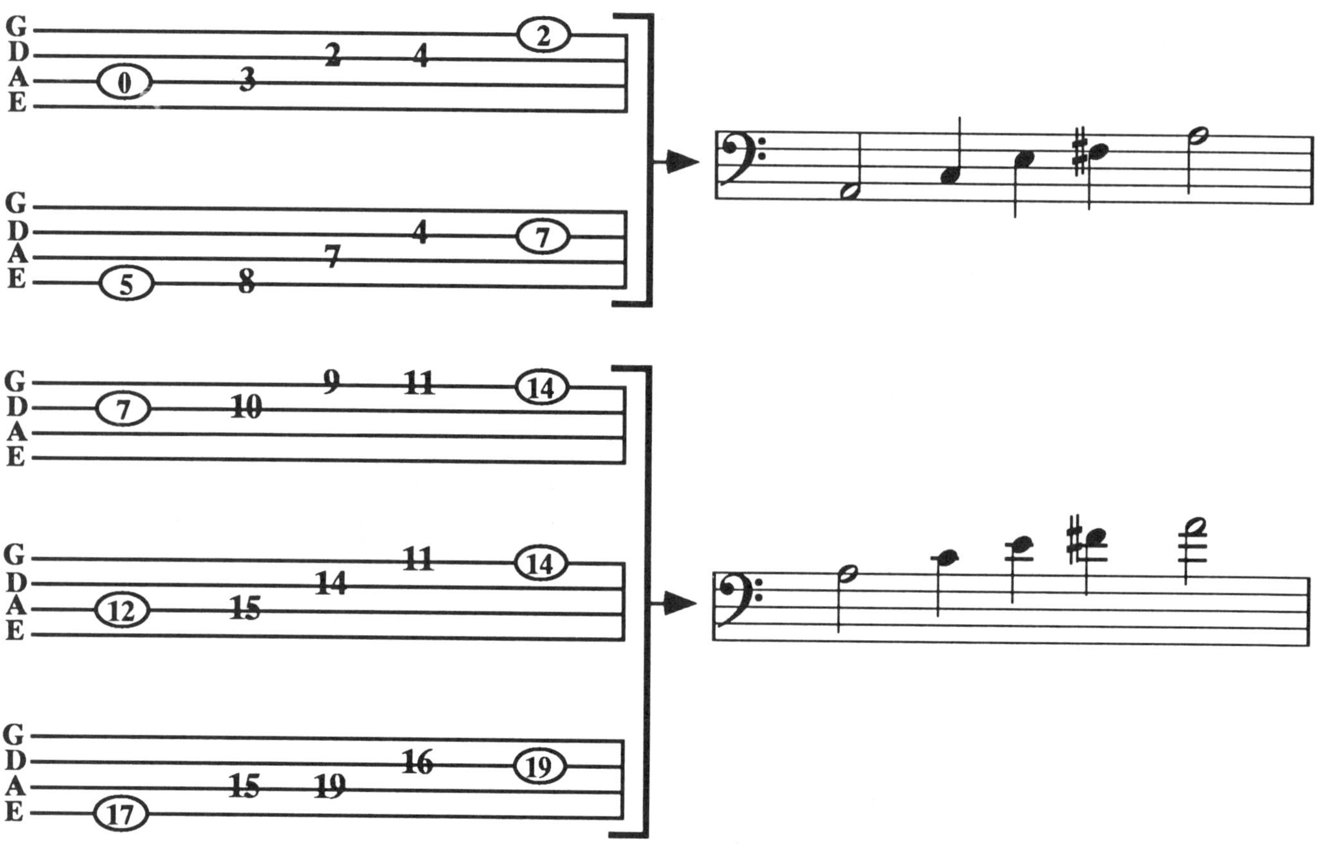

Riff

B MINOR 6TH

FORMULA - (B) Root (D) ♭3rd (F♯) 5th (G♯) 6th

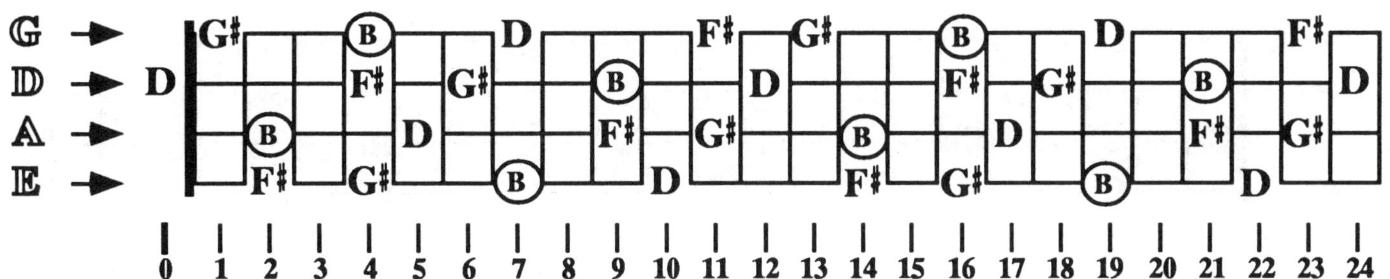

Positions

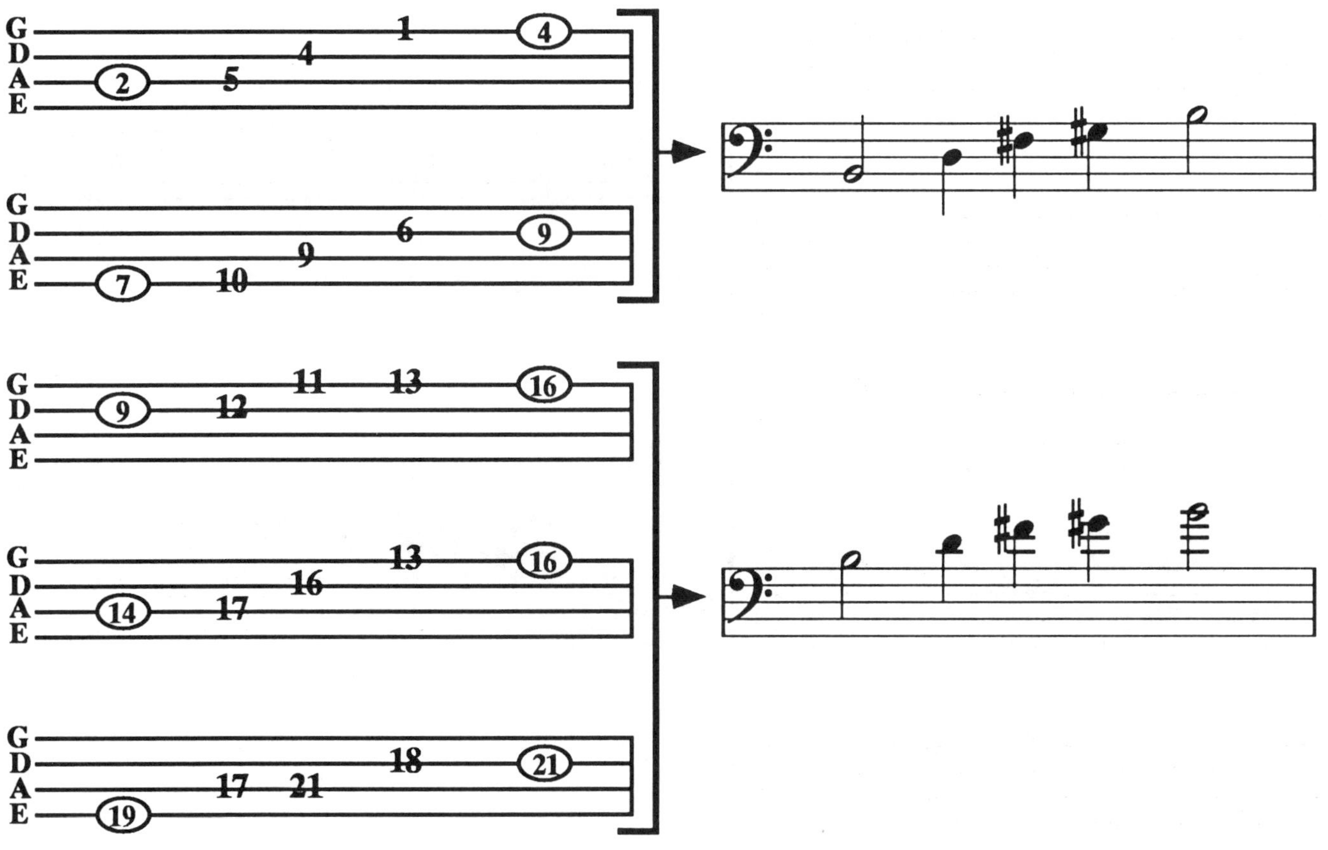

Riff

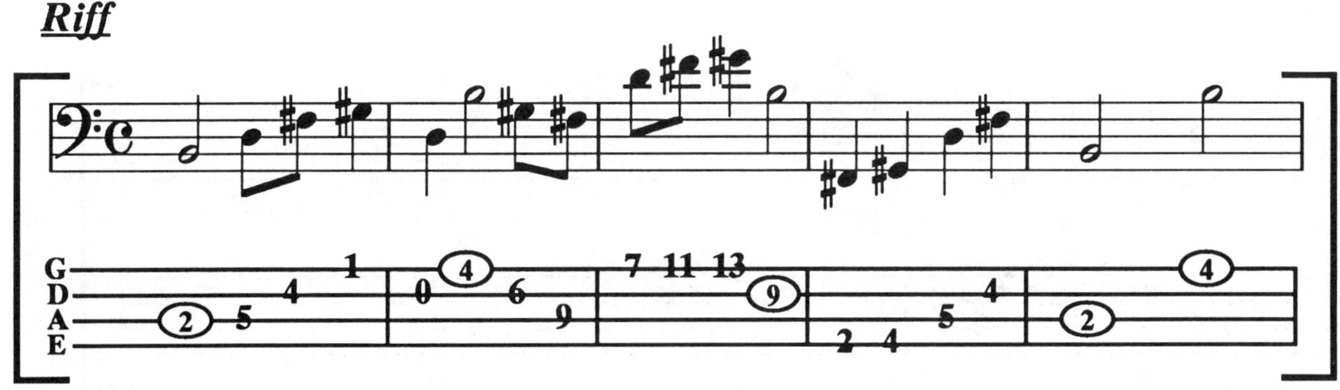

C MINOR 7TH

FORMULA - (C) Root (E♭) ♭3rd (G) 5th (B♭) ♭7th

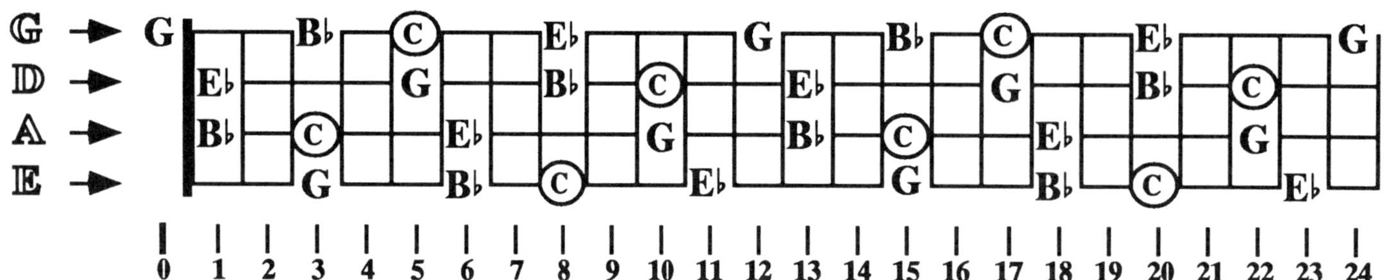

Positions

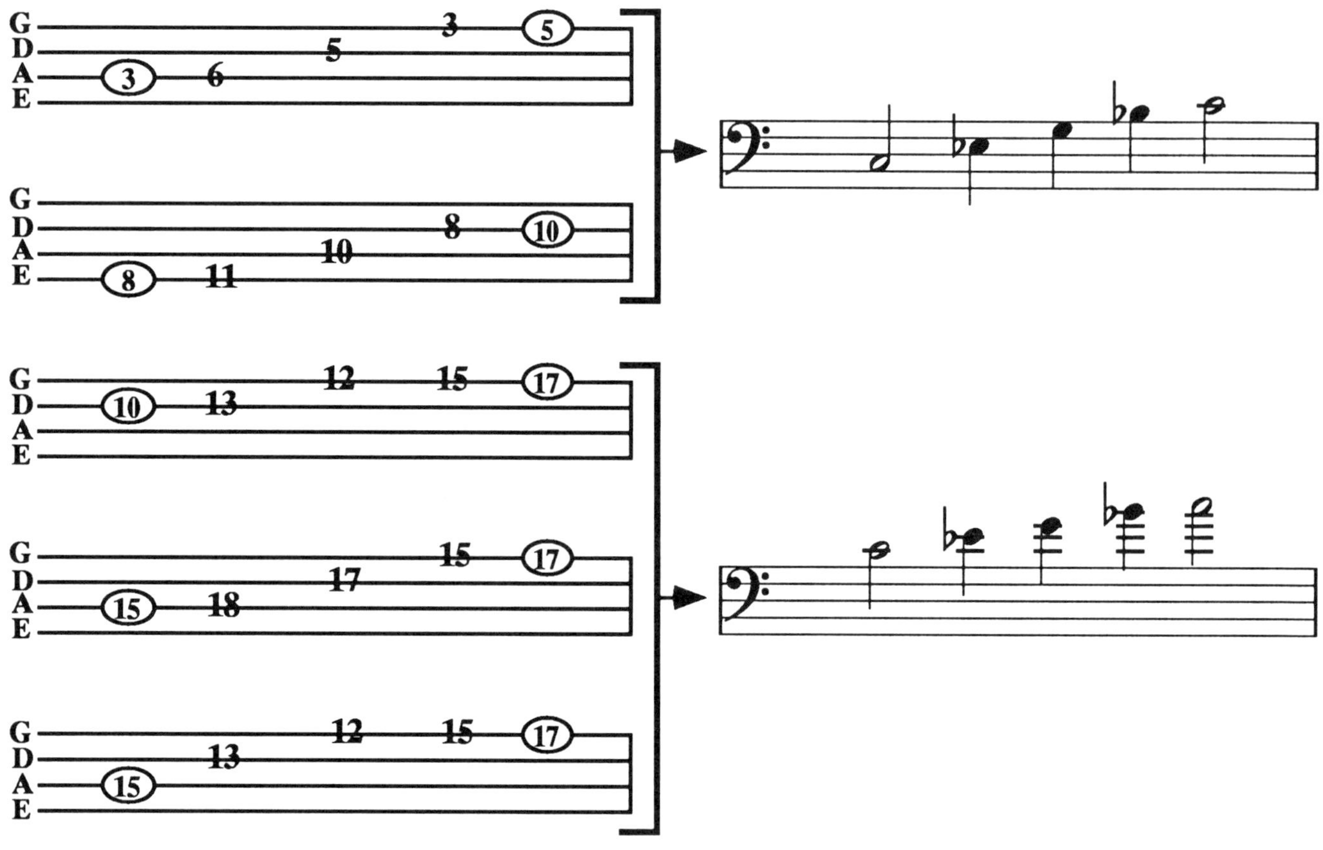

Riff

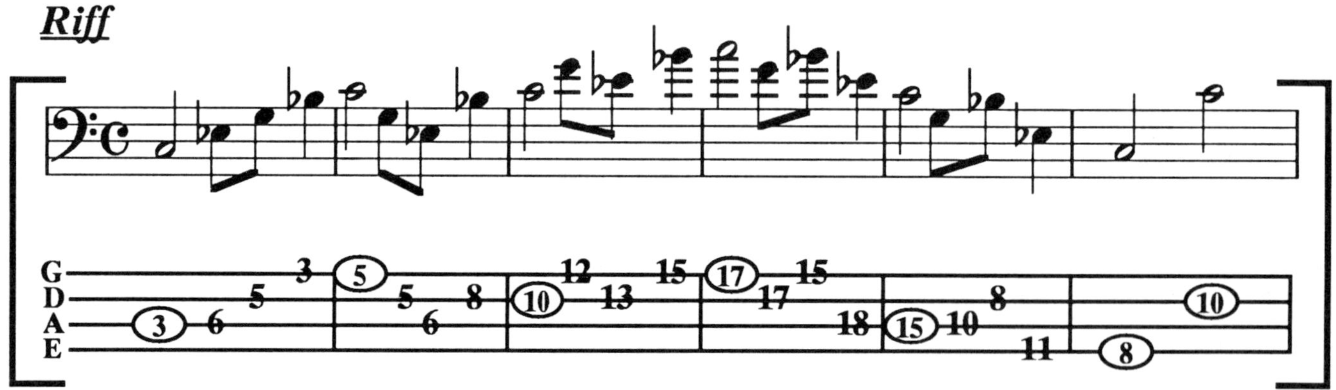

D MINOR 7TH

FORMULA - (D) Root (F) ♭3rd (A) 5th (C) ♭7th

Dm7

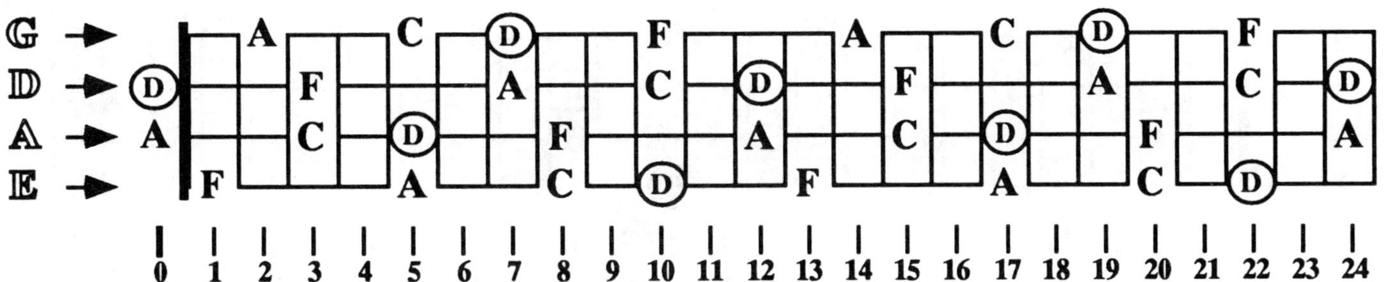

Positions

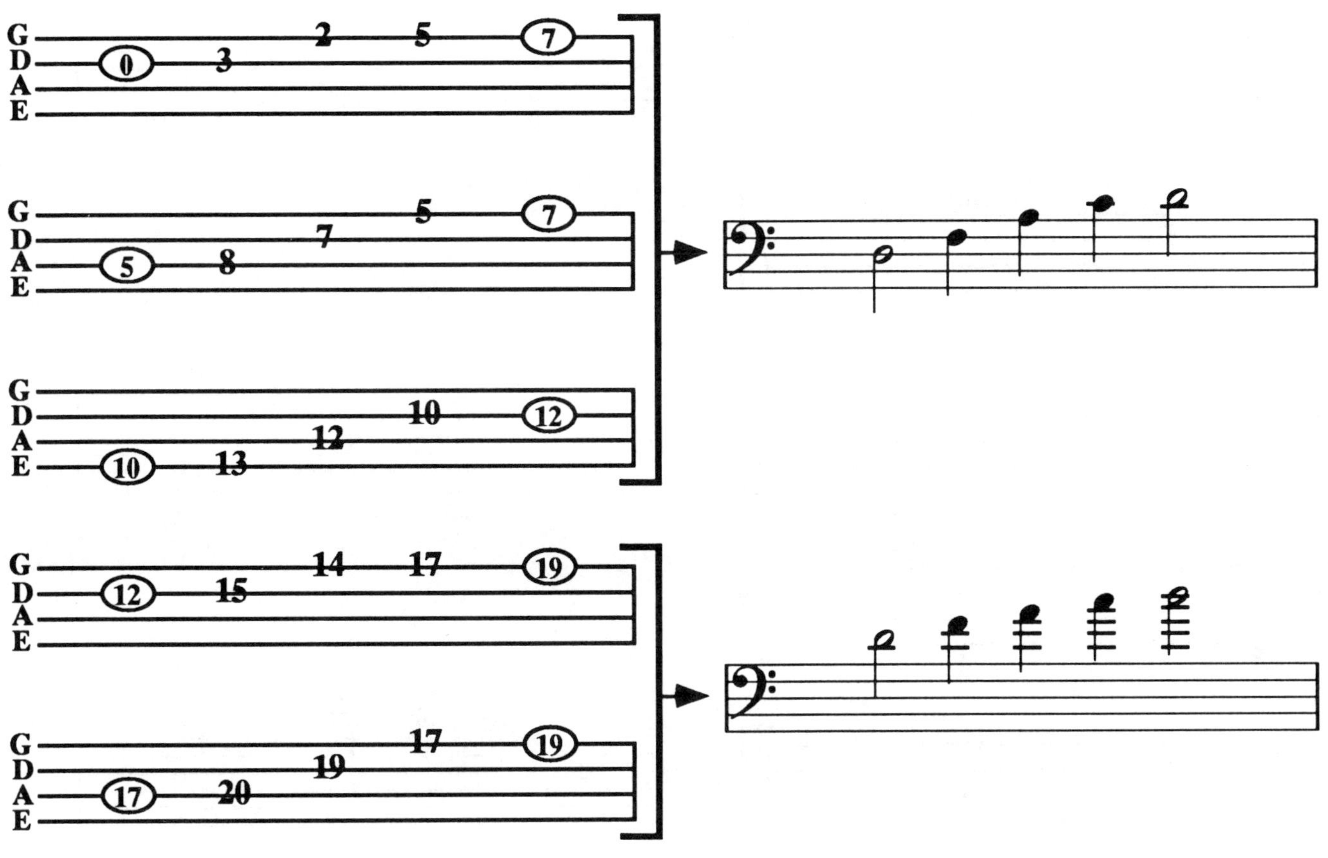

Riff

79

E MINOR 7TH

FORMULA - (E) Root (G) ♭3rd (B) 5th (D) ♭7th

Em7

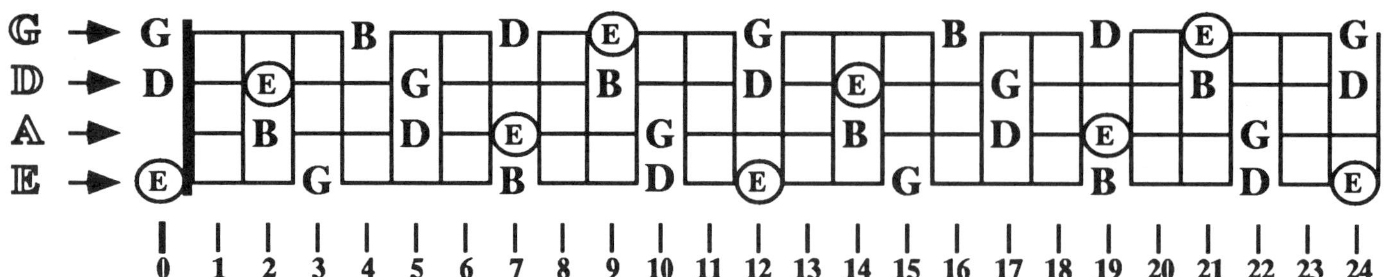

Positions

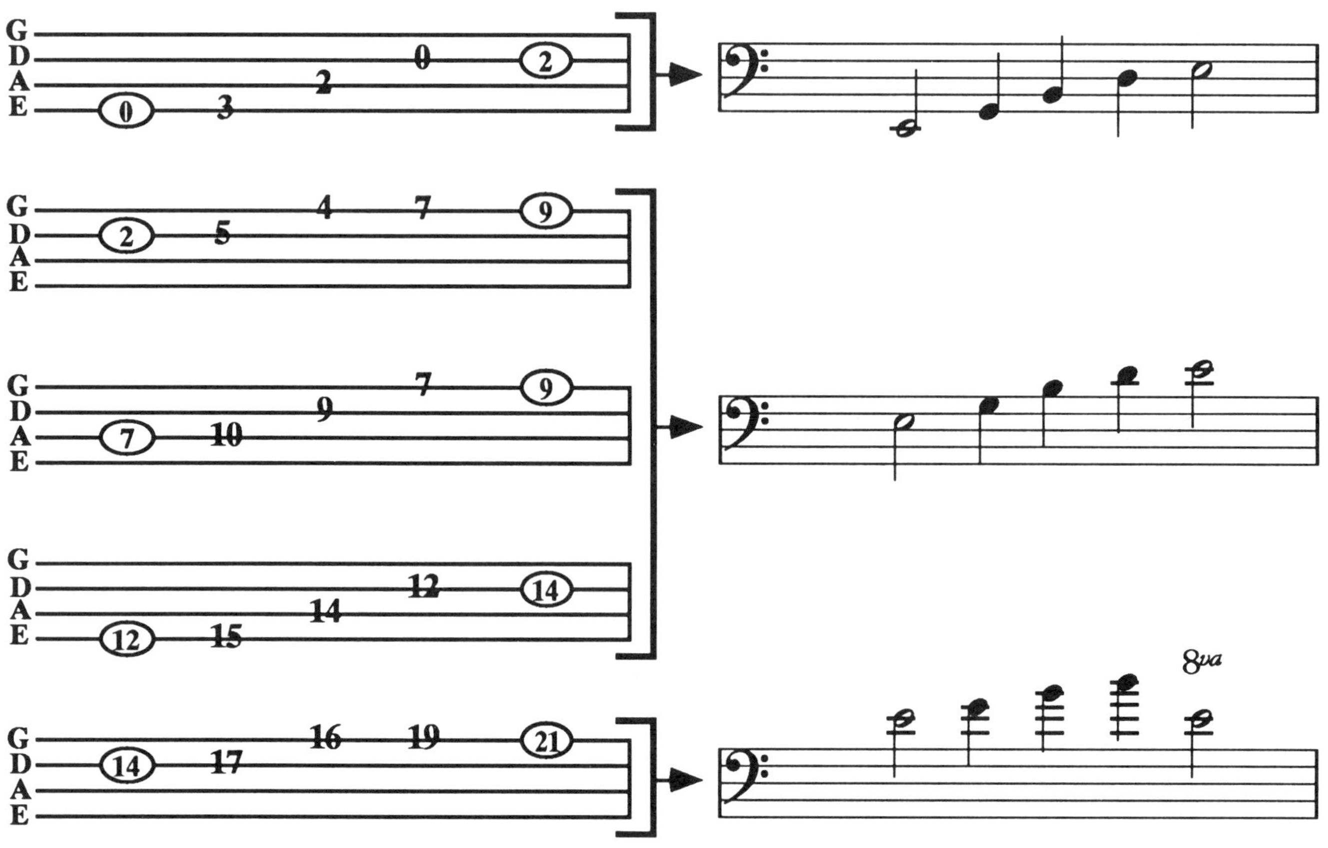

Riff

F MINOR 7TH

FORMULA - (F) Root (A♭) ♭3rd (C) 5th (E♭) ♭7th

Fm7

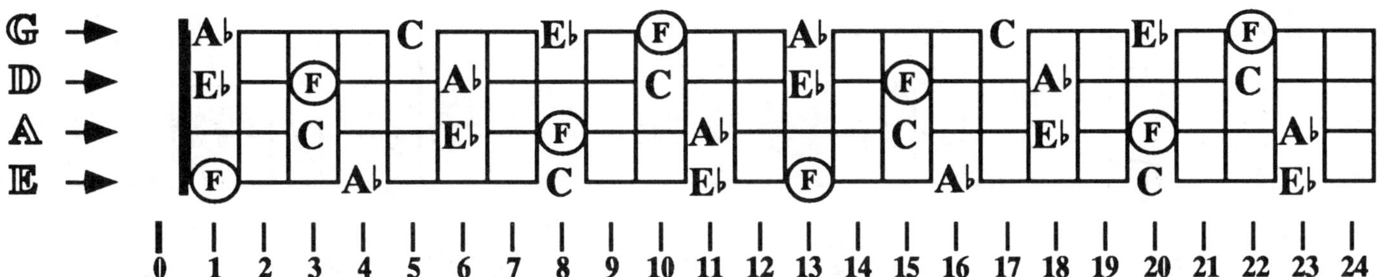

Positions

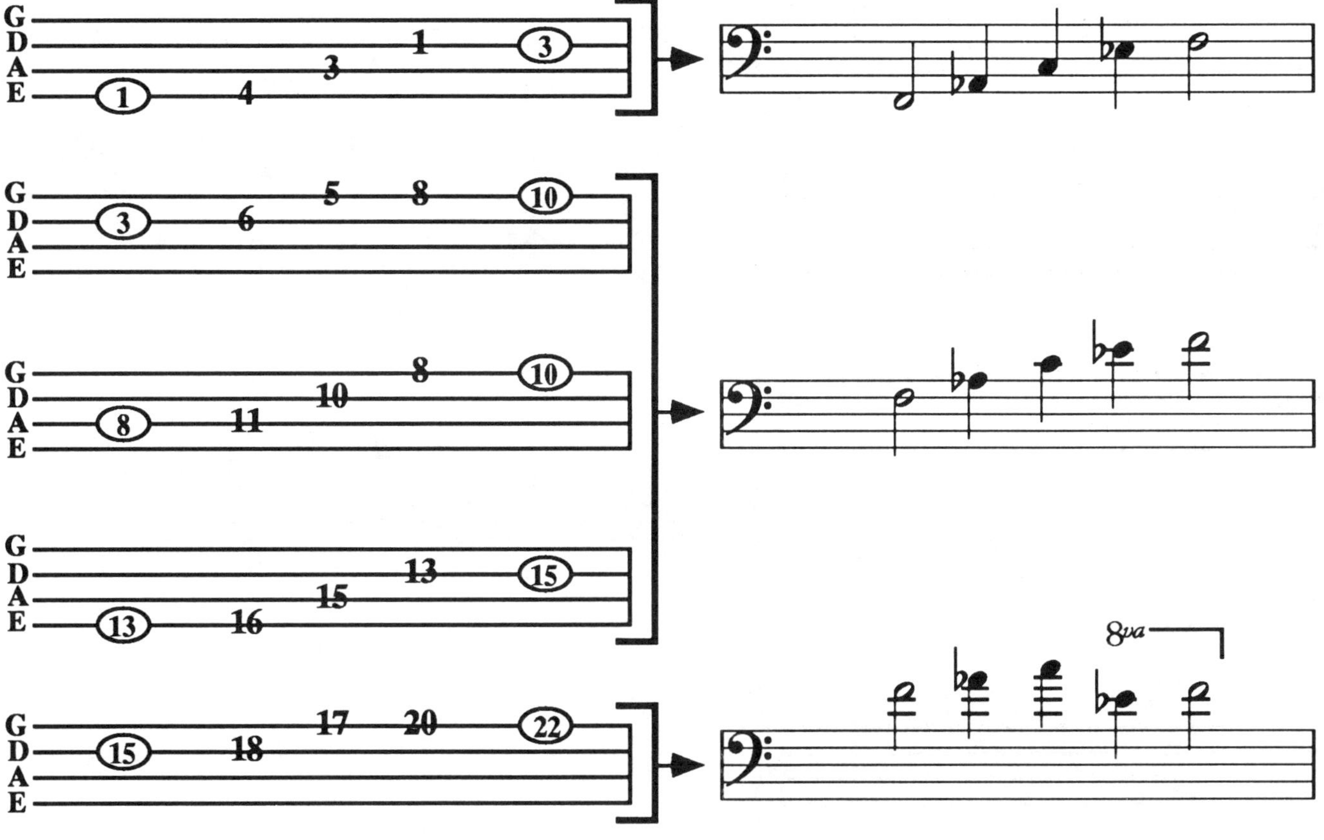

Riff

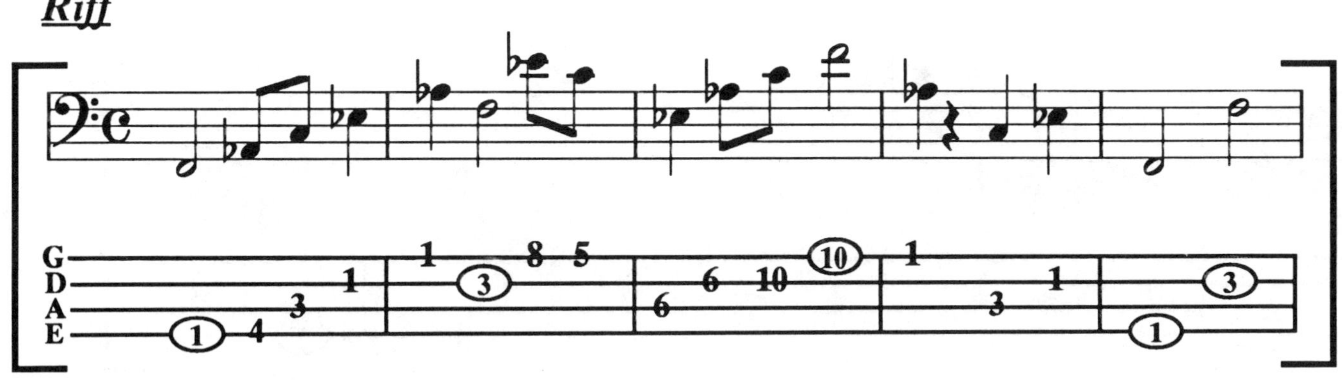

G MINOR 7TH

FORMULA - (G) Root (B♭) ♭3rd (D) 5th (F) ♭7th

Gm7

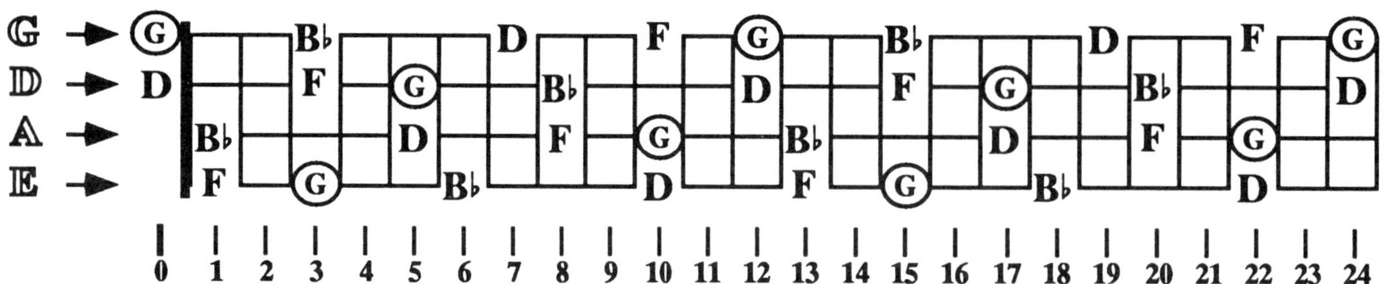

Positions

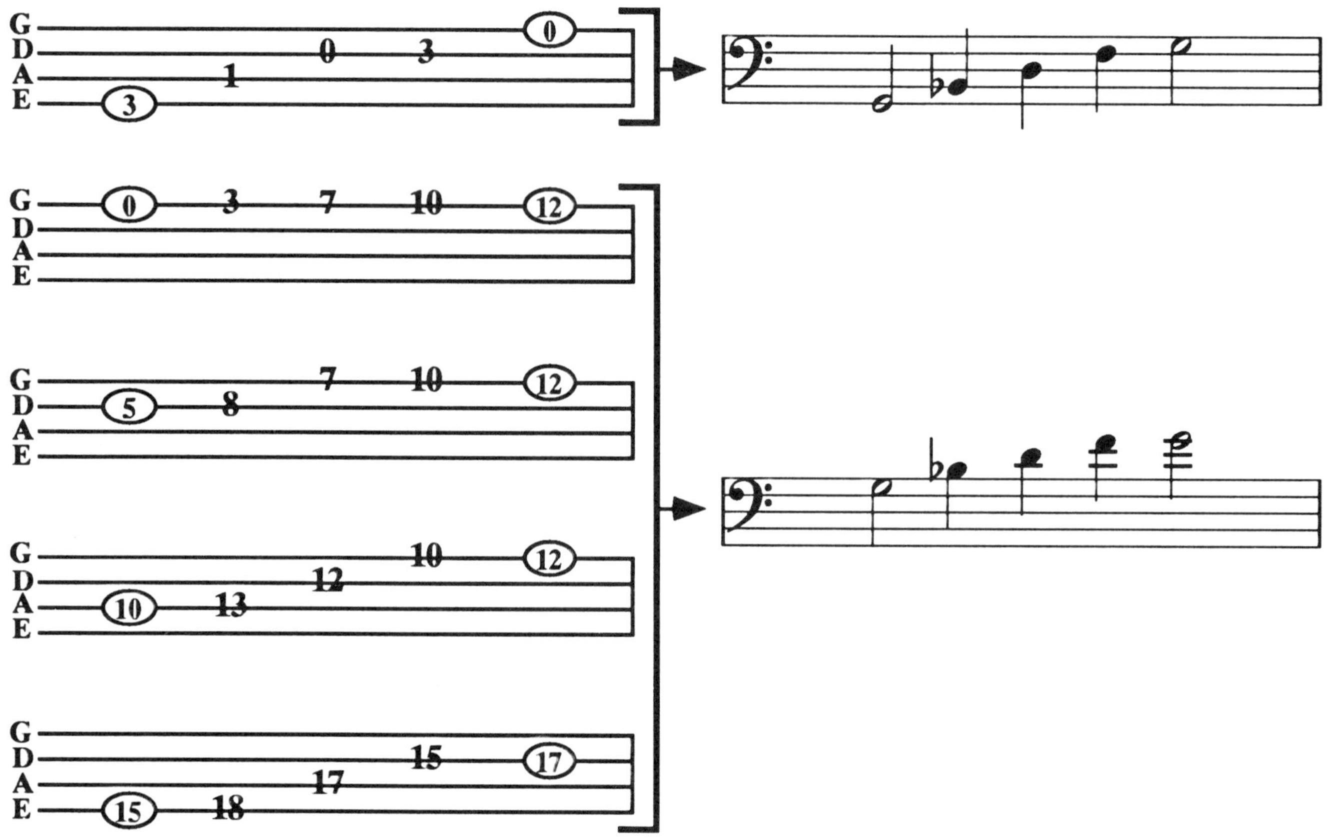

Riff

A MINOR 7TH

Am7

FORMULA - (A) Root (C) ♭3rd (E) 5th (G) ♭7th

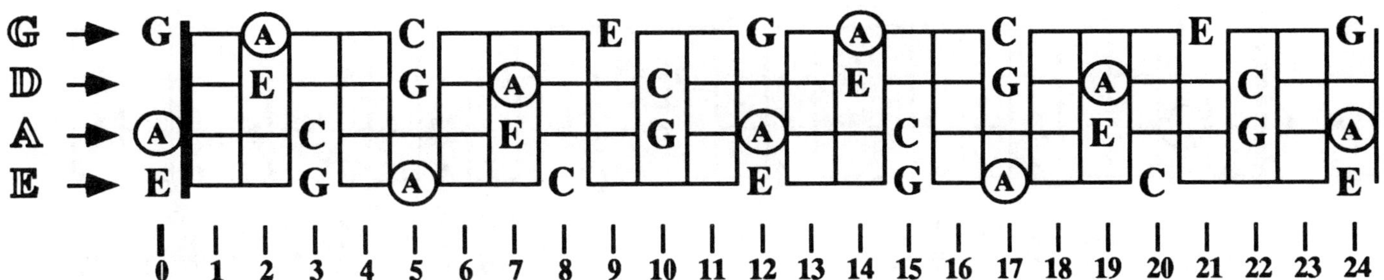

Positions

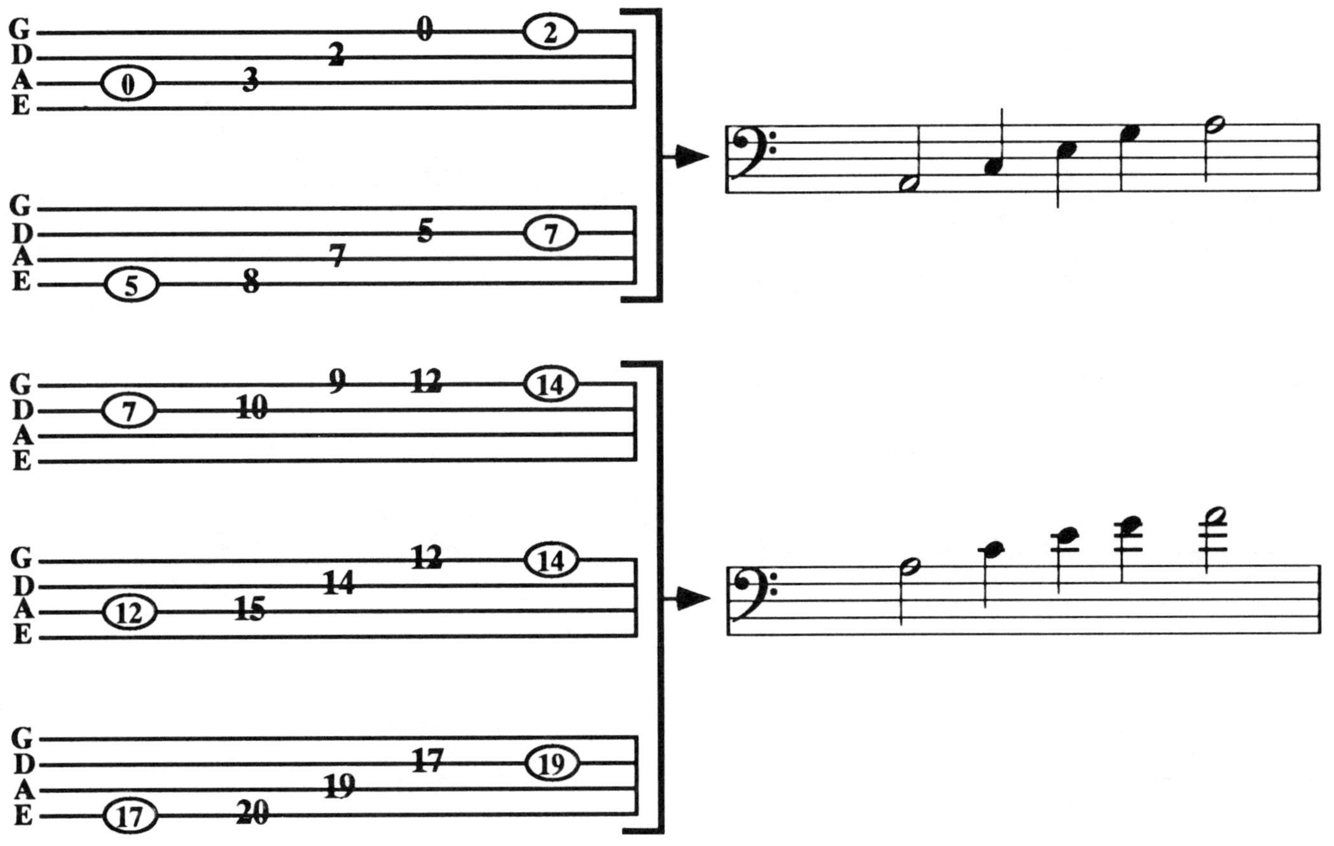

Riff

B MINOR 7TH

FORMULA - (B) Root (D) ♭3rd (F♯) 5th (A) ♭7th

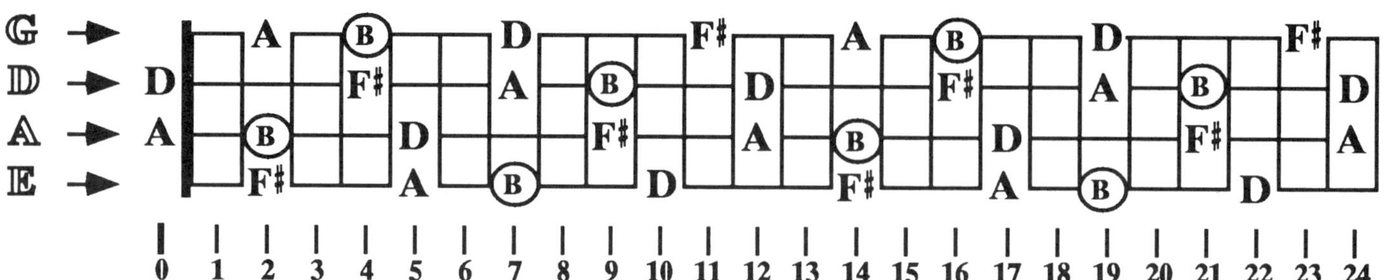

Positions

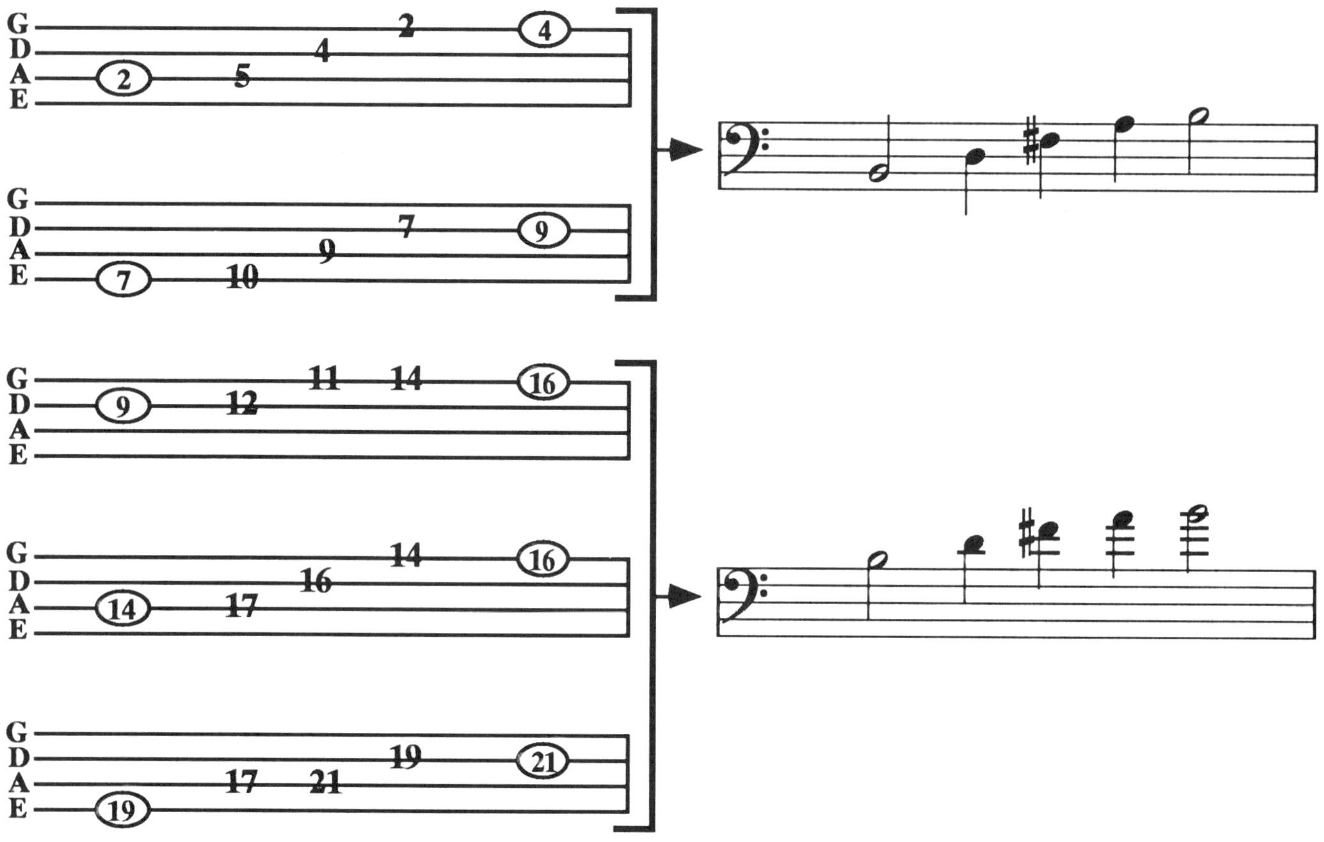

Riff

C MINOR 7TH ♭5TH

FORMULA - (C) Root (E♭) ♭3rd (G♭) ♭5th (B♭) ♭7th

Cm7-5

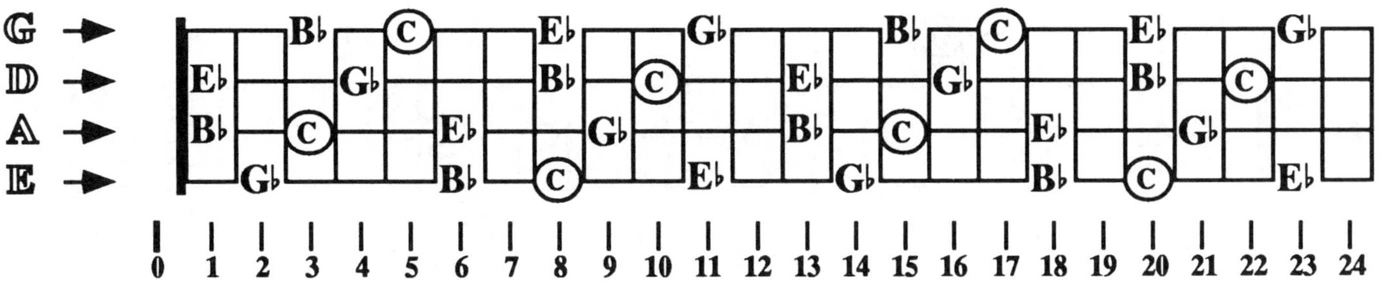

Positions

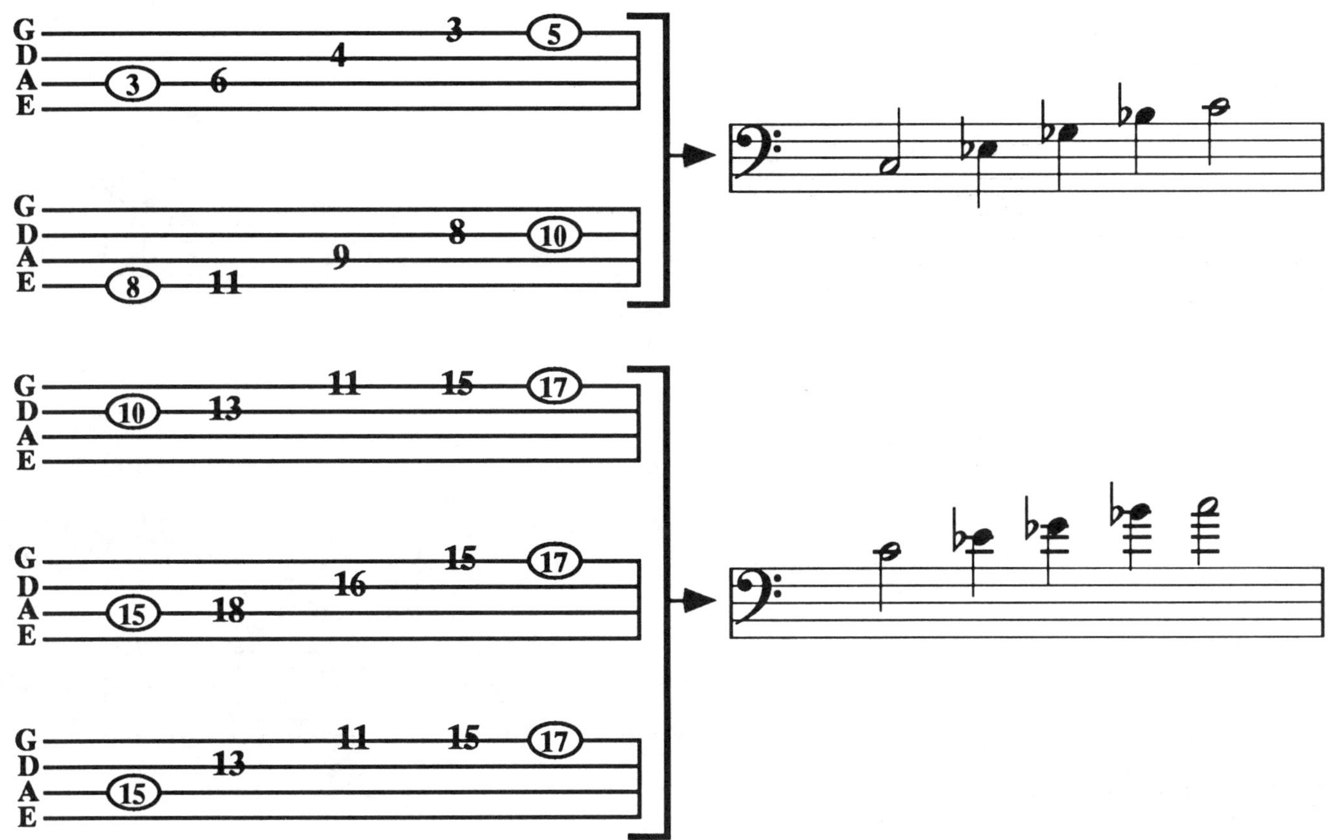

Riff

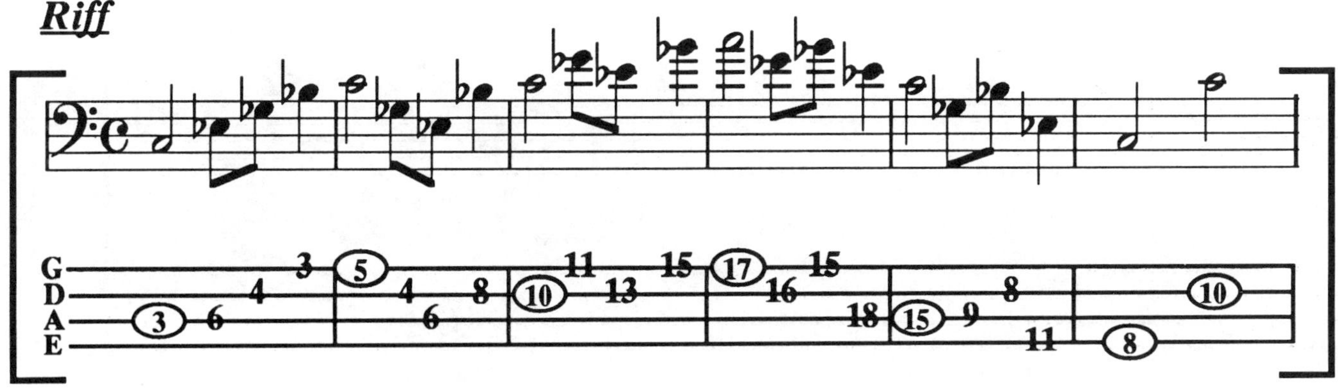

D MINOR 7TH ♭5TH

FORMULA - (D) Root (F) ♭3rd (A♭) ♭5th (C) ♭7th

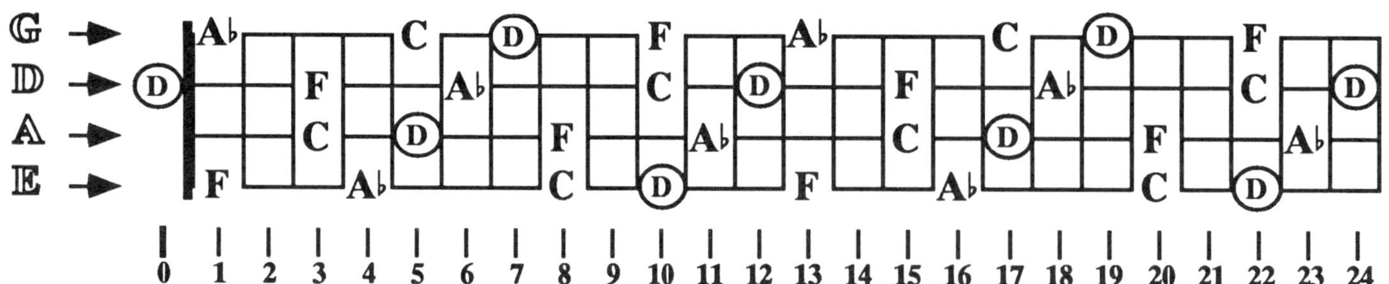

Positions

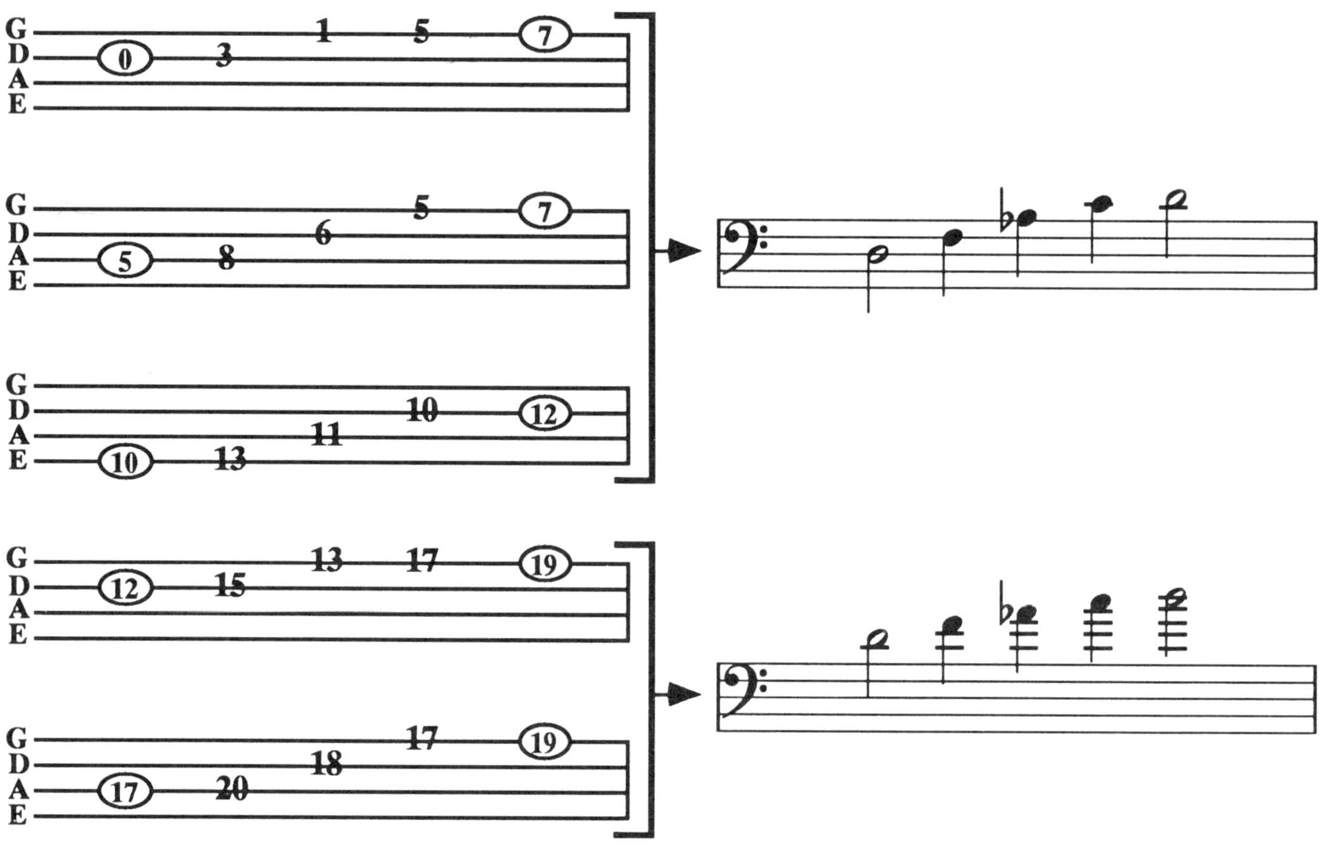

Riff

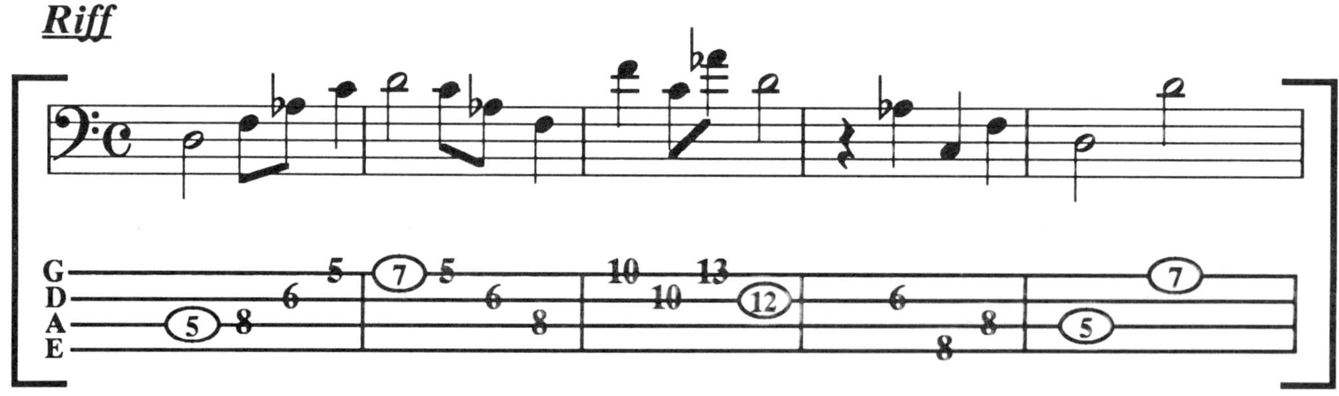

E MINOR 7TH ♭5TH
FORMULA - (E) Root (G) ♭3rd (B♭) ♭5th (D) ♭7th

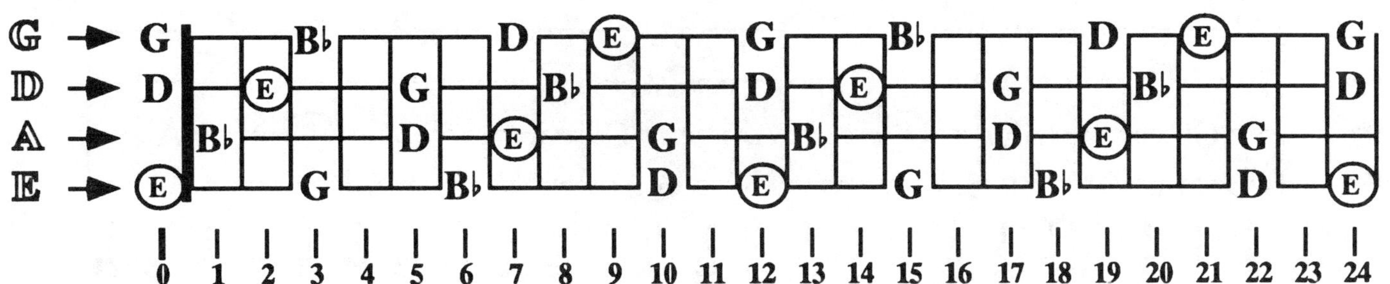

Positions

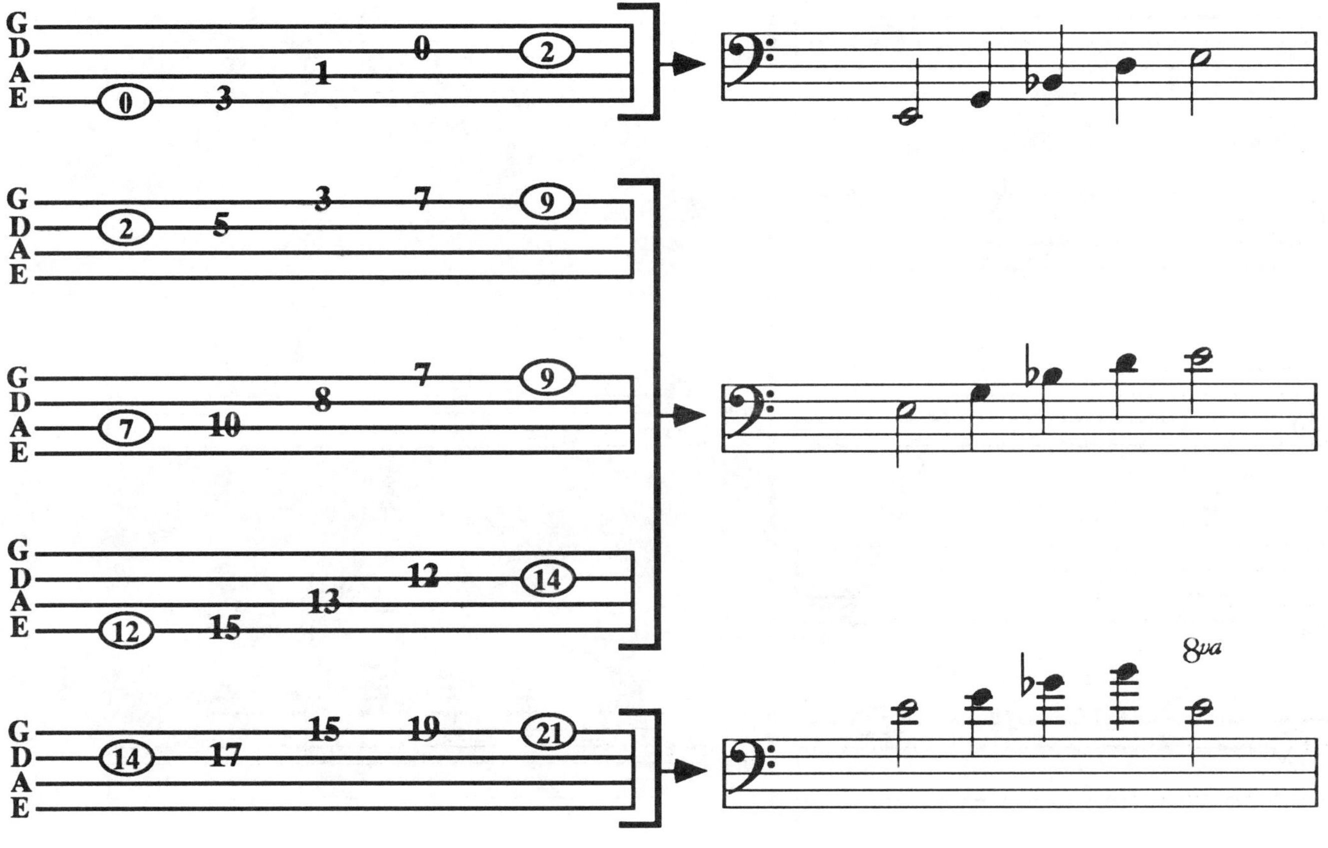

Riff

F MINOR 7TH ♭5TH

FORMULA - (F) Root (A♭) ♭3rd (C♭) ♭5th (E♭) ♭7th

Fm7-5

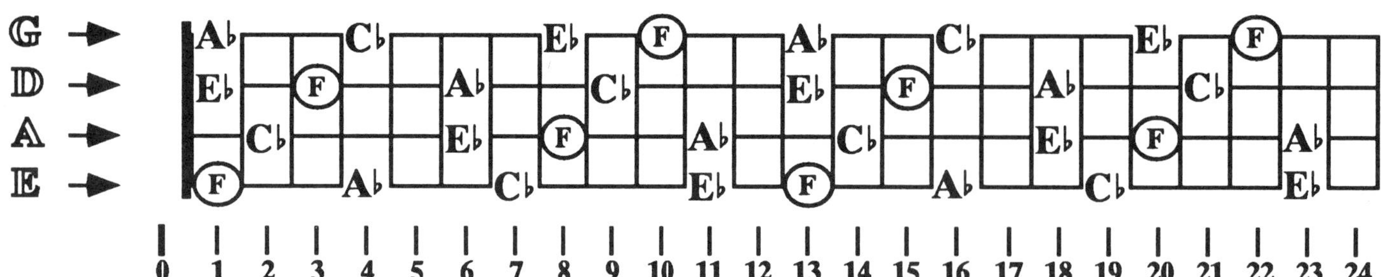

Positions

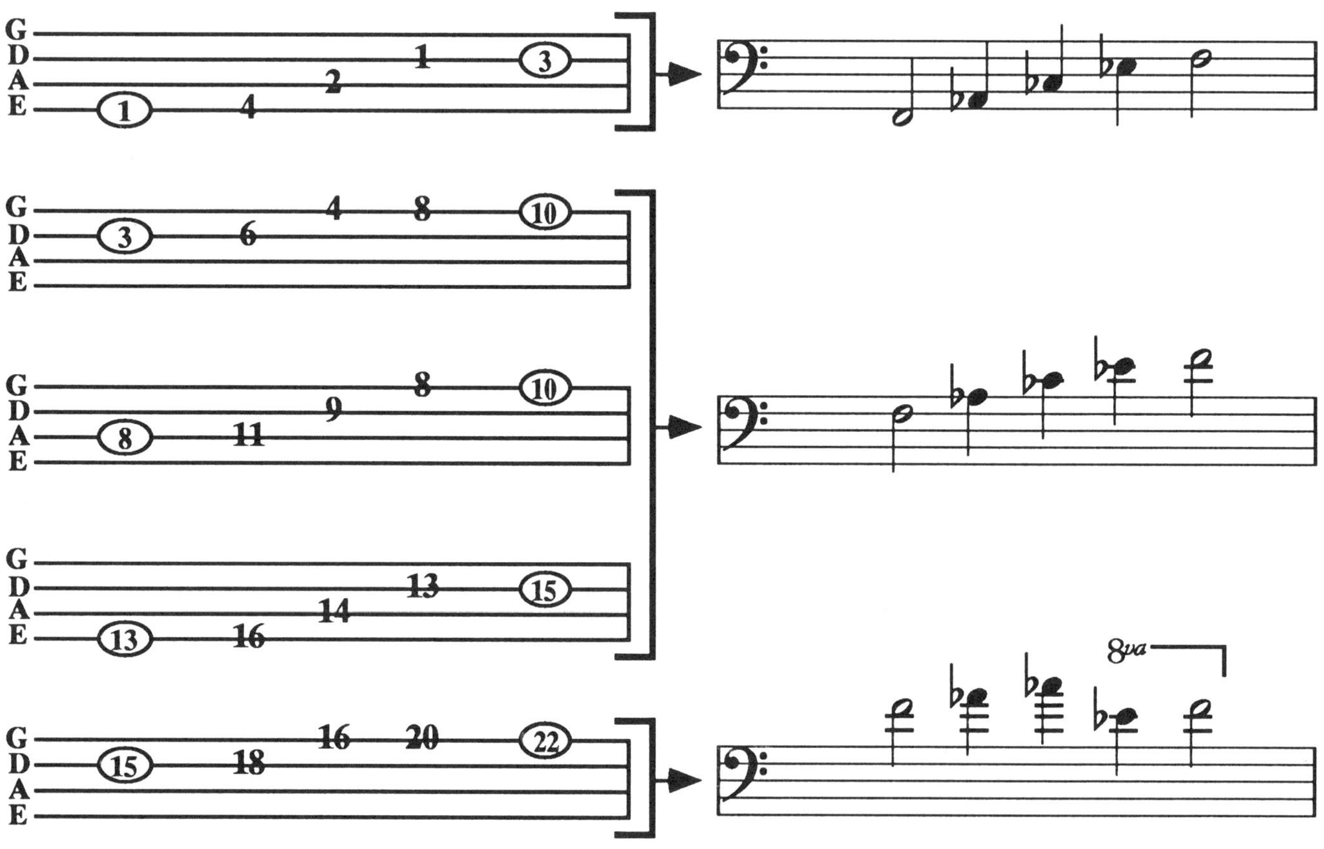

Riff

G MINOR 7TH ♭5TH

FORMULA - (G) Root (B♭) ♭3rd (D♭) ♭5th (F) ♭7th

Gm7-5

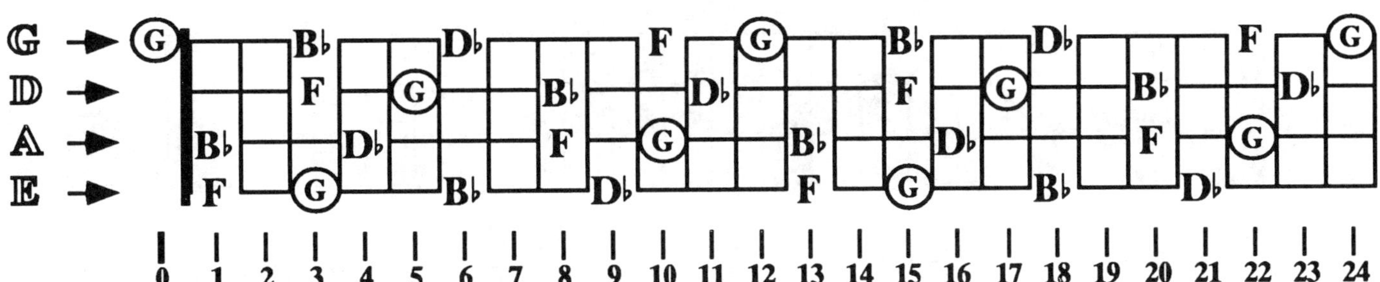

Positions

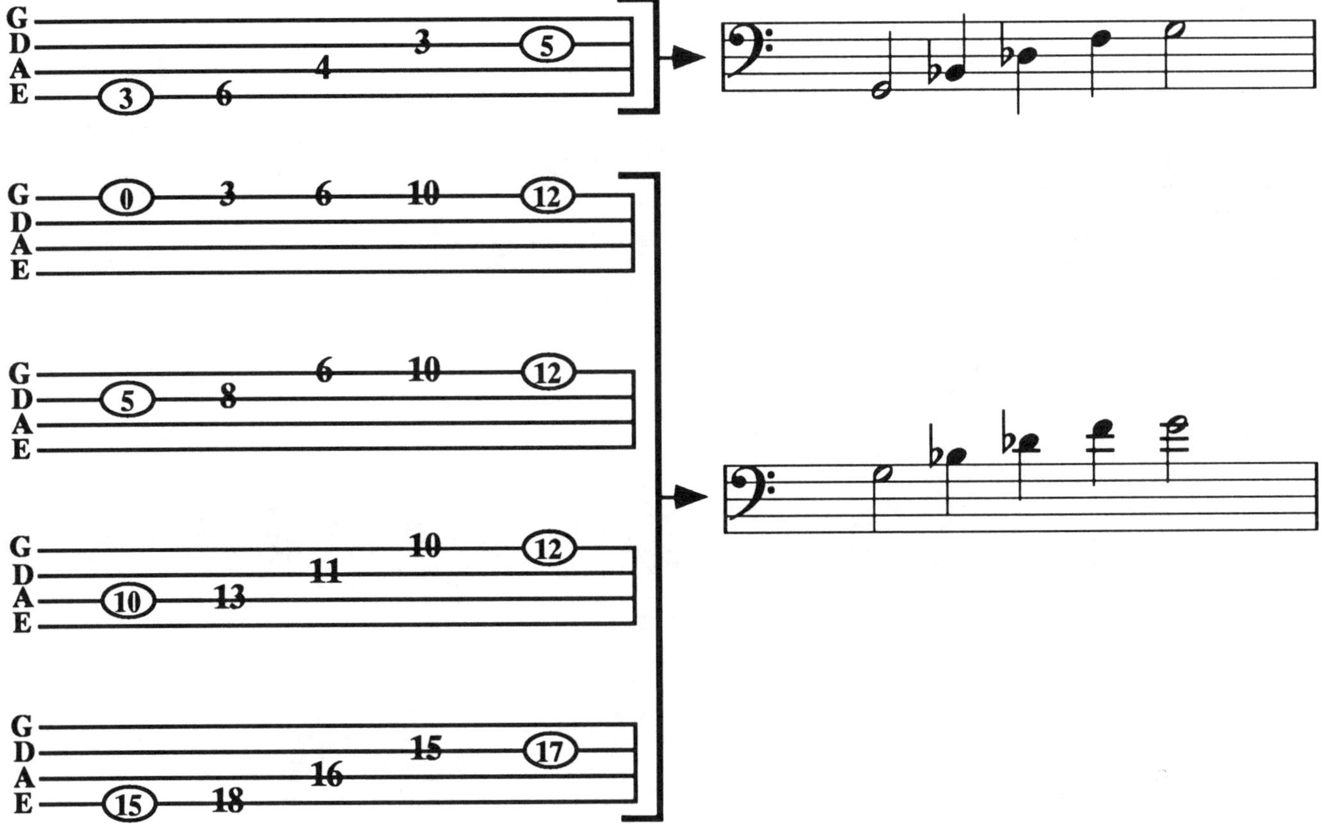

Riff

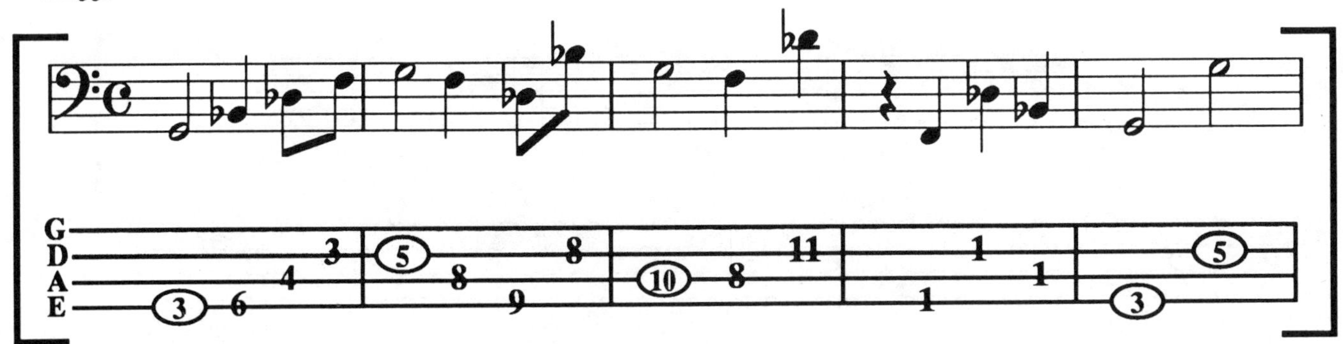

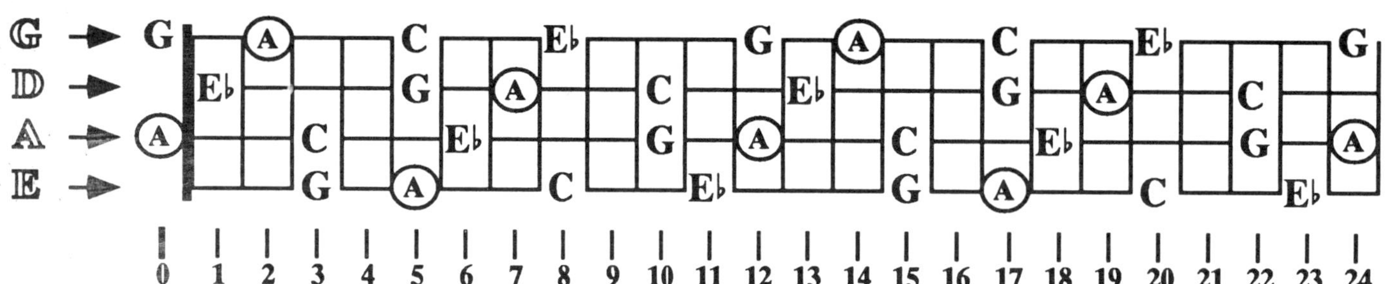

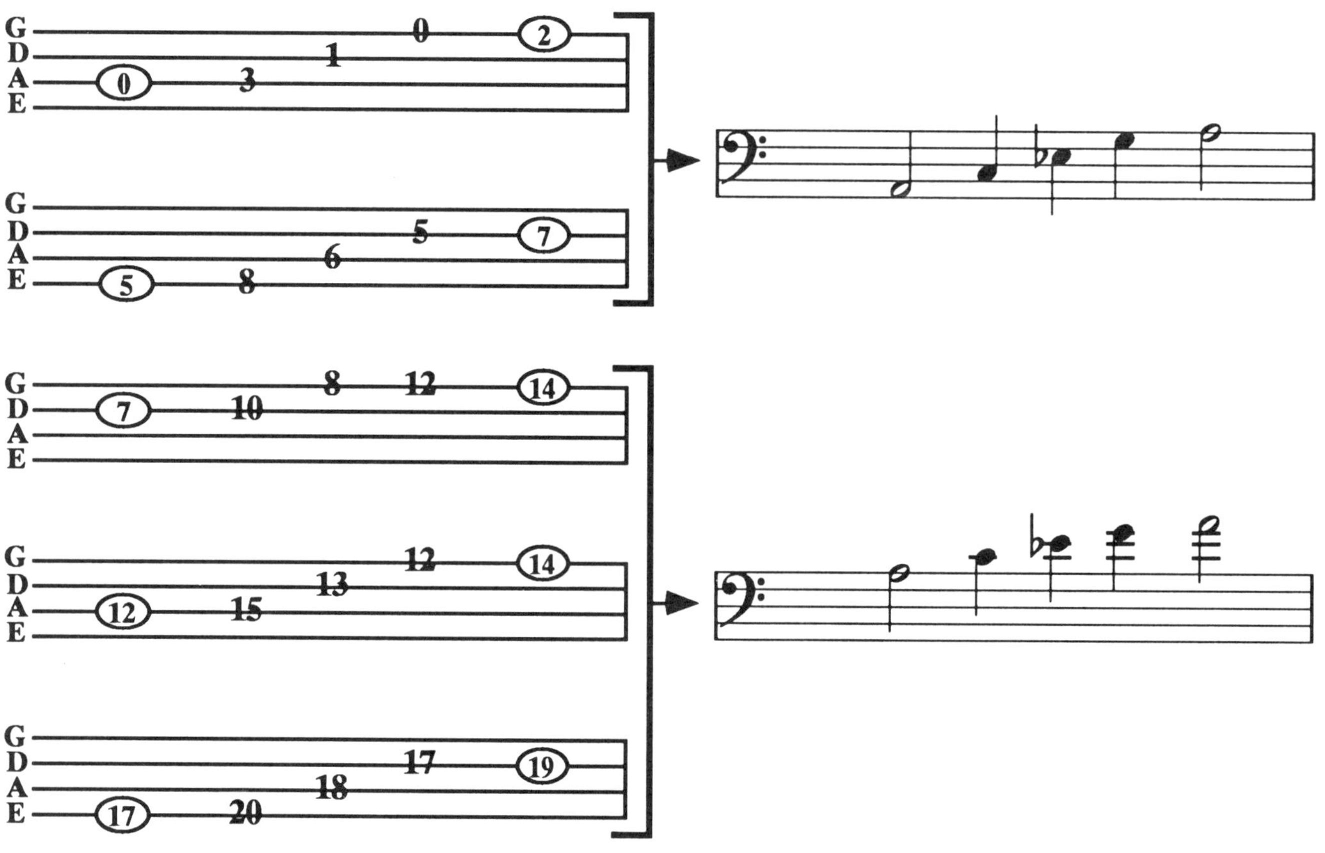

Positions

Riff

B MINOR 7TH ♭5TH

FORMULA - (B) Root (D) ♭3rd (F) ♭5th (A) ♭7th

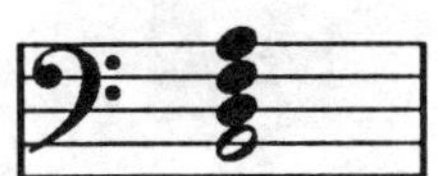

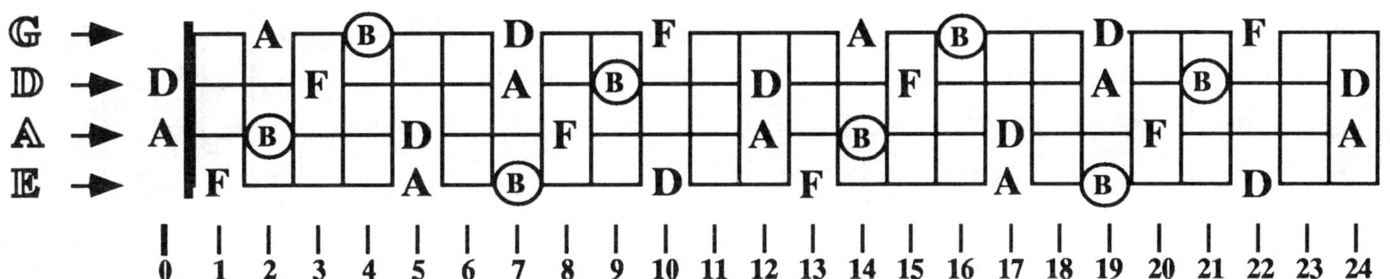

Positions

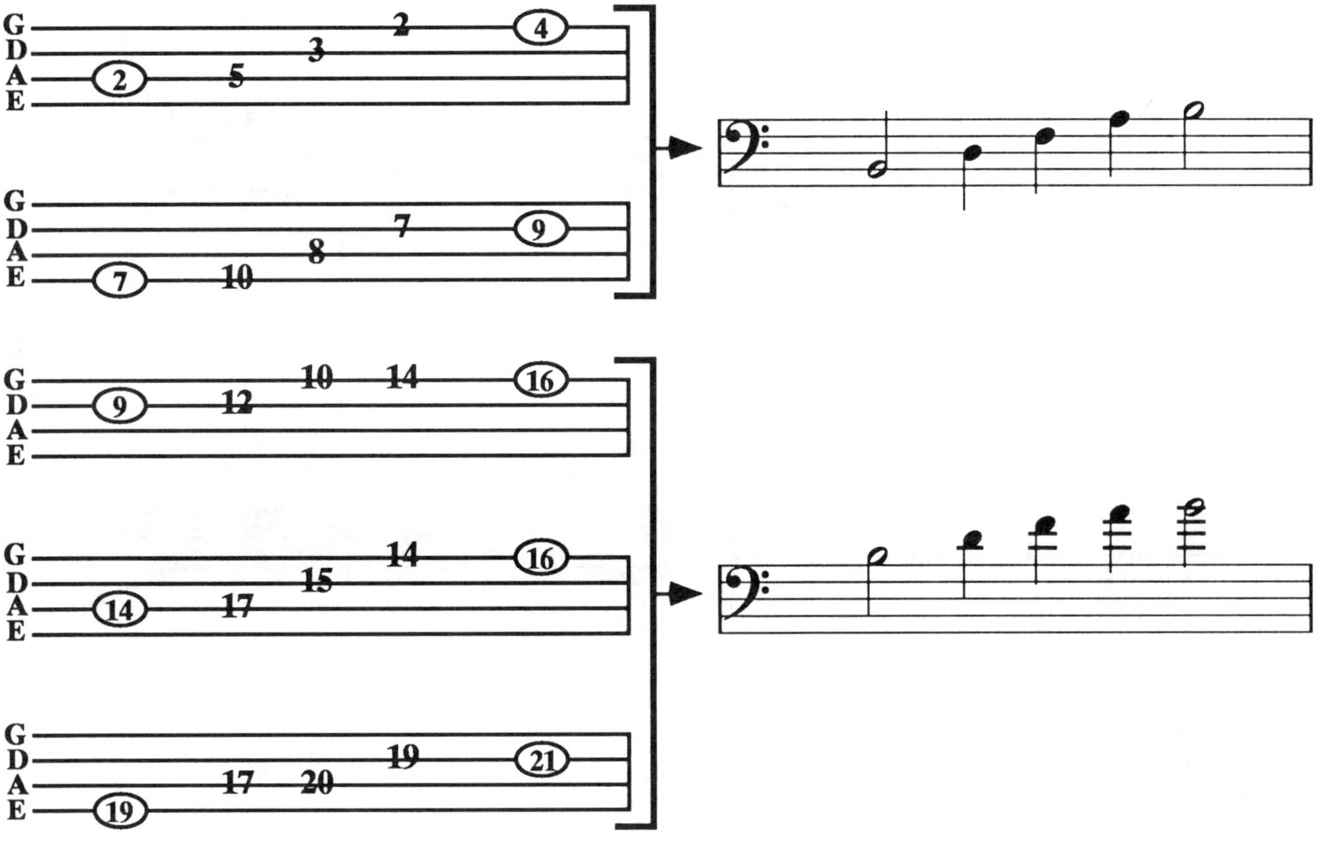

Riff

C MINOR 9TH

FORMULA - (C) Root (E♭) ♭3rd (G) 5th (B♭) ♭7th (D) 9th

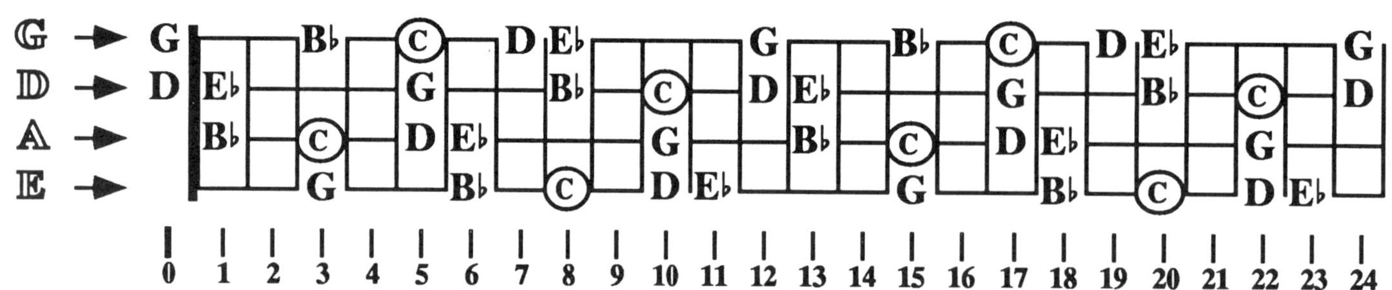

Positions

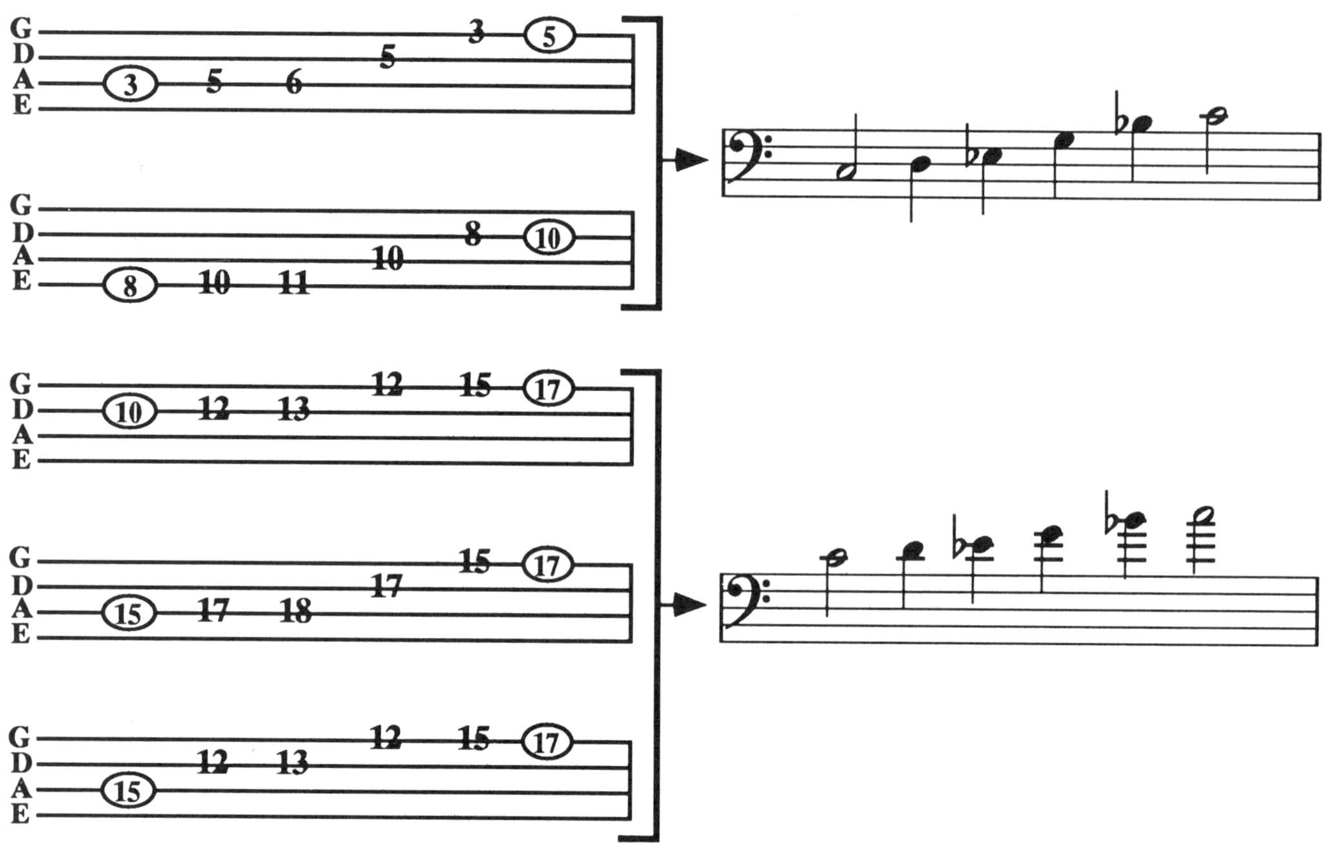

Riff

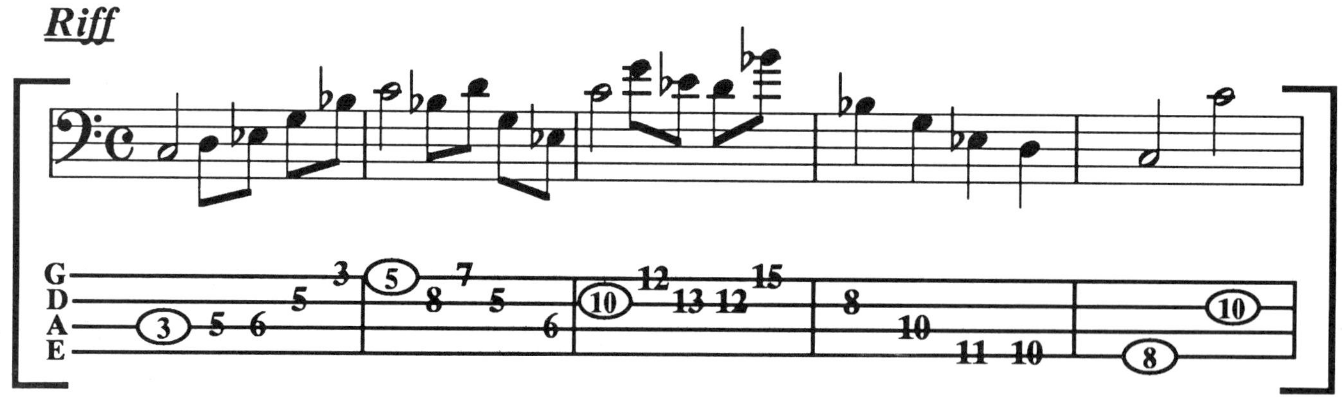

D MINOR 9TH

FORMULA - (D) Root (F) ♭3rd (A) 5th (C) ♭7th (E) 9th

Dm9

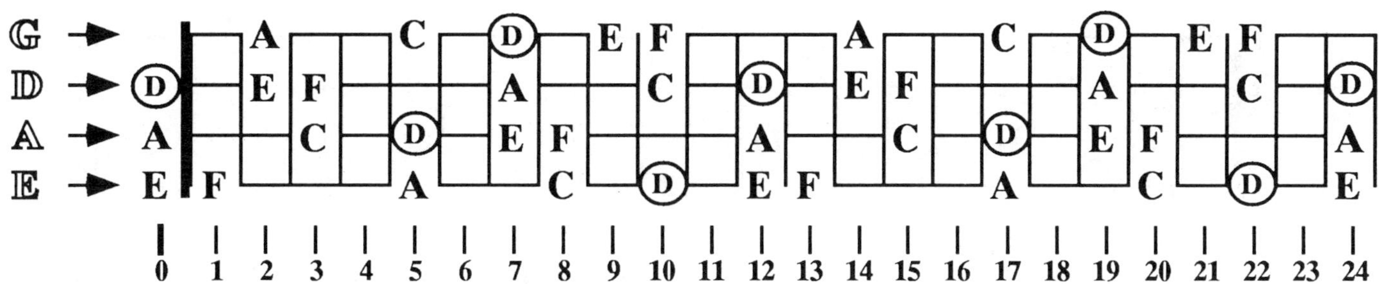

Positions

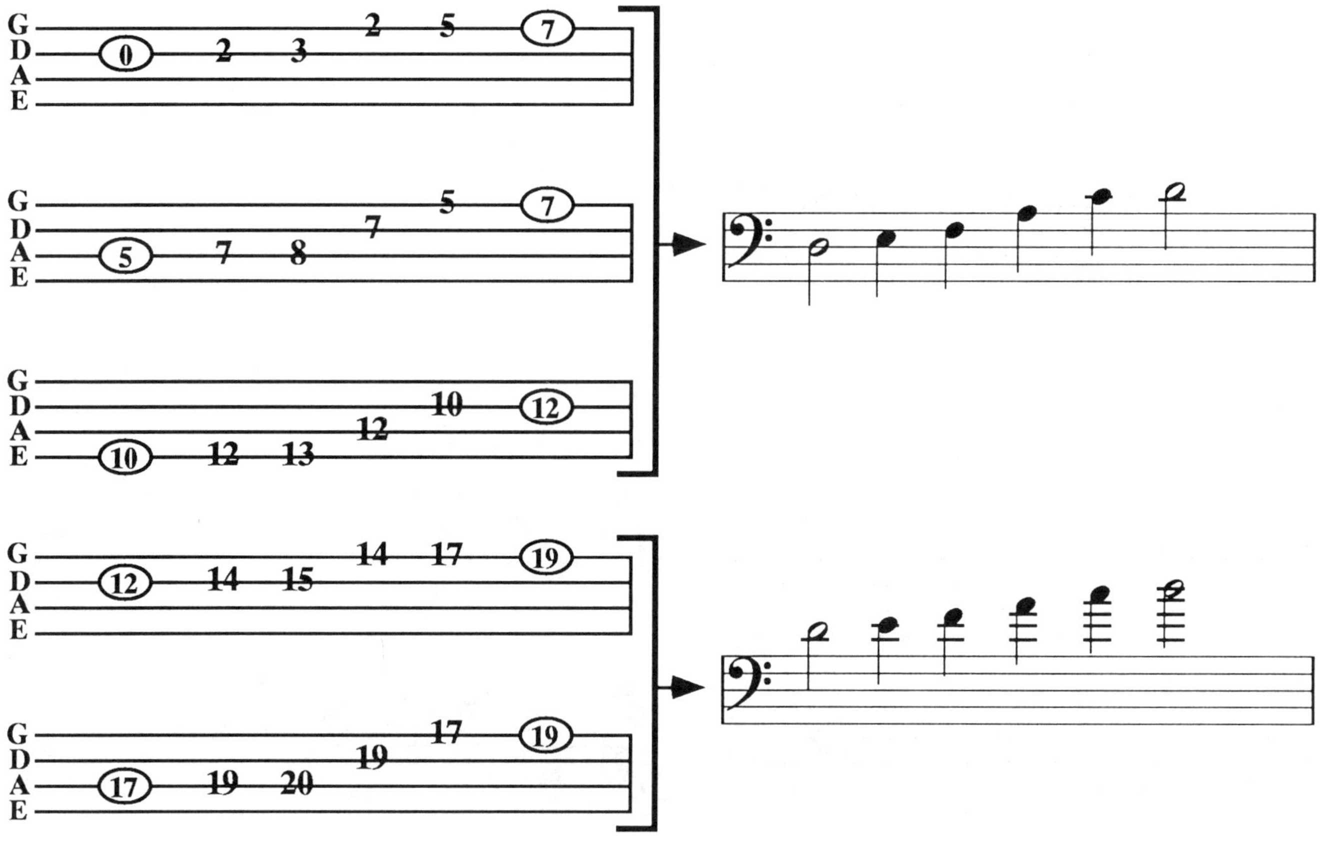

Riff

E MINOR 9TH

FORMULA - (E) Root (G) ♭3rd (B) 5th (D) ♭7th (F♯) 9th

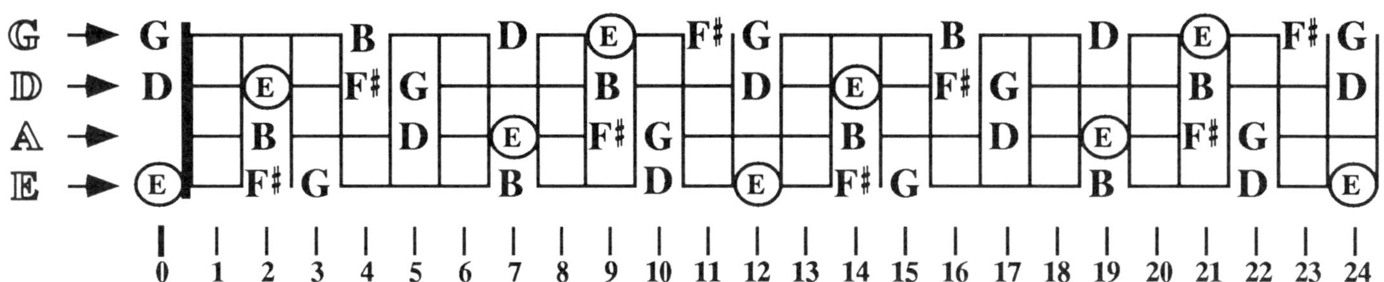

Positions

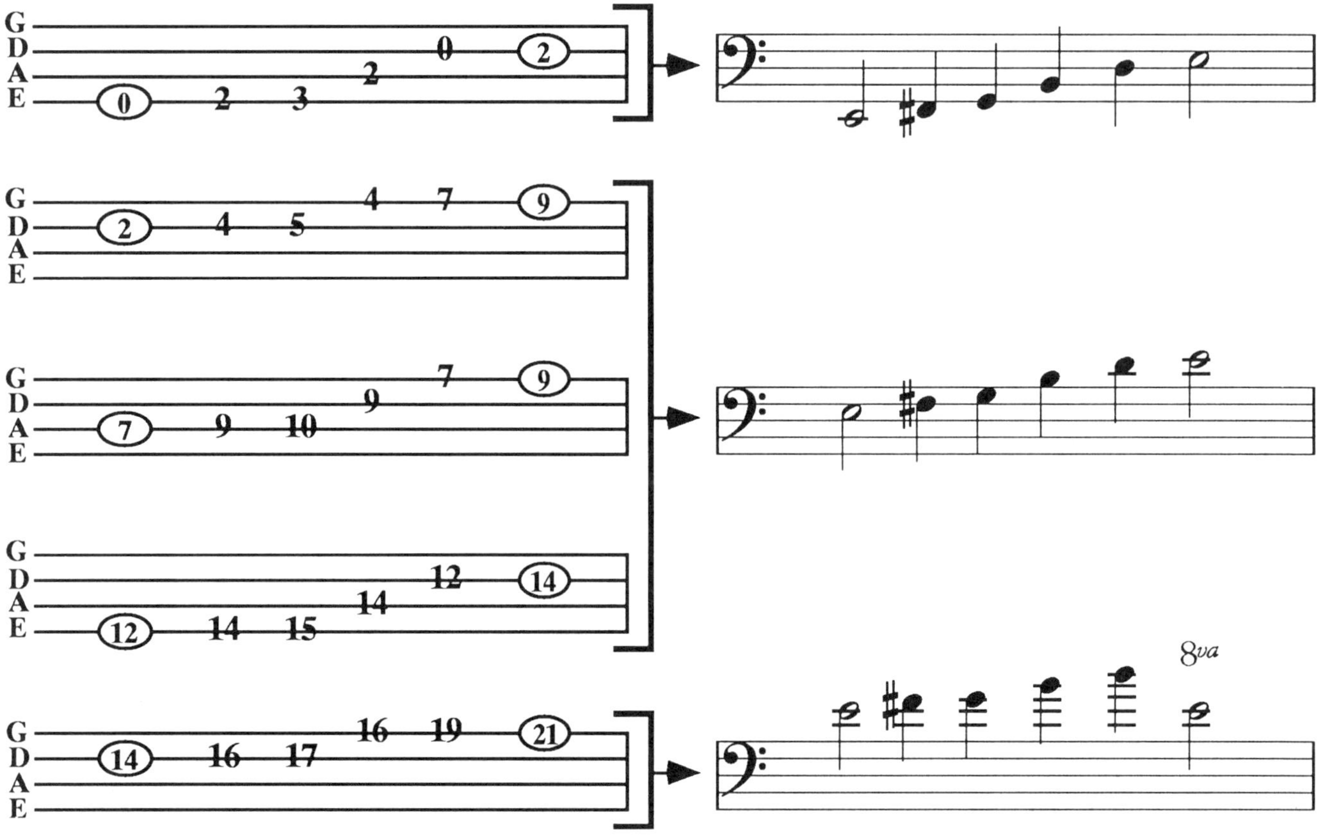

Riff

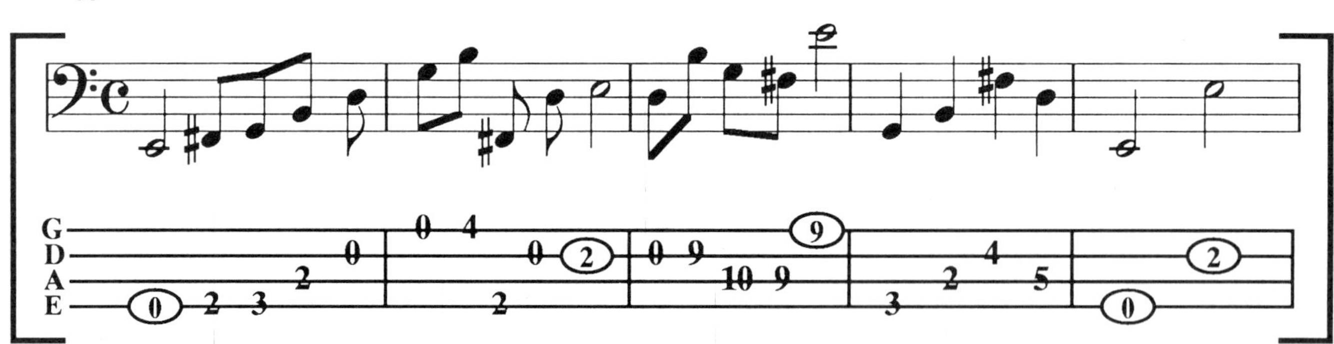

94

F MINOR 9TH

FORMULA - (F) Root (A♭) ♭3rd (C) 5th (E♭) ♭7th (G) 9th

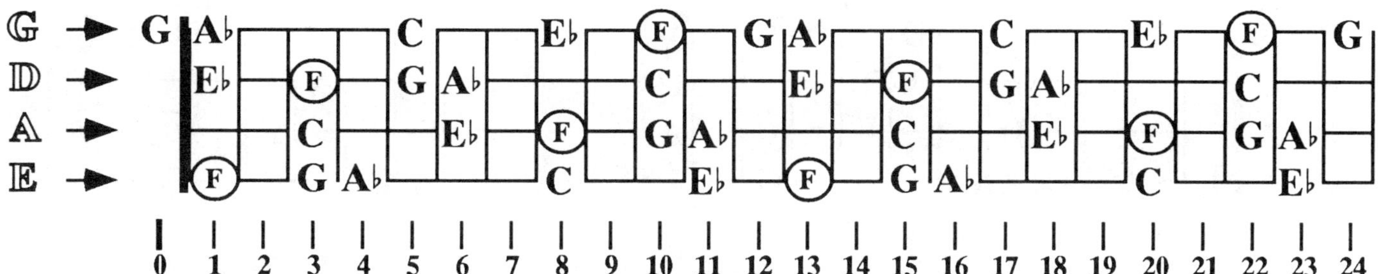

Positions

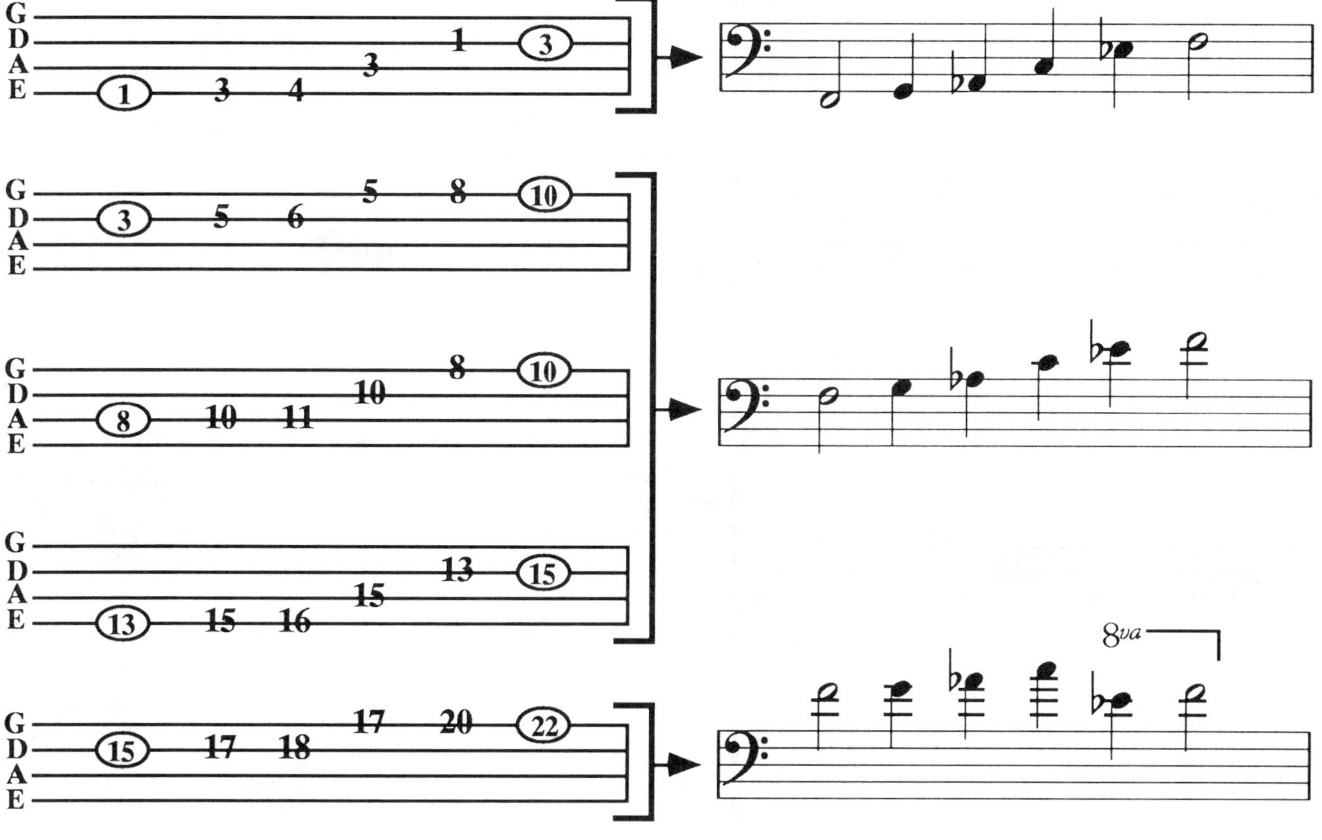

Riff

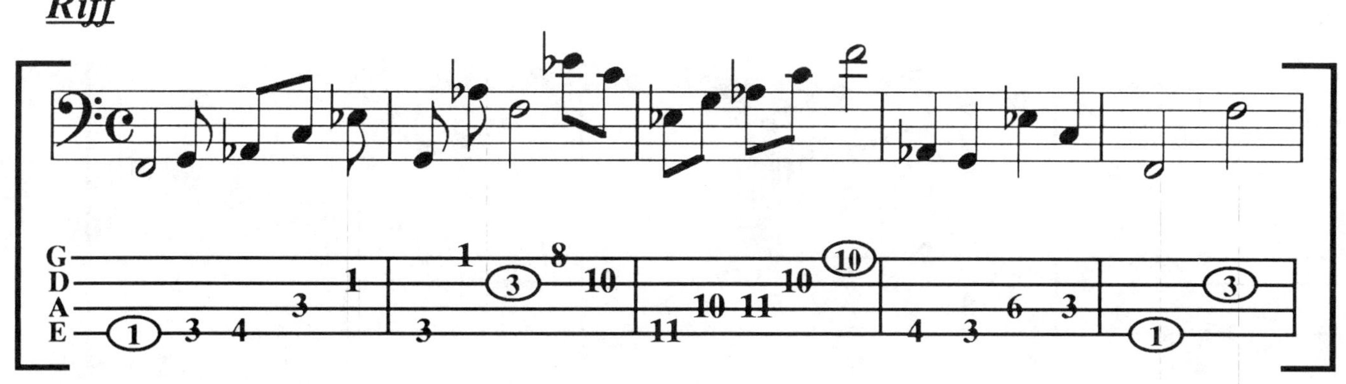

G   MINOR 9TH

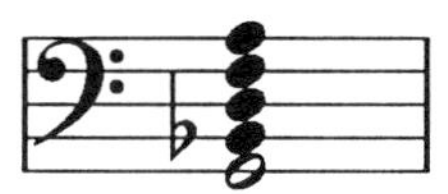

FORMULA - (G) Root (B♭) ♭3rd (D) 5th (F) ♭7th (A) 9th

Gm9

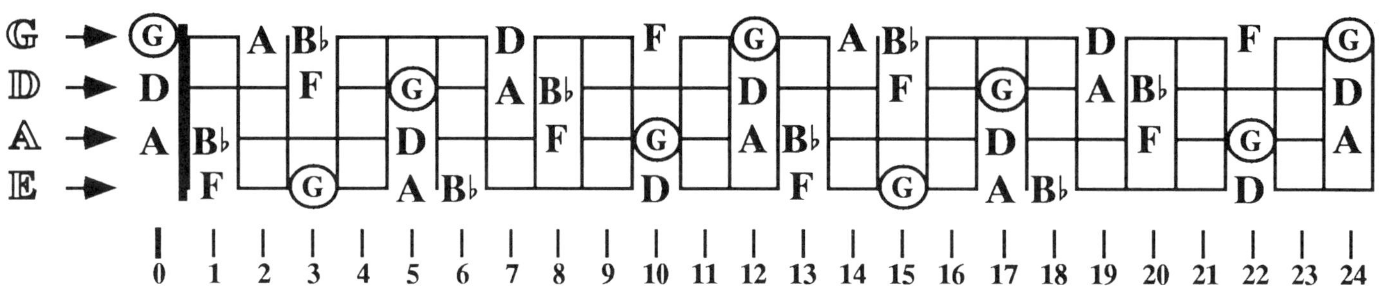

Positions

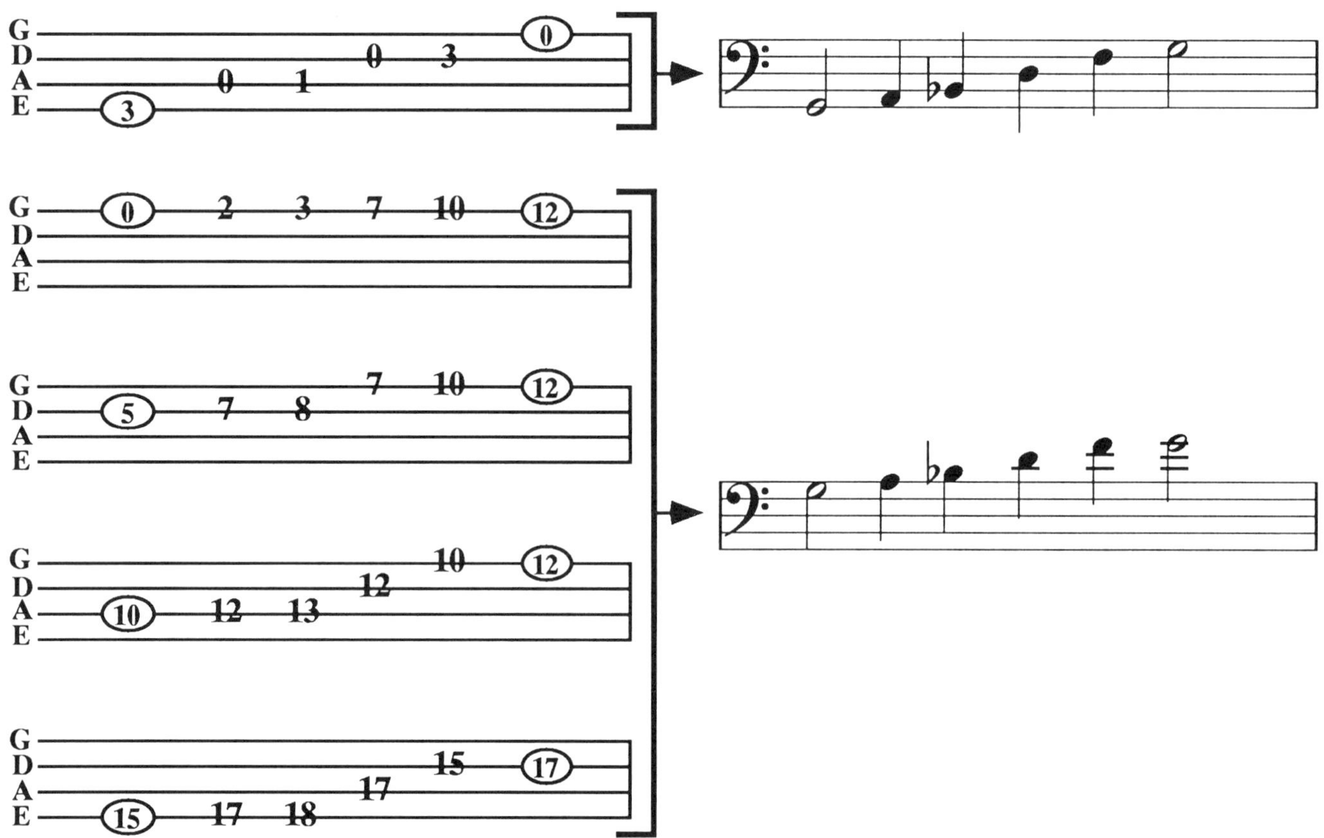

Riff

A MINOR 9TH

FORMULA - (A) Root (C) ♭3rd (E) 5th (G) ♭7th (B) 9th

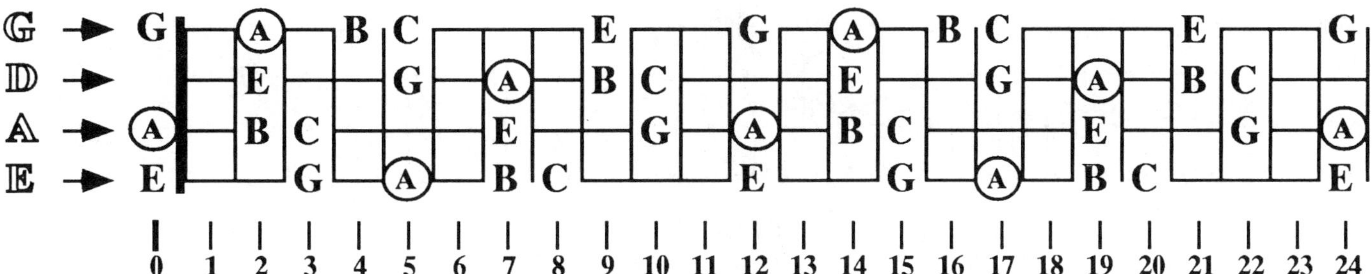

Positions

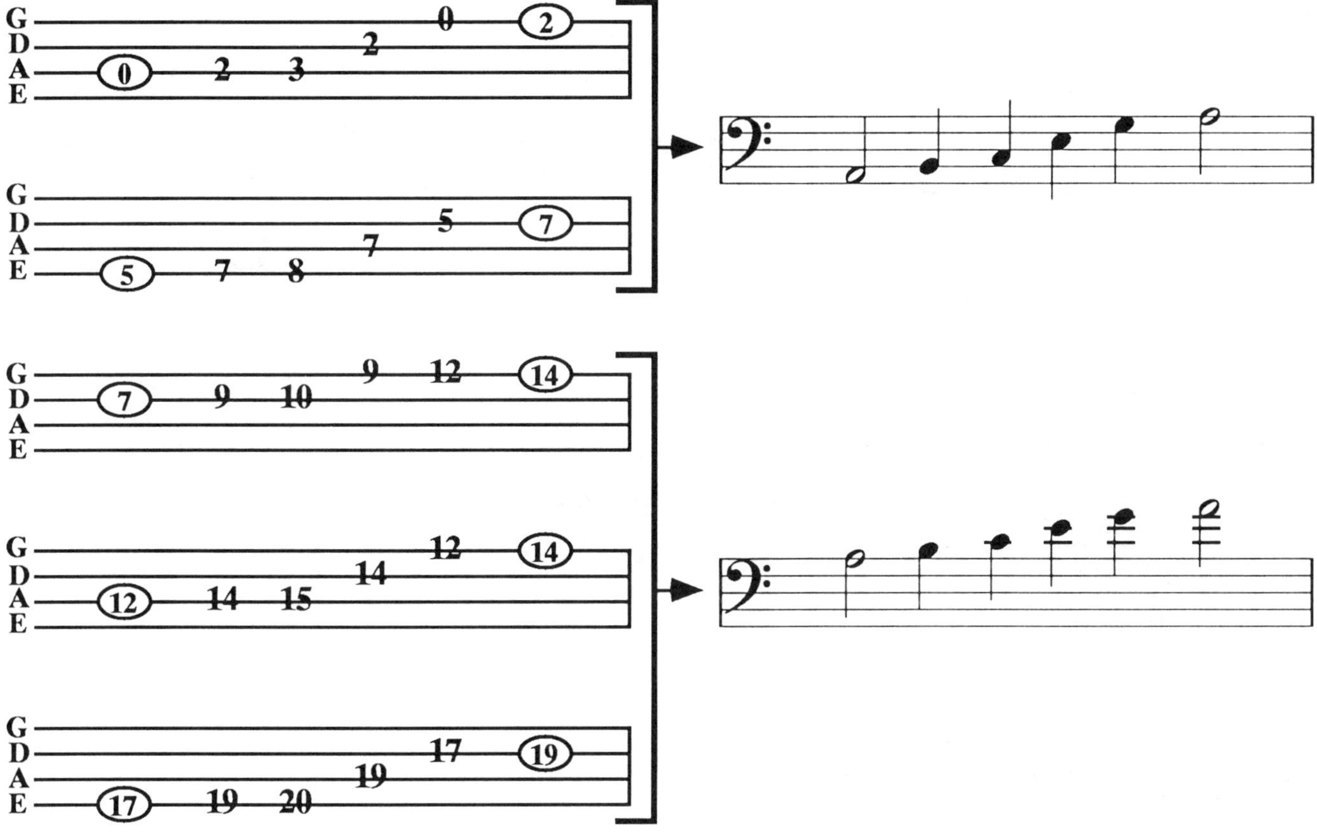

Riff

B MINOR 9TH

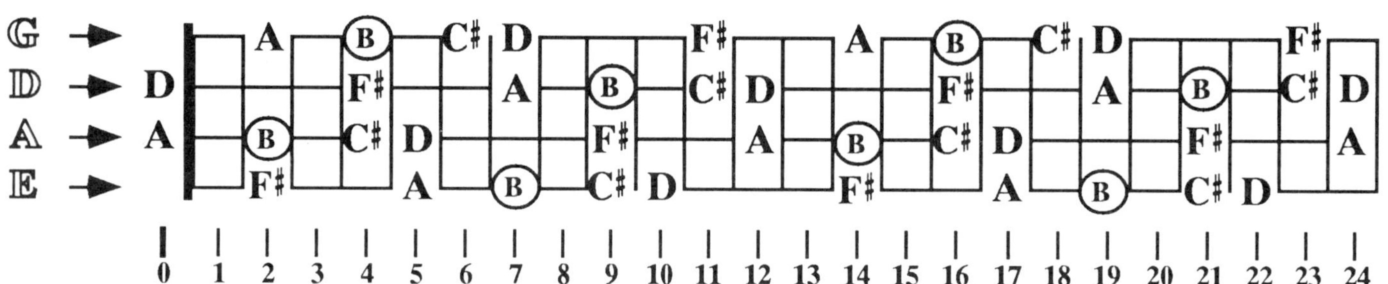

Positions

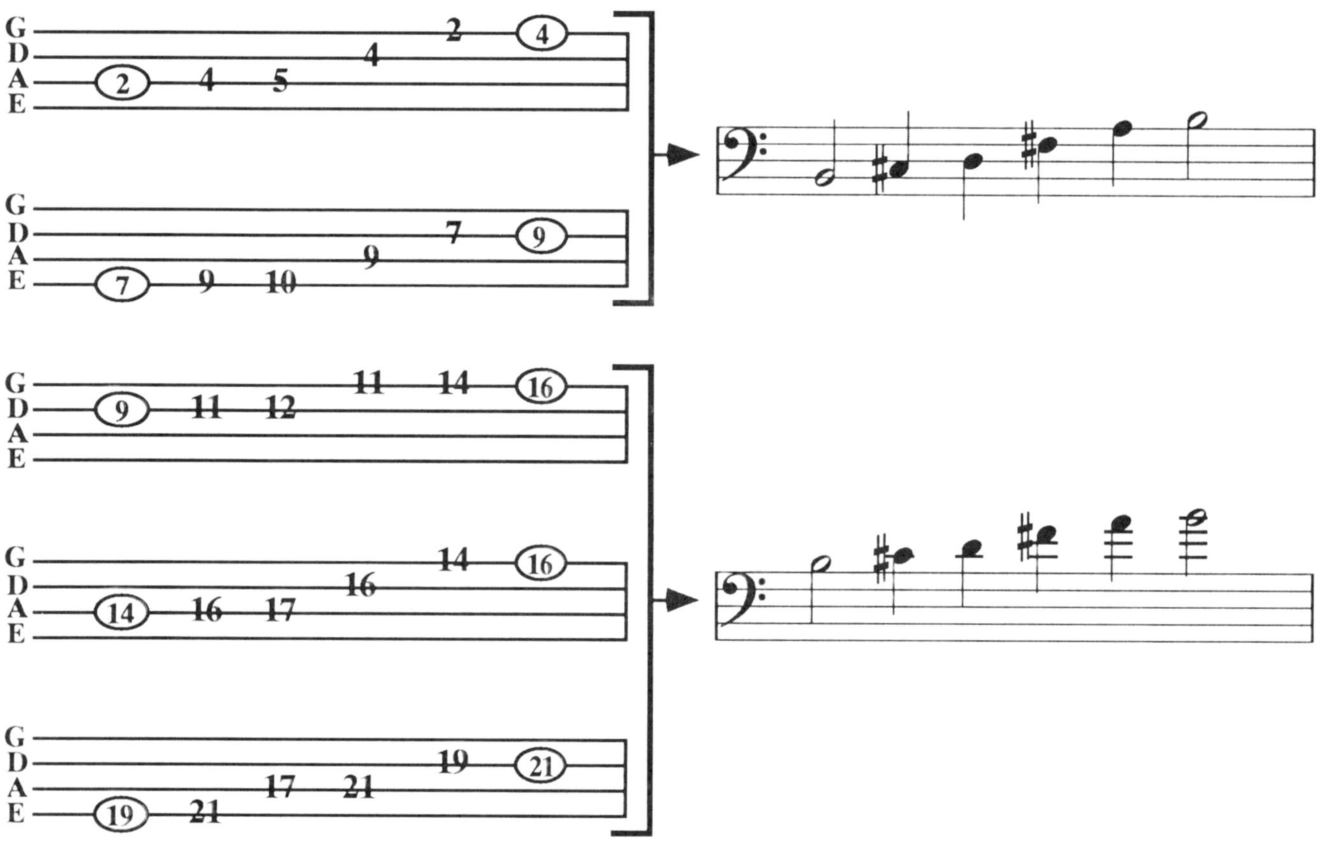

Riff

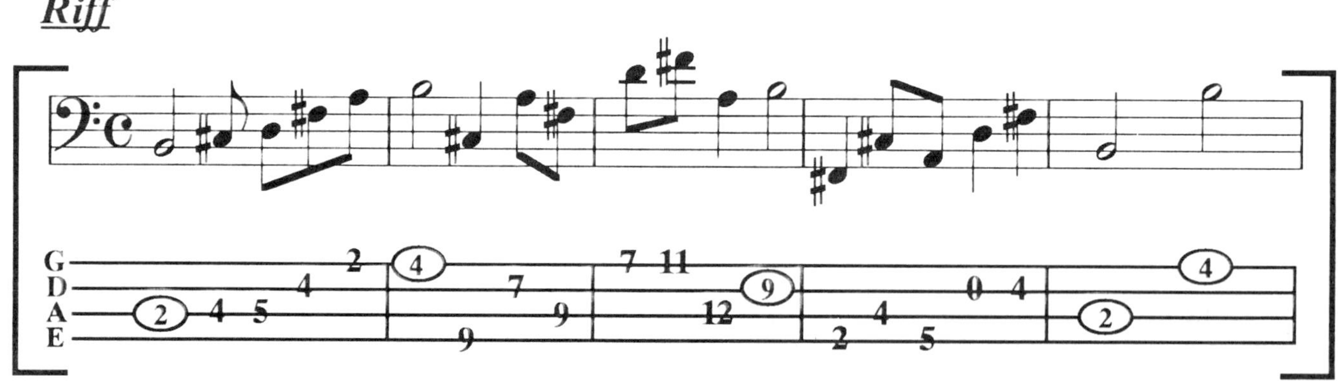

C MINOR 6TH-9TH

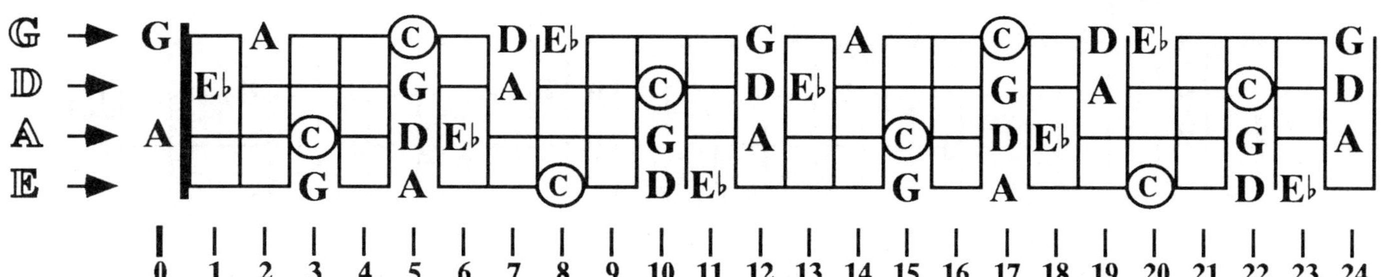

Positions

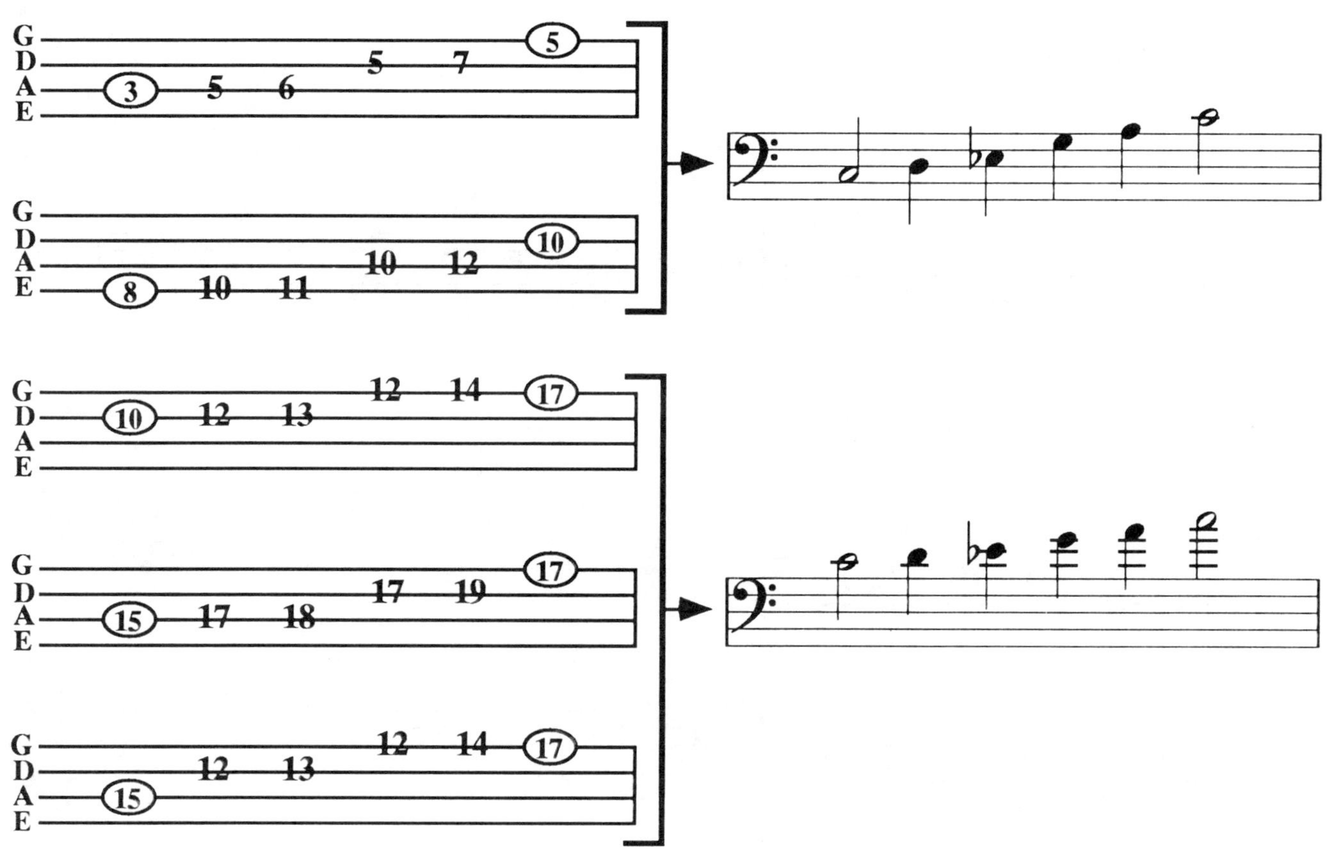

Riff

D MINOR 6TH-9TH

FORMULA - (D) Root (F) ♭3rd (A) 5th (B) 6th (E) 9th

Dm 6/9

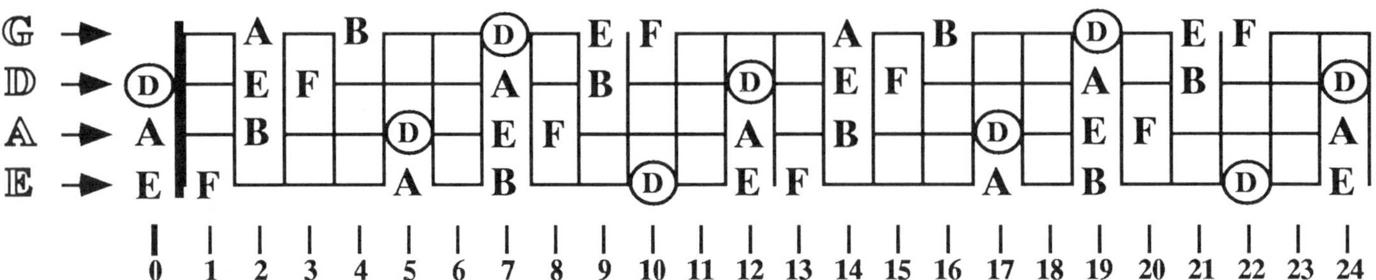

Positions

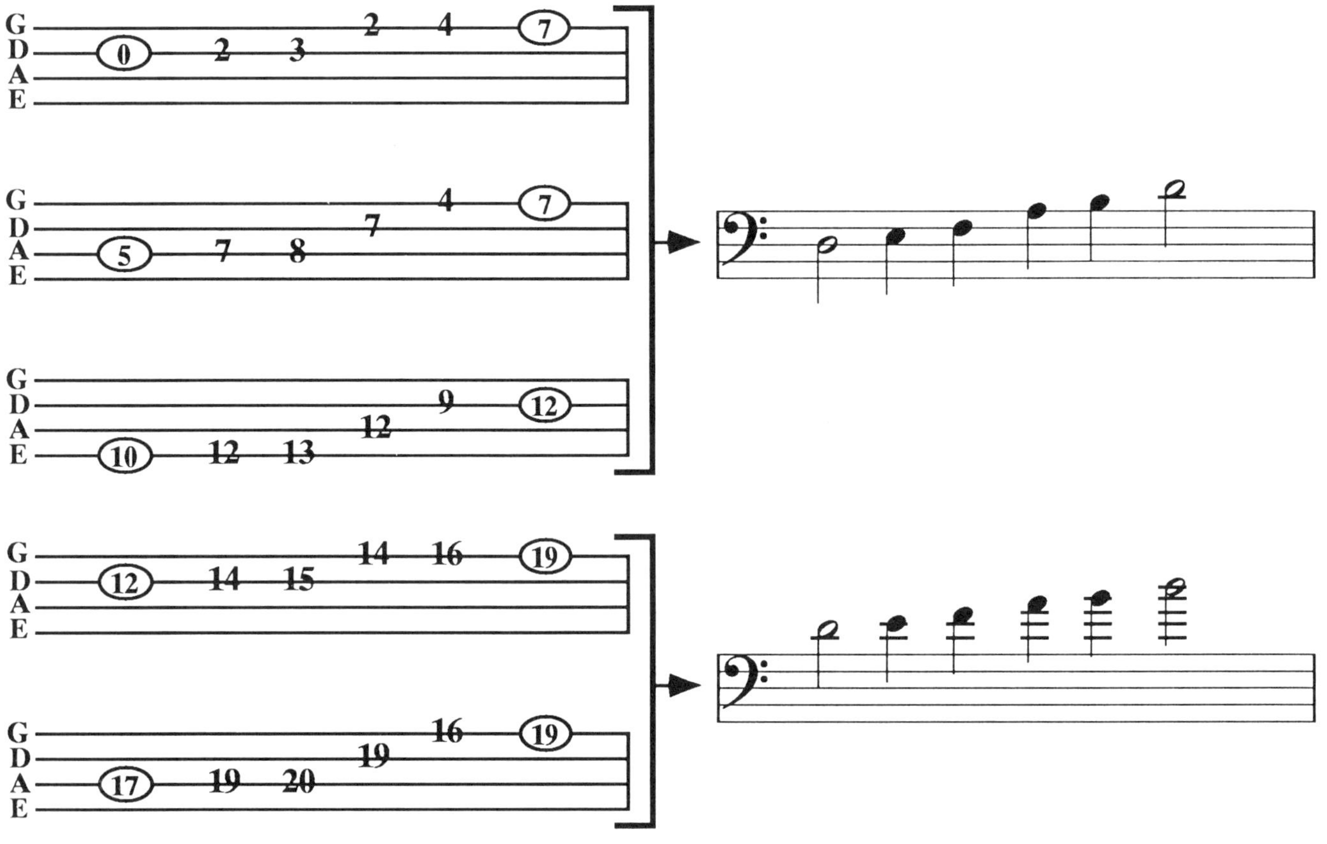

Riff

E MINOR 6TH-9TH

FORMULA - (E) Root (G) ♭3rd (B) 5th (C♯) 6th (F♯) 9th

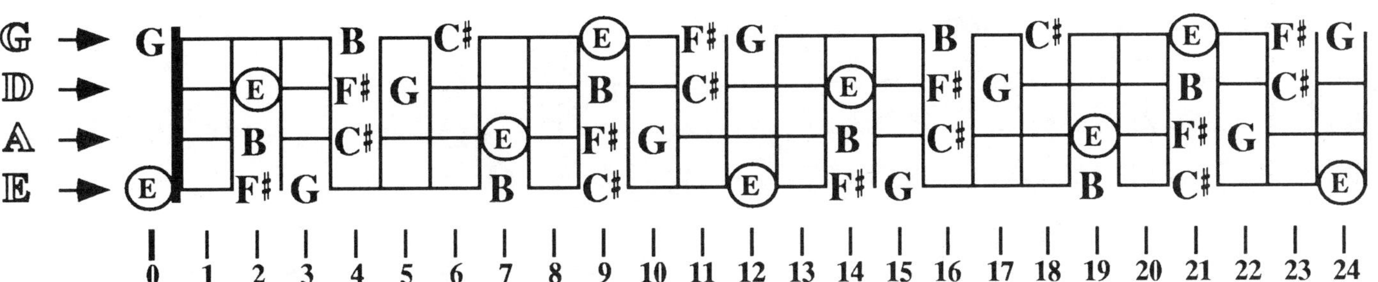

Positions

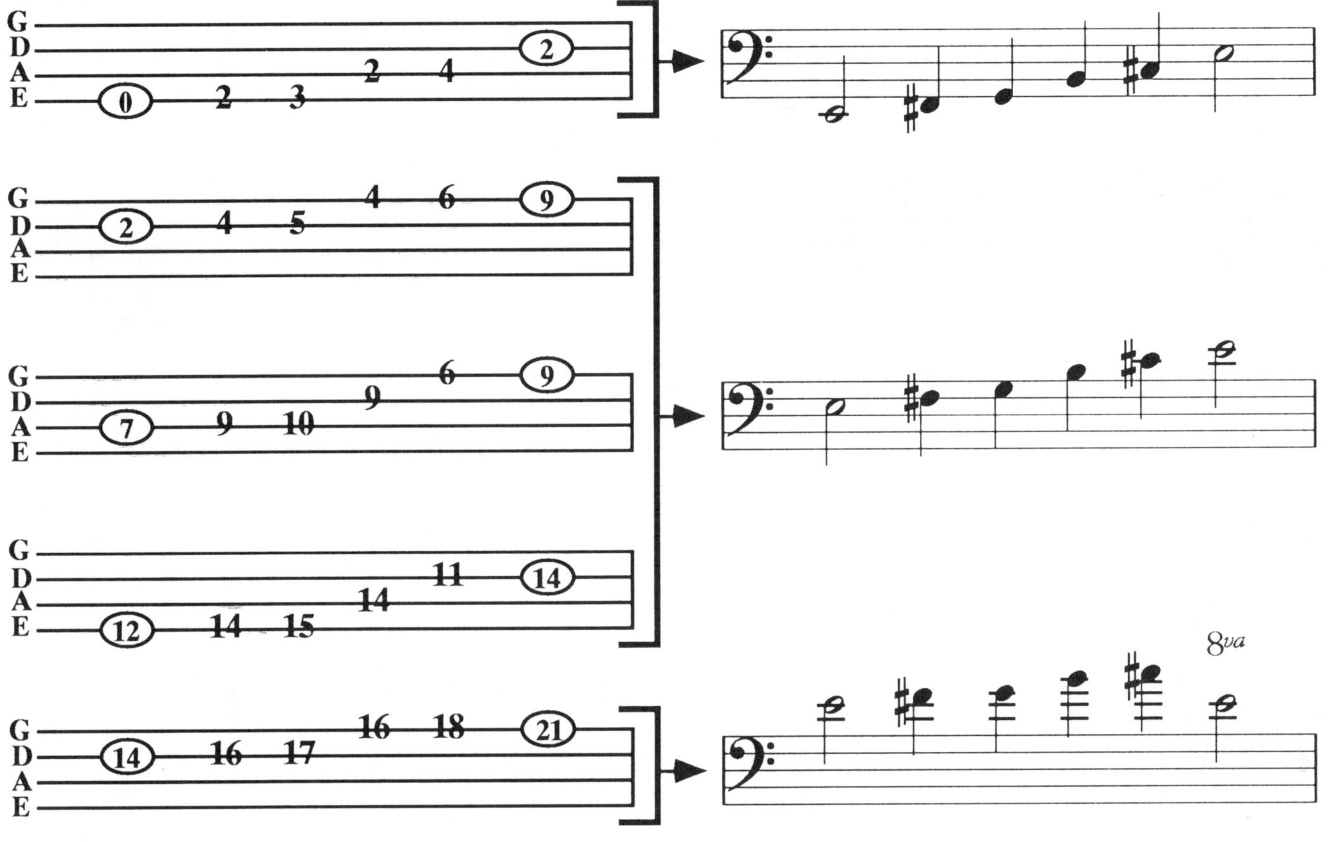

Riff

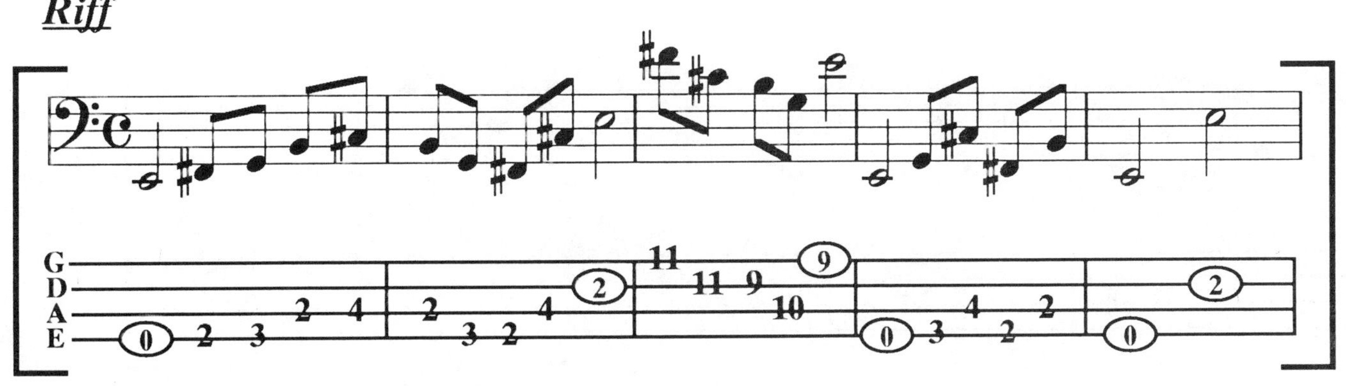

F   MINOR 6TH-9TH

FORMULA - (F) Root (A♭) ♭3rd (C) 5th (D) 6th (G) 9th

Fm 6/9

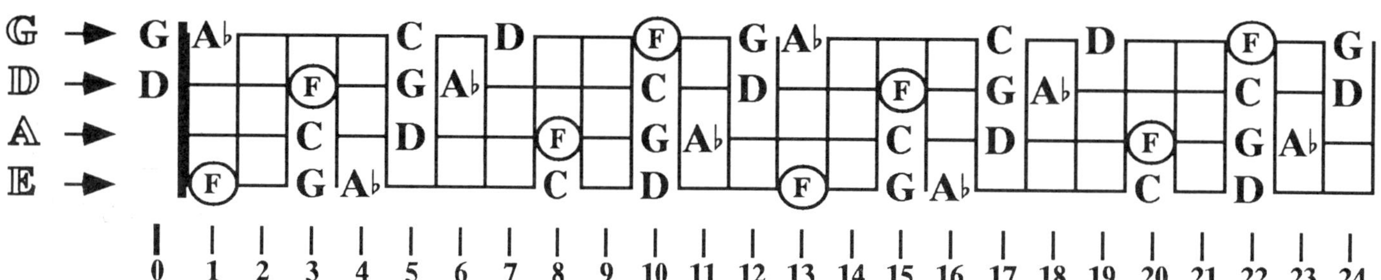

Positions

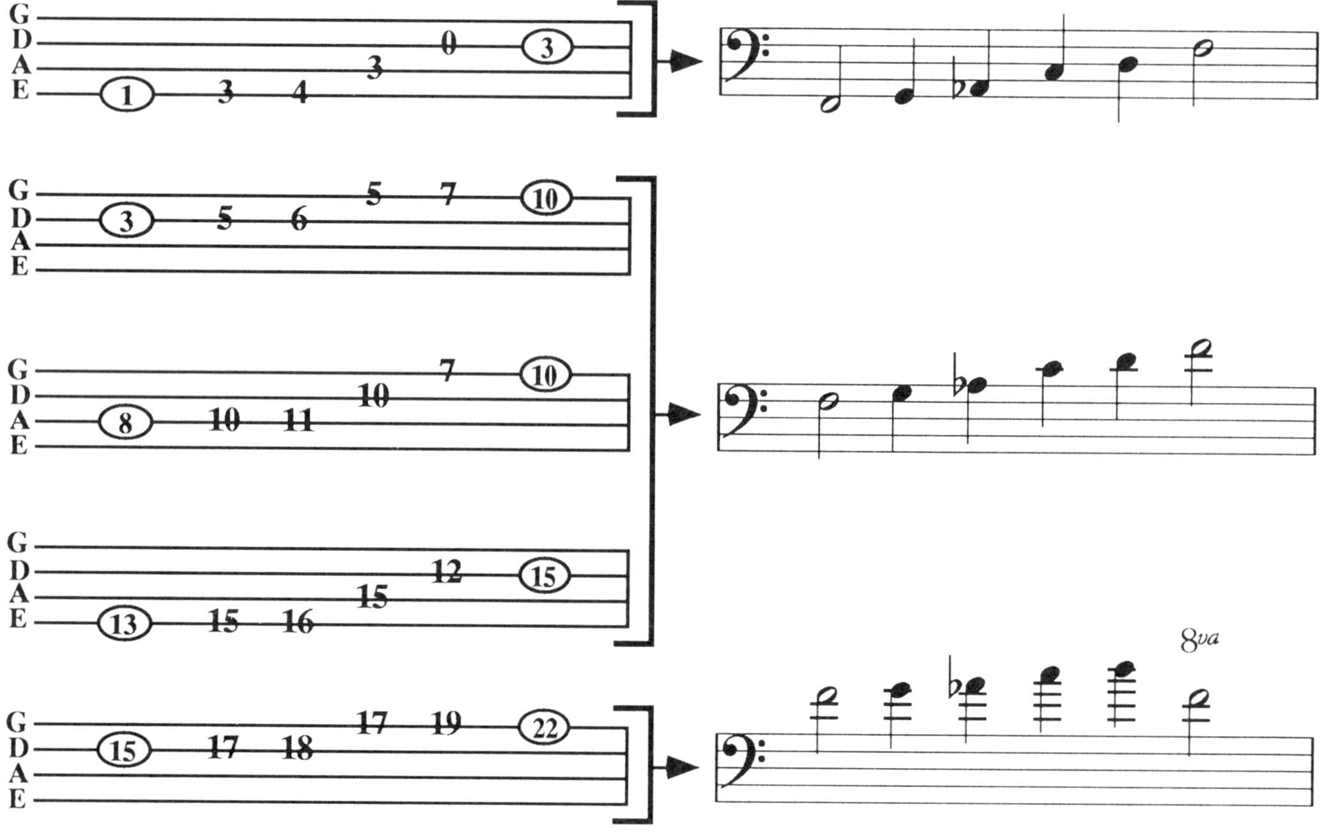

Riff

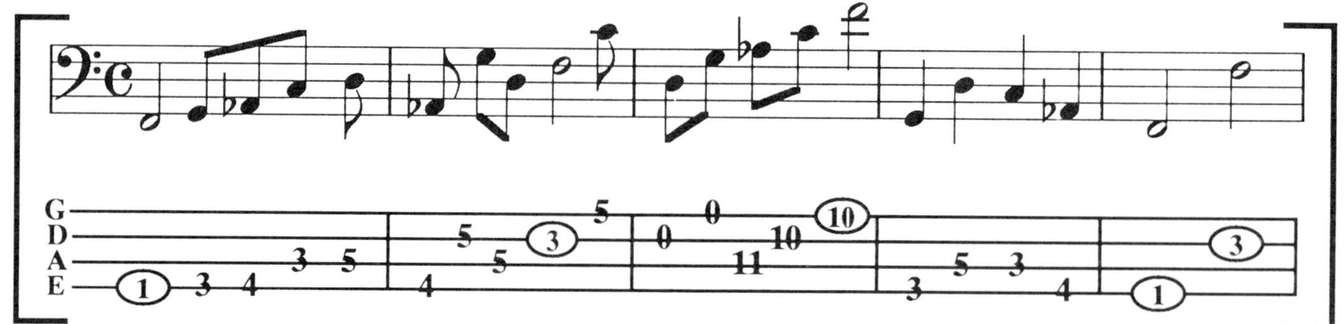

G MINOR 6TH-9TH

FORMULA - (G) Root (B♭) ♭3rd (D) 5th (E) 6th (A) 9th

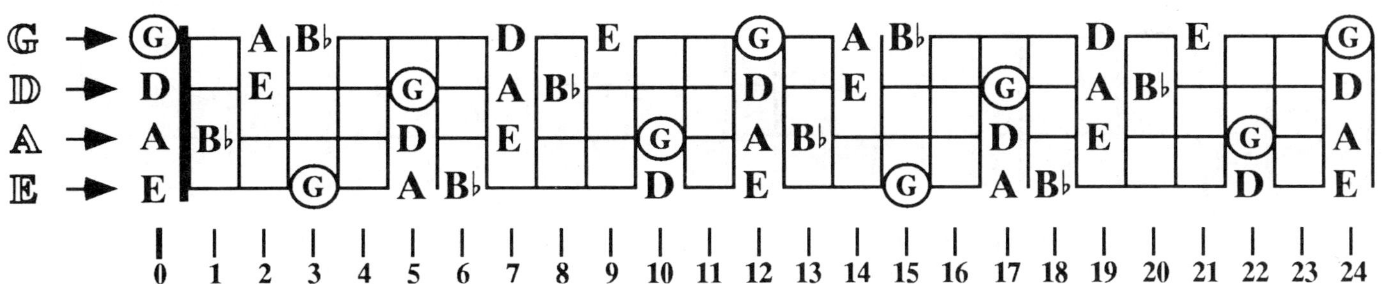

Positions

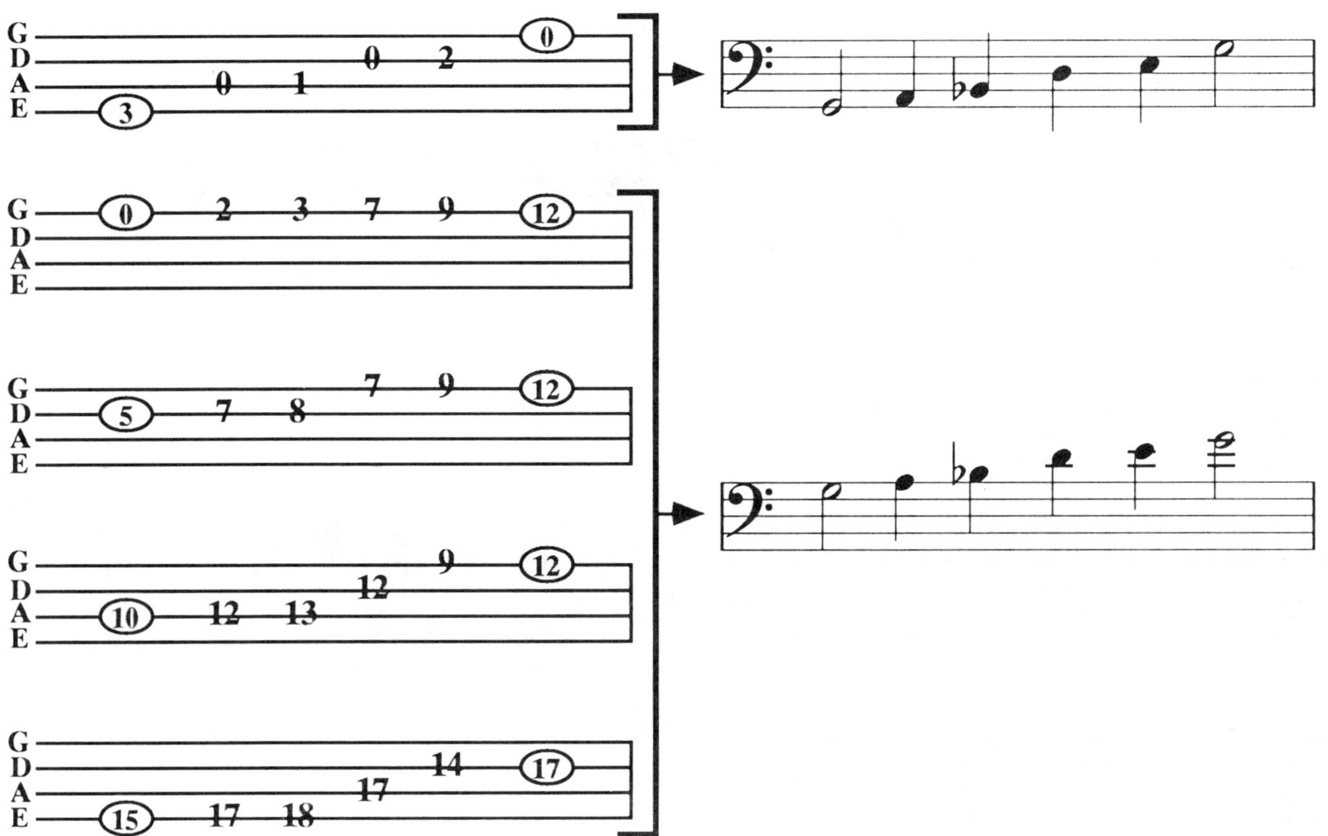

Riff

A MINOR 6TH-9TH

FORMULA - (A) Root (C) ♭3rd (E) 5th (F♯) 6th (B) 9th

Am 6/9

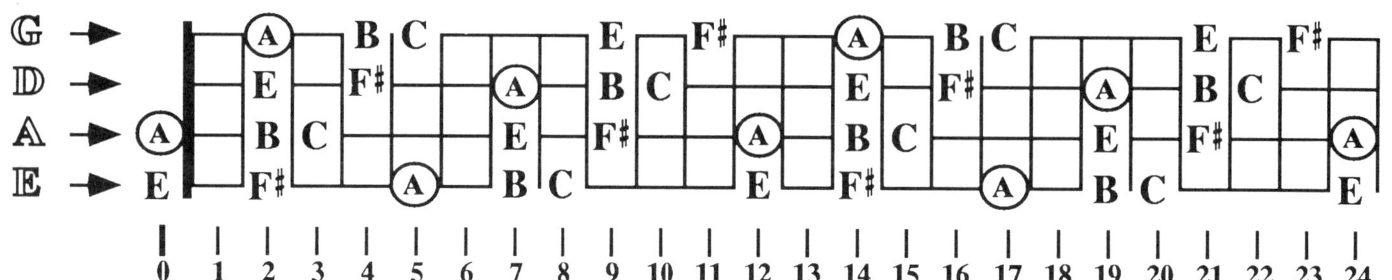

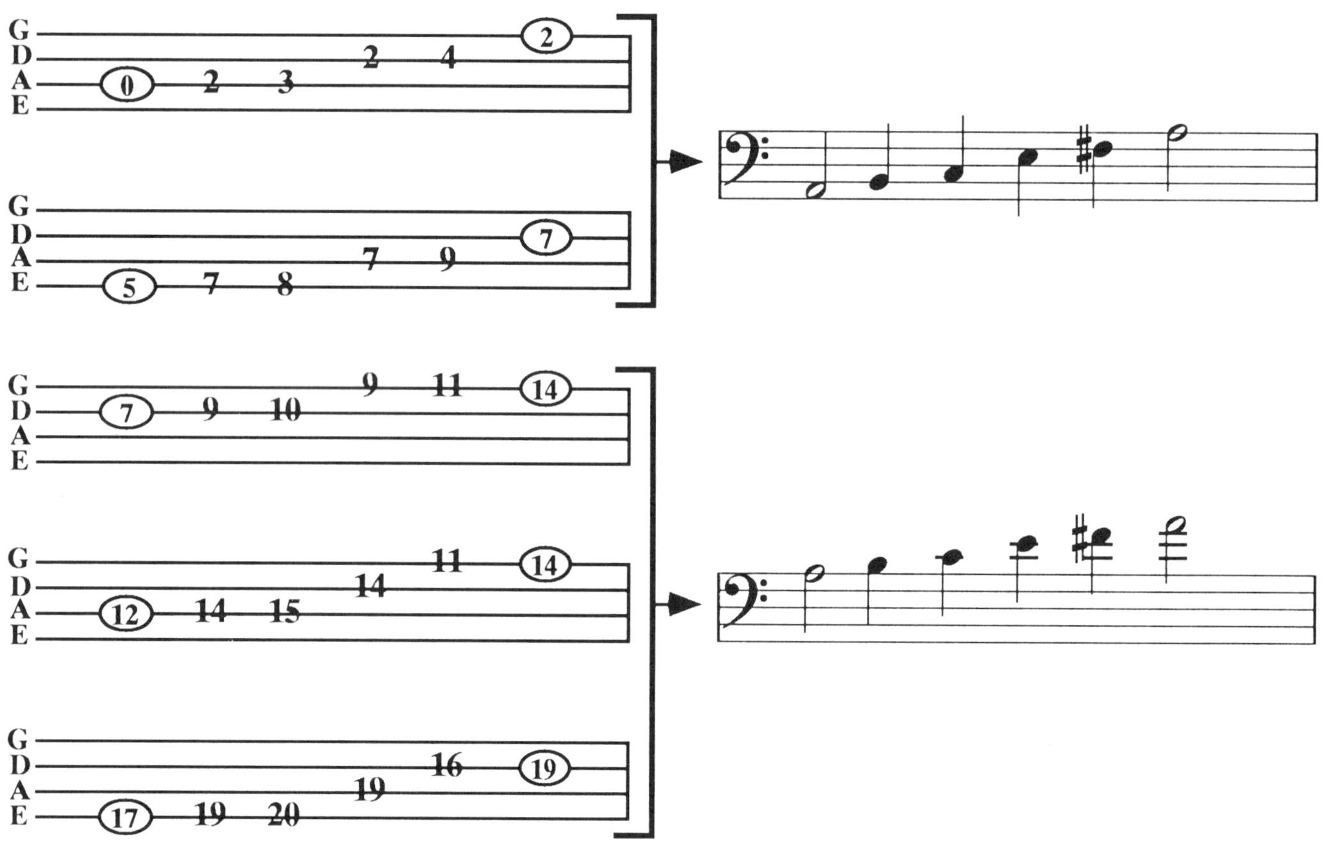

Positions

Riff

B MINOR 6TH-9TH

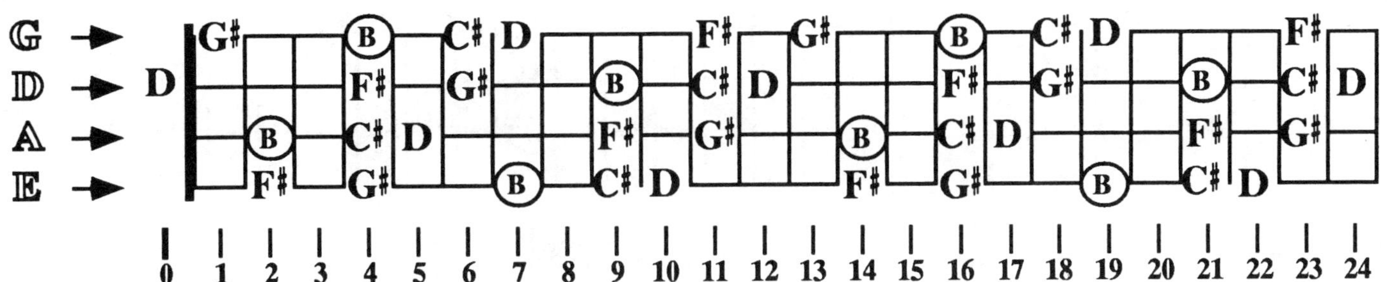

Positions

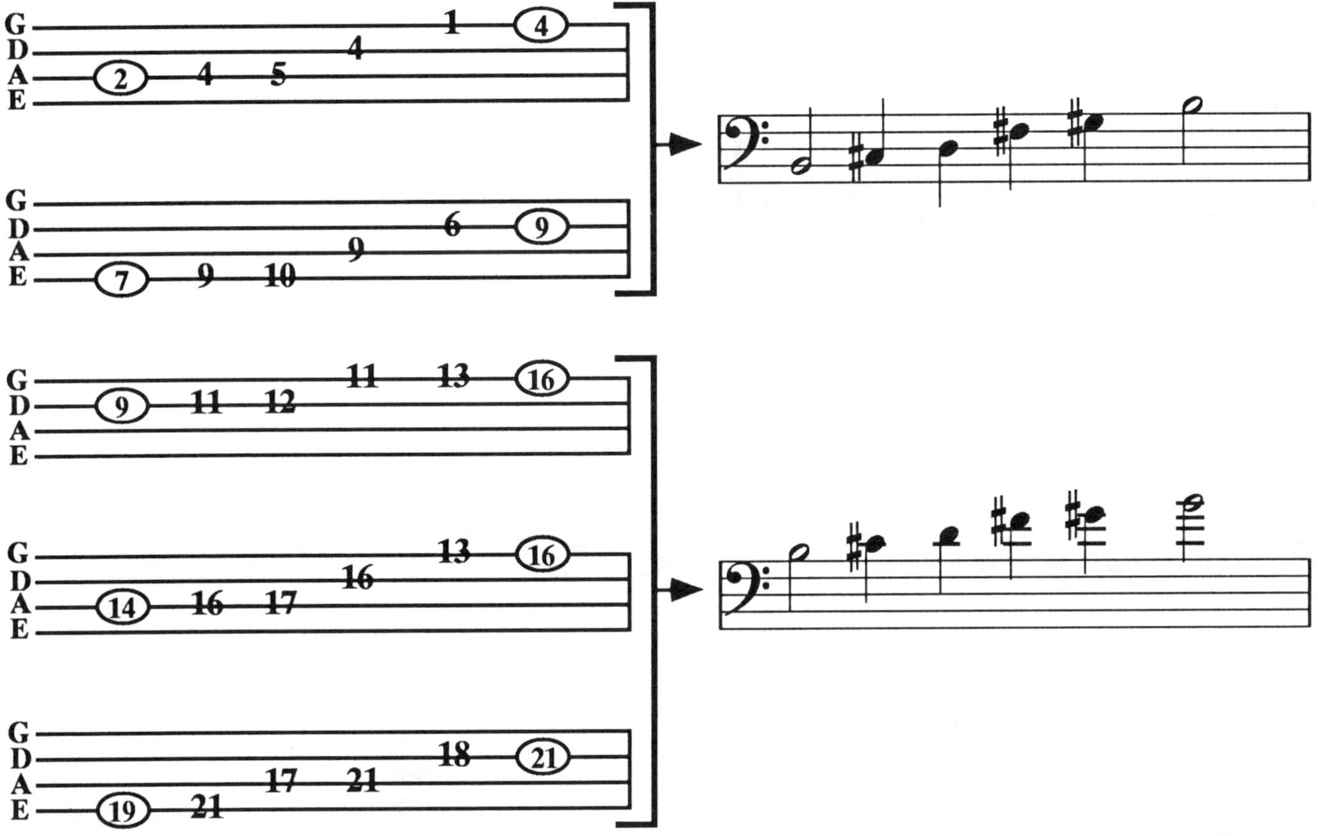

Riff

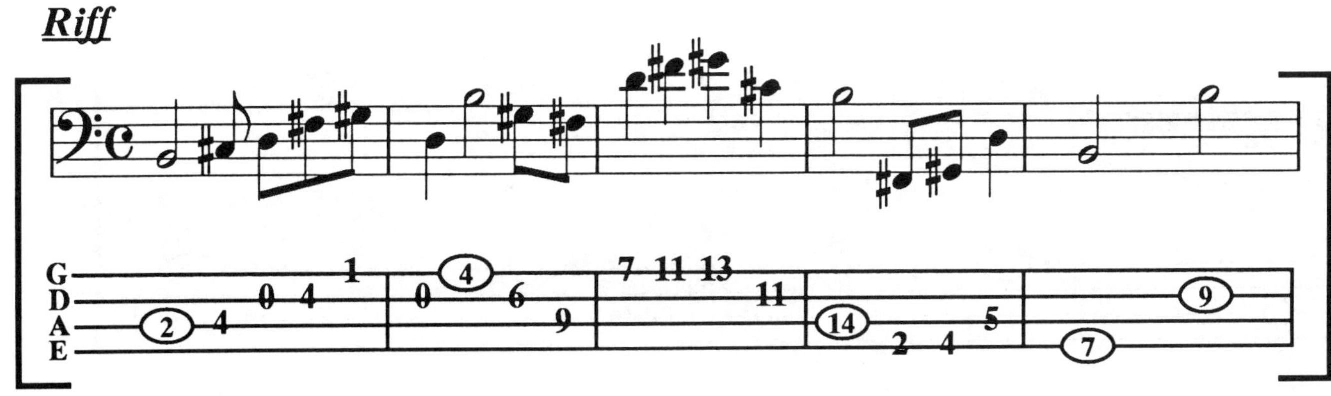

C MINOR 11TH

Cm11

FORMULA - (C) Root (E♭) ♭3rd (G) 5th (B♭) ♭7th (D) 9th (F) 11th

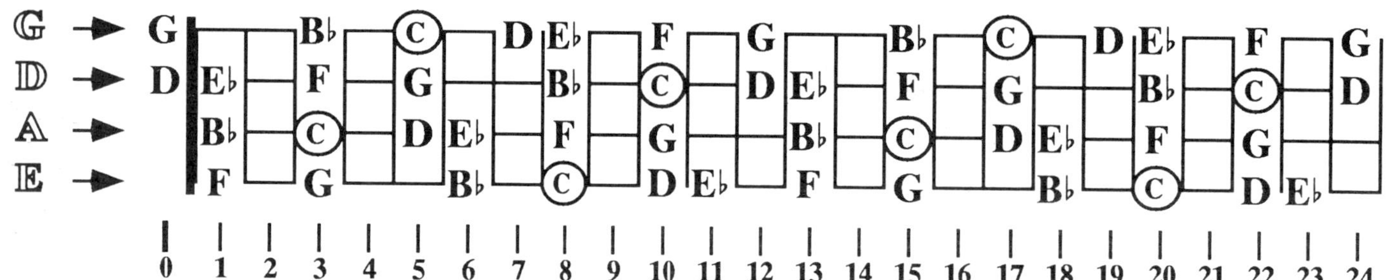

Positions

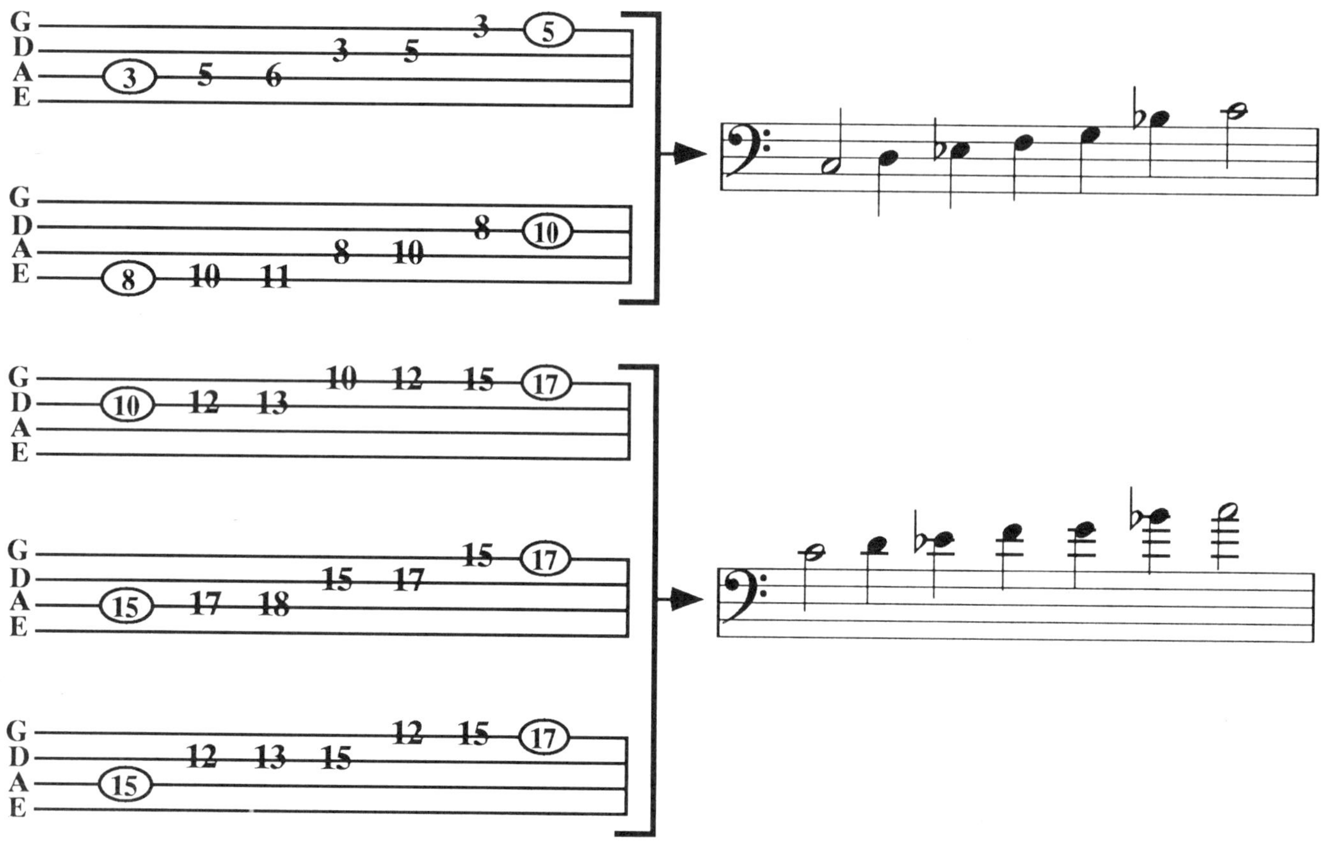

Riff

D MINOR 11TH

FORMULA - (D) Root (F) ♭3rd (A) 5th (C) ♭7th (E) 9th (G) 11th

Dm11

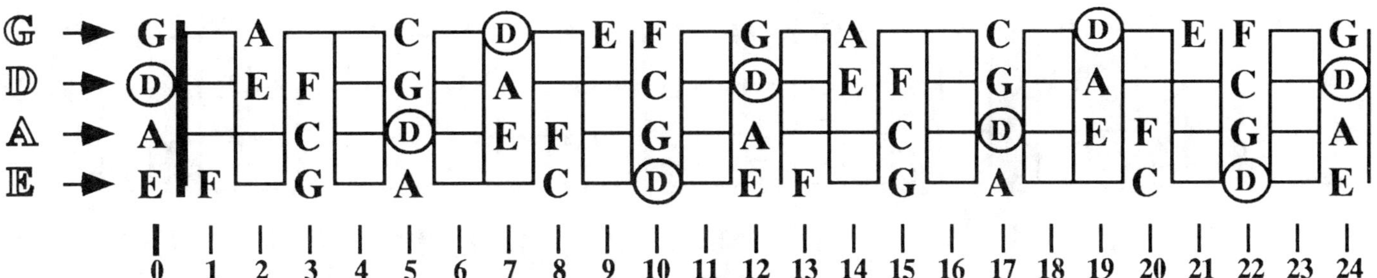

Positions

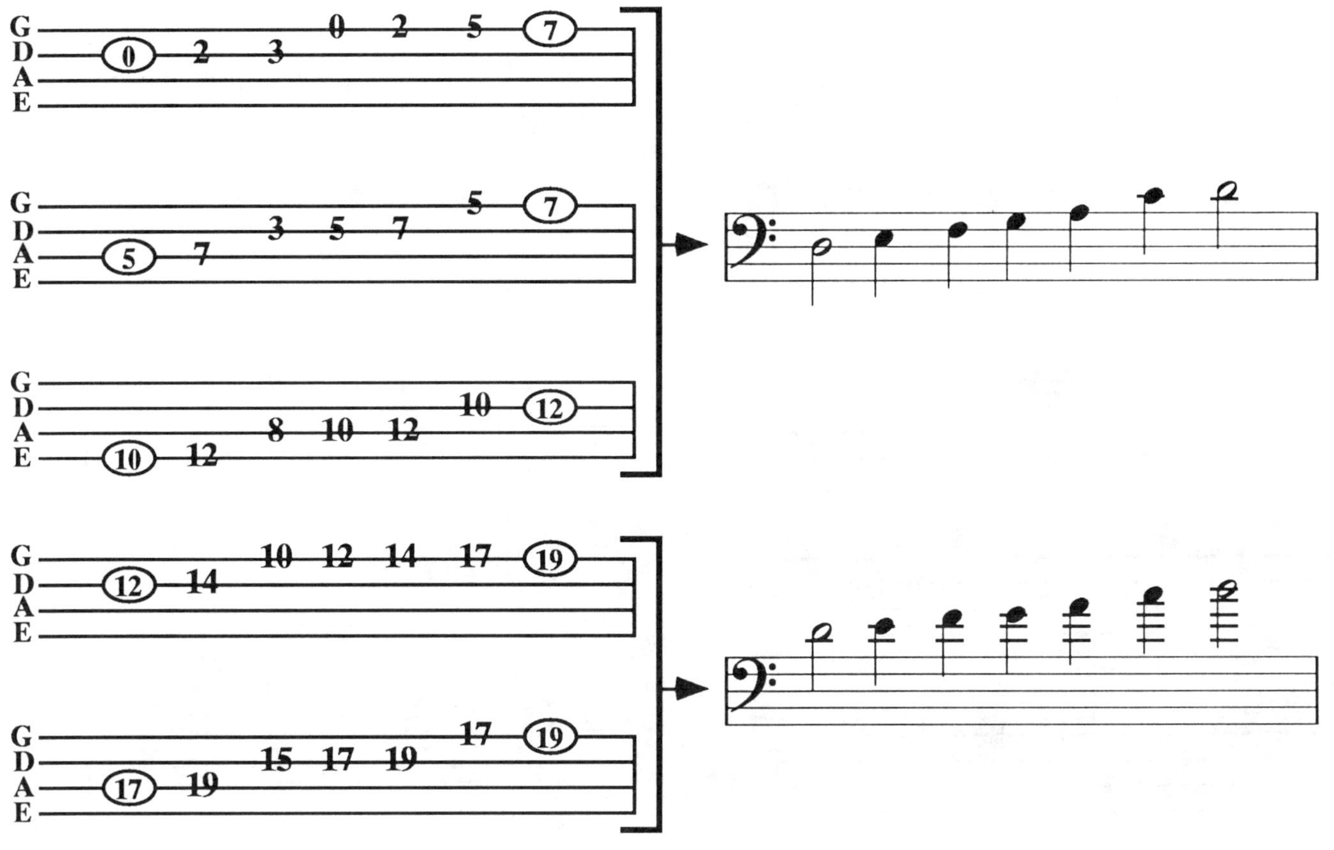

Riff

E MINOR 11TH

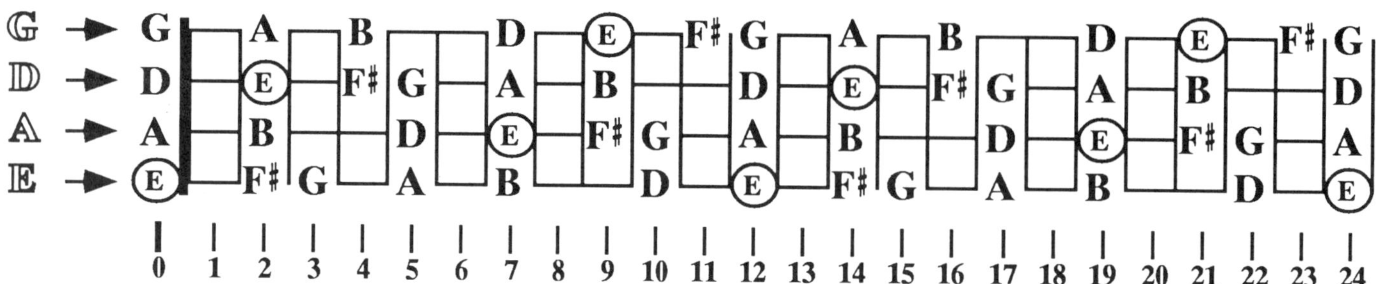

Positions

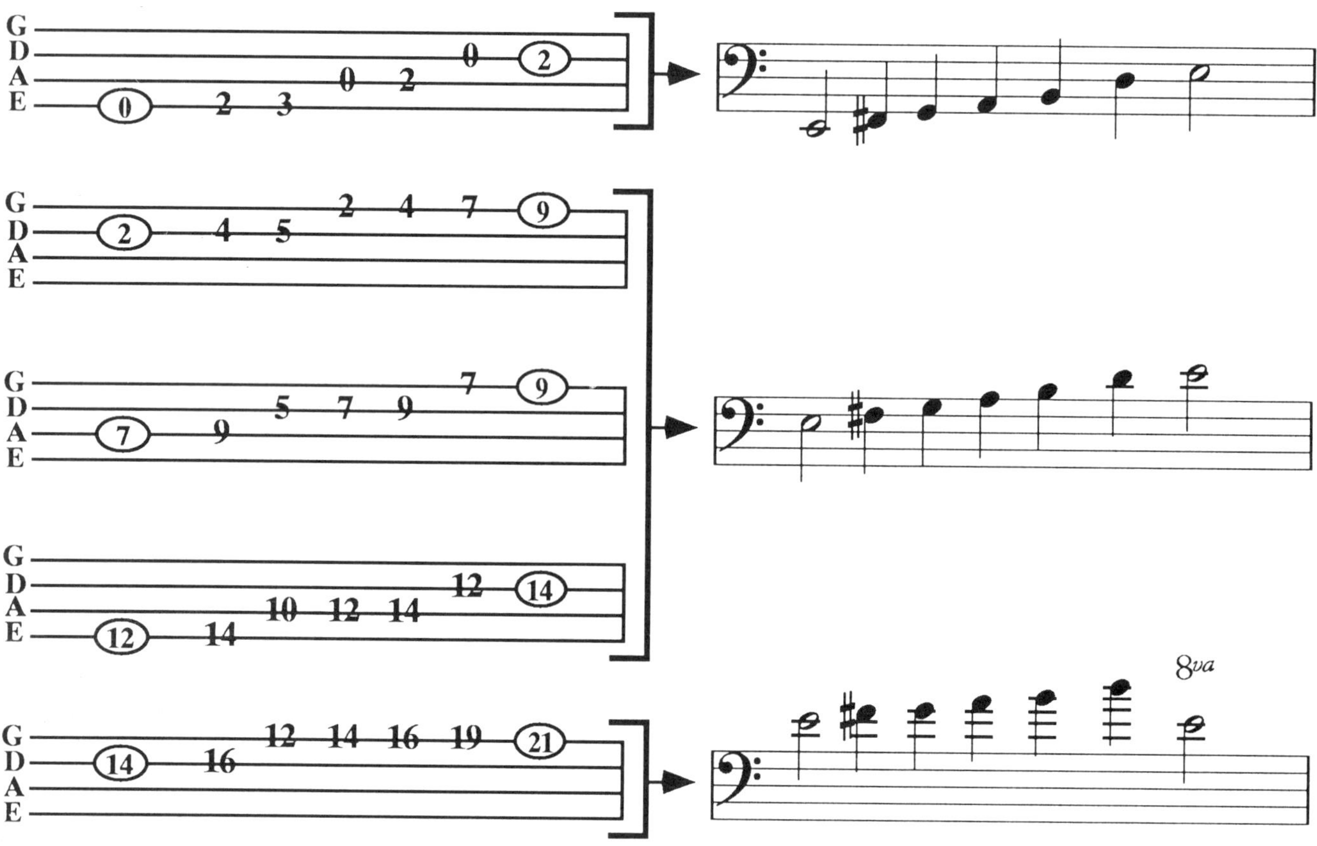

Riff

F MINOR 11TH

FORMULA - (F) Root (A♭) ♭3rd (C) 5th
(E♭) ♭7th (G) 9th (B♭) 11th

Fm11

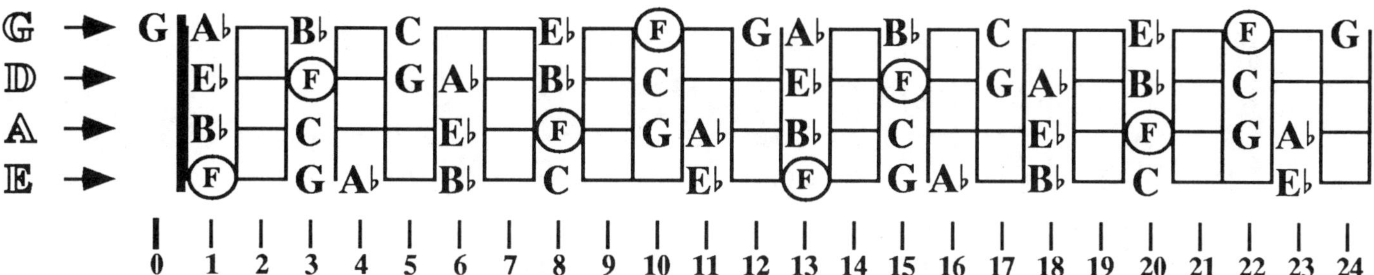

Positions

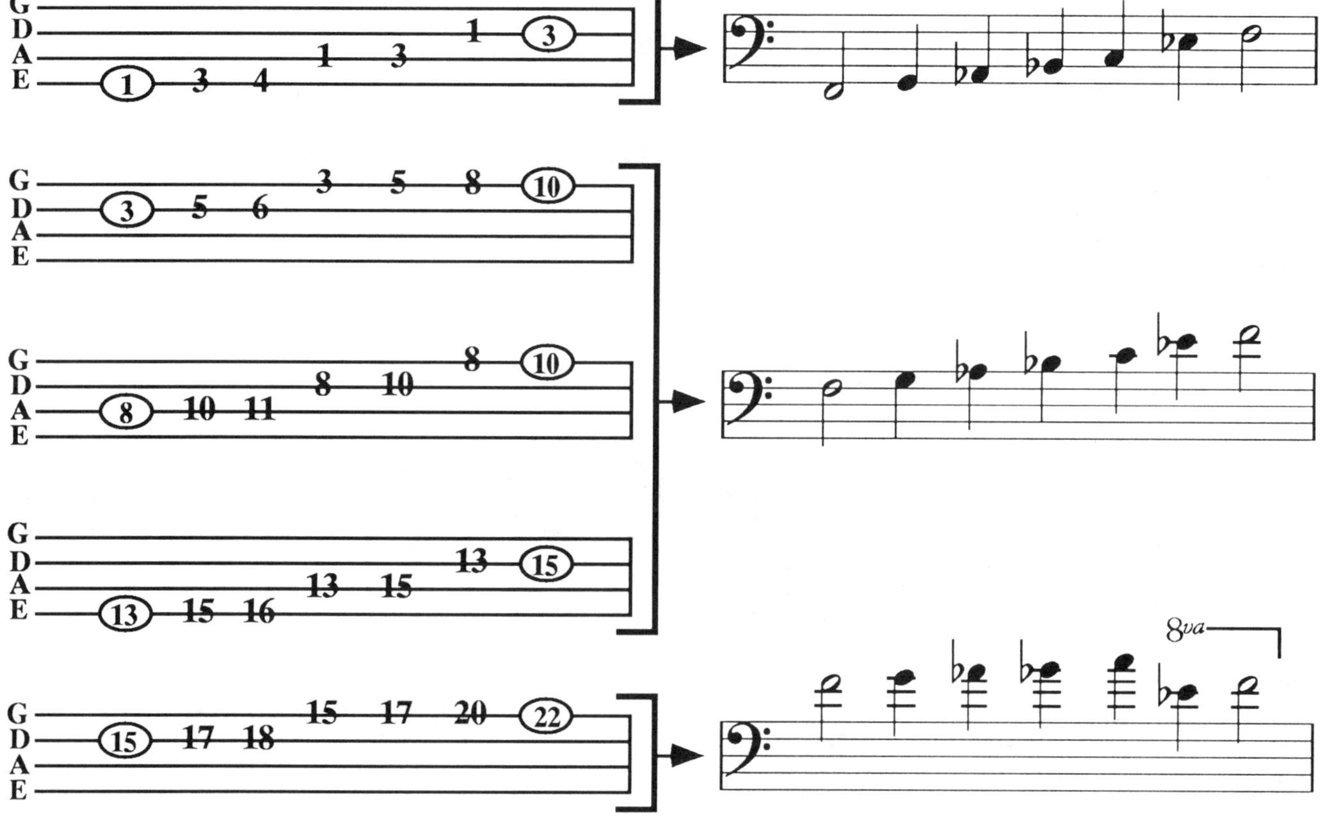

Riff

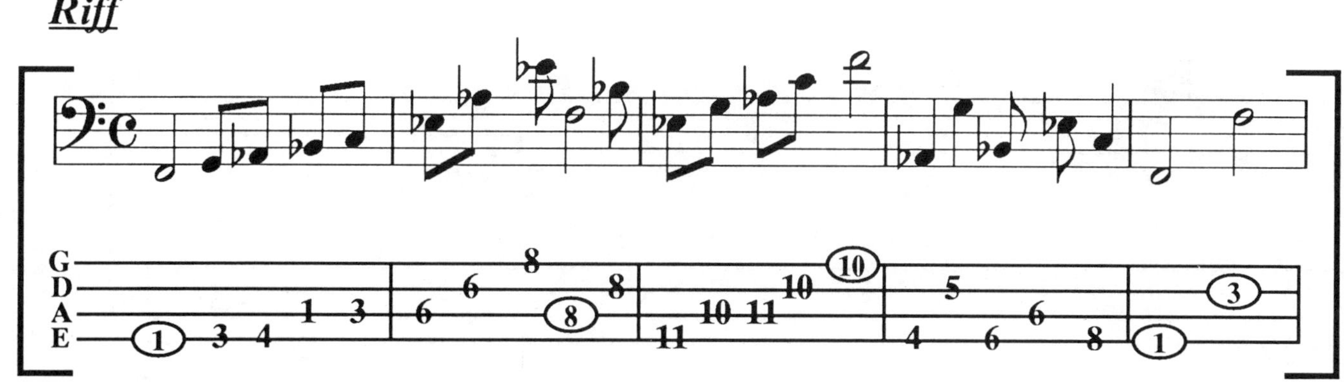

G MINOR 11TH

FORMULA - (G) Root (B♭) ♭3rd (D) 5th
(F) ♭7th (A) 9th (C) 11th

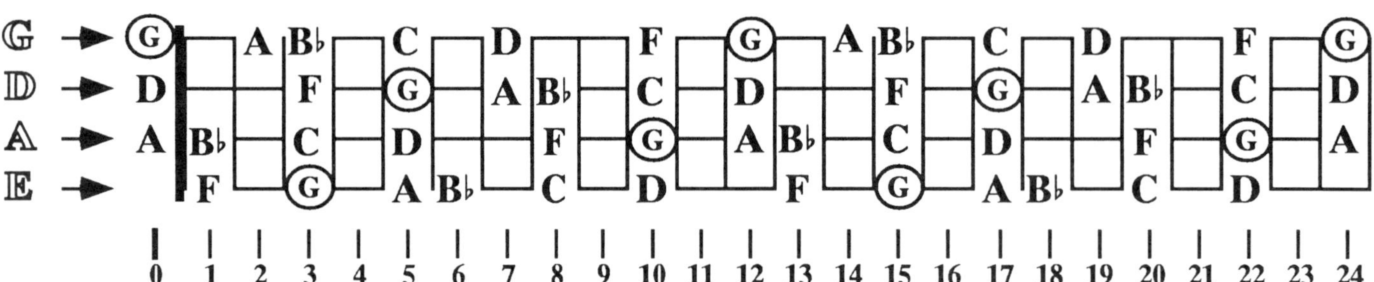

Positions

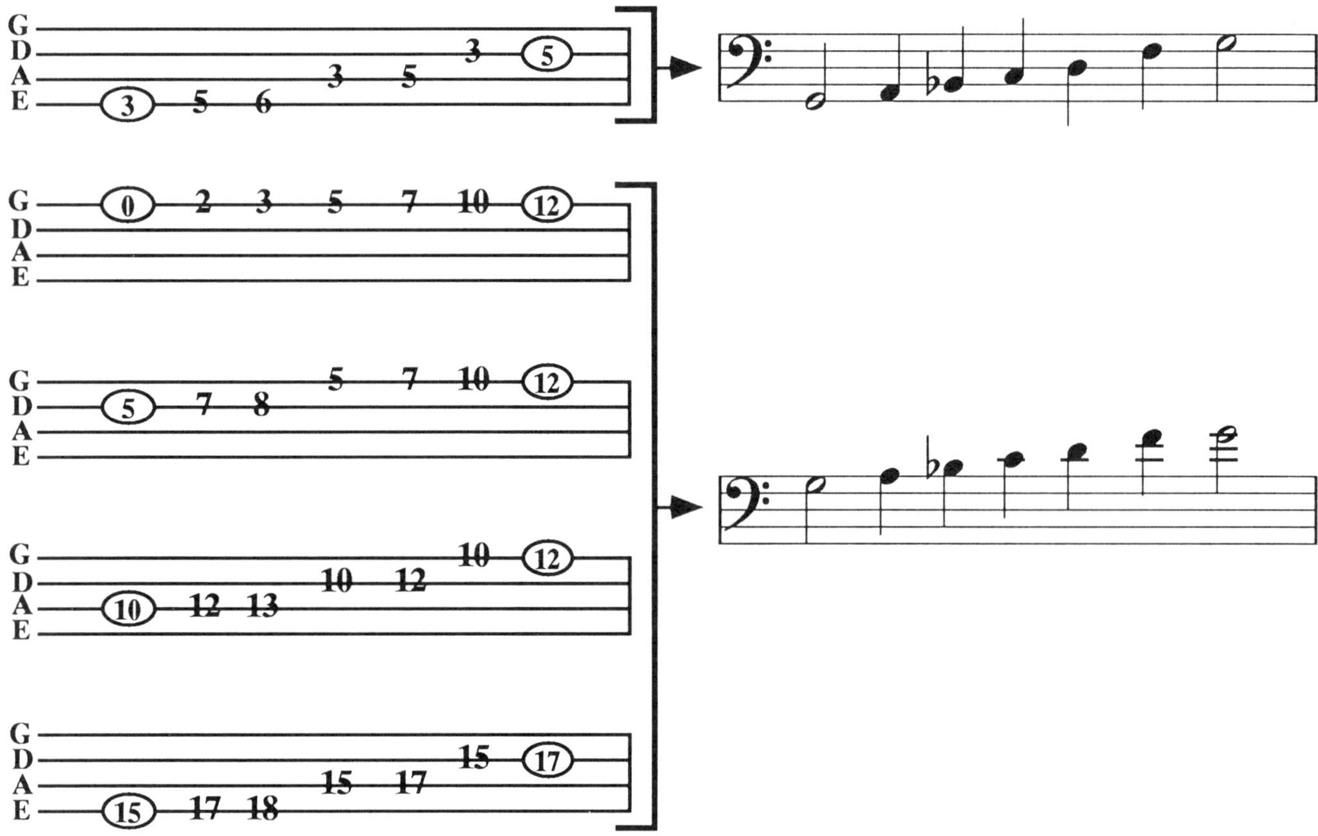

Riff

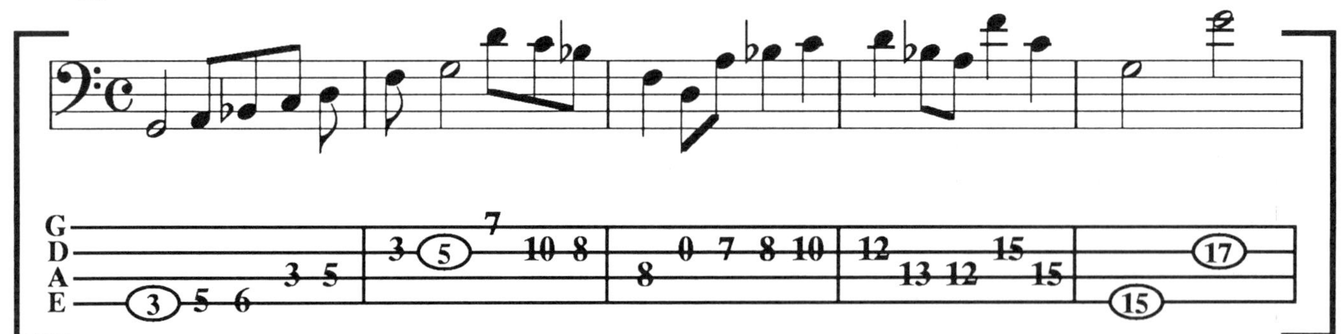

A MINOR 11TH

**FORMULA - (A) Root (C) ♭3rd (E) 5th
(G) ♭7th (B) 9th (D) 11th**

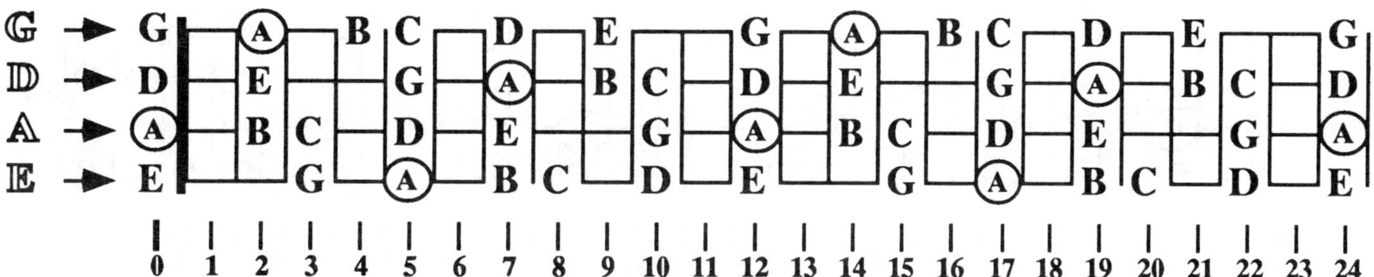

Positions

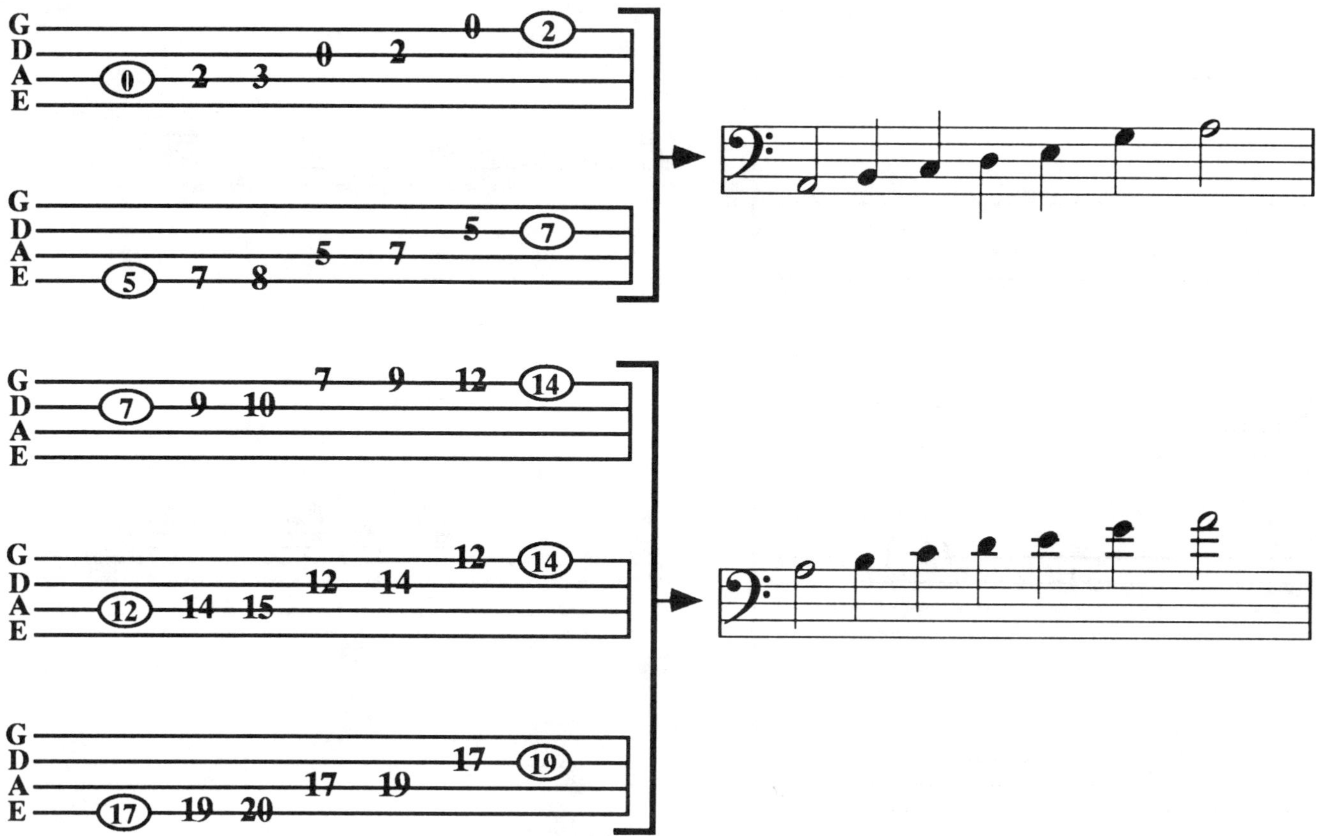

Riff

111

B MINOR 11TH

Bm11

FORMULA - (B) Root (D) ♭3rd (F♯) 5th
(A) ♭7th (C♯) 9th (E) 11th

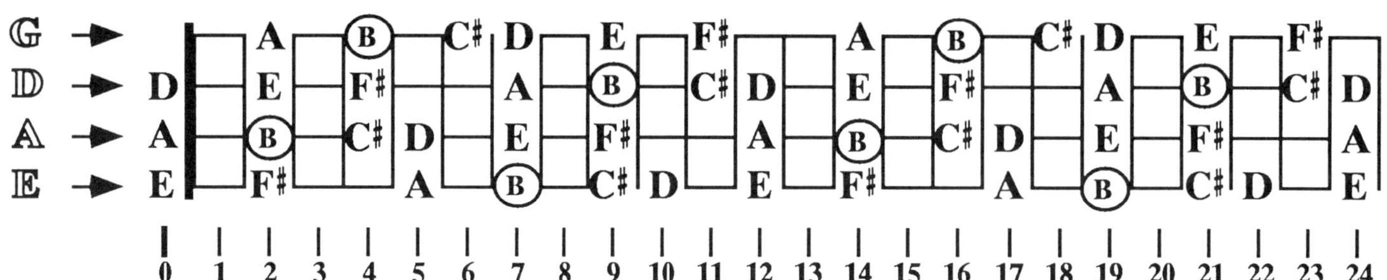

Positions

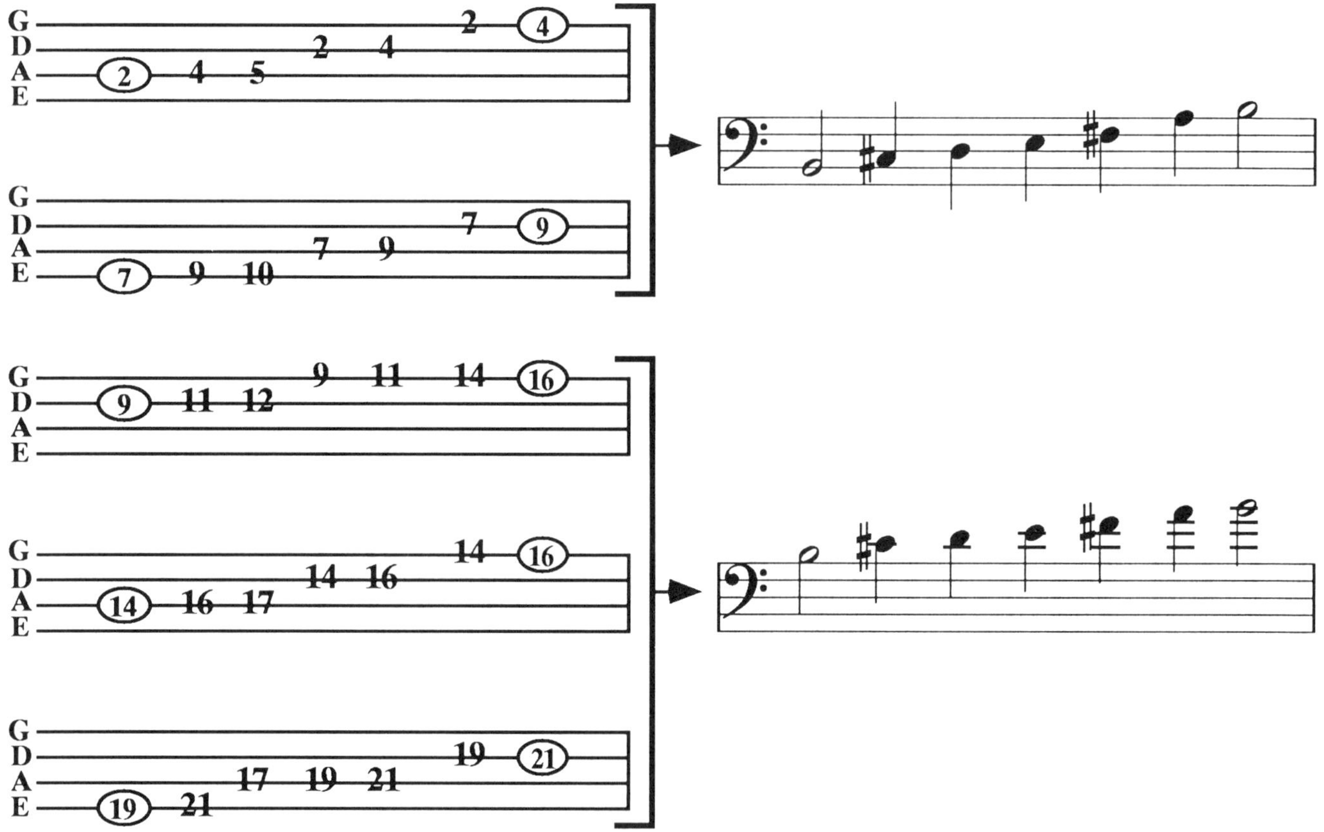

Riff

C MINOR - MAJOR 7TH

FORMULA - (C) Root (E♭) ♭3rd (G) 5th (B) 7th

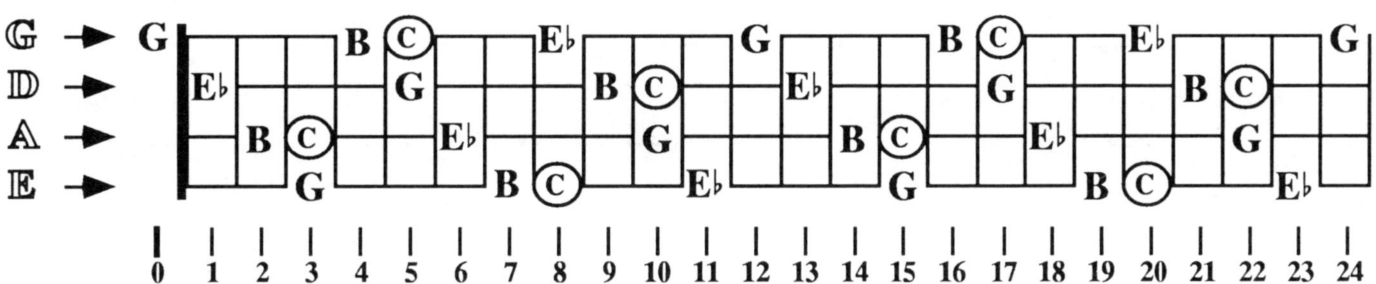

Positions

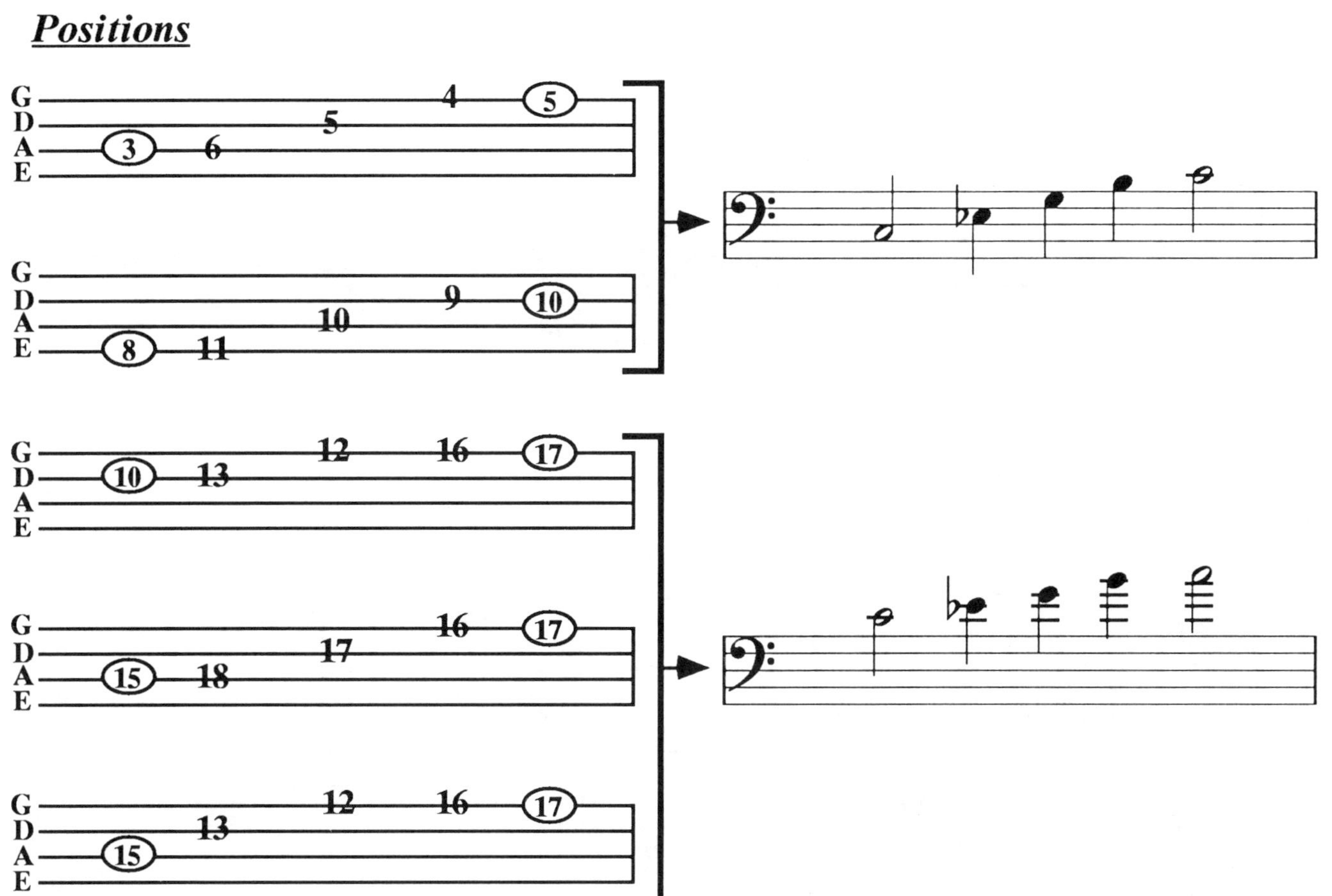

Riff

D   MINOR - MAJOR 7TH

D min. #7

FORMULA - (D) Root (F) ♭3rd (A) 5th (C♯) 7th

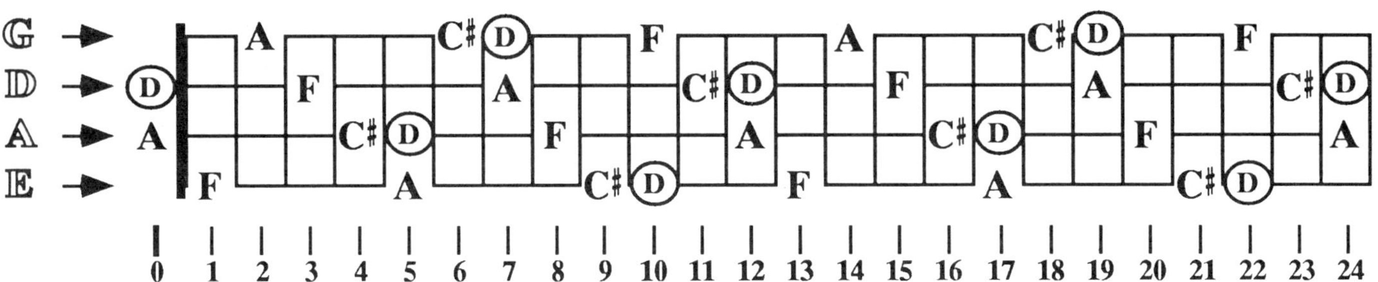

Positions

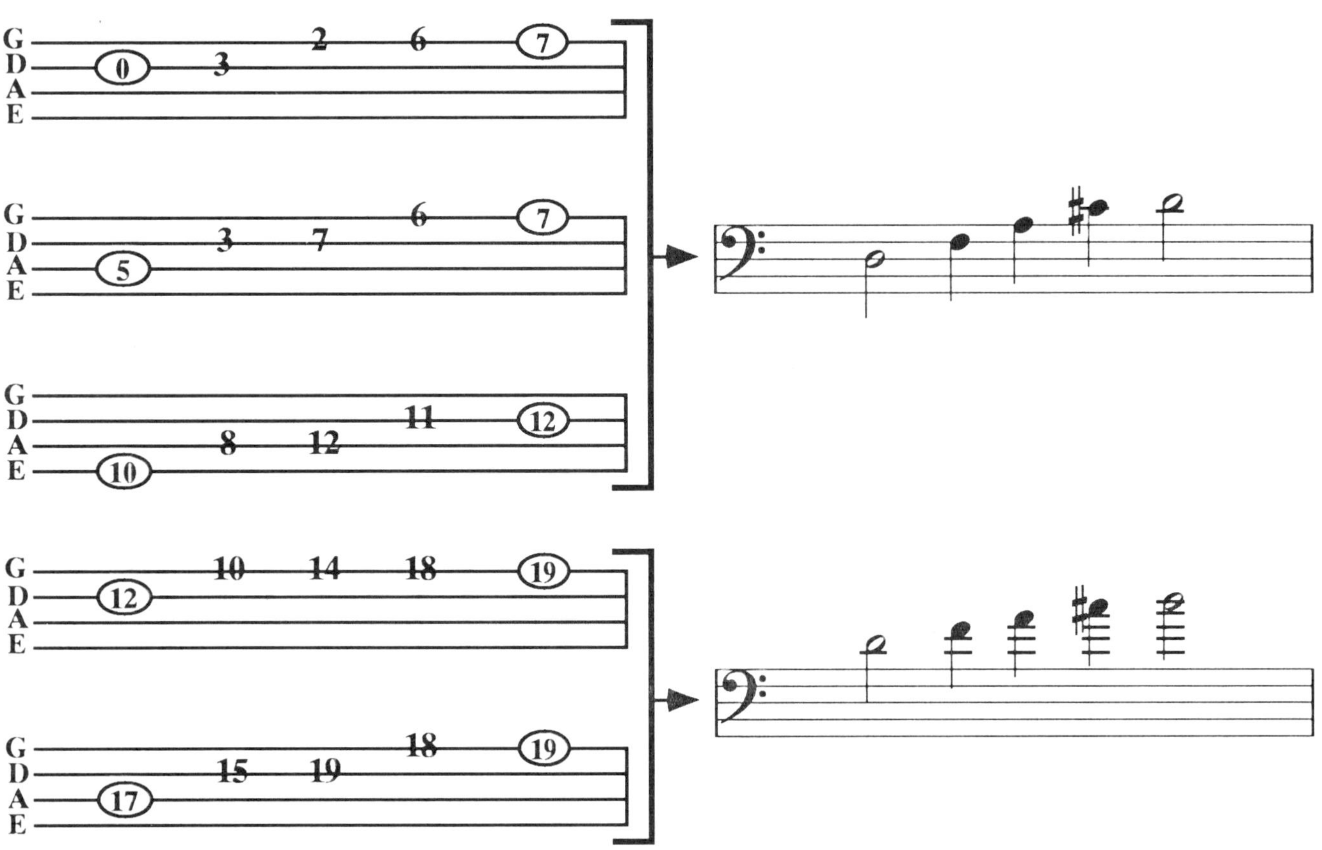

Riff

114

E   MINOR - MAJOR 7TH

FORMULA - (E) Root (G) ♭3rd (B) 5th (D♯) 7th

E min. #7

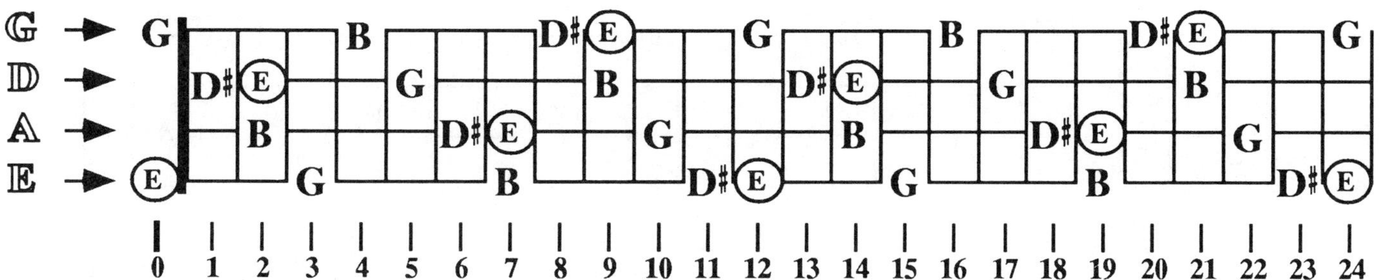

Positions

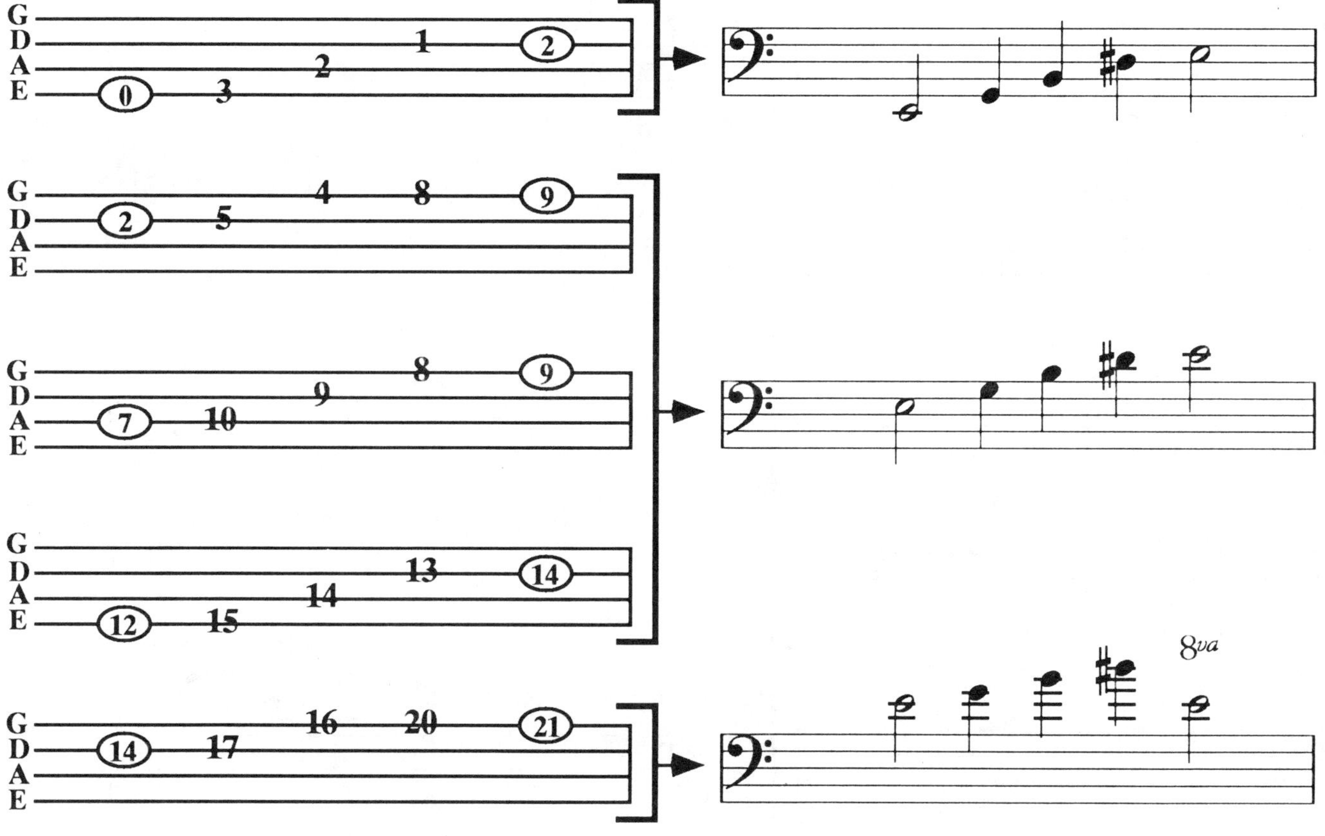

Riff

F MINOR - MAJOR 7TH

FORMULA - (F) Root (A♭) ♭3rd (C) 5th (E) 7th

F min. #7

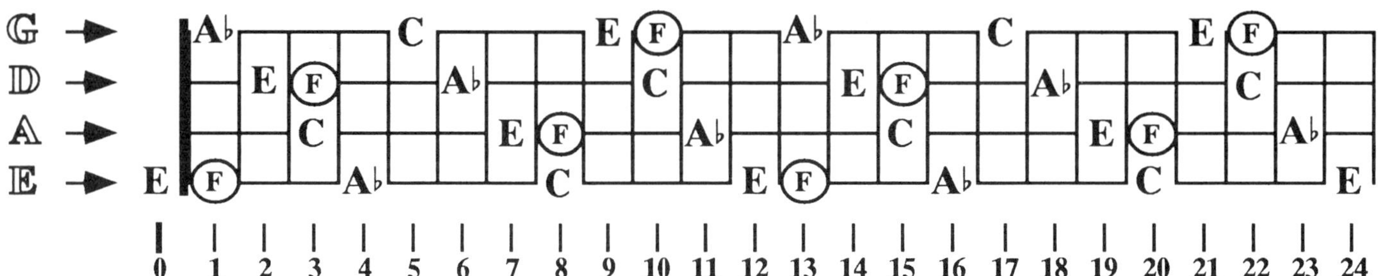

Positions

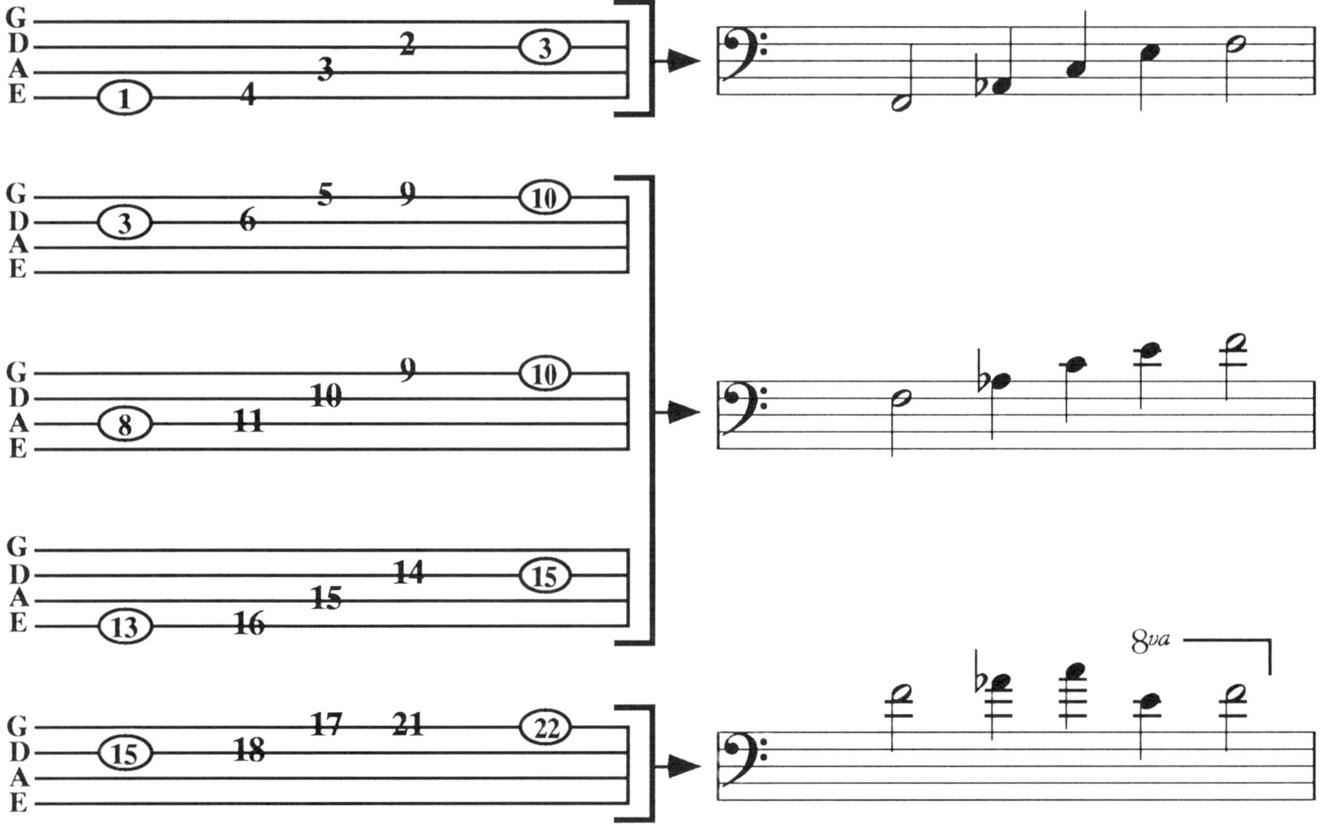

Riff

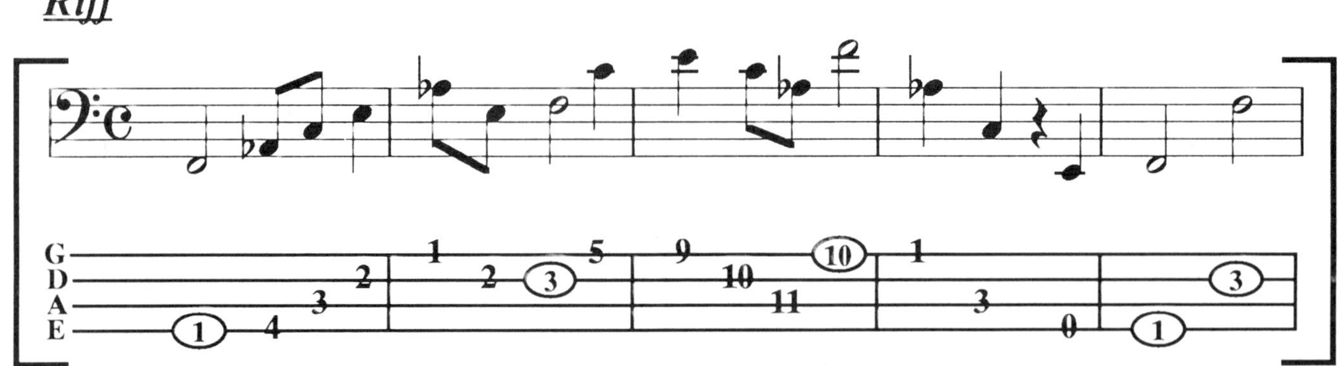

G MINOR - MAJOR 7TH

FORMULA - (G) Root (B♭) ♭3rd (D) 5th (F#) 7th

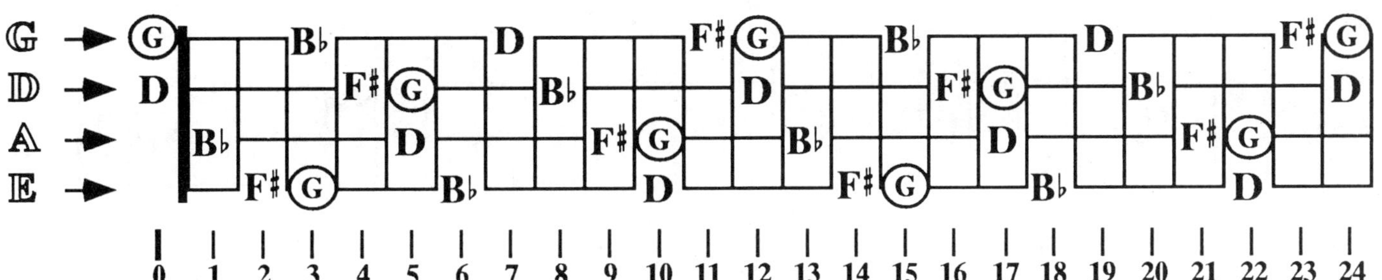

Positions

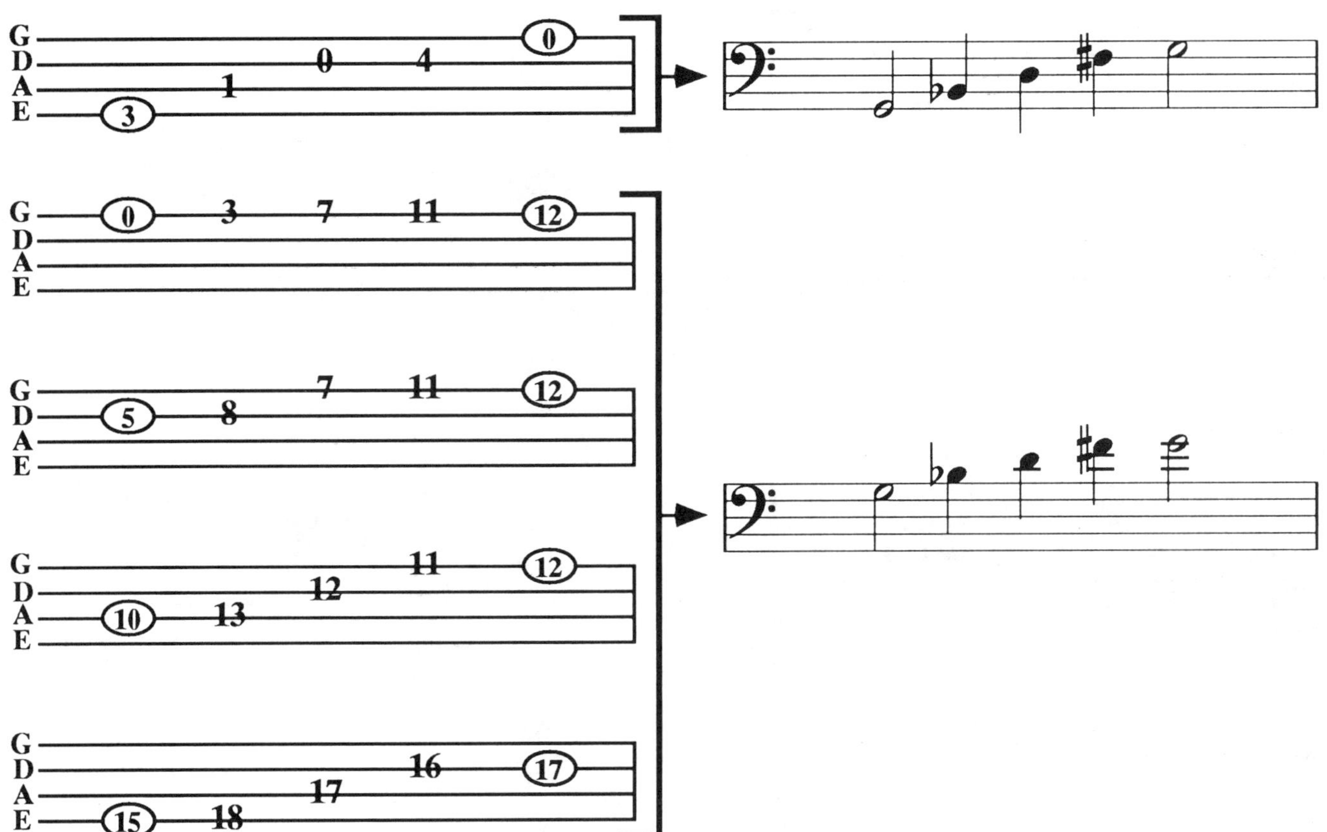

Riff

A MINOR - MAJOR 7TH

FORMULA - (A) Root (C) ♭3rd (E) 5th (G♯) 7th

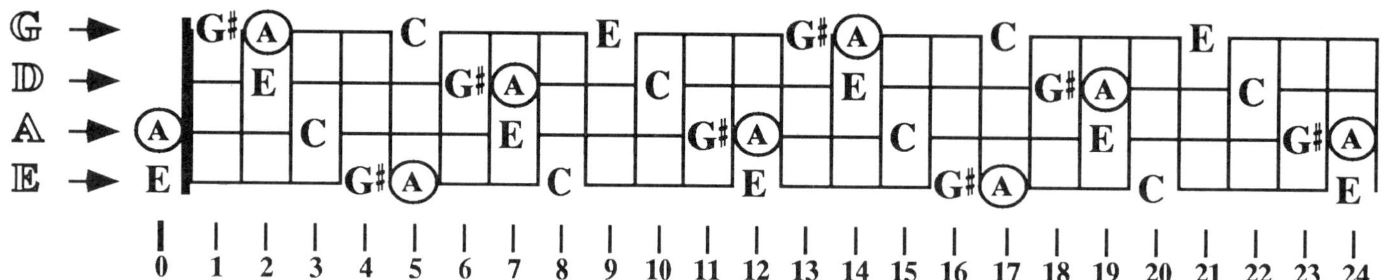

Positions

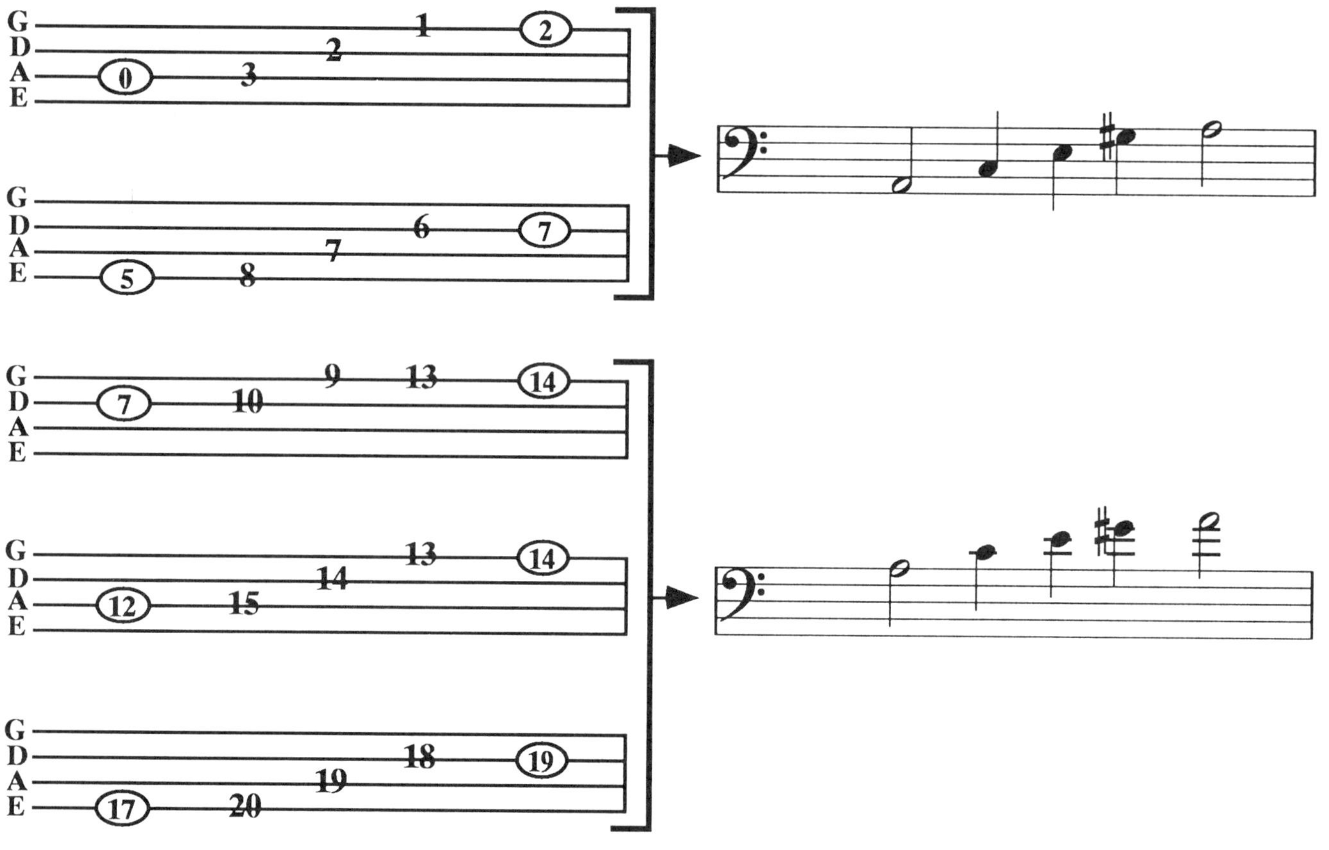

Riff

B MINOR - MAJOR 7TH

FORMULA - (B) Root (D) ♭3rd (F♯) 5th (A♯) 7th

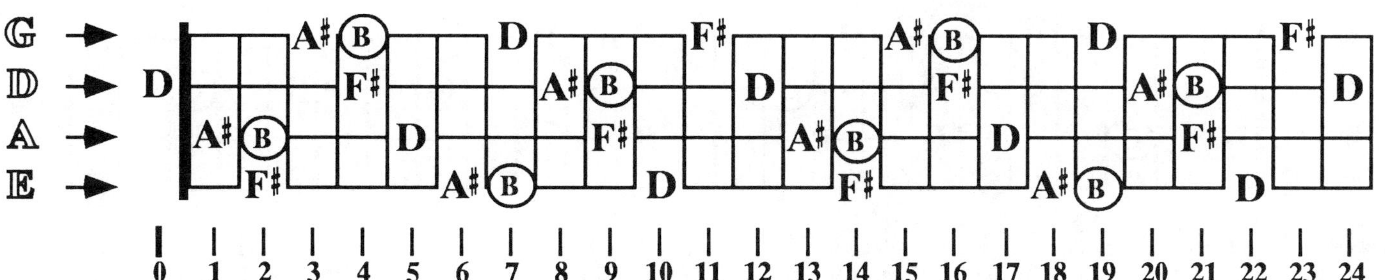

Positions

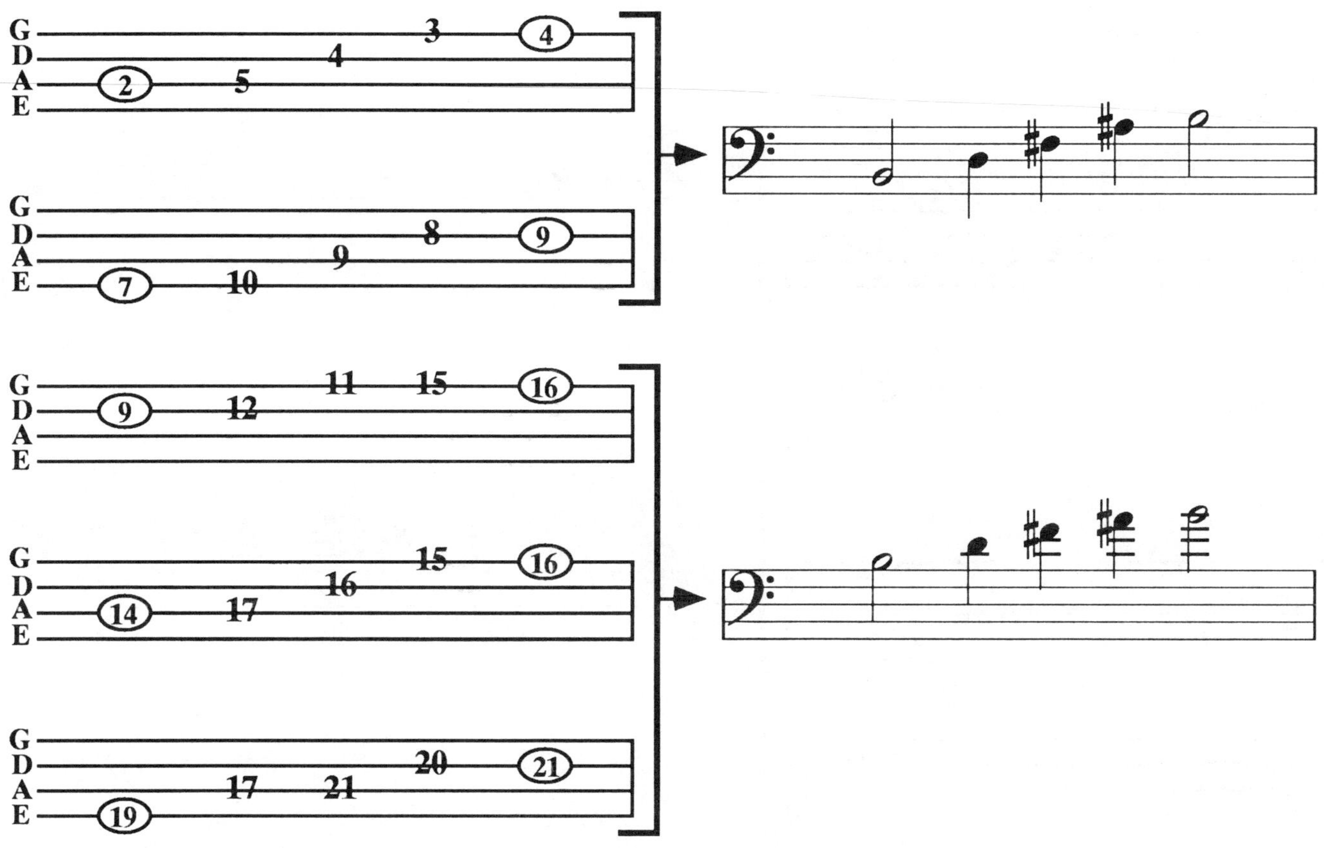

Riff

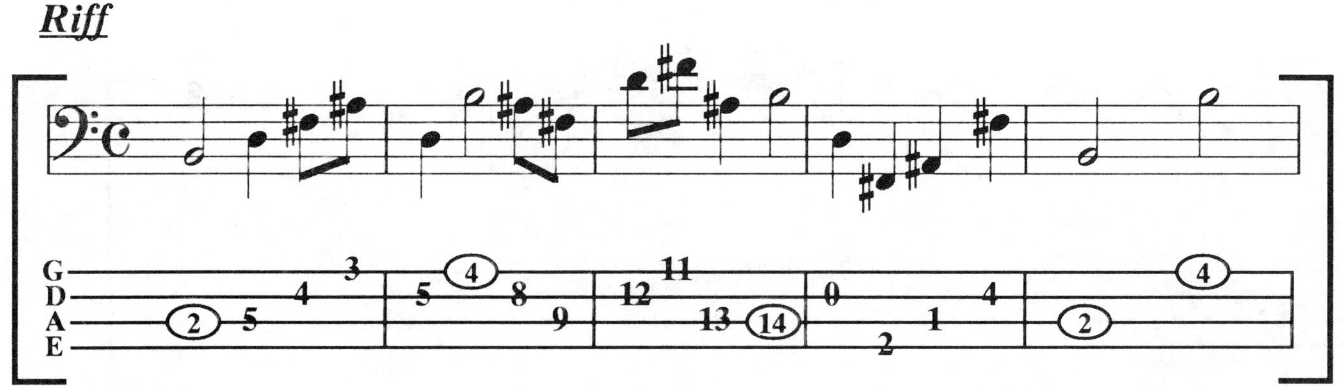

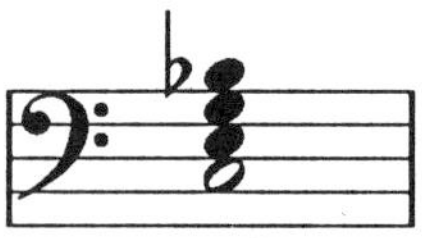

C SEVENTH

C7

FORMULA - (C) Root (E) 3rd (G) 5th (B♭) ♭7th

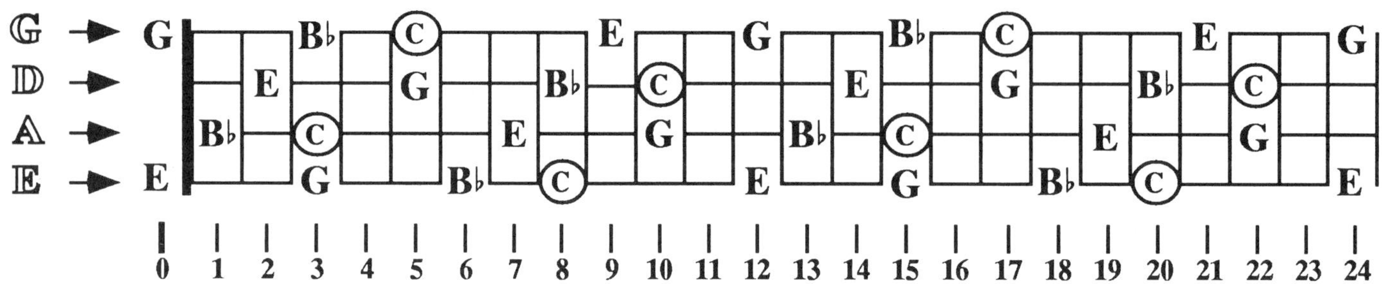

Positions

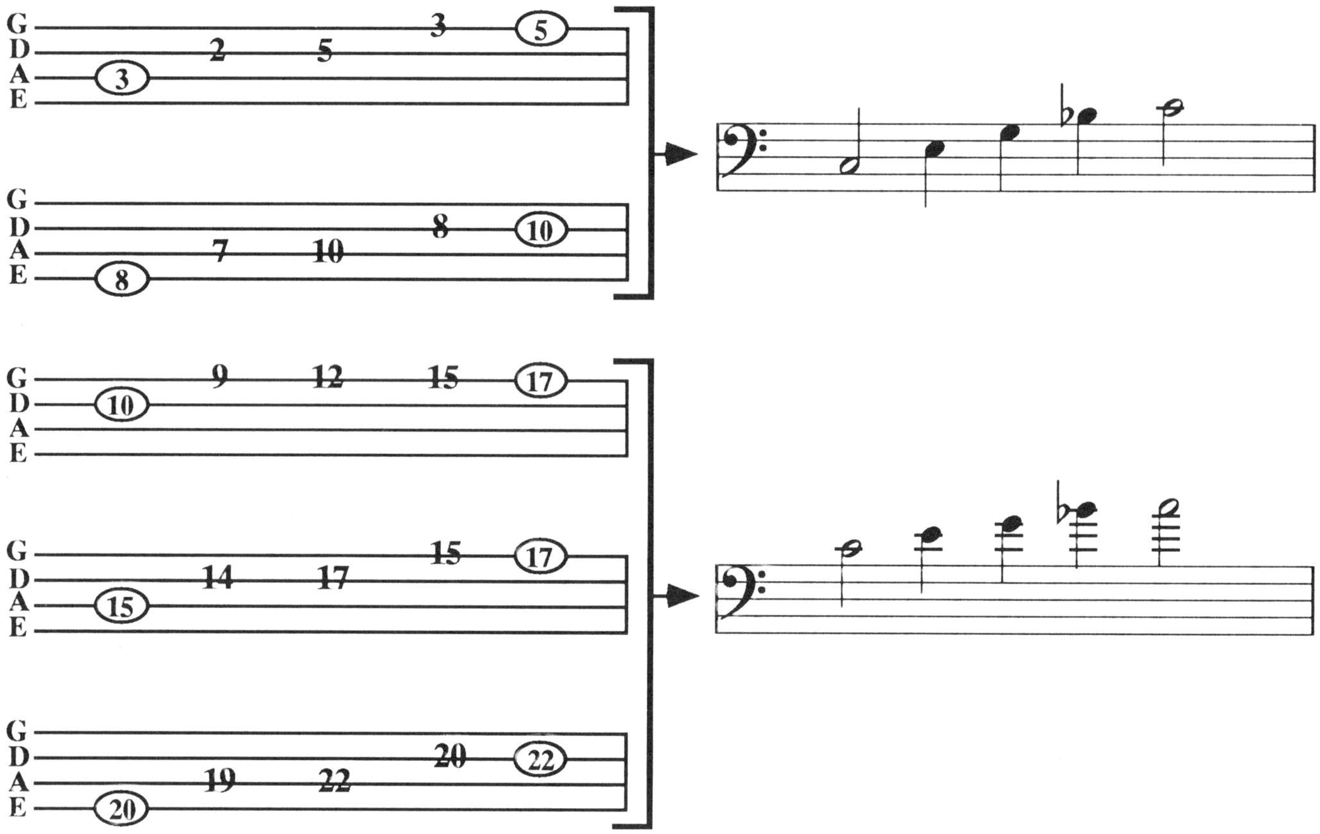

Riff

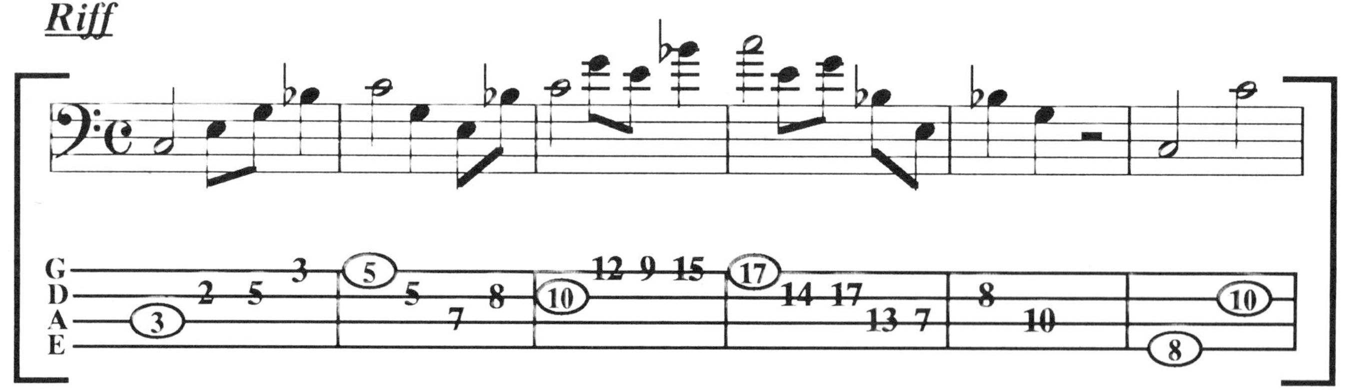

D SEVENTH

FORMULA - (D) Root (F♯) 3rd (A) 5th (C) ♭7th

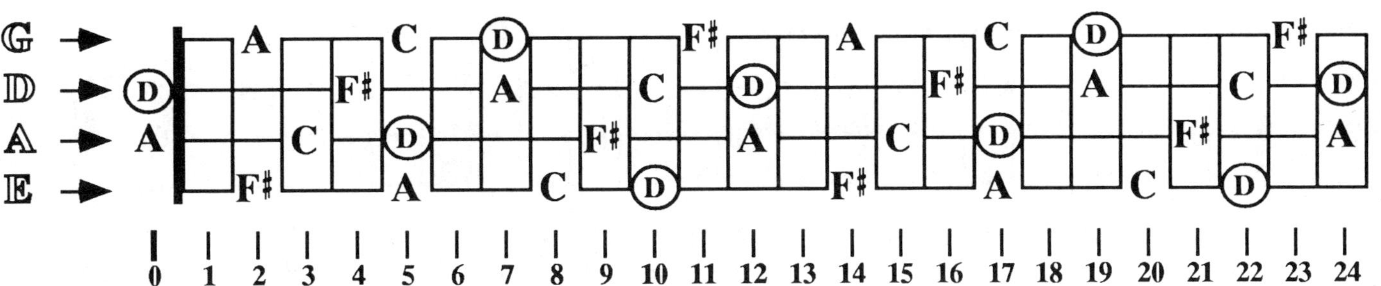

Positions

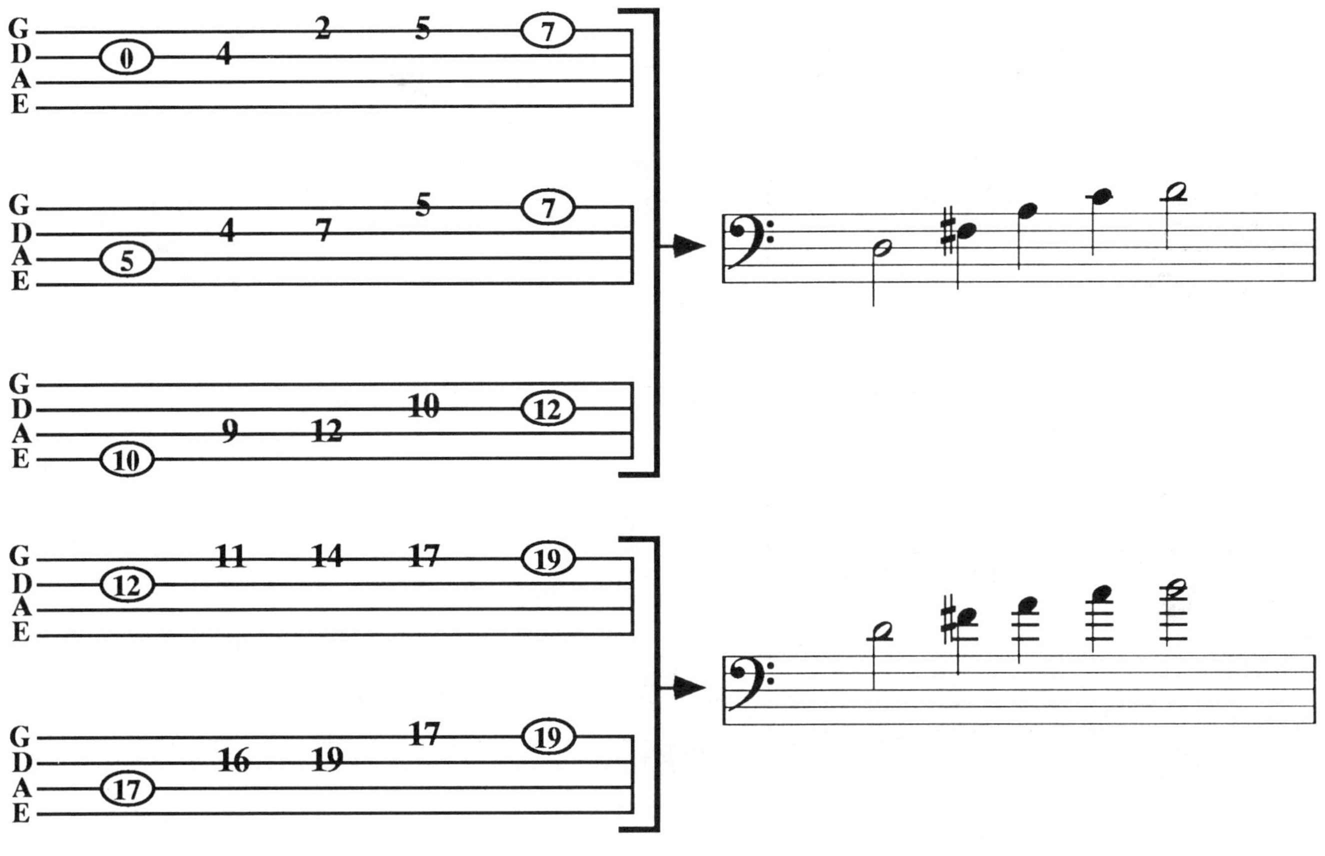

Riff

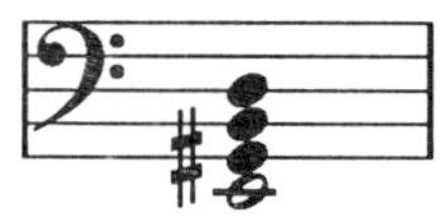

E SEVENTH

FORMULA - (E) Root (G♯) 3rd (B) 5th (D) ♭7th

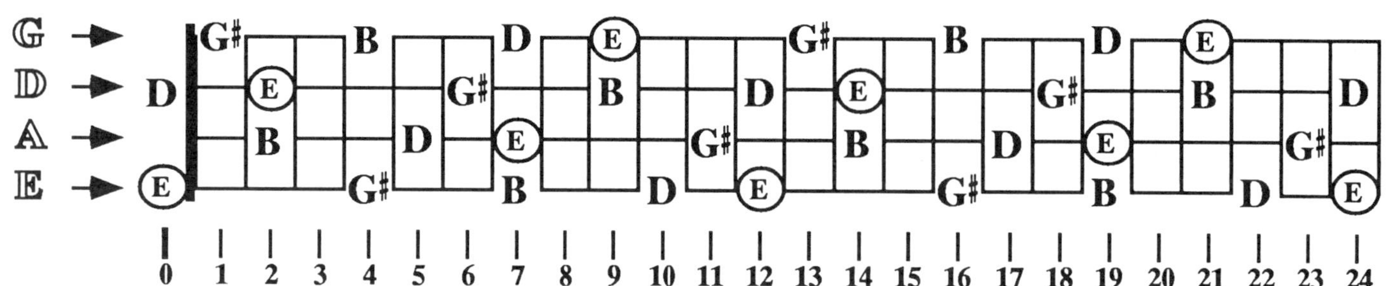

Positions

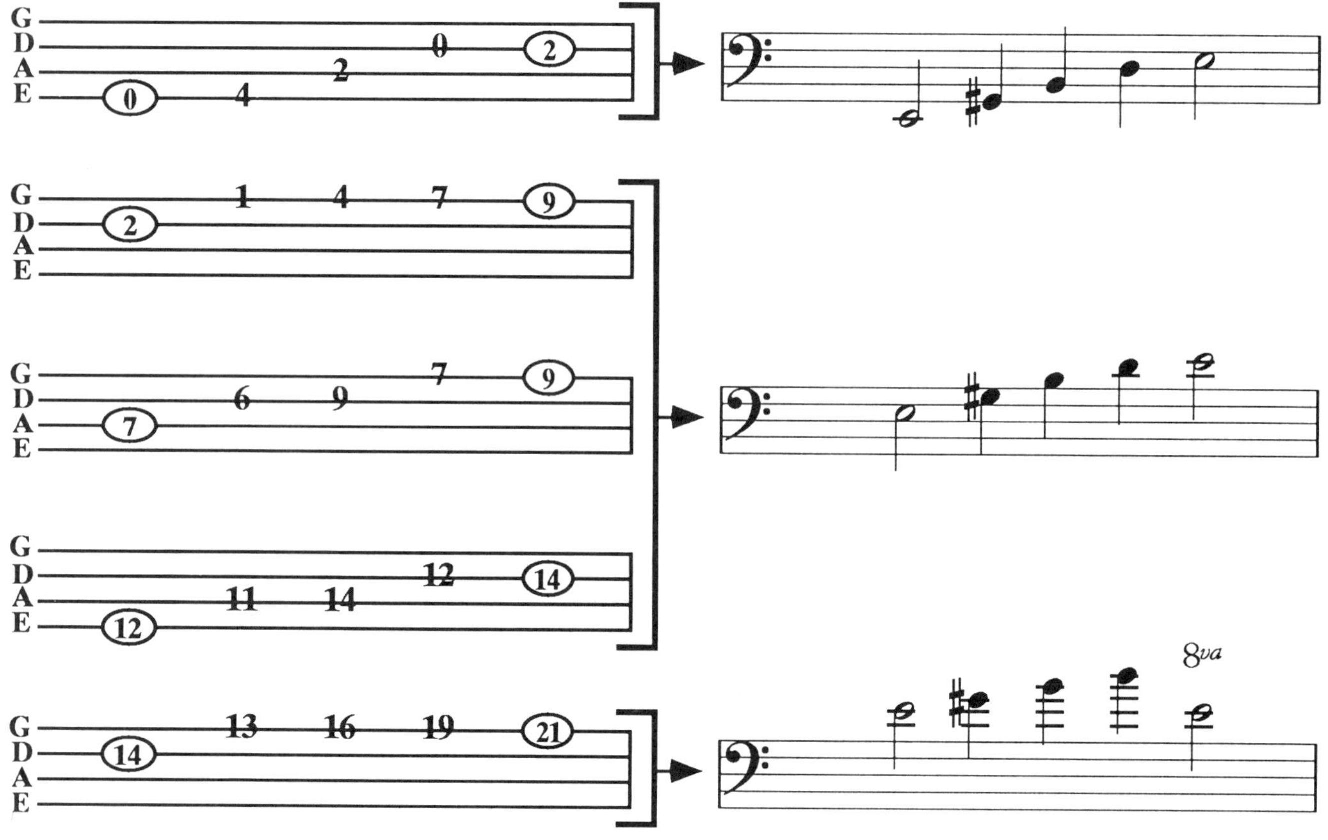

Riff

F SEVENTH
FORMULA - (F) Root (A) 3rd (C) 5th (E♭) ♭7th

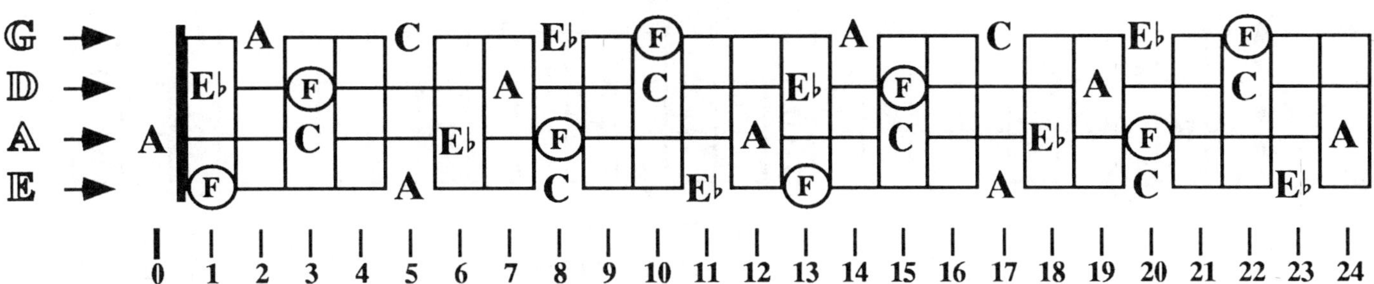

Positions

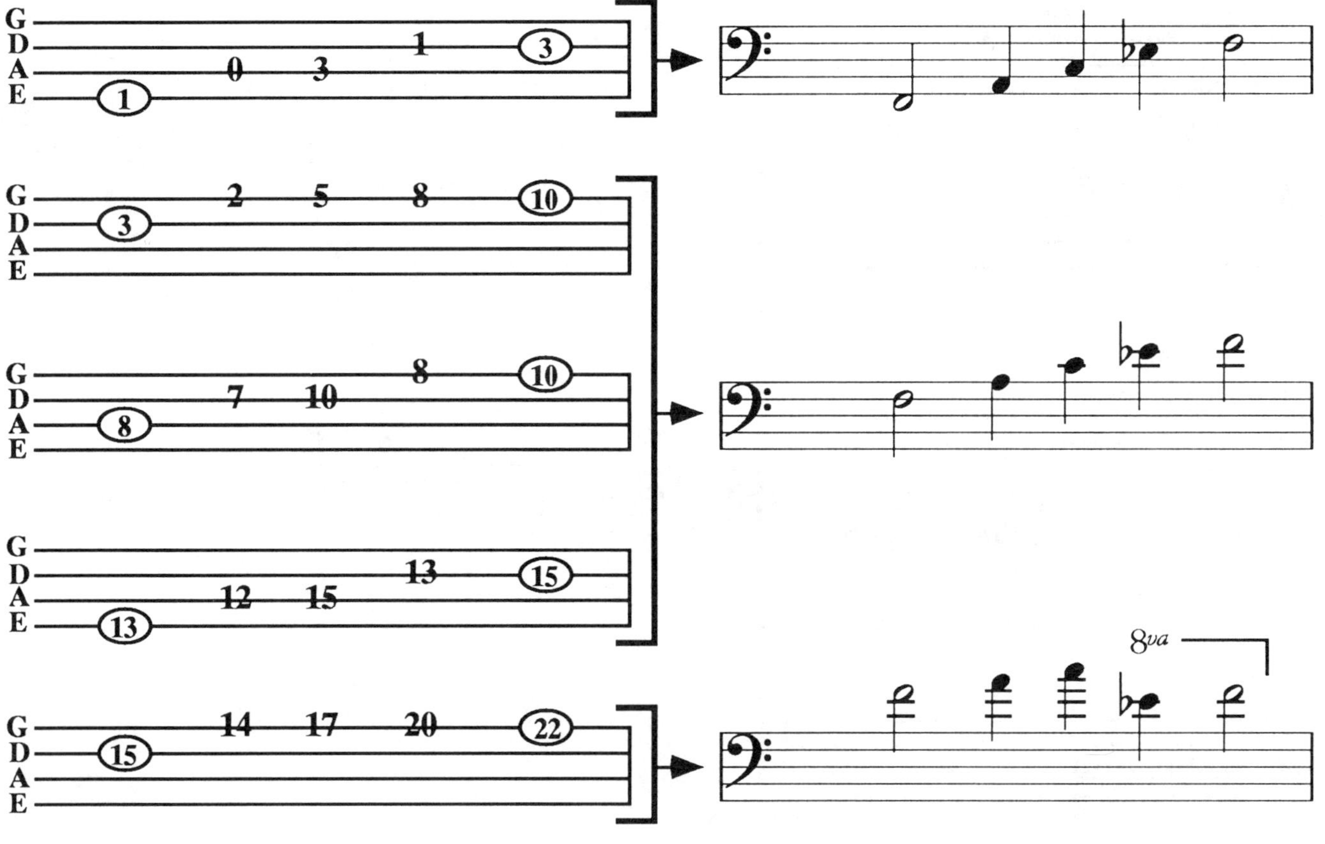

Riff

G SEVENTH

FORMULA - (G) Root (B) 3rd (D) 5th (F) ♭7th

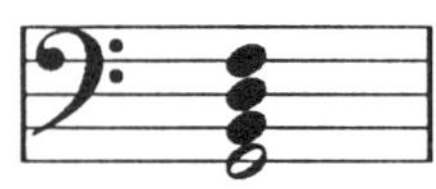

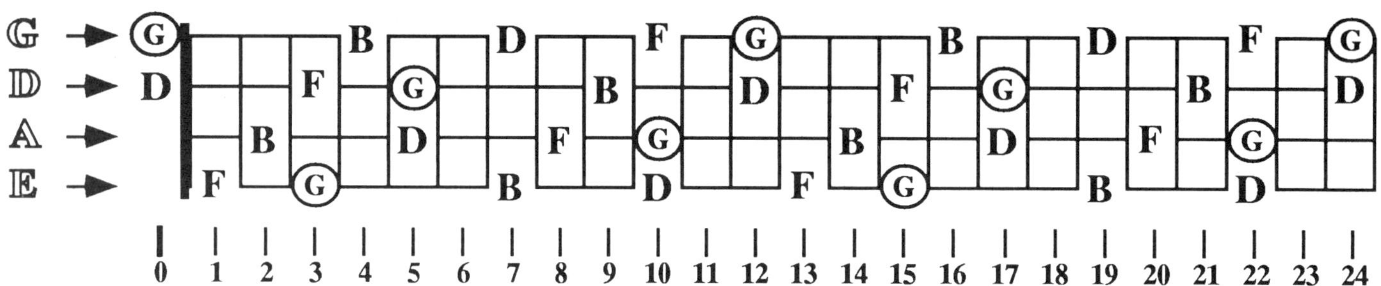

Positions

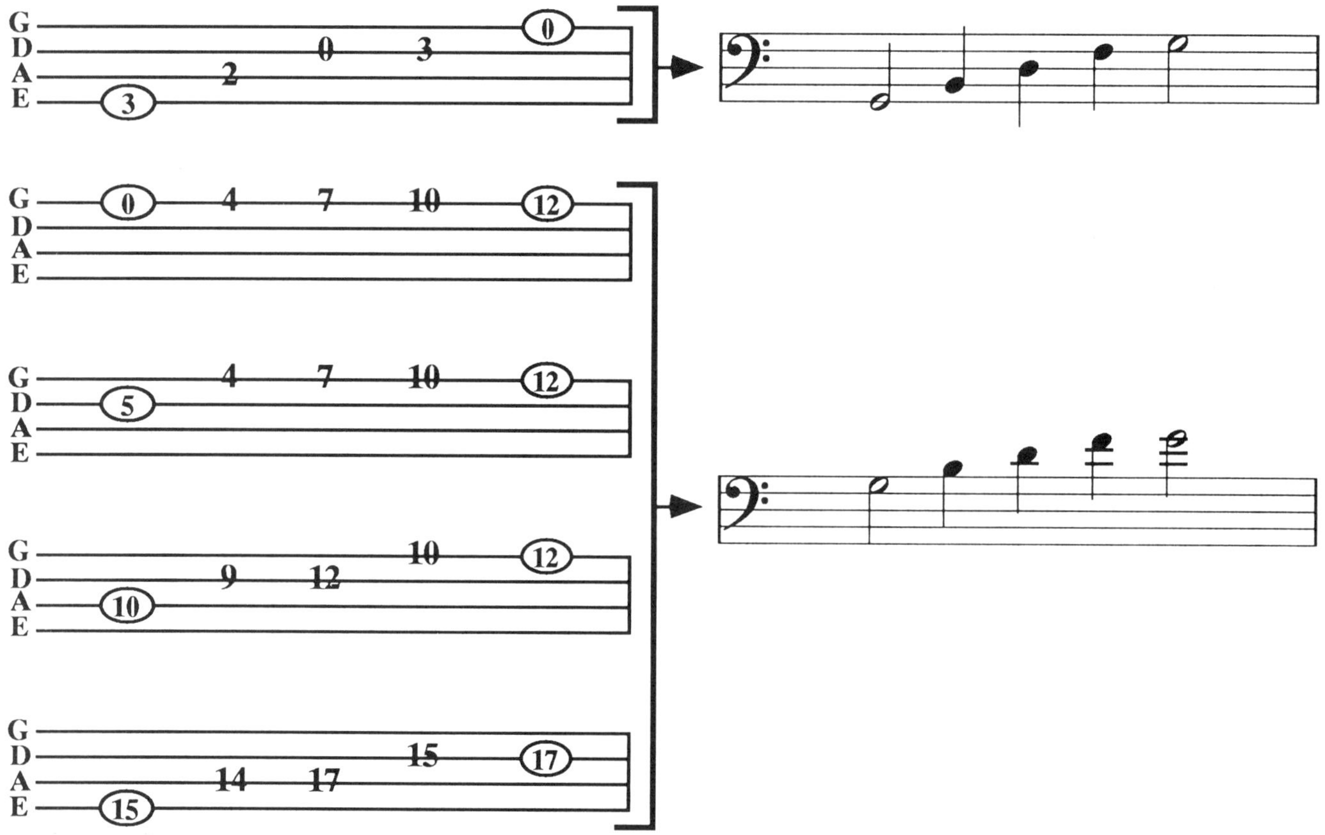

Riff

124

A SEVENTH

FORMULA - (A) Root (C♯) 3rd (E) 5th (G)♭7th

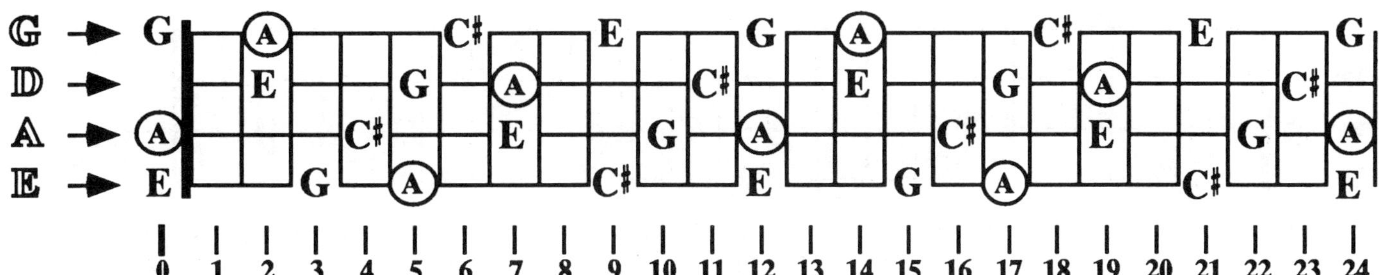

Positions

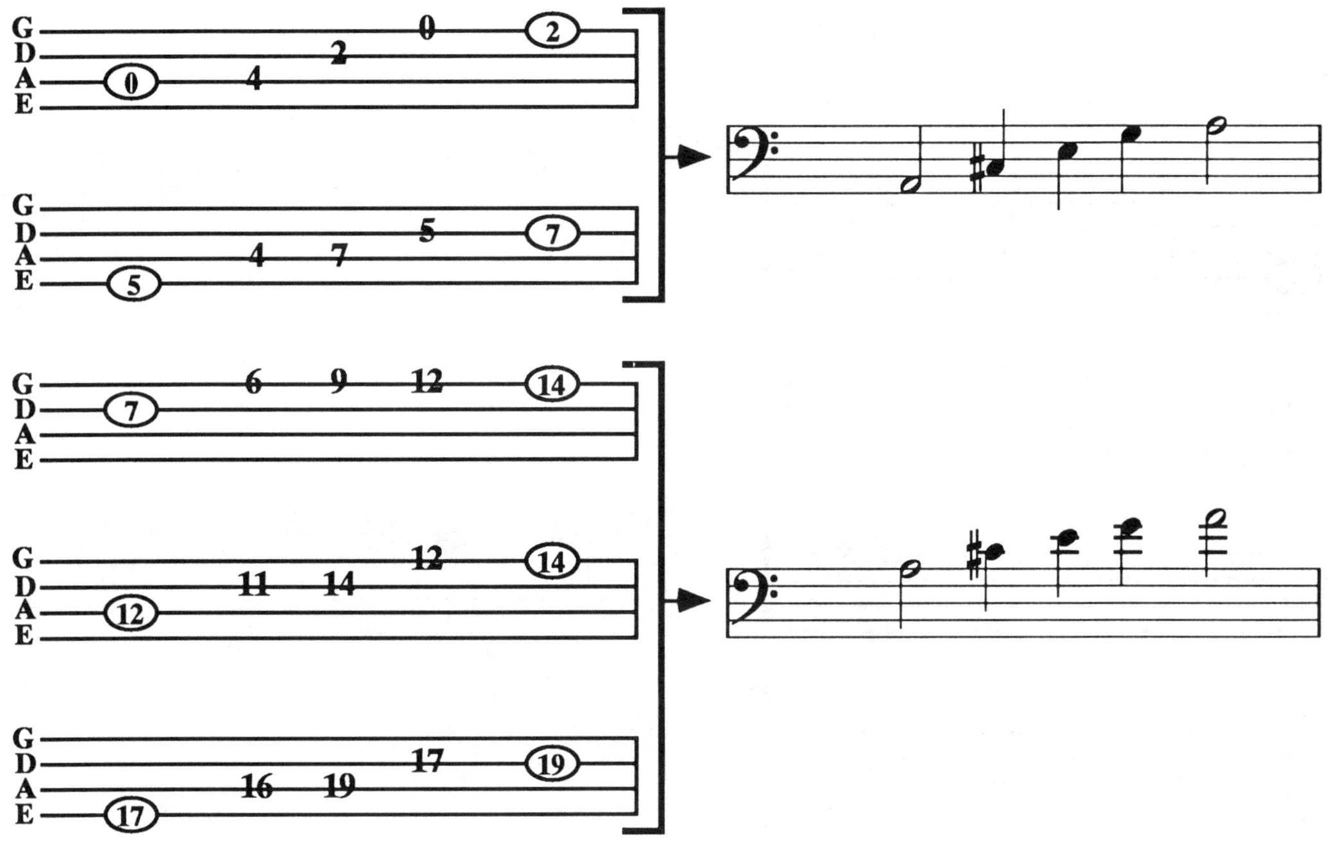

Riff

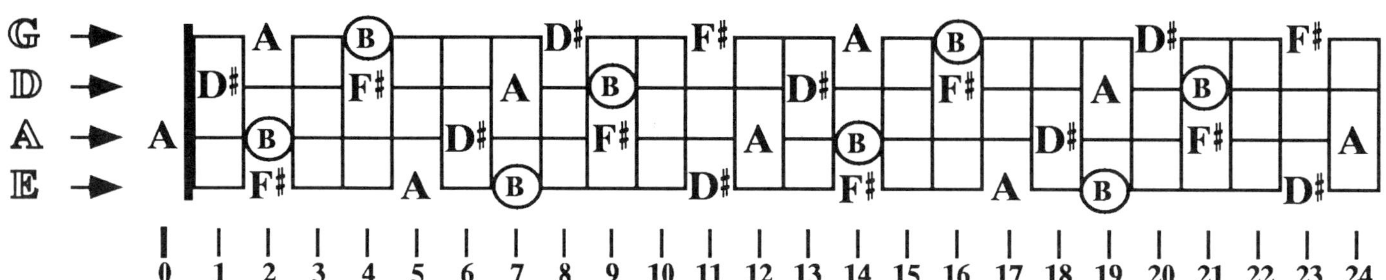

Positions

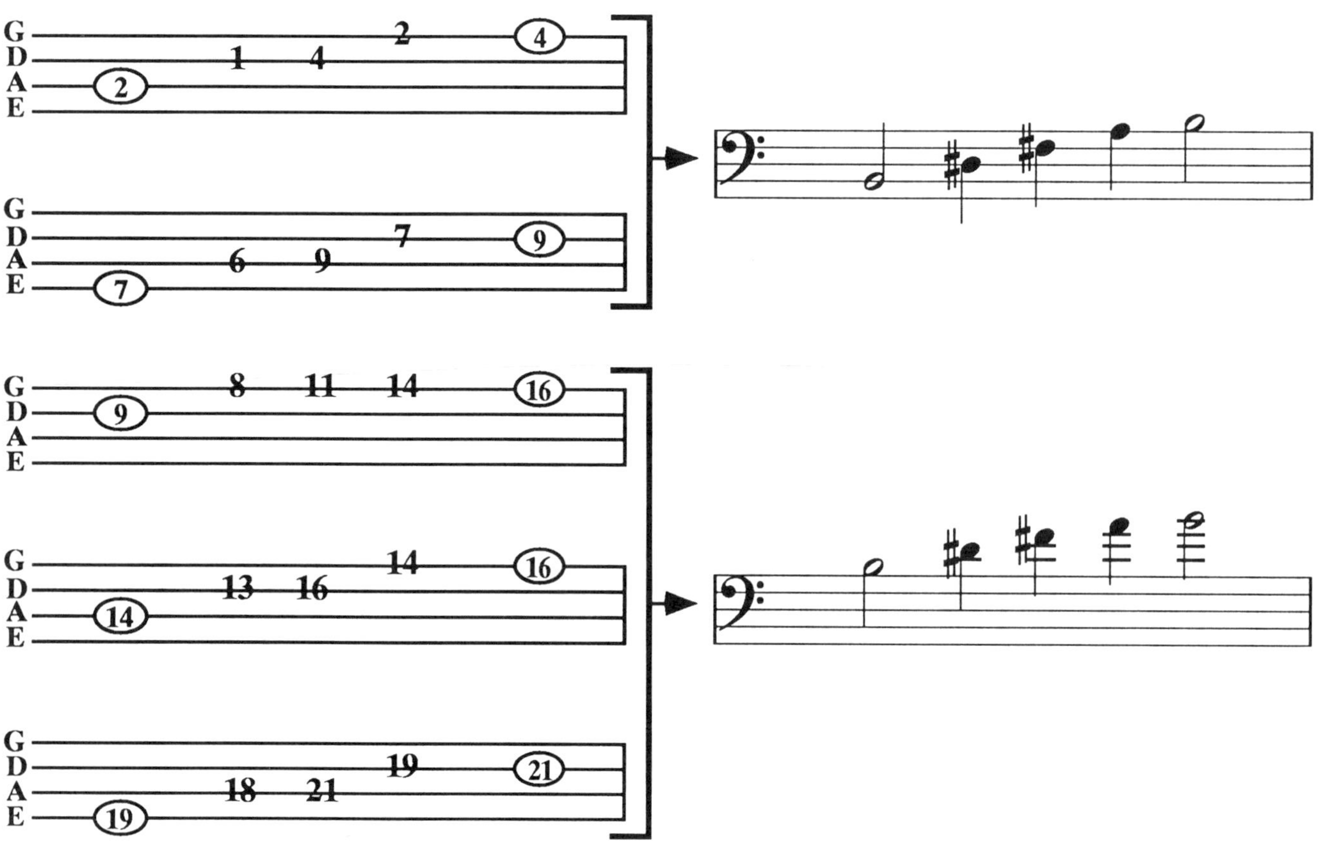

Riff

C SEVENTH ♭5TH

FORMULA - (C) Root (E) 3rd (G♭) ♭5th (B♭) ♭7th

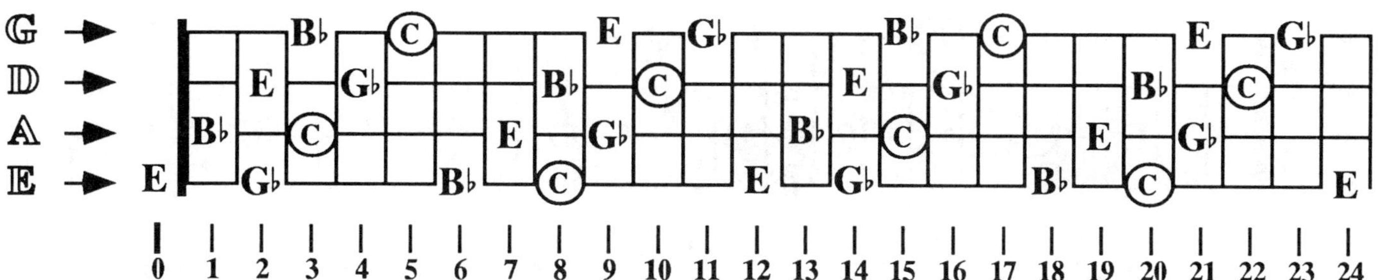

Positions

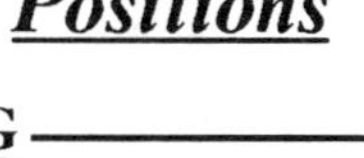

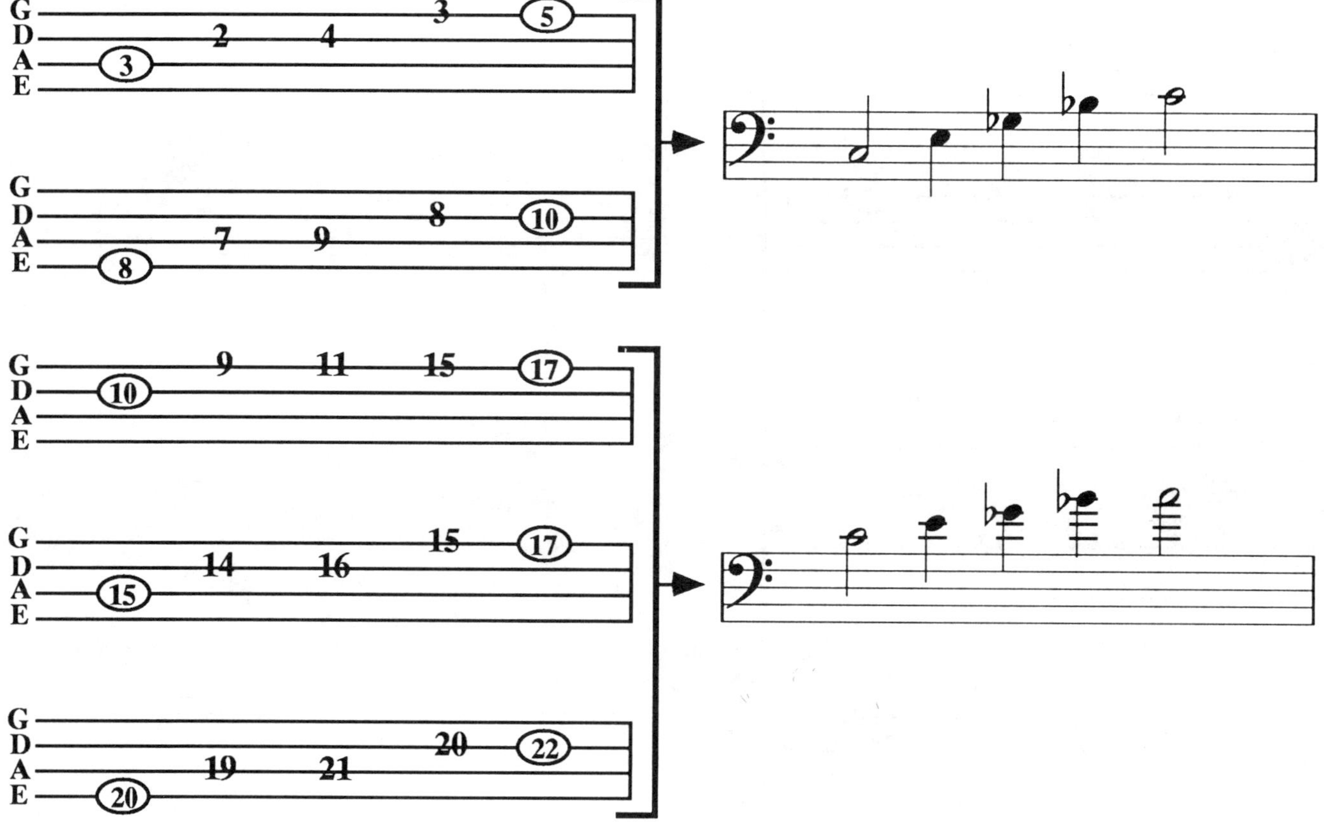

Riff

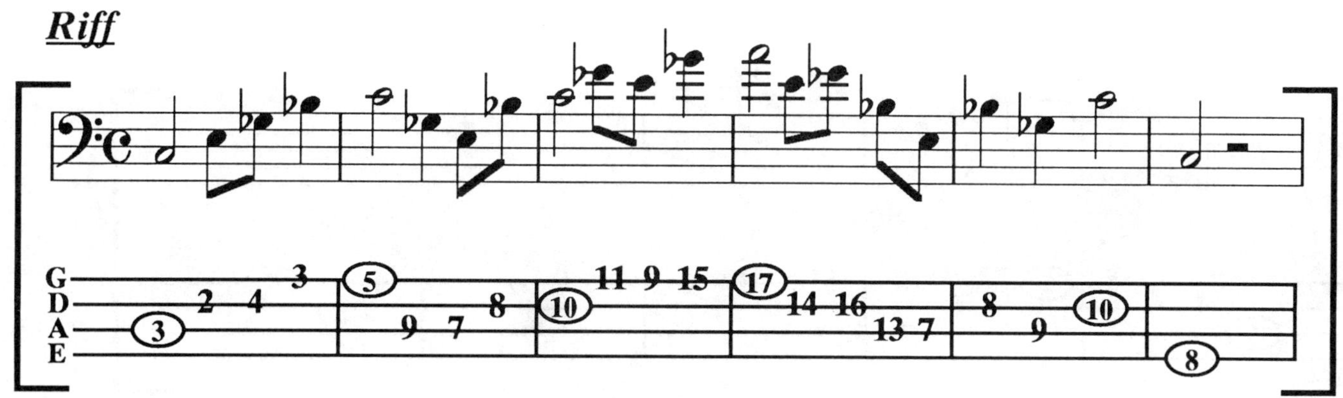

D SEVENTH ♭5TH

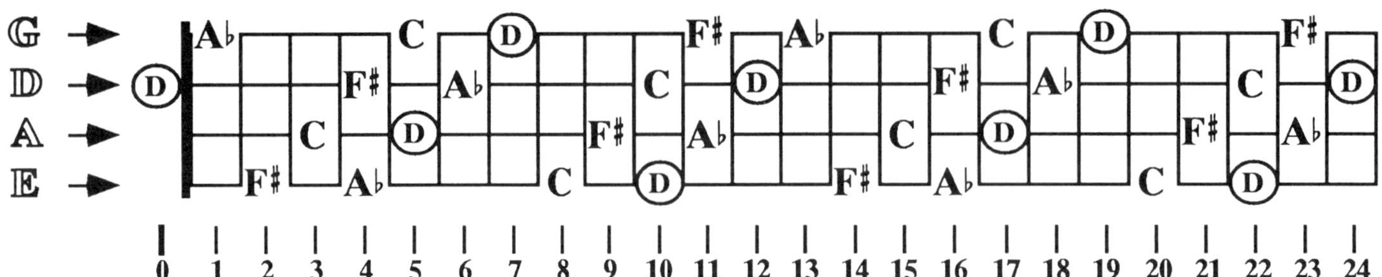

Positions

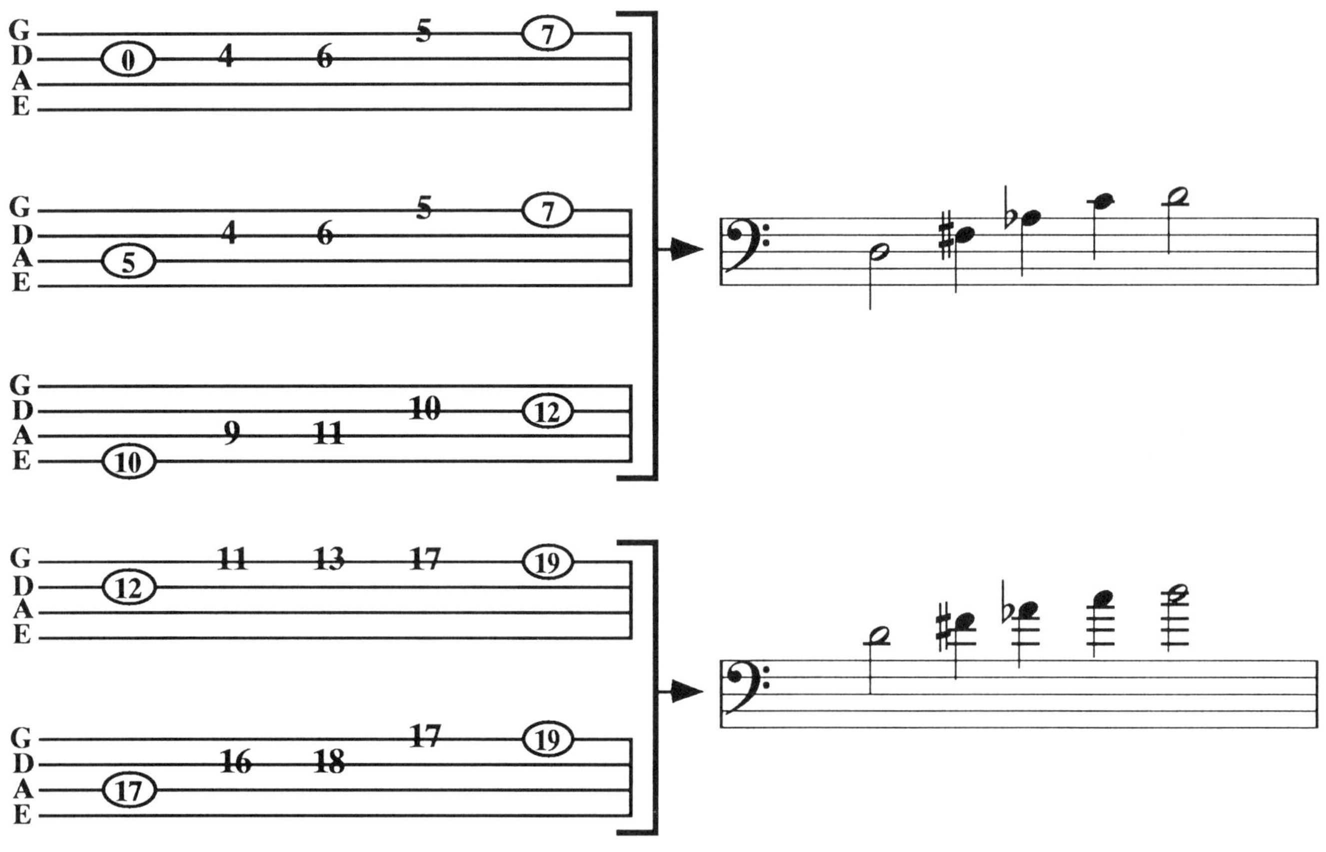

Riff

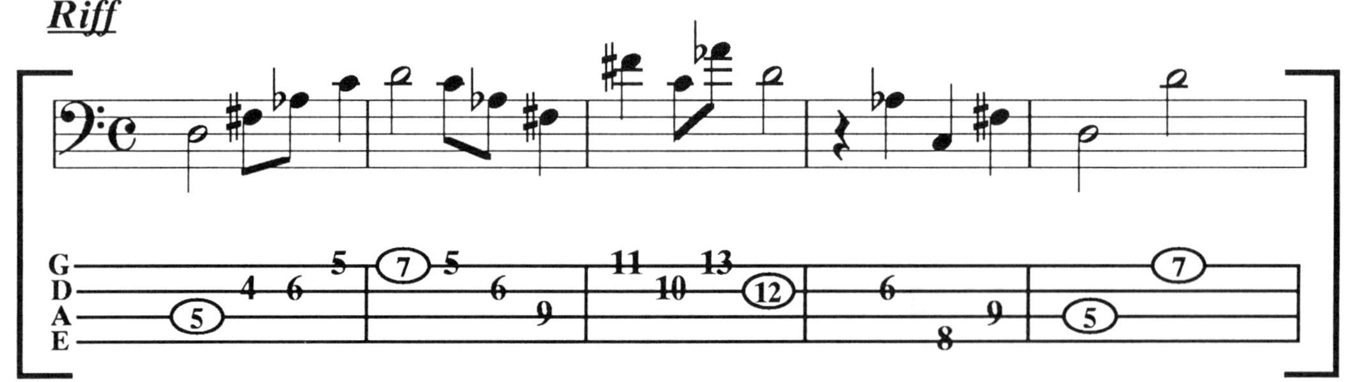

E SEVENTH ♭5TH

FORMULA - (E) Root (G♯) 3rd (B♭) ♭5th (D) ♭7th

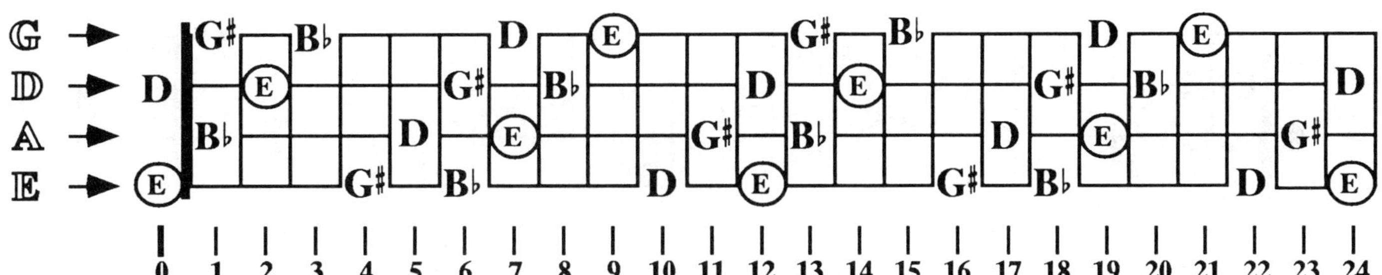

Positions

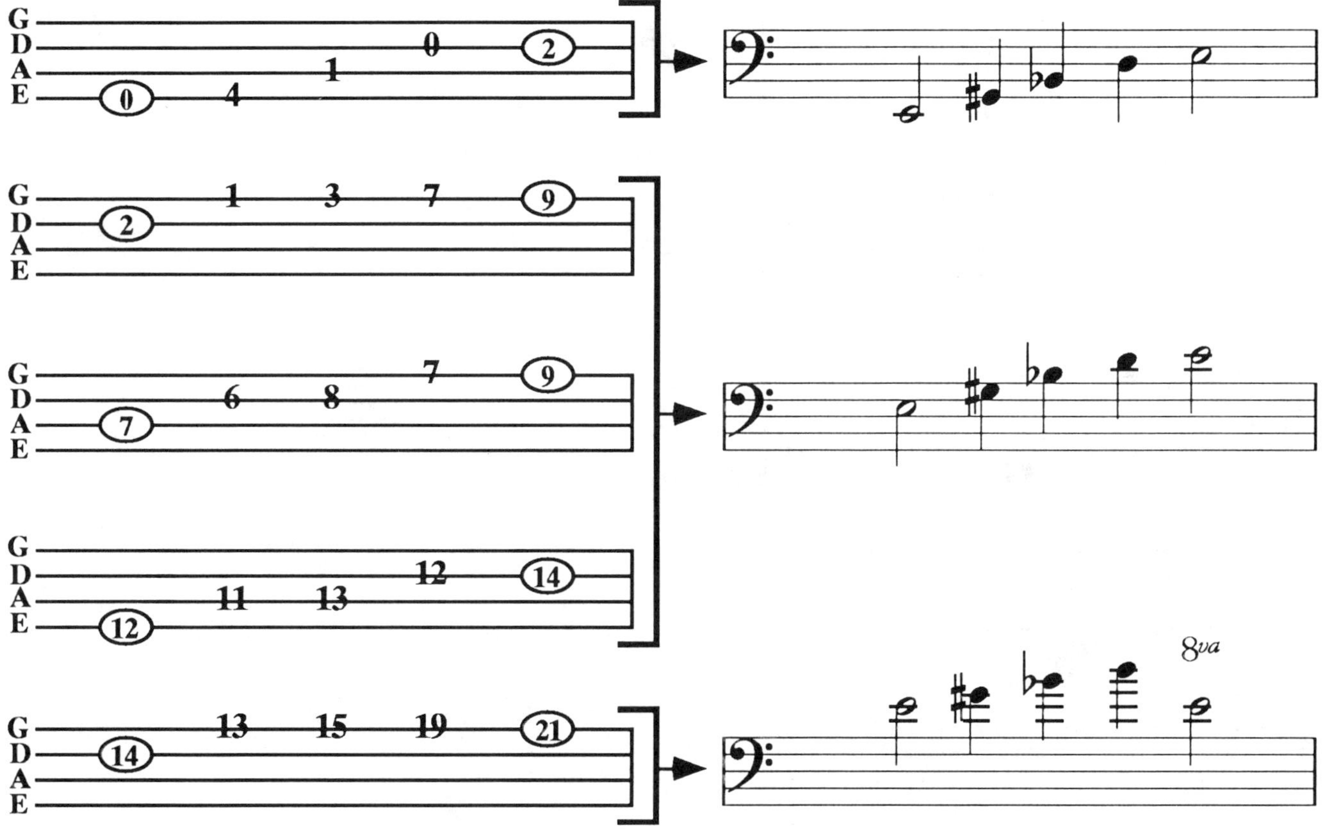

Riff

F SEVENTH ♭5TH

FORMULA - (F) Root (A) 3rd (C♭) ♭5th (E♭) ♭7th

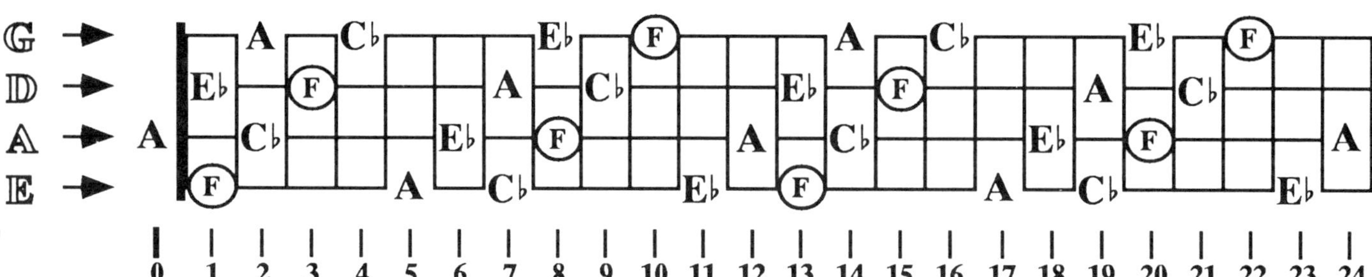

Positions

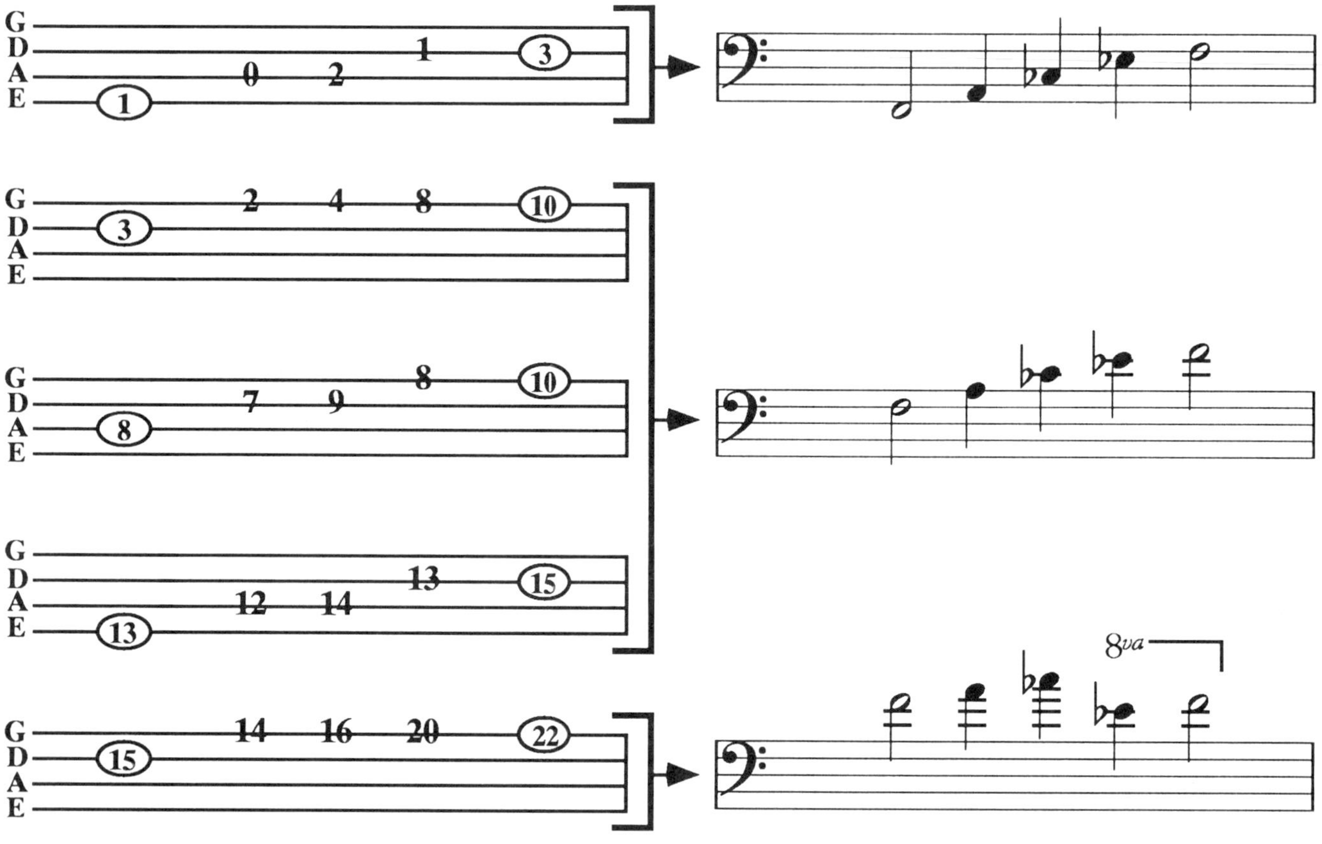

Riff

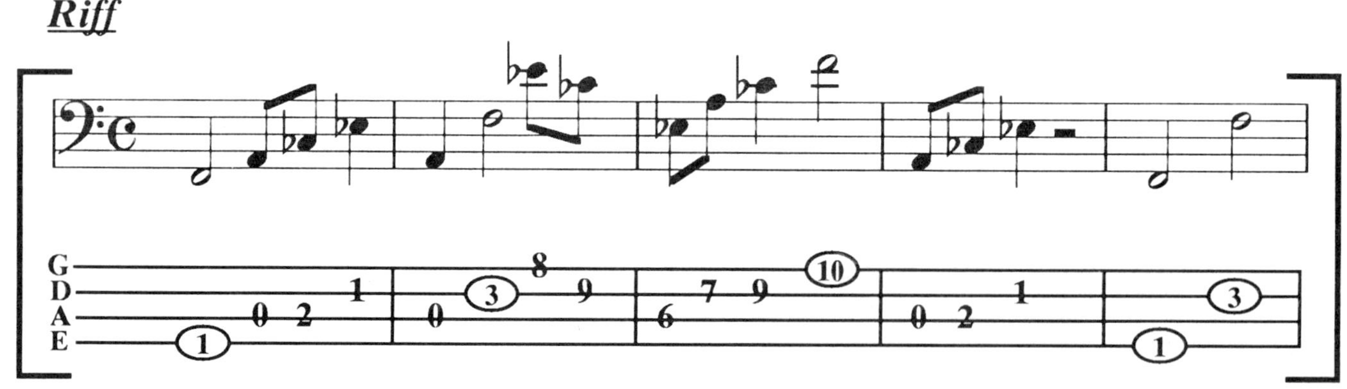

G SEVENTH ♭5TH

FORMULA - (G) Root (B) 3rd (D♭) ♭5th (F) ♭7th

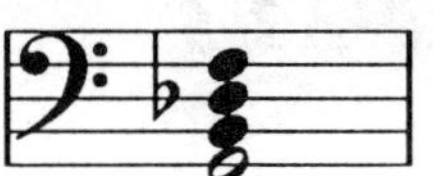

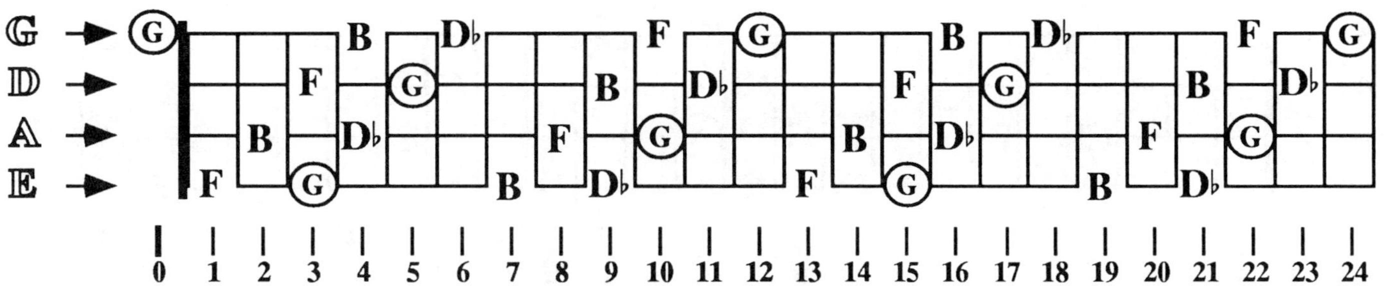

Positions

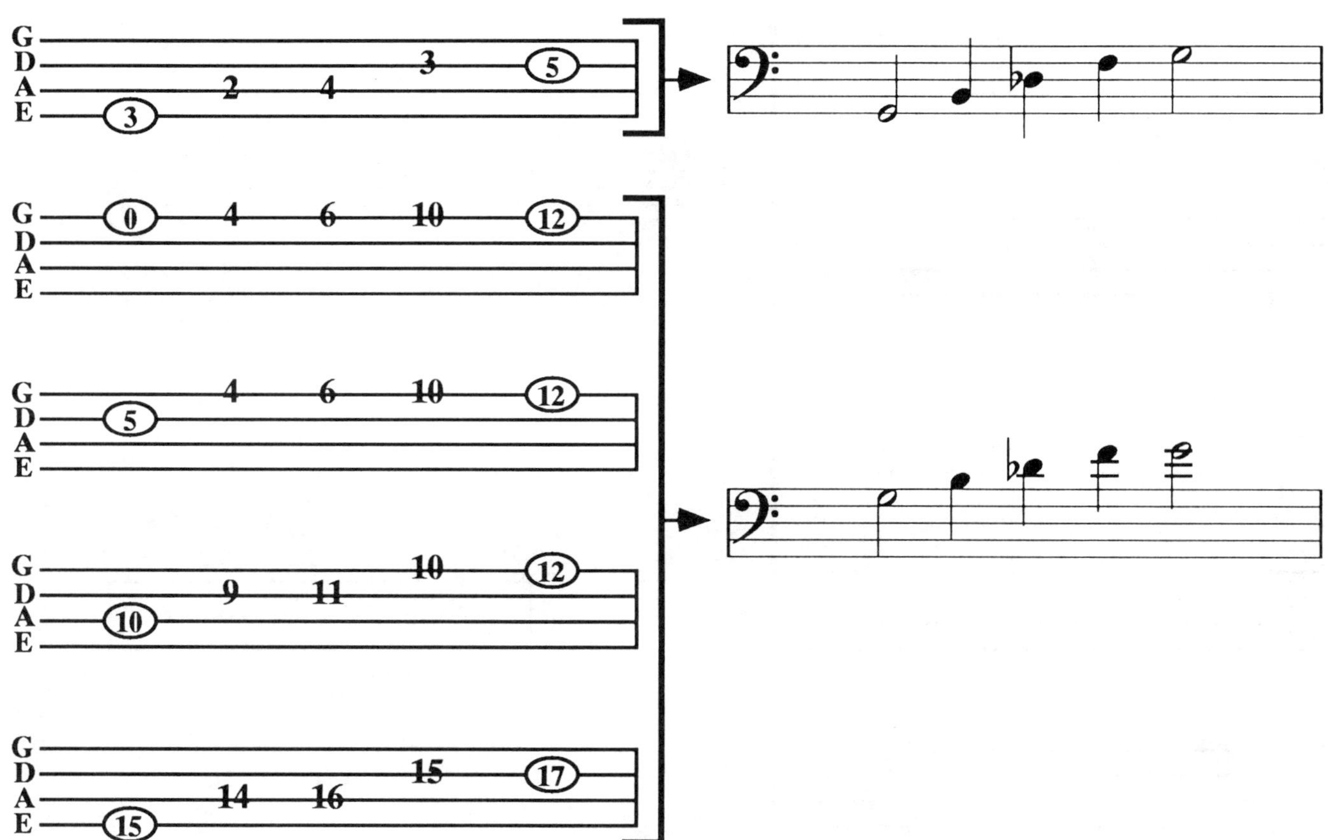

Riff

A SEVENTH ♭5TH

FORMULA - (A) Root (C♯) 3rd (E♭) ♭5th (G) ♭7th

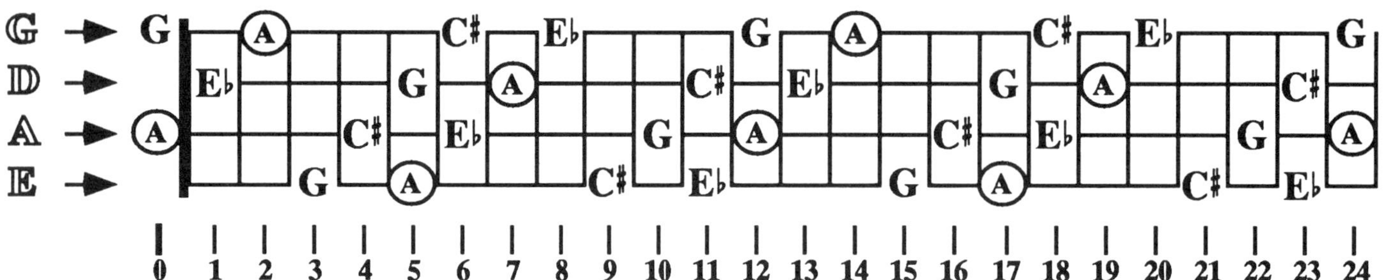

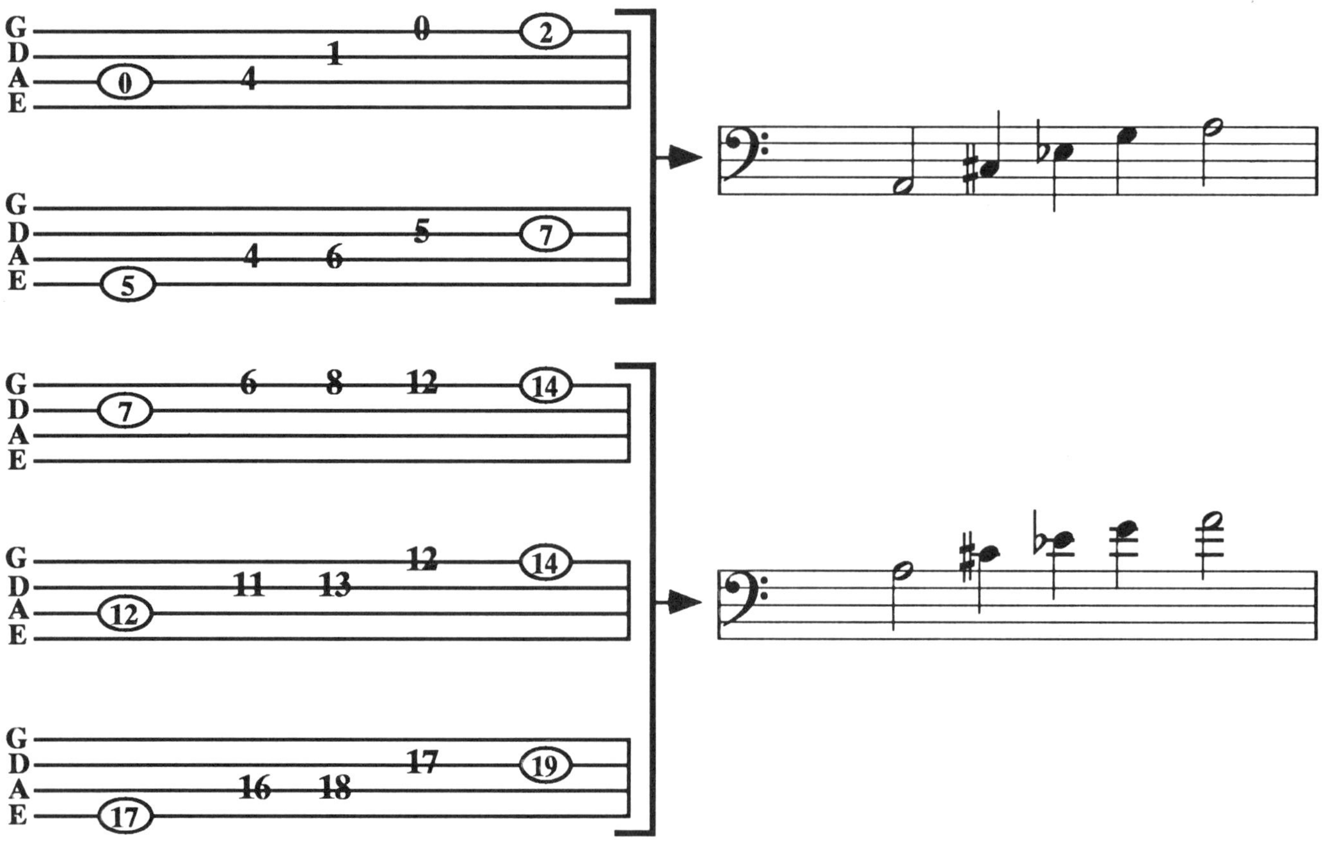

Positions

Riff

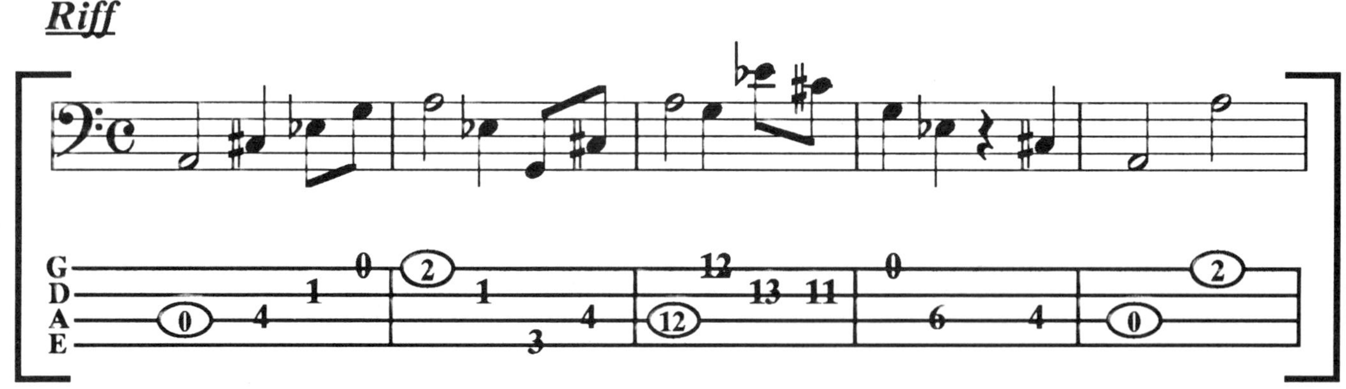

B SEVENTH ♭5TH

FORMULA - (B) Root (D♯) 3rd (F) ♭5th (A) ♭7th

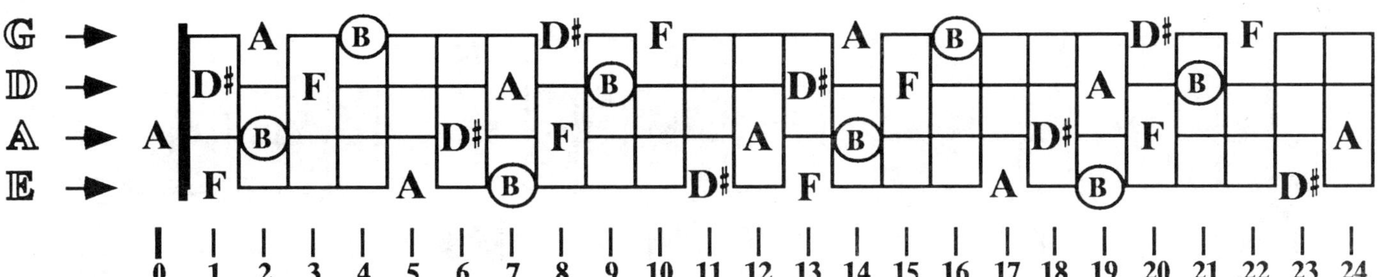

Positions

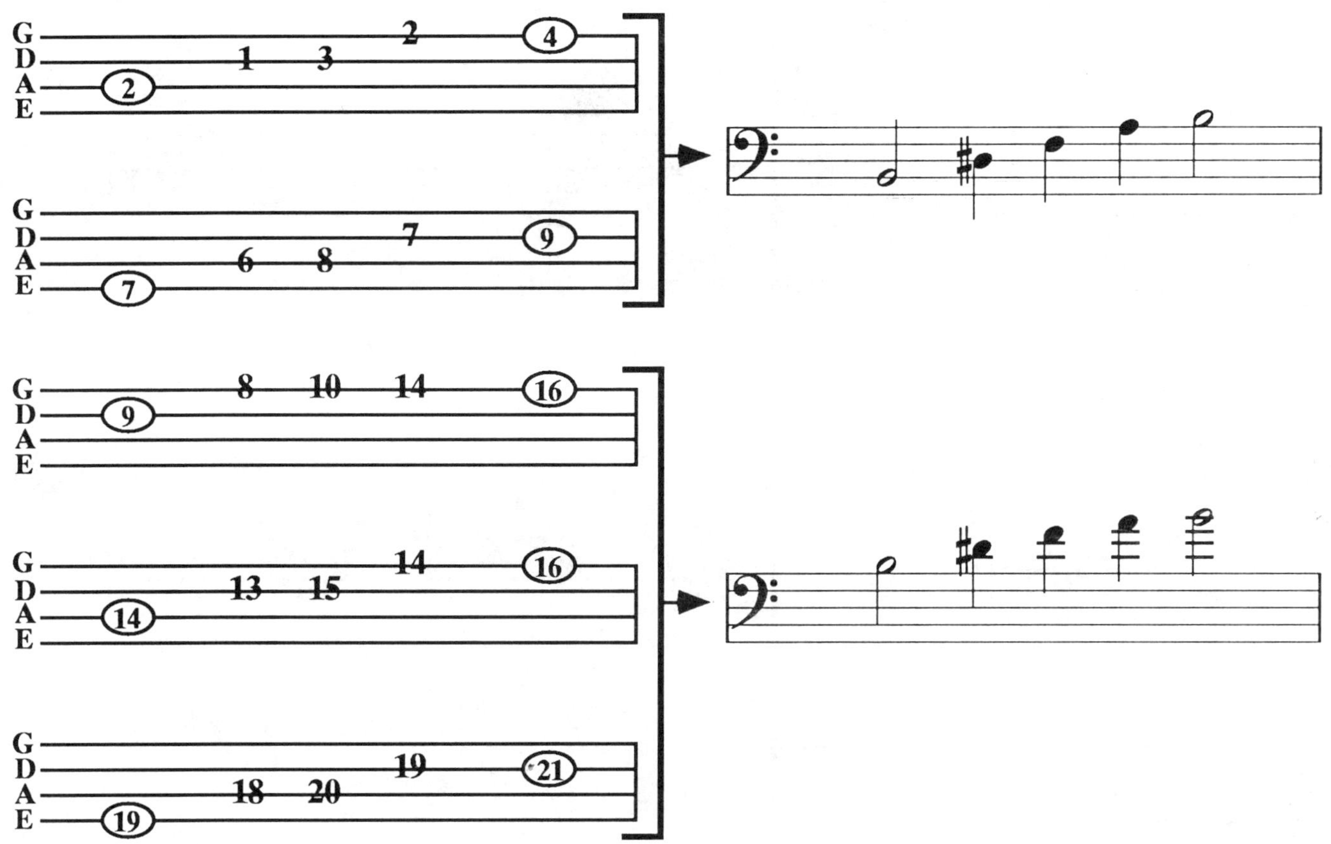

Riff

C   SEVENTH AUG 5TH

FORMULA - (C) Root (E) 3rd (G♯) ♯5th (B♭) ♭7th

C7+5

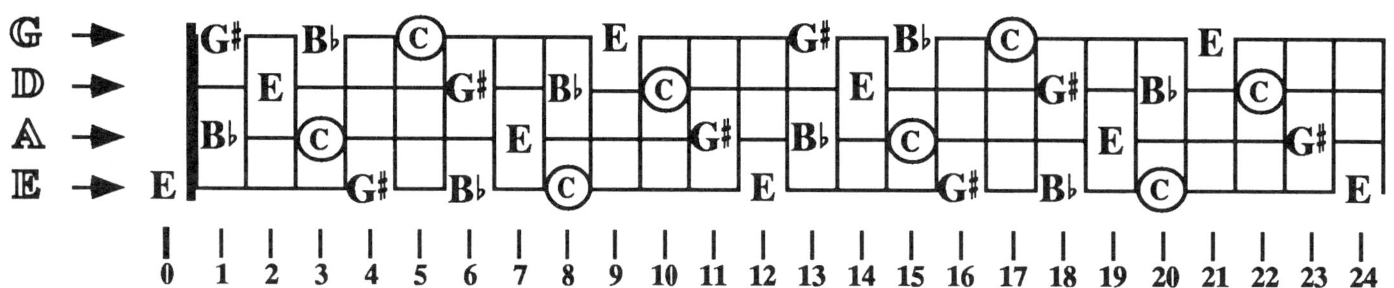

Positions

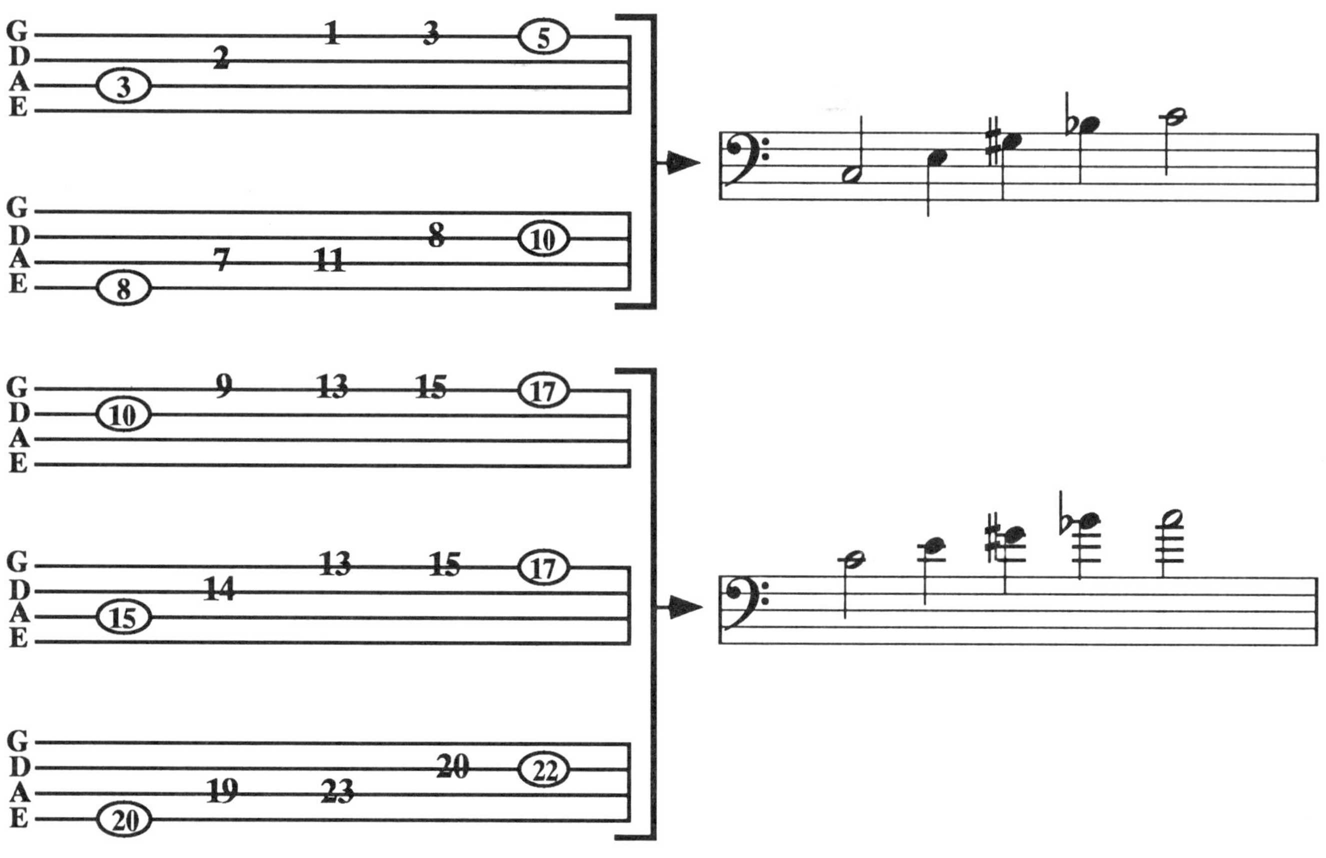

Riff

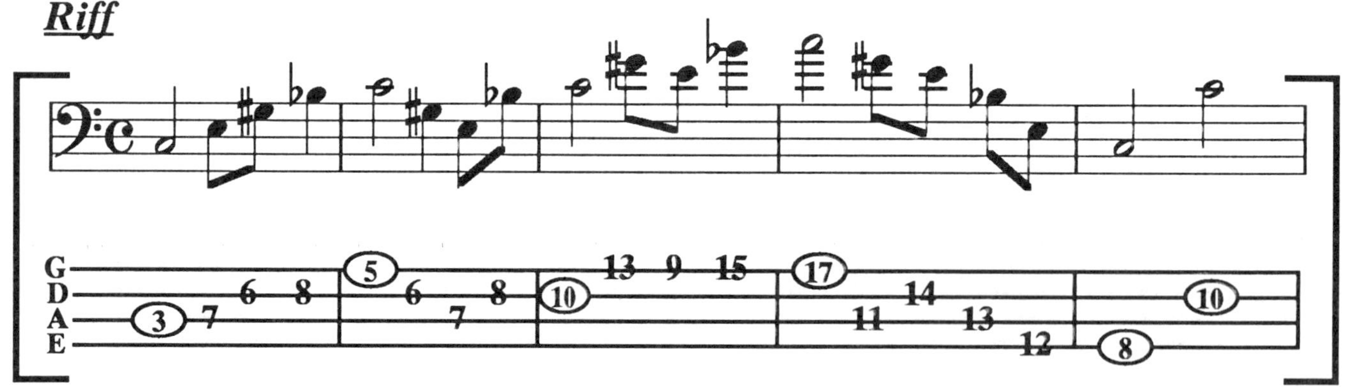

D SEVENTH AUG 5TH

FORMULA - (D) Root (F♯) 3rd (A♯) ♯5th (C) ♭7th

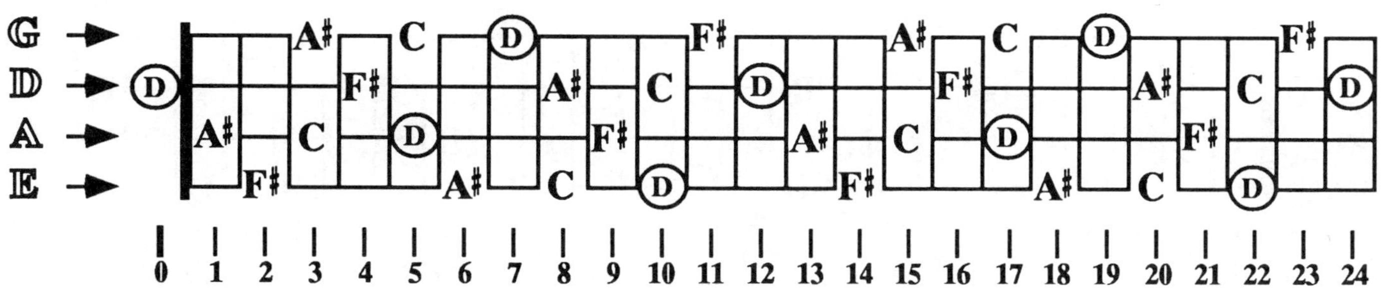

Positions

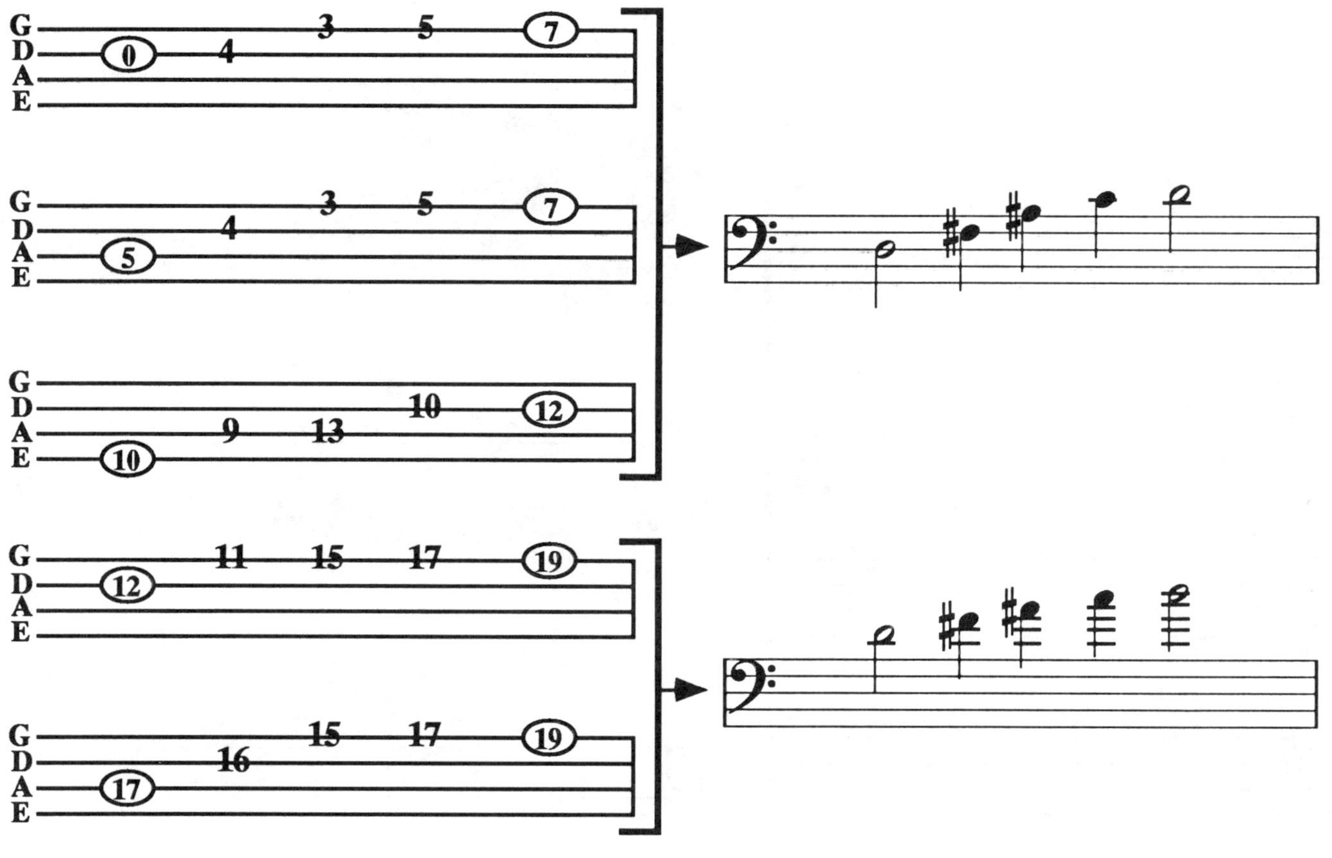

Riff

E SEVENTH AUG 5TH

FORMULA - (E) Root (G♯) 3rd (B♯) ♯5th (D) ♭7th

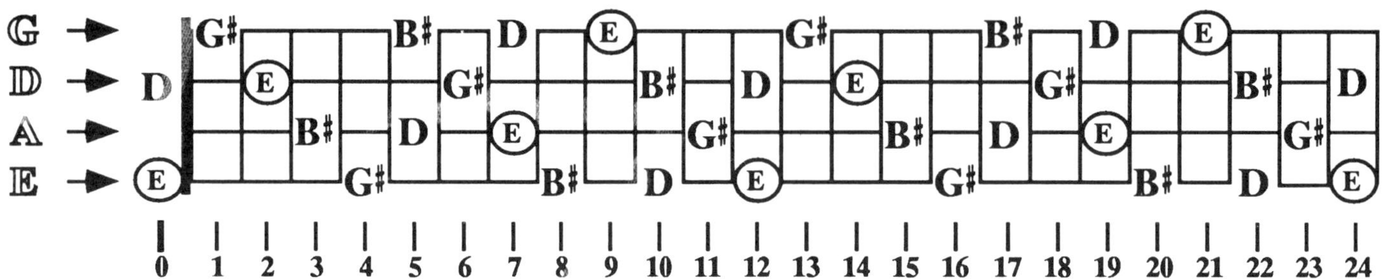

Positions

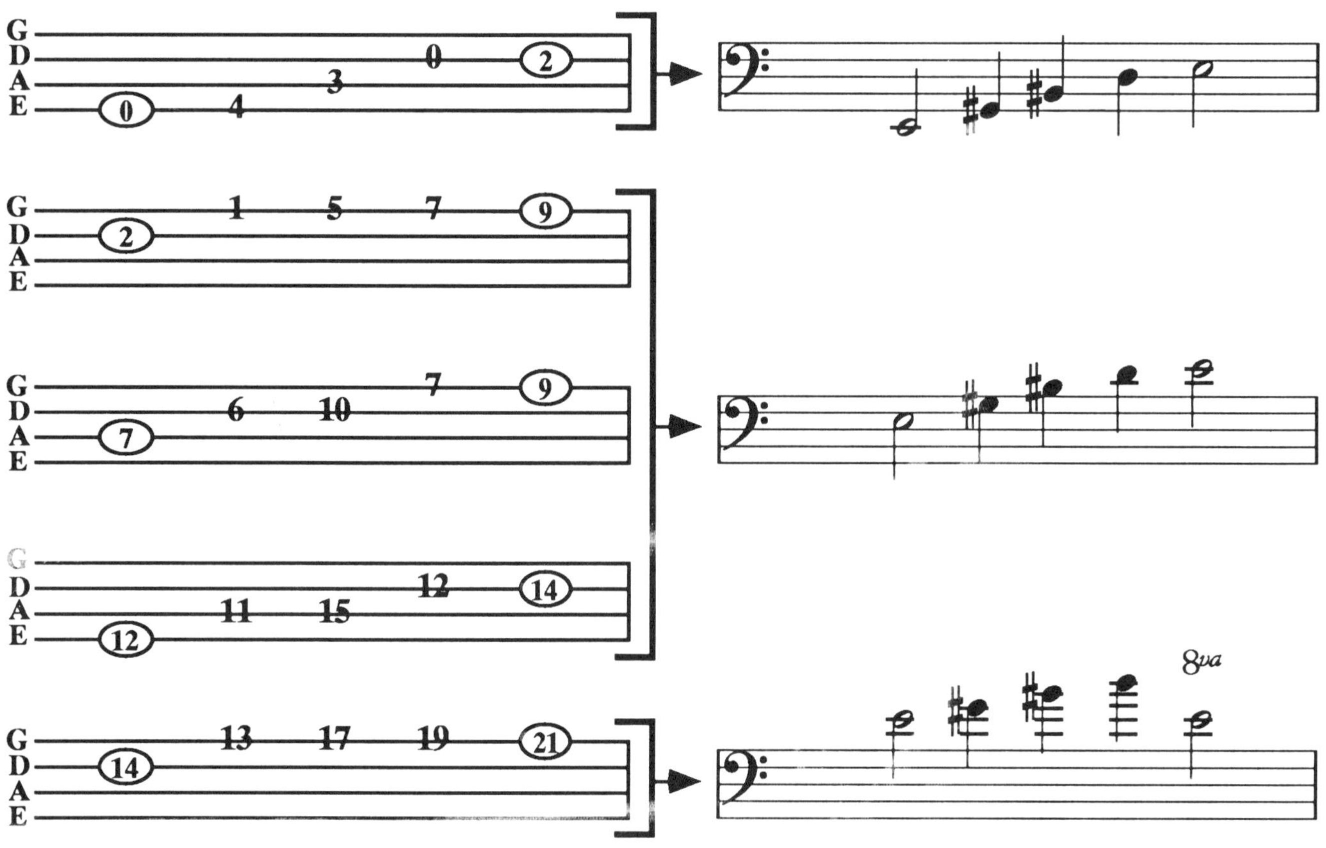

Riff

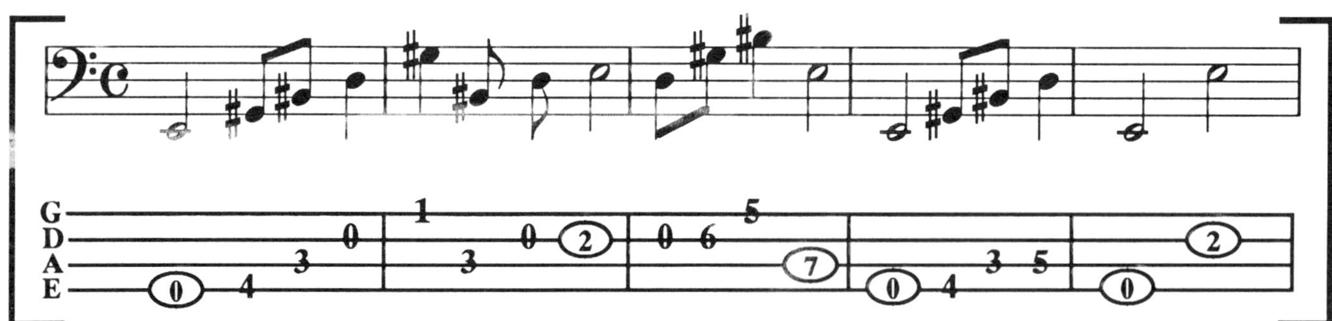

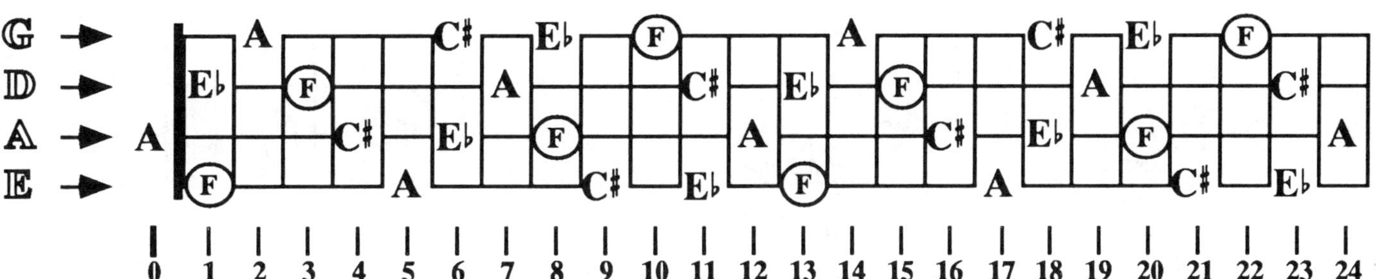

F SEVENTH AUG 5TH

FORMULA - (F) Root (A) 3rd (C♯) ♯5th (E♭) ♭7th

F7+5

Positions

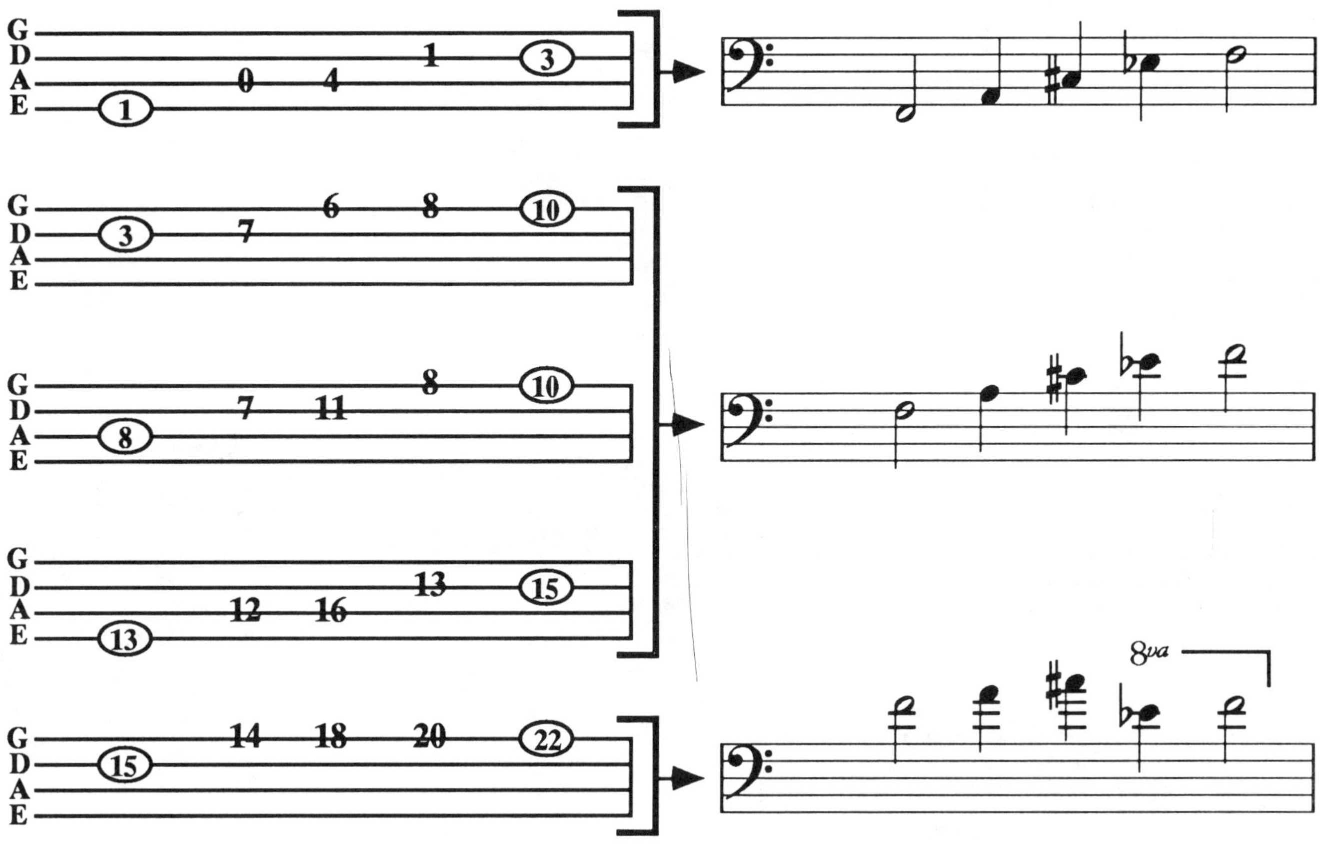

Riff

G SEVENTH AUG 5TH

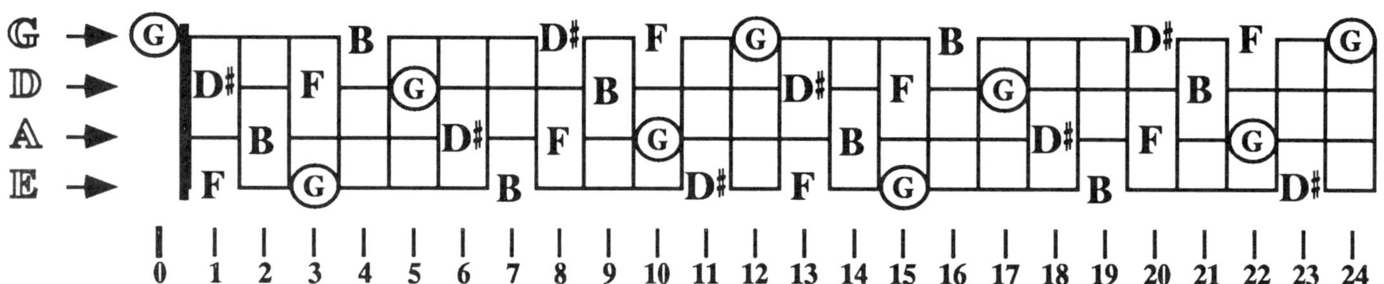

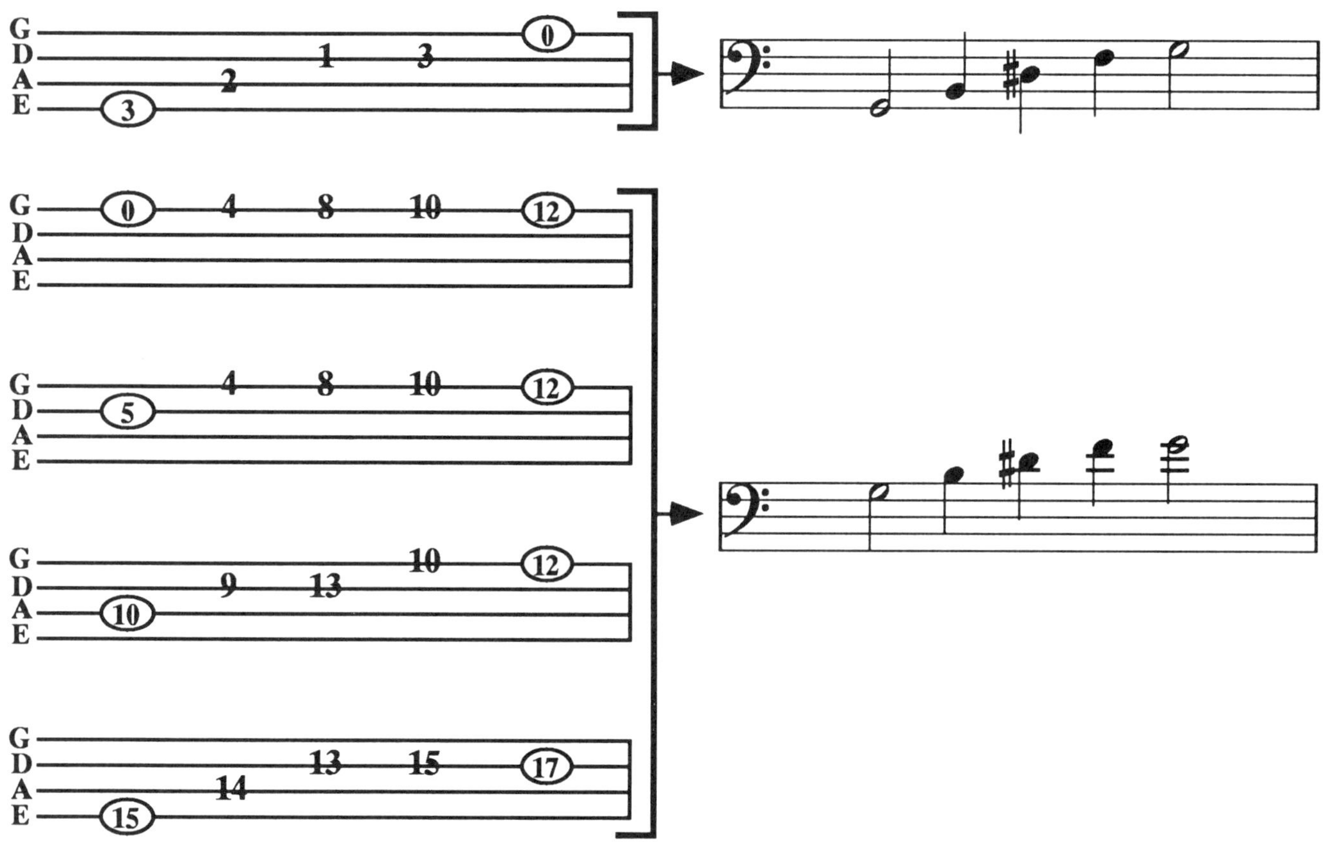

A SEVENTH AUG 5TH

FORMULA - (A) Root (C♯) 3rd (E♯) ♯5th (G) ♭7th

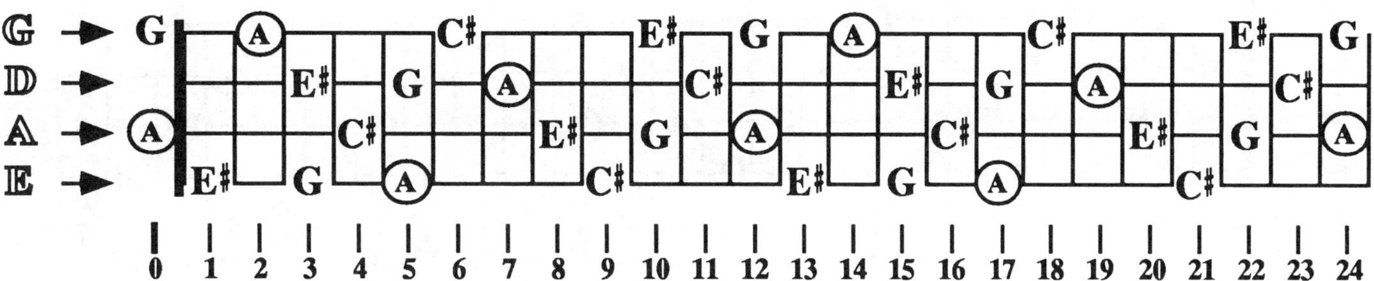

Positions

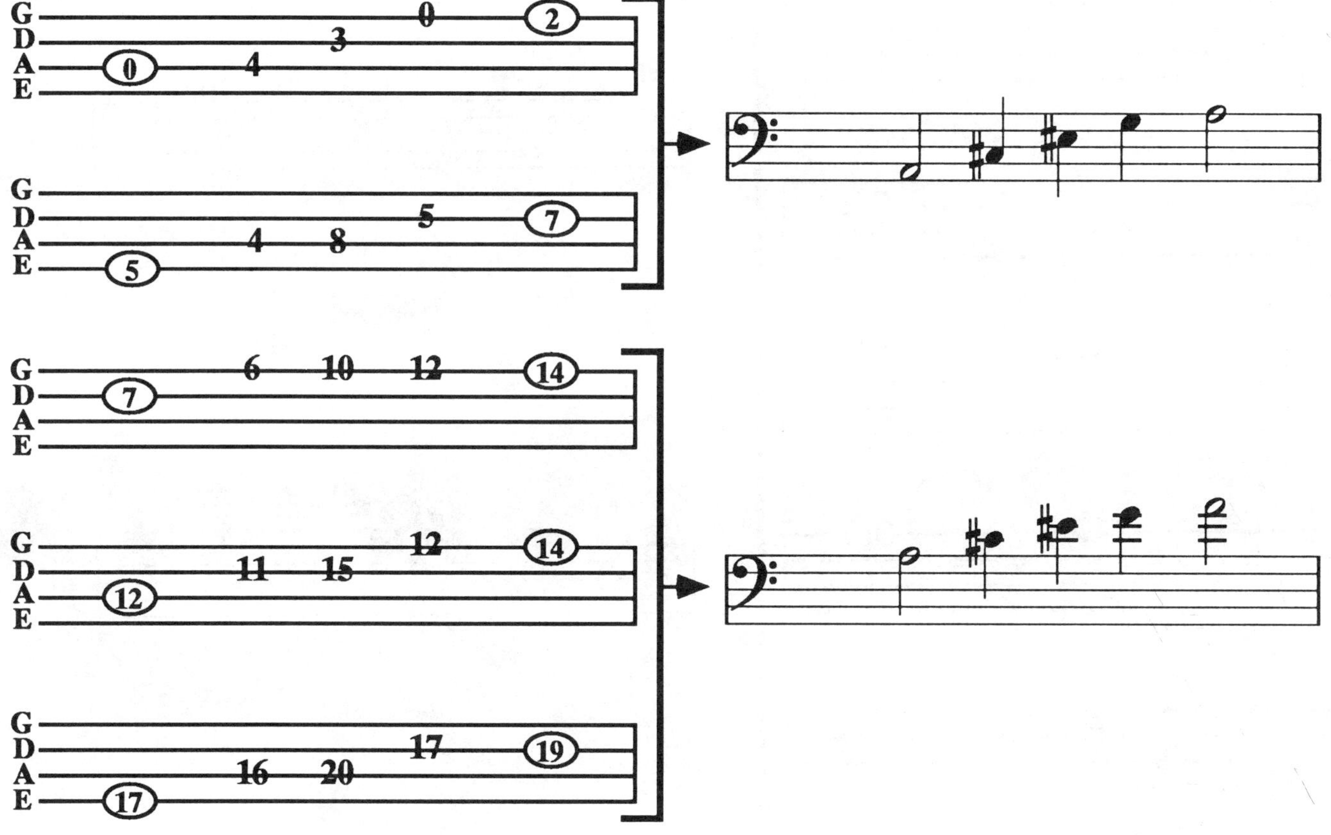

Riff

B SEVENTH AUG 5TH

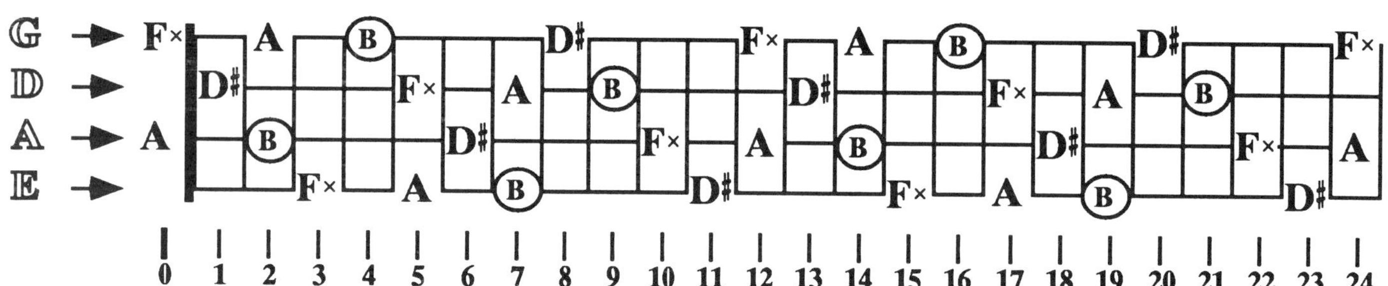

Positions

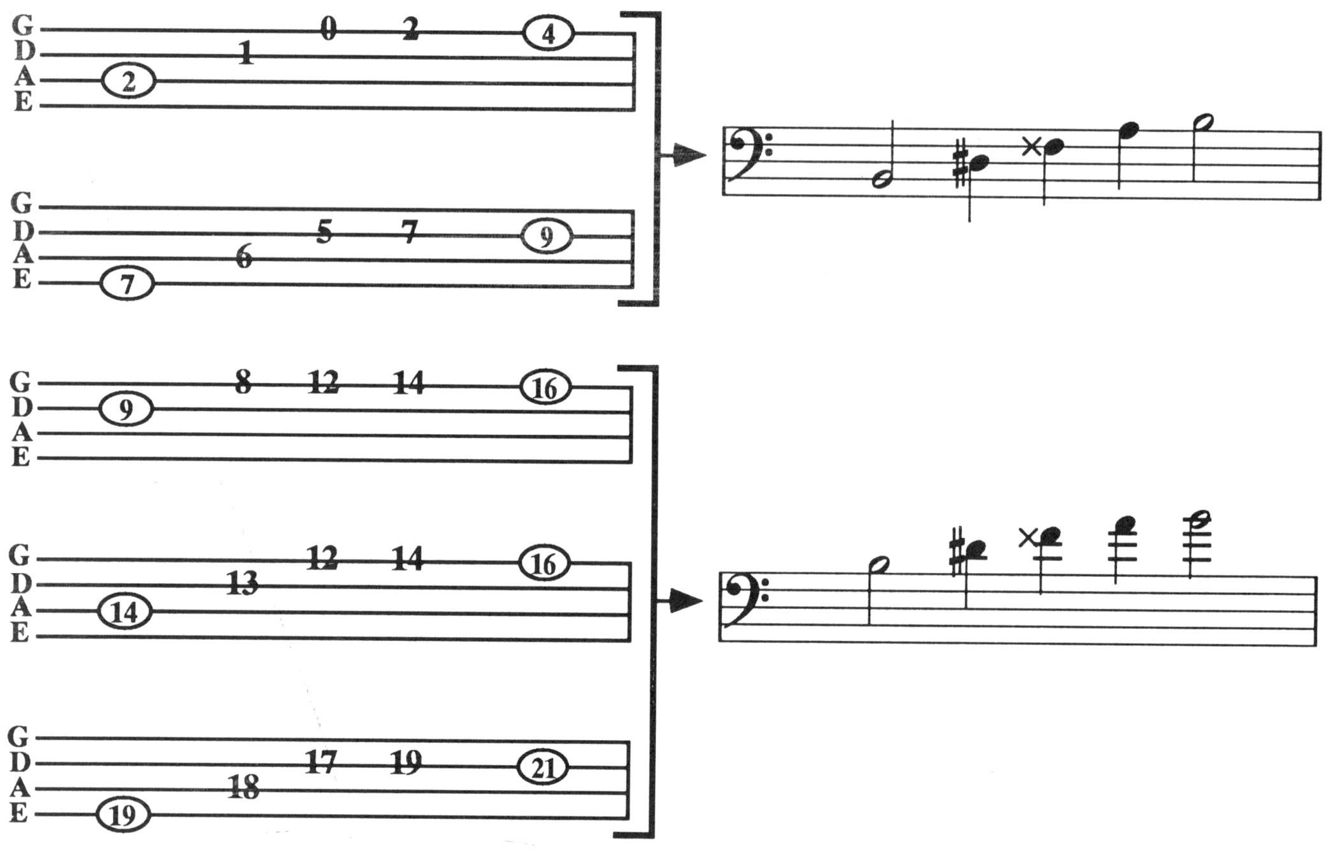

Riff

C NINTH

FORMULA - (C) Root (E) 3rd (G) 5th (B♭) ♭7th (D) 9th

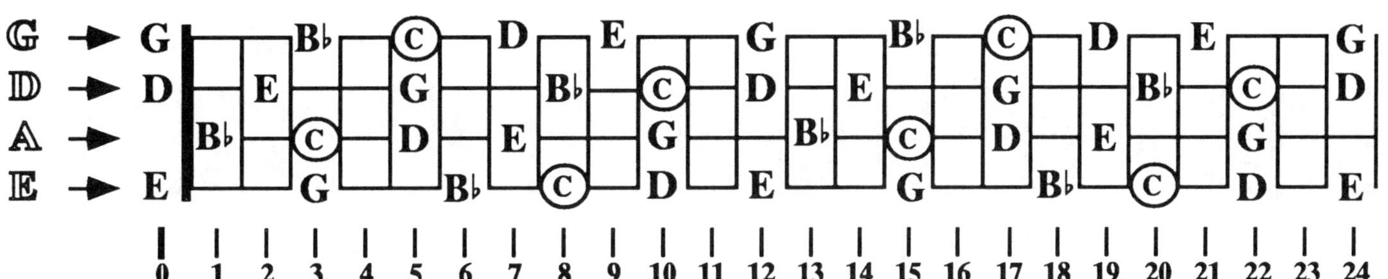

Positions

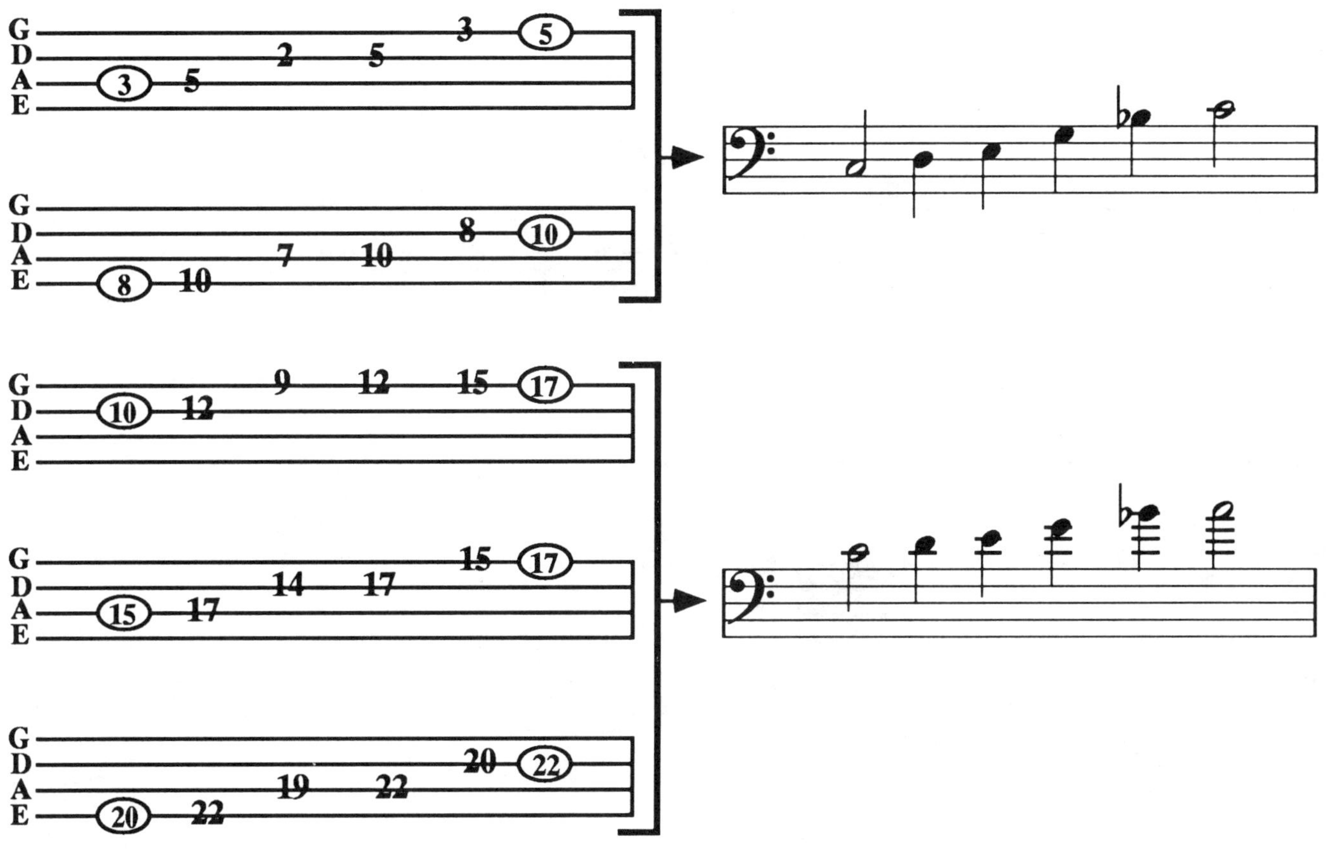

Riff

141

D NINTH

FORMULA - (D) Root (F♯) 3rd (A) 5th (C) ♭7th (E) 9th

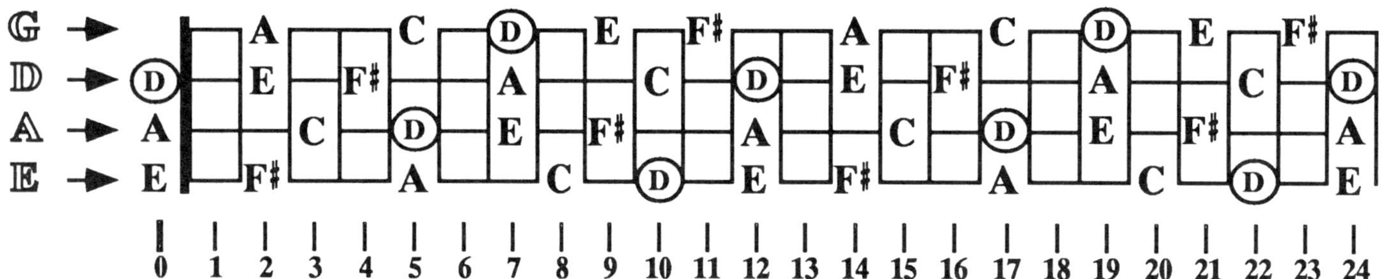

Positions

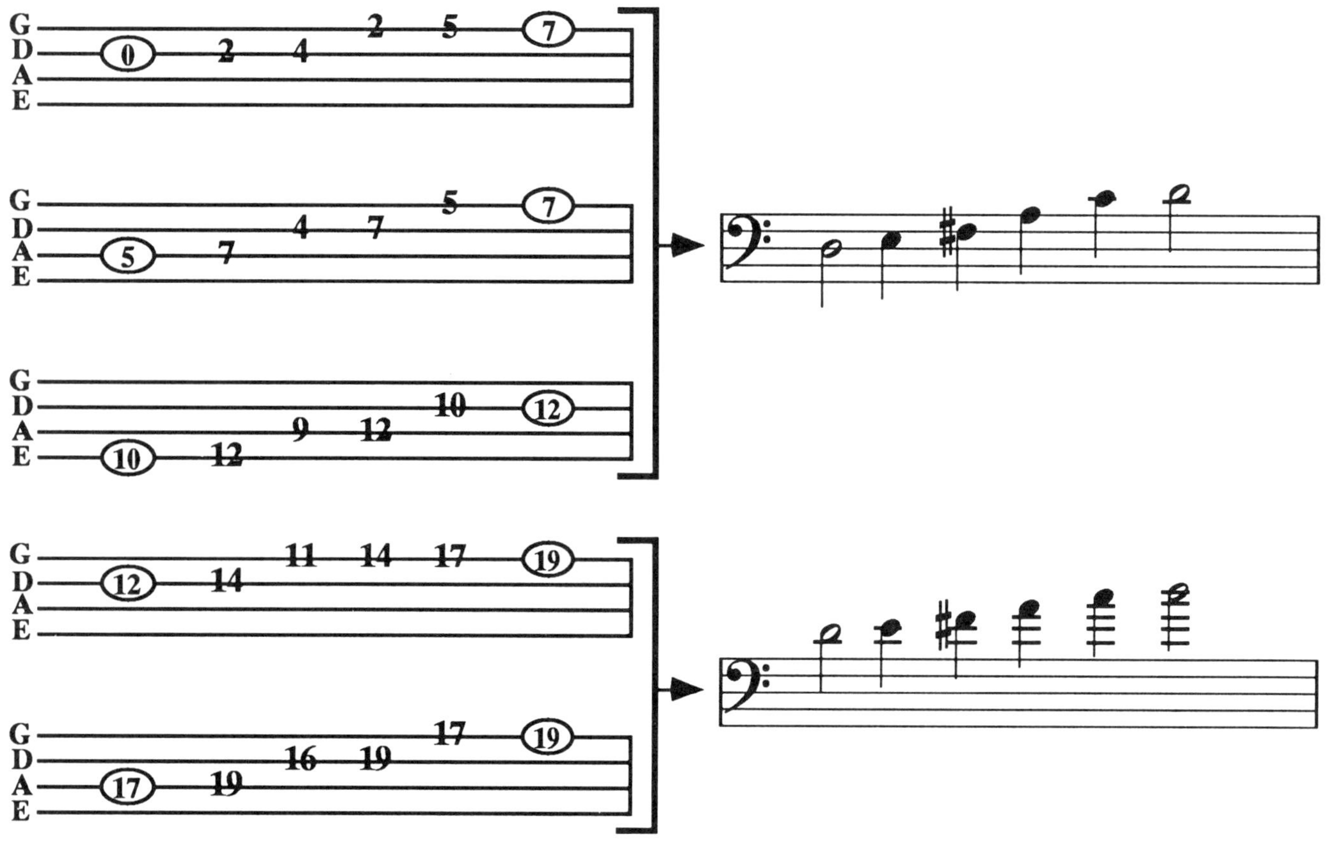

Riff

E NINTH

FORMULA - (E) Root (G♯) 3rd (B) 5th (D) ♭7th (F♯) 9th

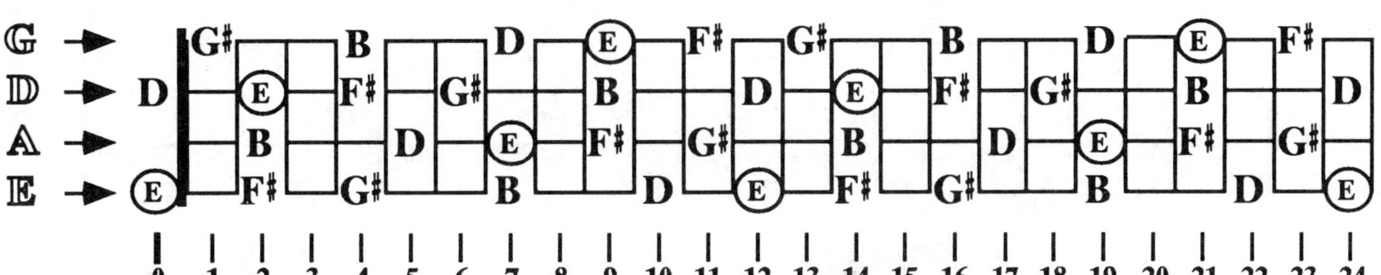

Positions

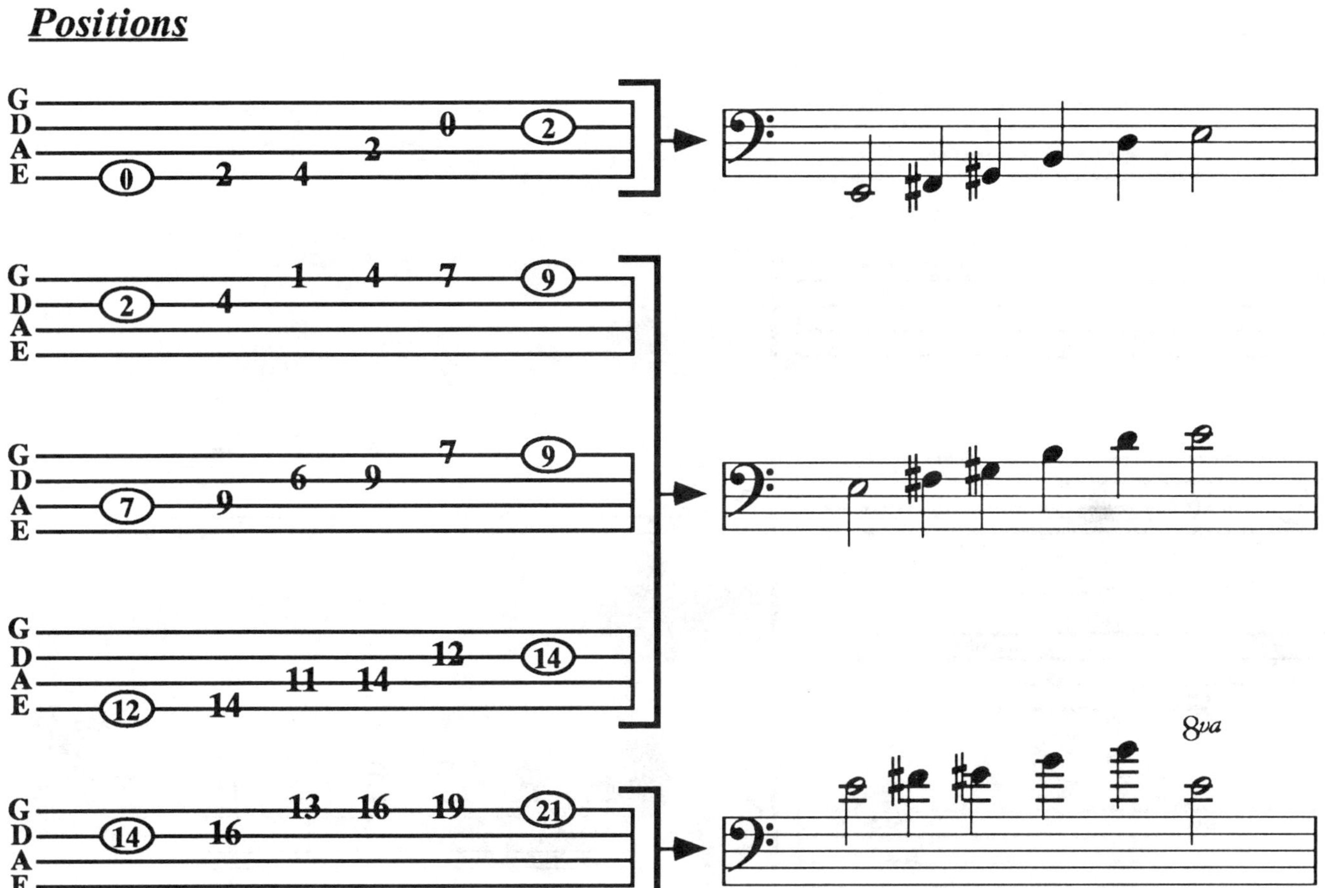

Riff

F NINTH

FORMULA - (F) Root (A) 3rd (C) 5th (E♭) ♭7th (G) 9th

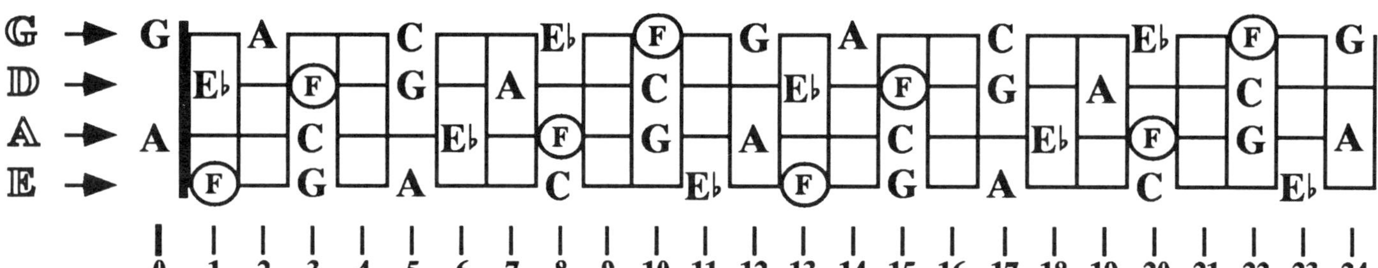

Positions

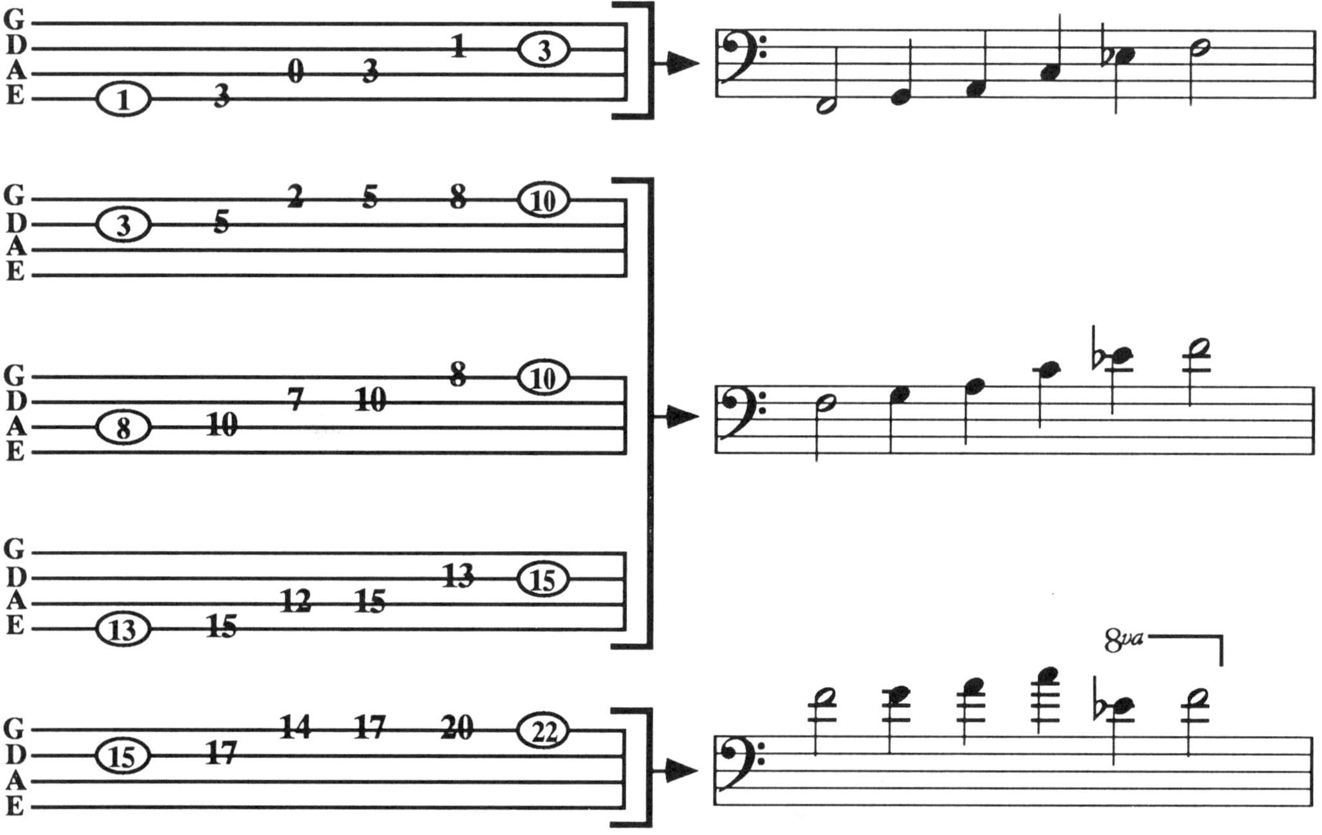

Riff

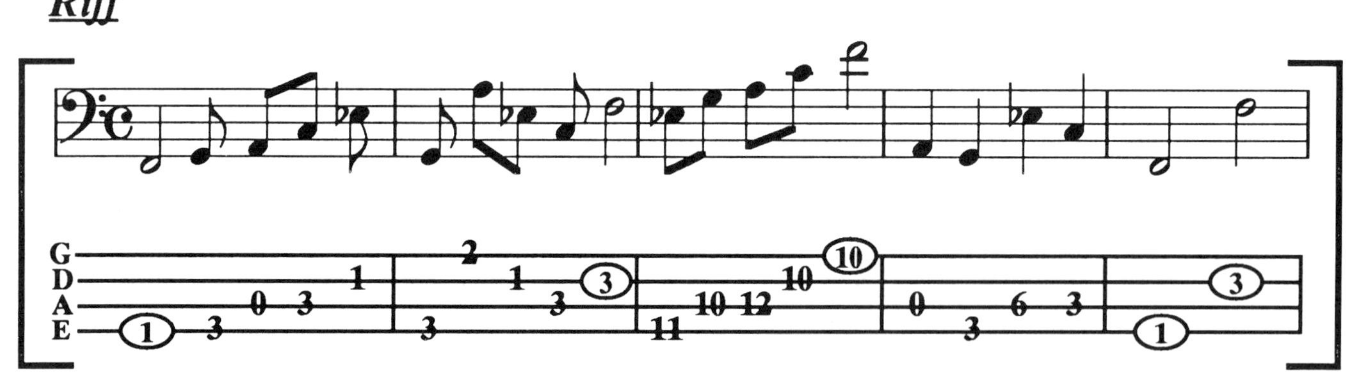

G NINTH

FORMULA - (G) Root (B) 3rd (D) 5th (F) ♭7th (A) 9th

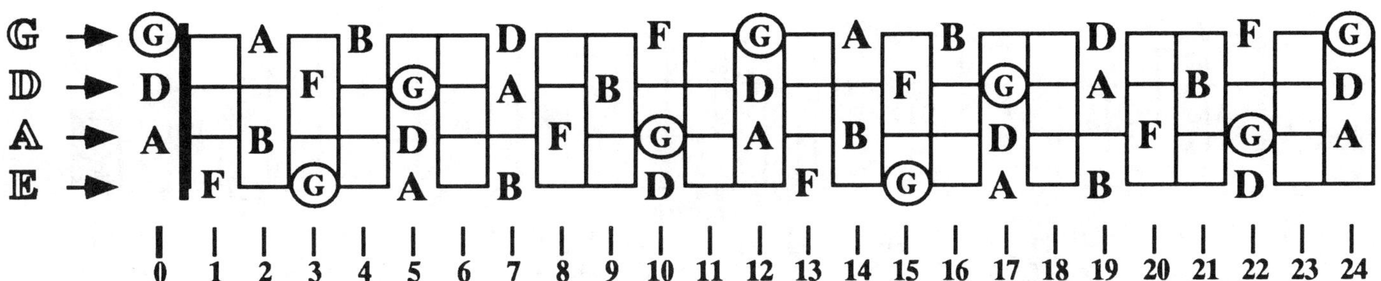

Positions

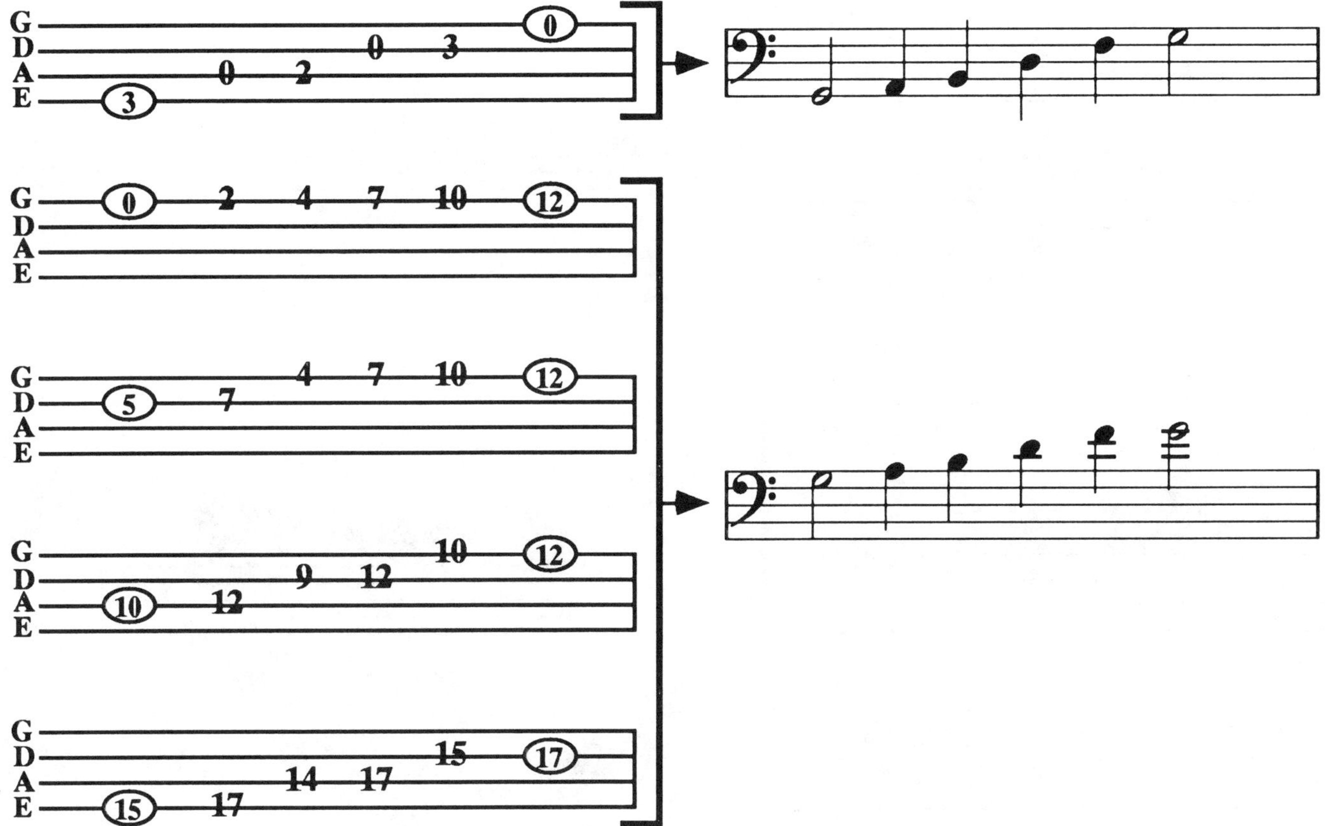

Riff

A NINTH

FORMULA - (A) Root (C♯) 3rd (E) 5th (G) ♭7th (B) 9th

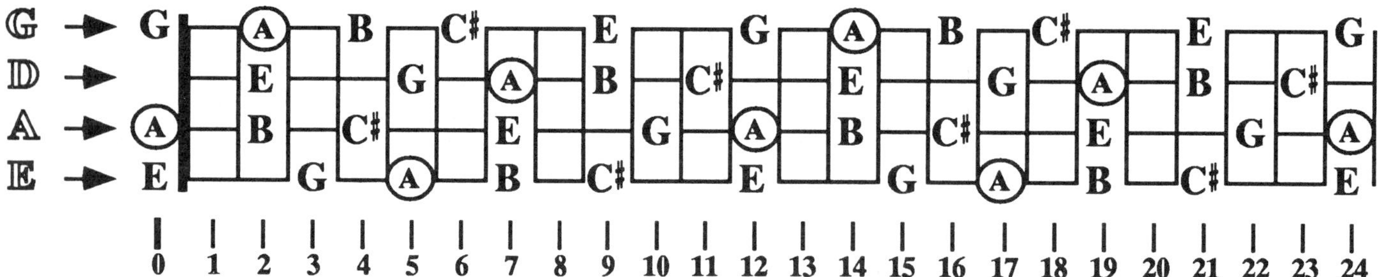

Positions

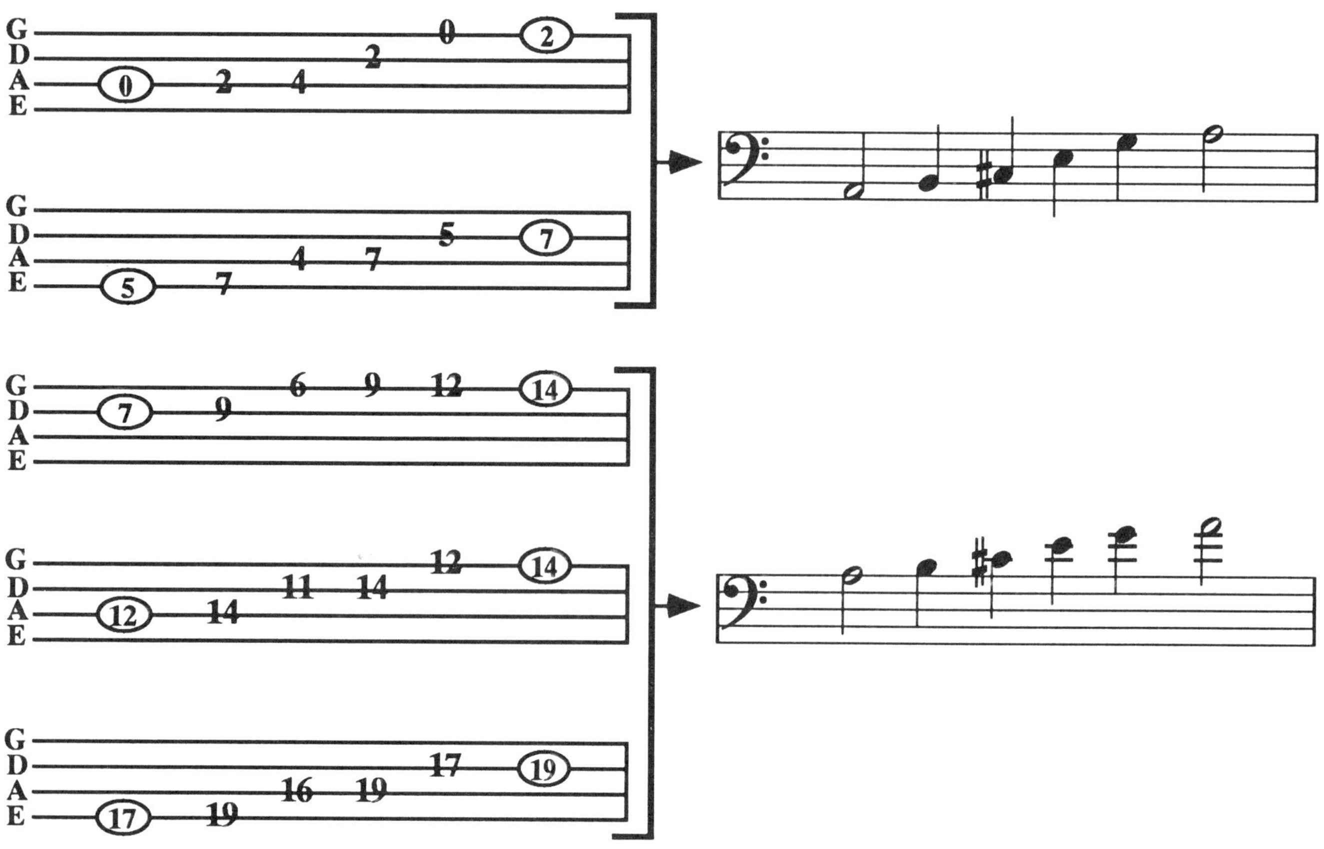

Riff

B NINTH

FORMULA - (B) Root (D♯) 3rd (F♯) 5th (A) ♭7th (C♯) 9th

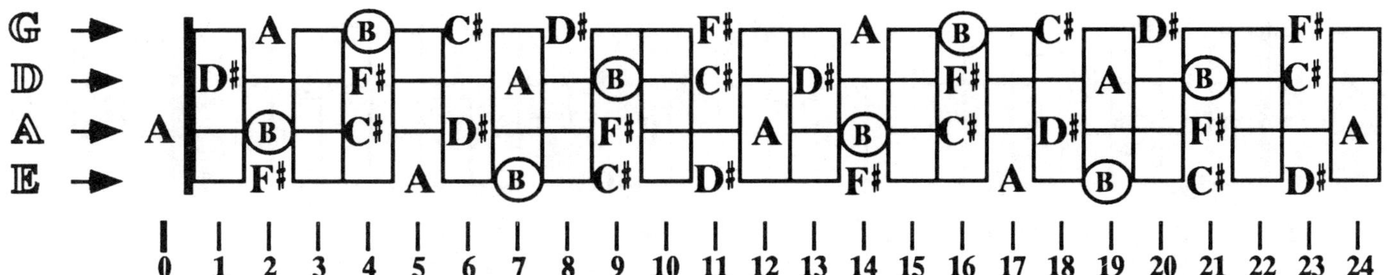

Positions

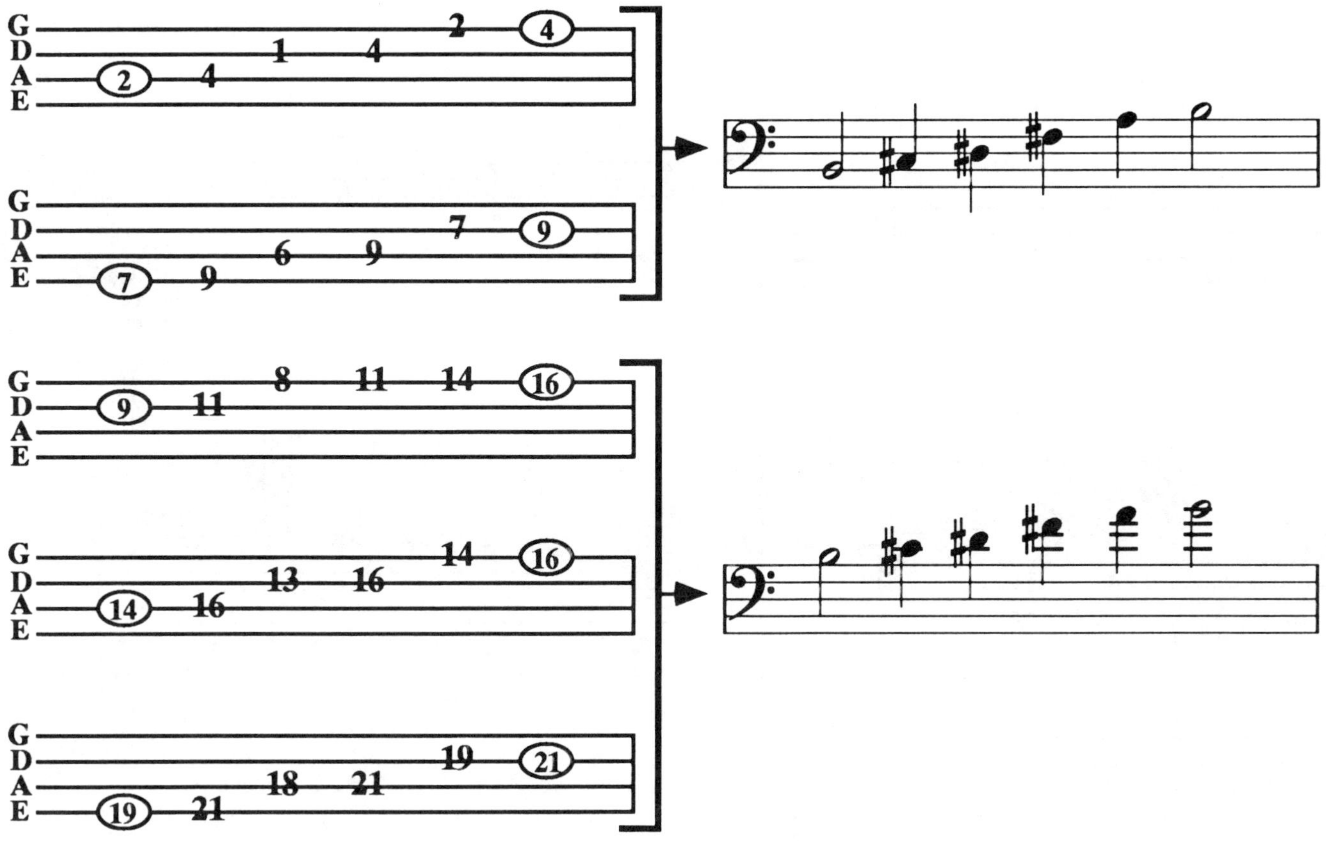

Riff

C NINTH ♭5TH

FORMULA - (C) Root (E) 3rd (G♭) ♭5th (B♭) ♭7th (D) 9th

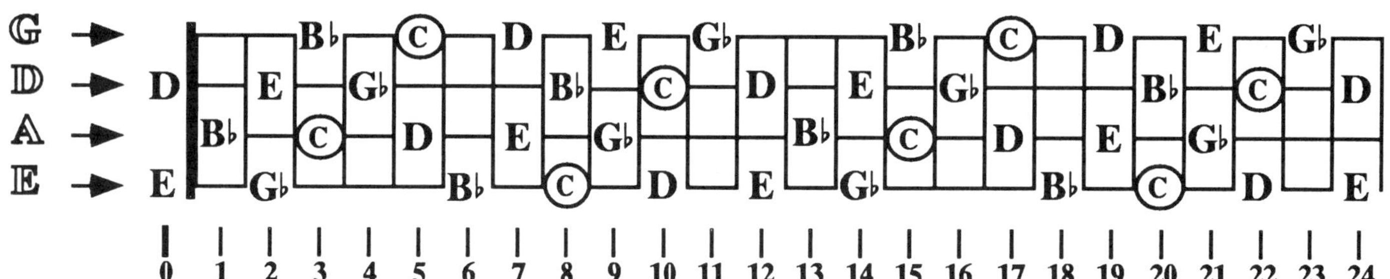

Positions

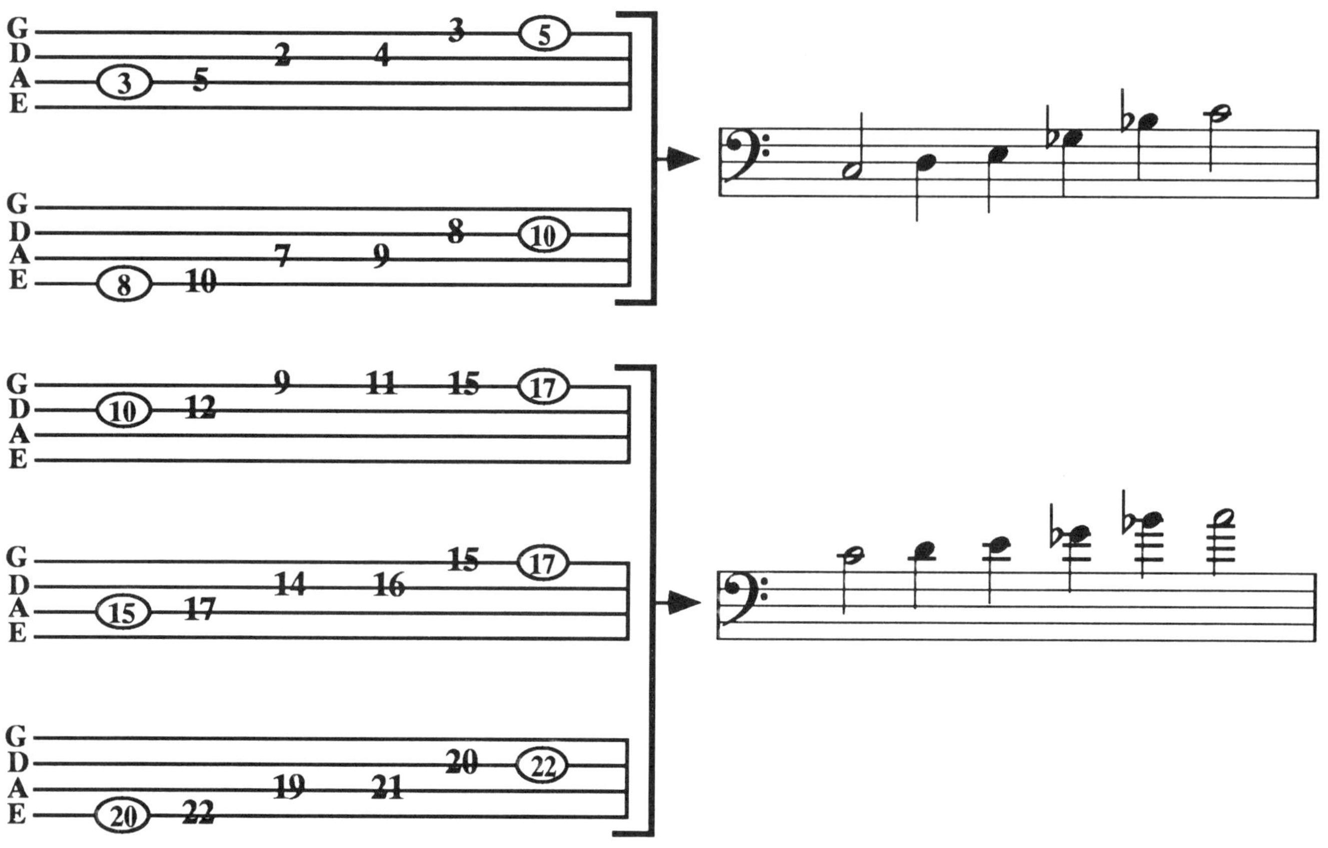

Riff

D NINTH ♭5TH

FORMULA - (D) Root (F♯) 3rd (A♭) ♭5th (C) ♭7th (E) 9th

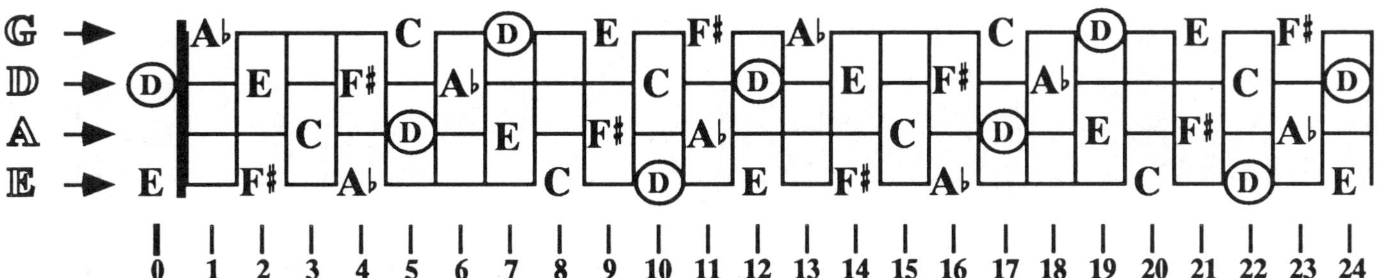

Positions

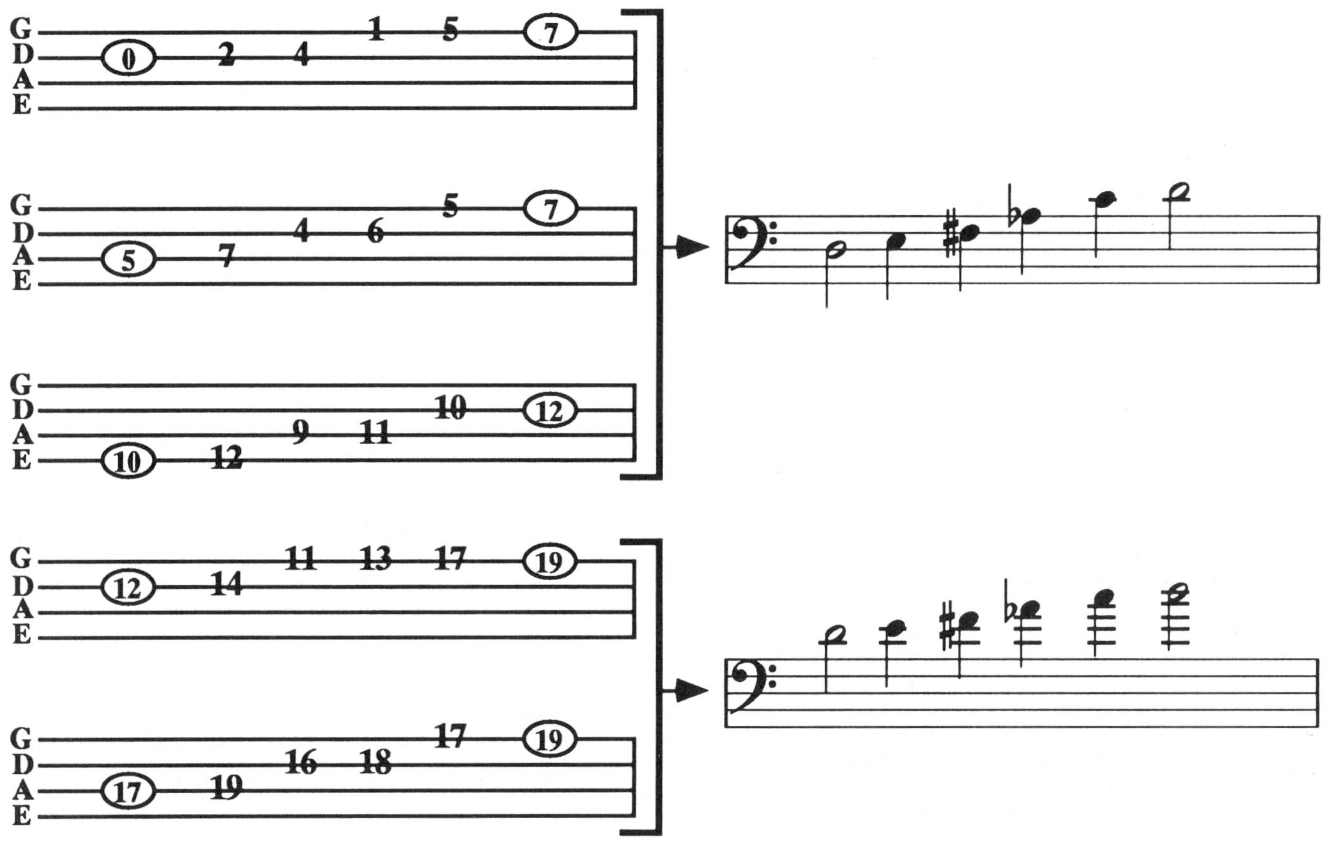

Riff

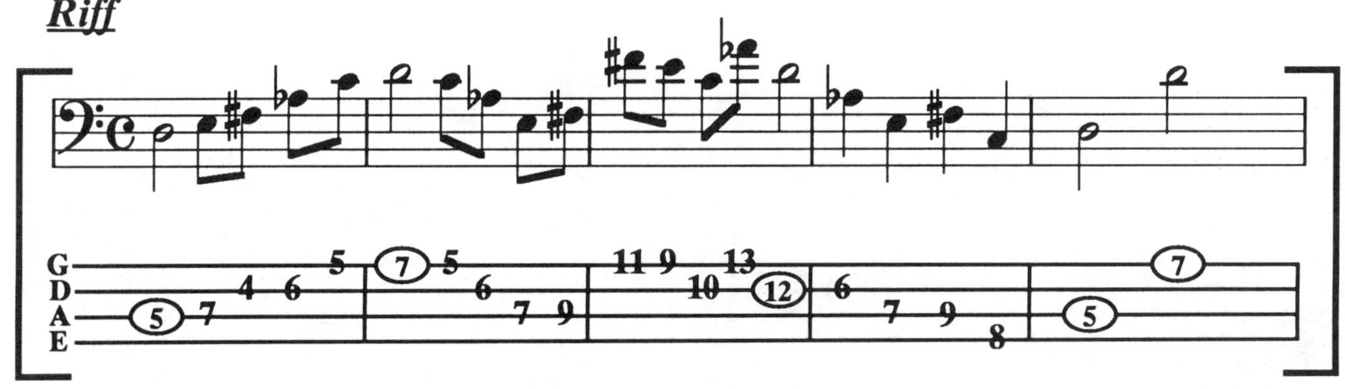

E NINTH ♭5TH
FORMULA - (E) Root (G♯) 3rd (B♭) ♭5th (D) ♭7th (F♯) 9th

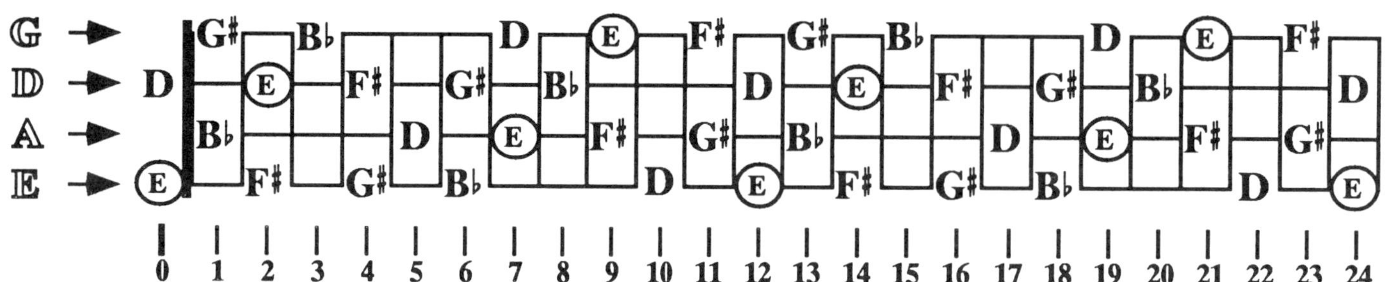

Positions

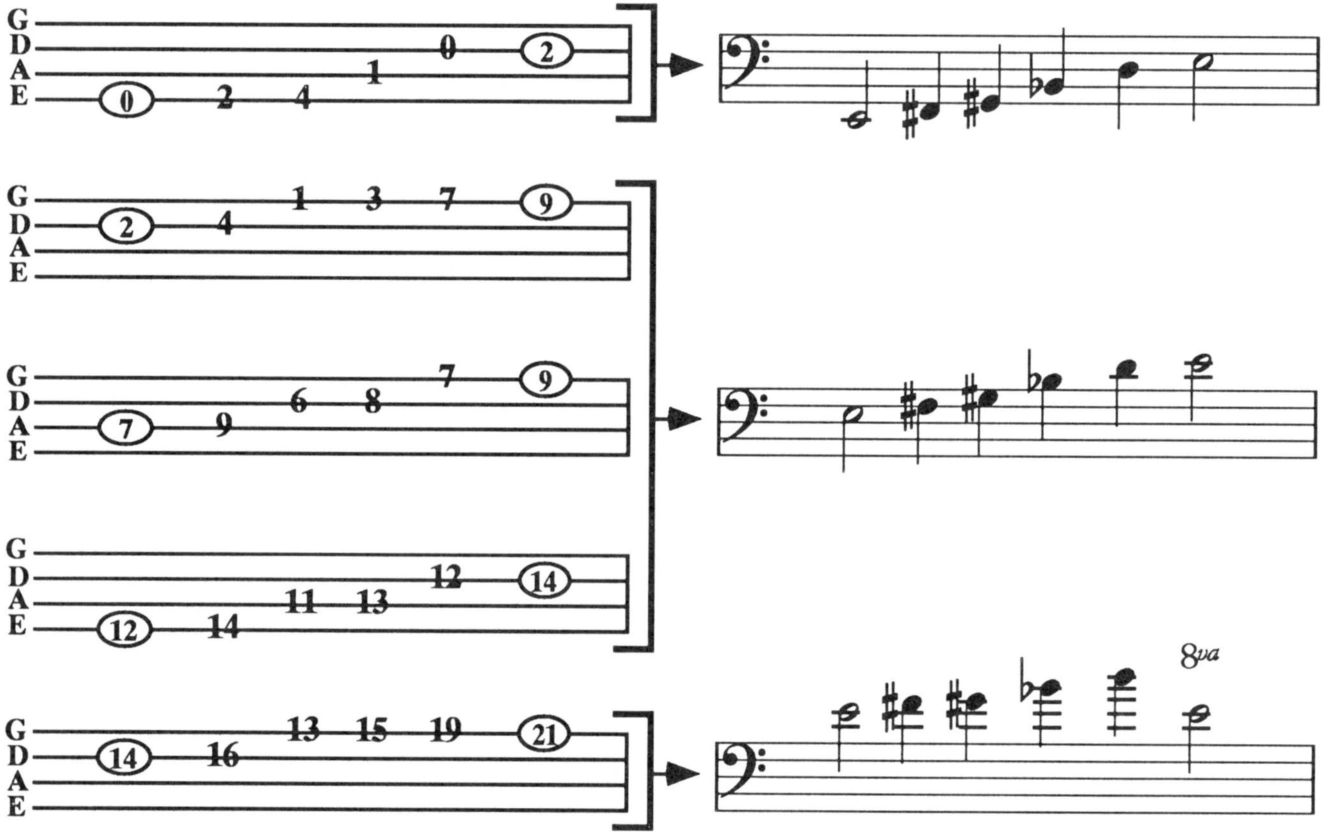

Riff

F NINTH ♭5TH

FORMULA - (F) Root (A) 3rd (C♭) ♭5th (E♭) ♭7th (G) 9th

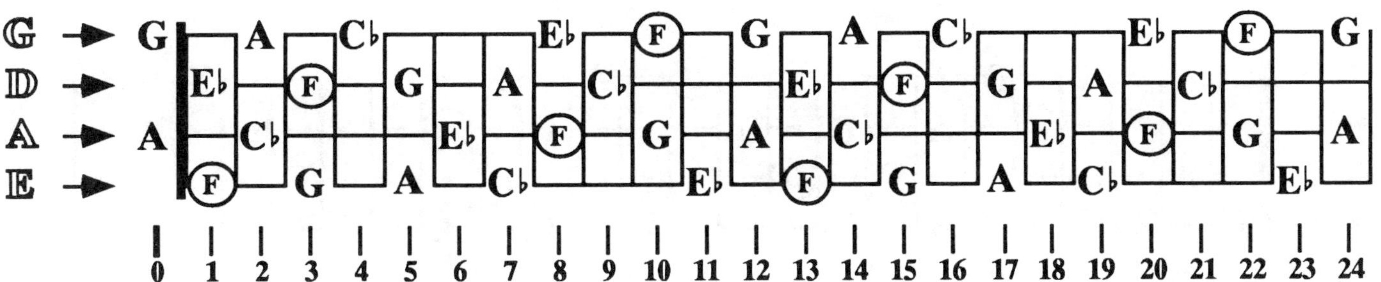

Positions

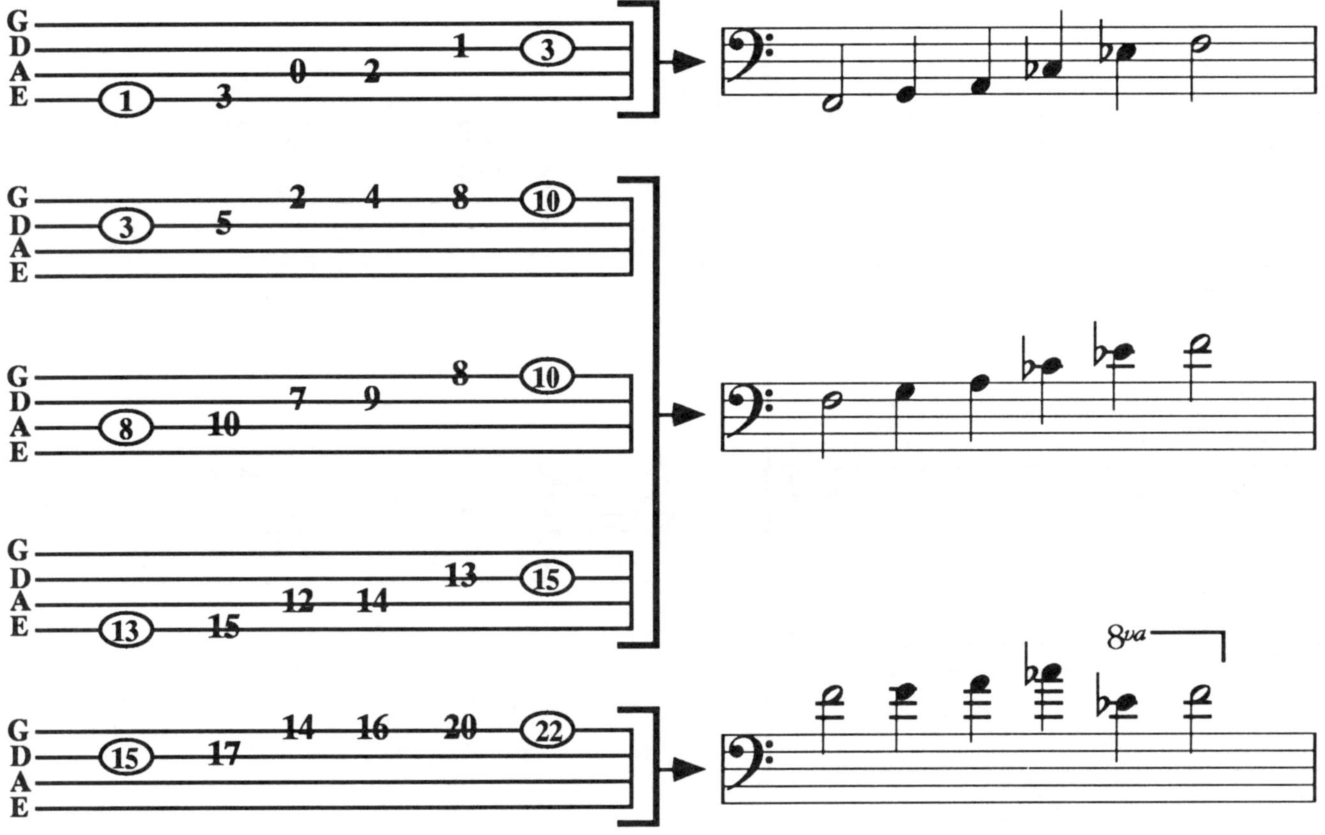

Riff

G NINTH ♭5TH

FORMULA - (G) Root (B) 3rd (D♭) ♭5th (F) ♭7th (A) 9th

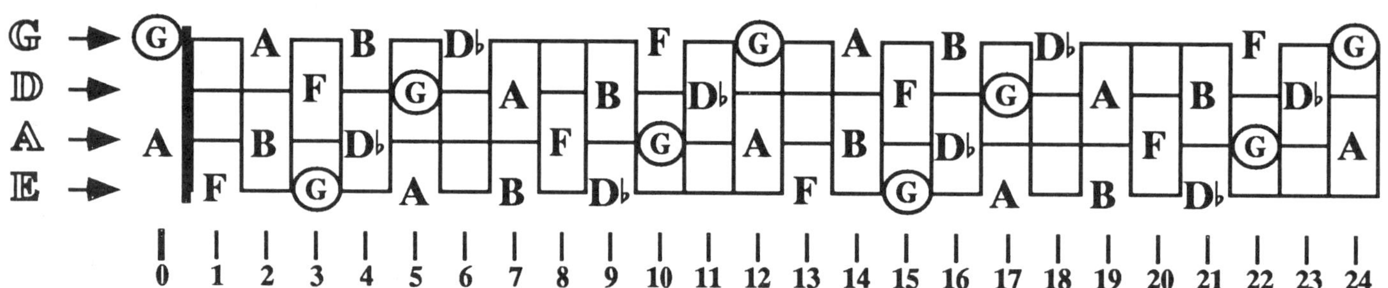

Positions

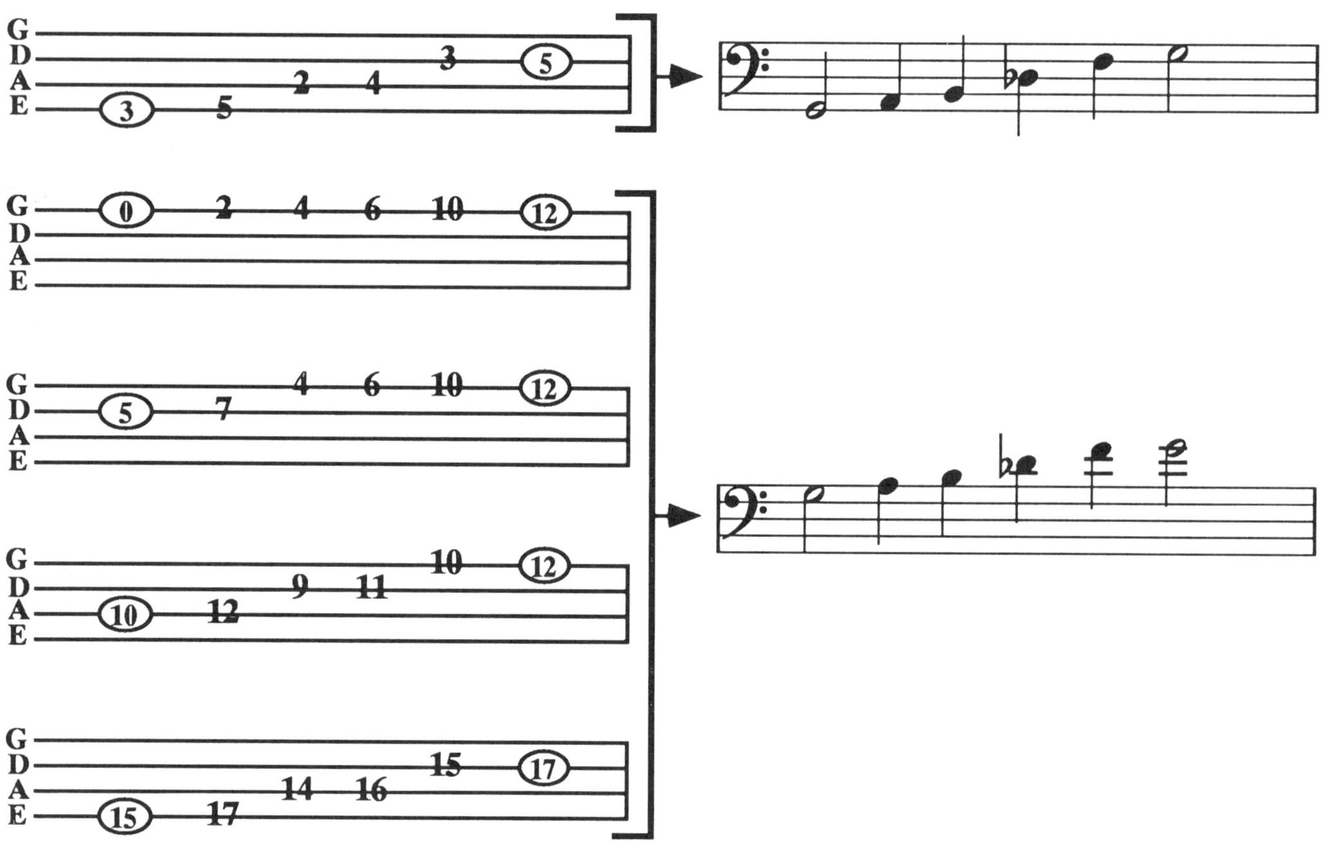

Riff

A NINTH♭5TH

FORMULA - (A) Root (C♯) 3rd (E♭) ♭5th (G) ♭7th (B) 9th

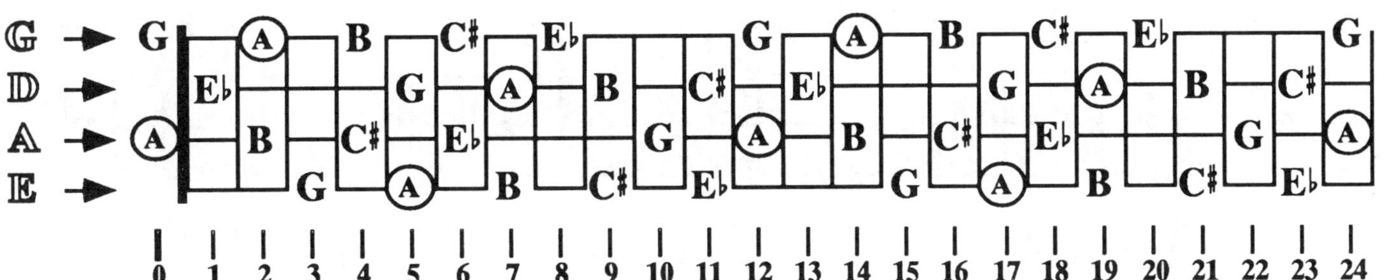

Positions

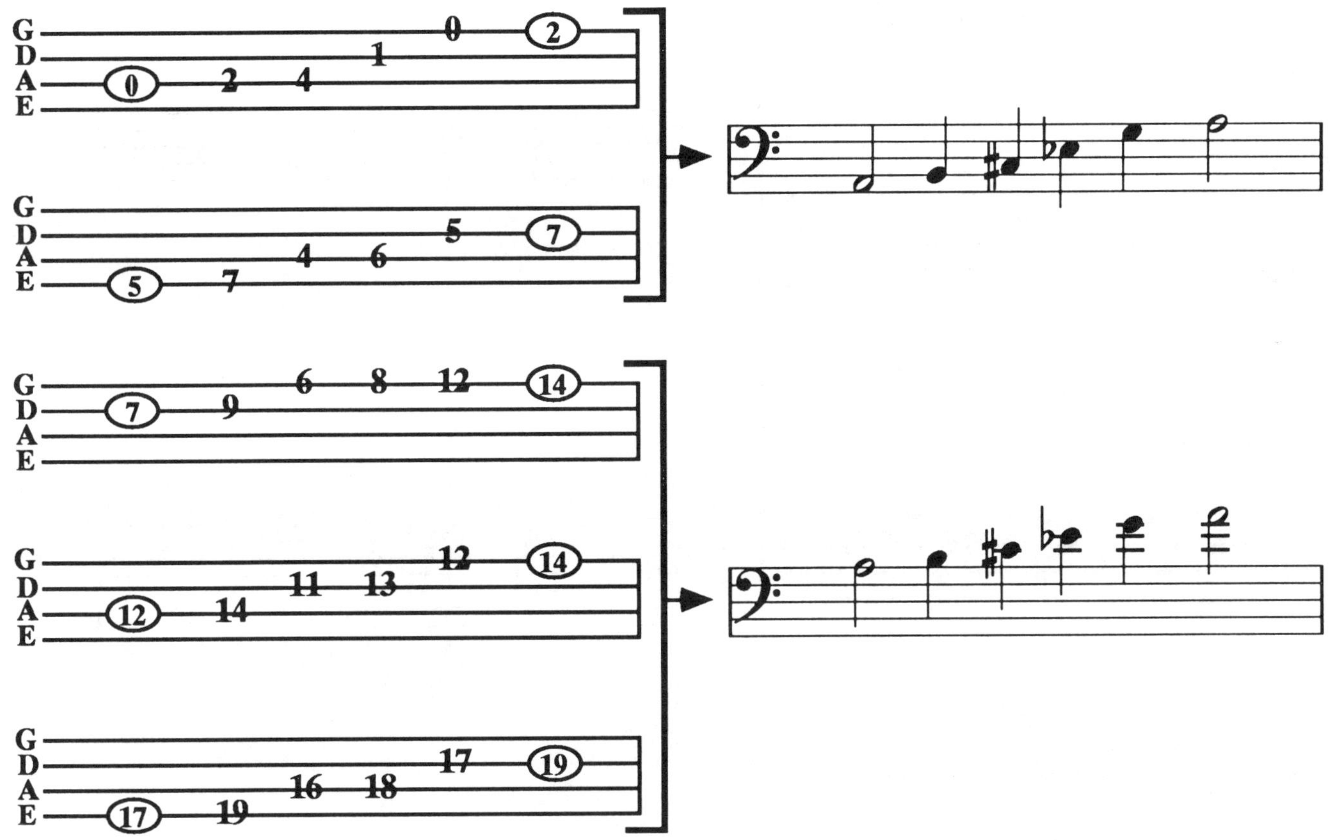

Riff

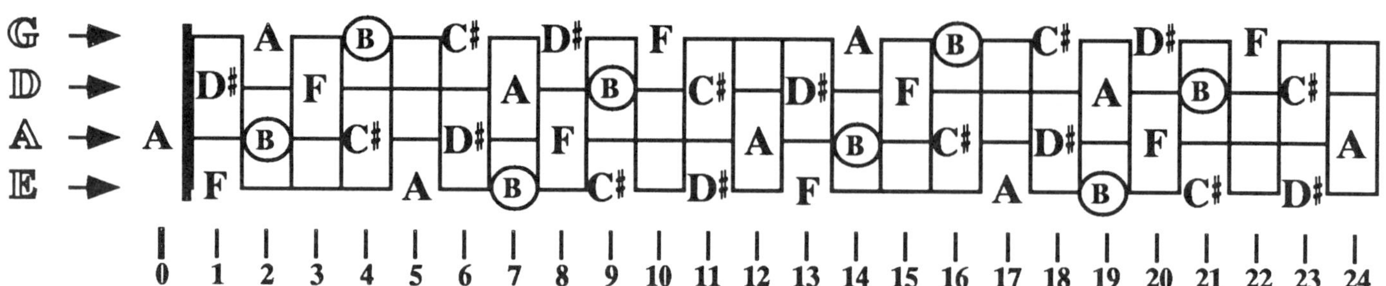

B NINTH ♭5TH

FORMULA - (B) Root (D♯) 3rd (F) ♭5th (A) ♭7th (C♯) 9th

Positions

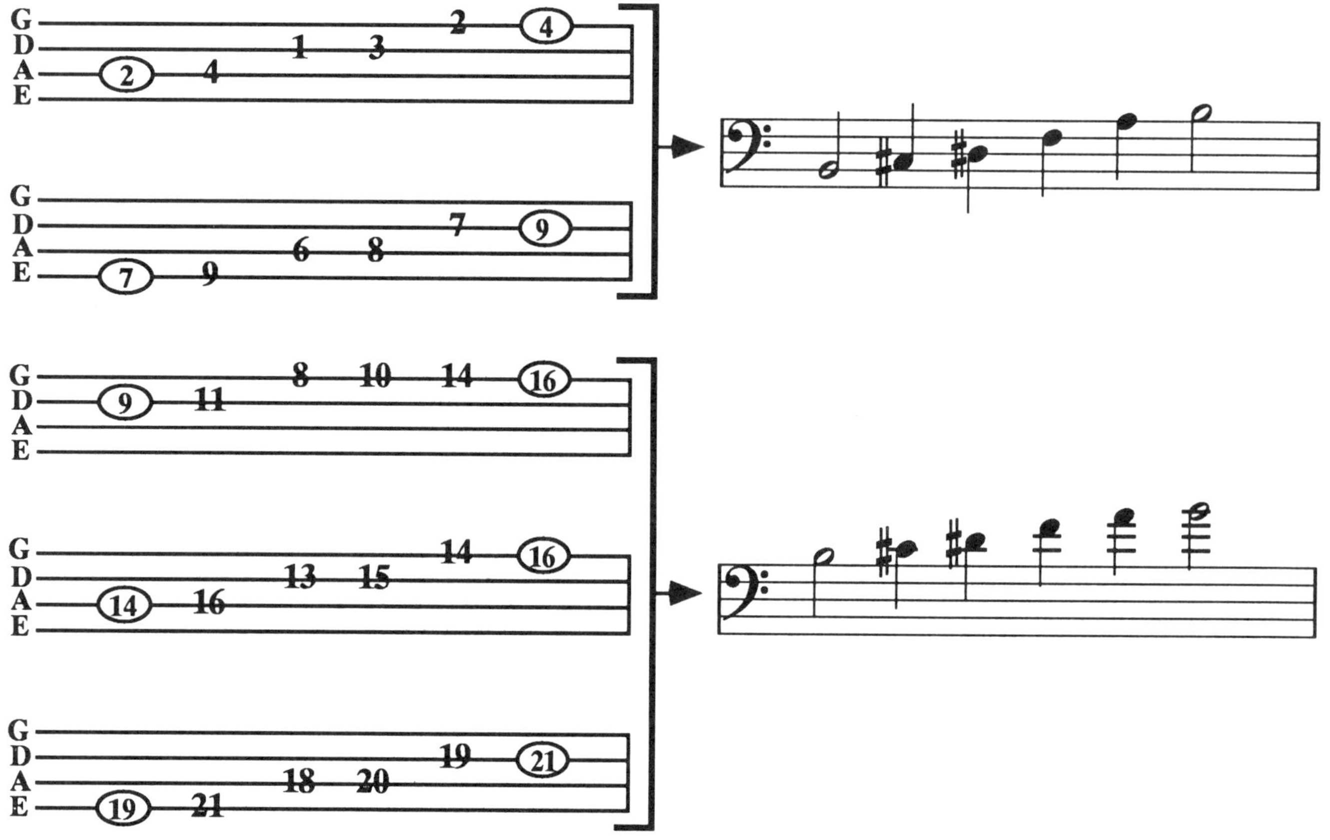

Riff

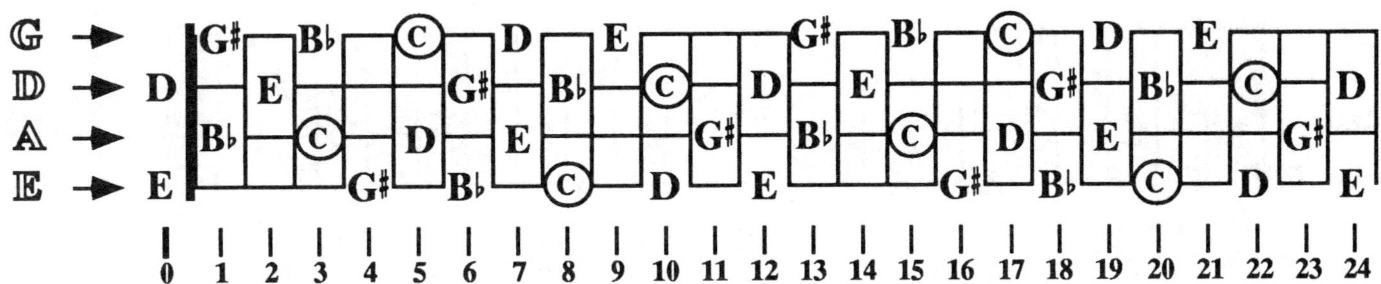

Positions

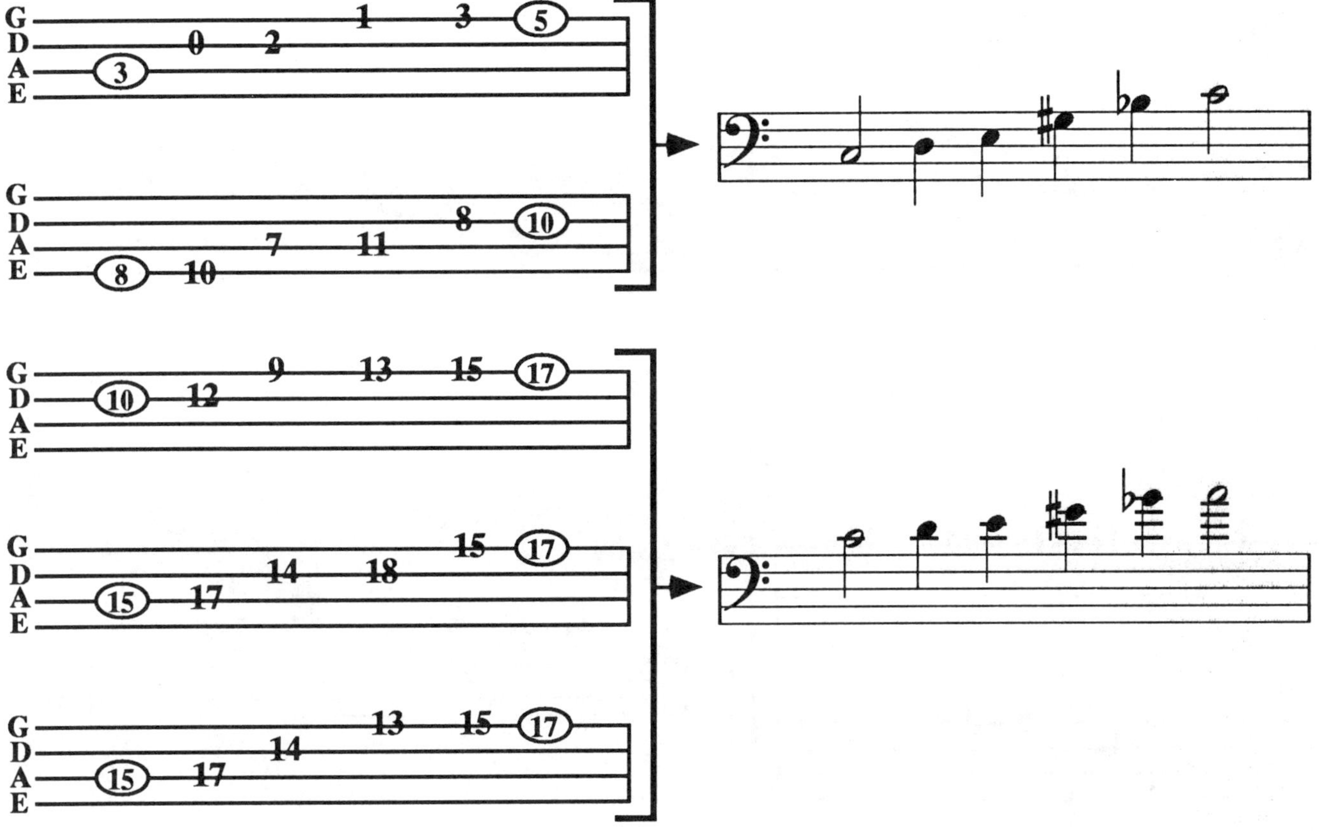

Riff

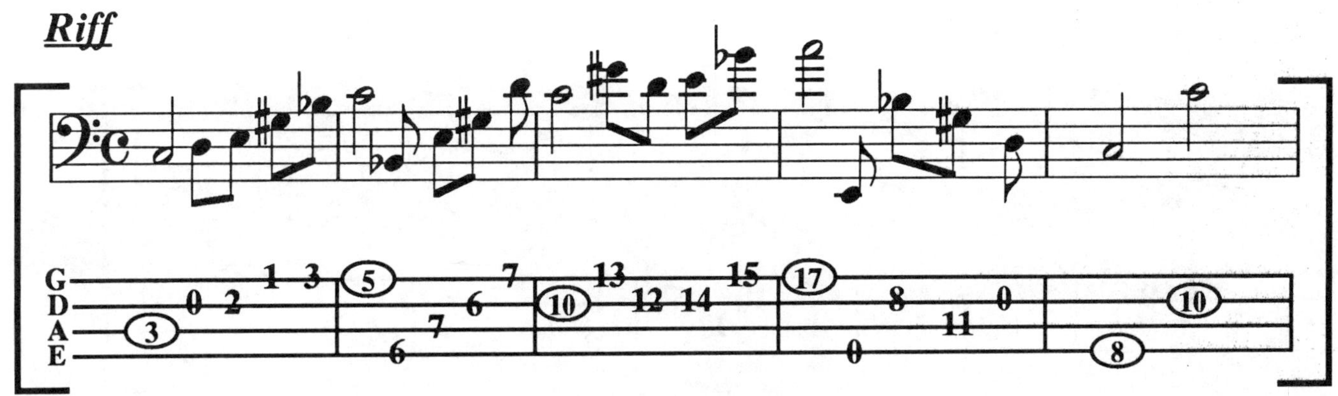

D NINTH AUG 5TH

FORMULA - (D) Root (F♯) 3rd (A♯) ♯5th (C) ♭7th (E) 9th

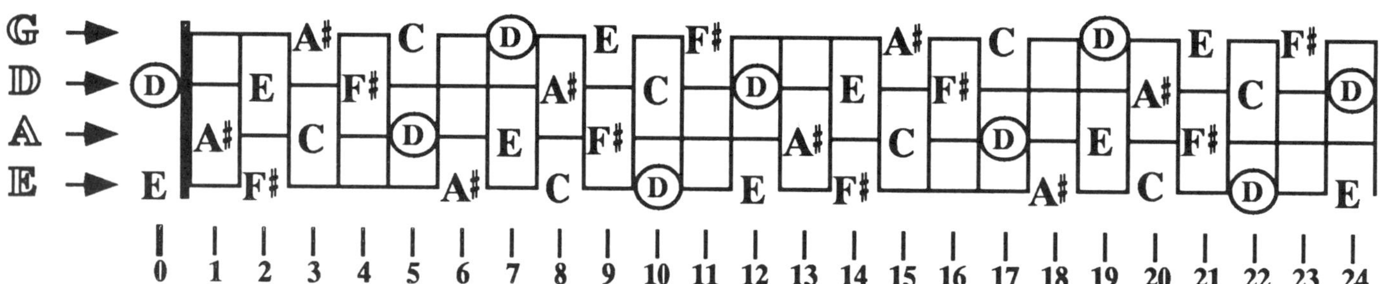

Positions

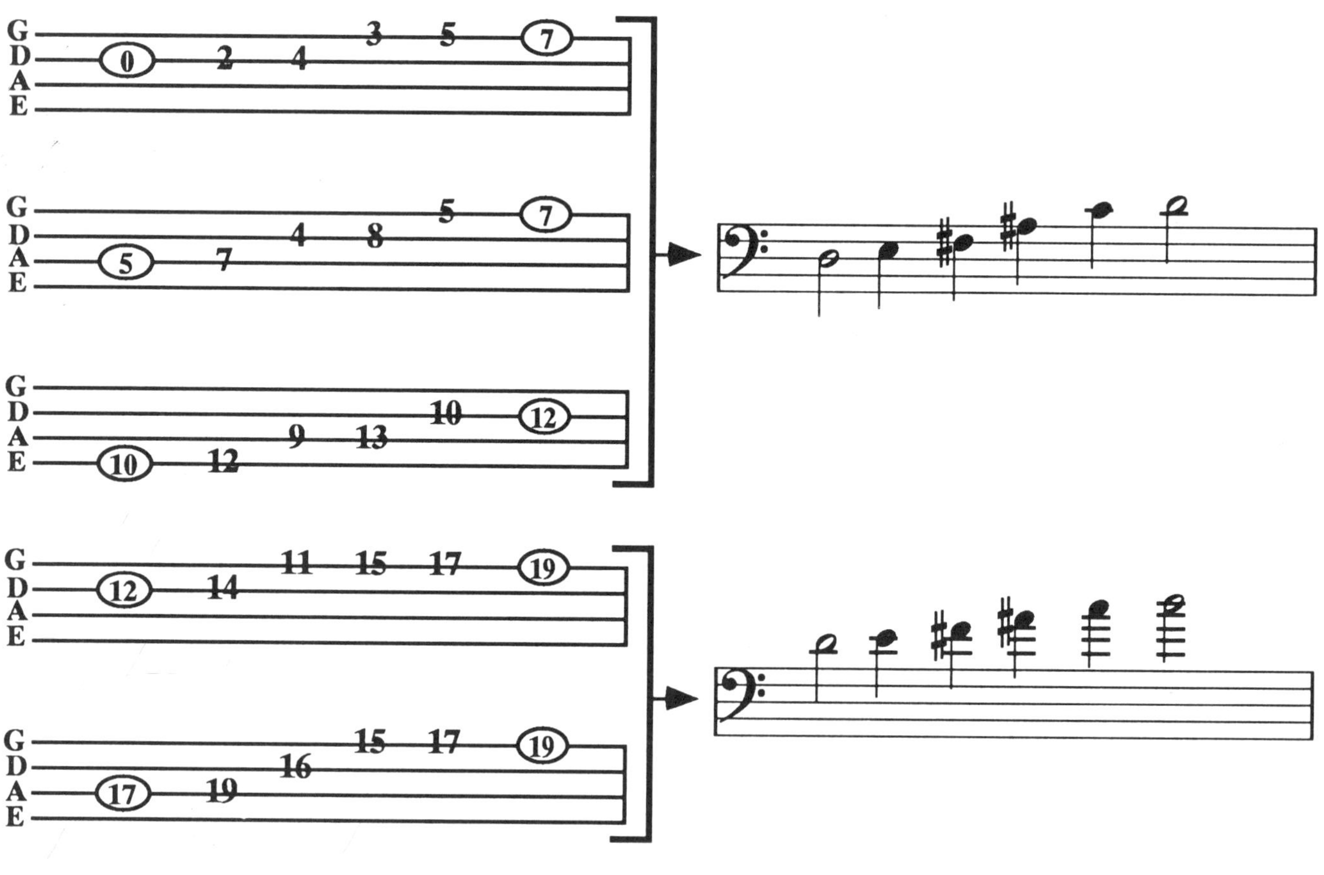

Riff

E NINTH AUG 5TH

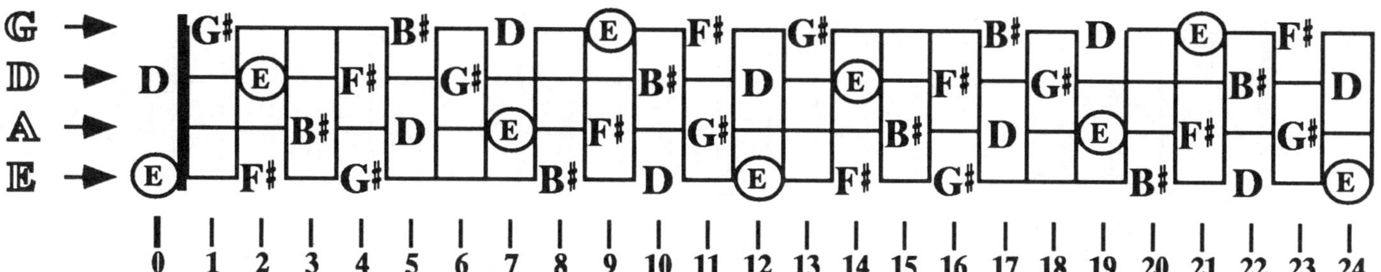

Positions

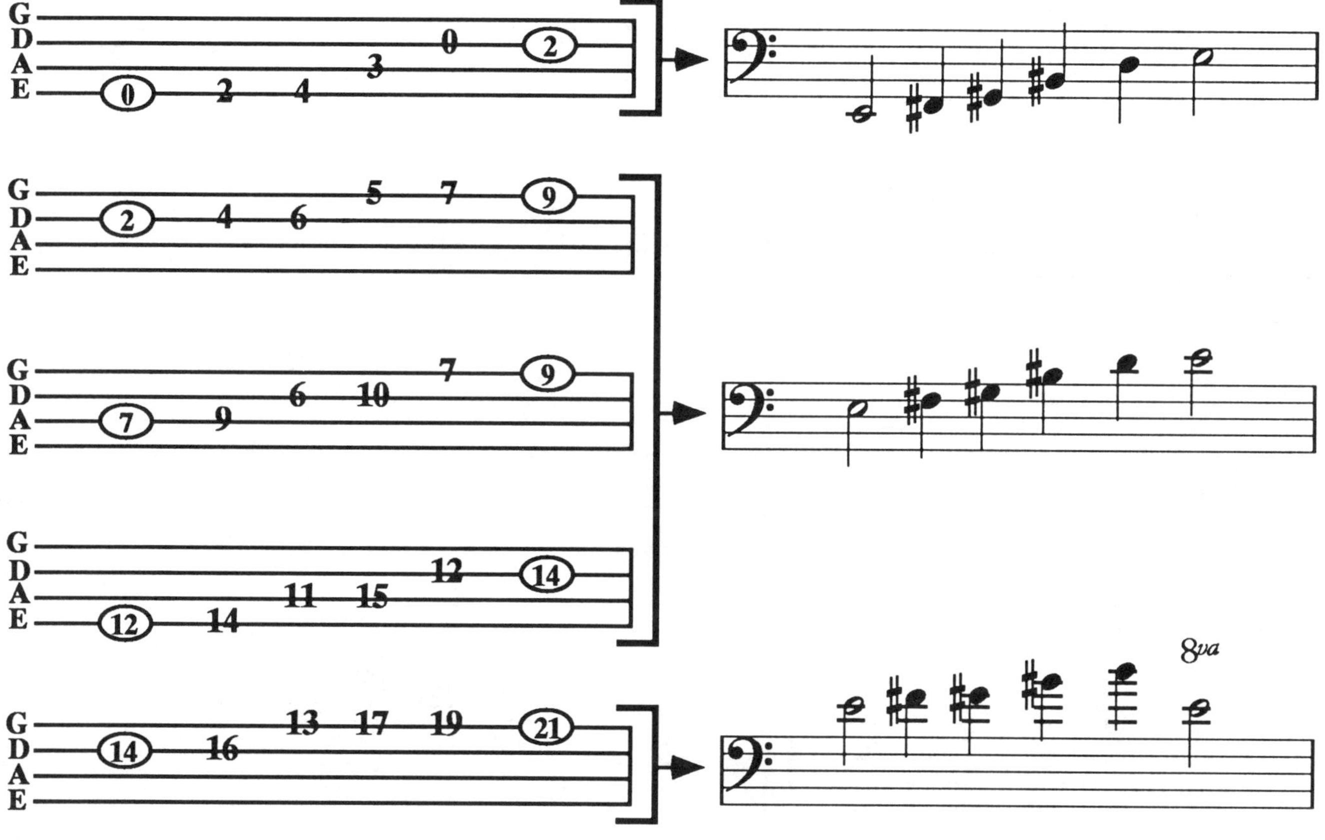

Riff

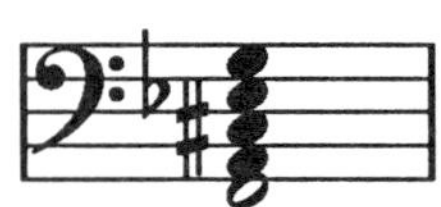

F NINTH AUG 5TH

FORMULA - (F) Root (A) 3rd (C♯) ♯5th (E♭) ♭7th (G) 9th

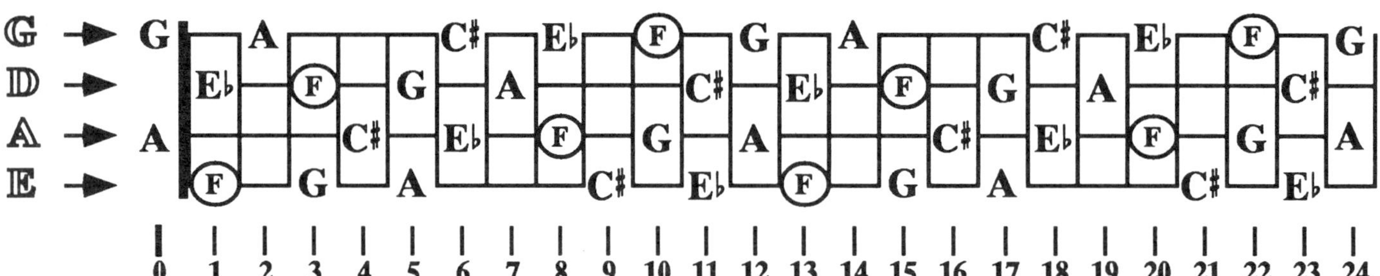

Positions

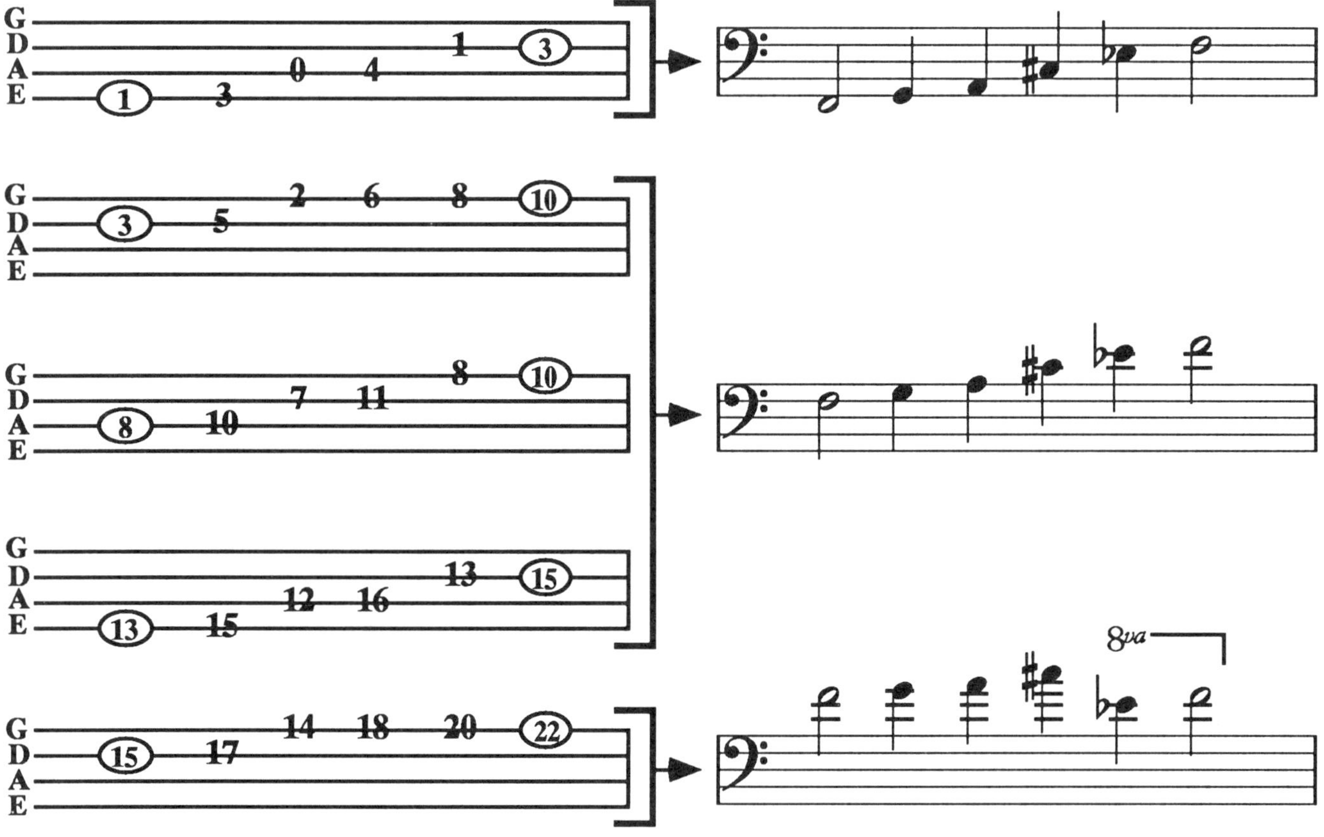

Riff

G NINTH AUG 5TH

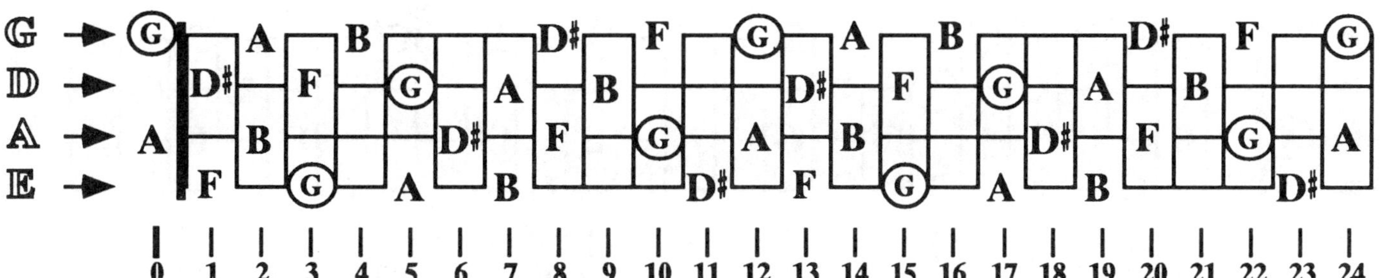

Positions

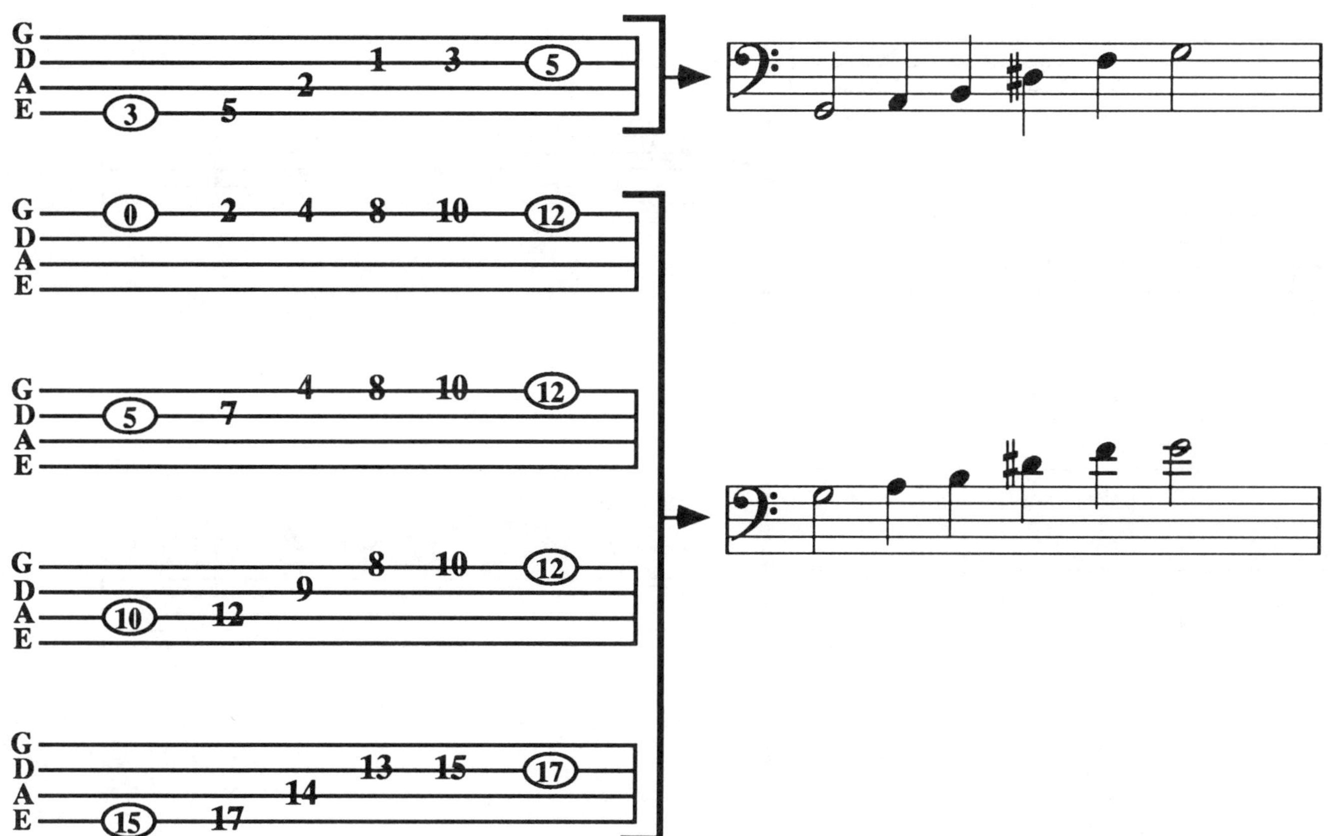

Riff

A   NINTH AUG 5TH

FORMULA - (A) Root (C♯) 3rd (E♯) ♯5th (G) ♭7th (B) 9th

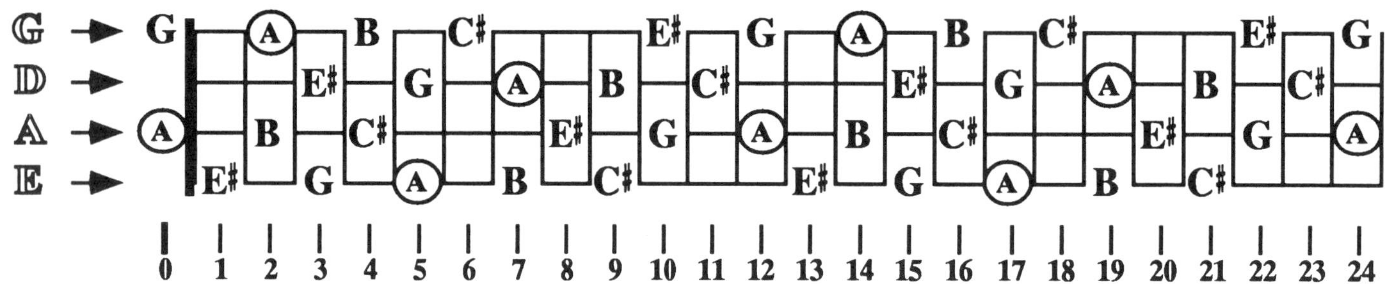

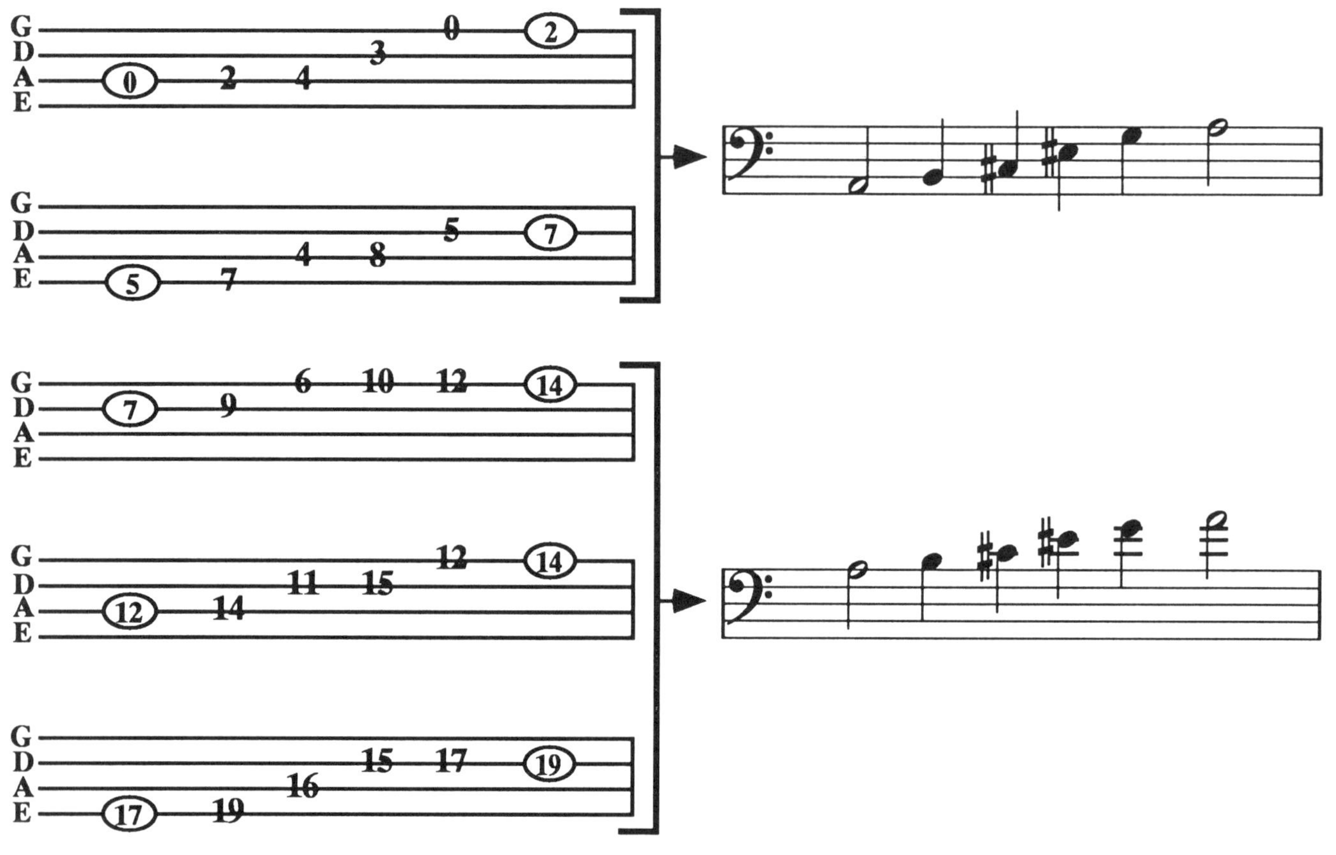

Positions

Riff

B NINTH AUG 5TH

FORMULA - (B) Root (D♯) 3rd (F×) ♯5th (A) ♭7th (C♯) 9th

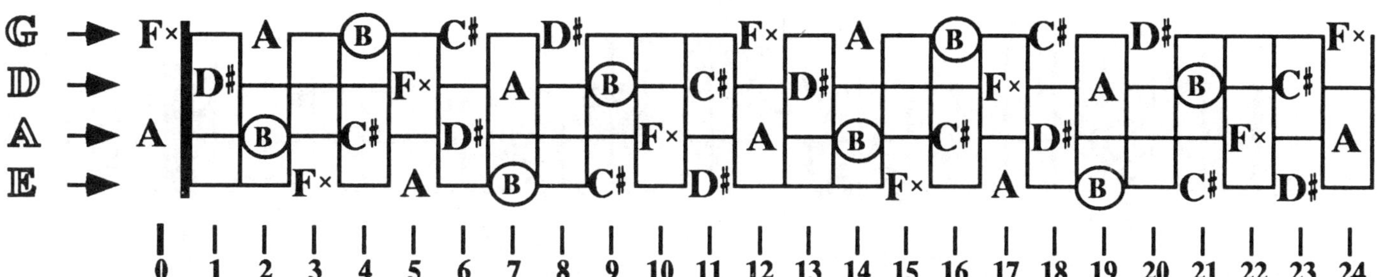

Positions

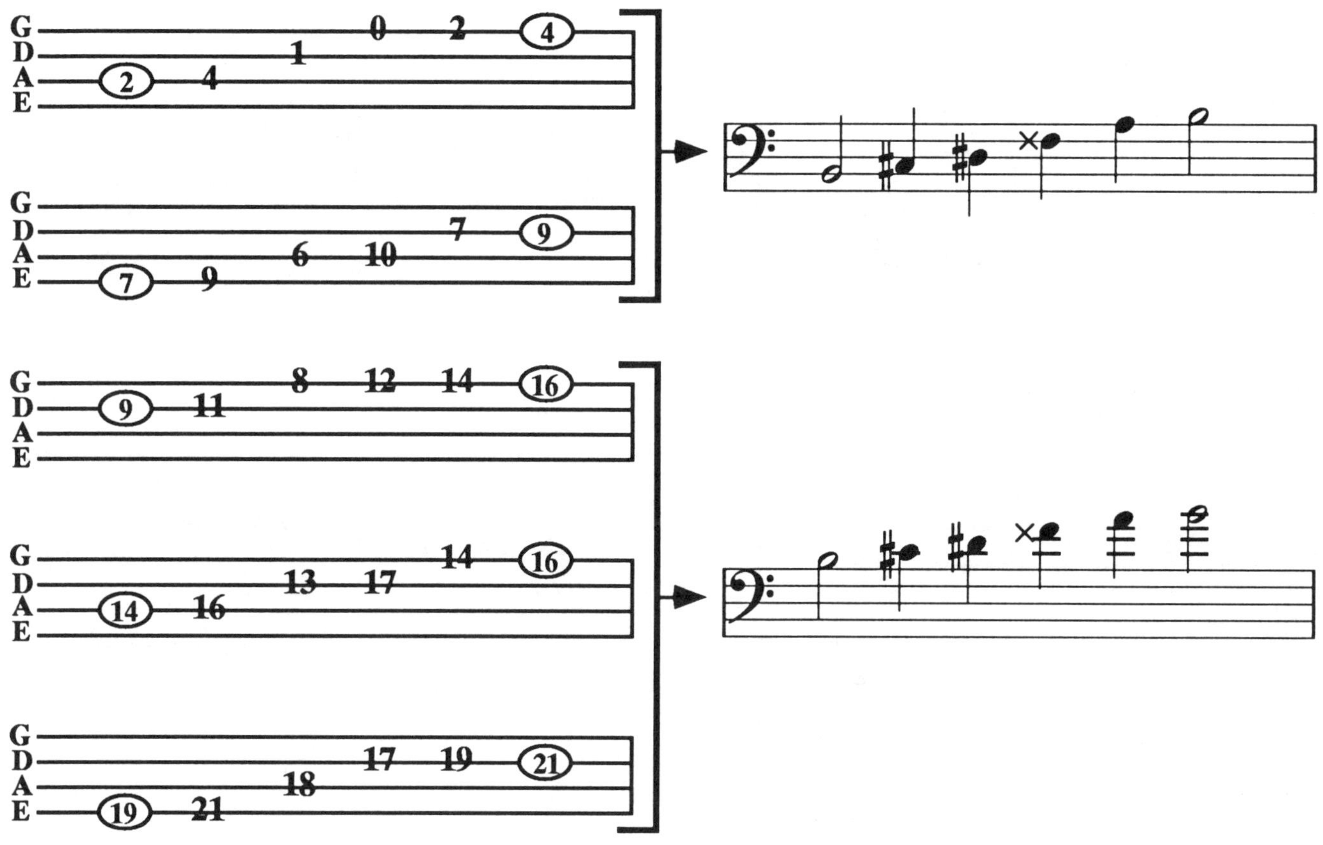

Riff

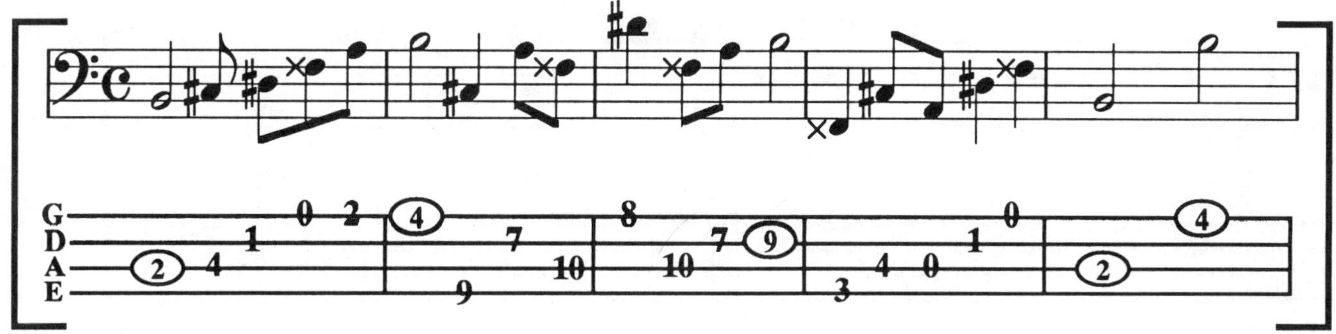

C SEVENTH ♭9TH

FORMULA - (C) Root (E) 3rd (G) 5th (B♭) ♭7th (D♭) ♭9th

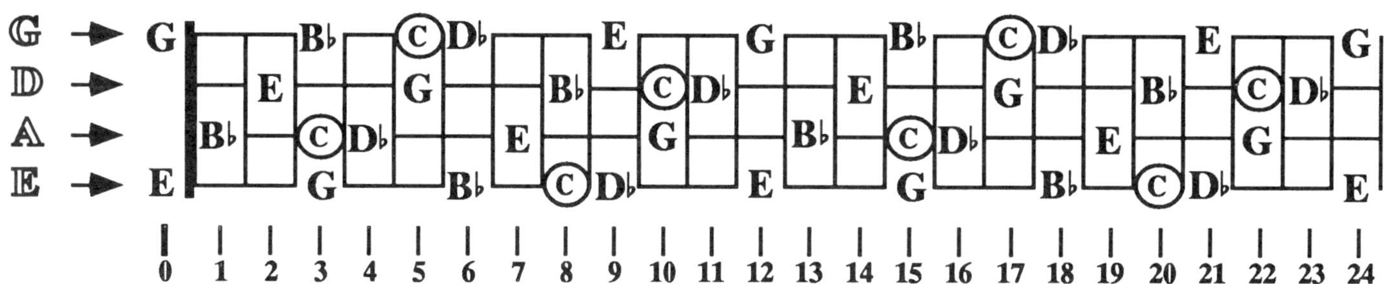

Positions

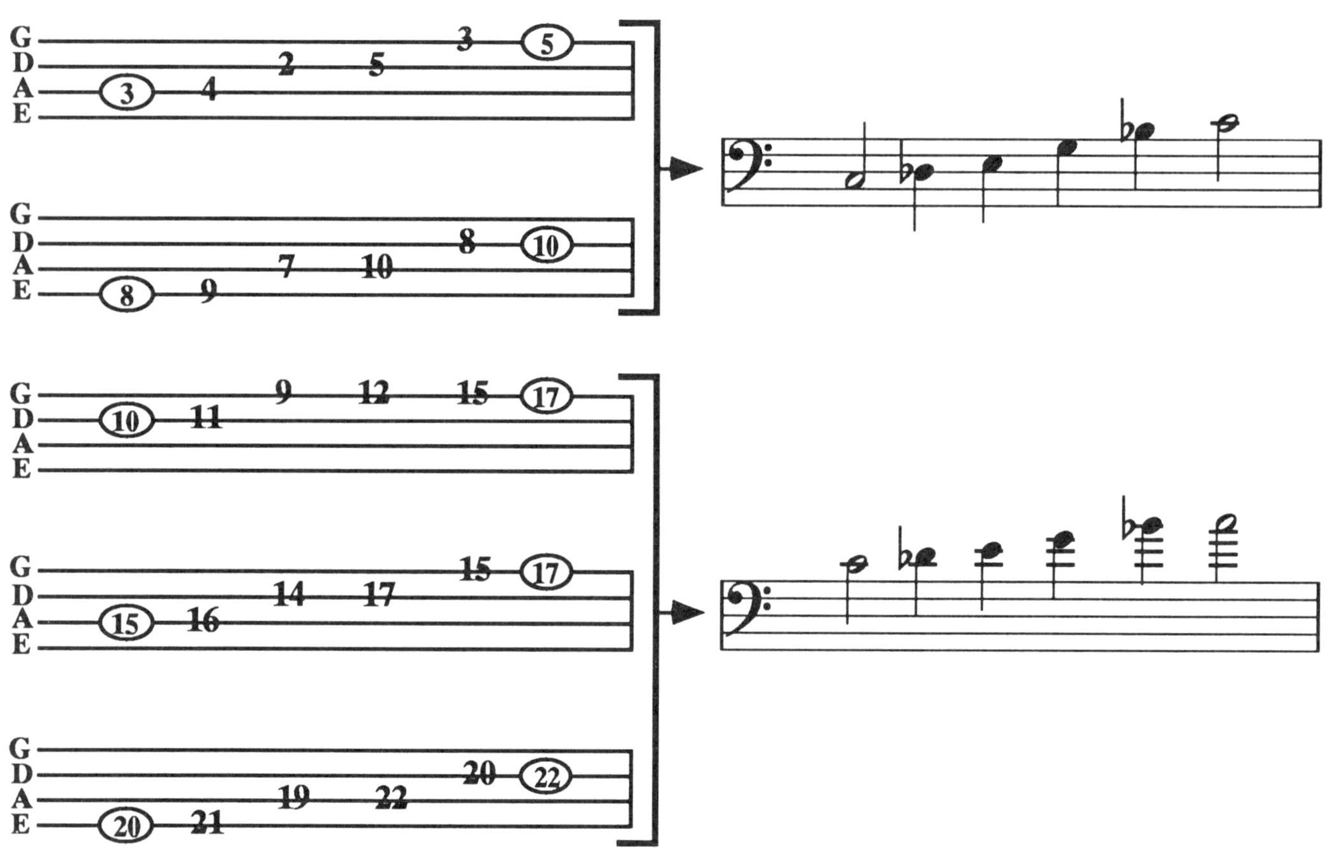

Riff

D SEVENTH ♭9TH

FORMULA - (D) Root (F♯) 3rd (A) 5th (C) ♭7th (E♭) ♭9th

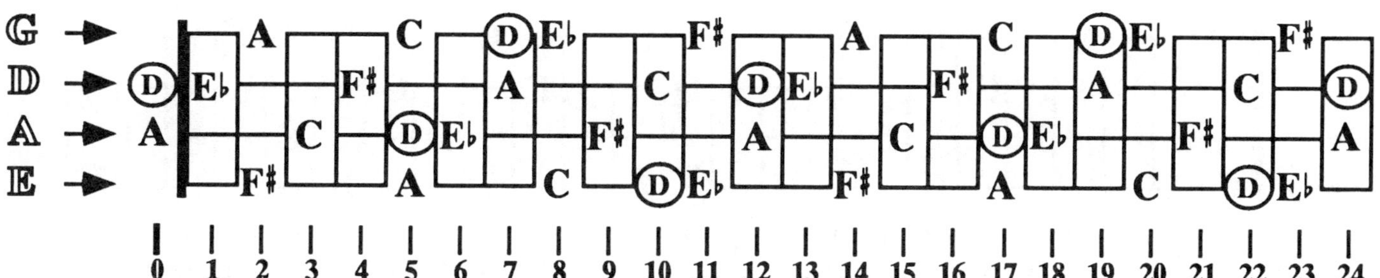

Positions

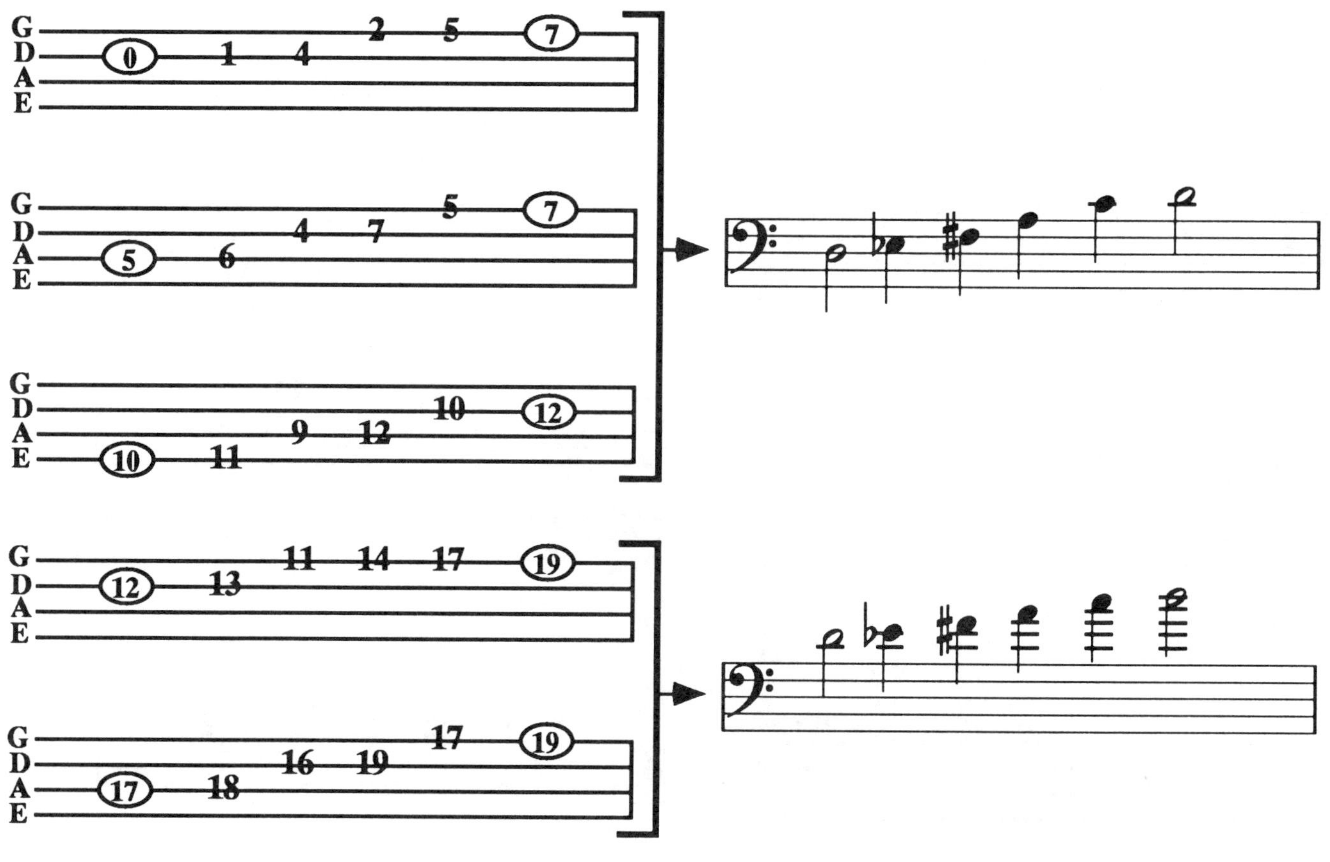

Riff

E SEVENTH ♭9TH

FORMULA - (E) Root (G♯) 3rd (B) 5th (D) ♭7th (F) ♭9th

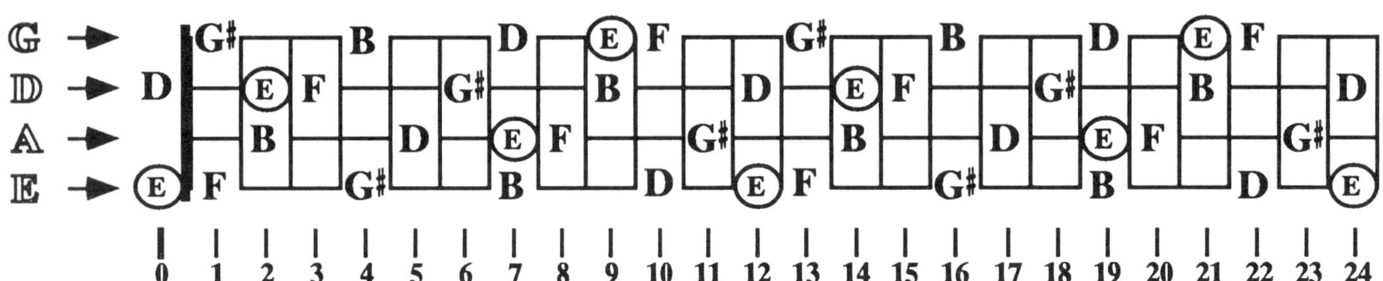

Positions

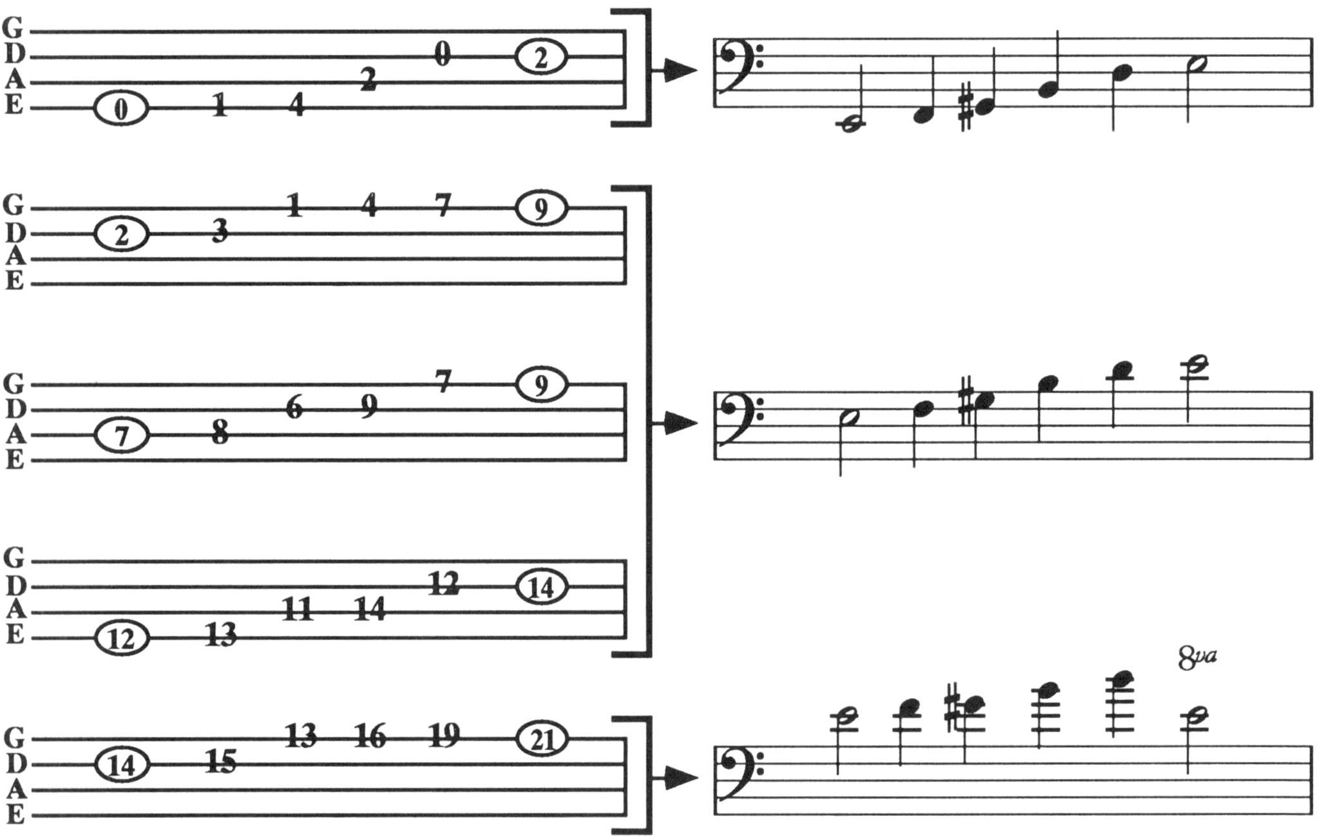

Riff

F SEVENTH ♭9TH

FORMULA - (F) Root (A) 3rd (C) 5th (E♭) ♭7th (G♭) ♭9th

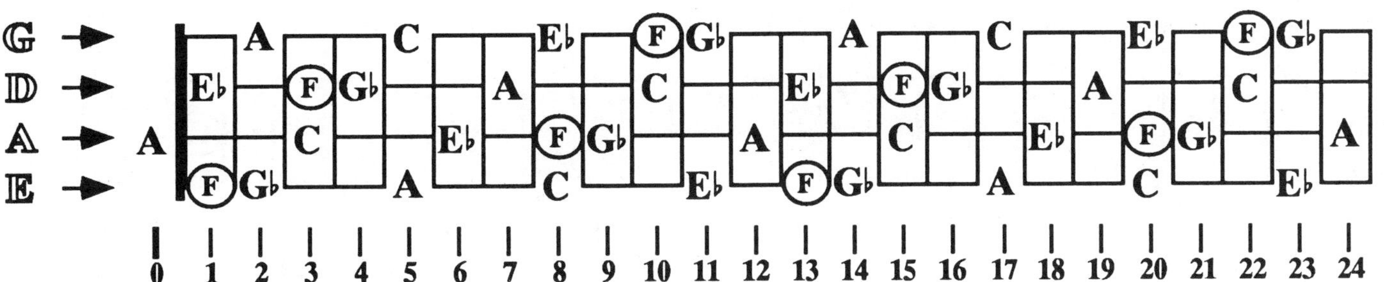

Positions

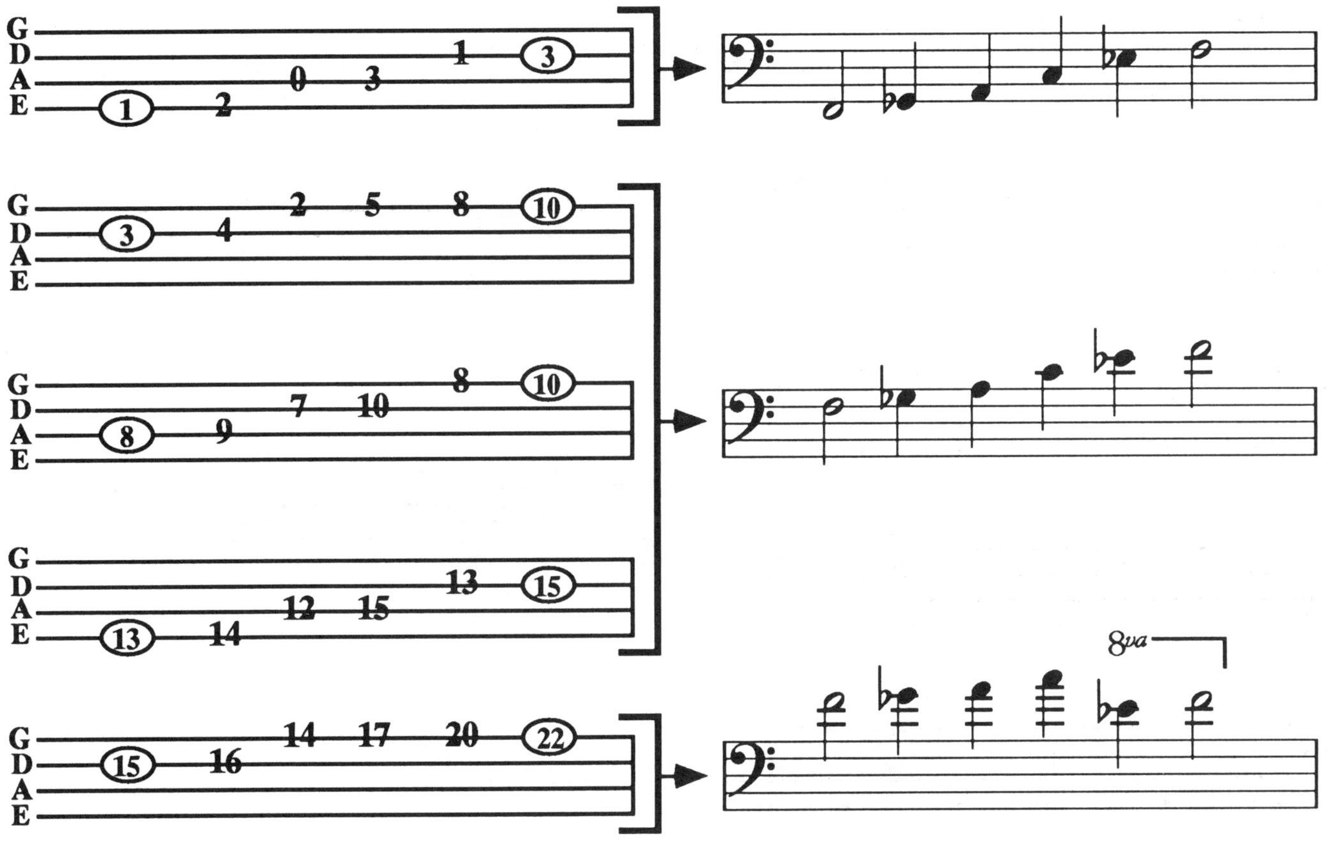

Riff

G SEVENTH♭9TH

FORMULA - (G) Root (B) 3rd (D) 5th (F) ♭7th (A♭) ♭9th

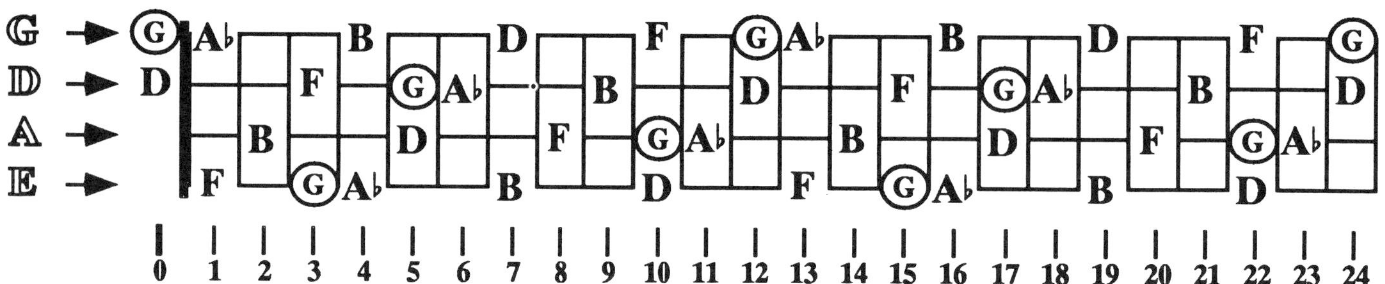

Positions

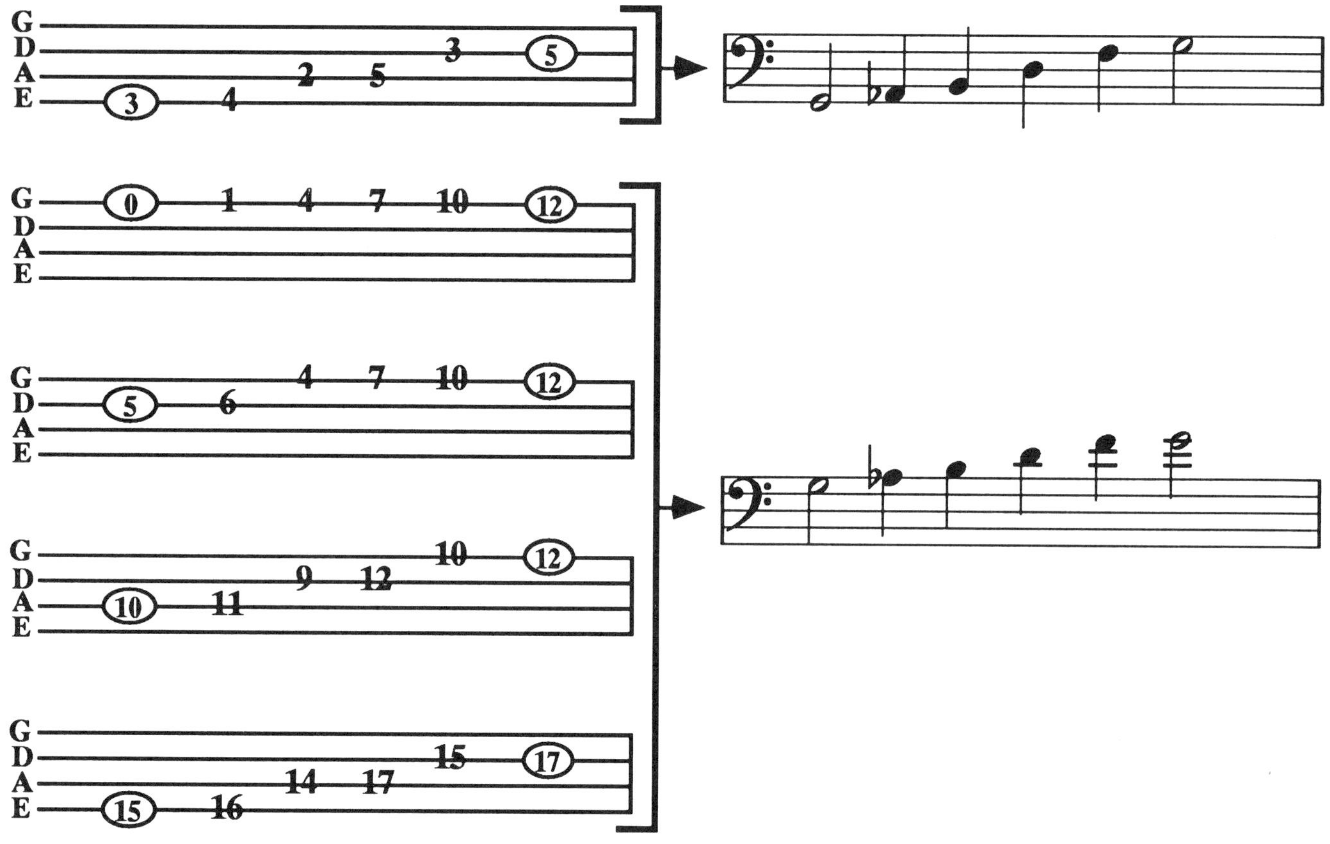

Riff

166

A SEVENTH ♭9TH

FORMULA - (A) Root (C♯) 3rd (E) 5th (G) ♭7th (B♭) ♭9th

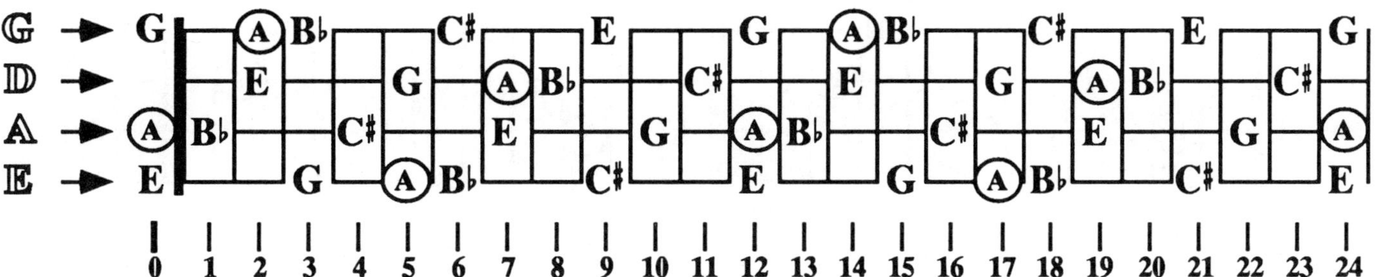

Positions

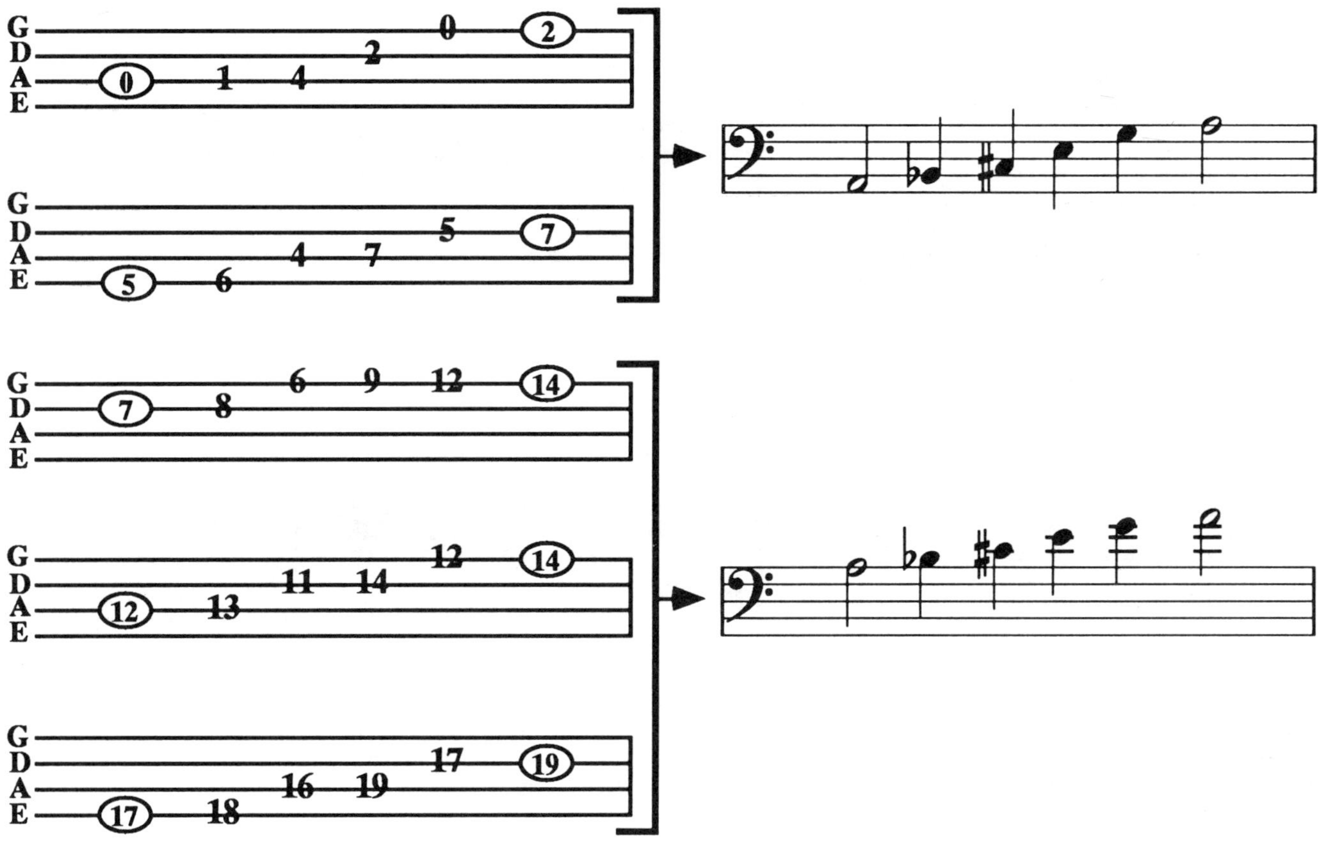

Riff

B SEVENTH ♭9TH

B7-9

FORMULA - (B) Root (D♯) 3rd (F♯) 5th (A) ♭7th (C) ♭9th

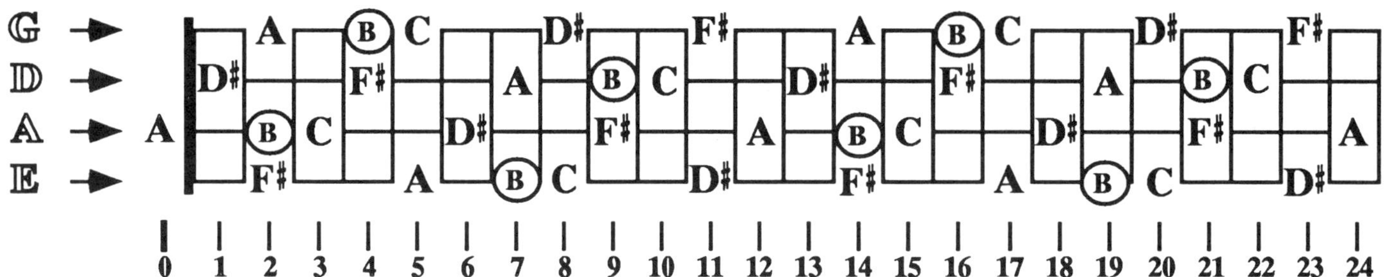

Positions

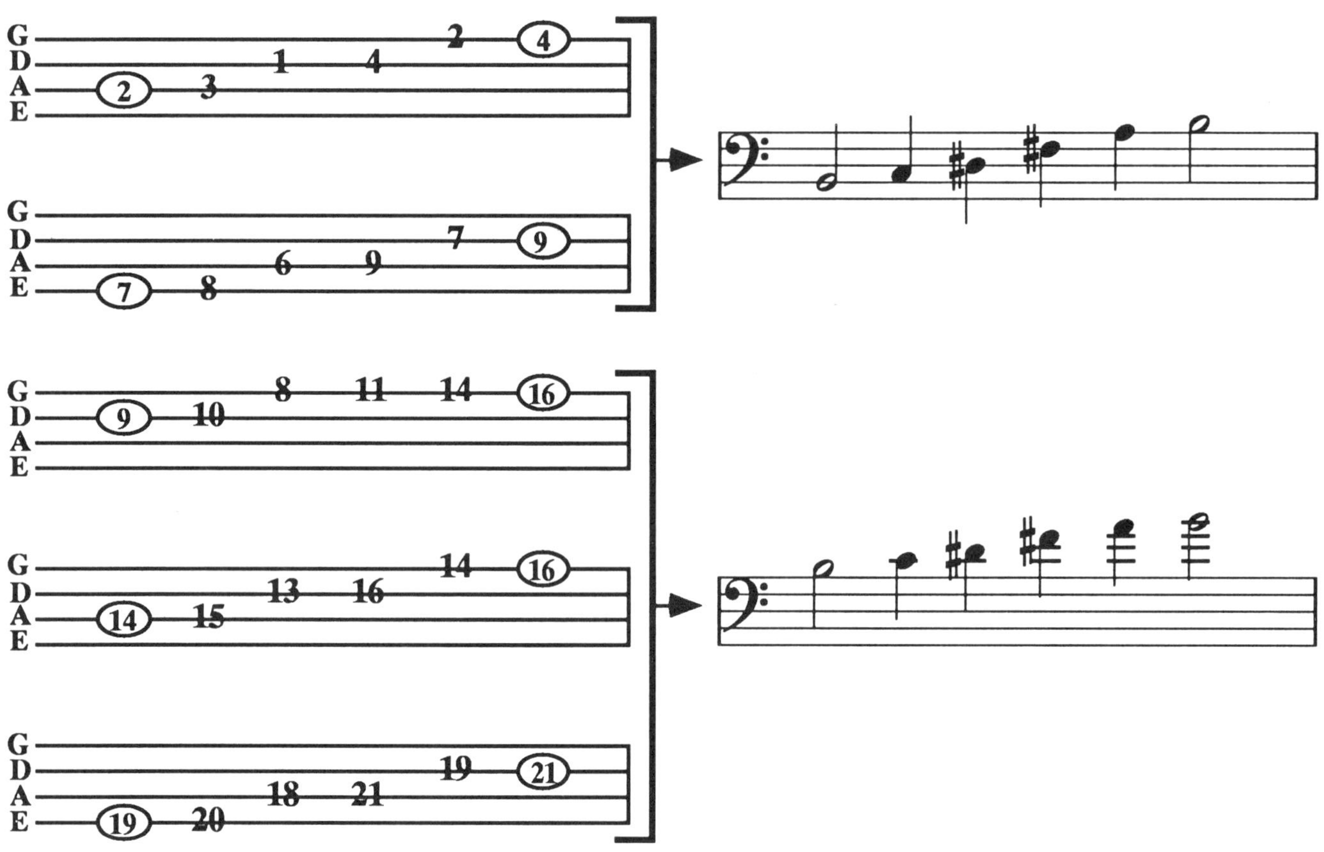

Riff

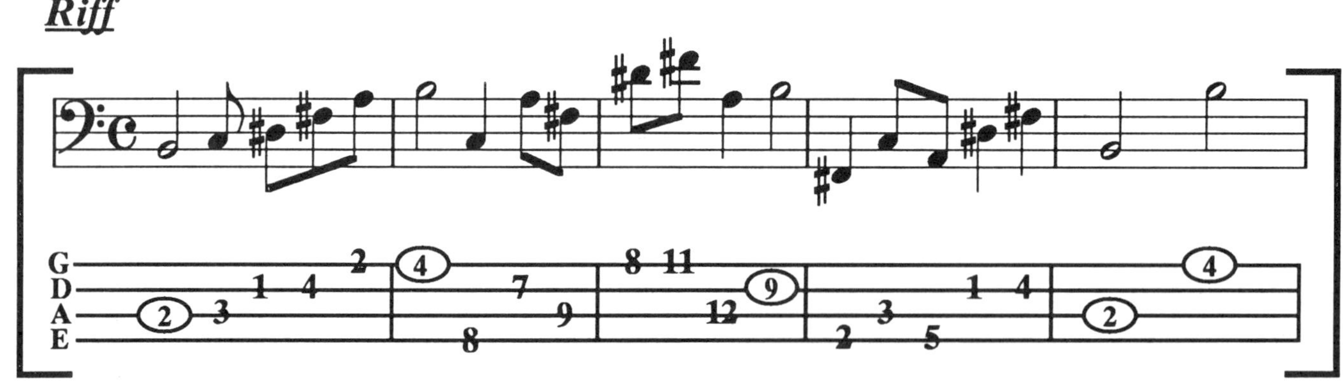

C SEVENTH ♭9TH ♭5TH

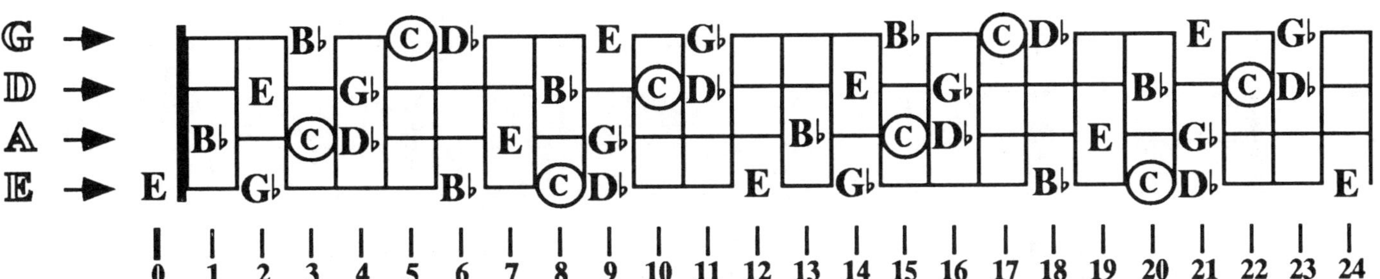

Positions

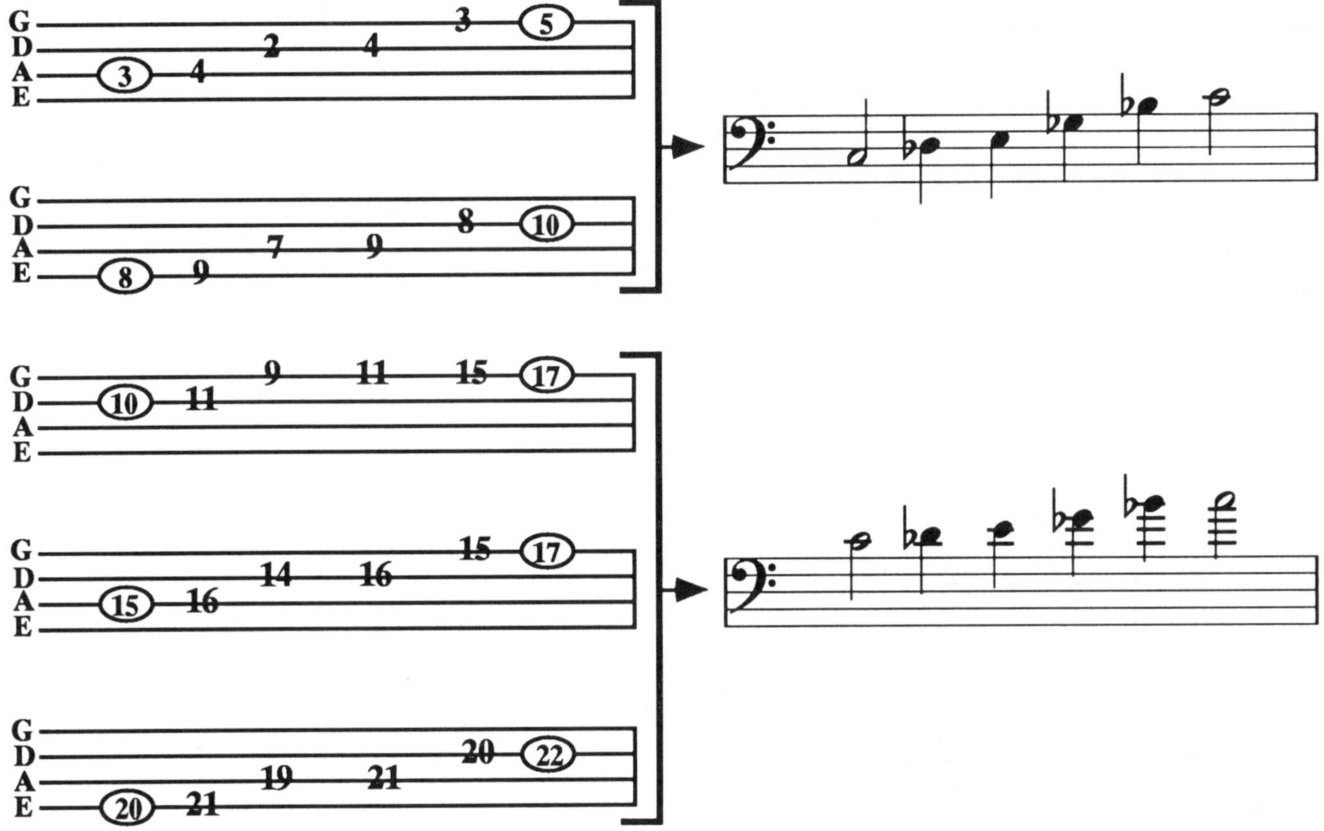

Riff

D SEVENTH ♭9TH ♭5TH
FORMULA - (D) Root (F♯) 3rd (A♭) ♭5th (C) ♭7th (E♭) ♭9th

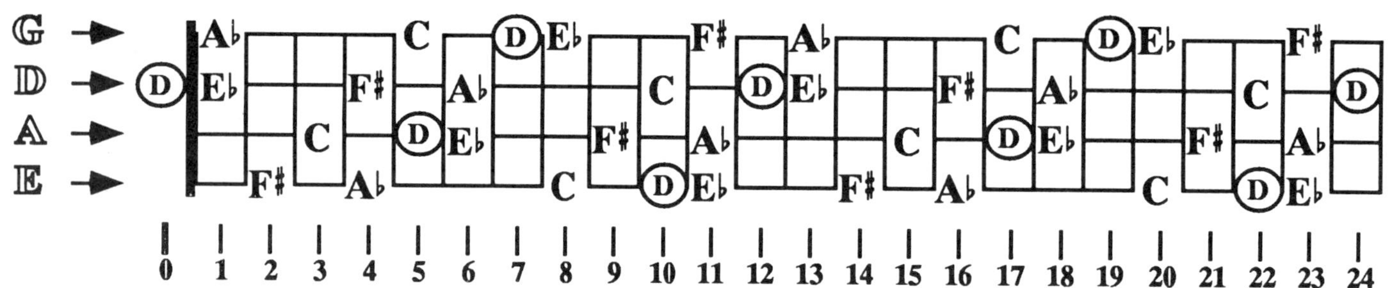

Positions

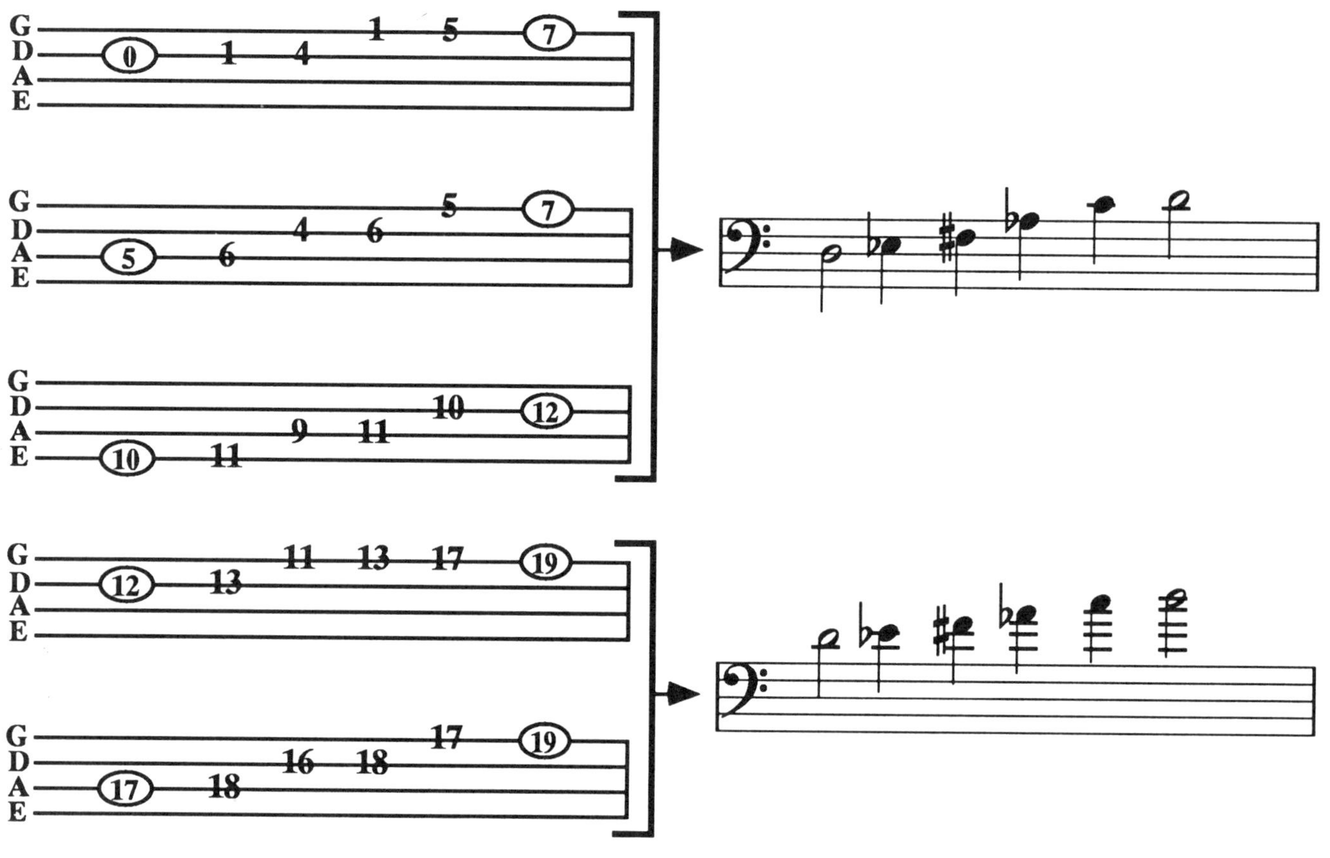

Riff

E SEVENTH ♭9TH ♭5TH

FORMULA - (E) Root (G♯) 3rd (B♭) ♭5th (D) ♭7th (F) ♭9th

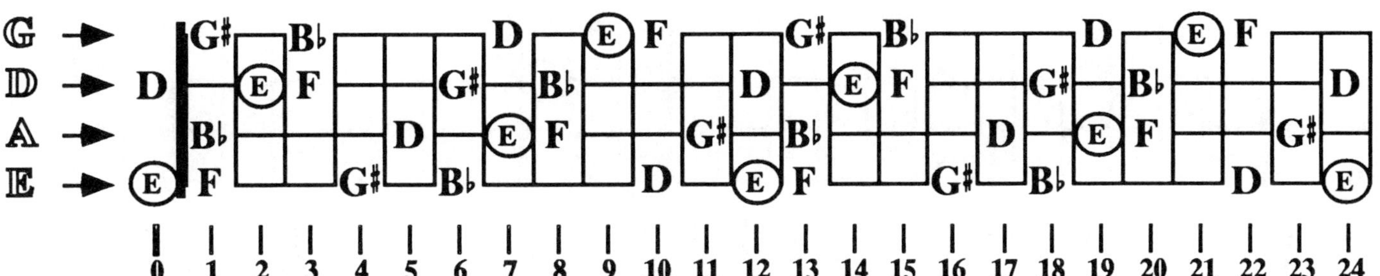

Positions

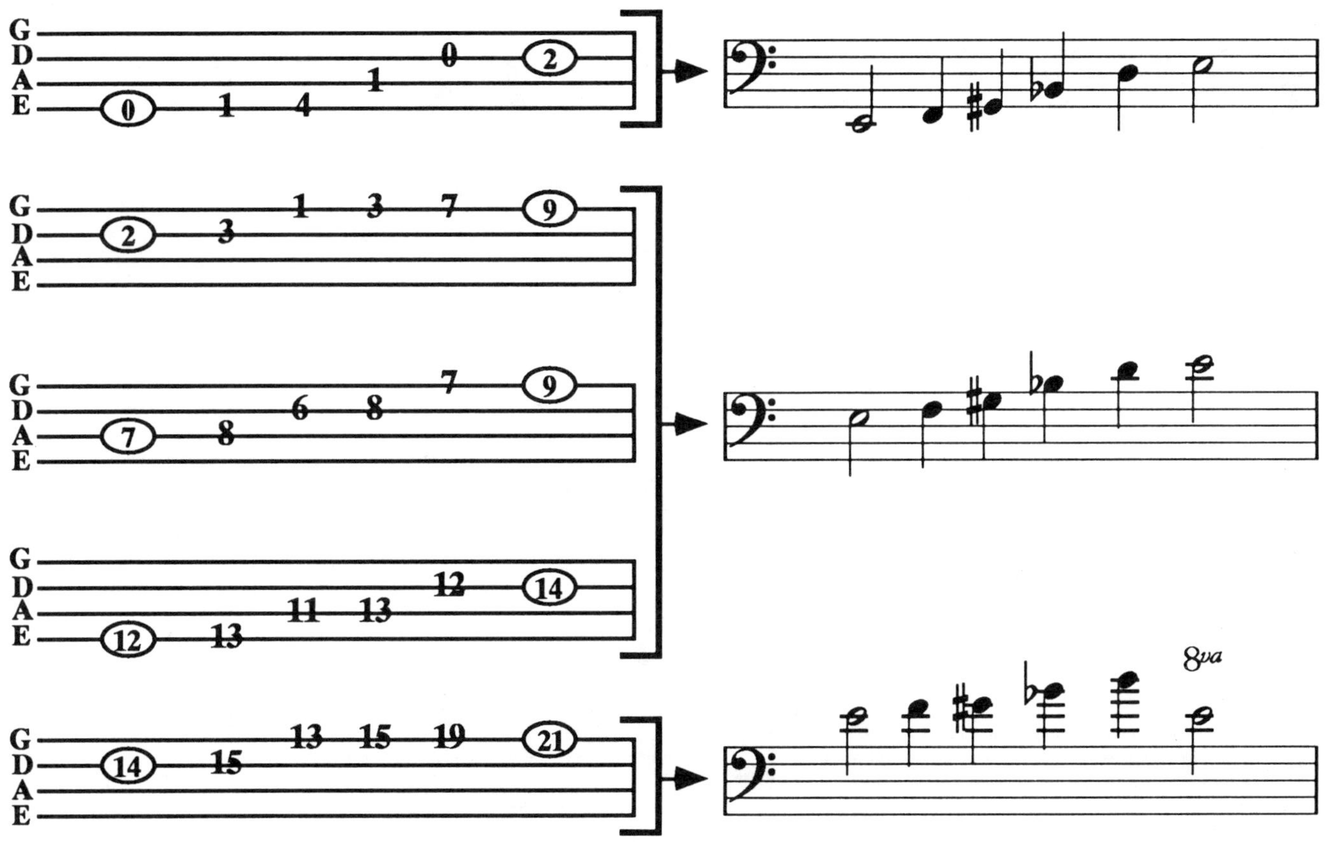

Riff

F SEVENTH ♭9TH ♭5TH
FORMULA - (F) Root (A) 3rd (C♭) ♭5th (E♭) ♭7th (G♭) ♭9th

F7-9-5

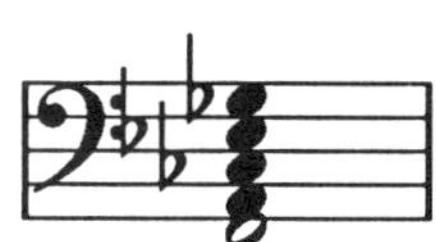

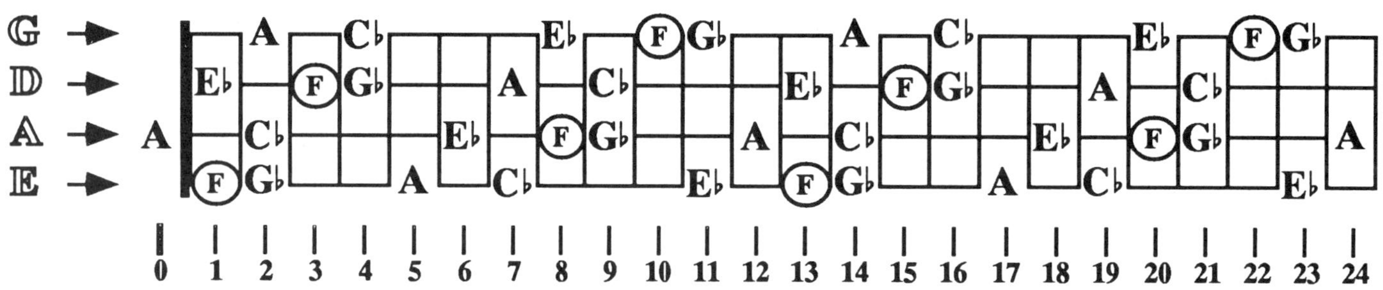

Positions

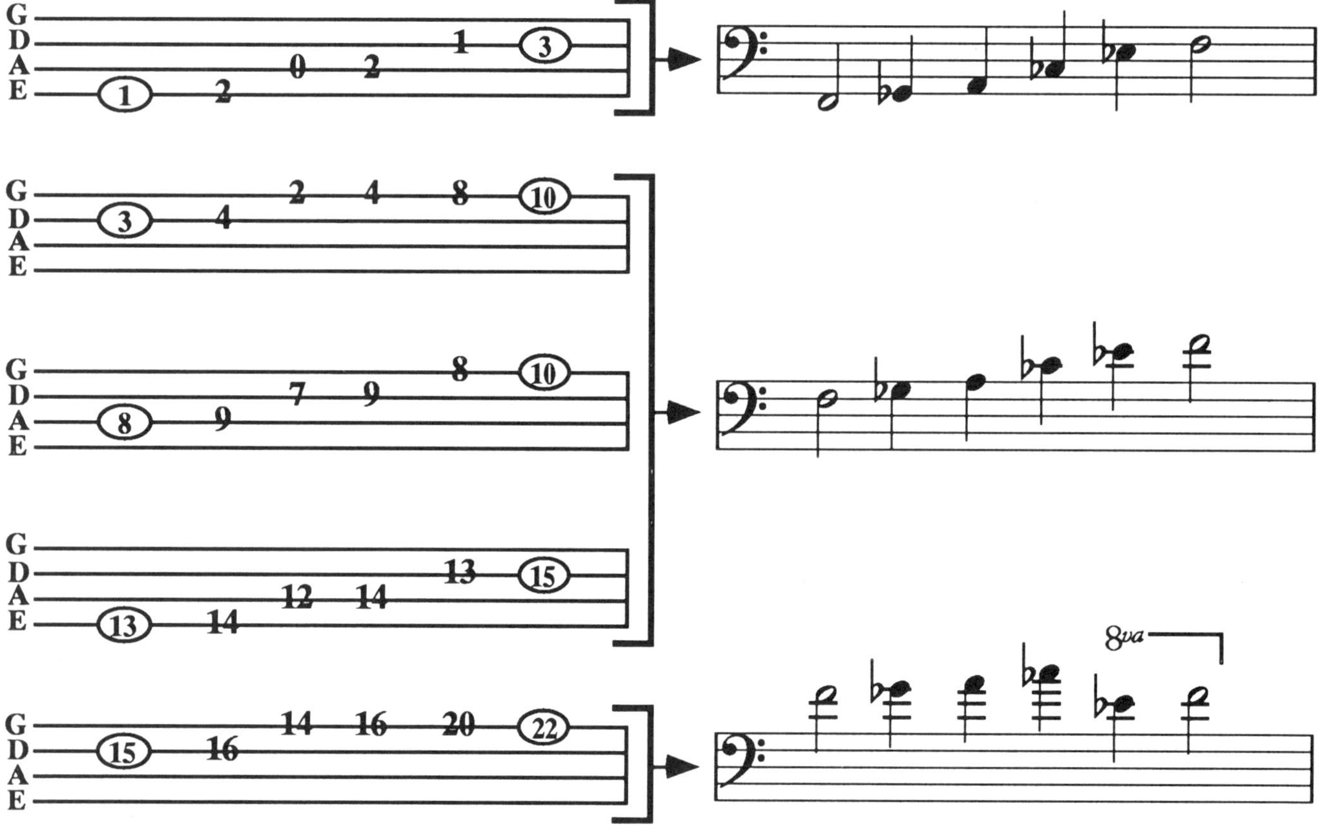

Riff

G SEVENTH ♭9TH ♭5TH

FORMULA - (G) Root (B) 3rd (D♭) ♭5th (F) ♭7th (A♭) ♭9th

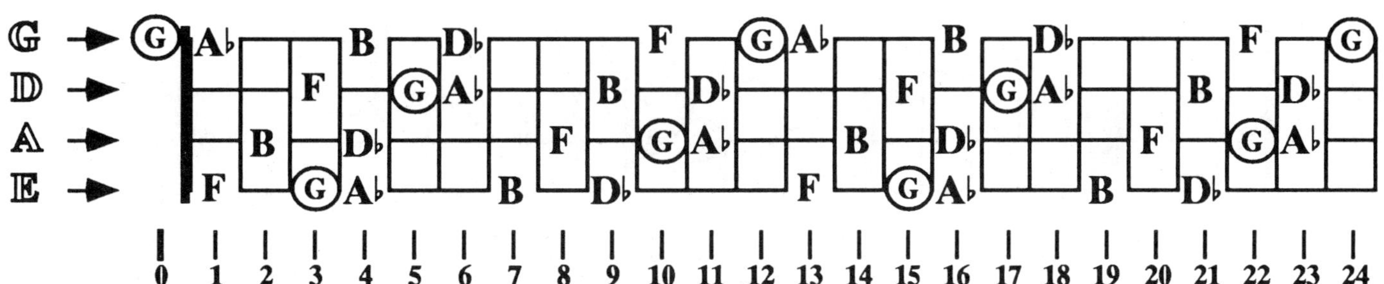

Positions

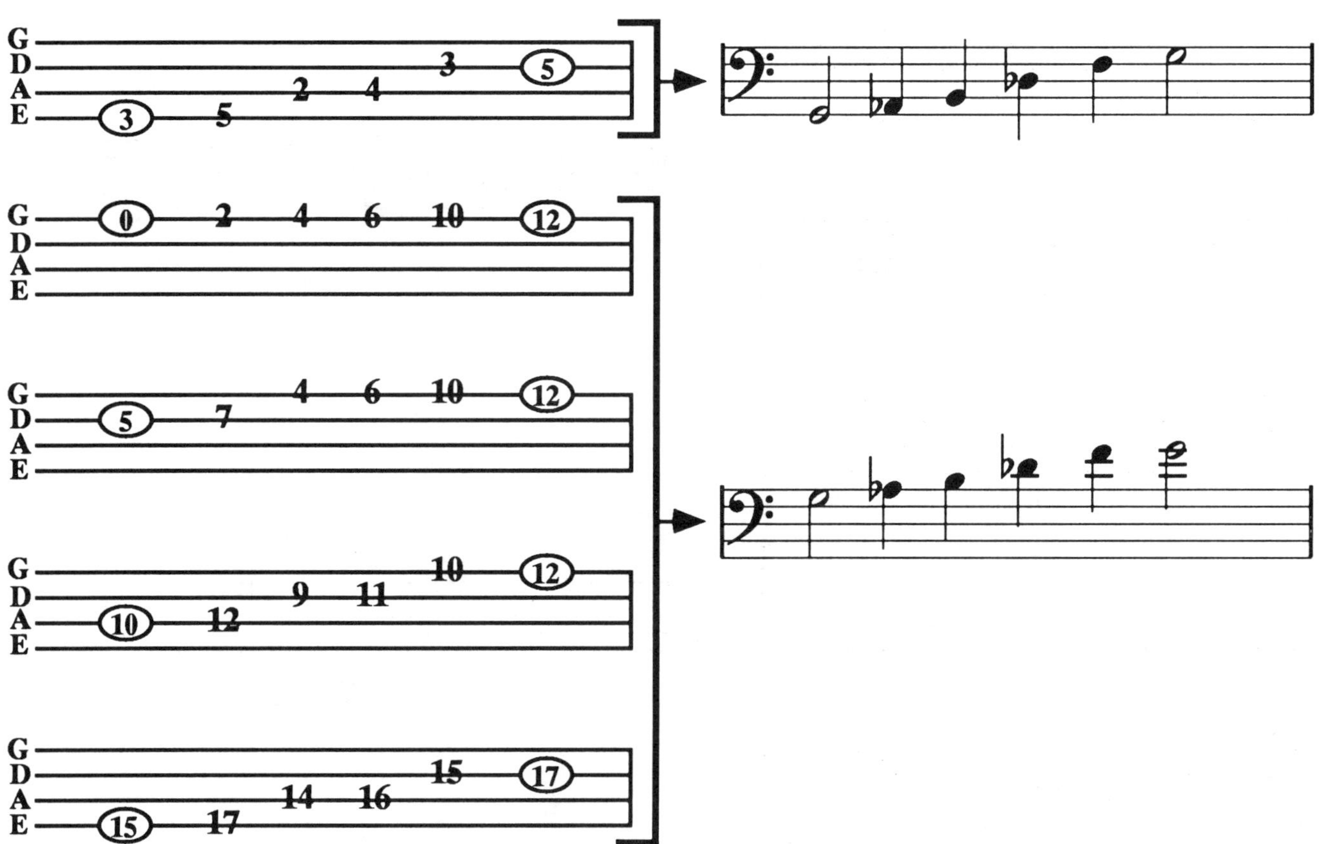

Riff

A SEVENTH ♭9TH ♭5TH

FORMULA - (A) Root (C♯) 3rd (E♭) ♭5th (G) ♭7th (B♭) ♭9th

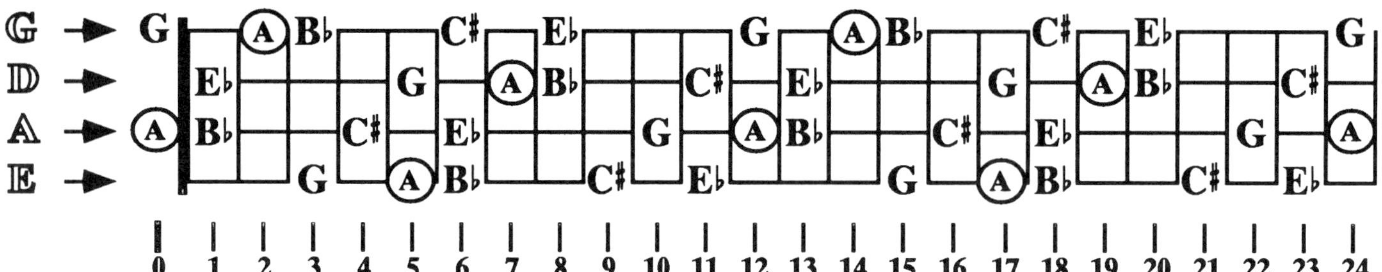

Positions

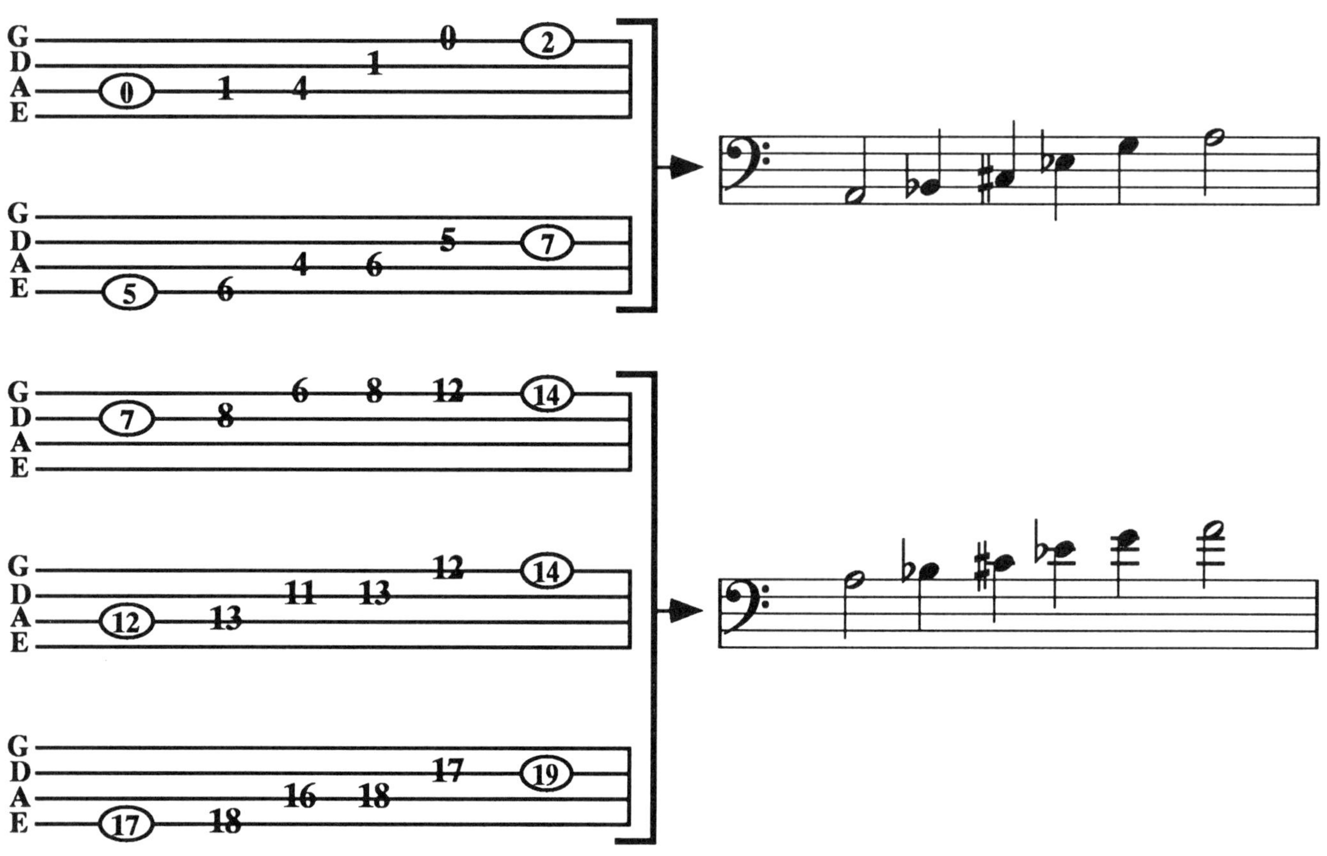

Riff

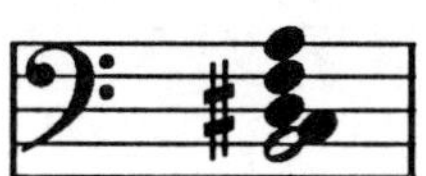

B SEVENTH ♭9TH ♭5TH

FORMULA - (B) Root (D♯) 3rd (F) ♭5th (A) ♭7th (C) ♭9th

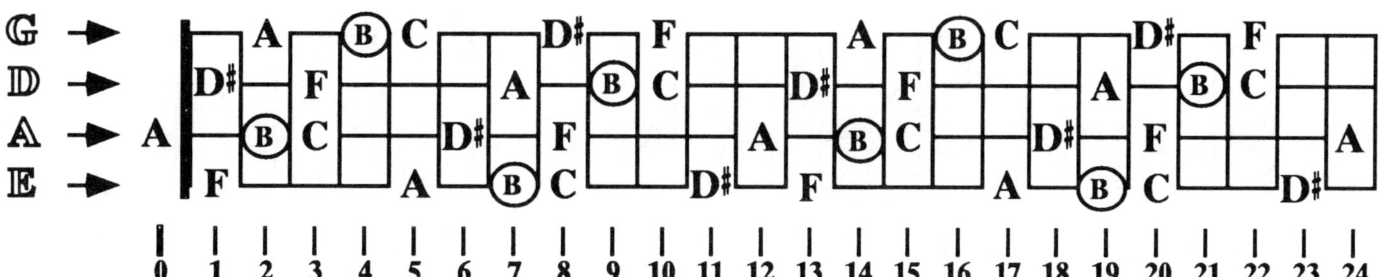

Positions

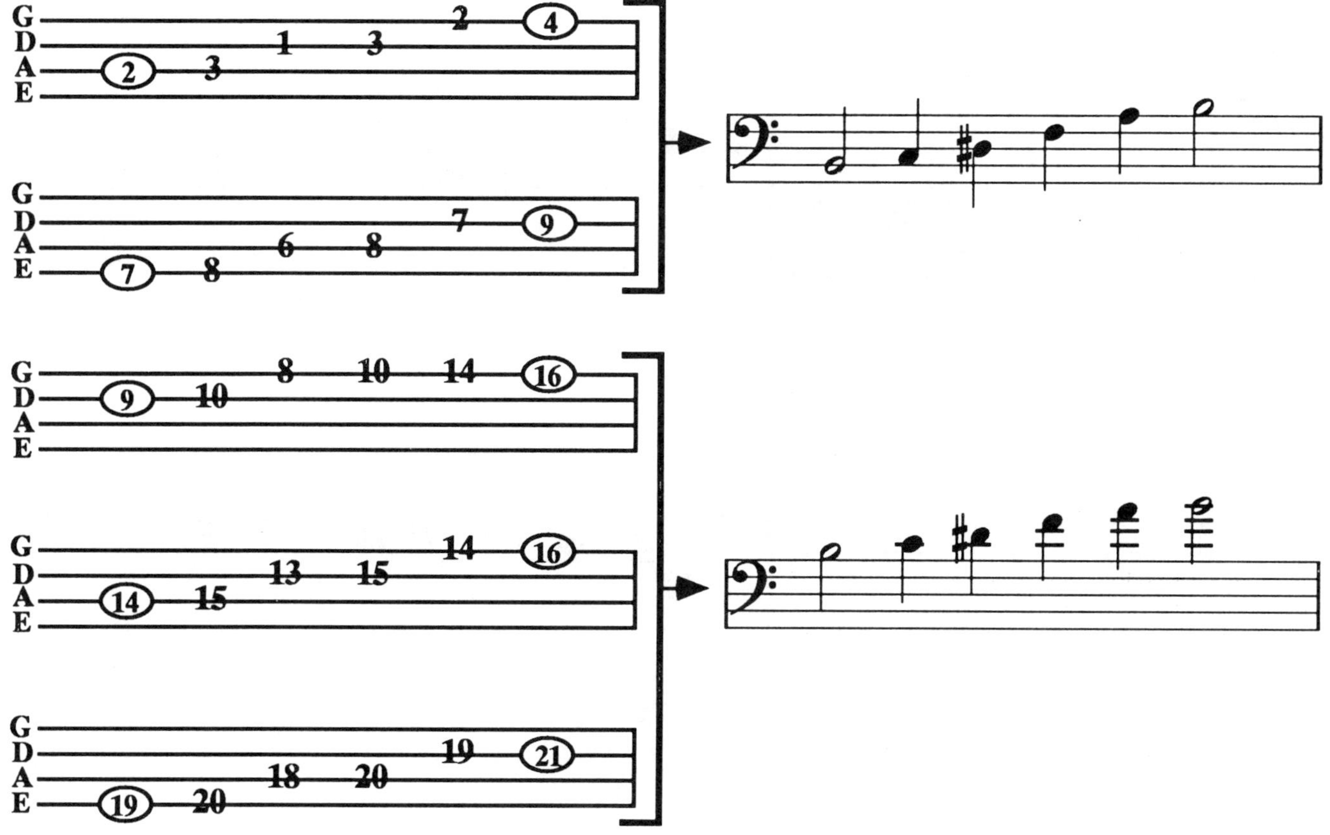

Riff

C SEVENTH ♭9TH AUG 5TH

C7-9+5

FORMULA - (C) Root (E) 3rd (G♯) ♯5th (B♭) ♭7th (D♭) ♭9th

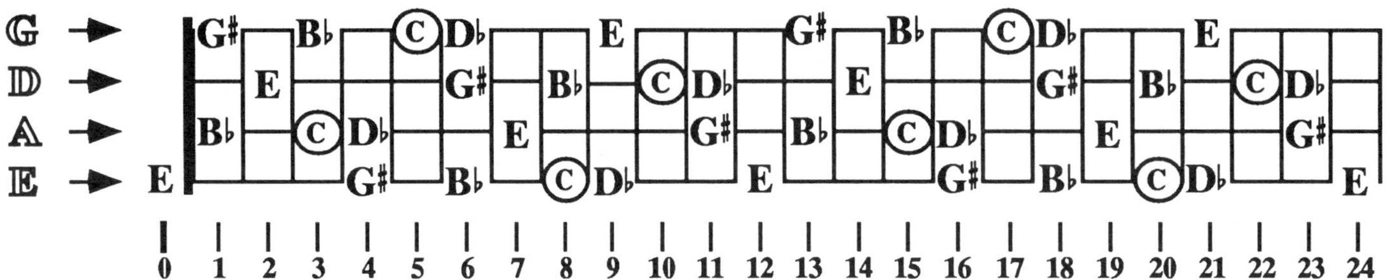

Positions

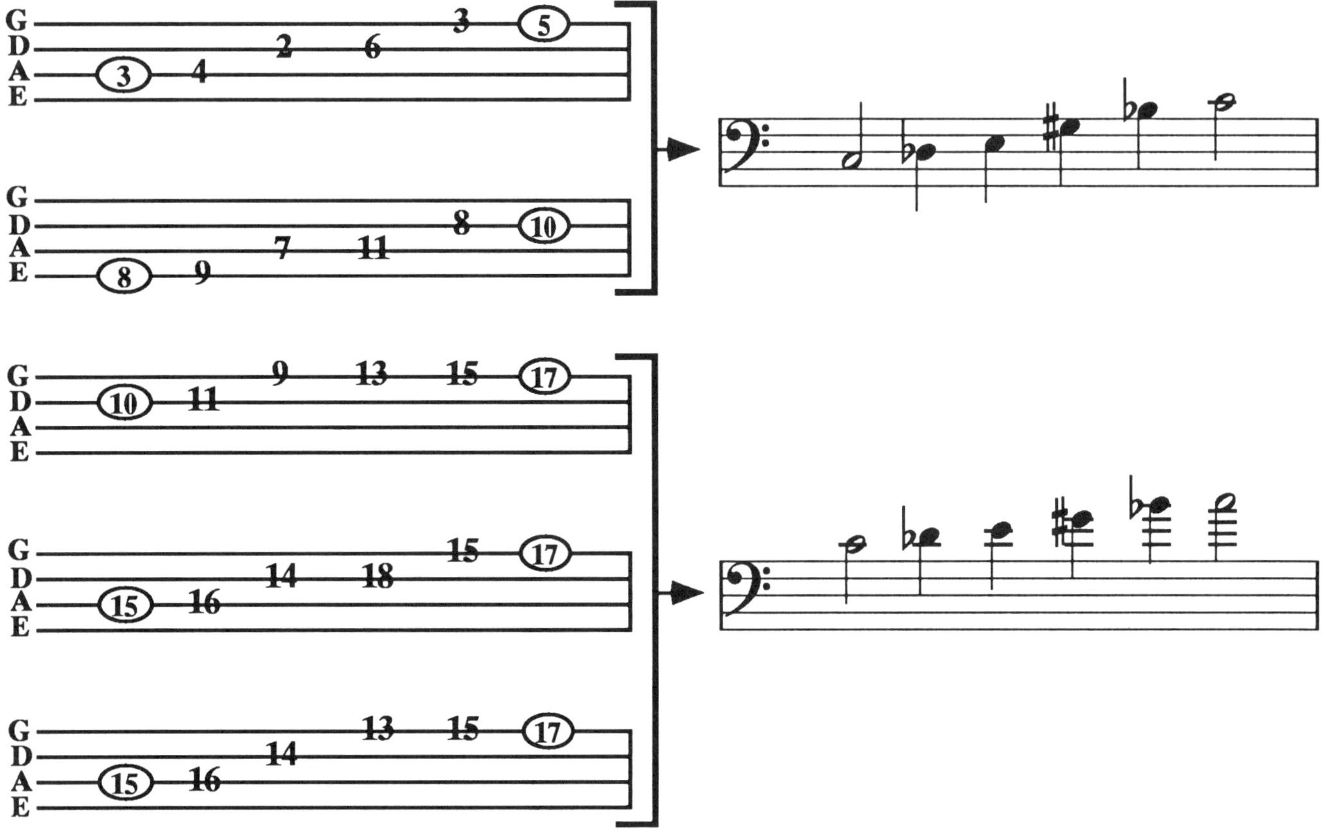

Riff

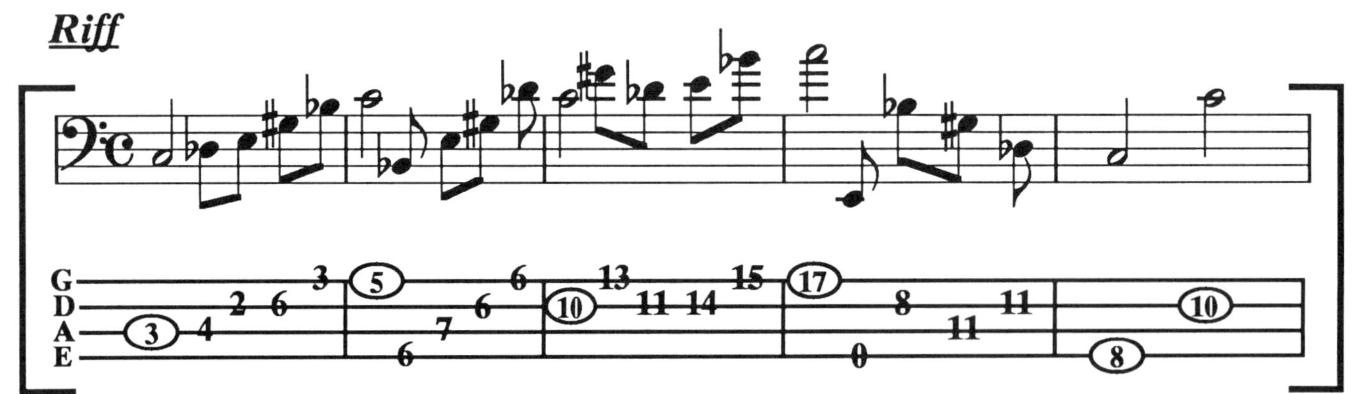

D SEVENTH ♭9TH AUG 5TH

FORMULA - (D) Root (F♯) 3rd (A♯) ♯5th (C) ♭7th (E♭) ♭9th

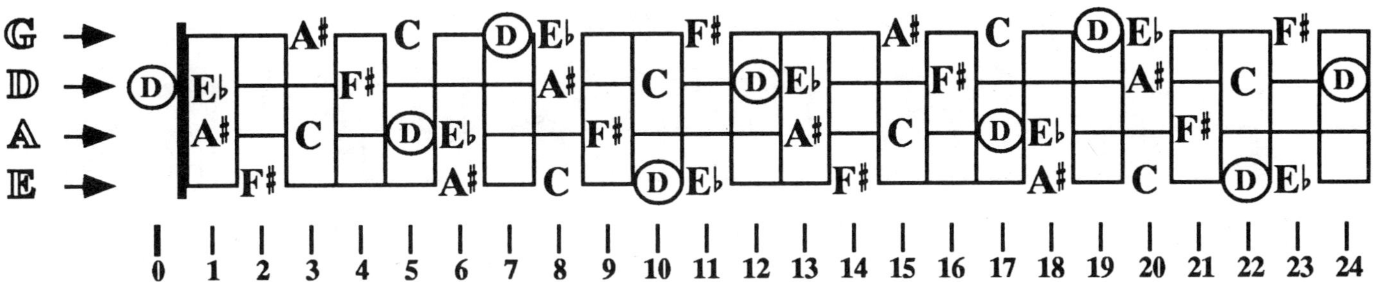

Positions

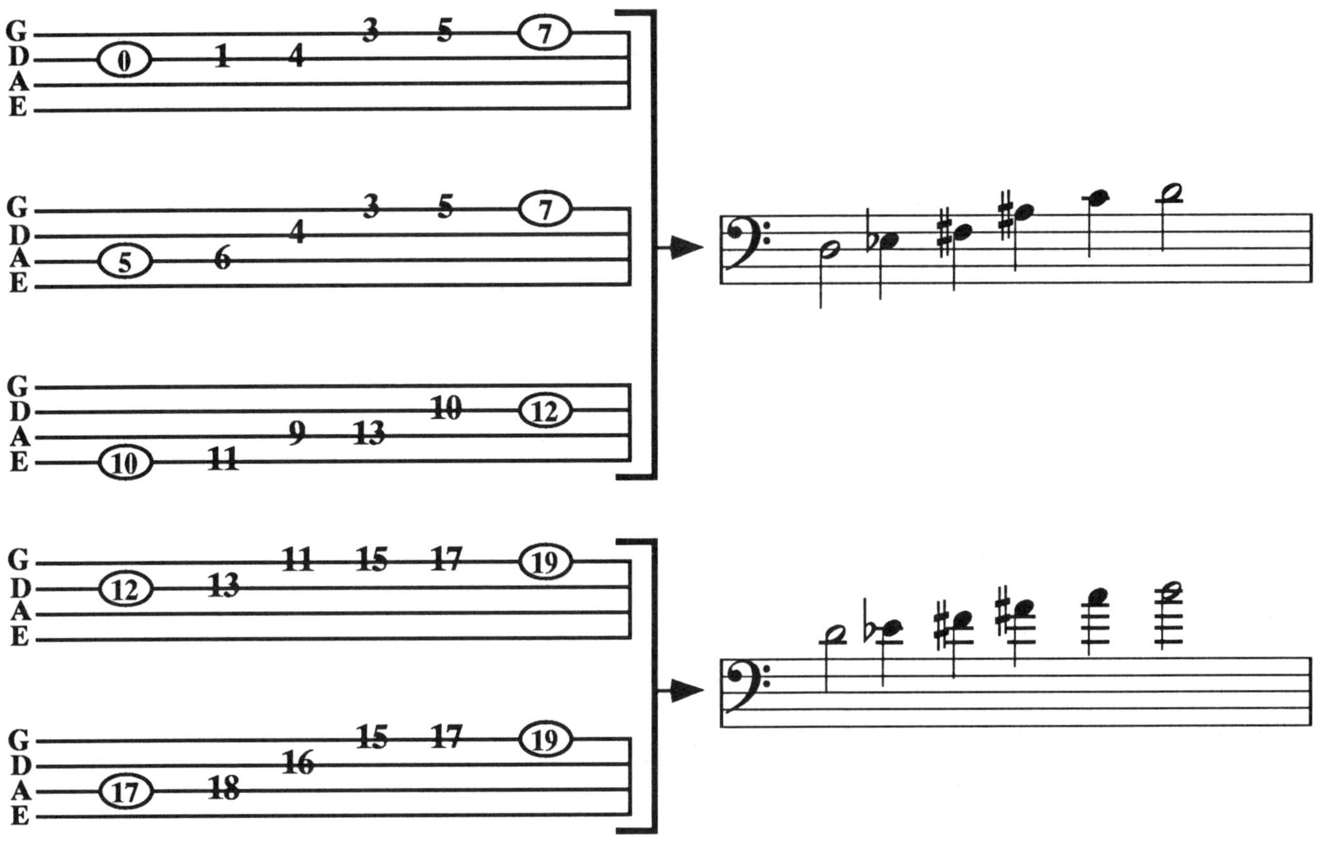

Riff

E SEVENTH ♭9TH AUG 5TH

FORMULA - (E) Root (G♯) 3rd (B♯) ♯5th (D) ♭7th (F) ♭9th

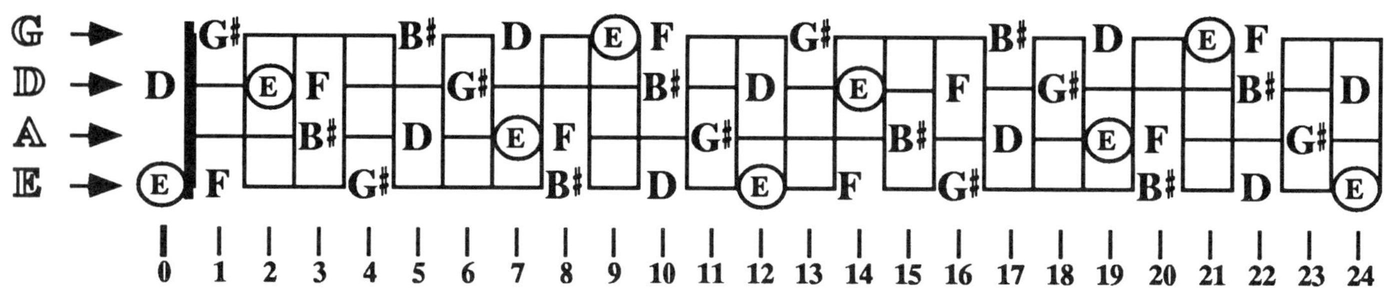

Positions

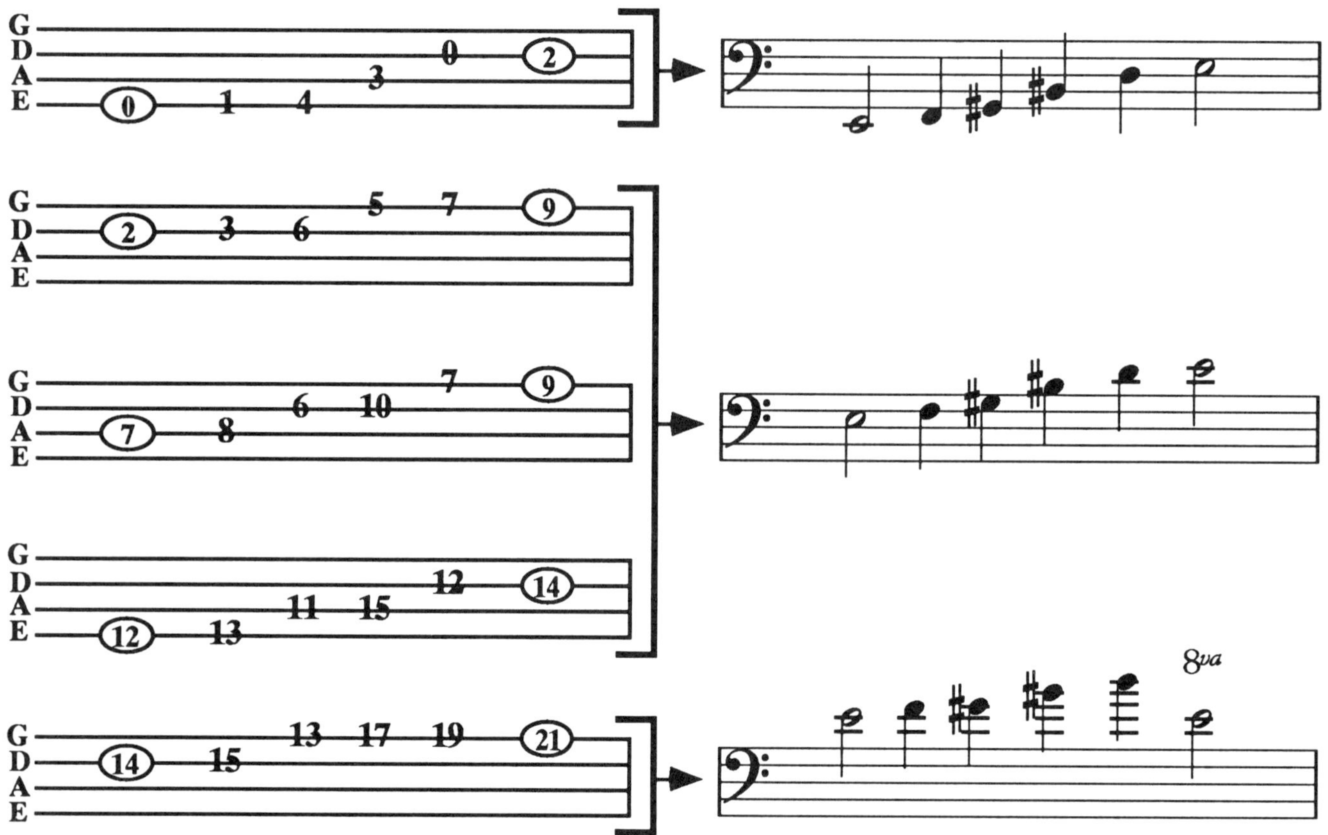

Riff

F SEVENTH ♭9TH AUG 5TH

FORMULA - (F) Root (A) 3rd (C♯) ♯5th (E♭) ♭7th (G♭) ♭9th

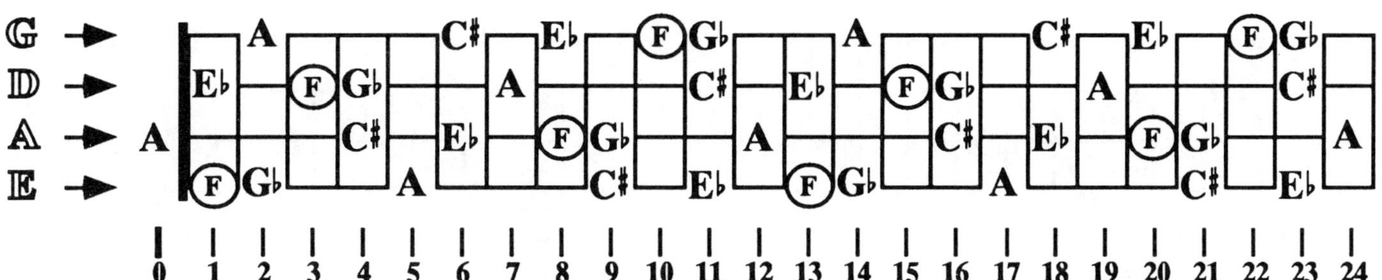

Positions

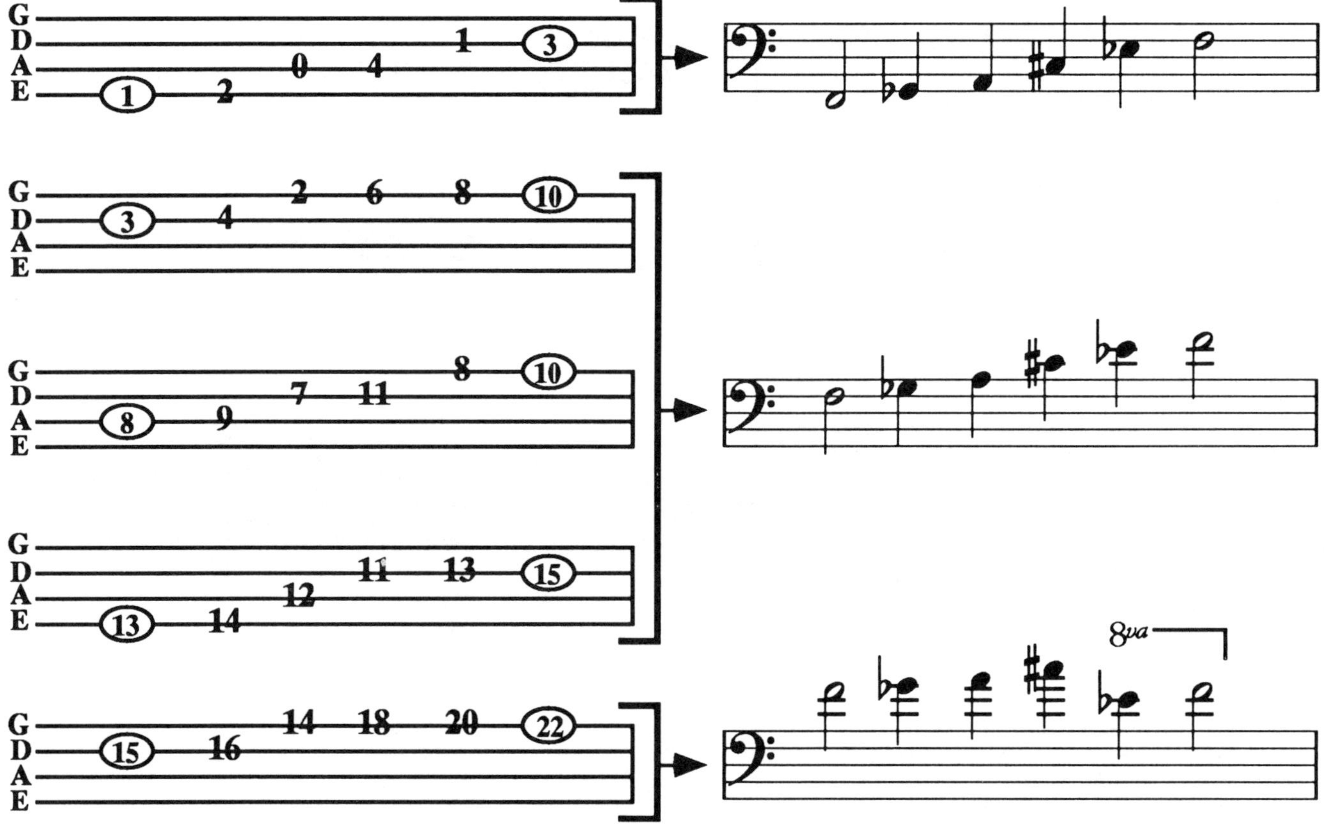

Riff

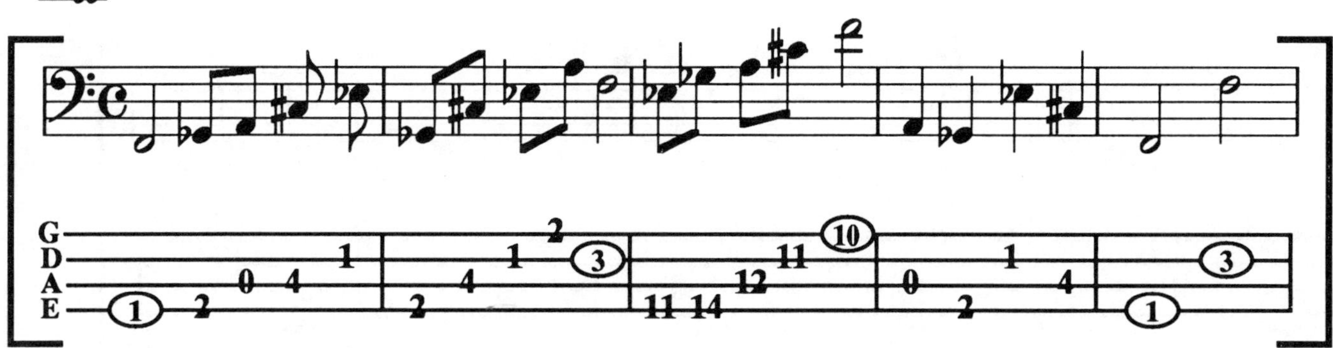

G SEVENTH ♭9TH AUG 5TH

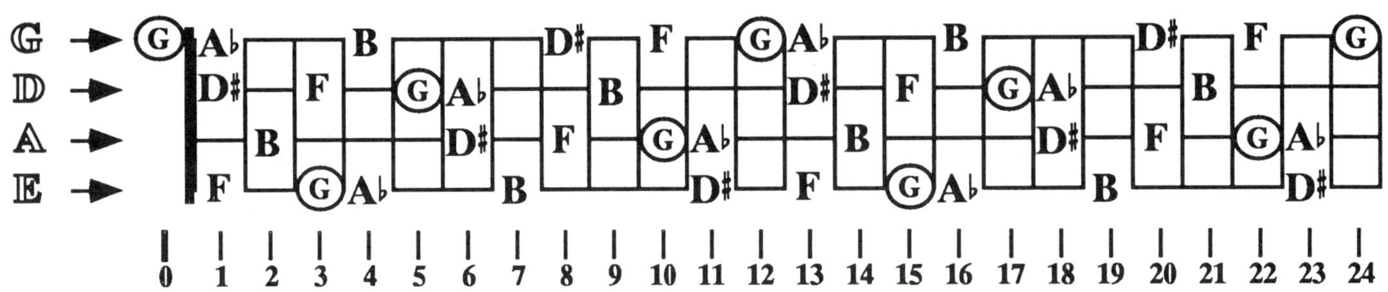

Positions

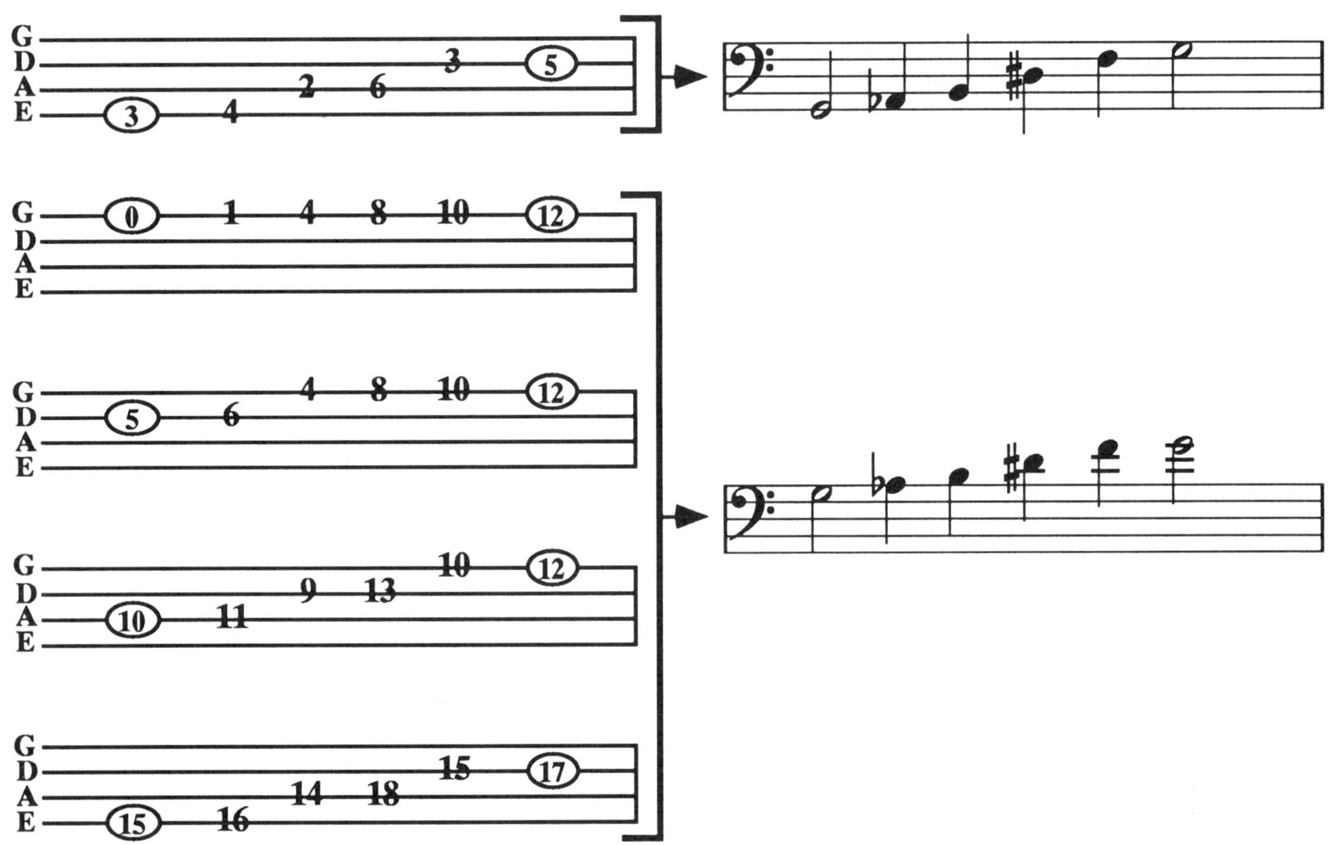

Riff

180

A   SEVENTH ♭9TH AUG 5TH

FORMULA - (A) Root (C♯) 3rd (E♯) ♯5th (G) ♭7th (B♭) ♭9th

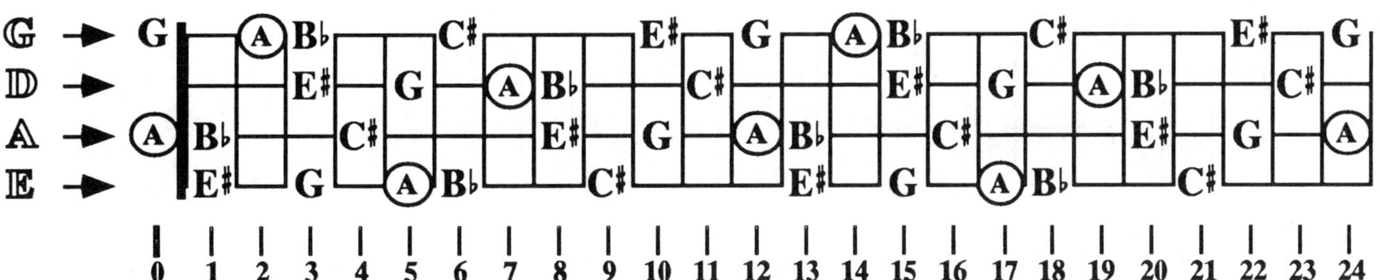

Positions

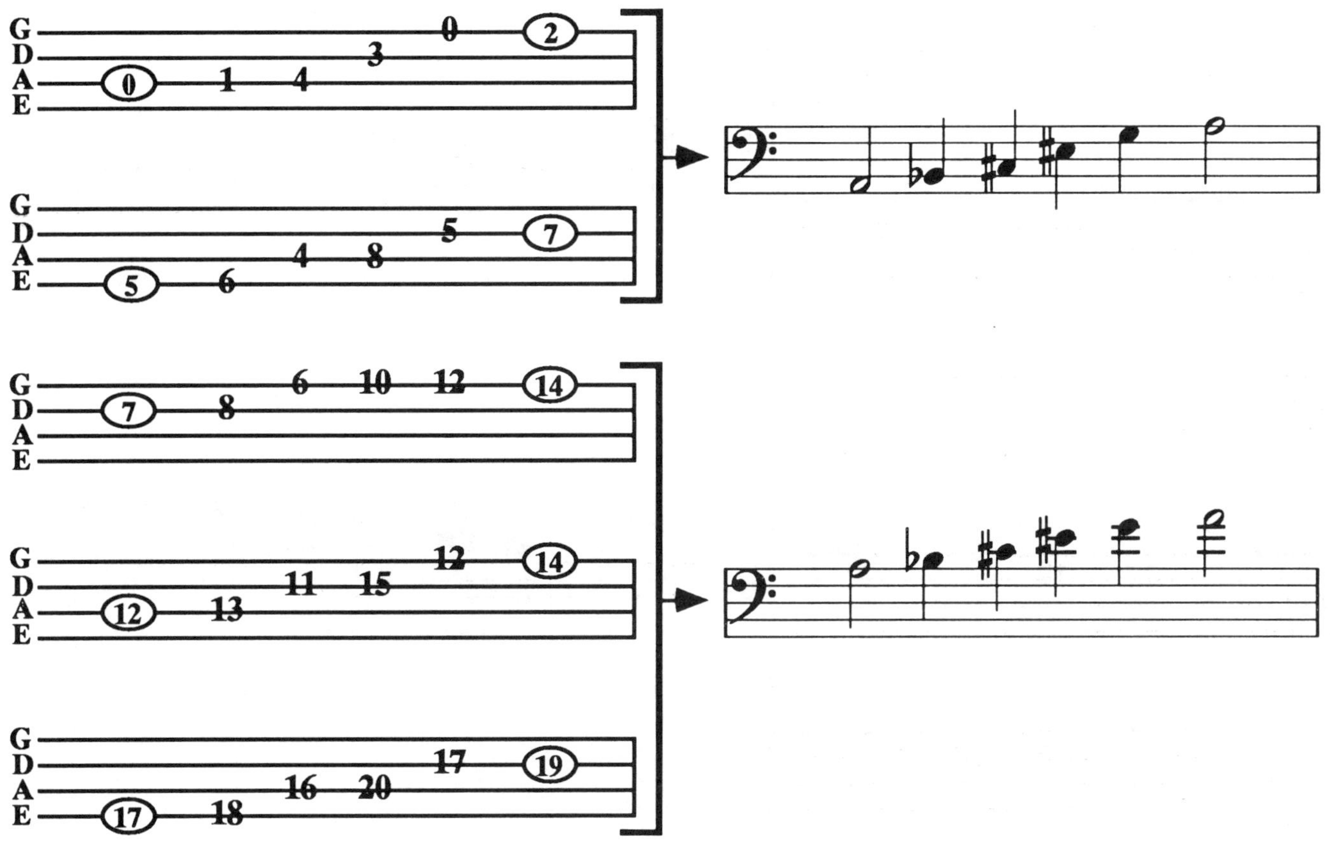

Riff

181

B SEVENTH ♭9TH AUG 5TH

FORMULA - (B) Root (D♯) 3rd (F×) ♯5th (A) ♭7th (C) ♭9th

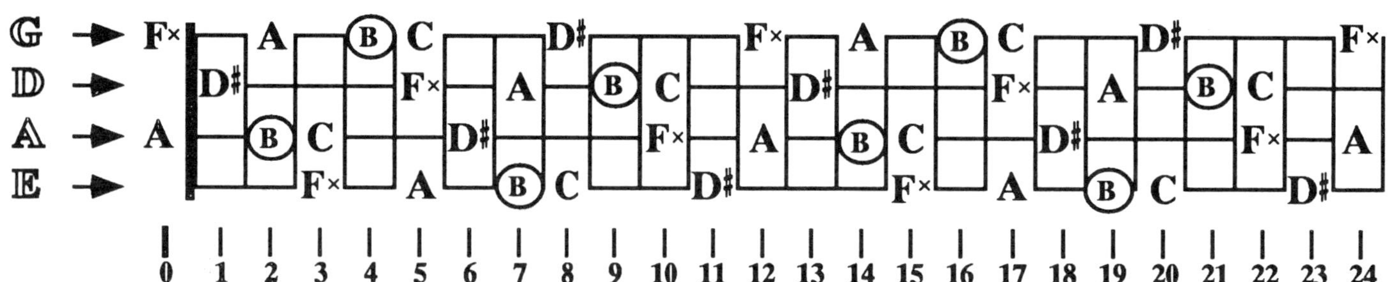

Positions

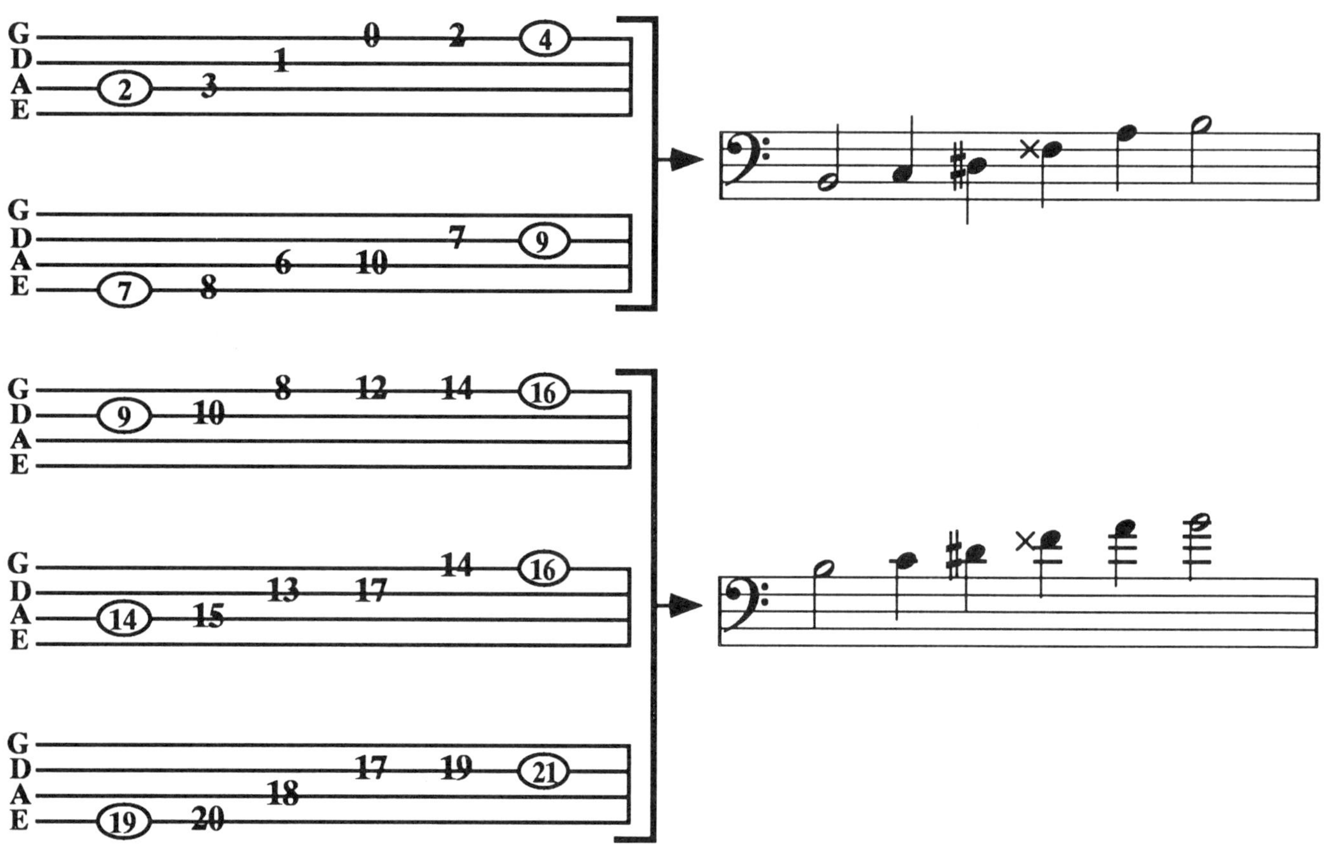

Riff

C SEVENTH AUG 9TH

FORMULA - (C) Root (E) 3rd (G) 5th (B♭) ♭7th (D♯) ♯9th

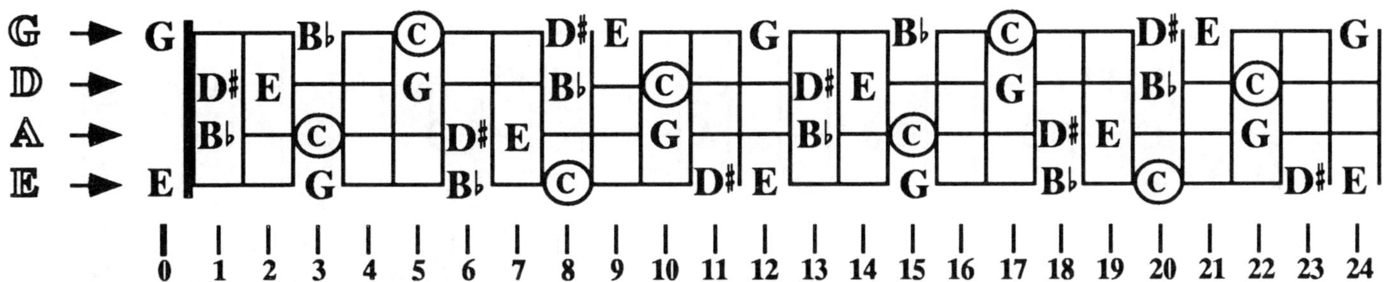

Positions

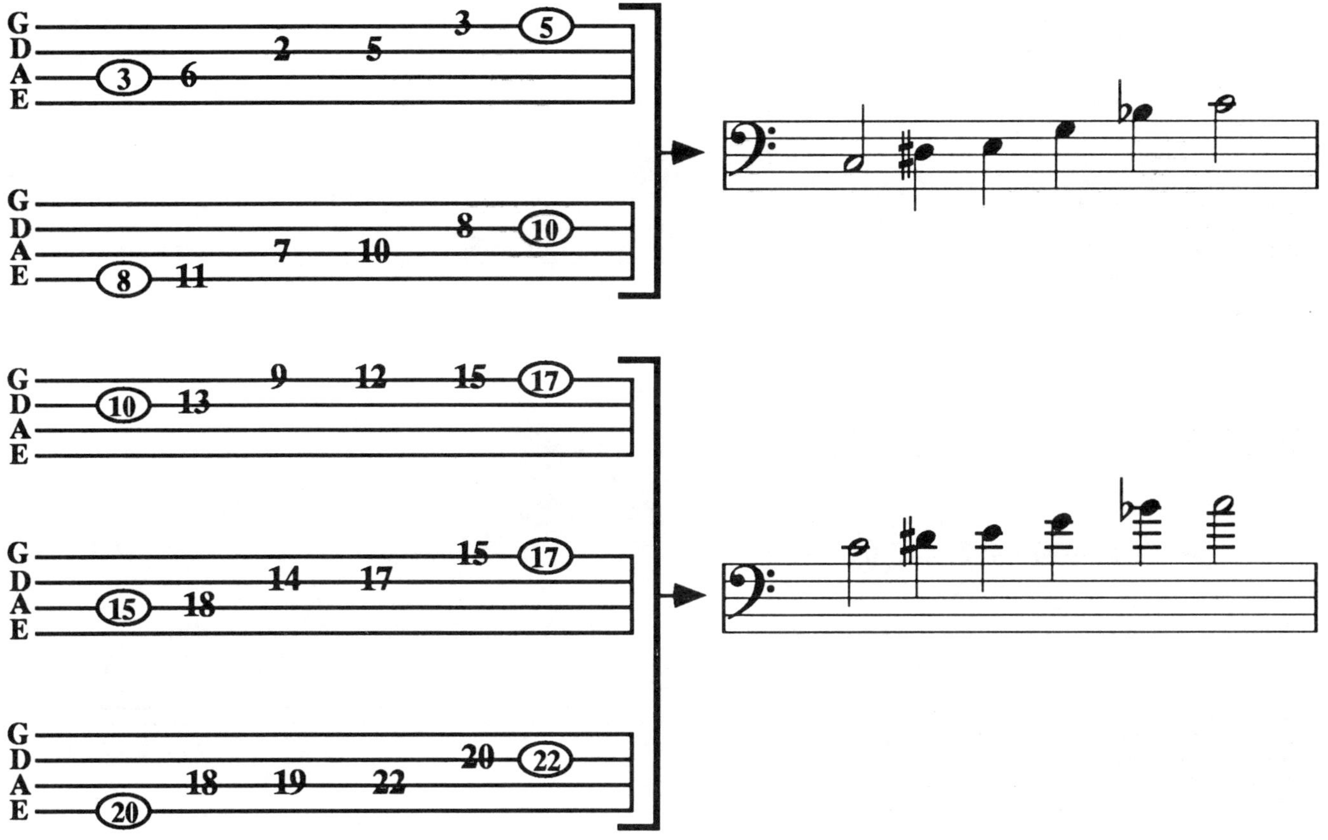

Riff

D   SEVENTH AUG 9TH

FORMULA - (D) Root (F♯) 3rd (A) 5th (C) ♭7th (E♯) ♯9th

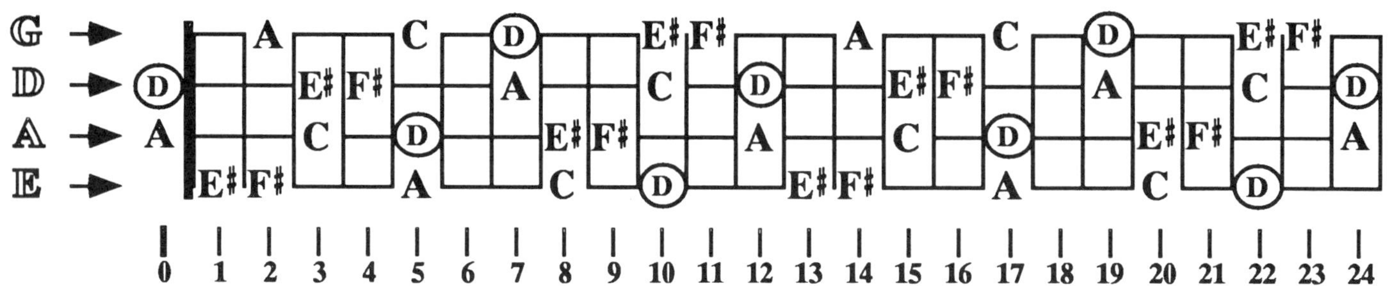

Positions

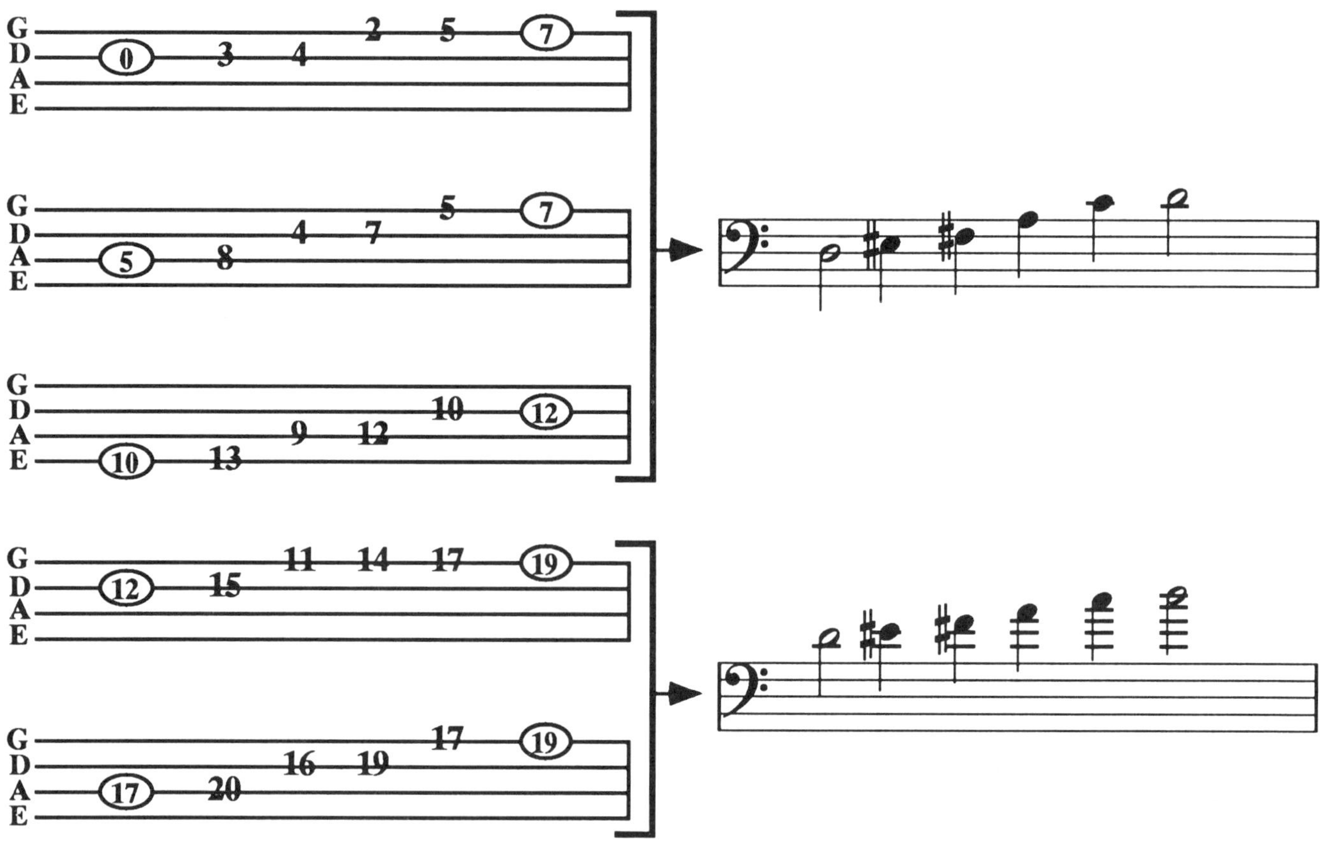

Riff

E   SEVENTH AUG 9TH

FORMULA - (E) Root (G♯) 3rd (B) 5th (D) ♭7th (F×) ×9th

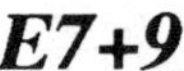

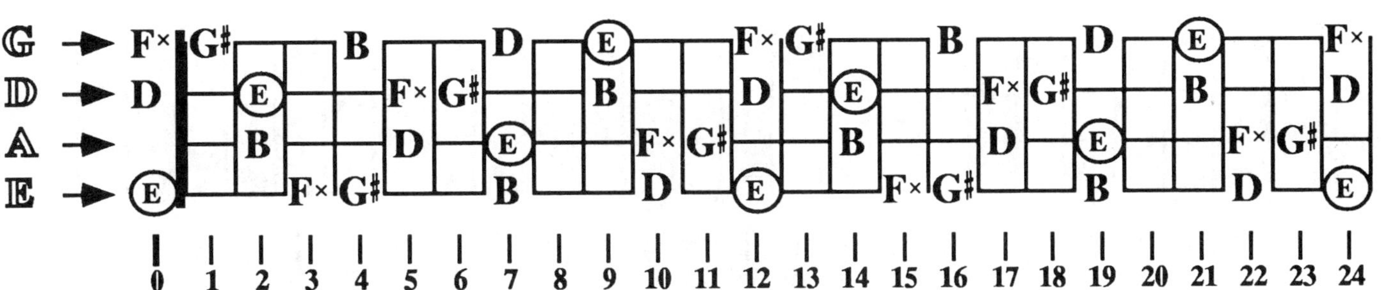

Positions

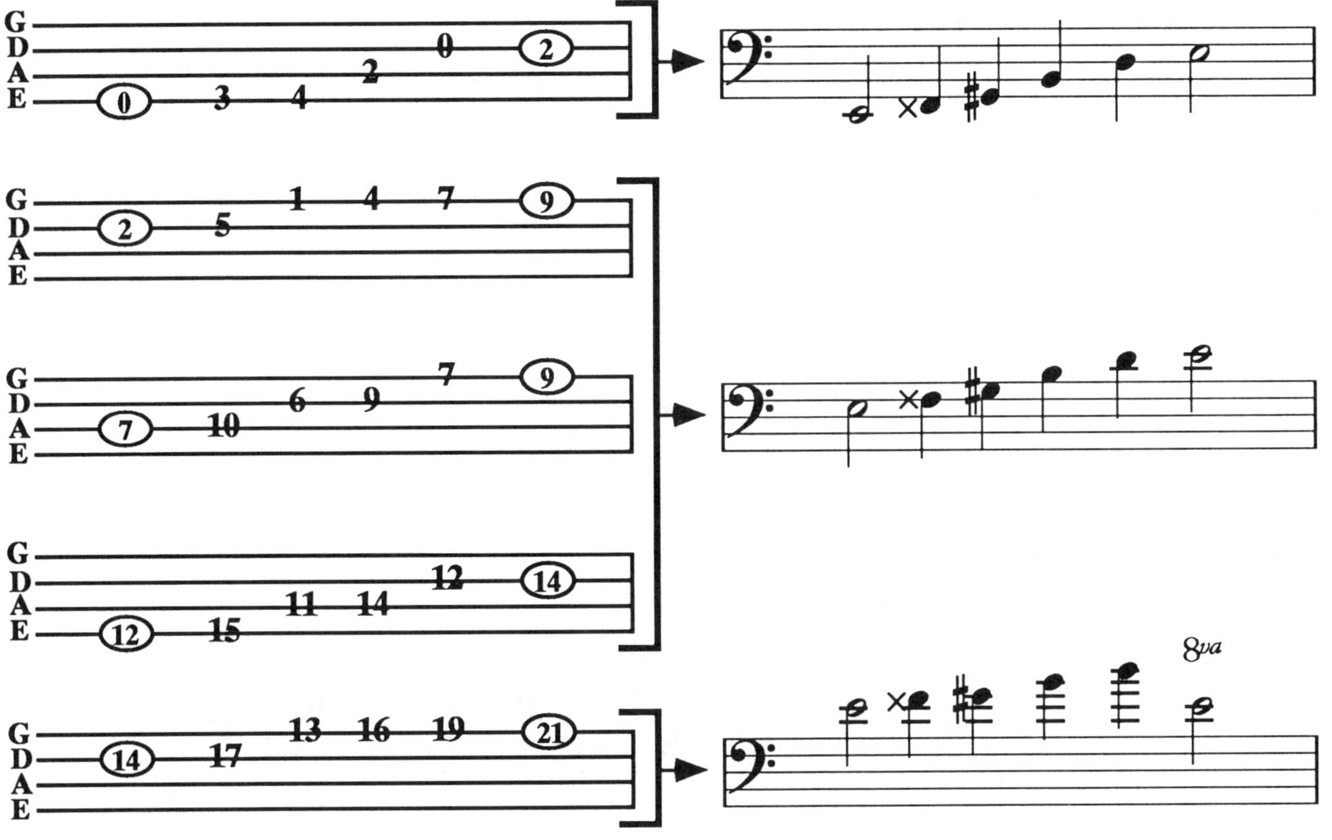

Riff

F SEVENTH AUG 9TH

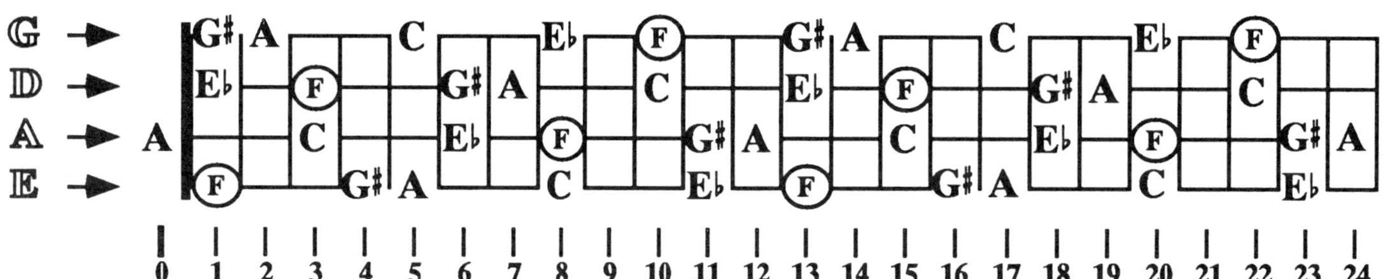

Positions

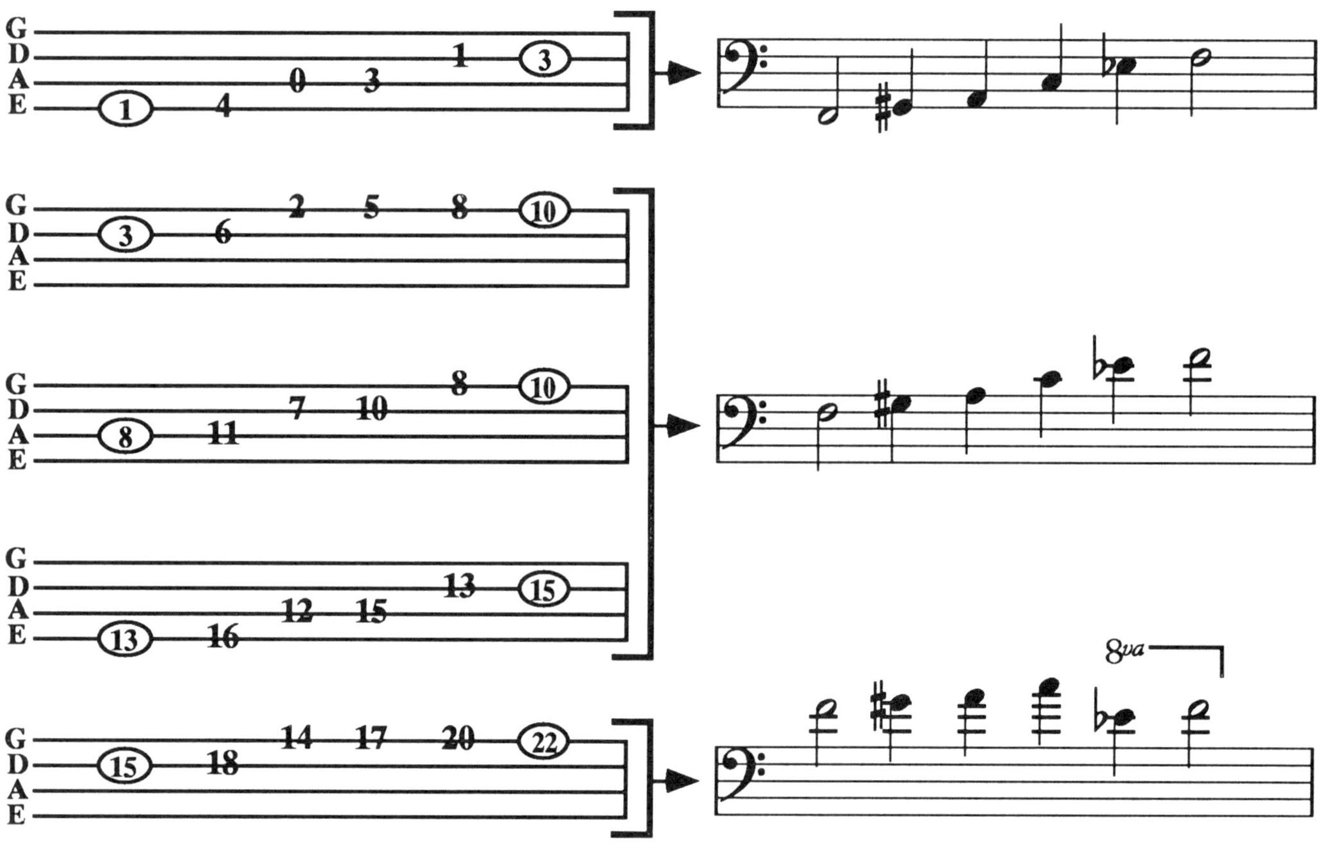

Riff

G SEVENTH AUG 9TH

FORMULA - (G) Root (B) 3rd (D) 5th (F) ♭7th (A♯) ♯9th

G7+9

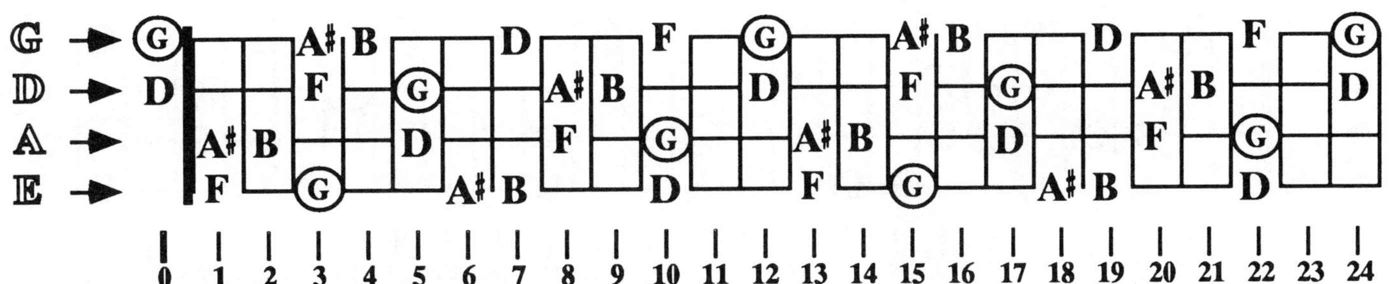

Positions

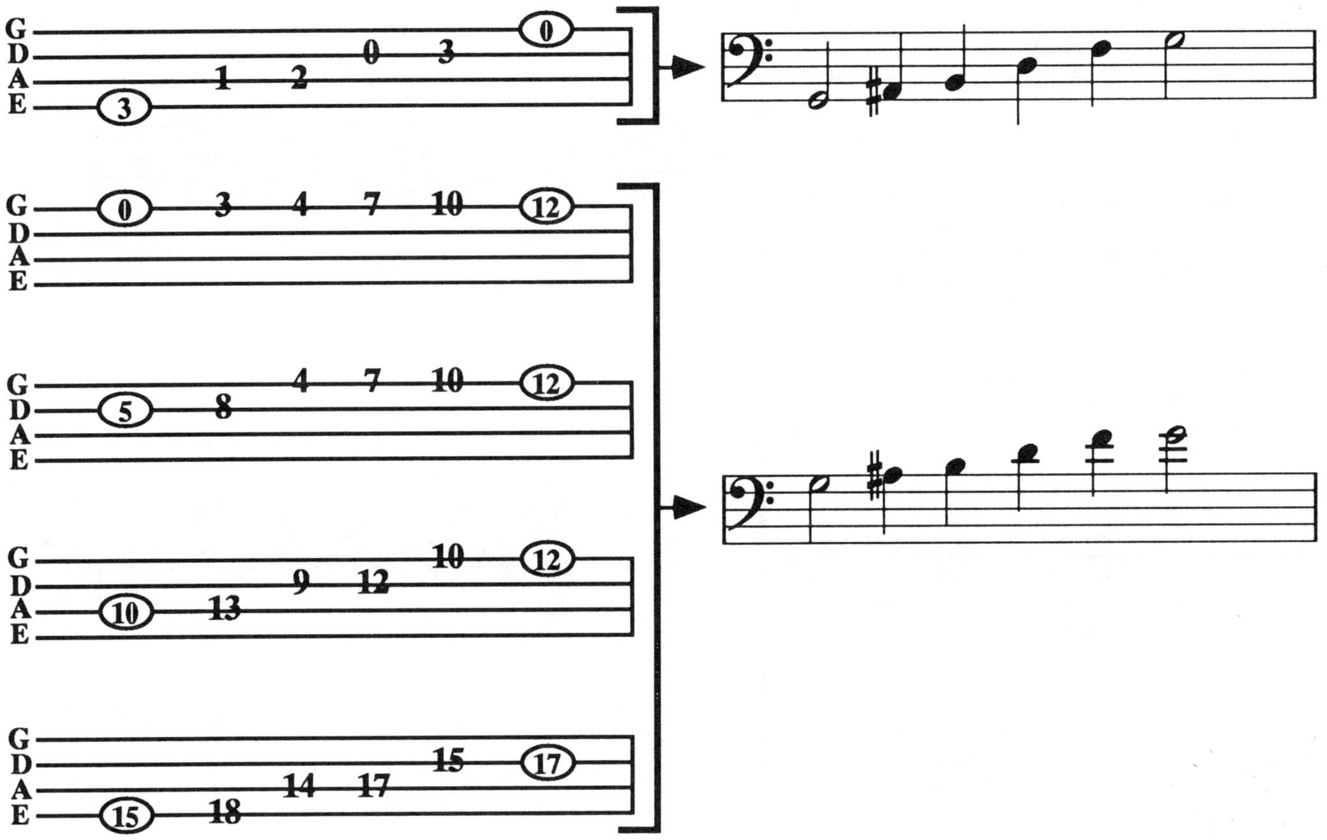

Riff

A SEVENTH AUG 9TH

FORMULA - (A) Root (C♯) 3rd (E) 5th (G) ♭7th (B♯) ♯9th

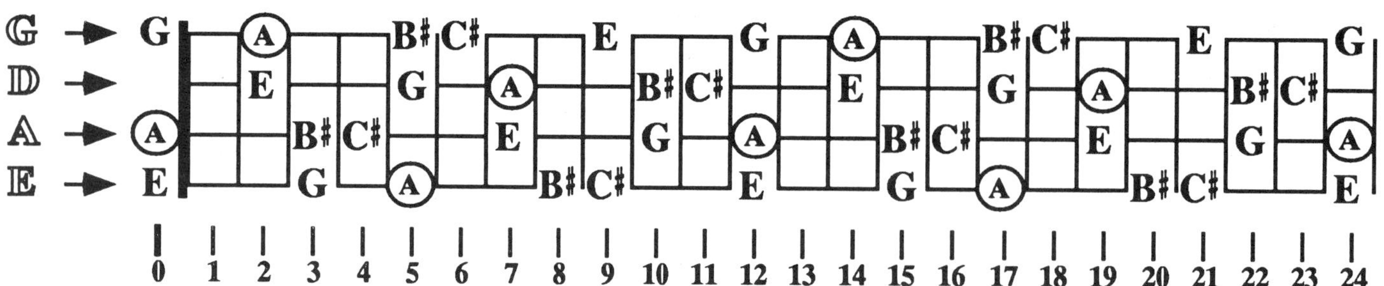

Positions

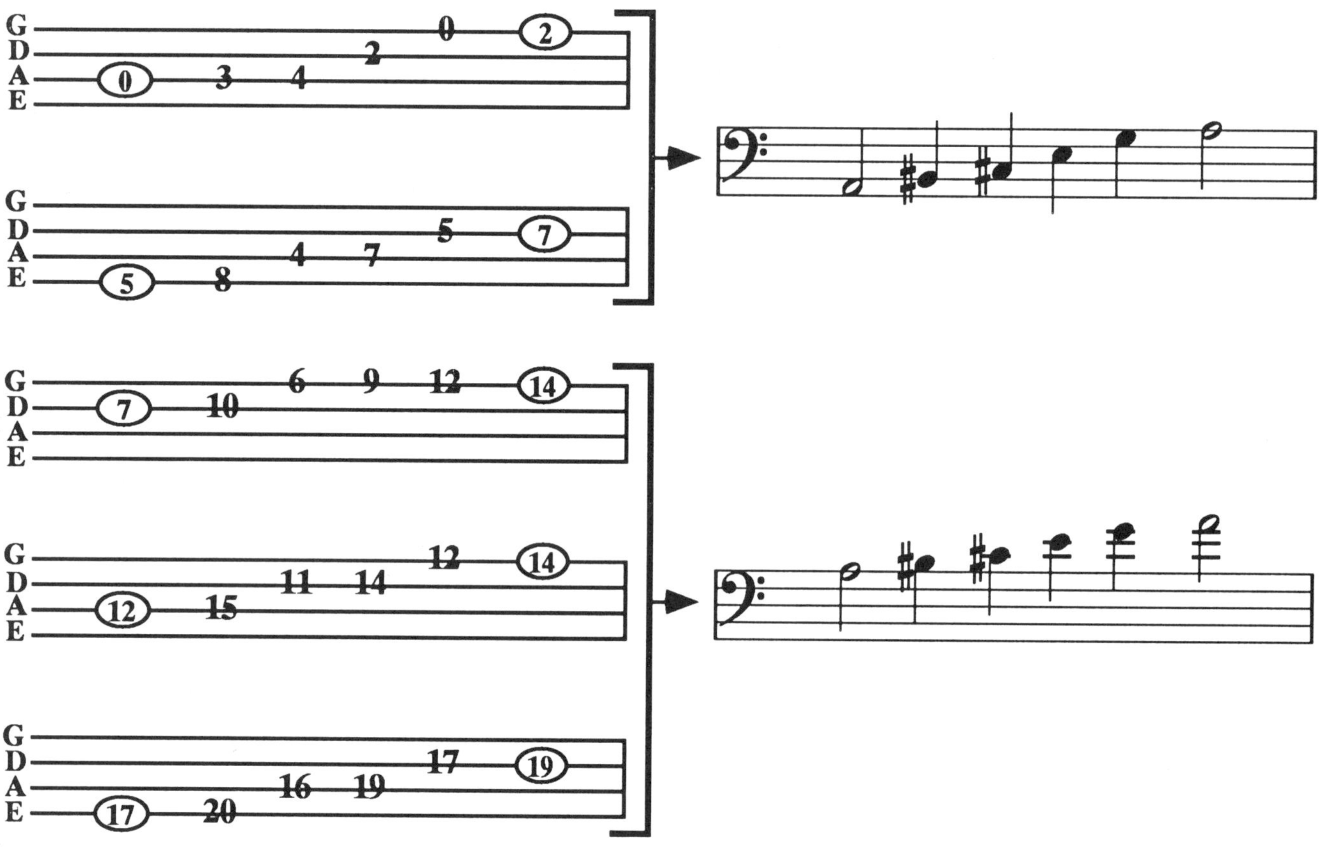

Riff

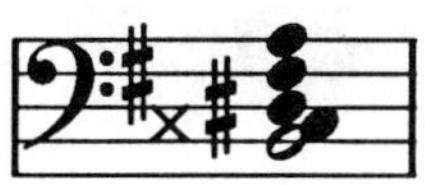

B SEVENTH AUG 9TH

FORMULA - (B) Root (D♯) 3rd (F♯) 5th (A) ♭7th (C×) ♯9th

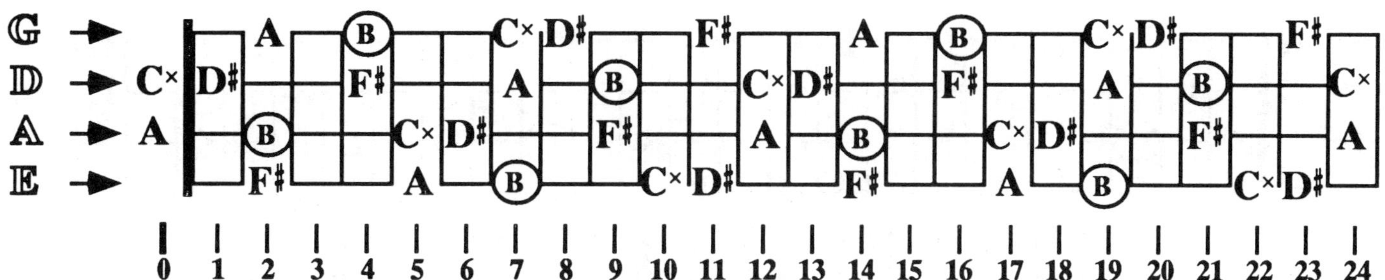

Positions

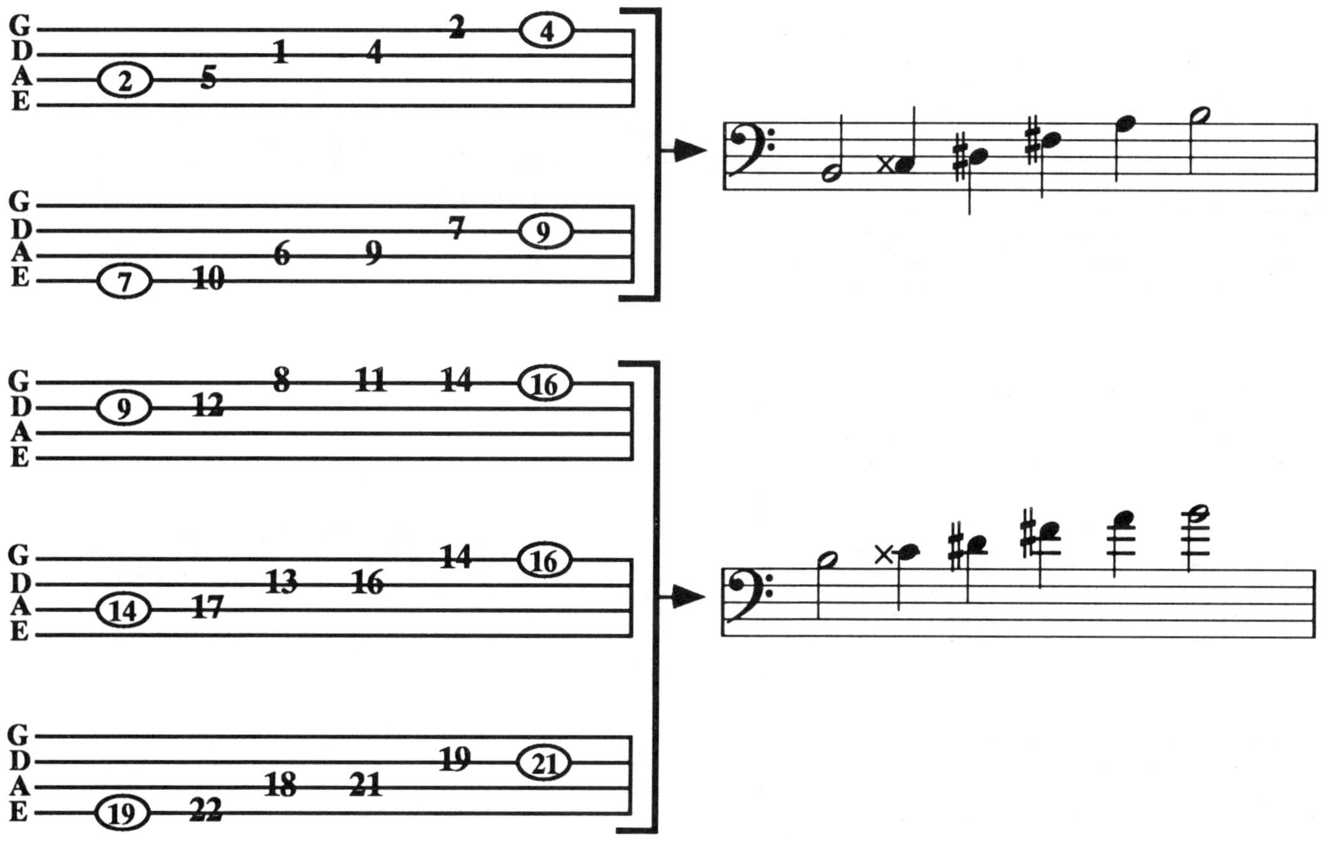

Riff

C ELEVENTH
FORMULA - (C) Root (E) 3rd (G) 5th
(B♭) ♭7th (D) 9th (F) 11th

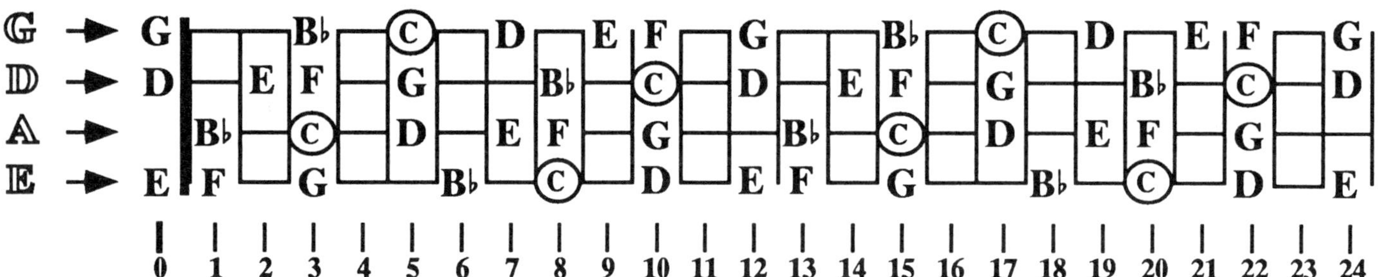

Positions

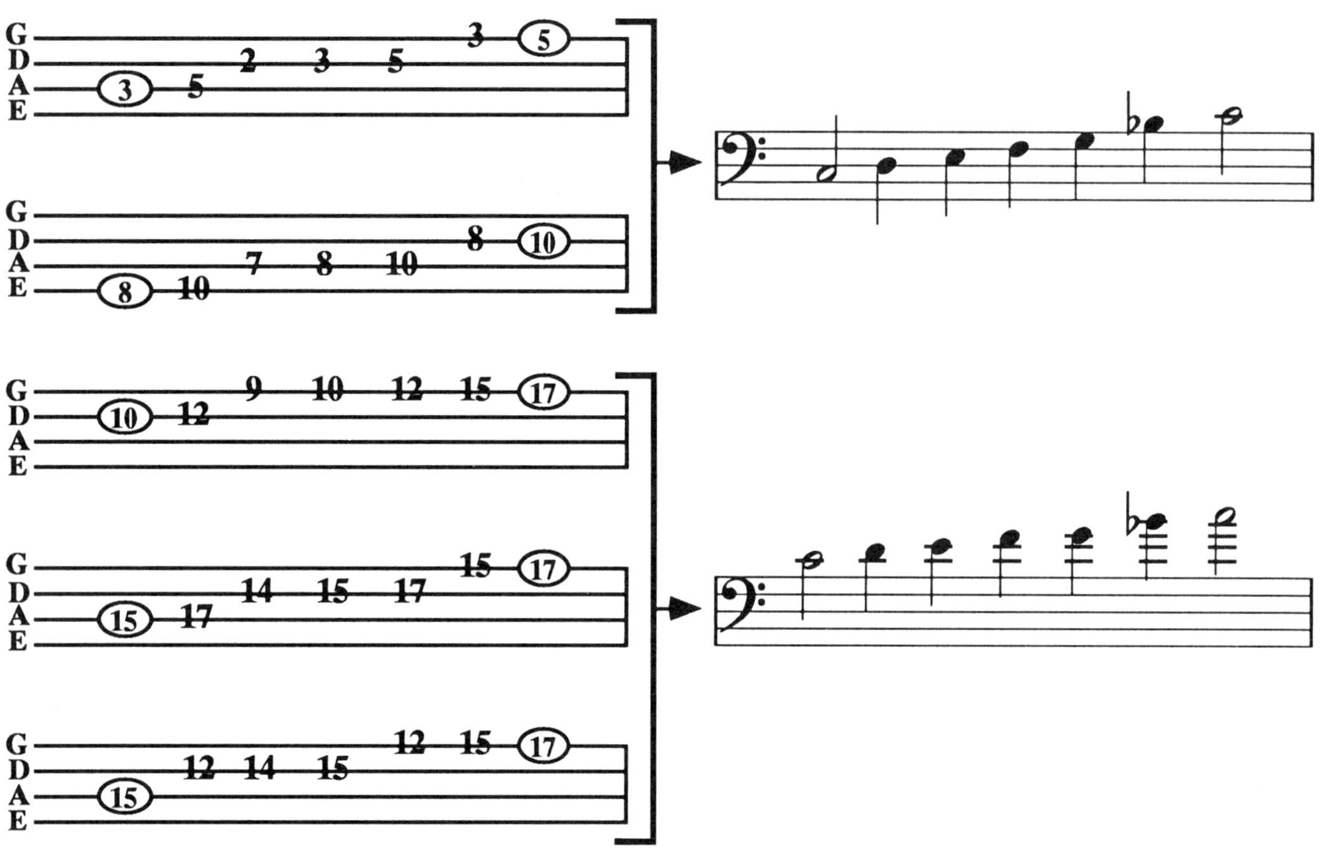

Riff

D ELEVENTH

FORMULA - (D) Root (F♯) 3rd (A) 5th (C) ♭7th (E) 9th (G) 11th

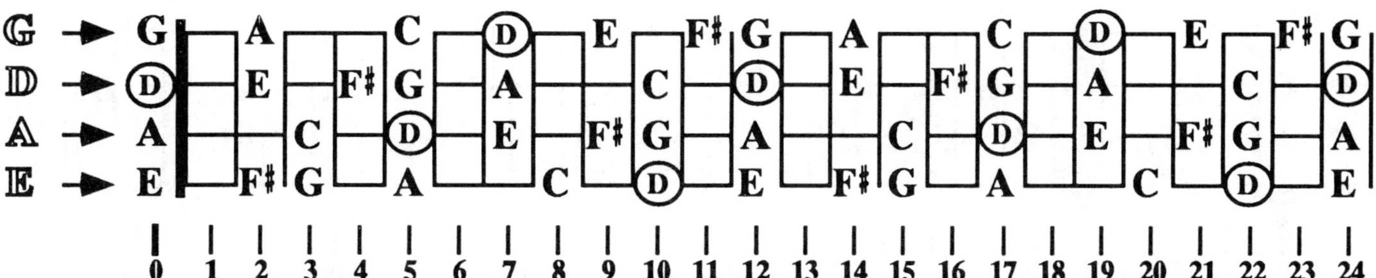

Positions

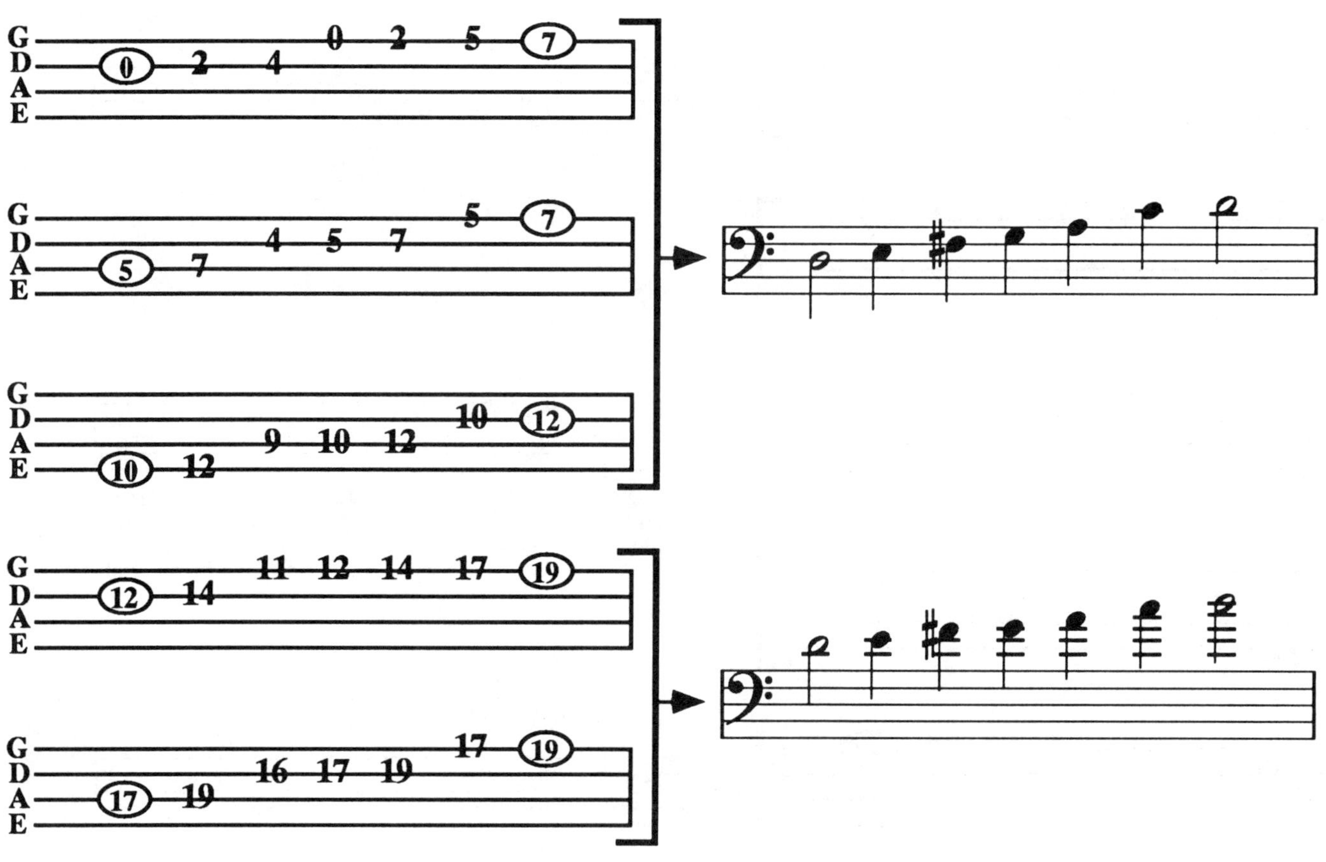

Riff

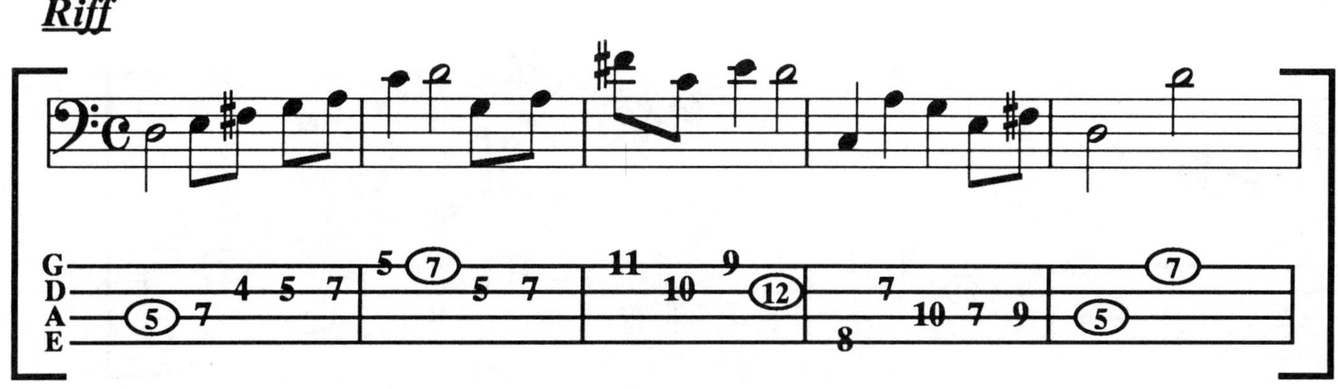

E ELEVENTH

**FORMULA - (E) Root (G♯) 3rd (B) 5th
(D) ♭7th (F♯) 9th (A) 11th**

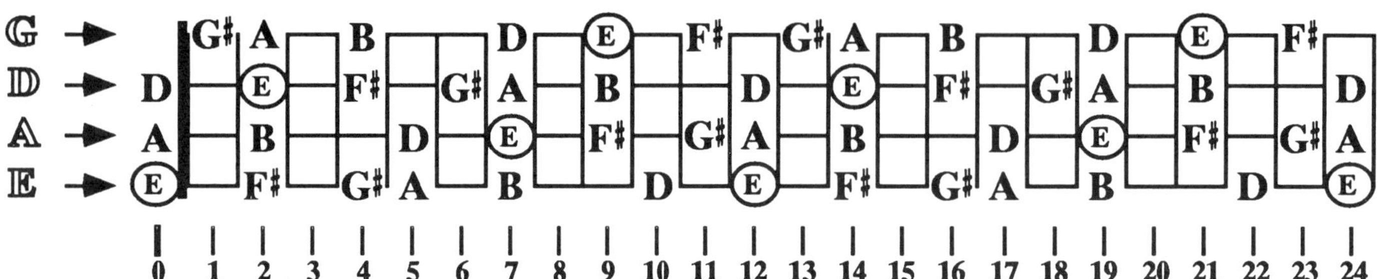

Positions

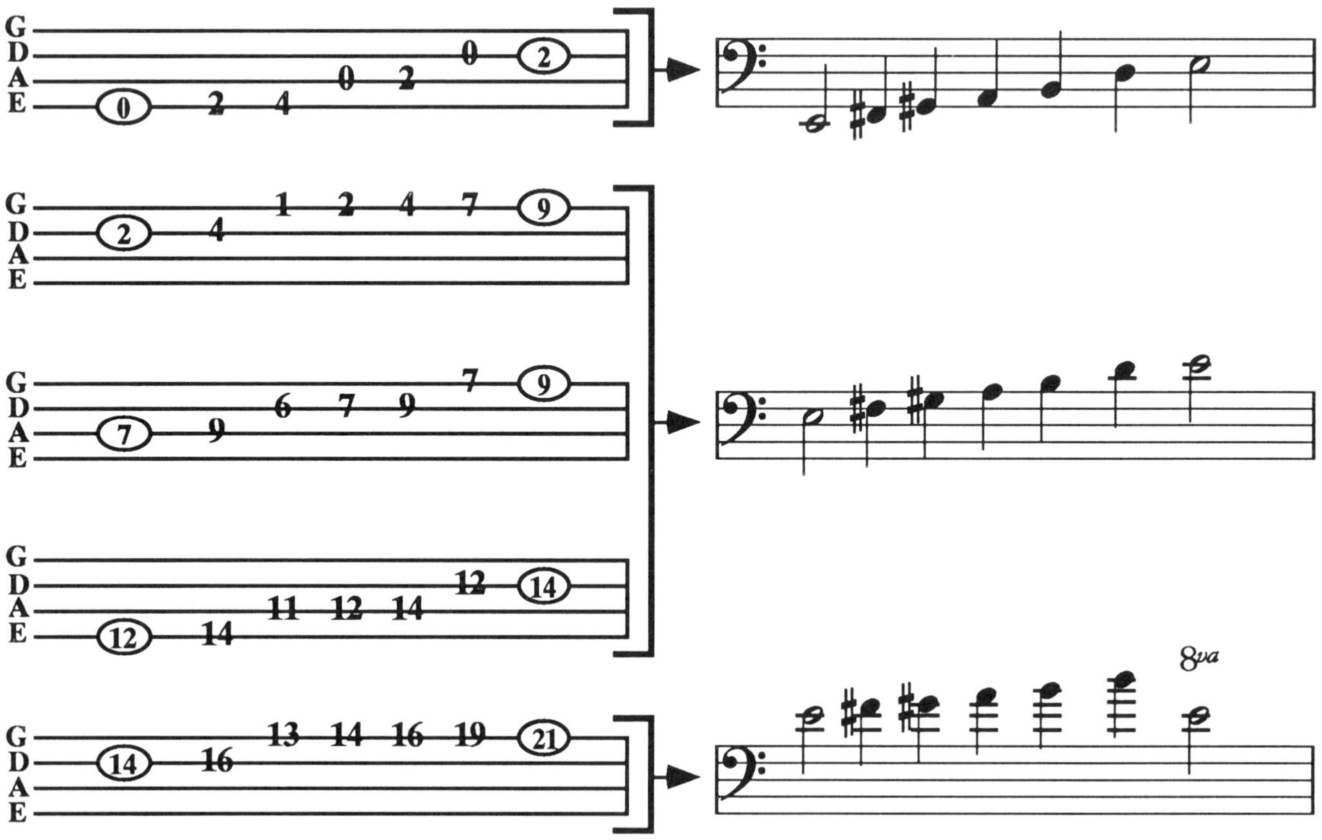

Riff

F ELEVENTH

FORMULA - (F) Root (A) 3rd (C) 5th
(E♭) ♭7th (G) 9th (B♭) 11th

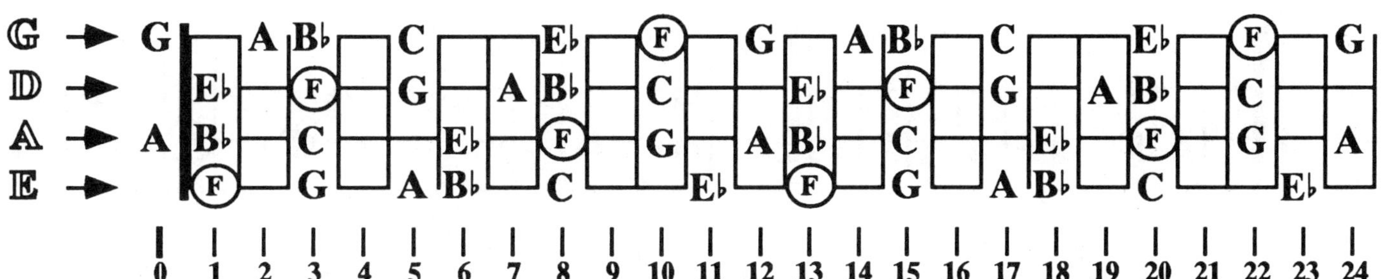

Positions

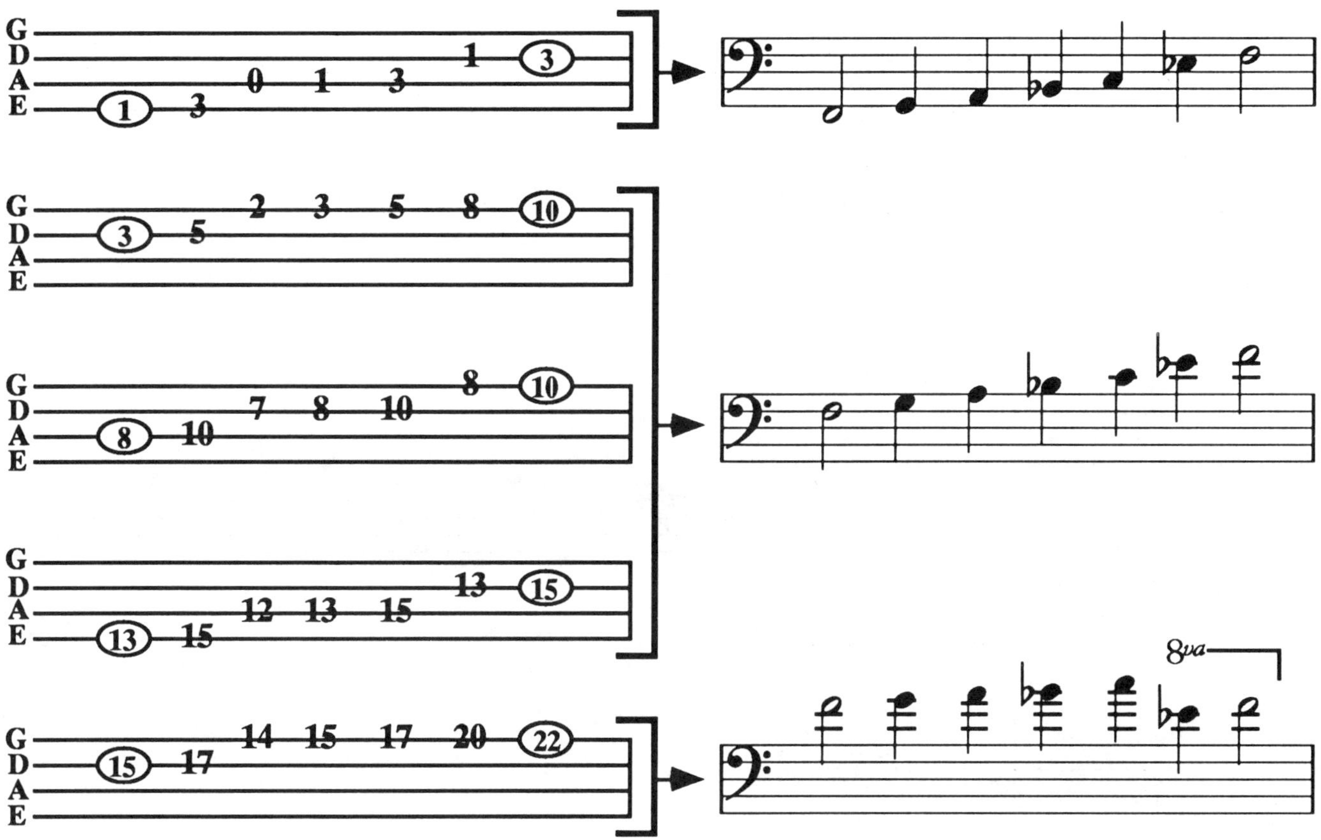

Riff

G ELEVENTH

FORMULA - (G) Root (B) 3rd (D) 5th
(F) ♭7th (A) 9th (C) 11th

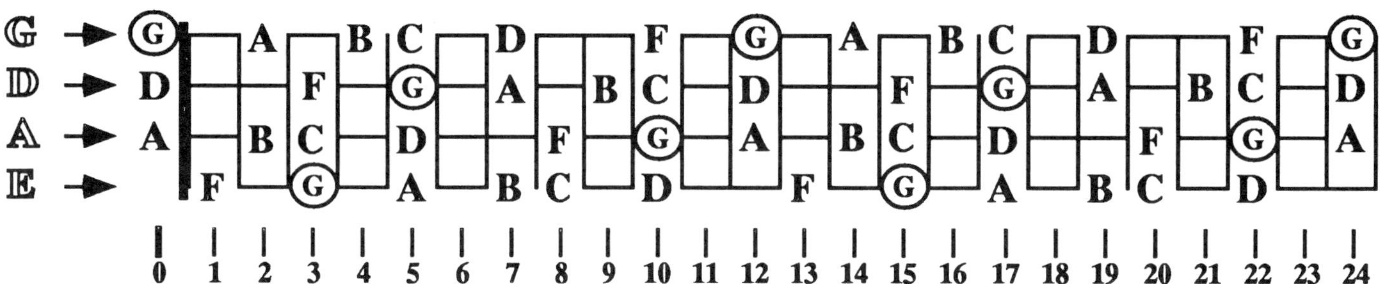

Positions

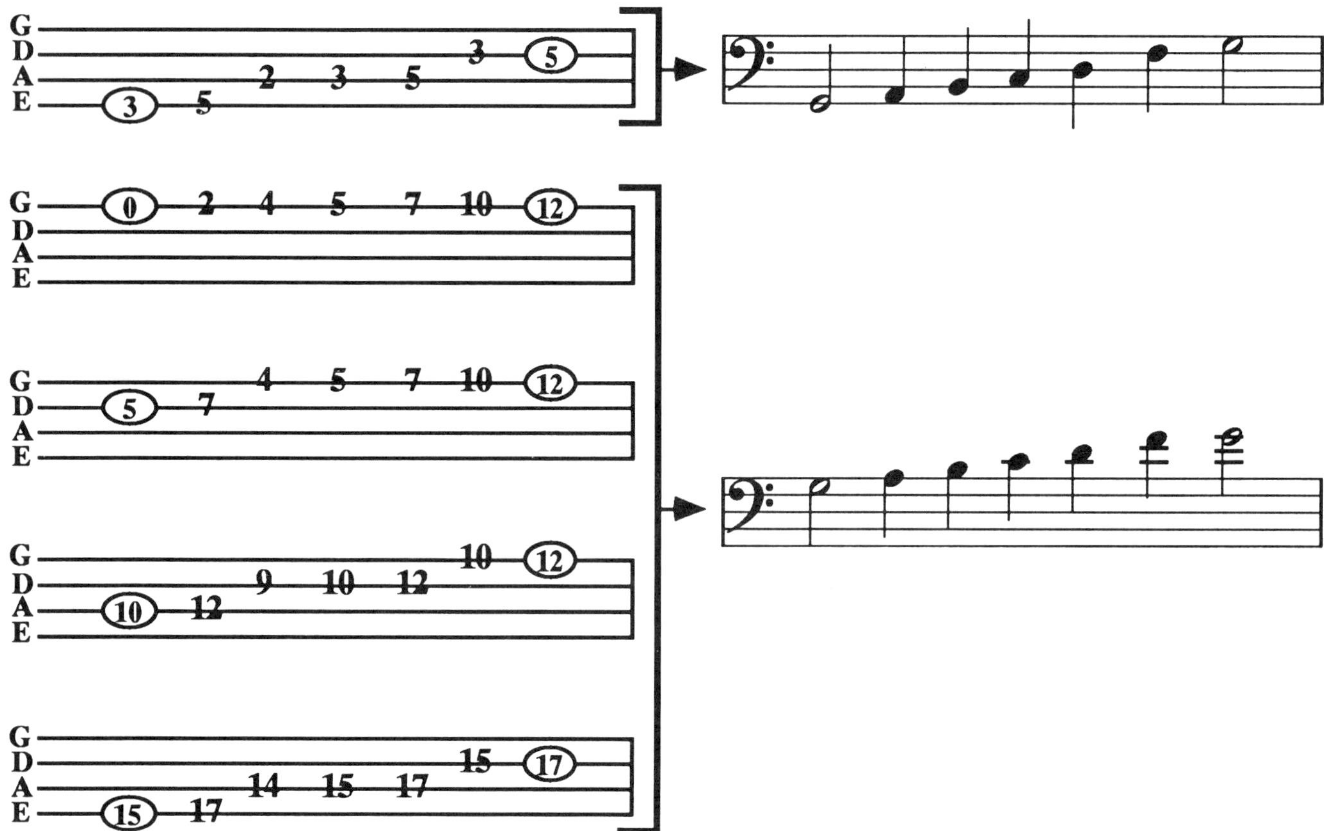

Riff

A ELEVENTH

FORMULA - (A) Root (C♯) 3rd (E) 5th
(G)♭7th (B) 9th (D) 11th

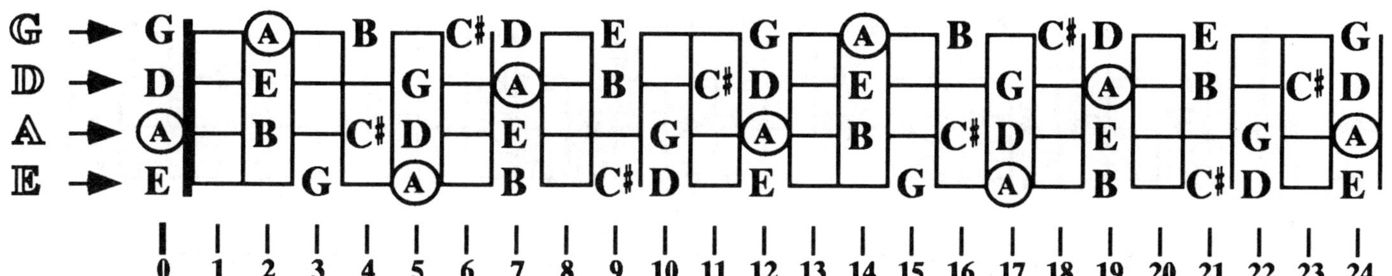

Positions

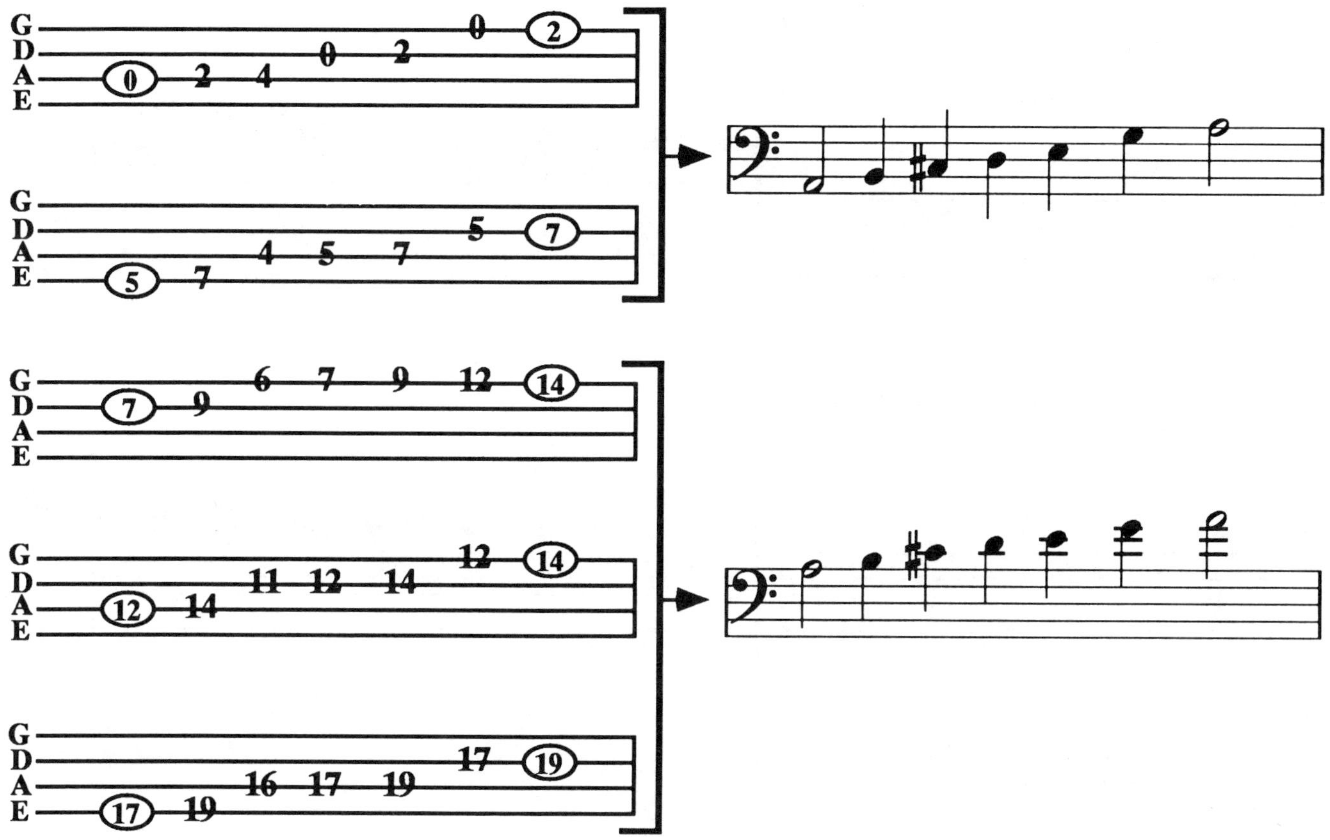

Riff

B ELEVENTH

**FORMULA - (B) Root (D#) 3rd (F#) 5th
(A)♭7th (C#) 9th (E) 11th**

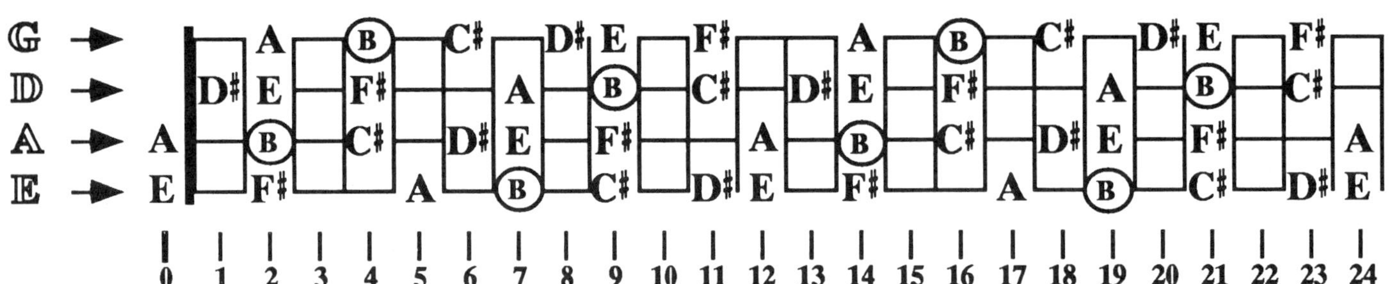

Positions

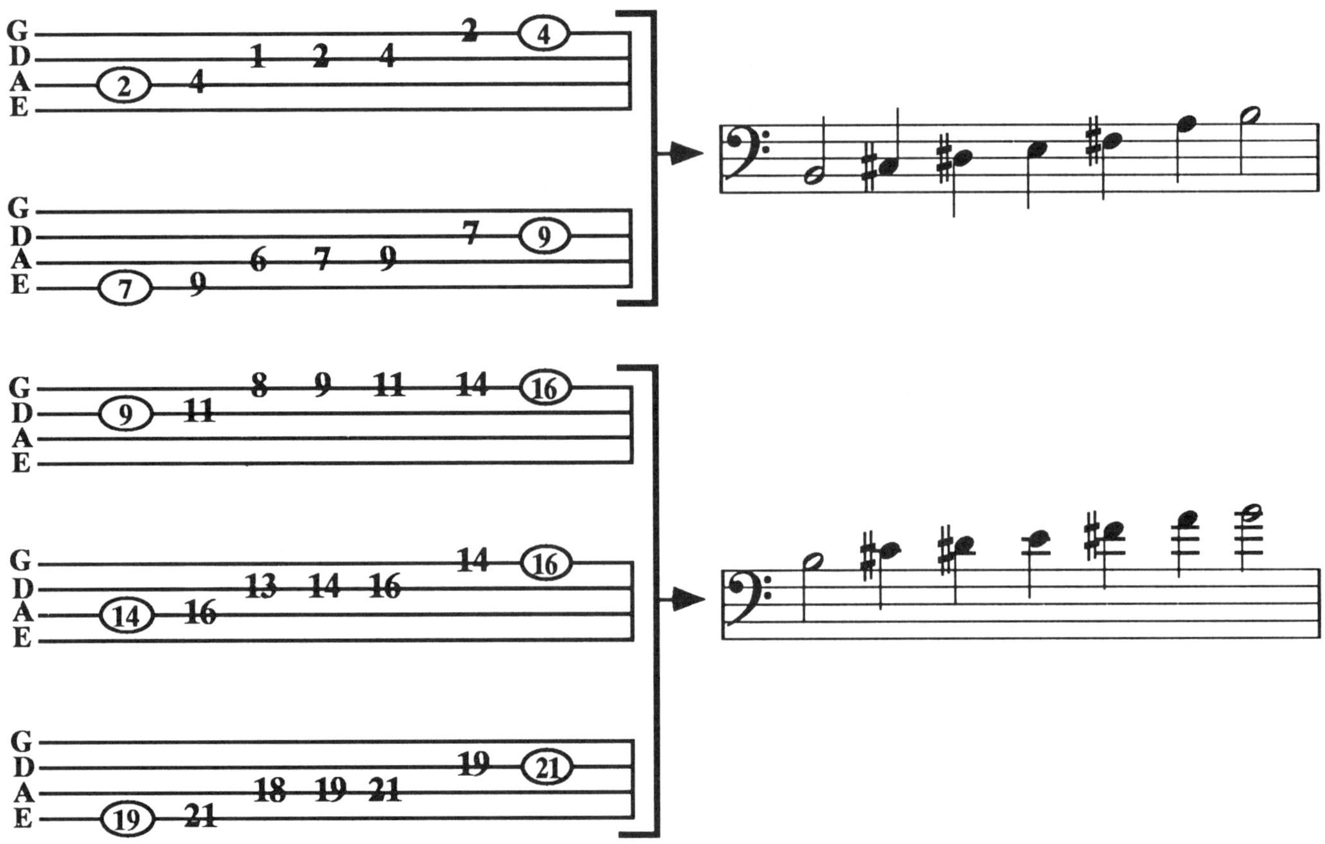

Riff

C   SEVENTH SUSPENDED 4TH   *C7sus4*

FORMULA - (C) Root (F) 4th (G) 5th (B♭) ♭7th

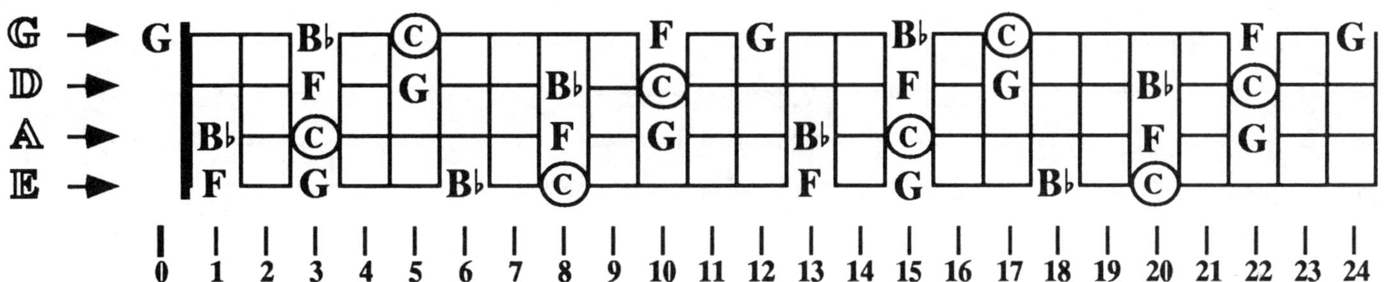

Positions

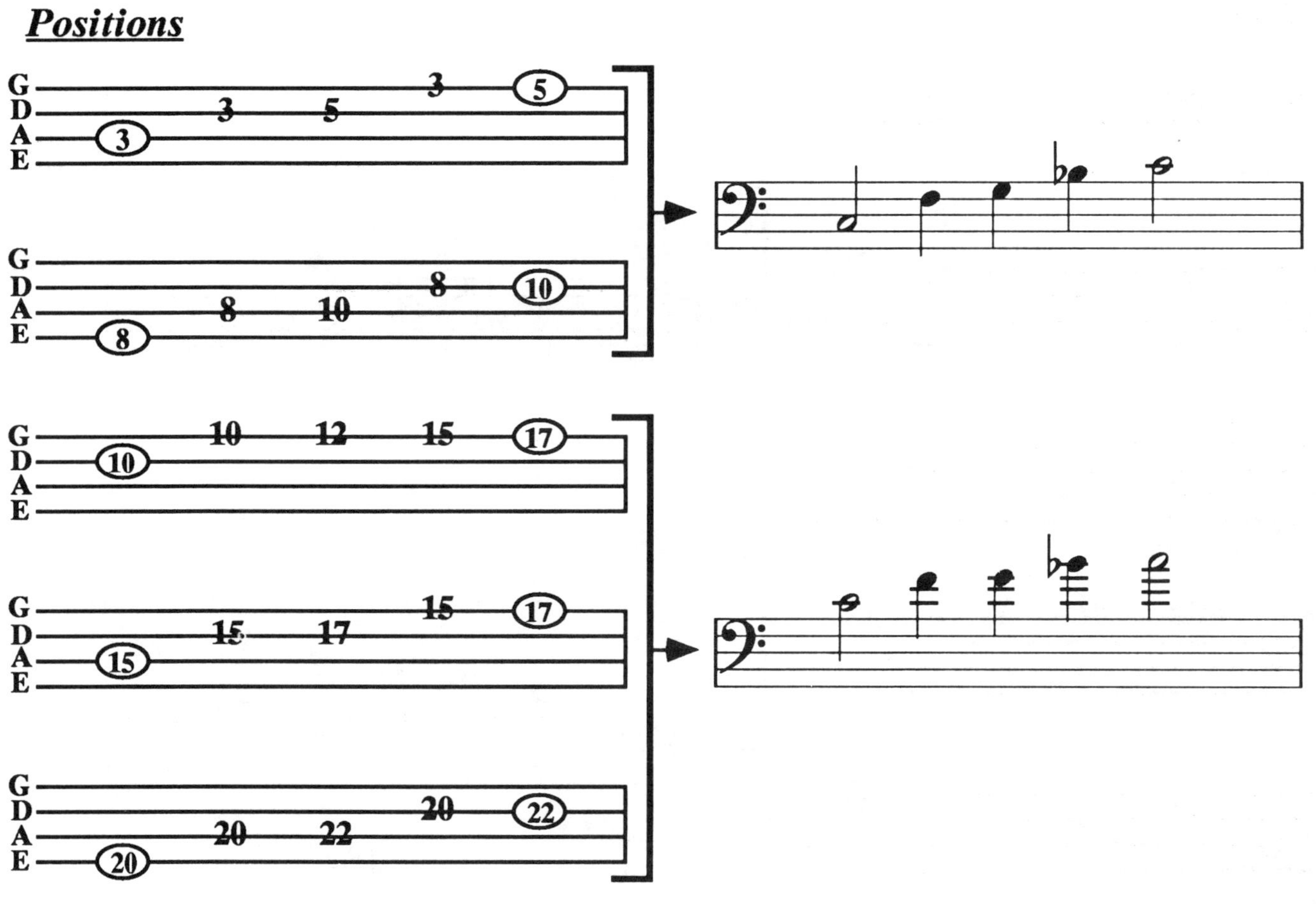

Riff

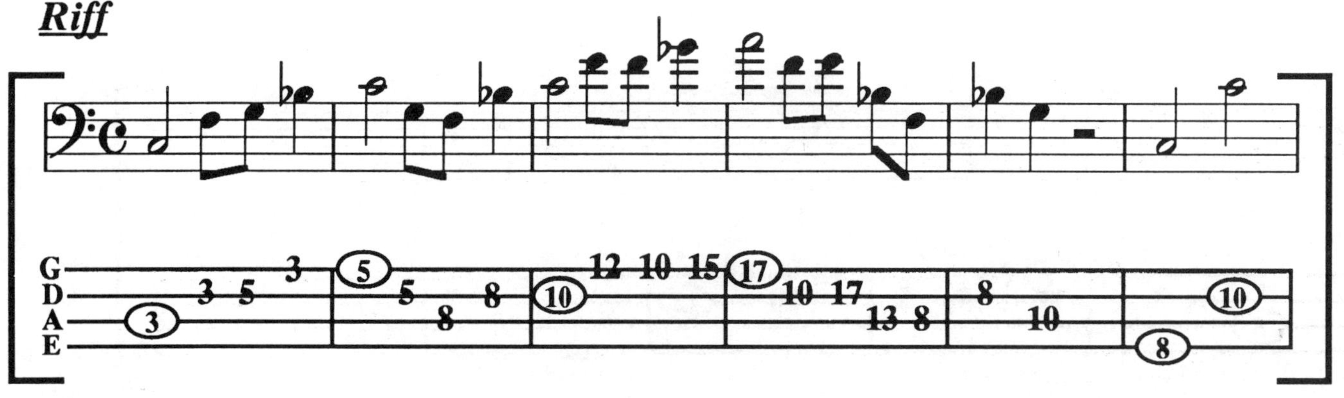

D SEVENTH SUSPENDED 4TH

FORMULA - (D) Root (G) 4th (A) 5th (C) ♭7th

D7sus4

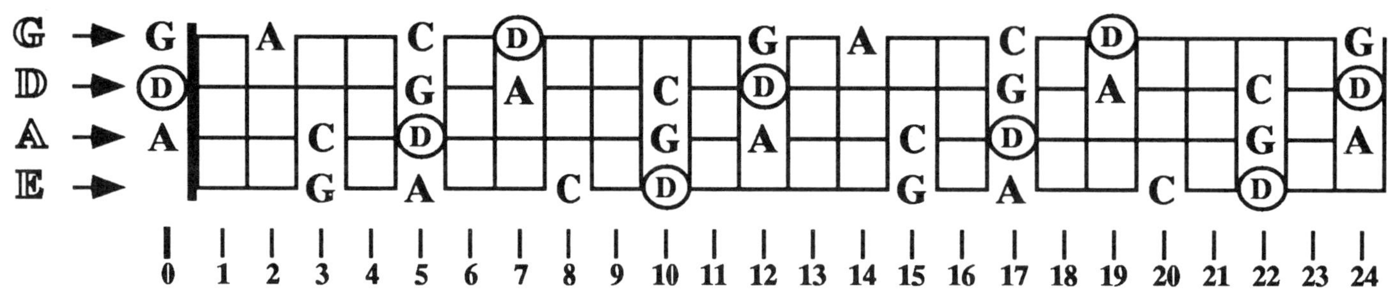

Positions

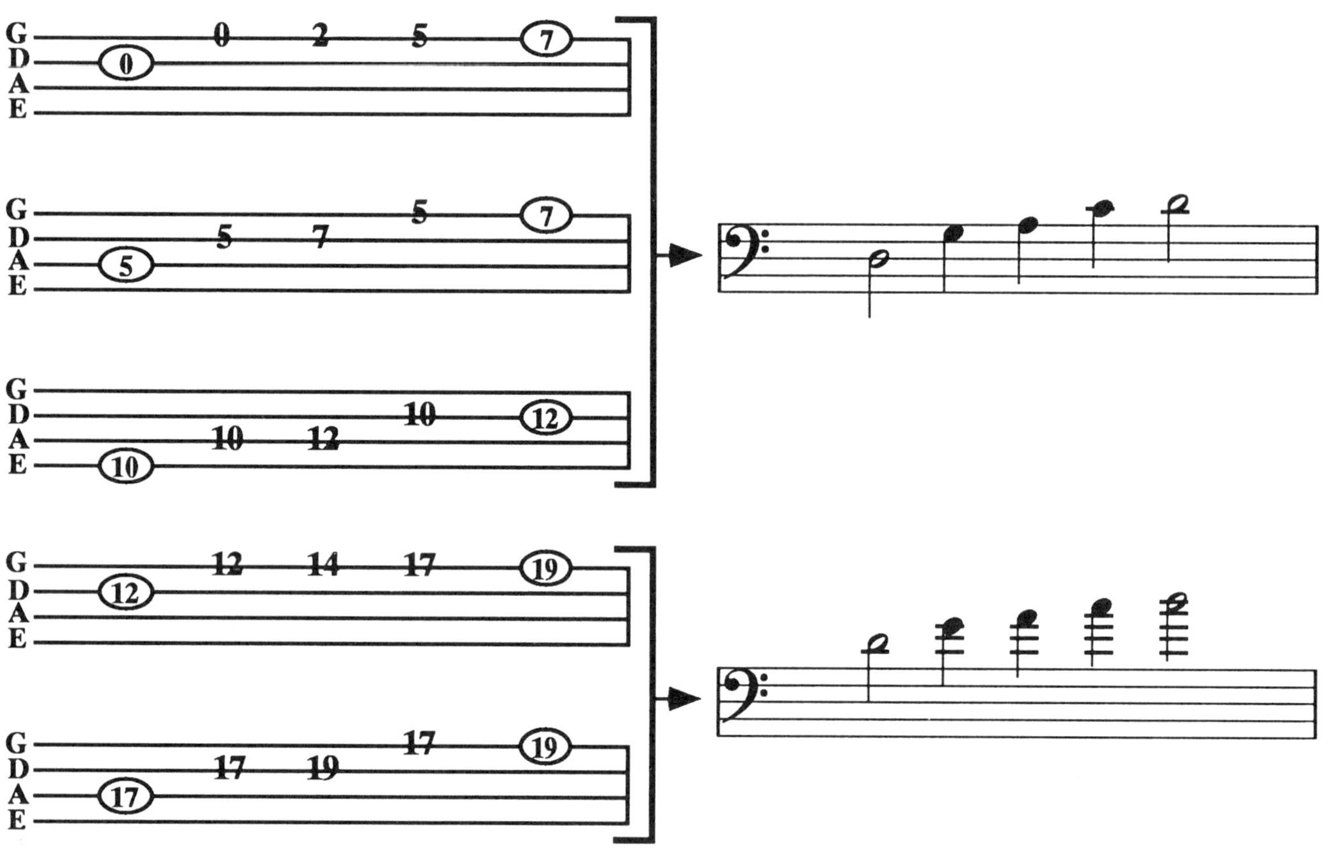

Riff

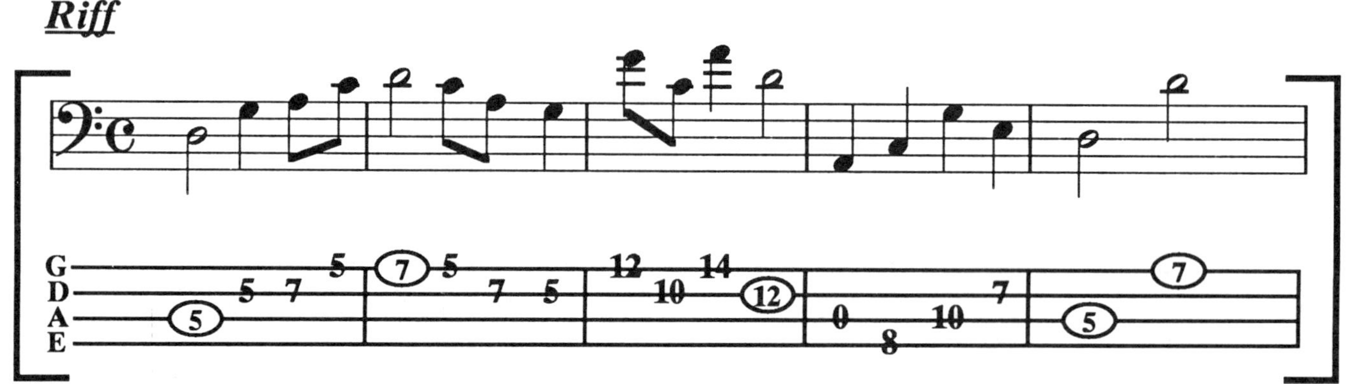

198

E SEVENTH SUSPENDED 4TH

E7sus4

FORMULA - (E) Root (A) 4th (B) 5th (D) ♭7th

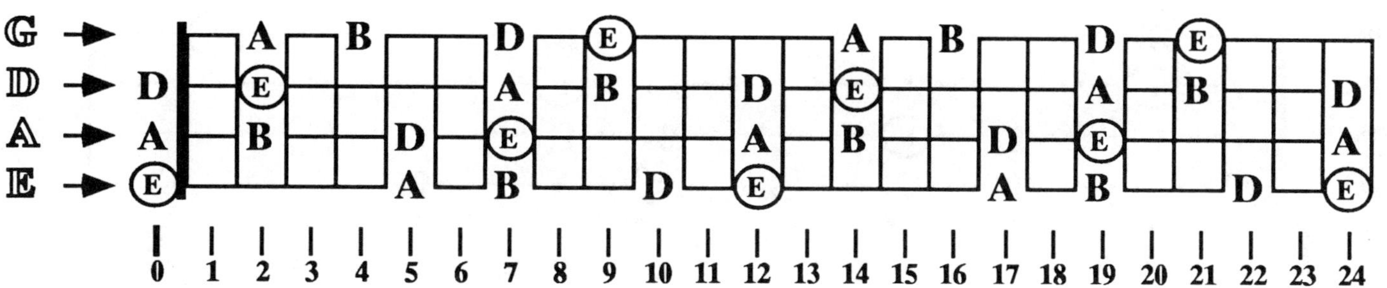

Positions

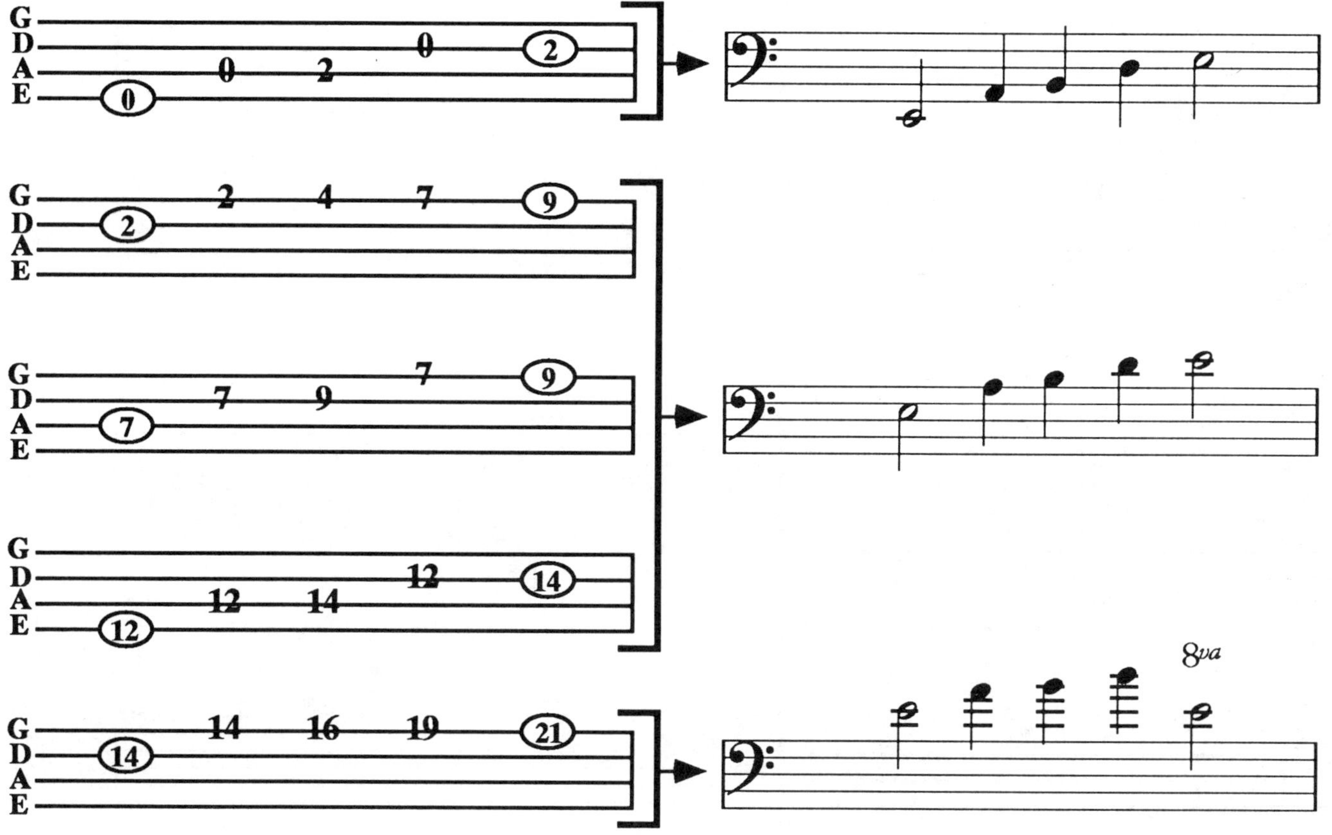

Riff

F SEVENTH SUSPENDED 4TH

FORMULA - (F) Root (B♭) 4th (C) 5th (E♭) ♭7th

F7sus4

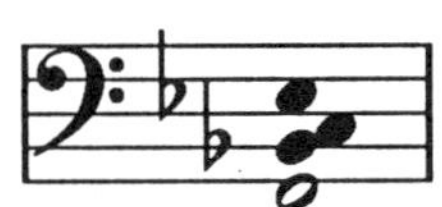

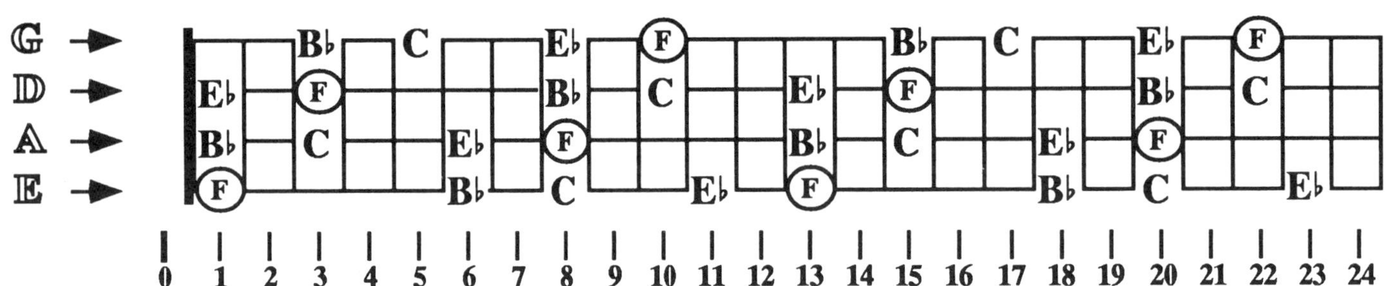

Positions

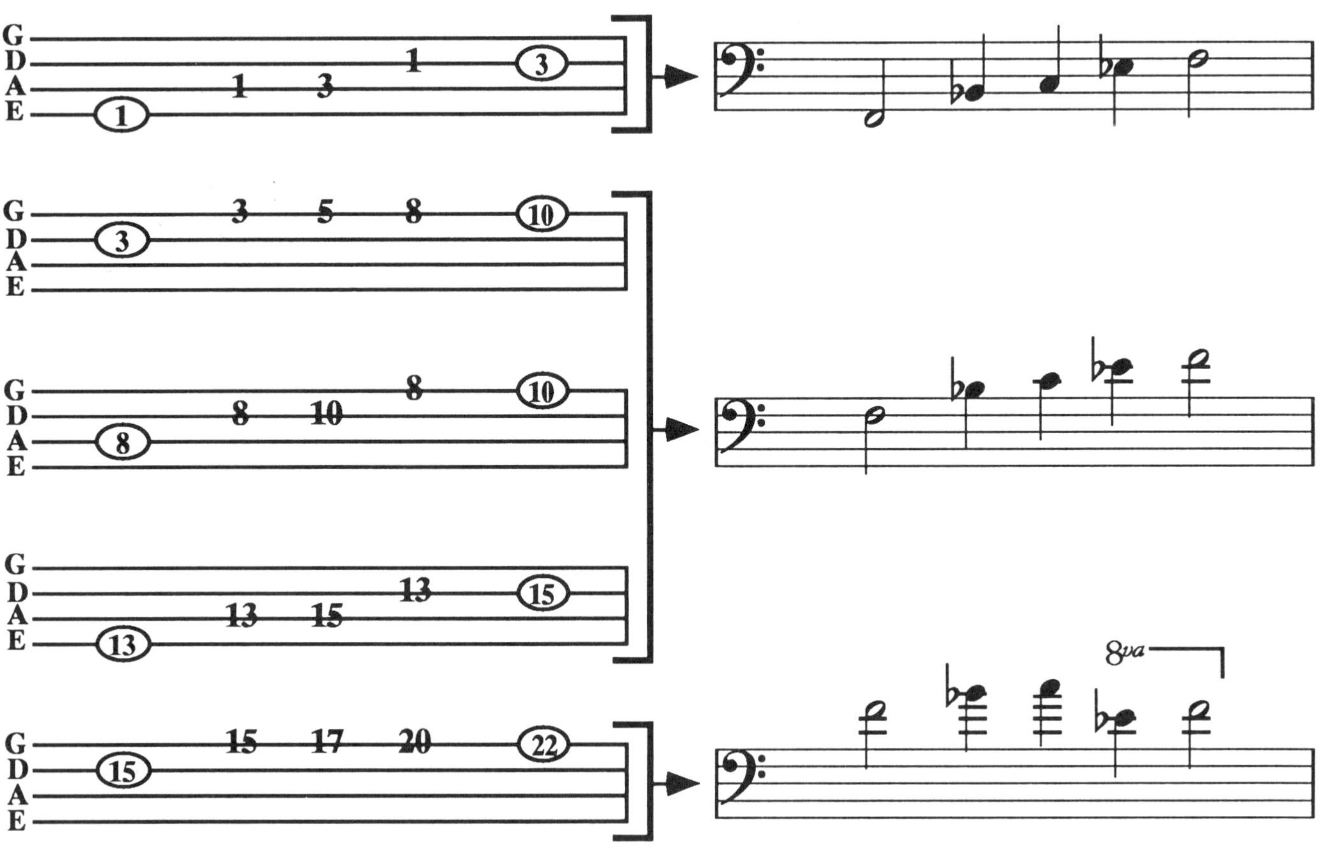

Riff

G   SEVENTH SUSPENDED 4TH   *G7sus4*
FORMULA - (G) Root (C) 4th (D) 5th (F) ♭7th

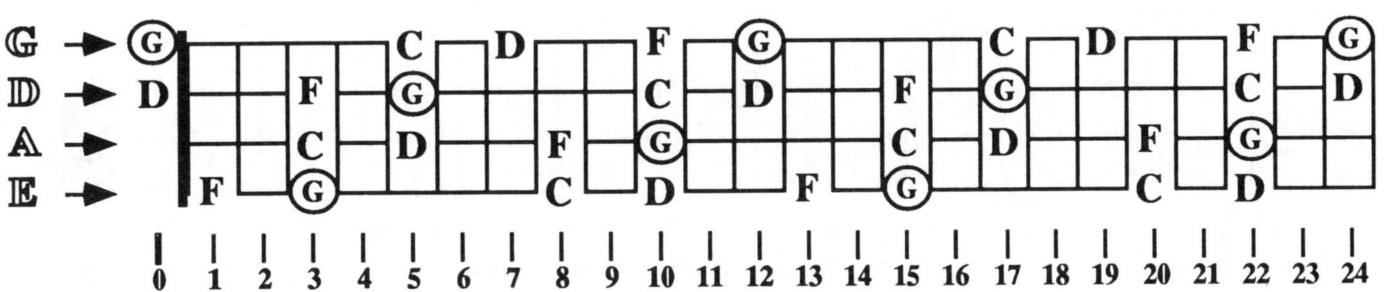

Positions

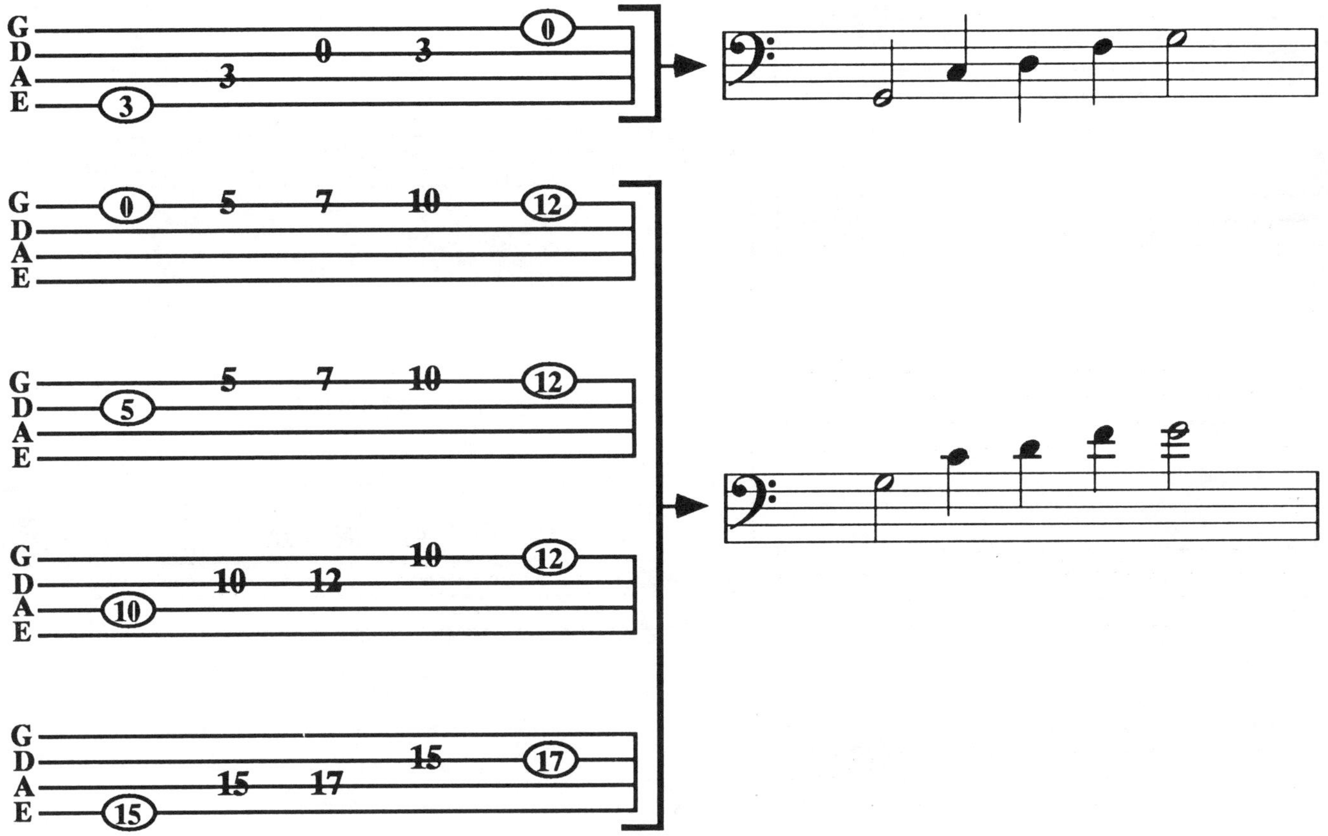

Riff

A SEVENTH SUSPENDED 4TH
FORMULA - (A) Root (D) 4th (E) 5th (G) ♭7th

A7sus4

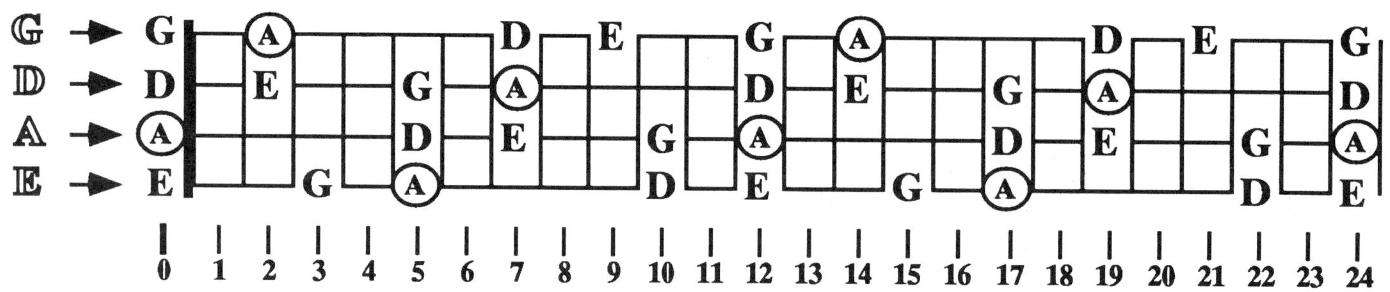

Positions

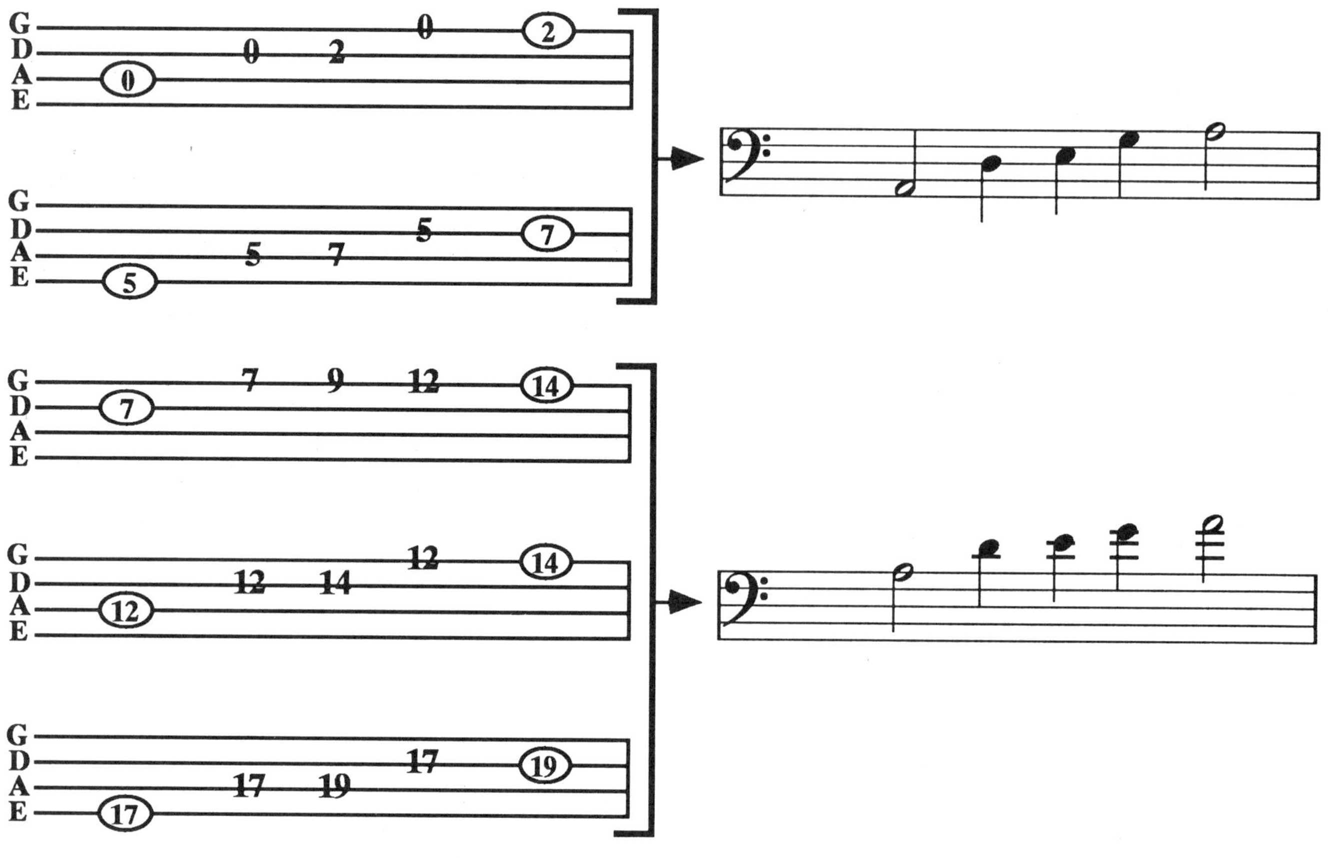

Riff

B SEVENTH SUSPENDED 4TH

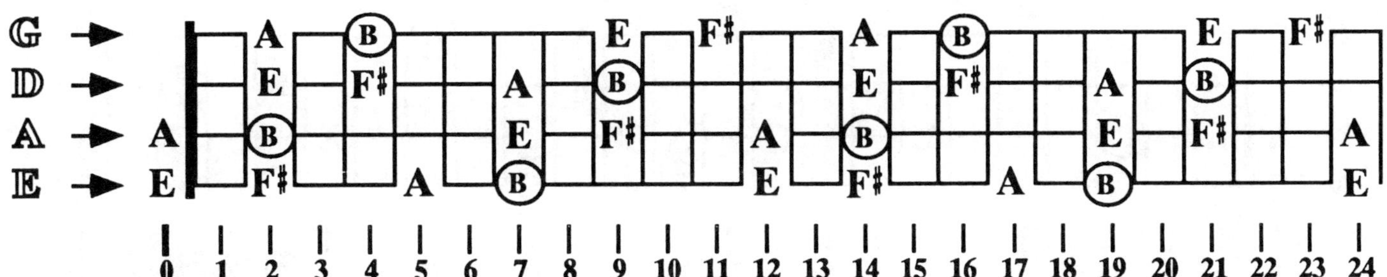

Positions

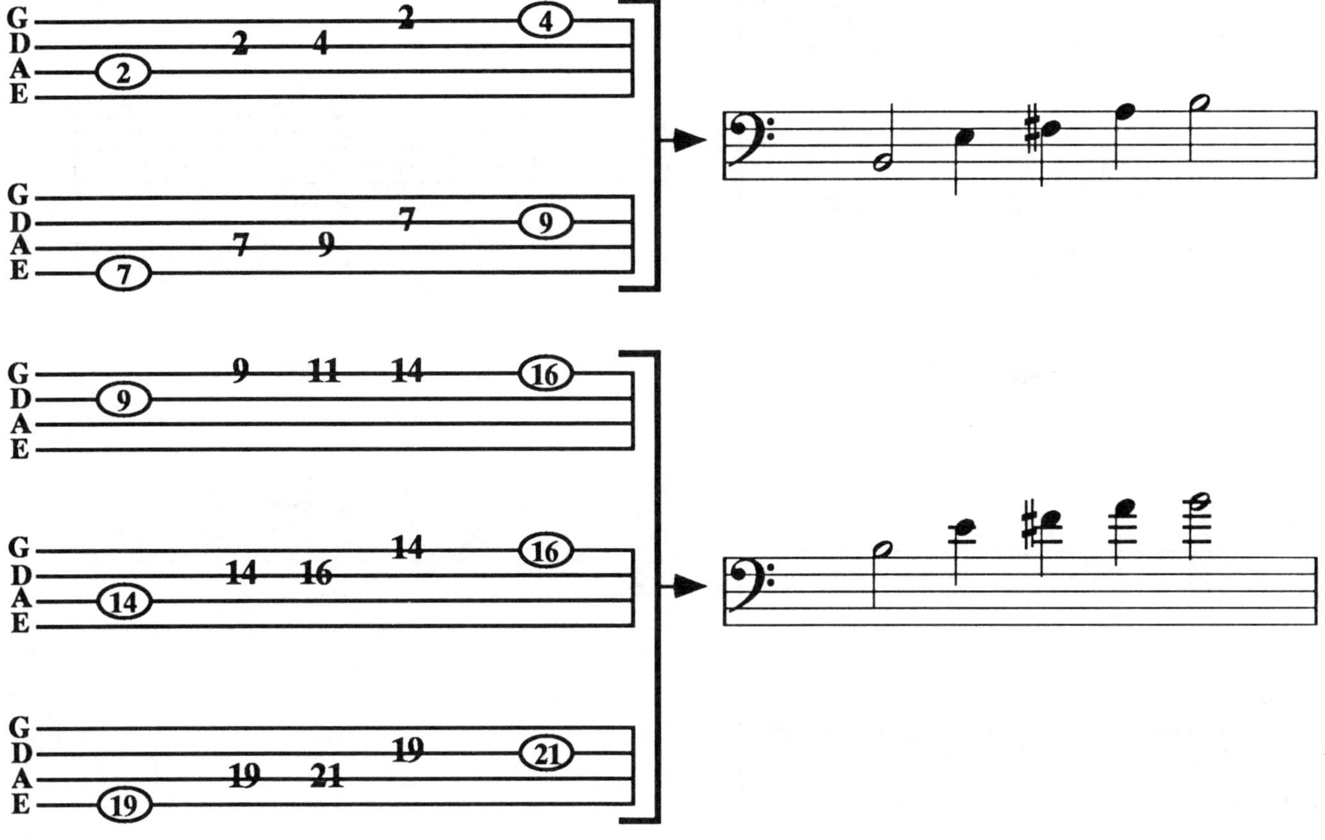

Riff

C THIRTEENTH

FORMULA - (C) Root (E) 3rd (G) 5th (A) 13th (B♭) ♭7th

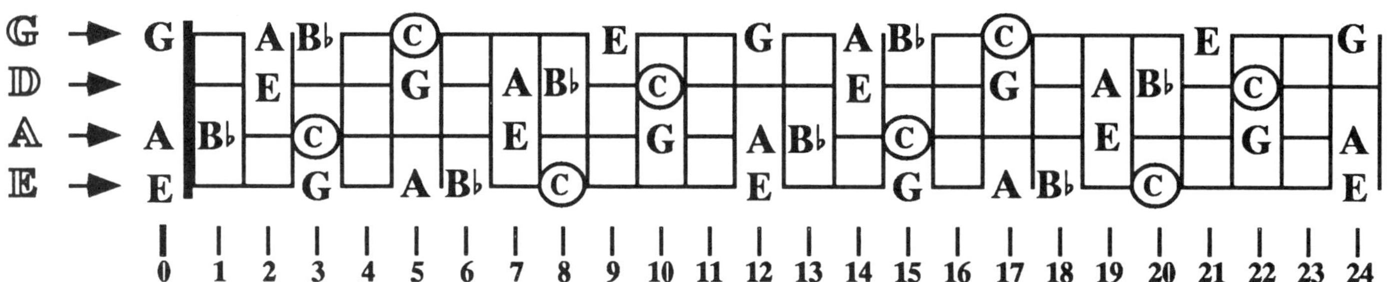

Positions

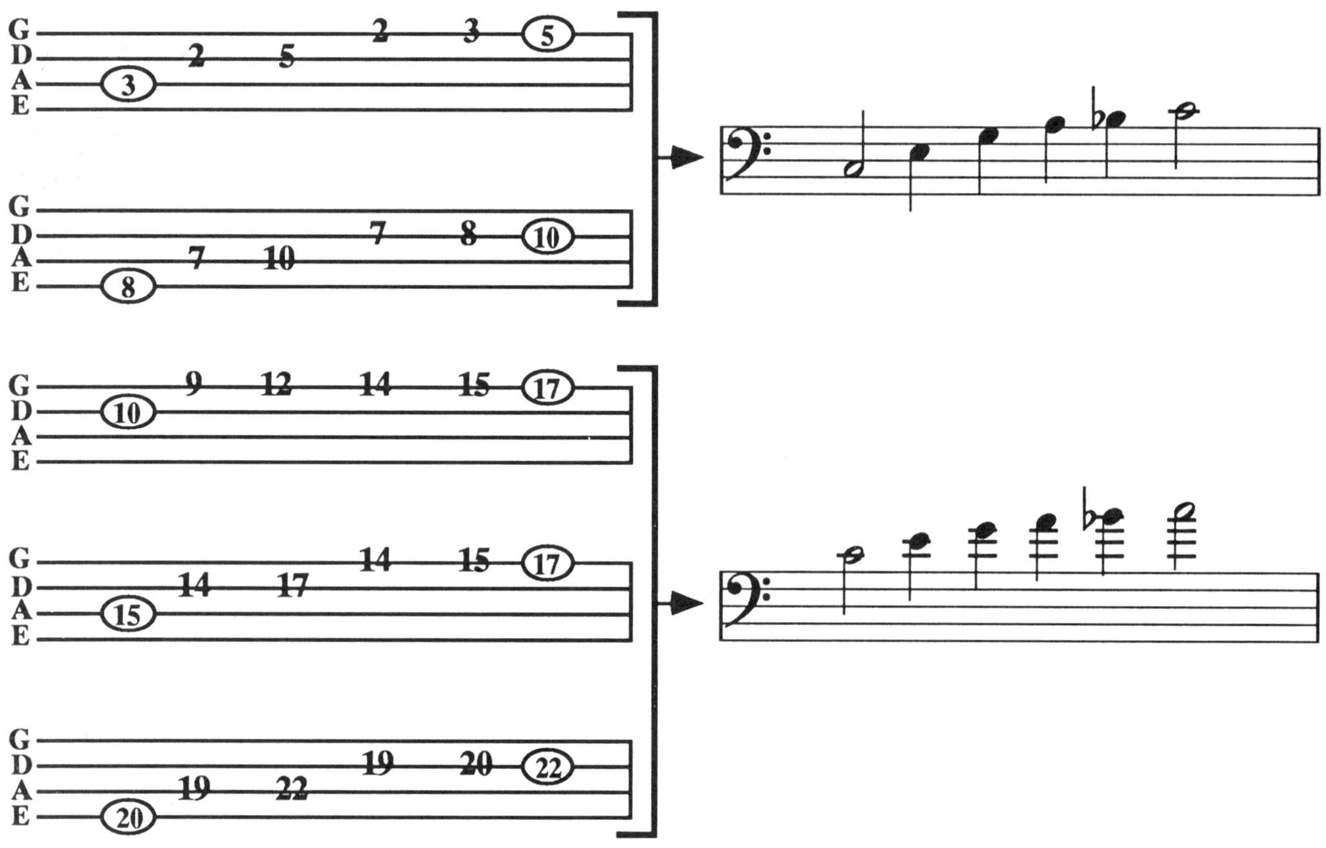

Riff

D THIRTEENTH

FORMULA - (D) Root (F♯) 3rd (A) 5th (B) 13th (C) ♭7th

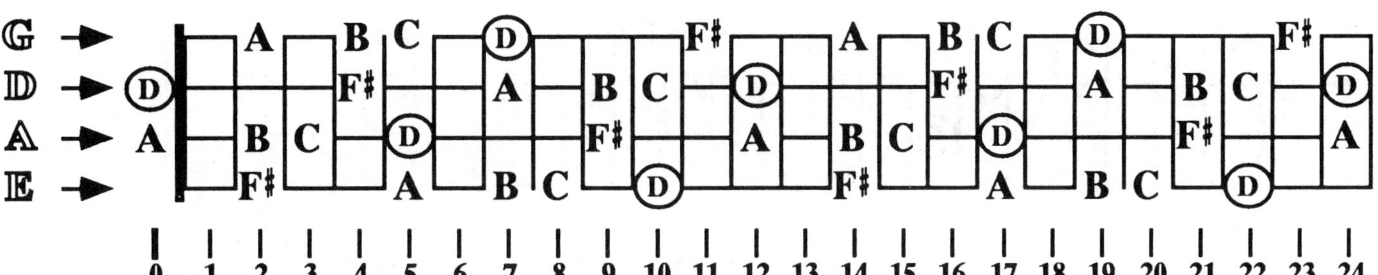

Positions

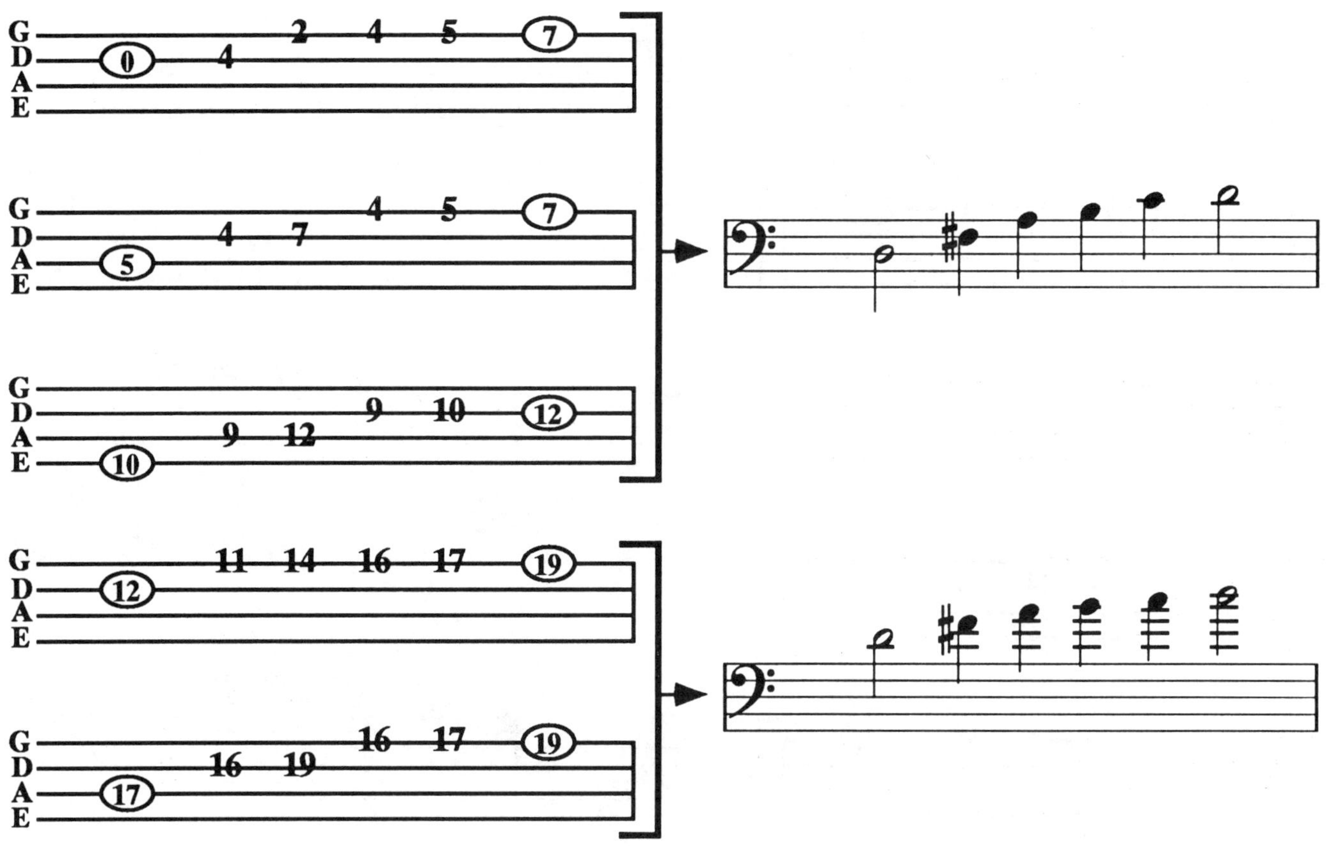

Riff

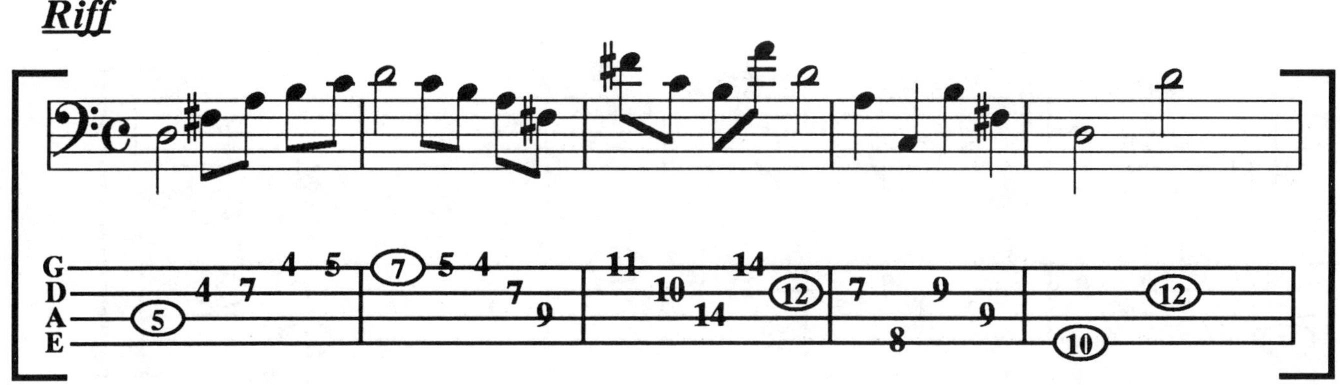

E THIRTEENTH

FORMULA - (E) Root (G♯) 3rd (B) 5th (C♯) 13th (D) ♭7th

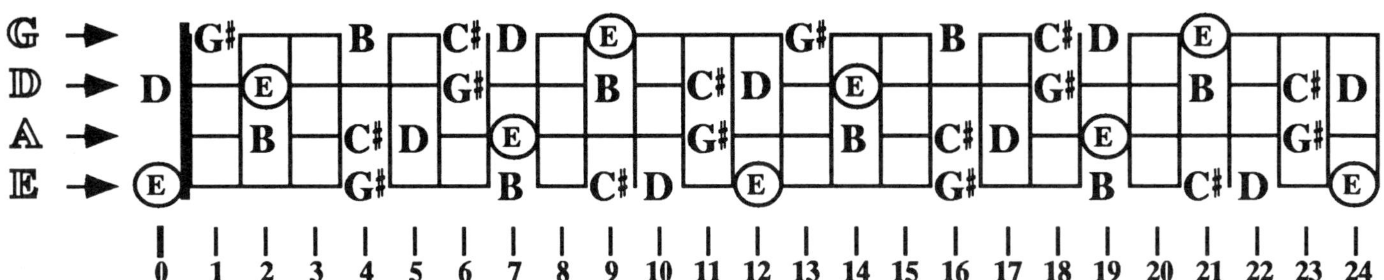

Positions

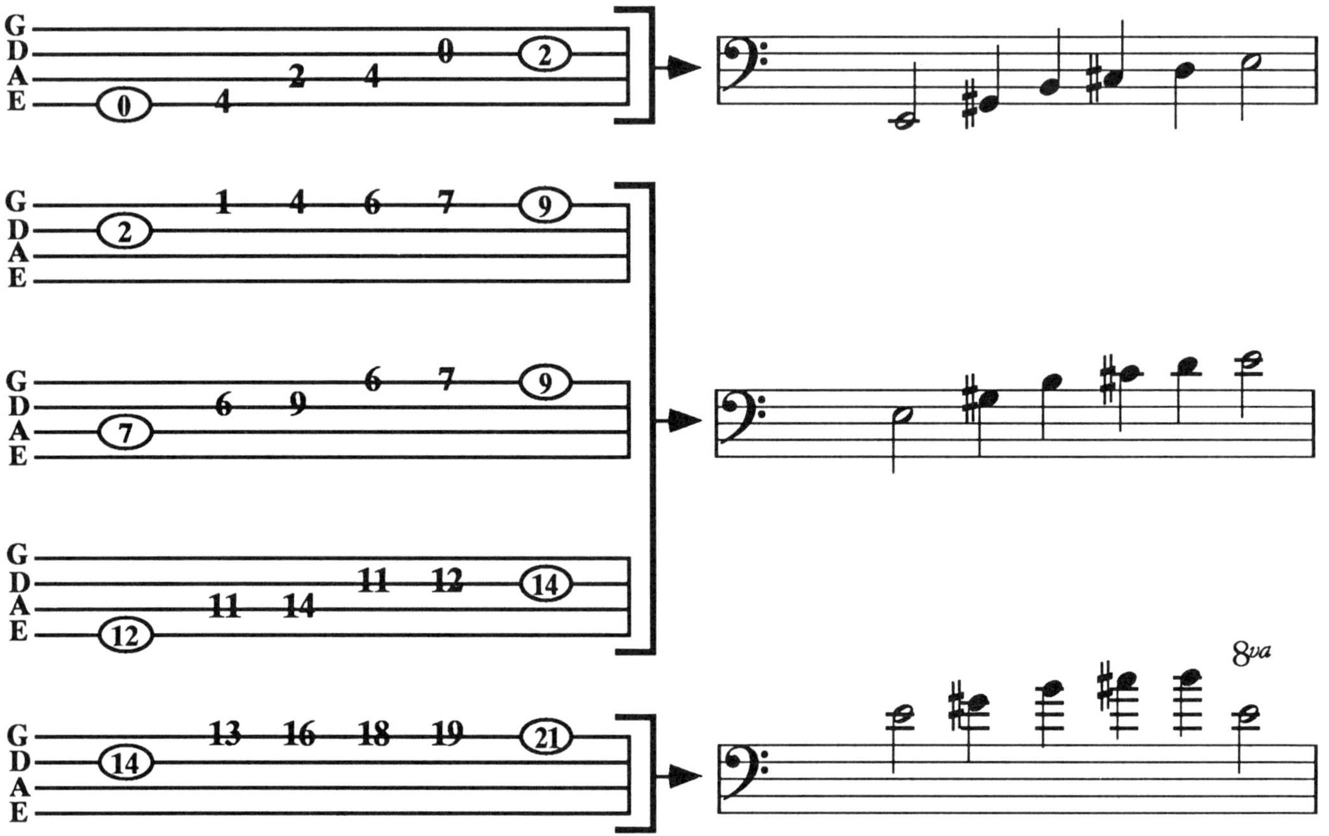

Riff

F THIRTEENTH

FORMULA - (F) Root (A) 3rd (C) 5th (D) 13th (E♭) ♭7th

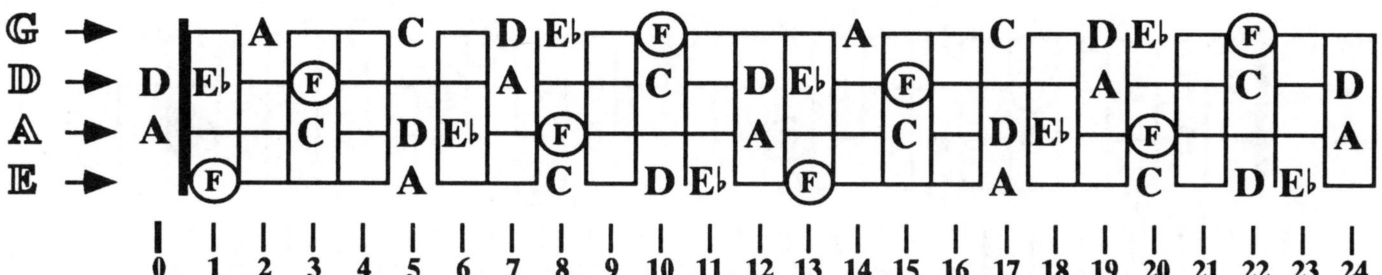

Positions

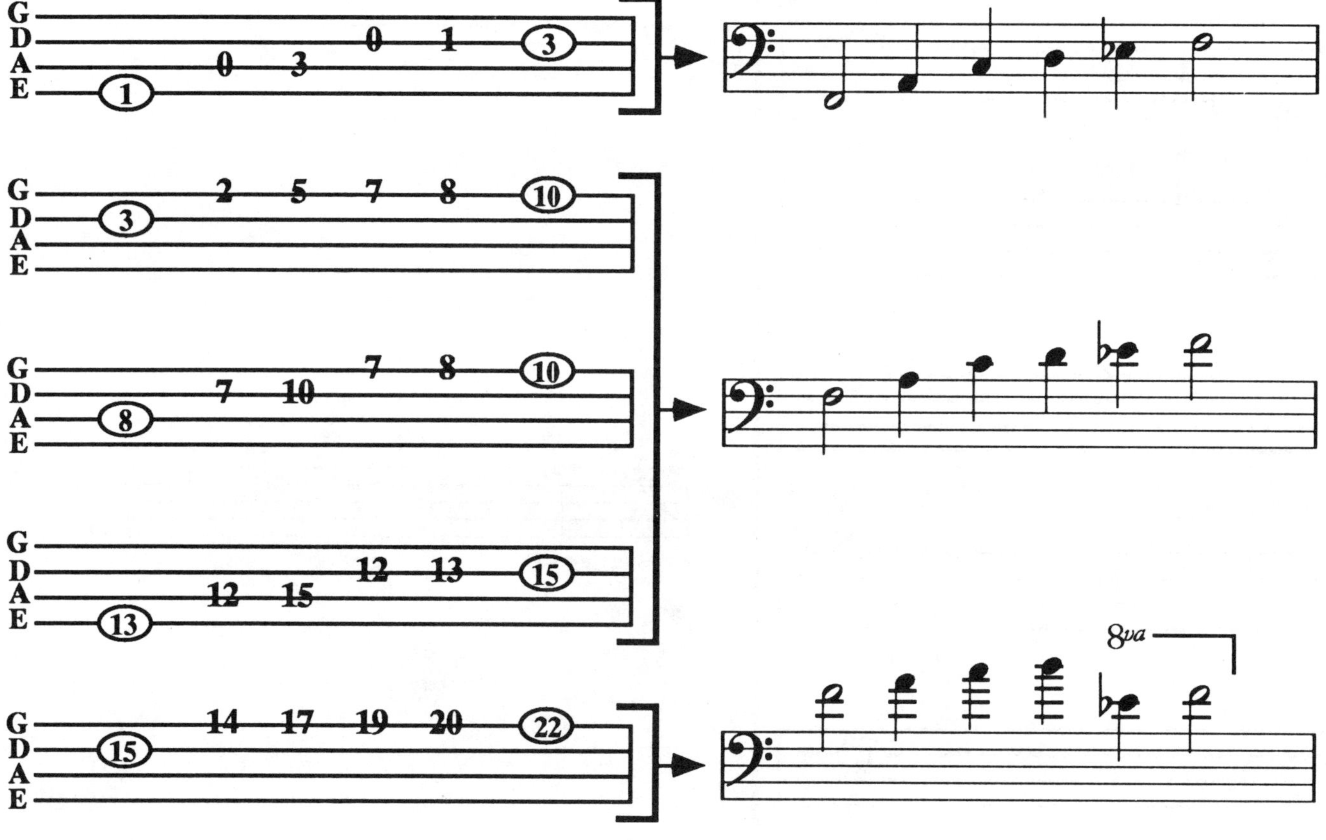

Riff

G THIRTEENTH

FORMULA - (G) Root (B) 3rd (D) 5th (E) 13th (F) ♭7th

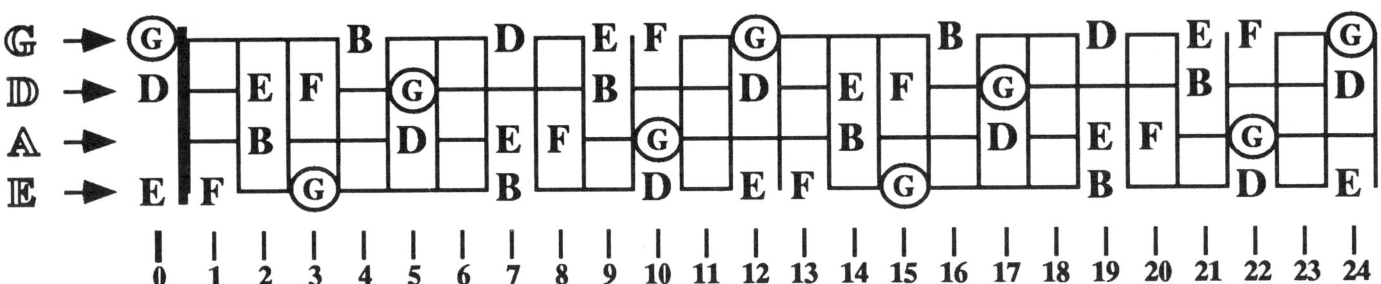

Positions

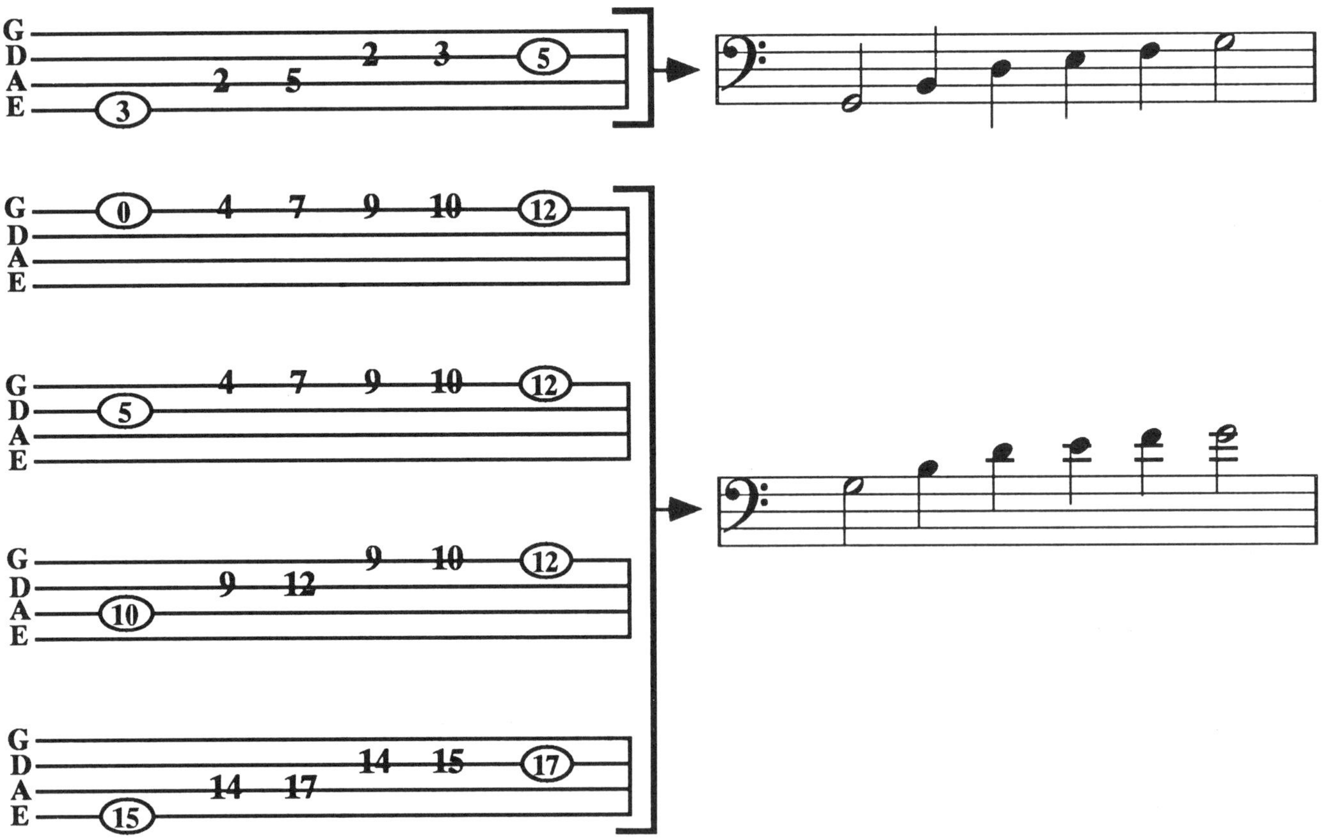

Riff

A THIRTEENTH

FORMULA - (A) Root (C♯) 3rd (E) 5th (F♯)13th (G) ♭9th

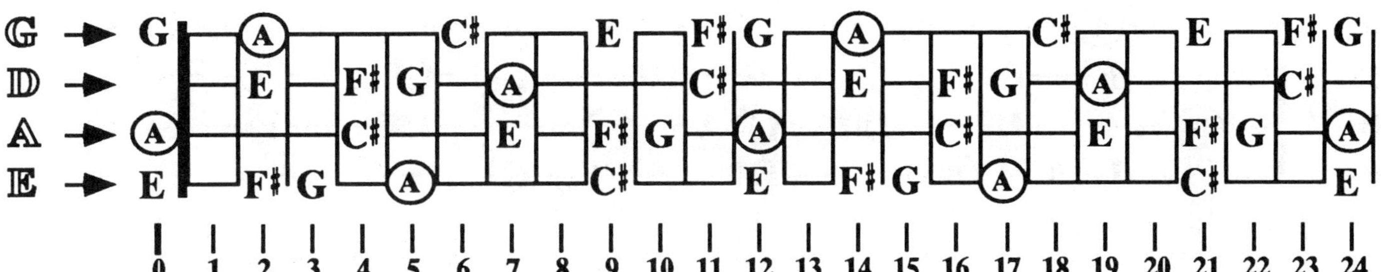

Positions

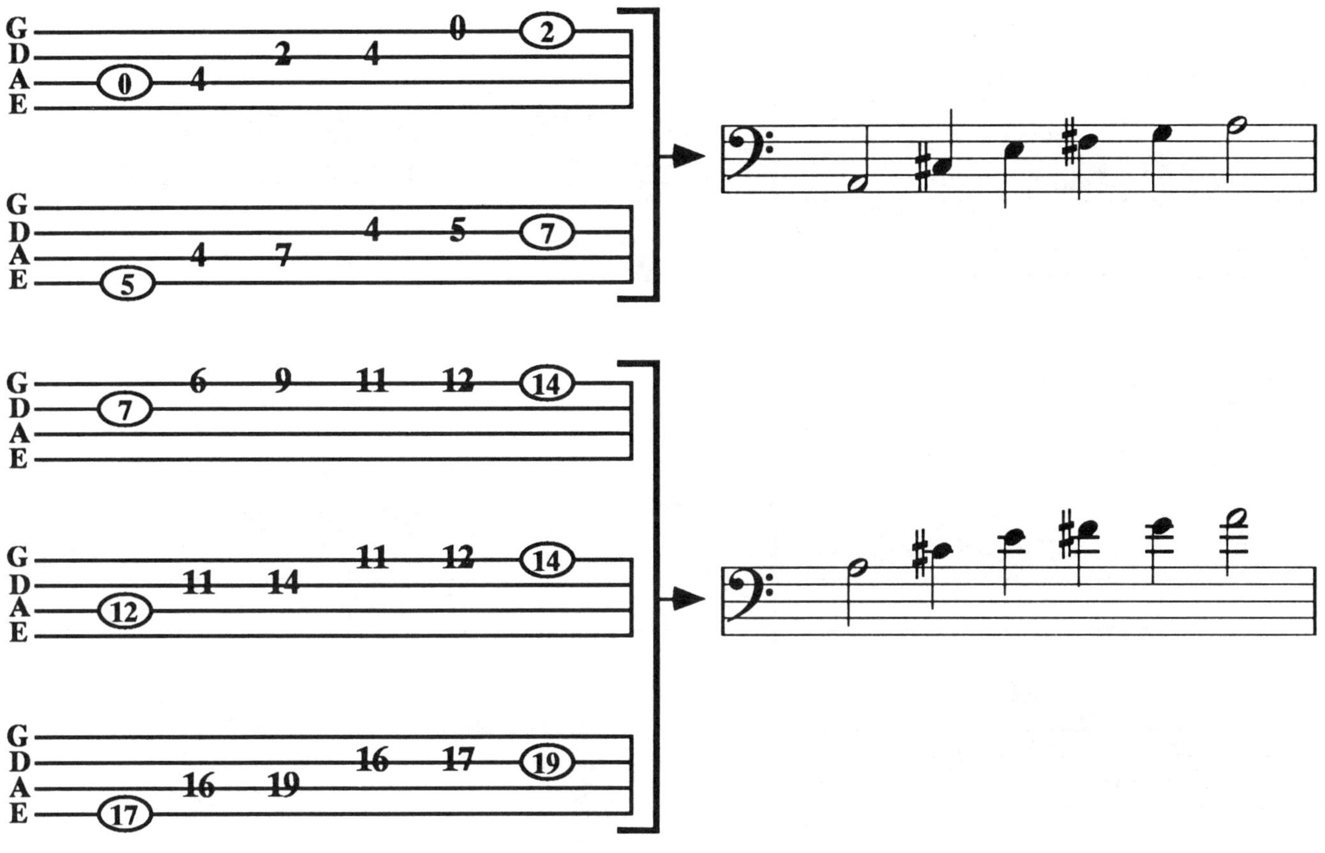

Riff

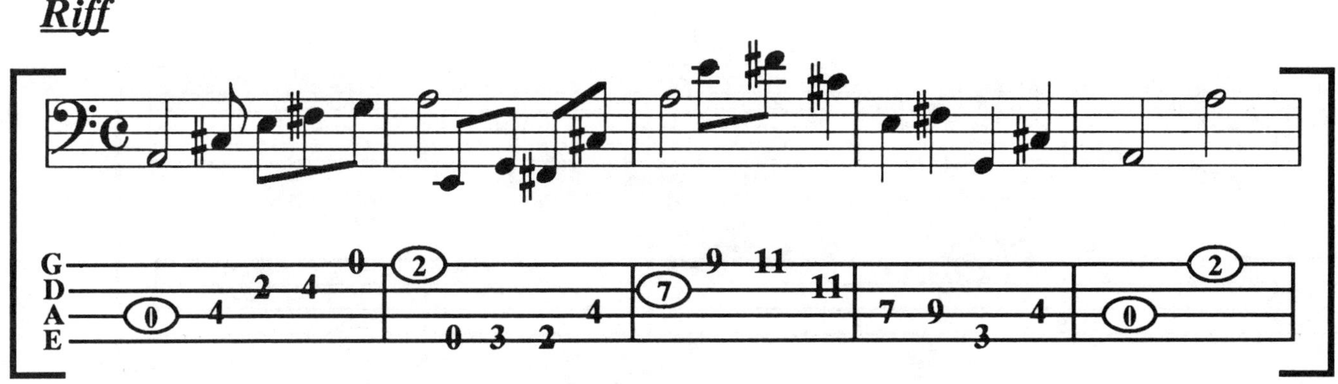

B THIRTEENTH

FORMULA - (B) Root (D♯) 3rd (F♯) 5th (G♯) 13th (A) ♭7th

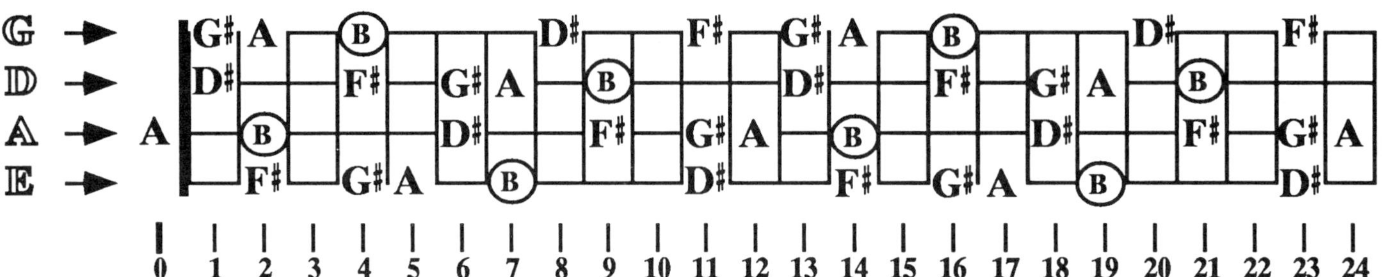

Positions

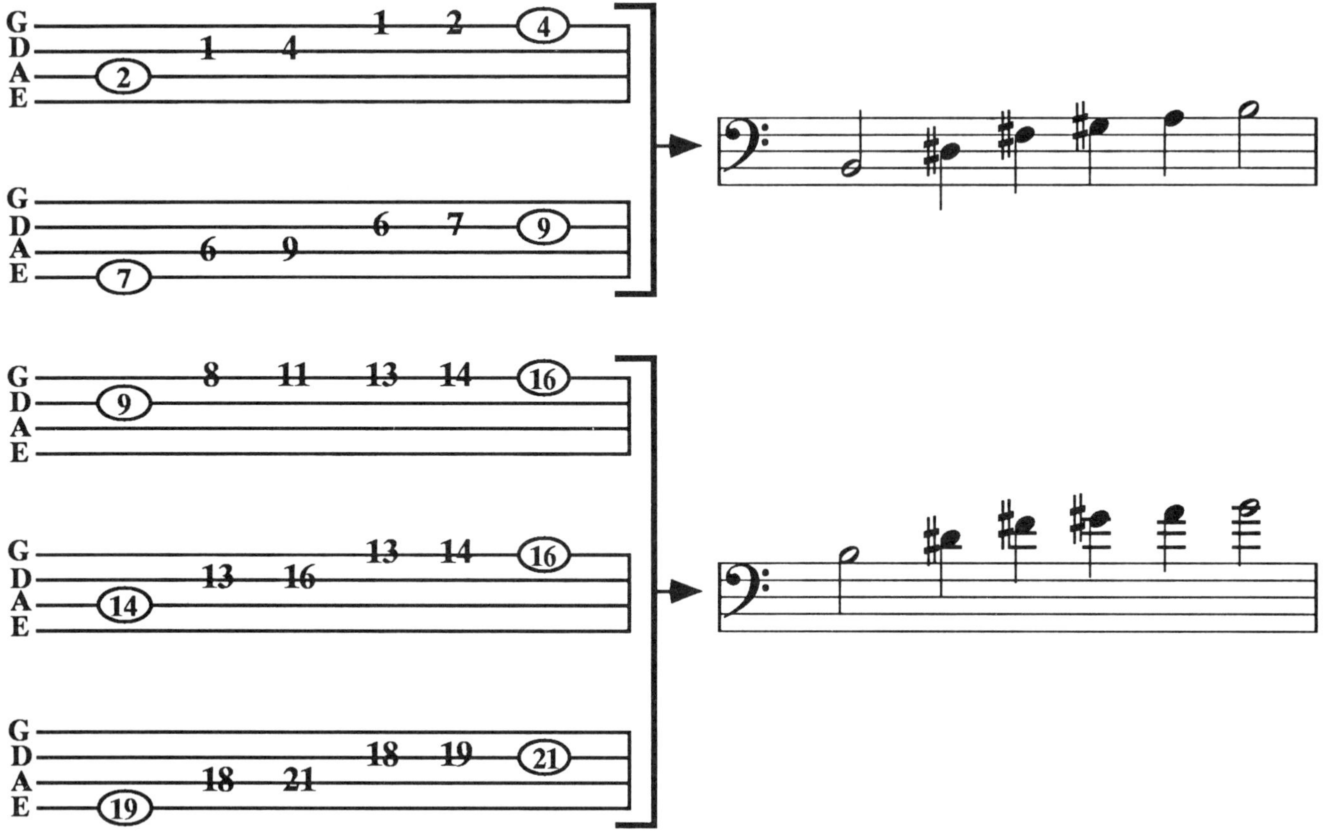

Riff

C THIRTEENTH ♭9TH

FORMULA - (C) Root (E) 3rd (G) 5th
(A) 13th (B♭) ♭7th (D♭) ♭9th

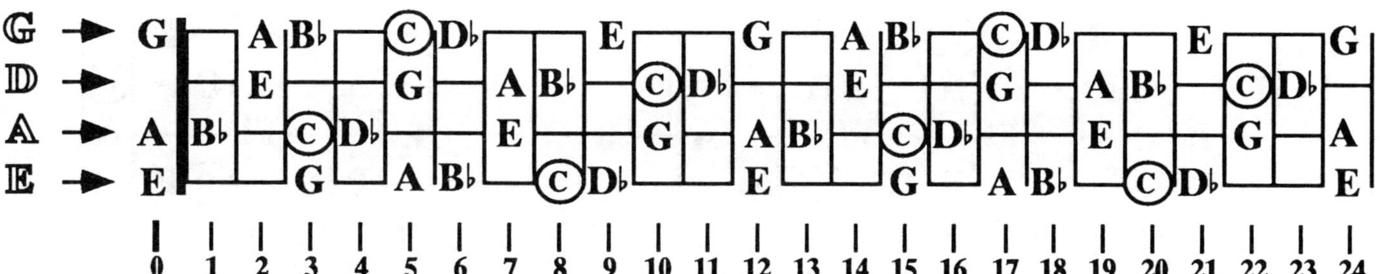

Positions

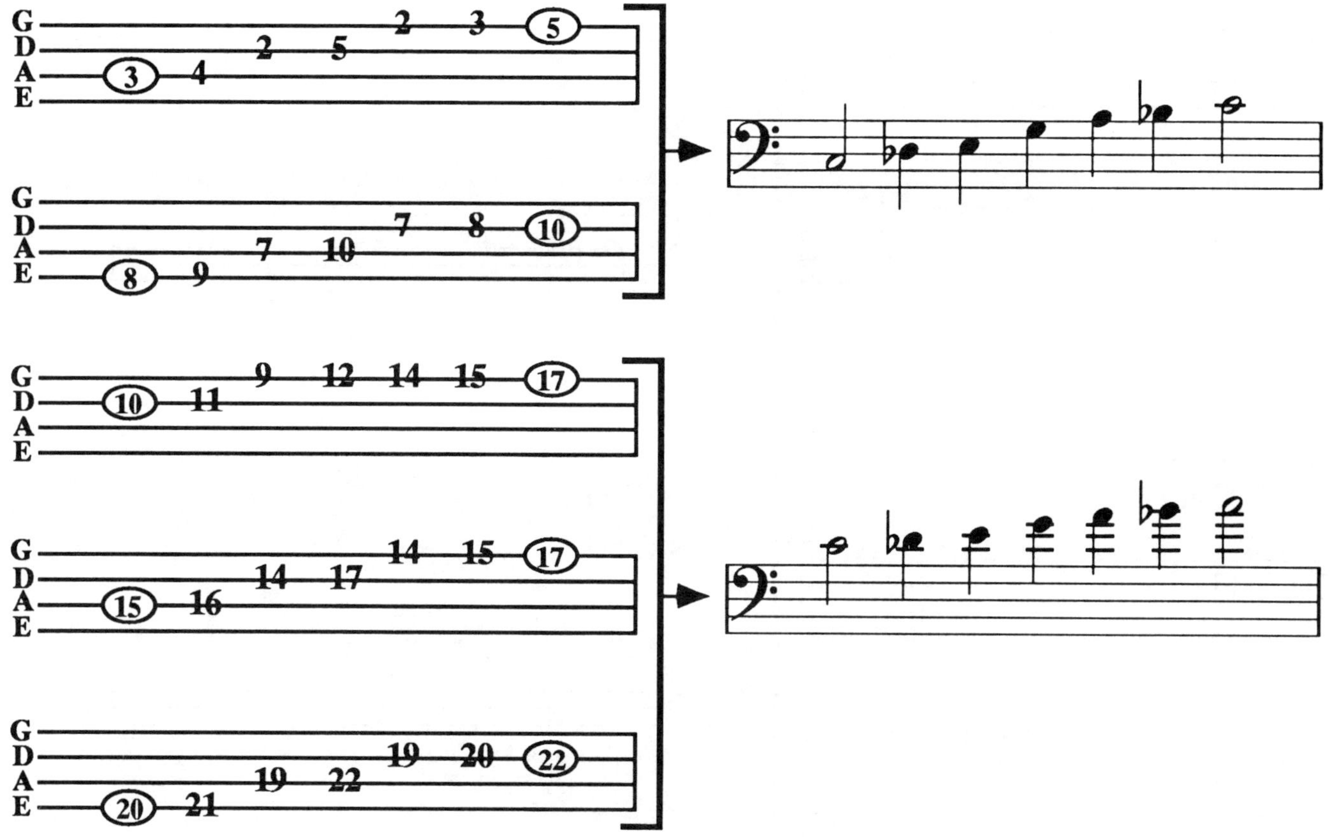

Riff

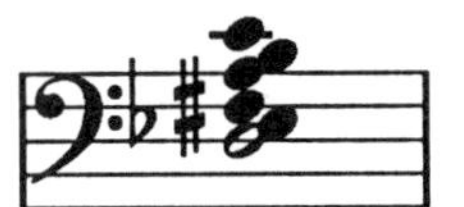

D THIRTEENTH ♭9TH

FORMULA - (D) Root (F♯) 3rd (A) 5th (B)13th (C) ♭7th (E♭) ♭9th

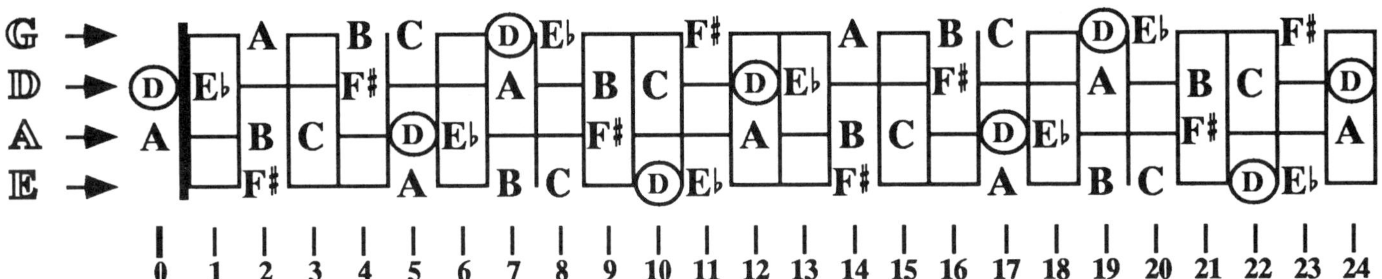

Positions

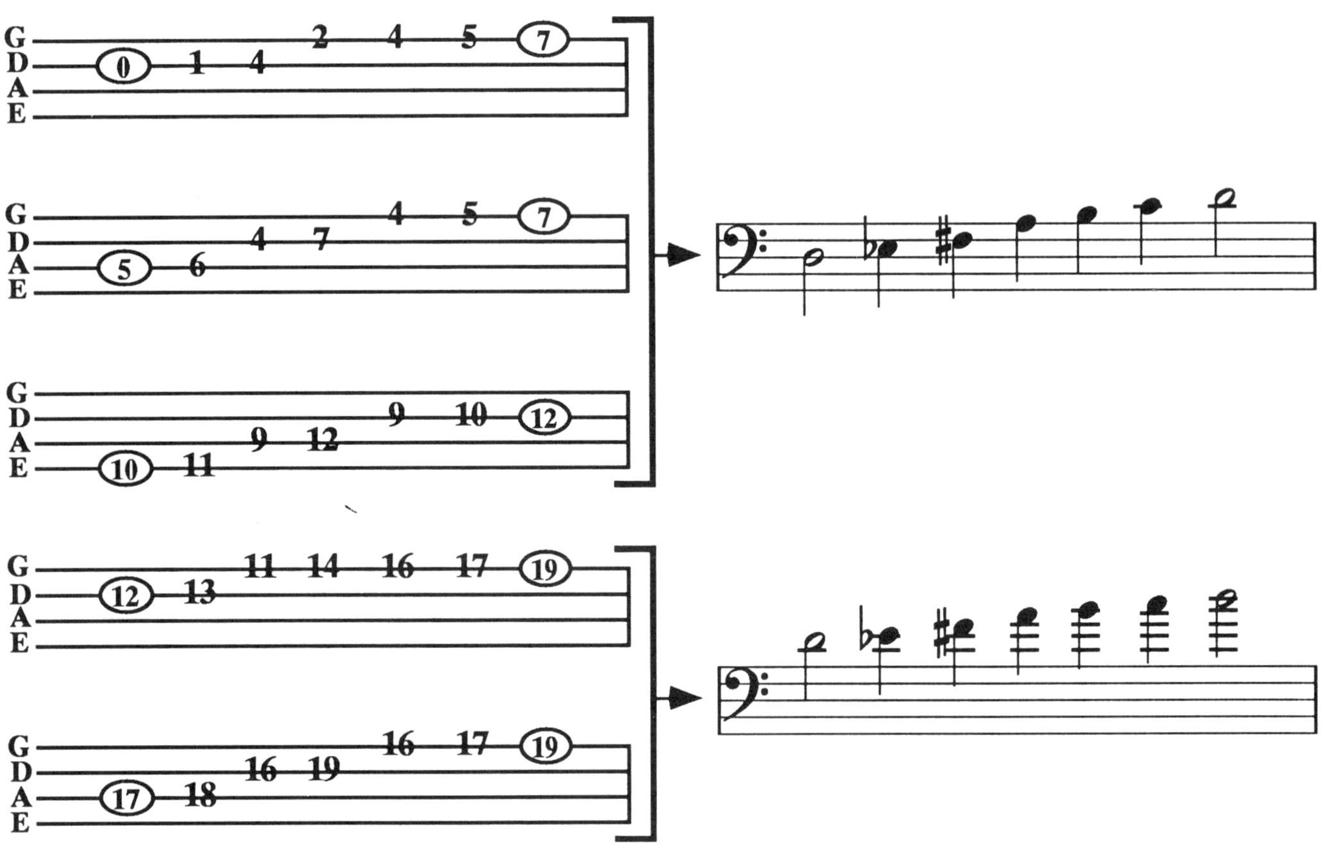

Riff

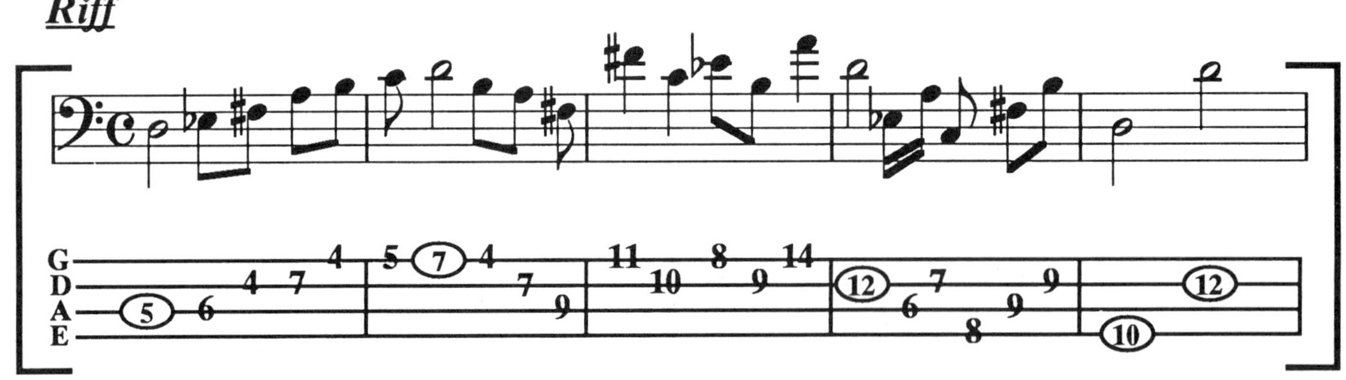

E THIRTEENTH ♭9TH

FORMULA - (E) Root (G♯) 3rd (B) 5th (C♯) 13th (D) ♭7th (F) ♭9th

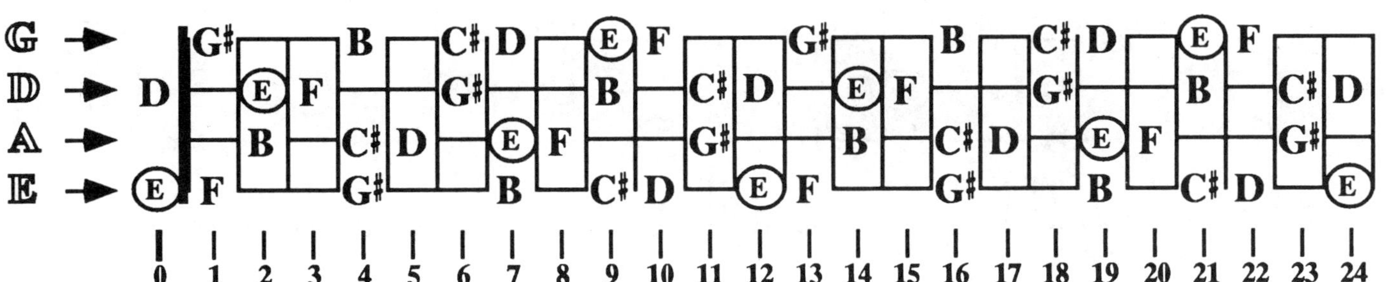

Positions

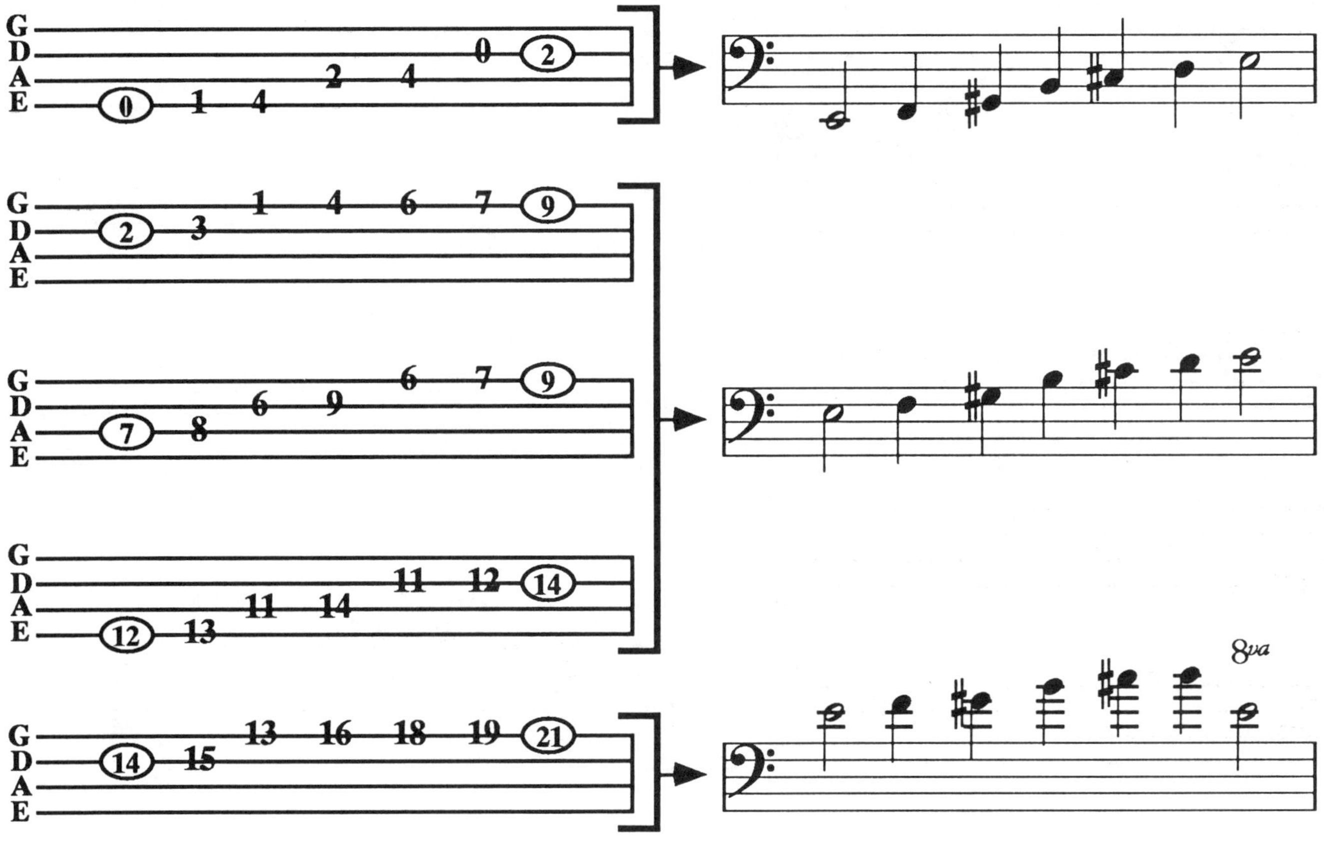

Riff

F THIRTEENTH ♭9TH

FORMULA - (F) Root (A) 3rd (C) 5th
(D) 13th (E♭) ♭7th (G♭) ♭9th

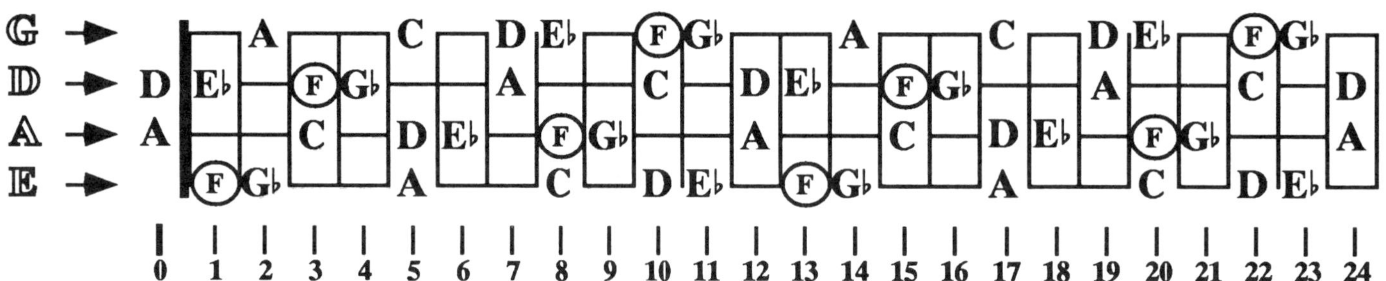

Positions

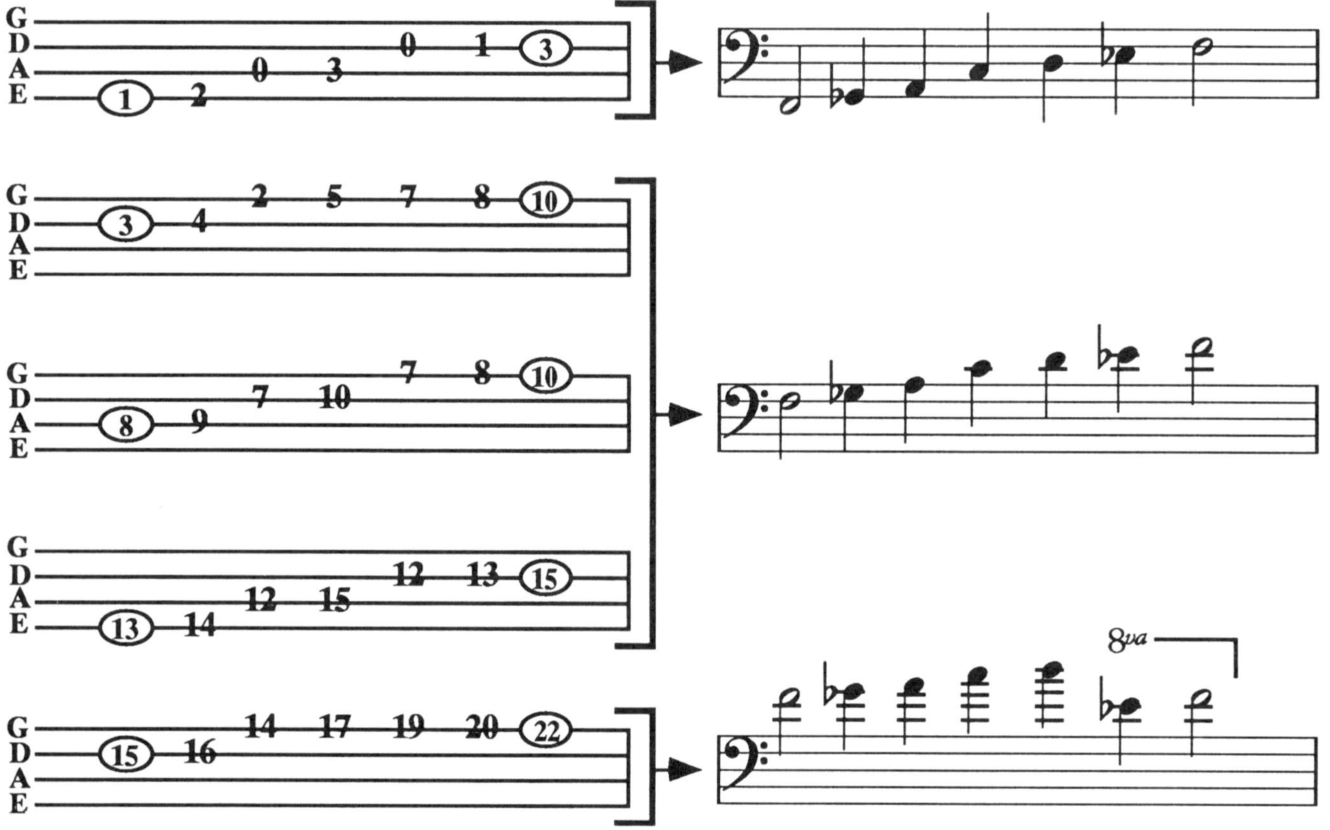

Riff

G   THIRTEENTH ♭9TH

FORMULA - (G) Root (B) 3rd (D) 5th
(E) 13th (F) ♭7th (A♭) ♭9th

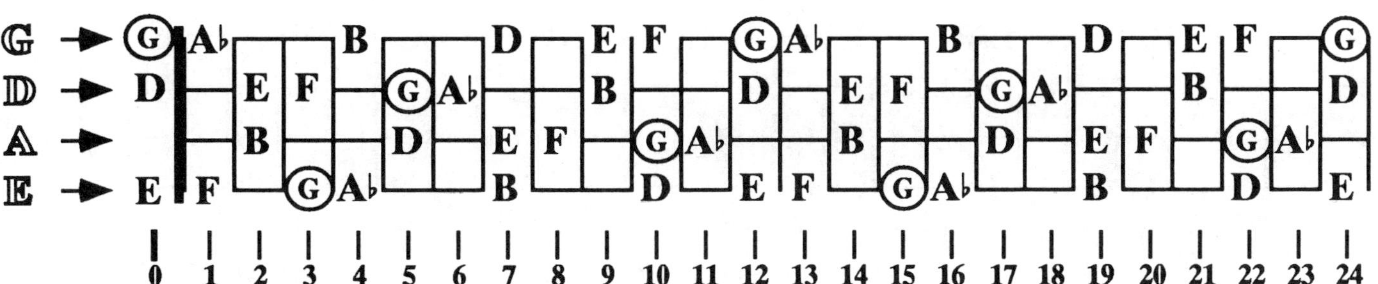

Positions

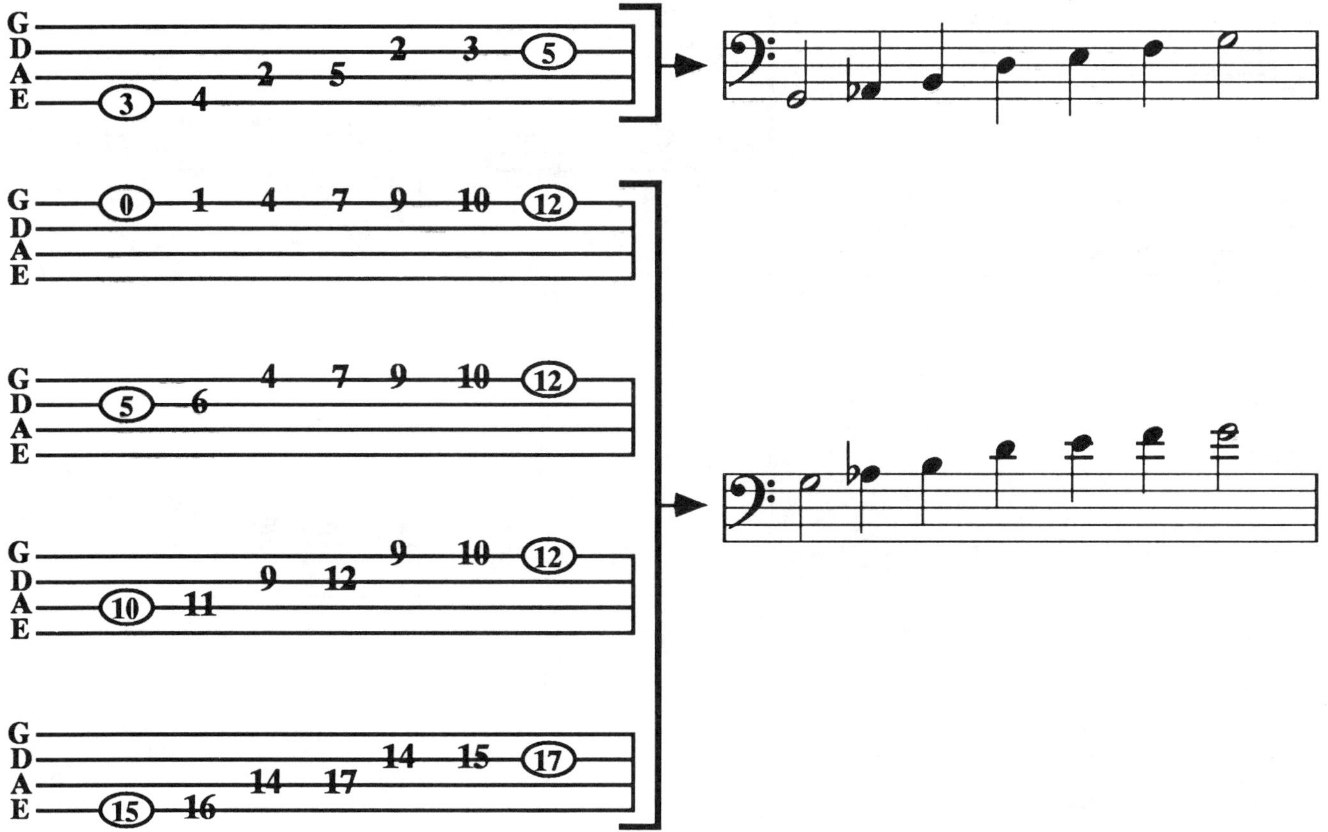

Riff

A THIRTEENTH ♭9TH

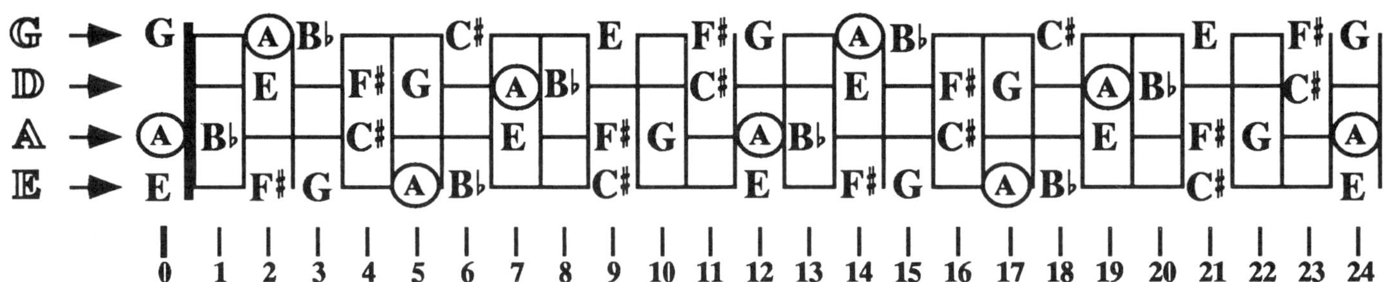

FORMULA - (A) Root (C♯) 3rd (E) 5th (F♯)13th (G) ♭7th (B♭) ♭9th

A13-9

Positions

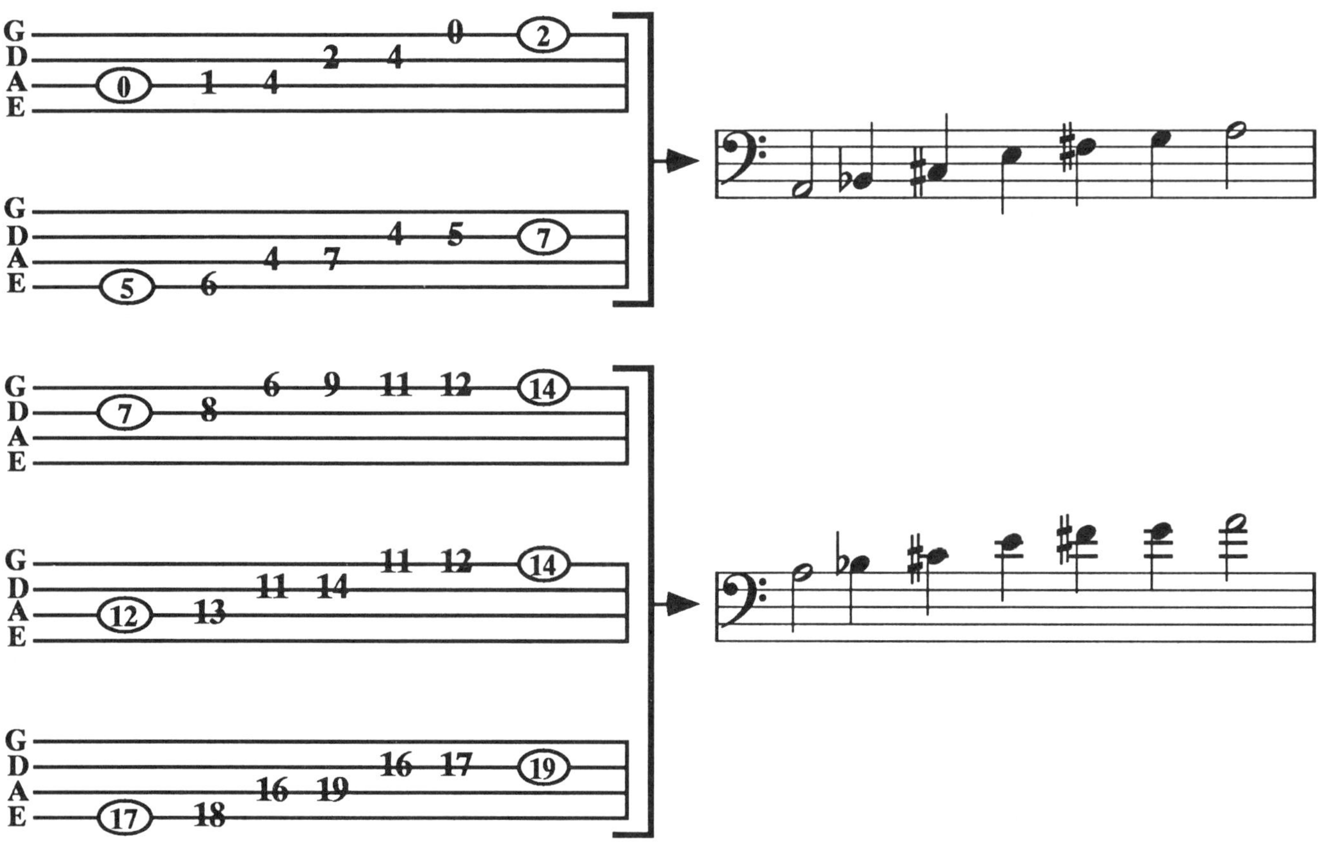

Riff

B THIRTEENTH ♭9TH

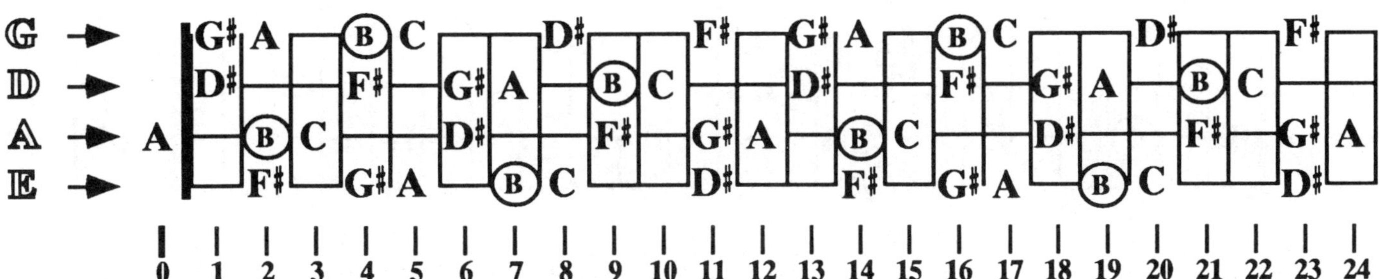

Positions

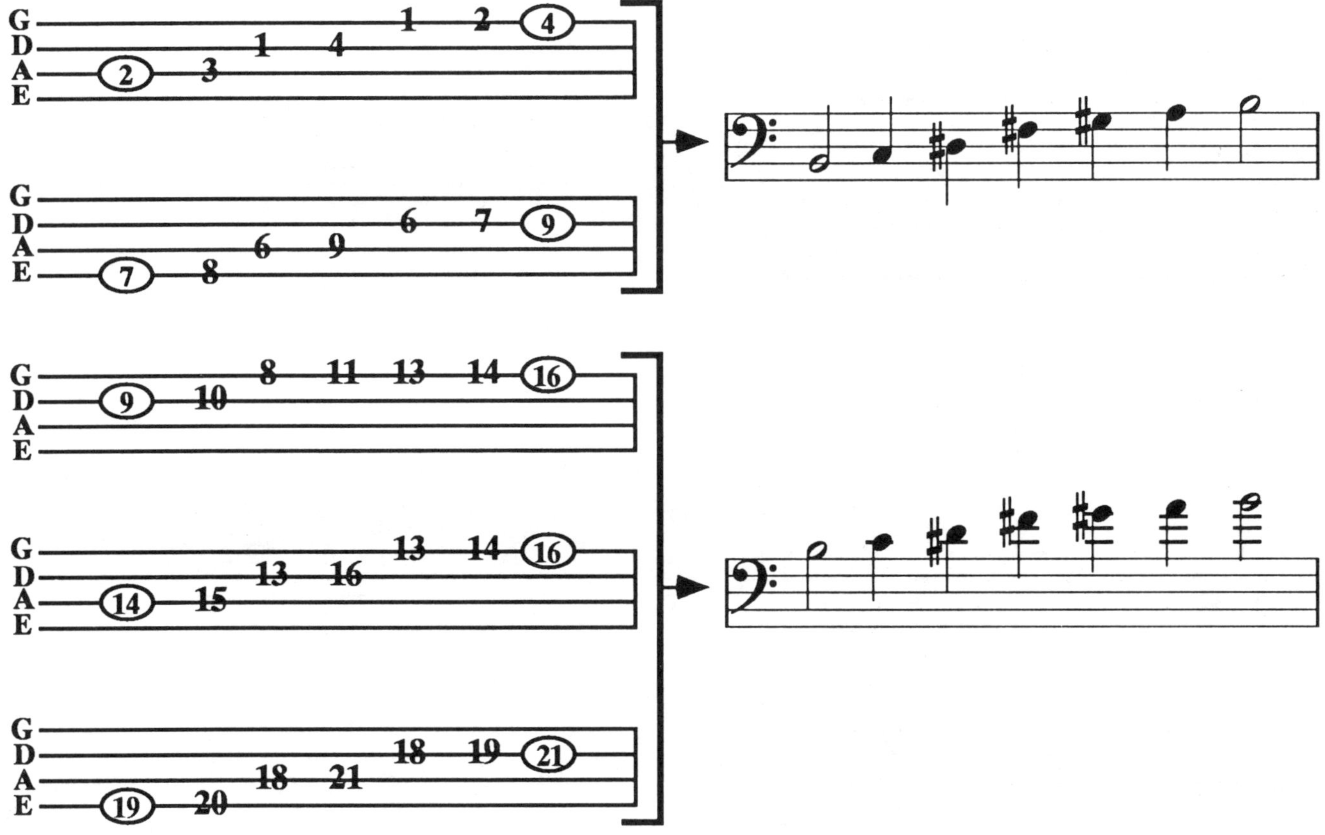

Riff

C THIRTEENTH ♭9TH ♭5TH

FORMULA - (C) Root (E♭) ♭3rd (G♭) ♭5th
(A) 13th (B♭) ♭7th (D♭) ♭9th

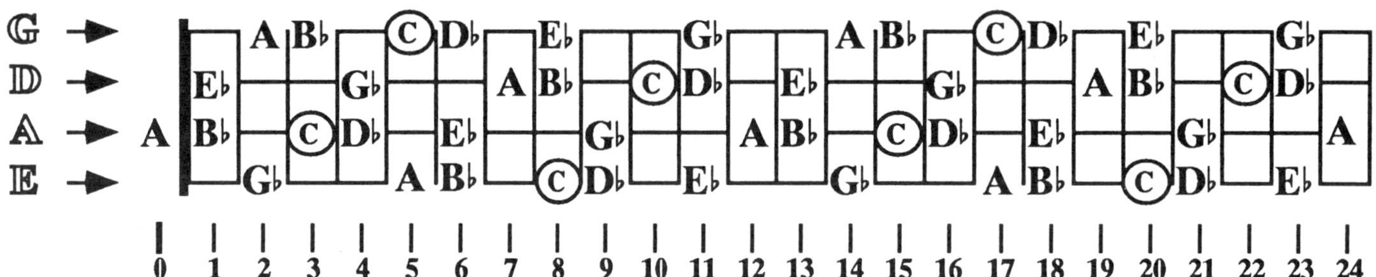

Positions

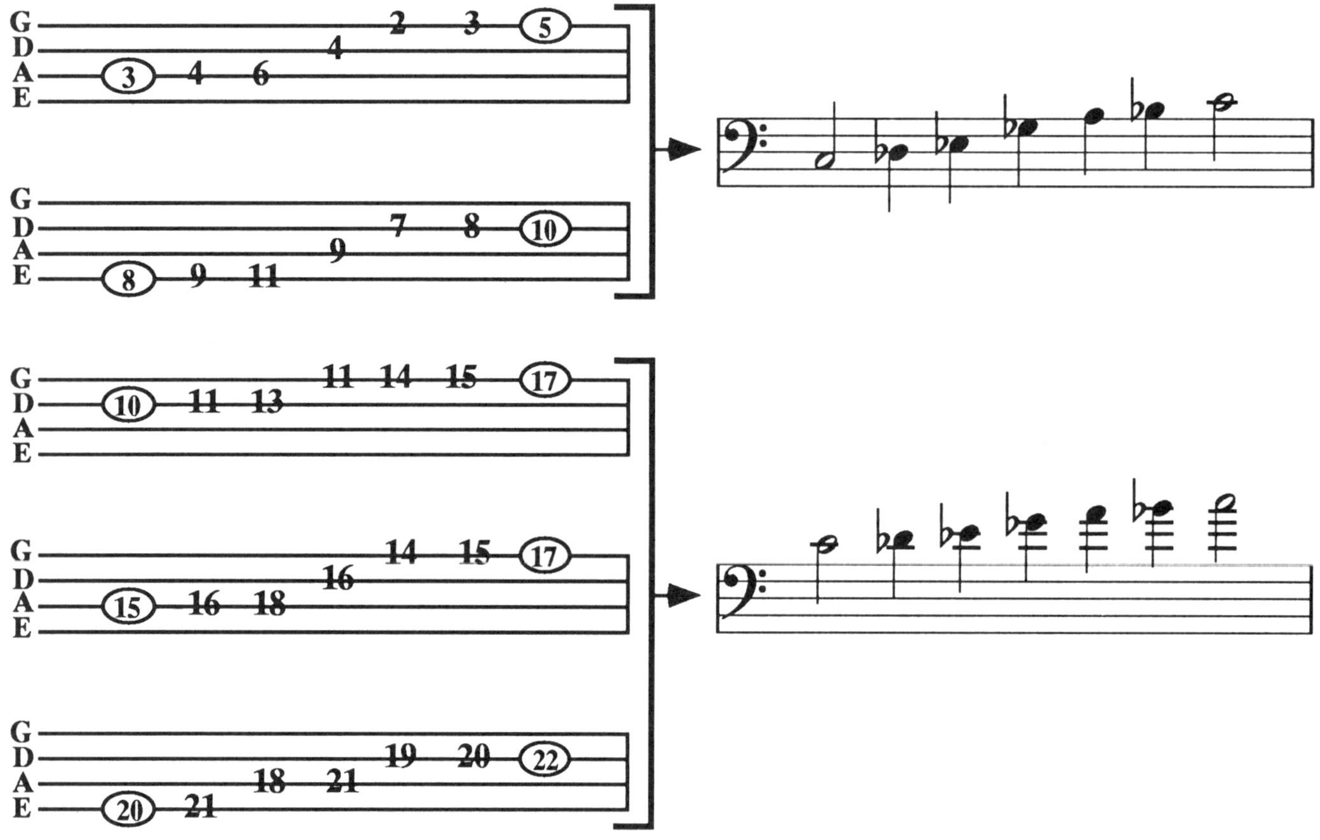

Riff

D THIRTEENTH ♭9TH ♭5TH

FORMULA - (D) Root (F♯) 3rd (A♭) ♭5th
(B)13th (C) ♭7th (E♭)♭9th

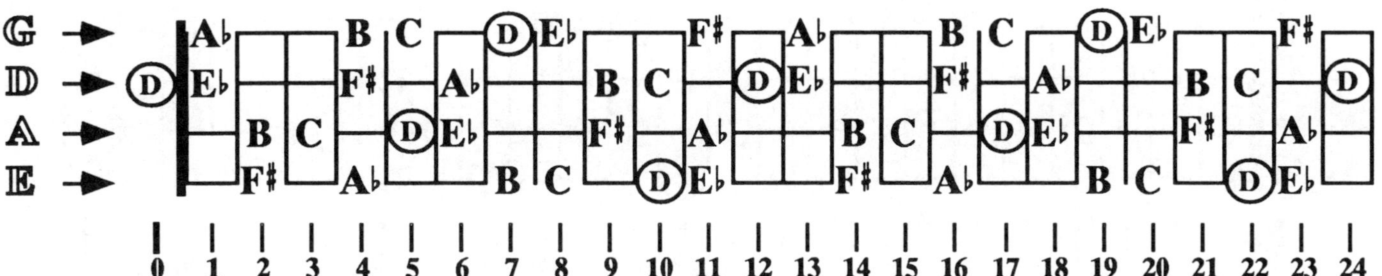

Positions

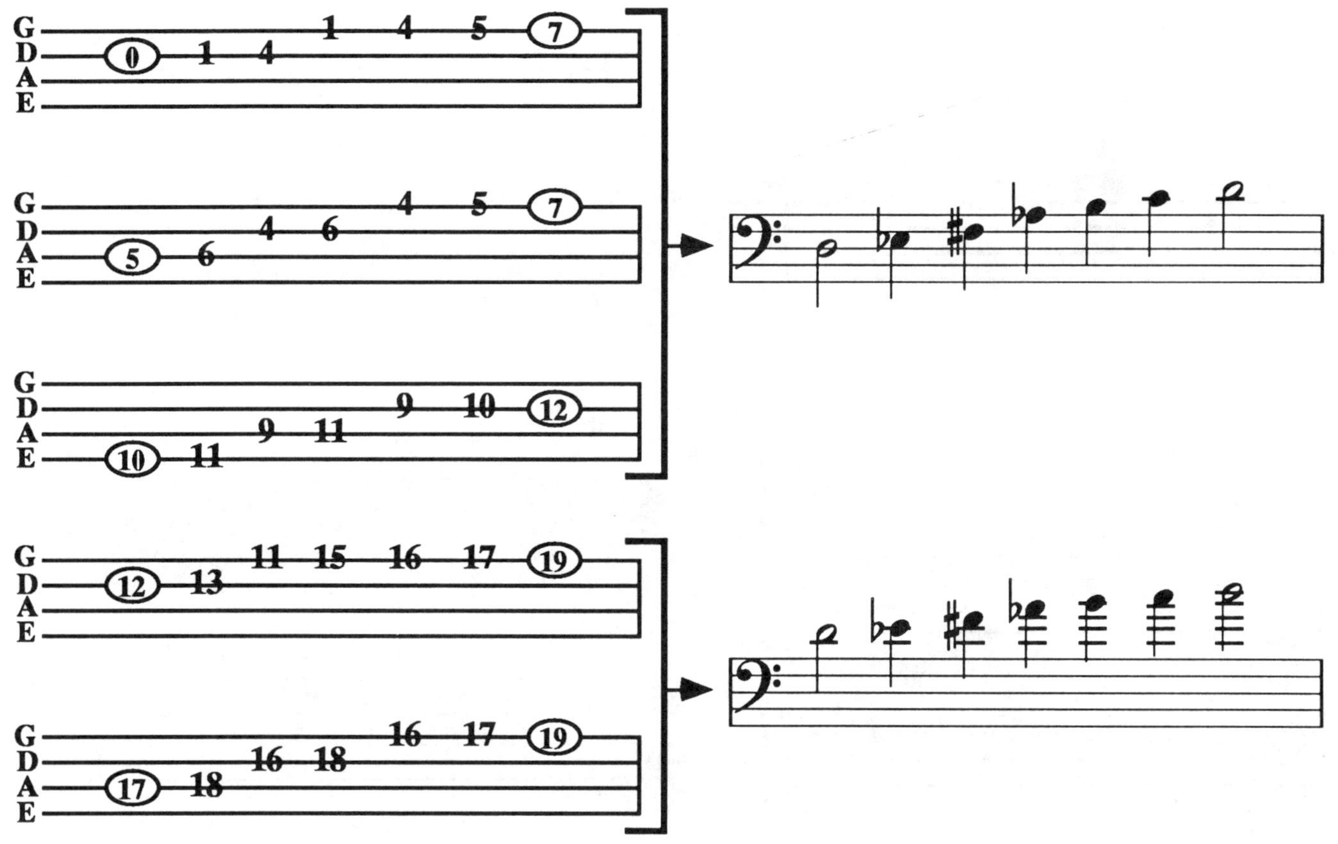

Riff

E THIRTEENTH ♭9TH ♭5TH

FORMULA - (E) Root (G♯) 3rd (B♭) ♭5th (C♯) 13th (D) ♭7th (F) ♭9th

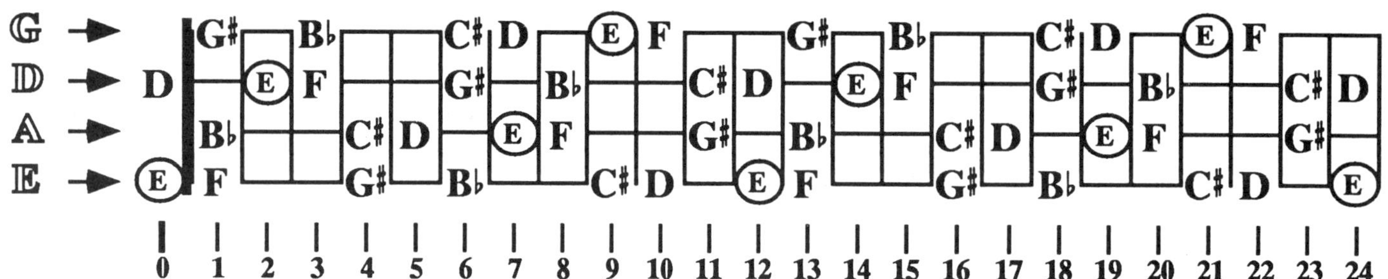

Positions

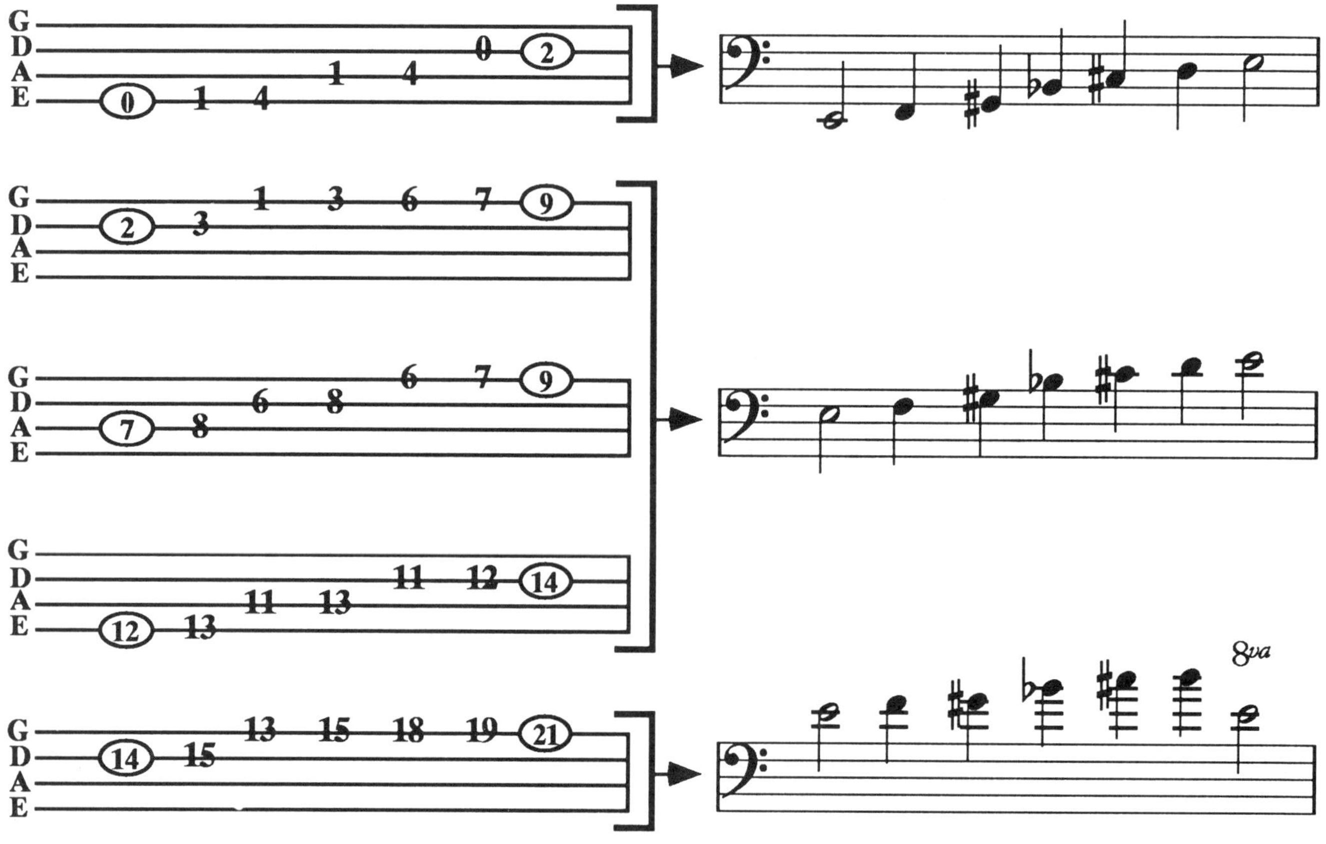

Riff

F THIRTEENTH ♭9TH ♭5TH

FORMULA - (F) Root (A) 3rd (C♭) ♭5th (D) 13th (E♭) ♭7th (G♭) ♭9th

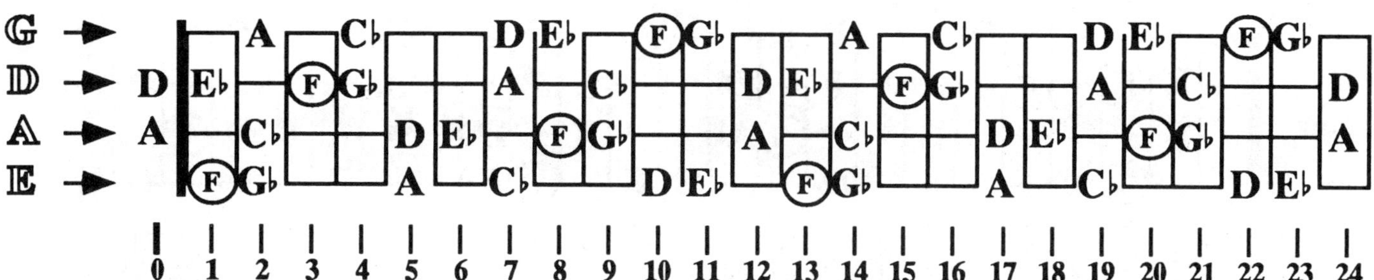

Positions

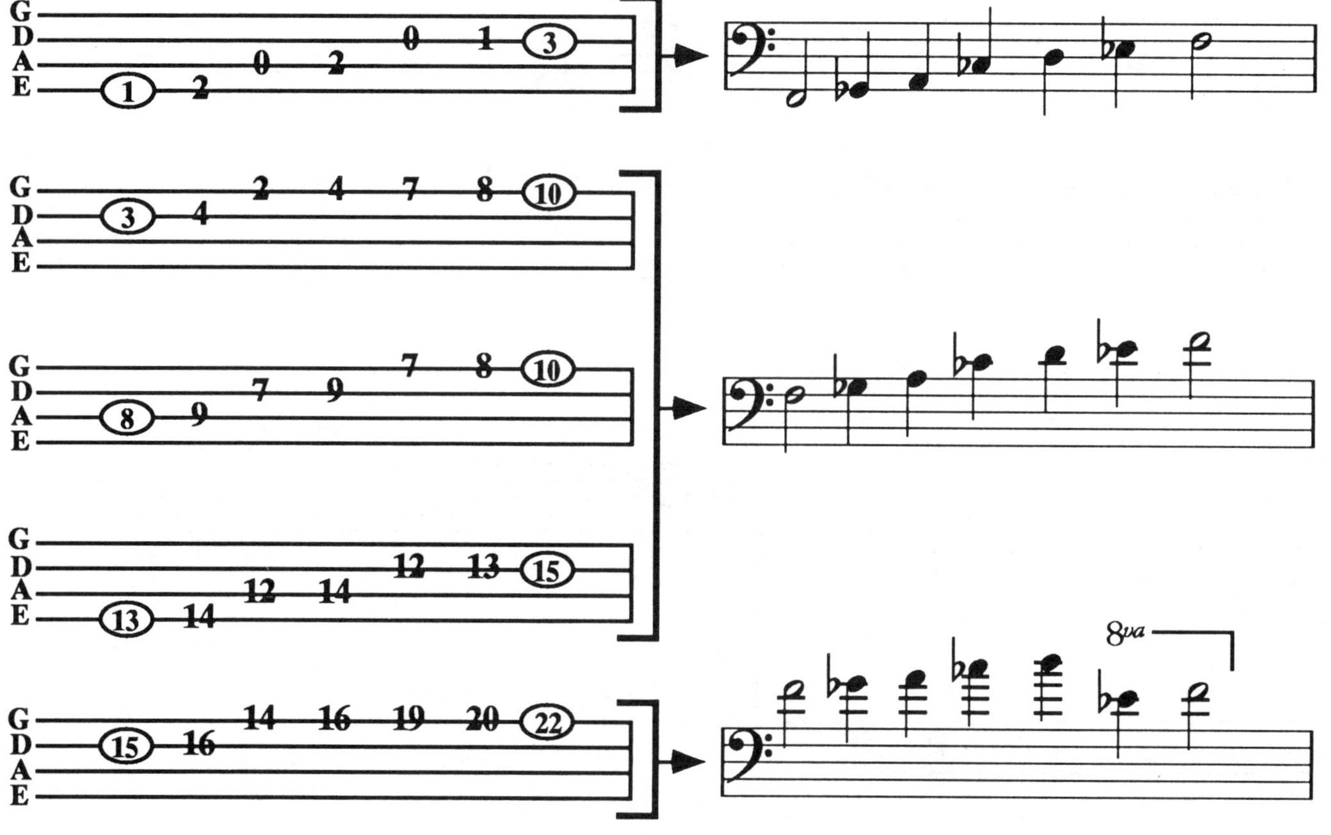

Riff

G THIRTEENTH ♭9TH ♭5TH

FORMULA - (G) Root (B) 3rd (D♭) ♭5th
(E) 13th (F) ♭7th (A♭) ♭9th

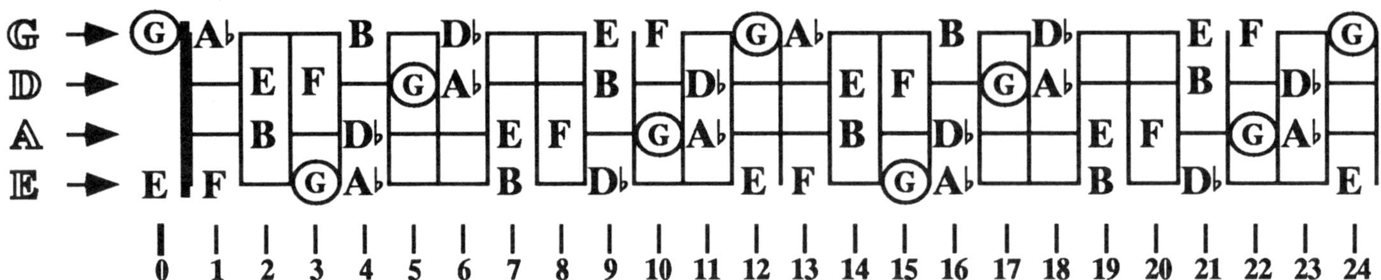

Positions

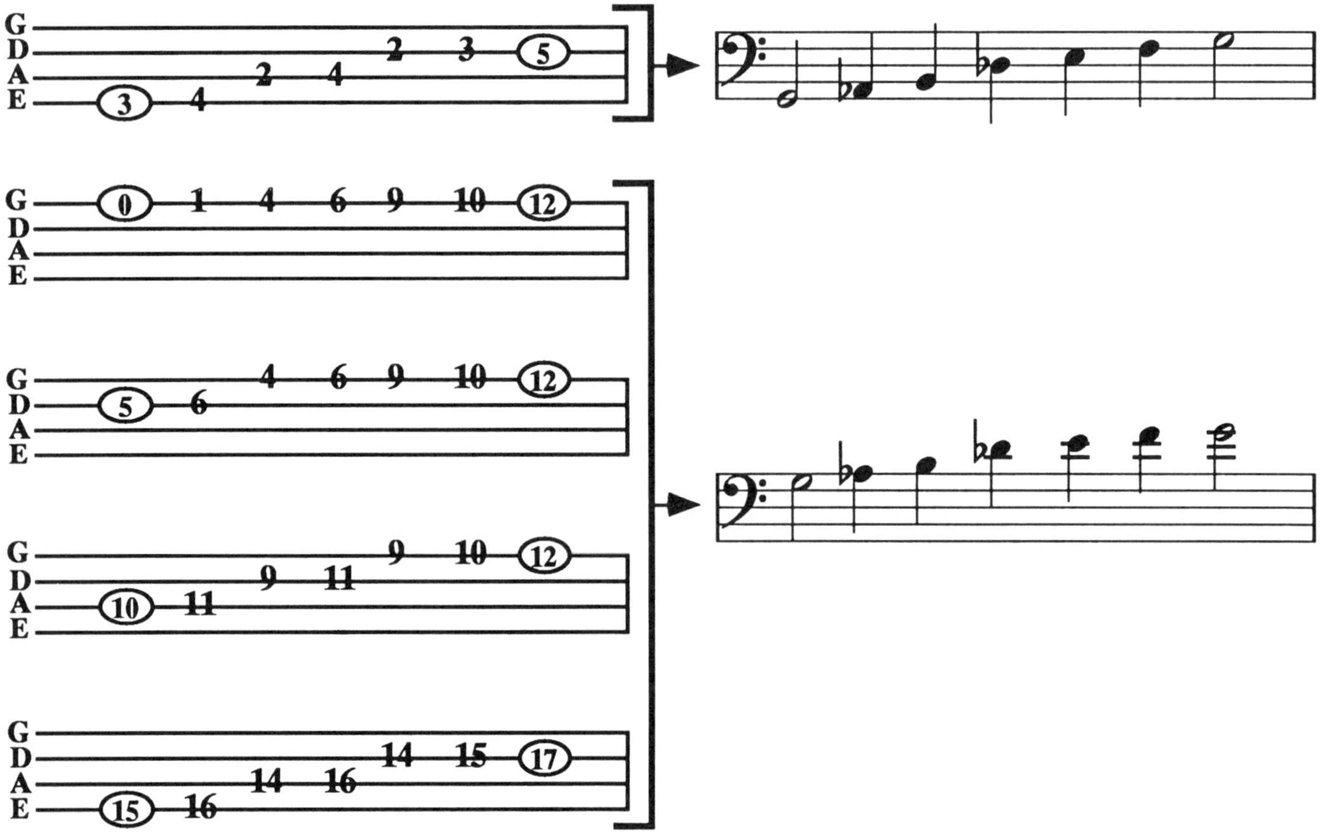

Riff

A THIRTEENTH ♭9TH ♭5TH

FORMULA - (A) Root (C♯) 3rd (E♭) ♭5th (F♯)13th (G) ♭7th (B♭) ♭9th

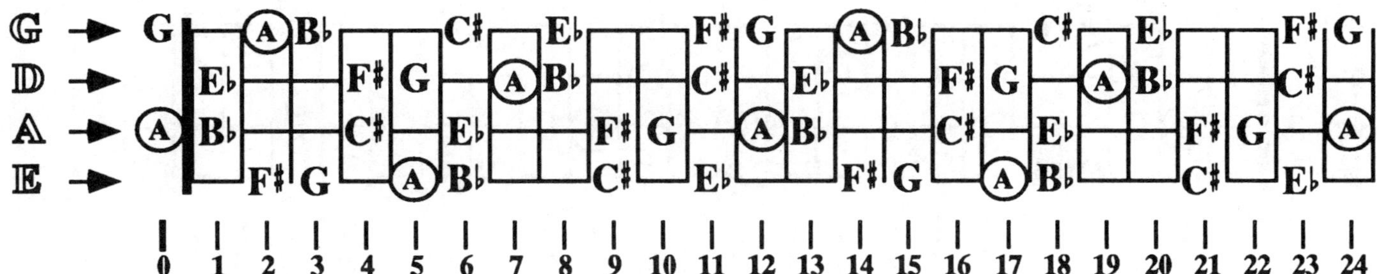

Positions

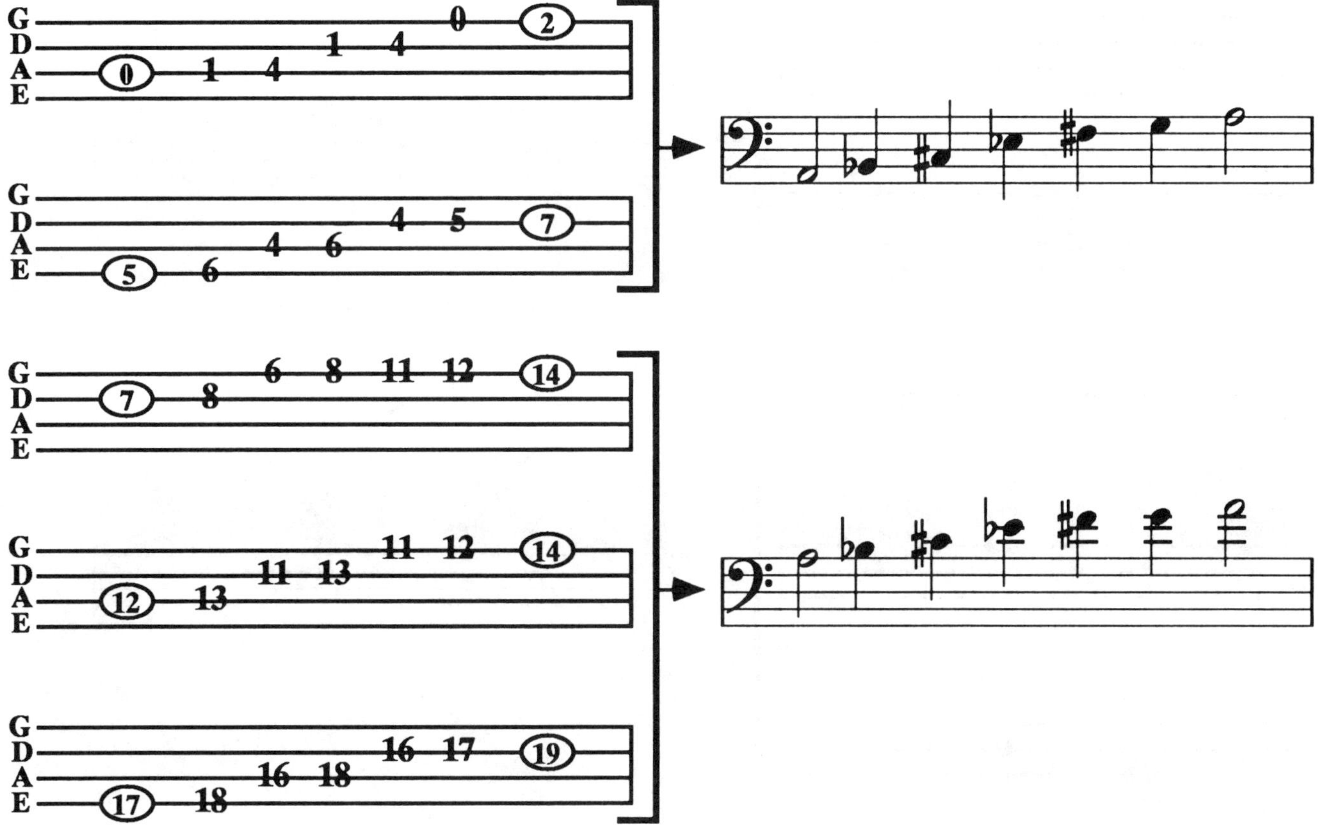

Riff

B THIRTEENTH ♭9TH ♭5TH

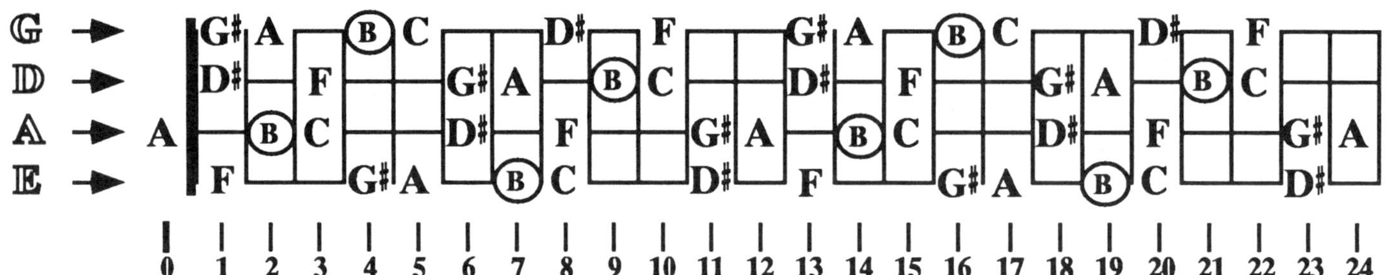

Positions

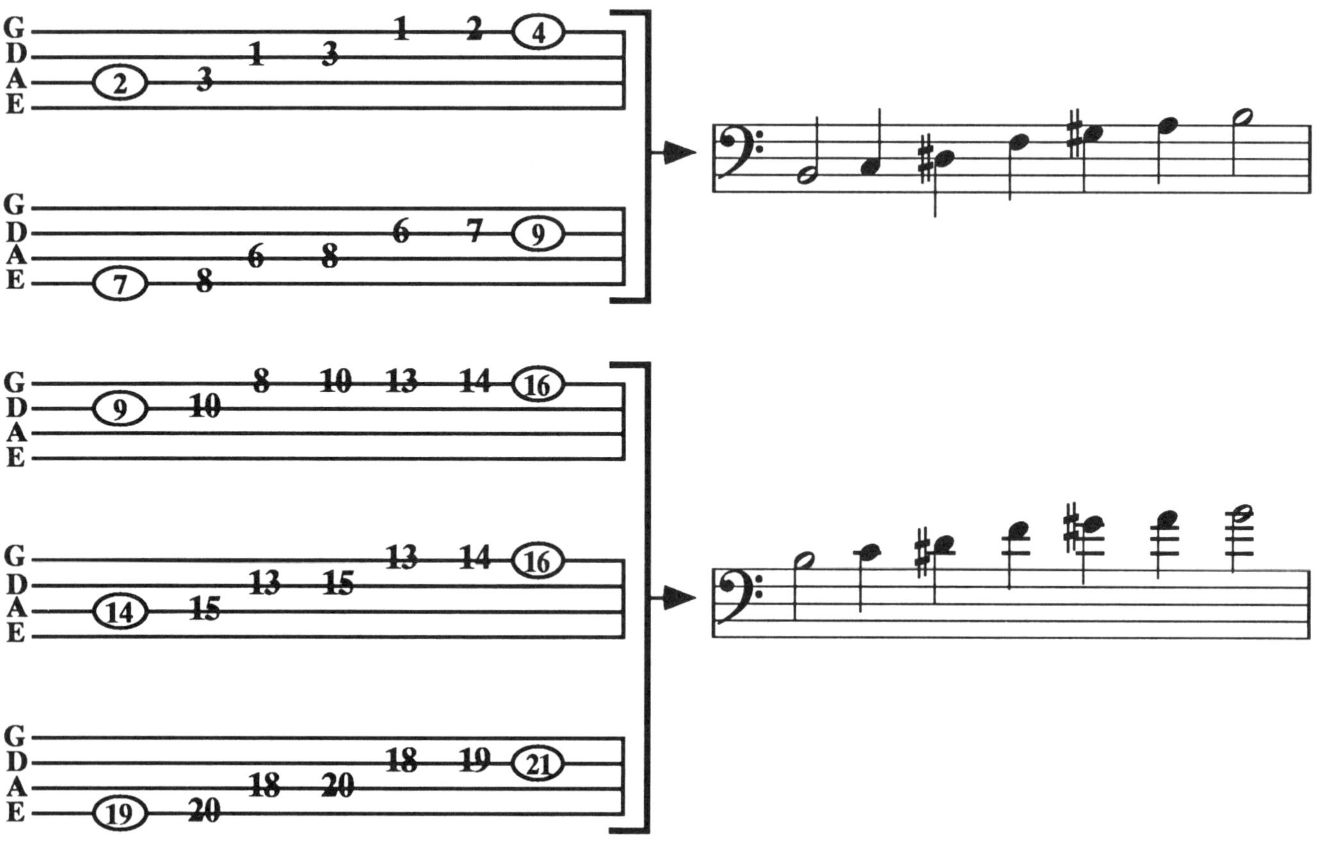

Riff

C DIMINISHED
FORMULA - (C) Root (E♭) ♭3rd (G♭) ♭5th

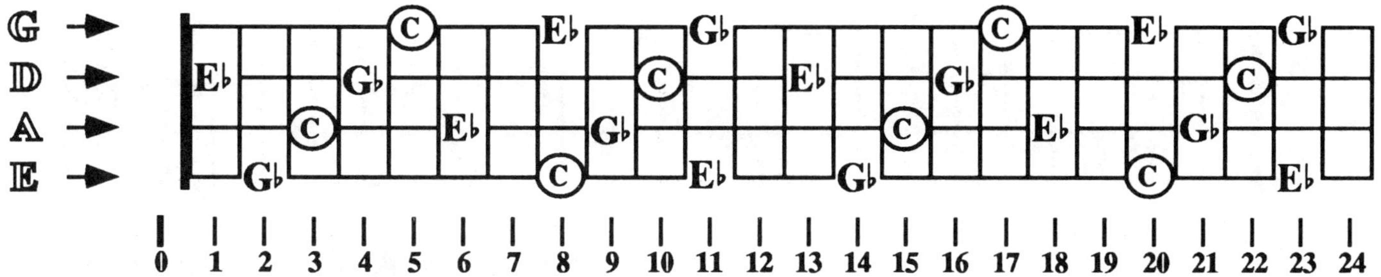

Positions

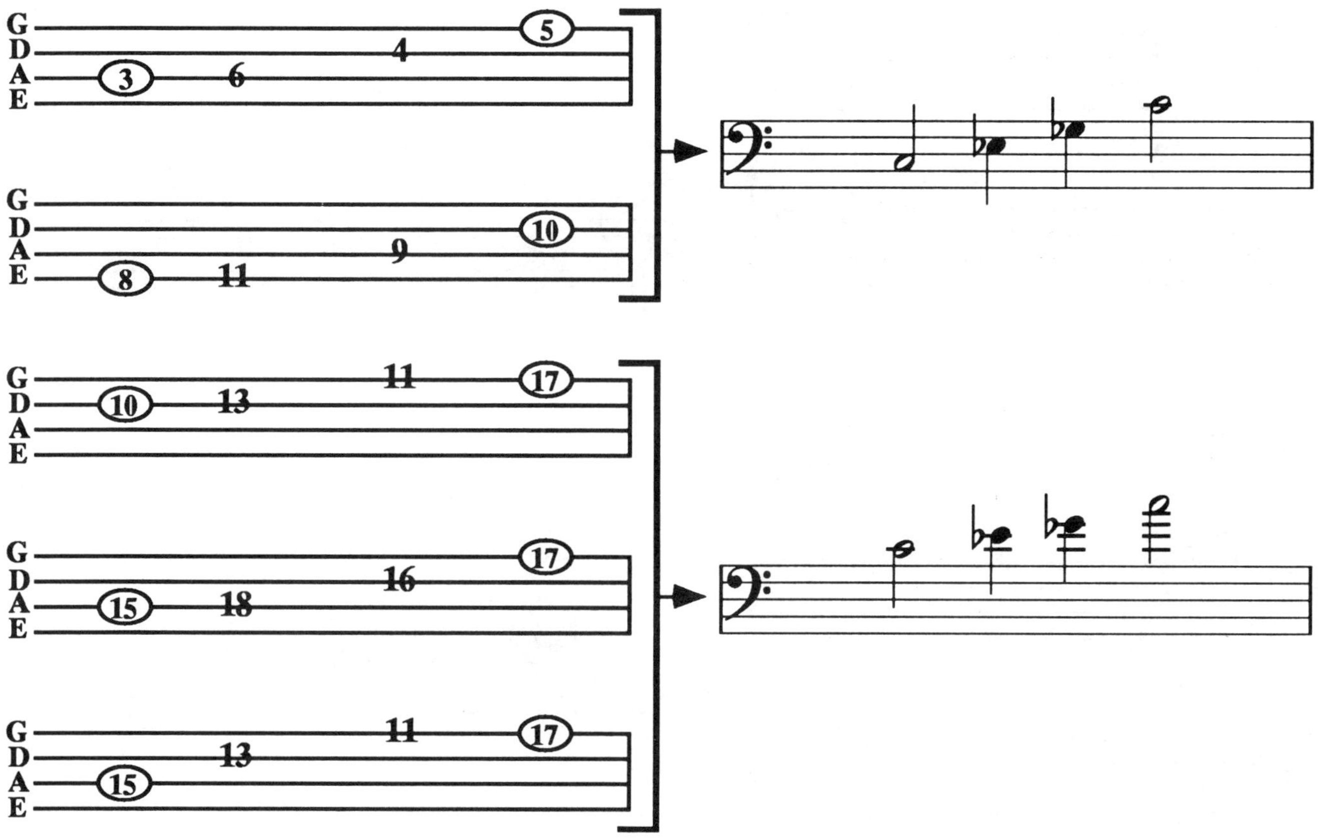

Riff

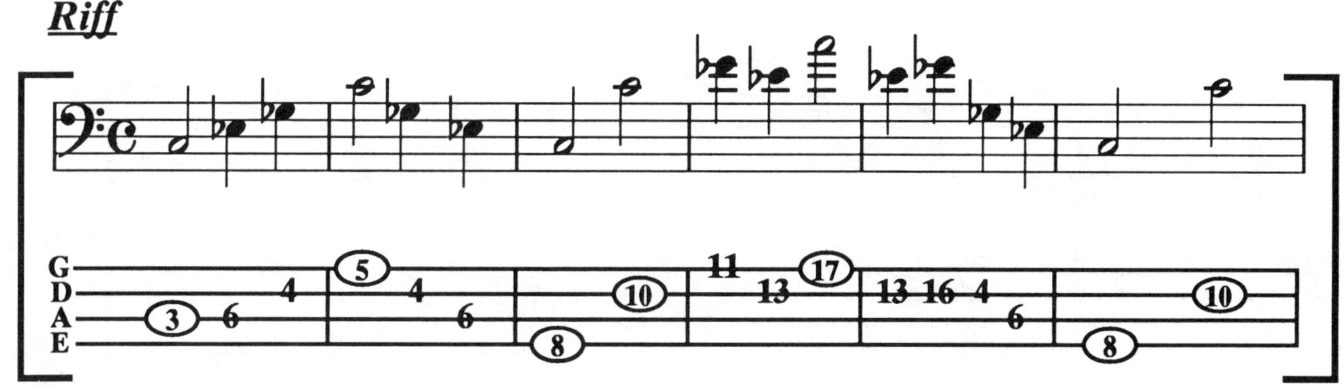

D DIMINISHED

FORMULA - (D) Root (F) ♭3rd (A♭) ♭5th

D°

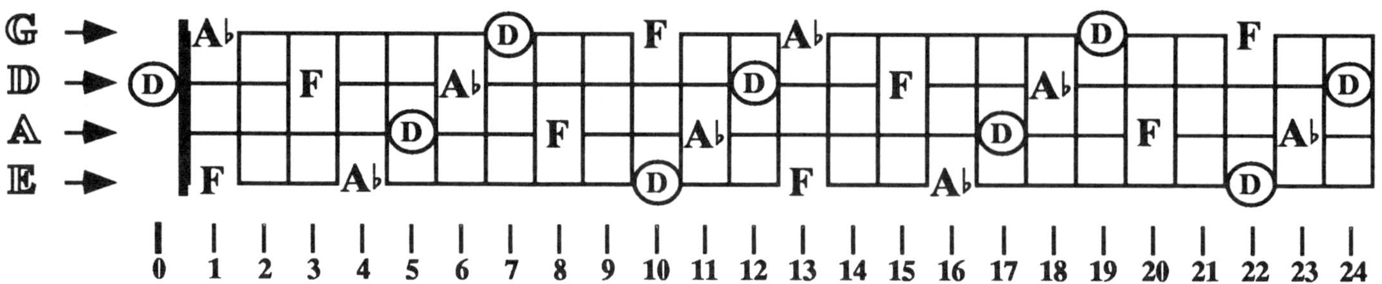

Positions

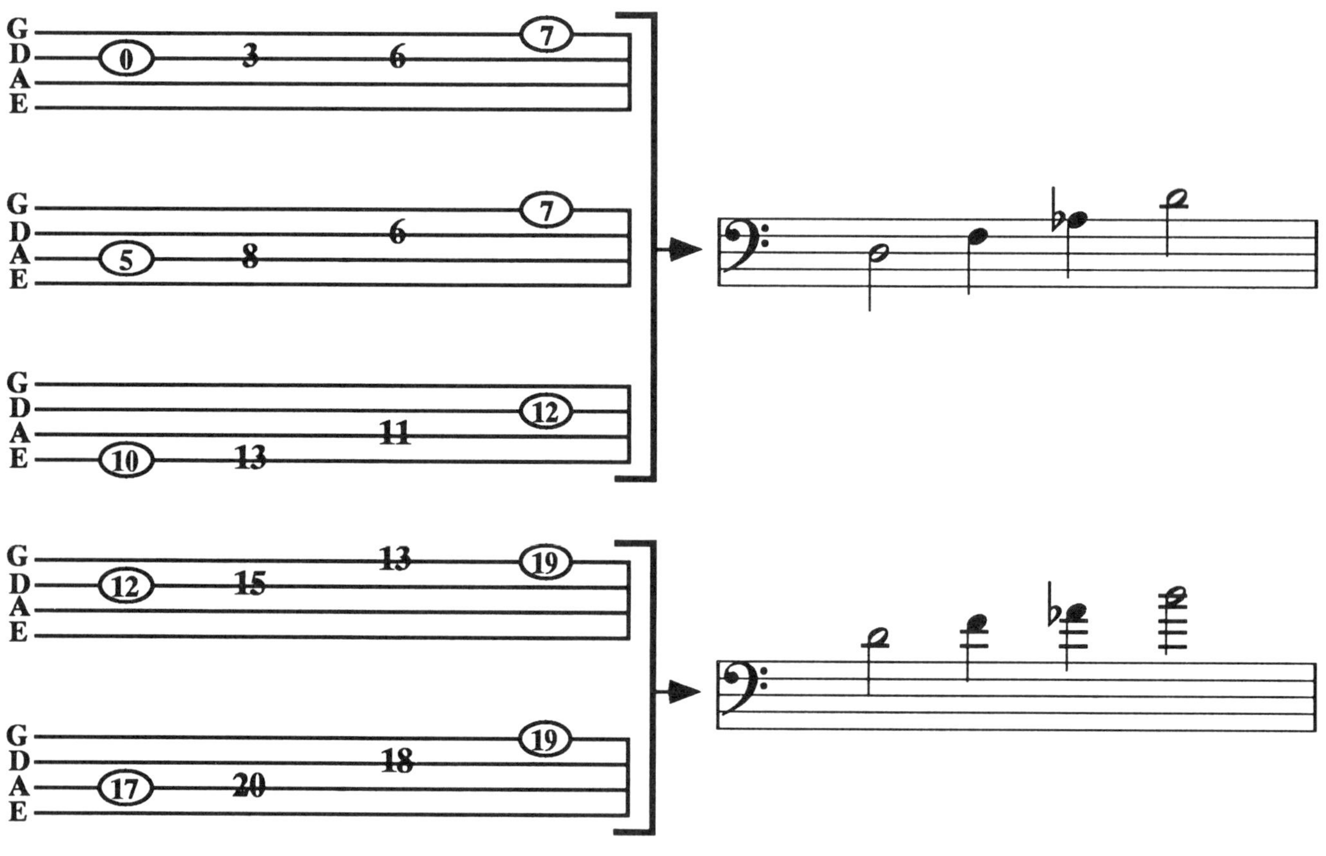

Riff

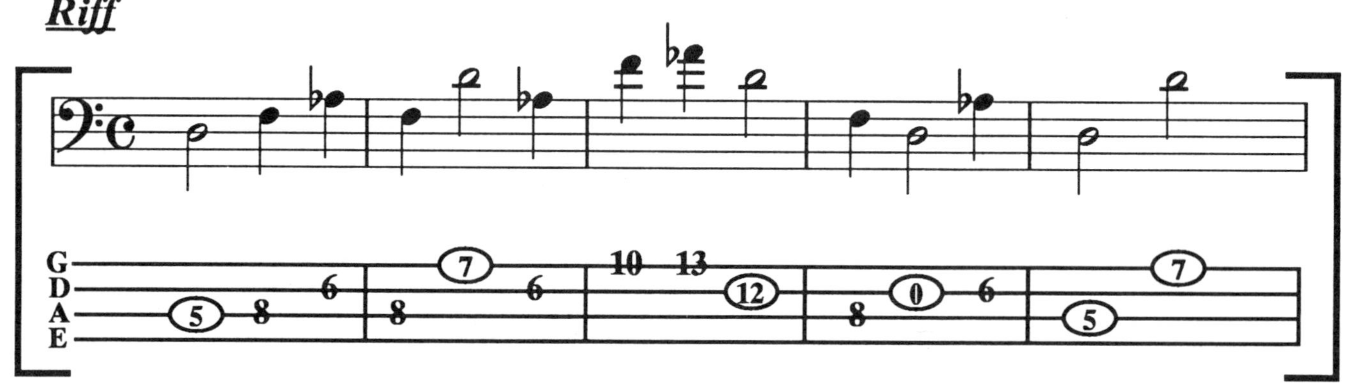

E DIMINISHED

FORMULA - (E) Root (G) ♭3rd (B♭) ♭5th

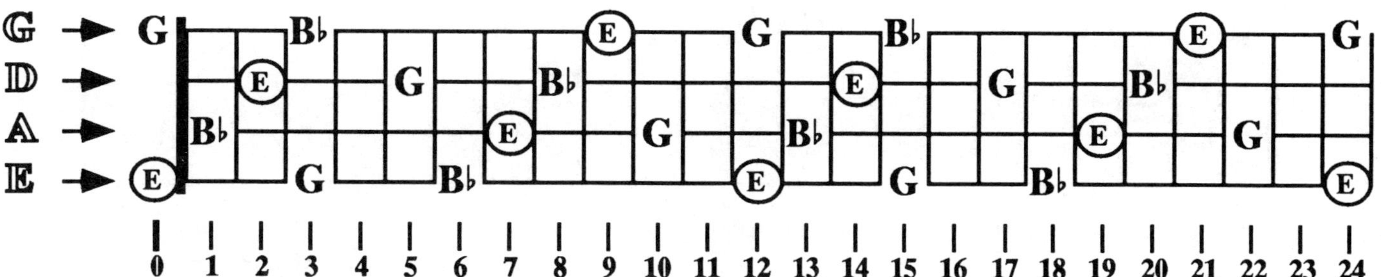

Positions

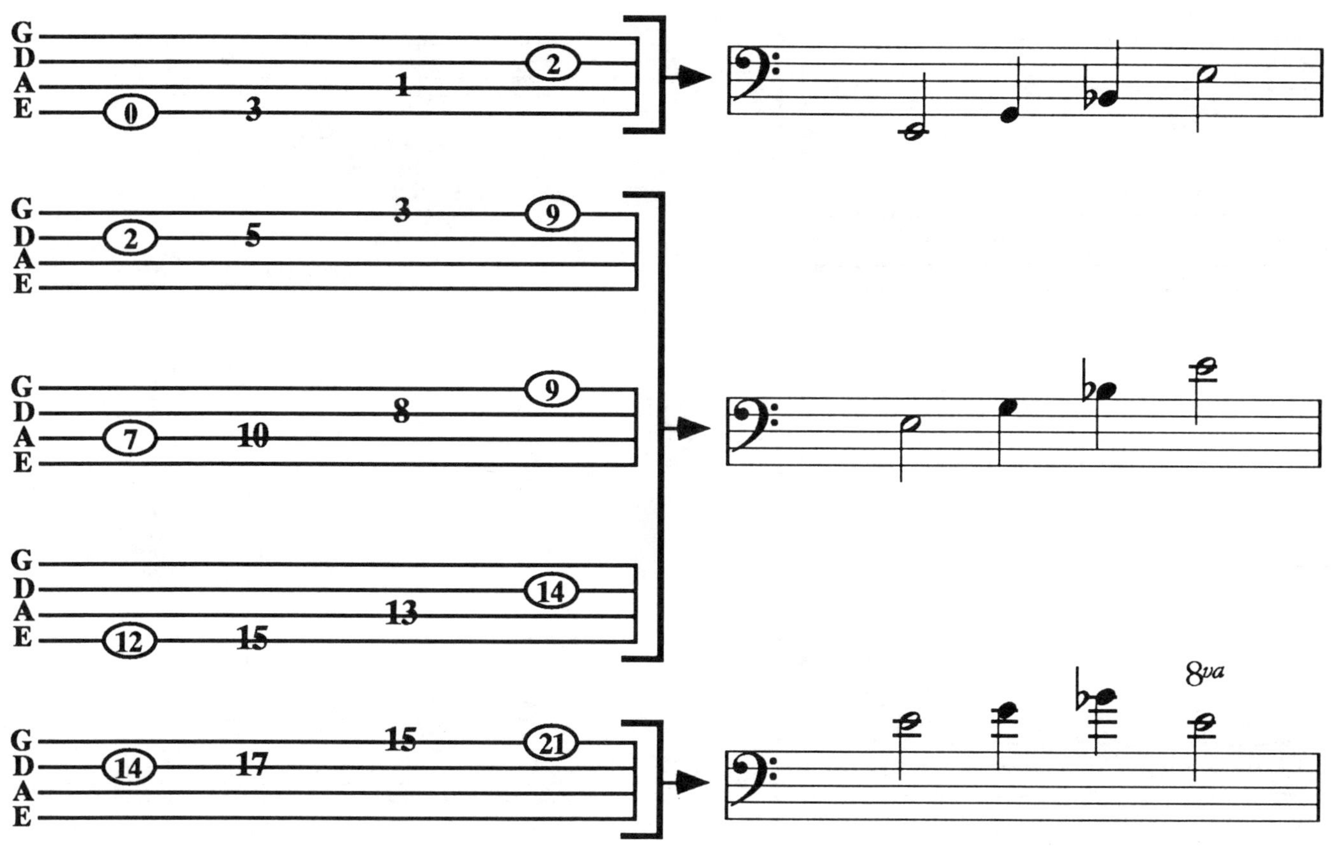

Riff

F DIMINISHED

FORMULA - (F) Root (A♭) ♭3rd (C♭) ♭5th

F°

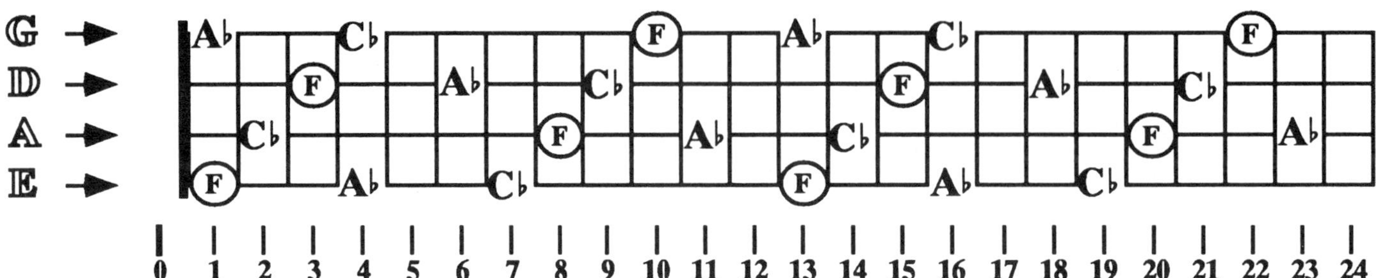

Positions

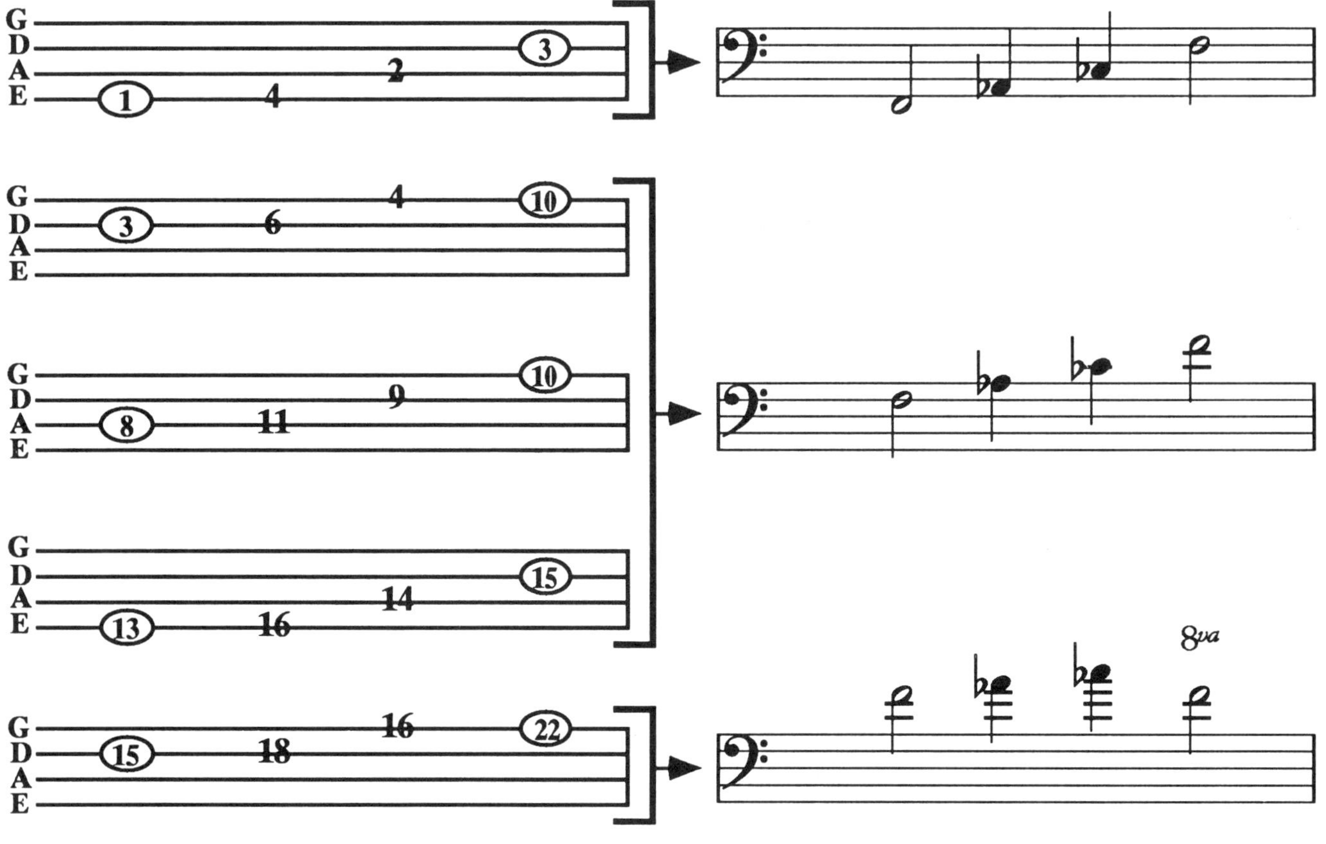

Riff

G DIMINISHED

FORMULA - (G) Root (B♭) ♭3rd (D♭) ♭5th

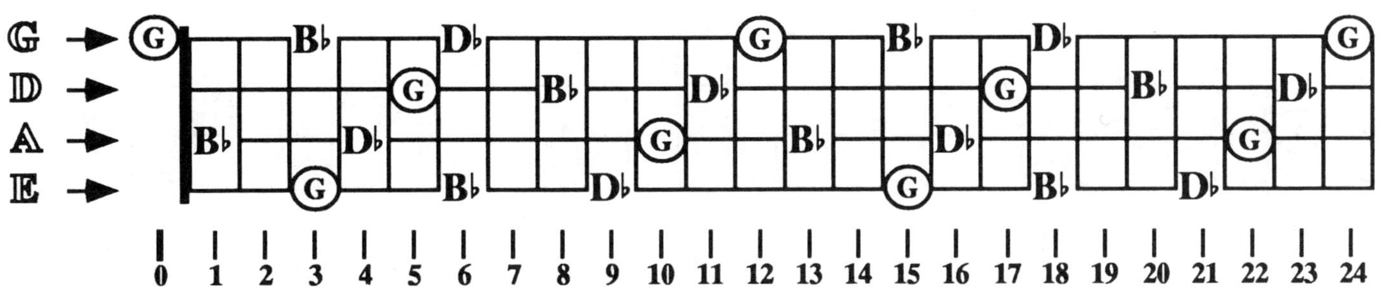

Positions

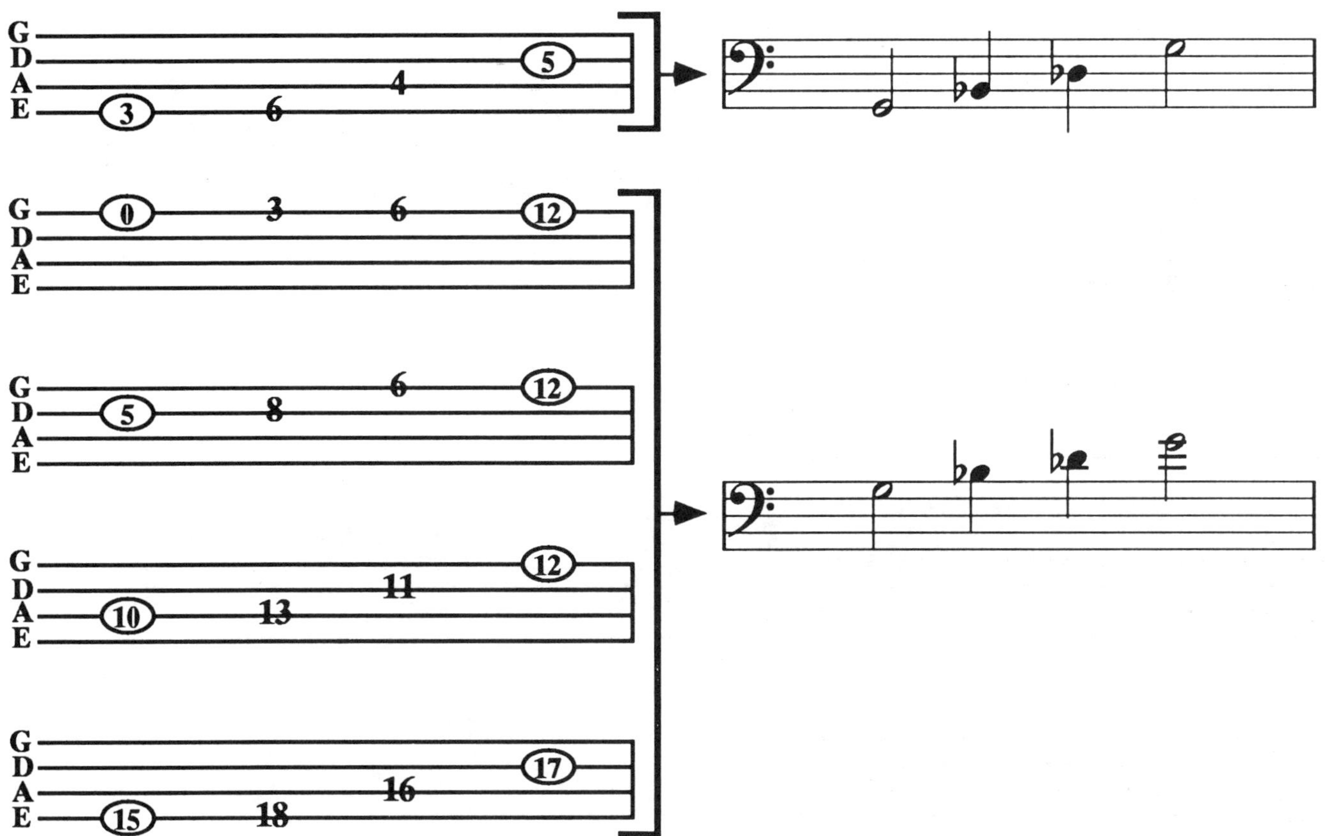

Riff

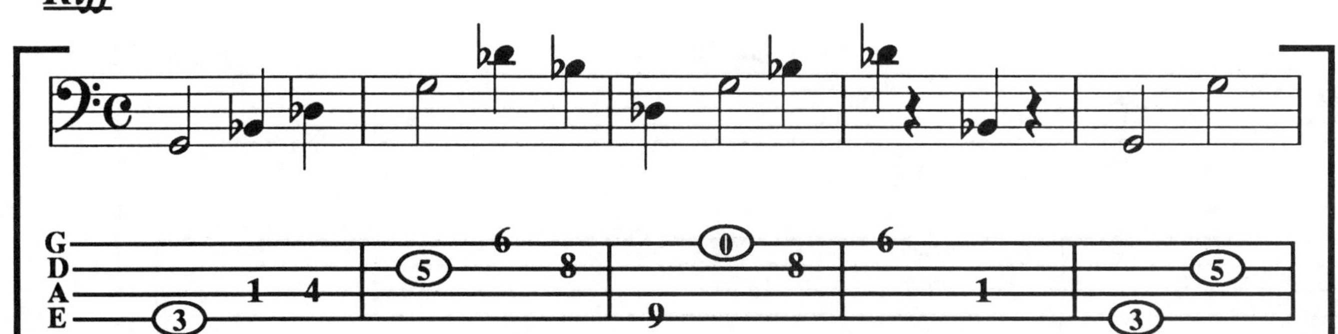

A DIMINISHED

FORMULA - (A) Root (C) ♭3rd (E♭) ♭5th

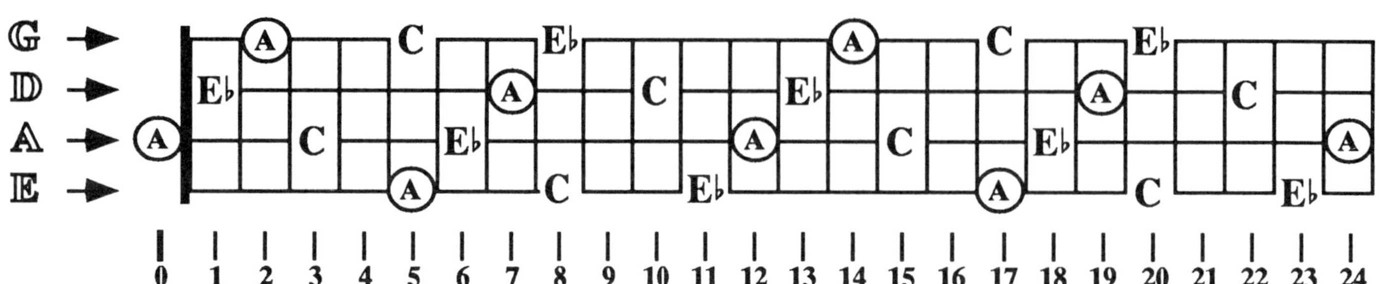

Positions

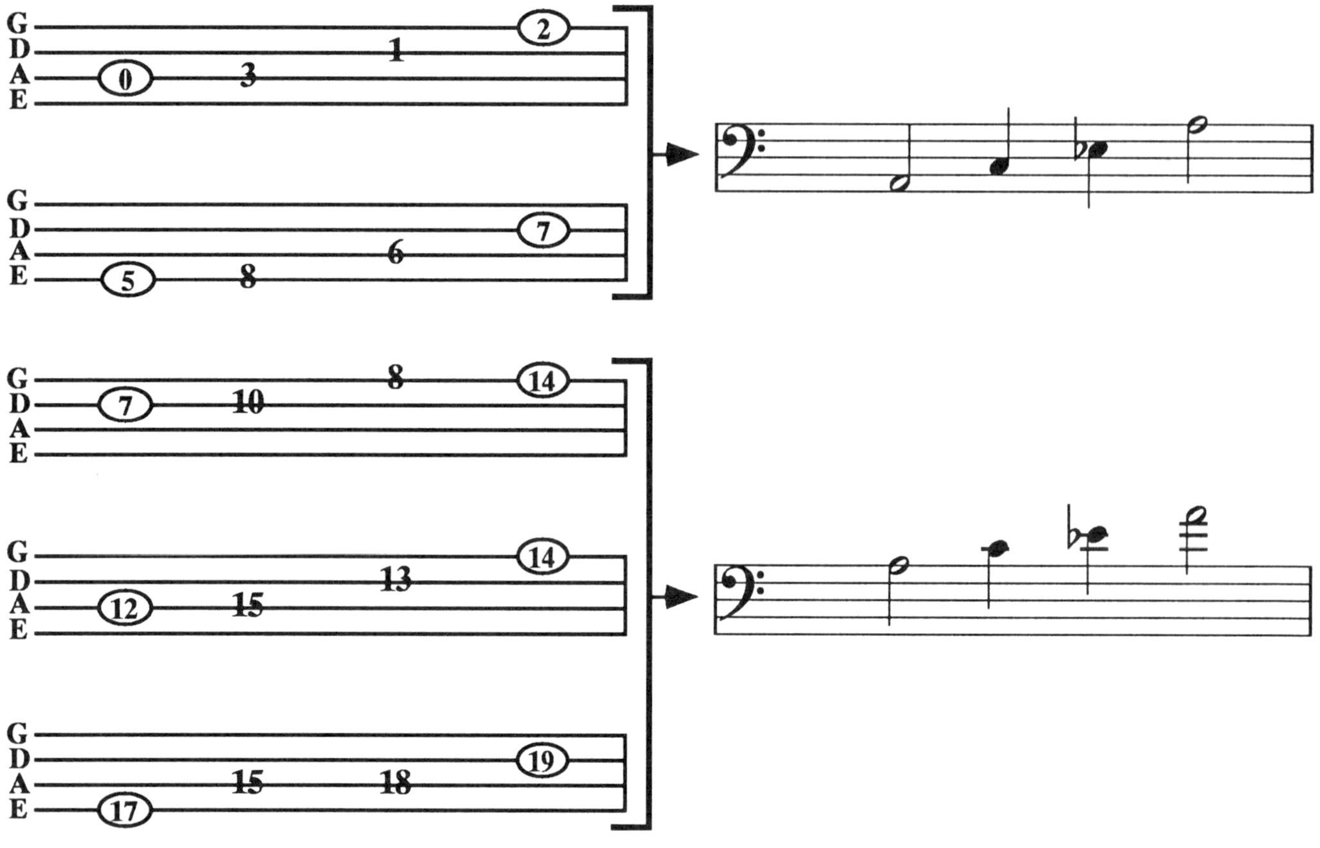

Riff

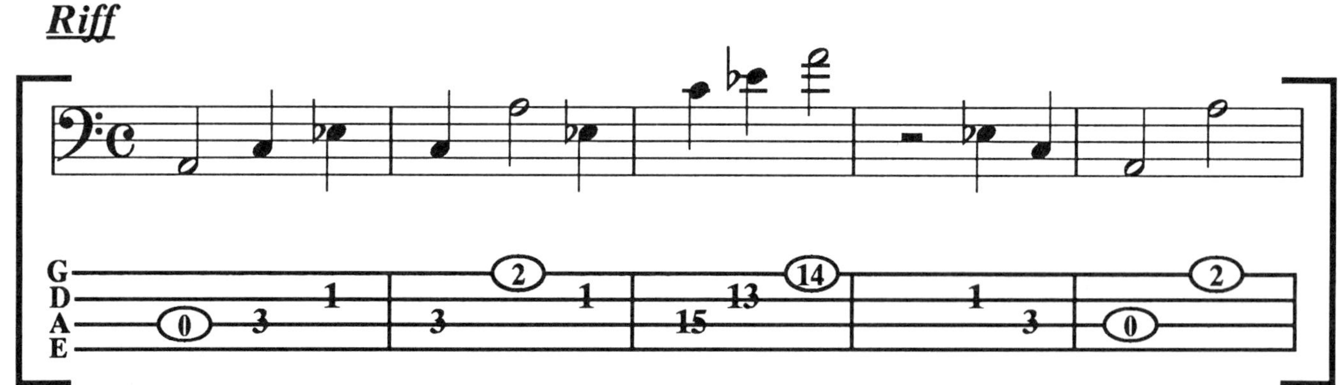

B DIMINISHED

FORMULA - (B) Root (D) ♭3rd (F) ♭5th

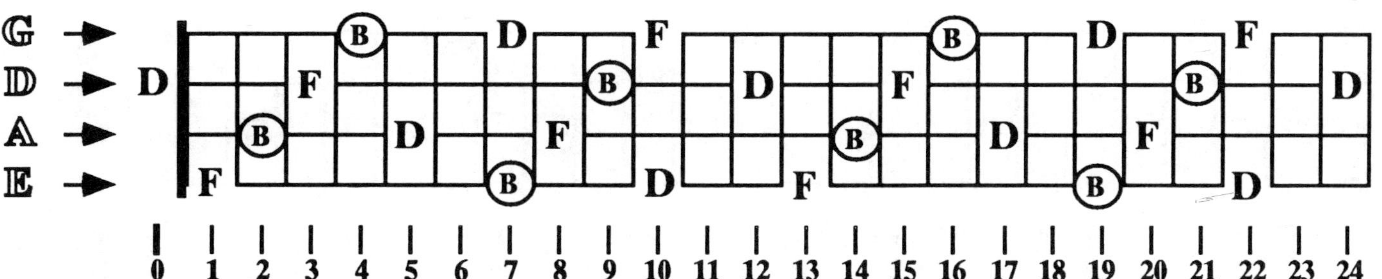

Positions

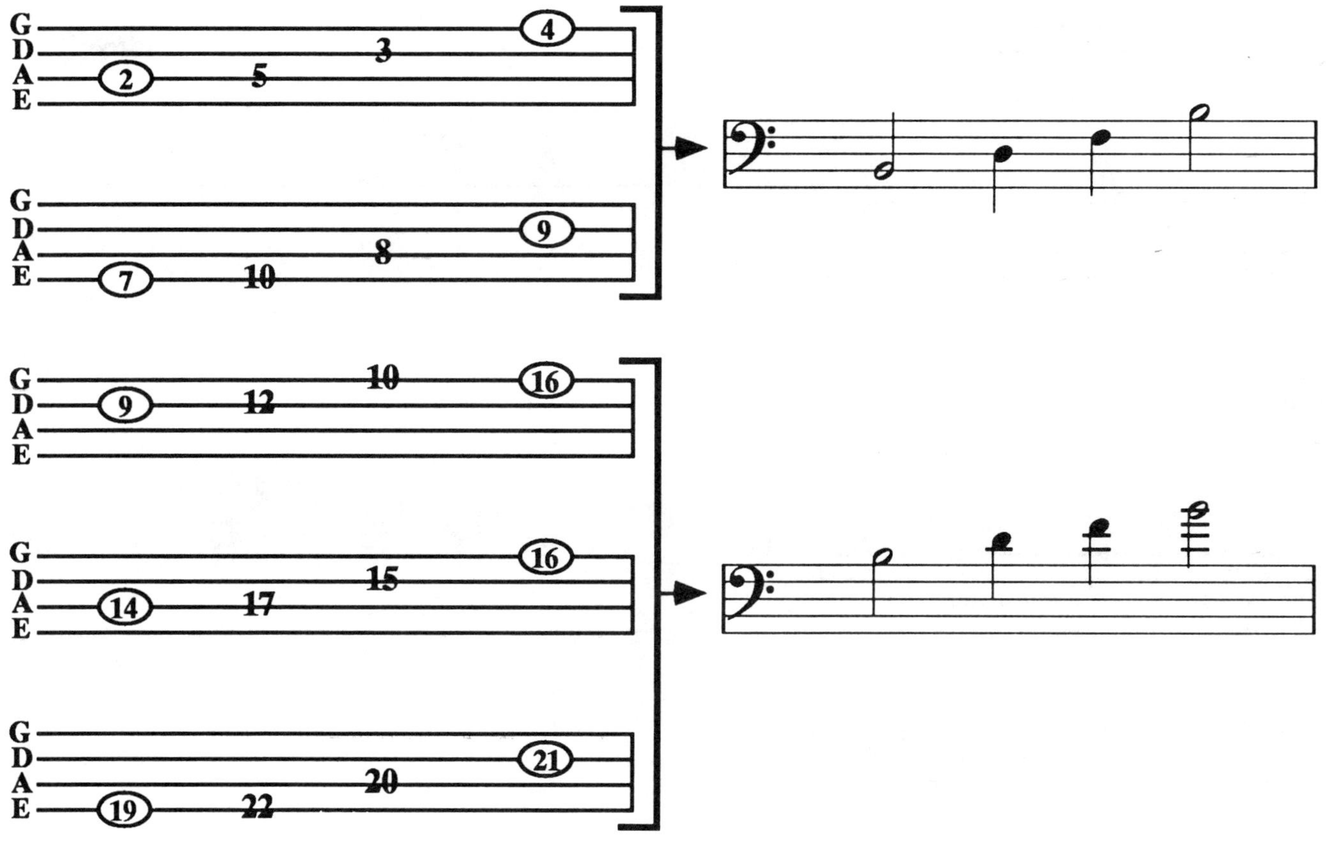

Riff

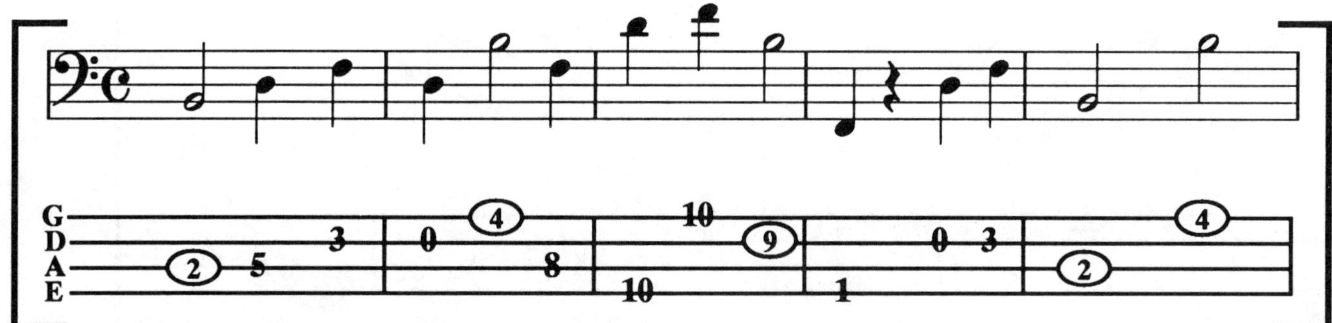

231

C DIMINISHED 7TH

FORMULA - (C) Root (E♭) ♭3rd (G♭) ♭5th (B♭♭) ♭♭7th

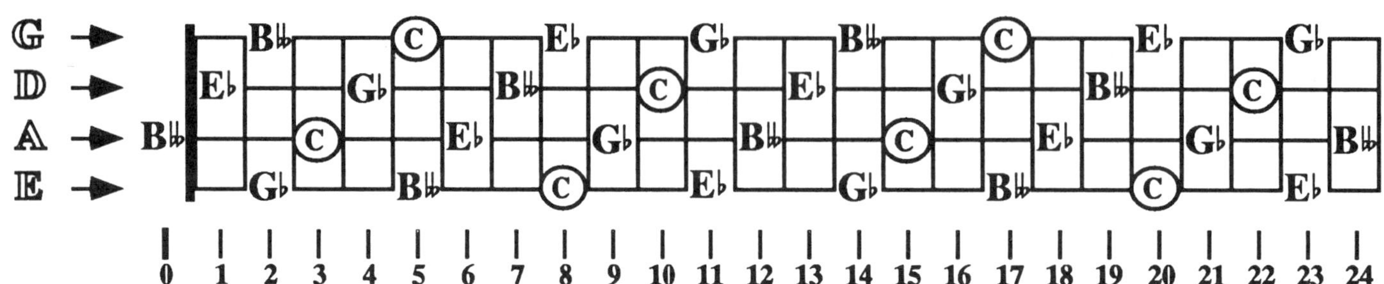

Positions

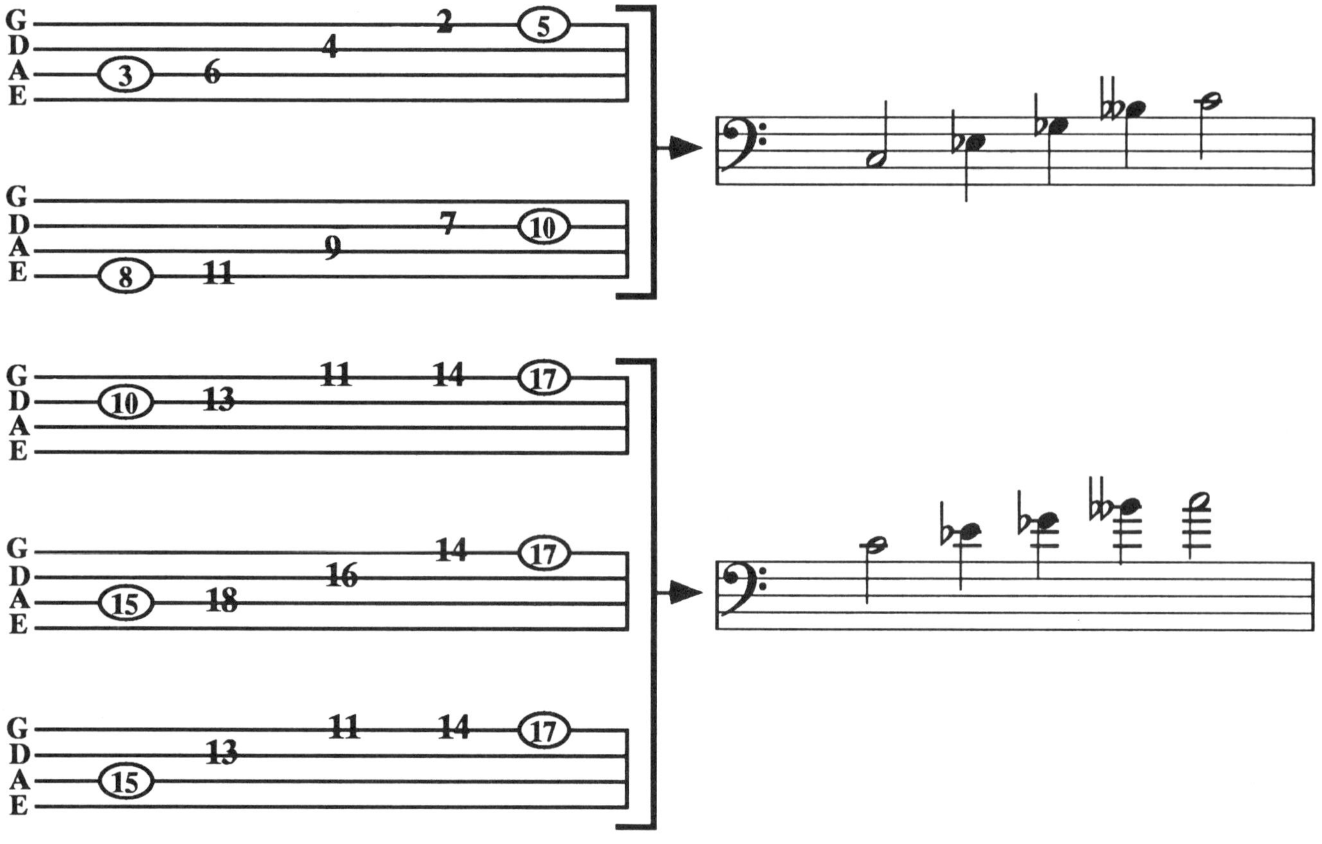

Riff

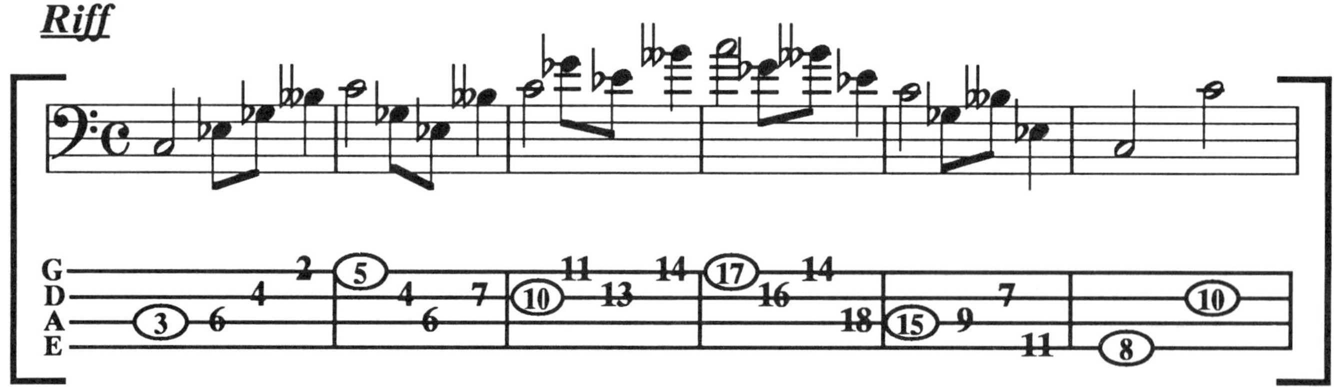

D DIMINISHED 7TH

FORMULA - (D) Root (F) ♭3rd (A♭) ♭5th (C♭) ♭♭7th

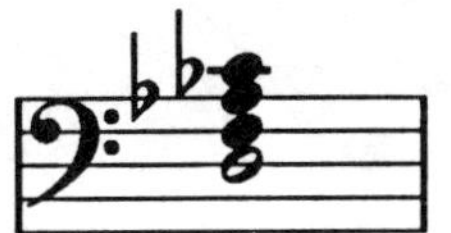

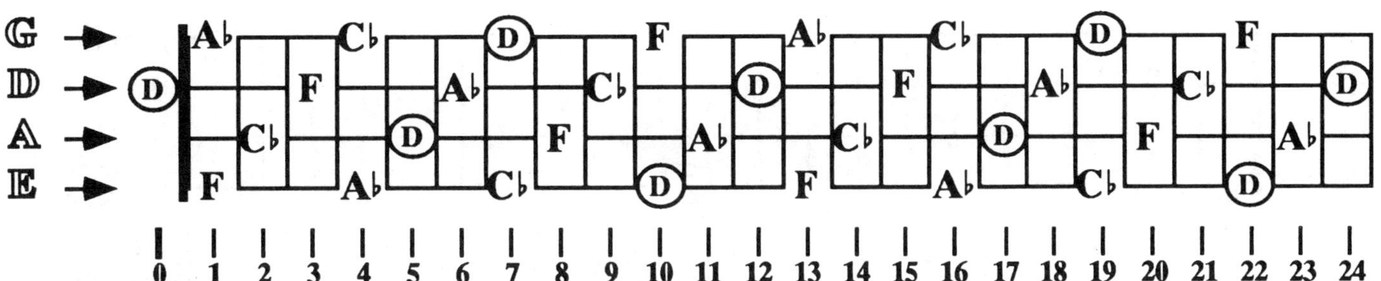

Positions

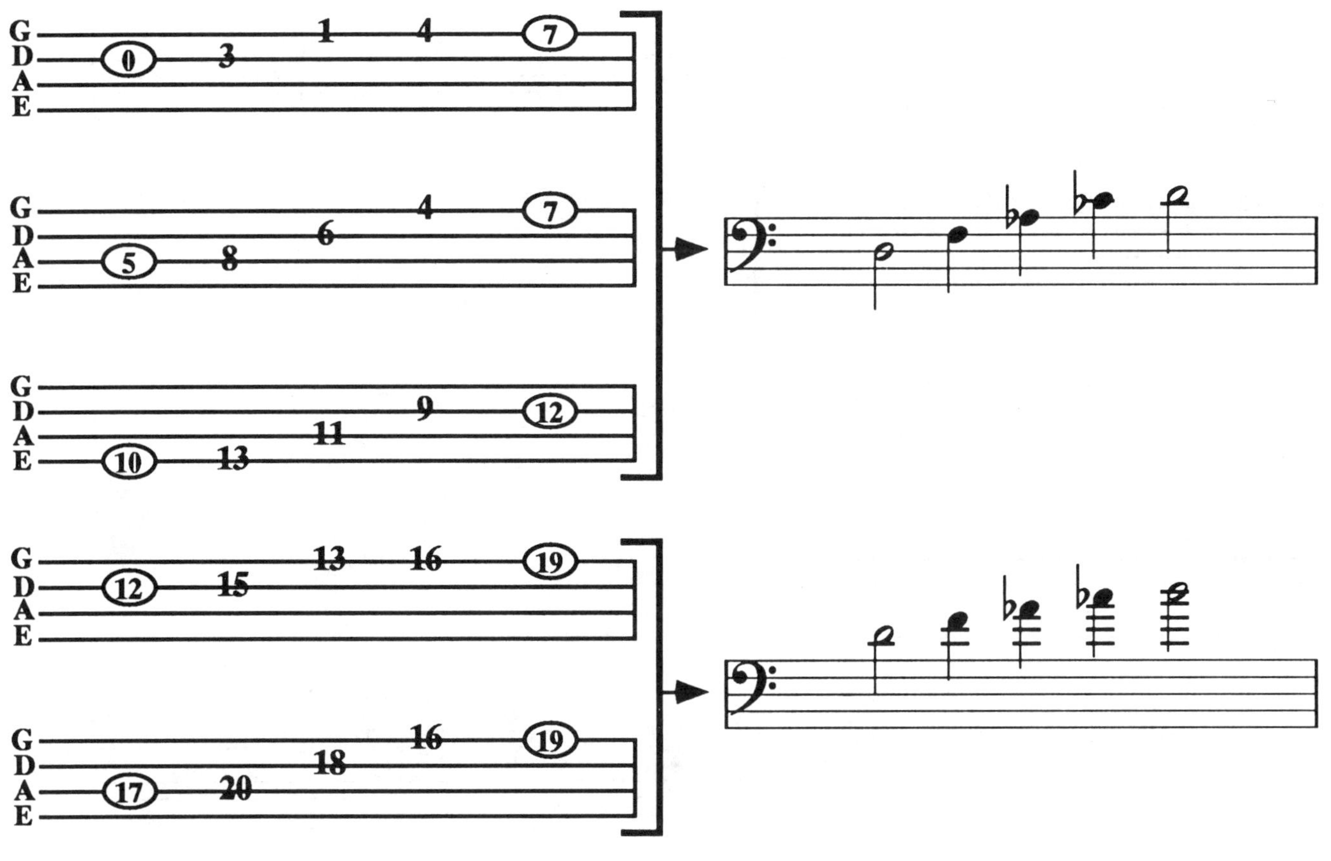

Riff

E DIMINISHED 7TH
FORMULA - (E) Root (G) ♭3rd (B♭) ♭5th (D♭) ♭♭7th

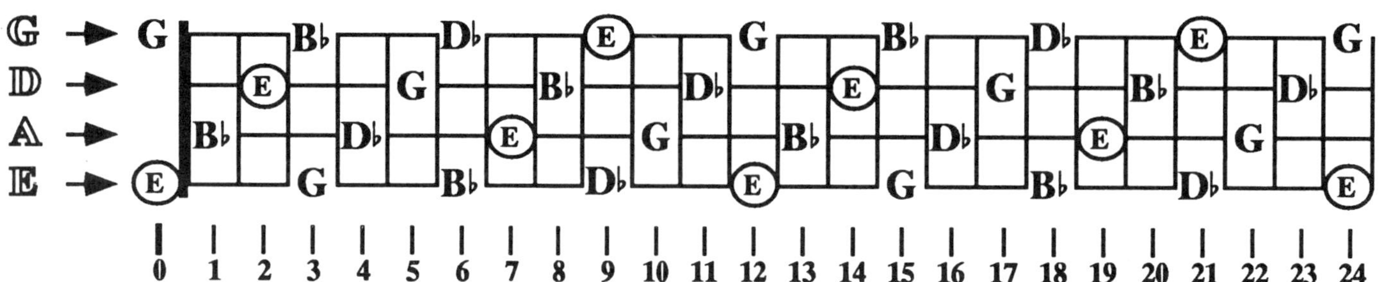

Positions

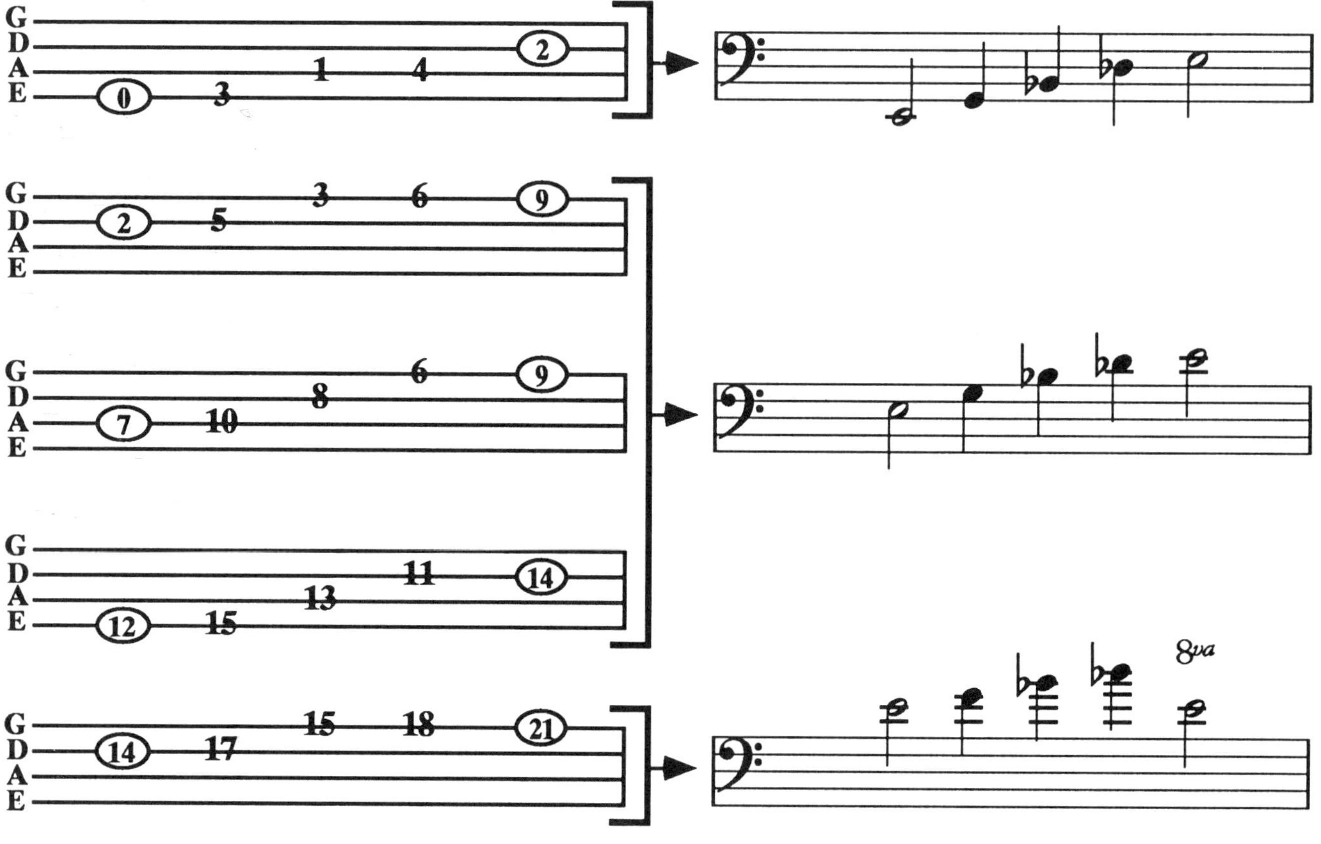

Riff

F DIMINISHED 7TH

FORMULA - (F) Root (A♭) ♭3rd (C♭) ♭5th (E♭♭)♮7th

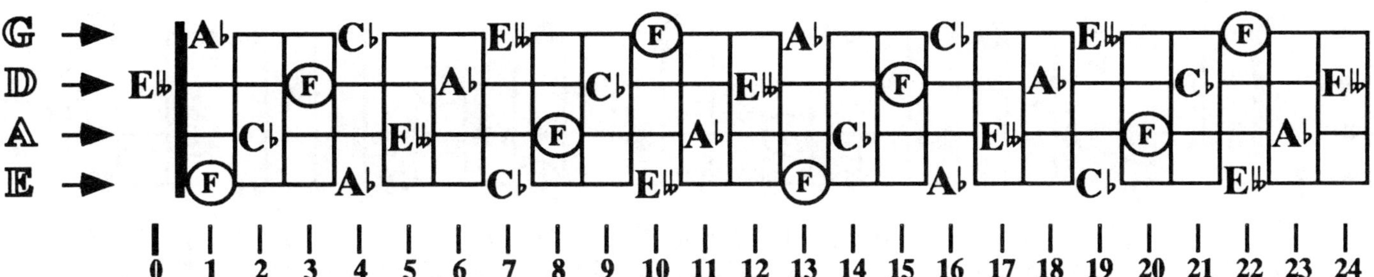

Positions

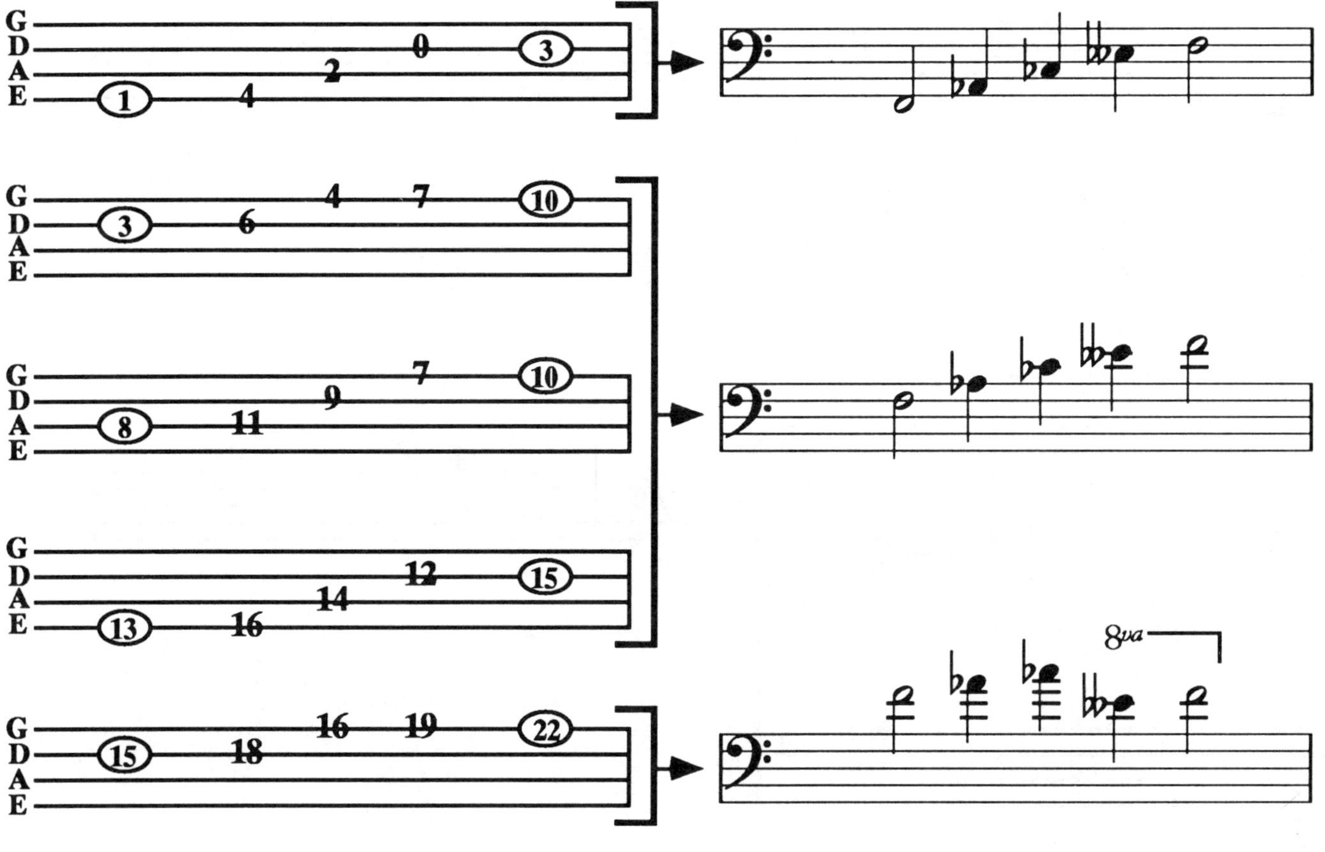

Riff

G   DIMINISHED 7TH

FORMULA - (G) Root (B♭) ♭3rd (D♭) ♭5th (F♭)♭♭7th

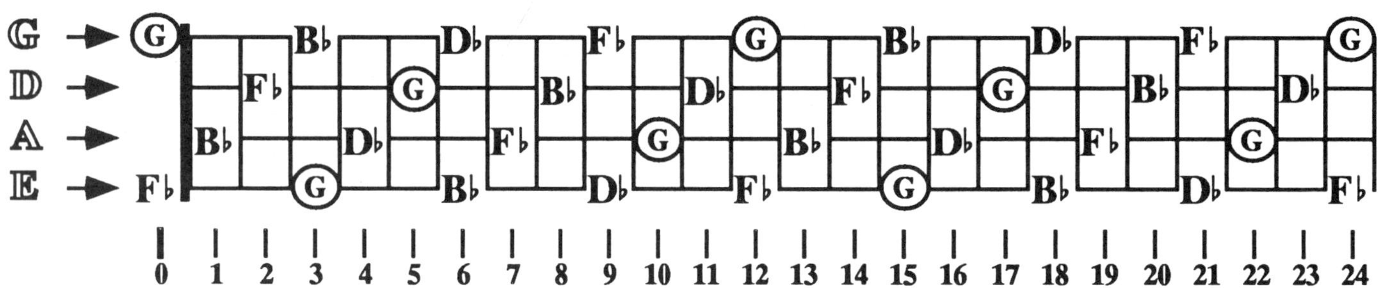

Positions

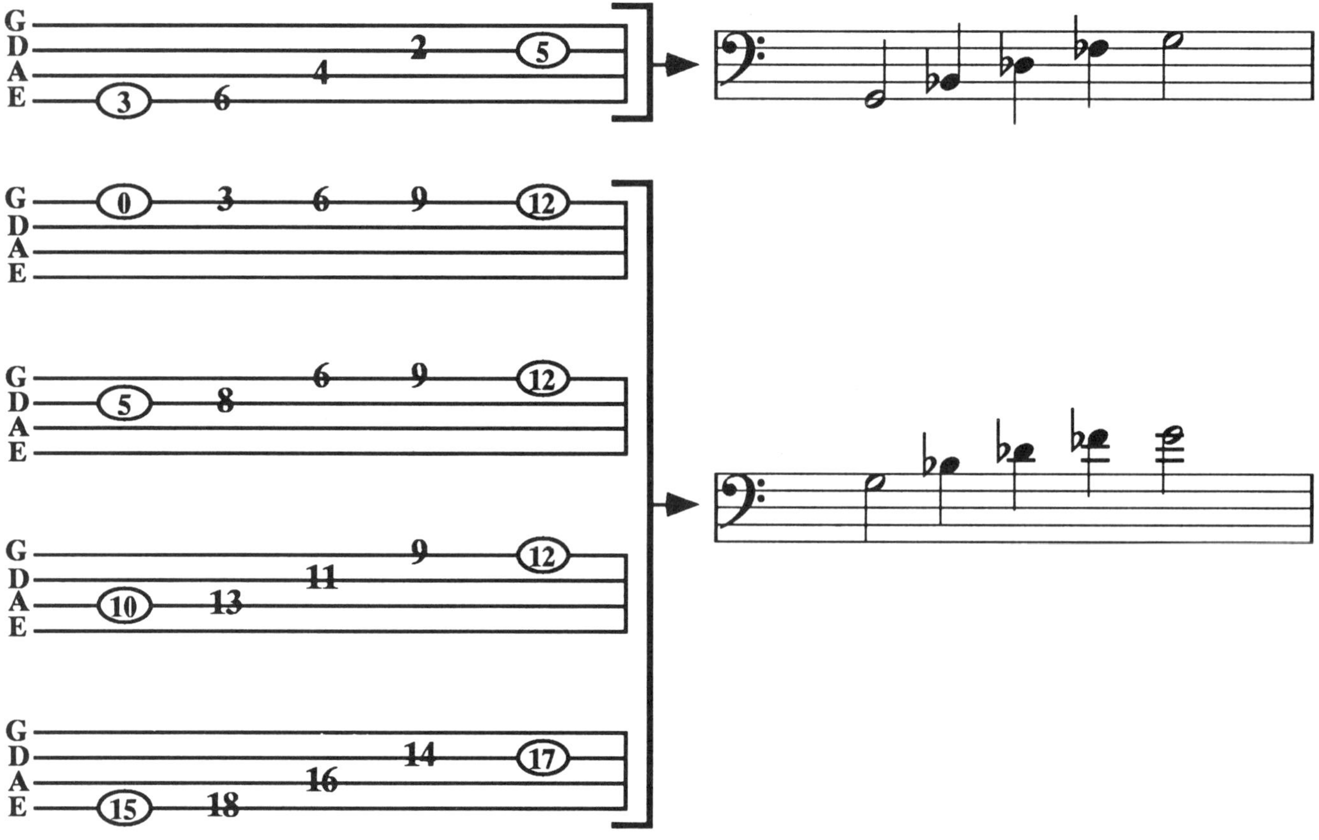

Riff

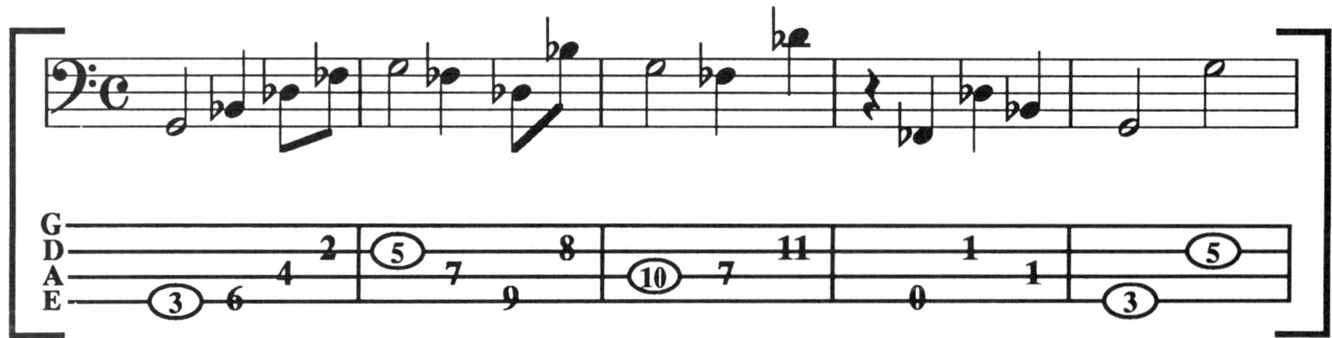

A DIMINISHED 7TH

FORMULA - (A) Root (C) ♭3rd (E♭) ♭5th (G♭) ♮7th

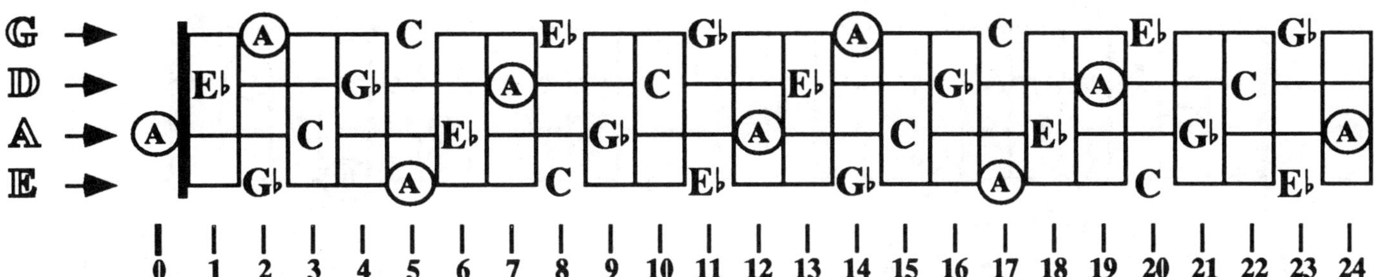

Positions

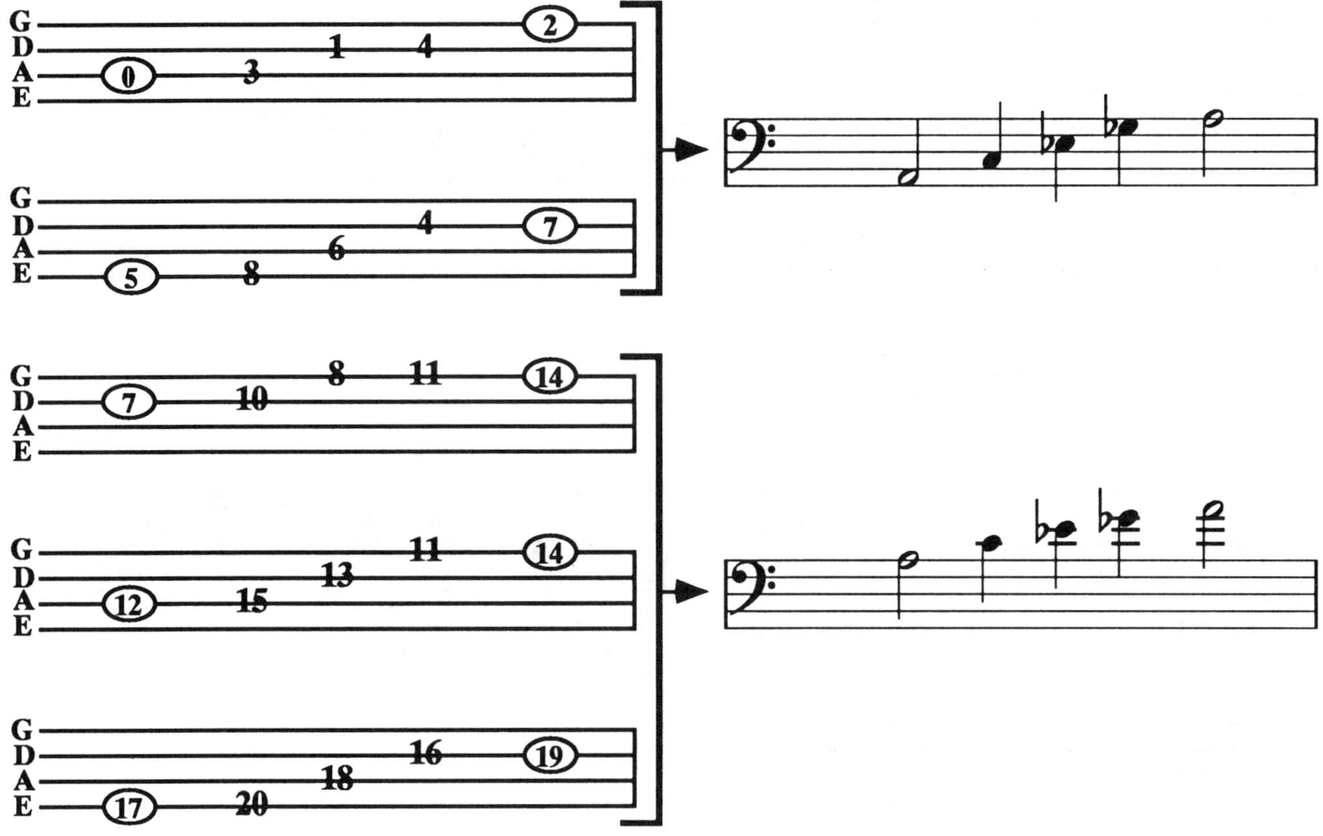

Riff

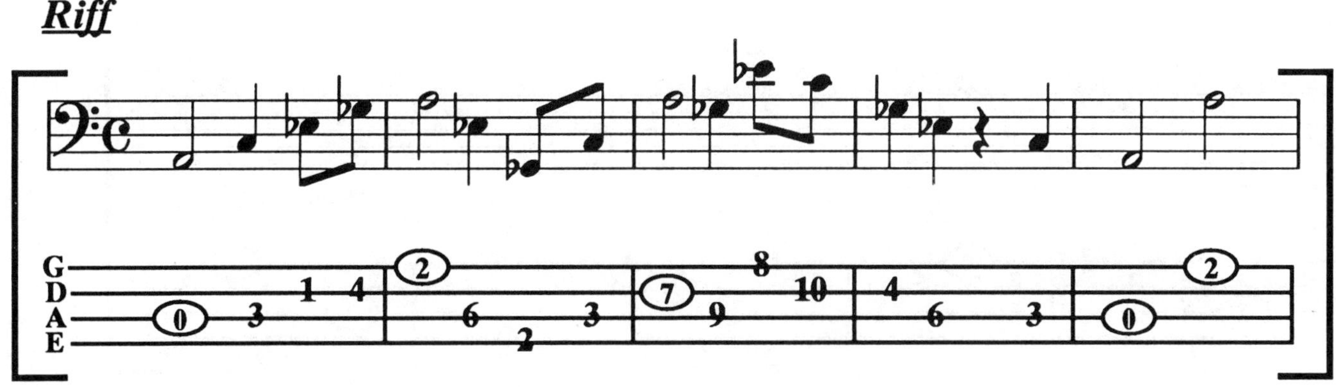

B DIMINISHED 7TH

FORMULA - (B) Root (D) ♭3rd (F) ♭5th (A♭) ♮7th

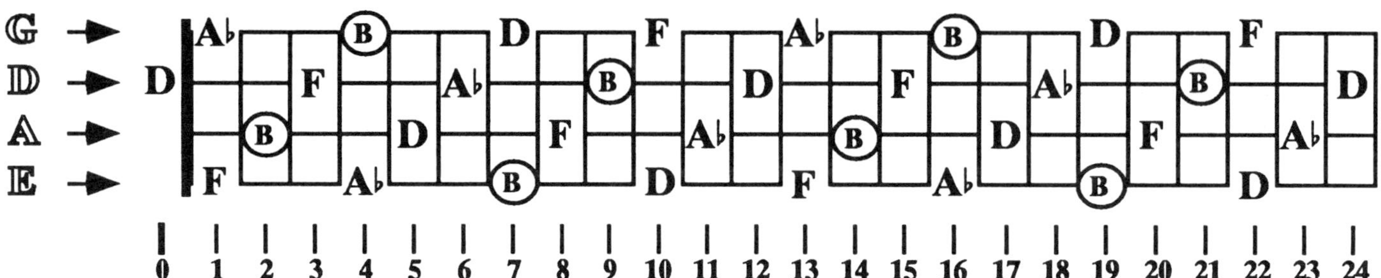

Positions

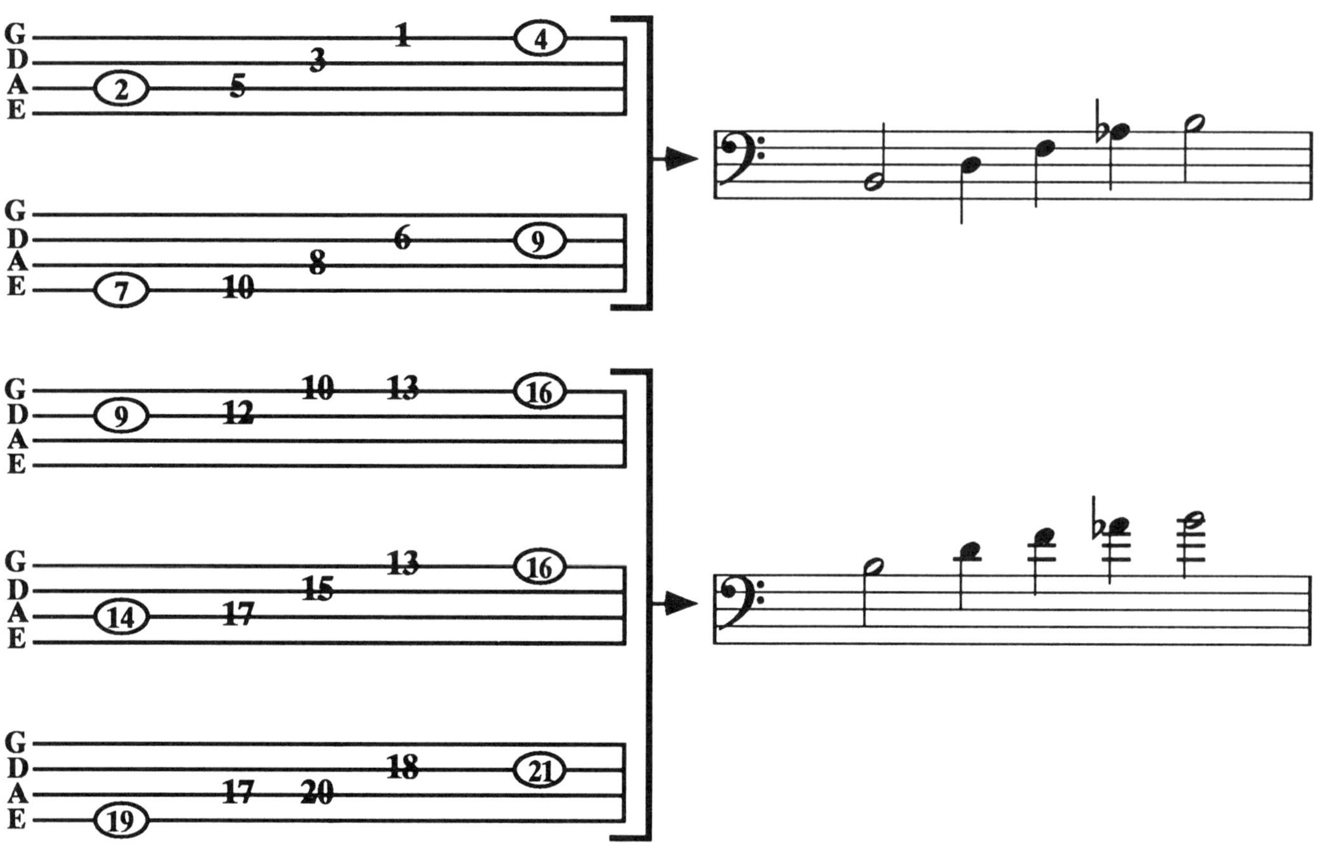

Riff

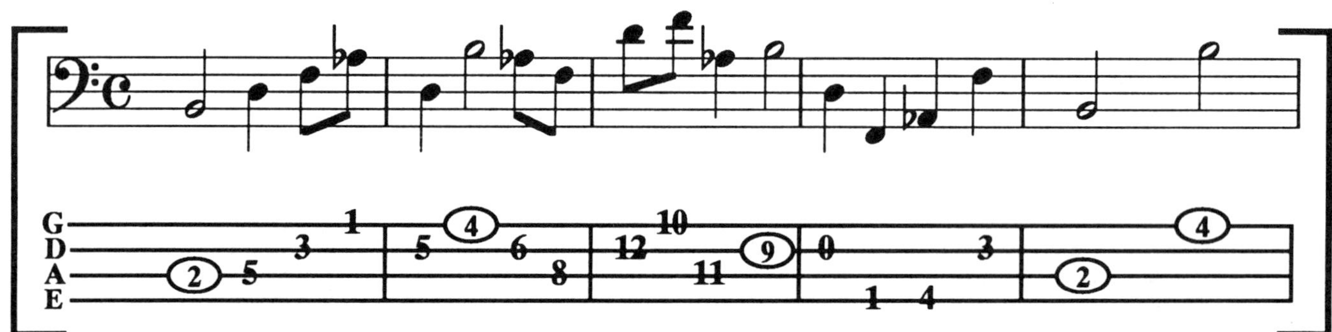

238

C HALF-DIMINISHED 7TH

FORMULA - (C) Root (E♭) ♭3rd (G♭) ♭5th (B♭) ♭7th

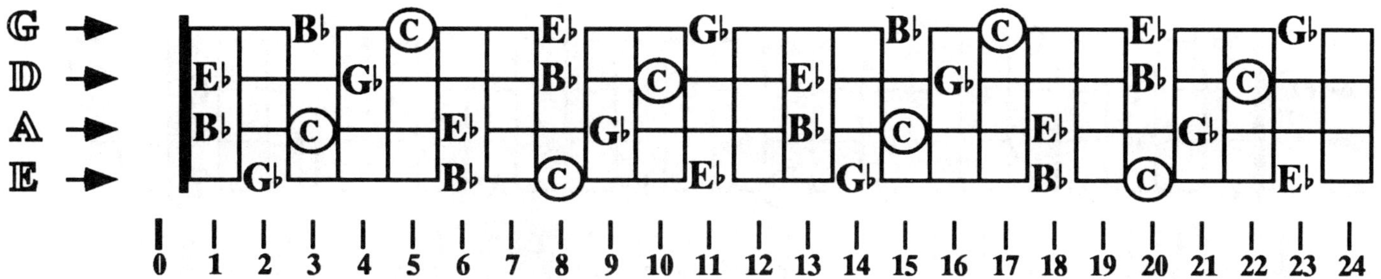

Positions

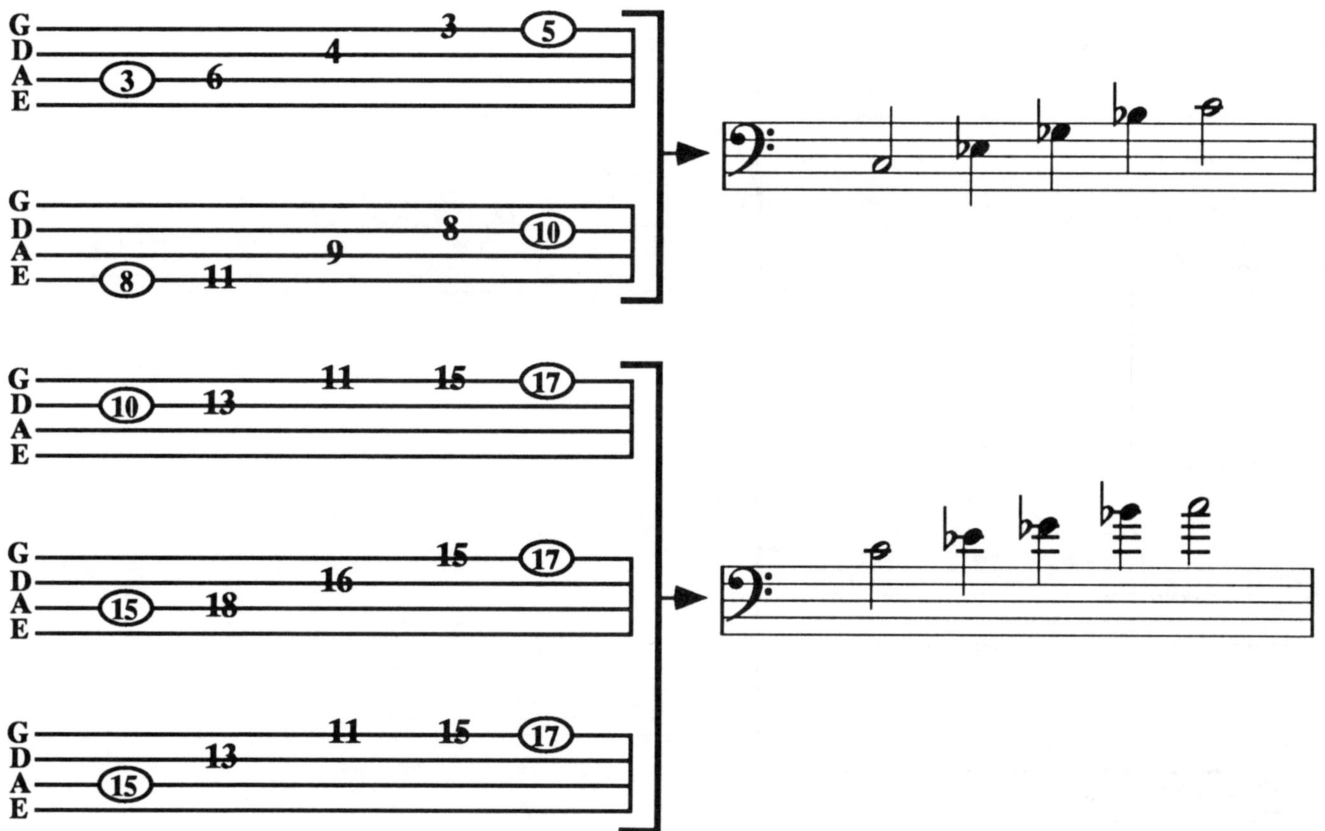

Riff

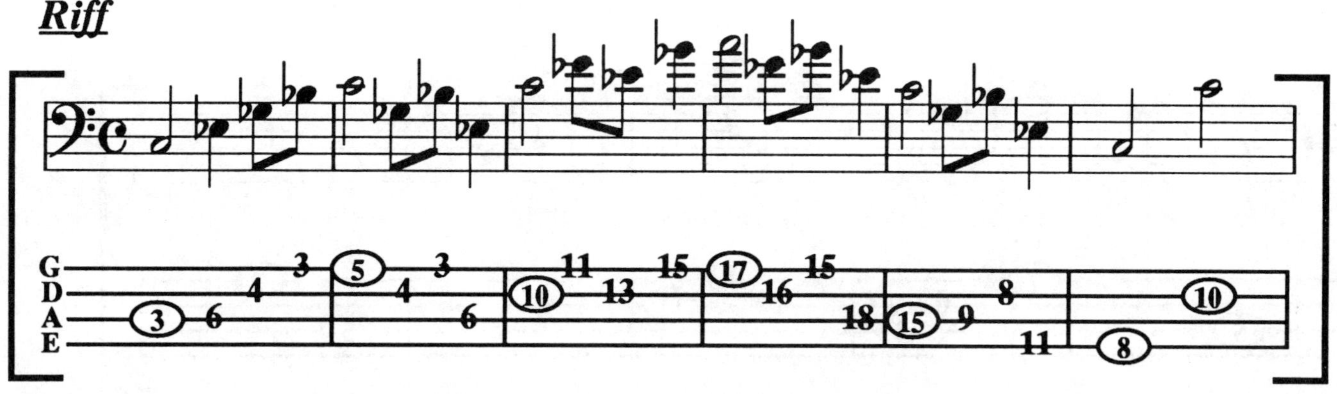

D HALF-DIMINISHED 7TH
FORMULA - (D) Root (F) ♭3rd (A♭) ♭5th (C) ♭7th

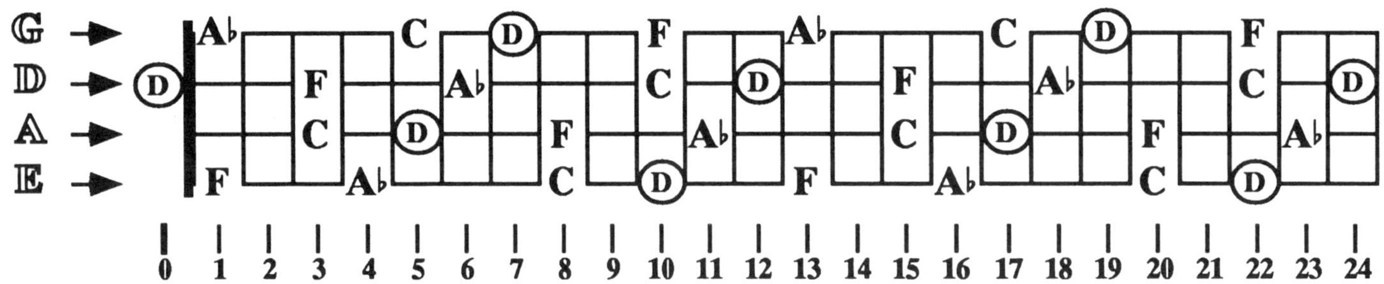

Positions

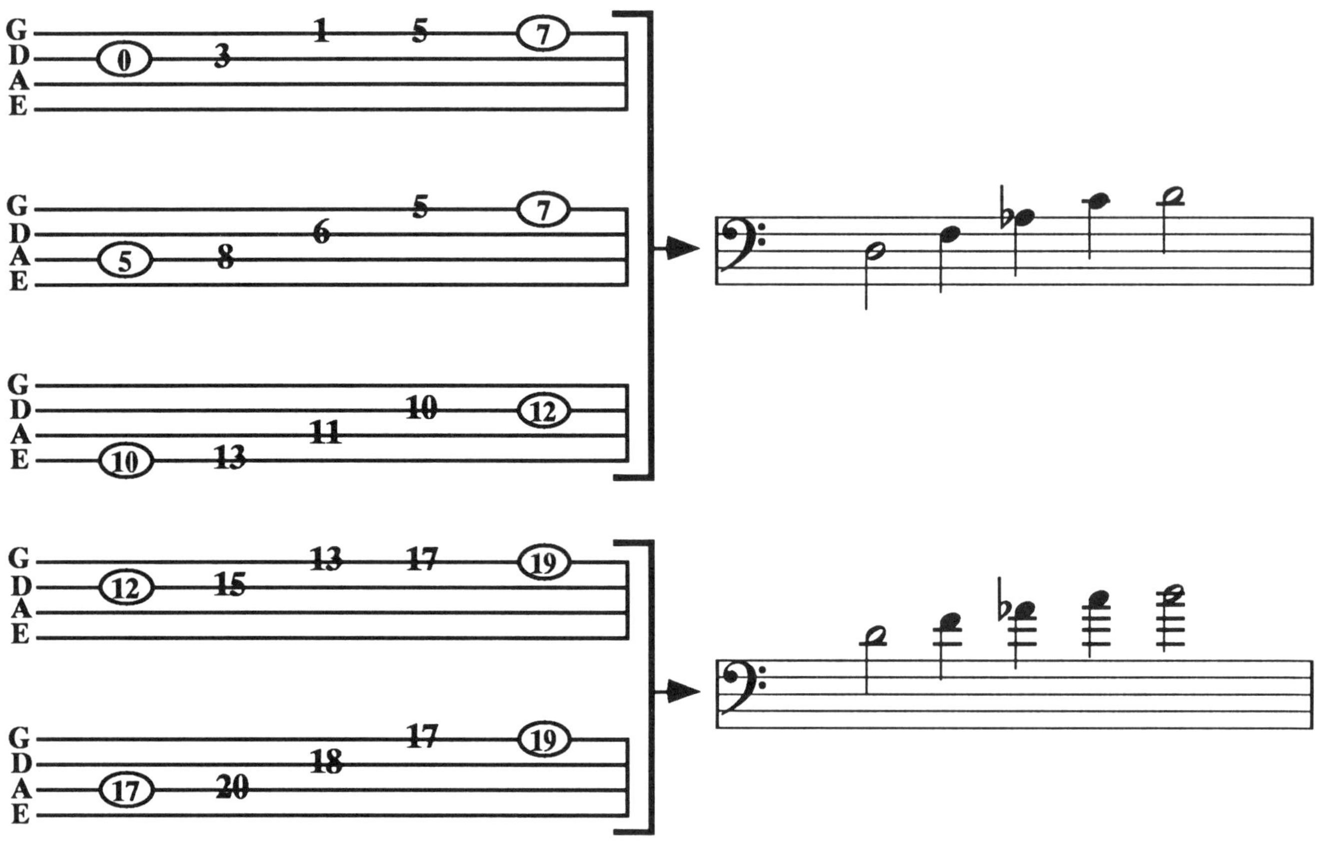

Riff

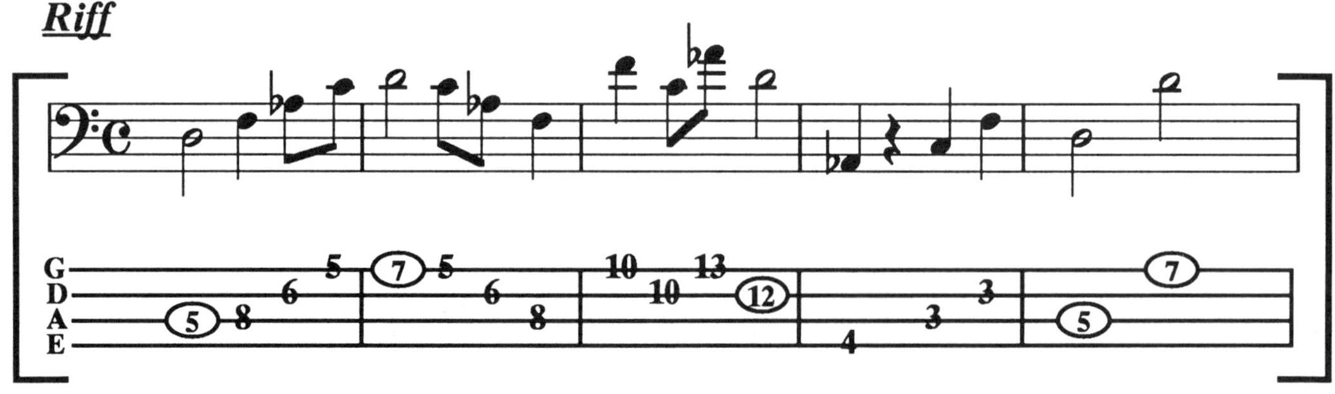

240

E   HALF-DIMINISHED 7TH

FORMULA - (E) Root (G) ♭3rd (B♭) ♭5th (D) ♭7th

Eø7

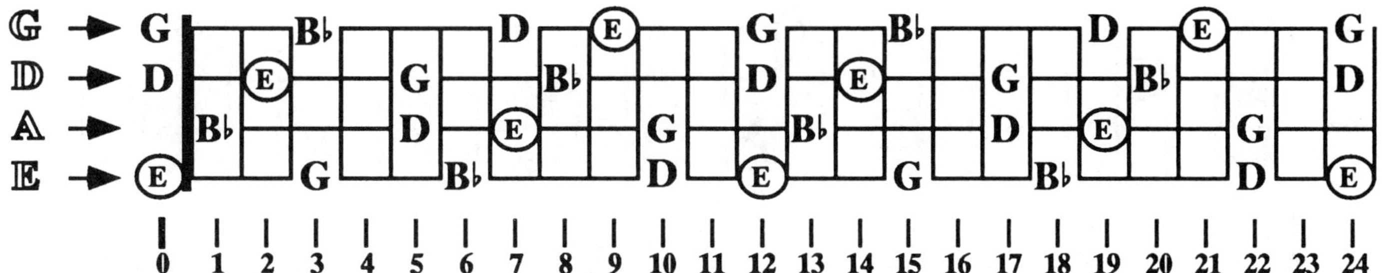

Positions

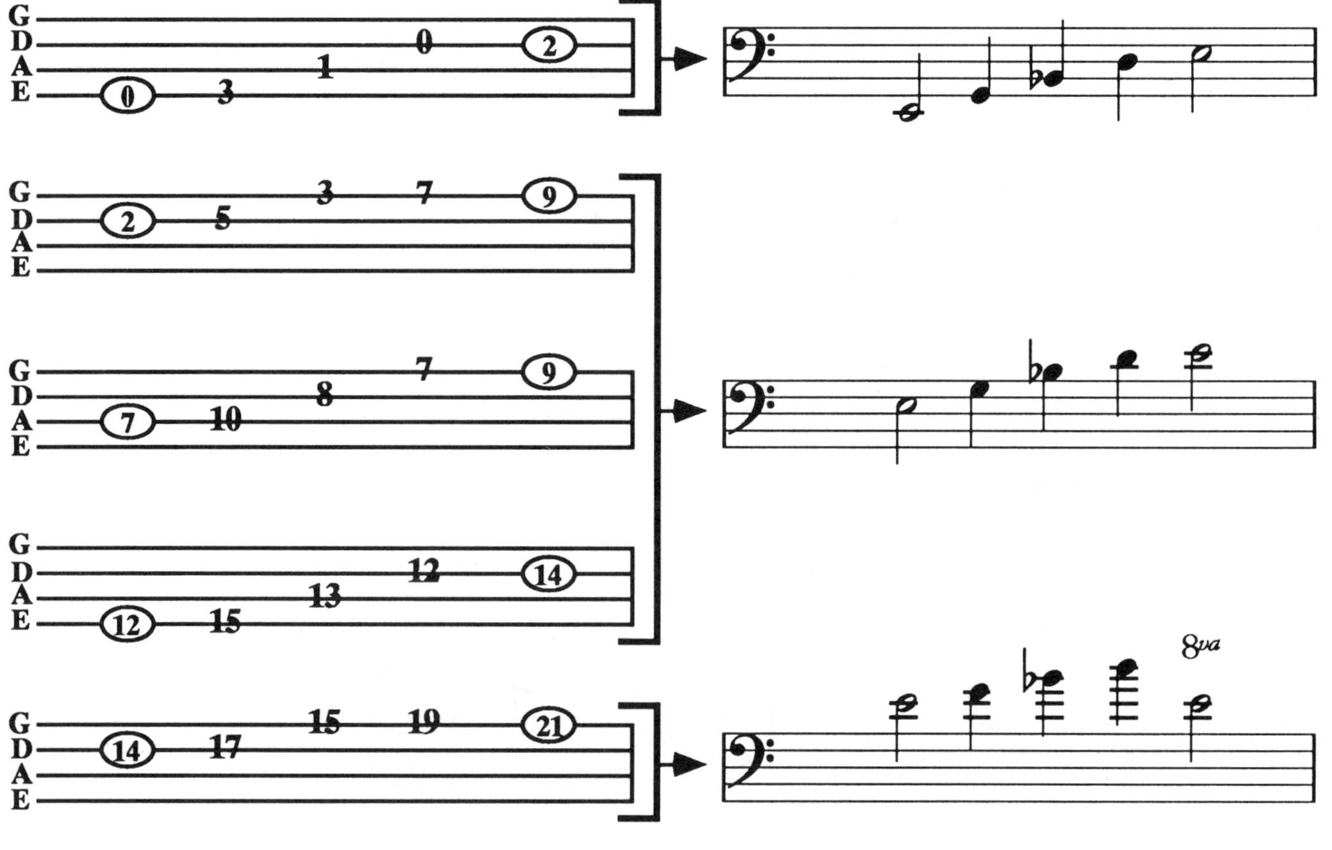

Riff

F   HALF-DIMINISHED 7TH

FORMULA - (F) Root (A♭) ♭3rd (C♭) ♭5th (E♭) ♭7th

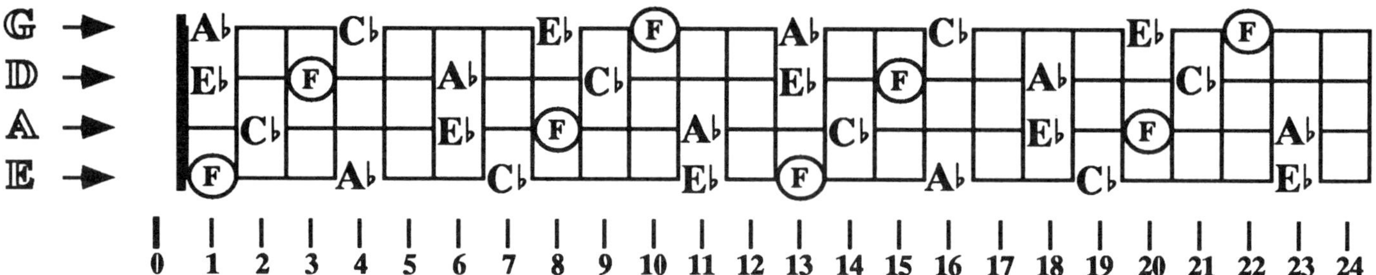

Positions

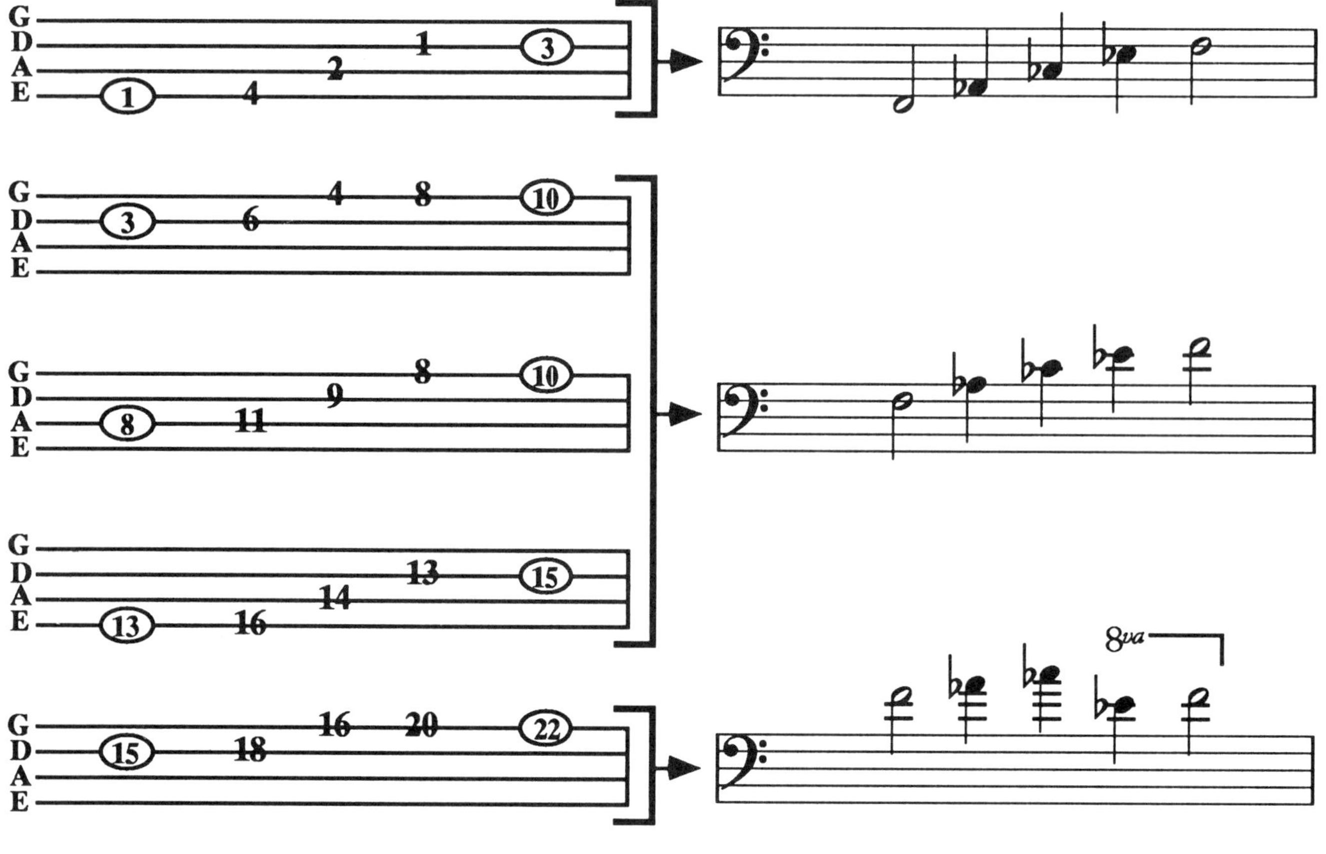

Riff

G   HALF-DIMINISHED 7TH

FORMULA - (G) Root (B♭) ♭3rd (D♭) ♭5th (F) ♭7th

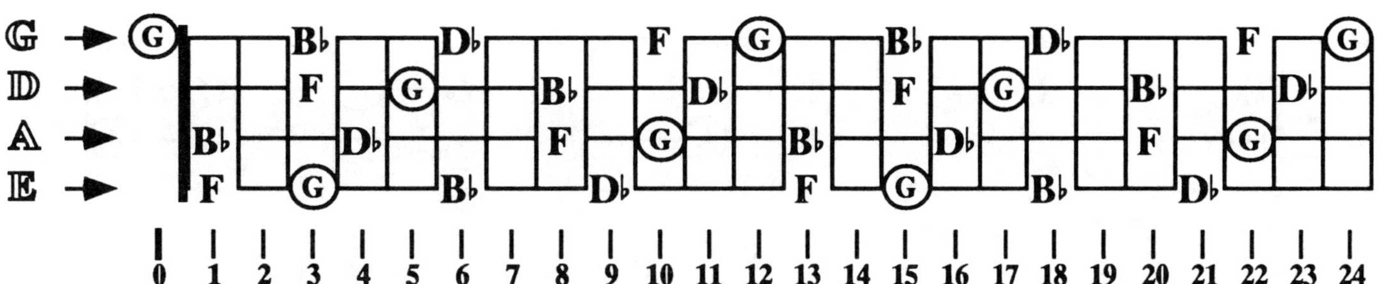

Positions

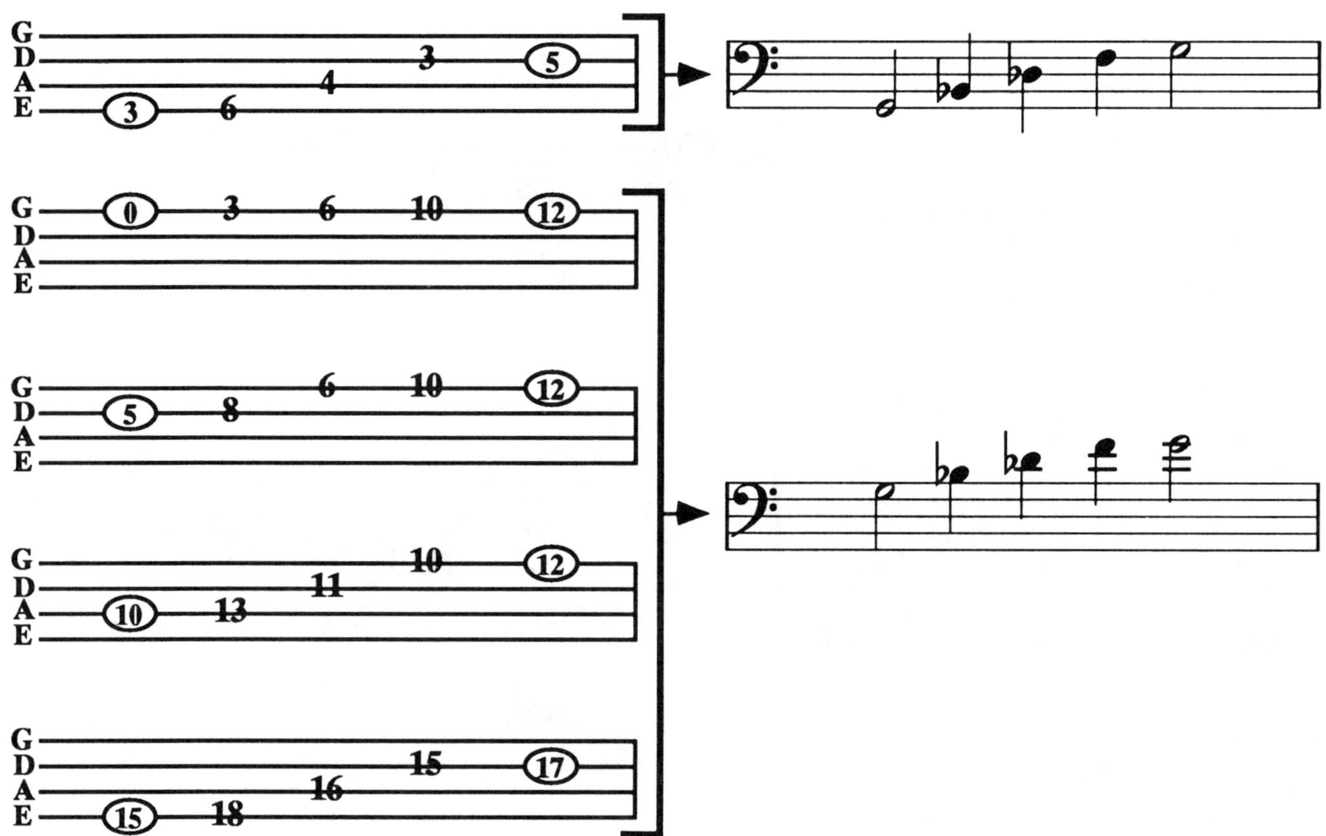

Riff

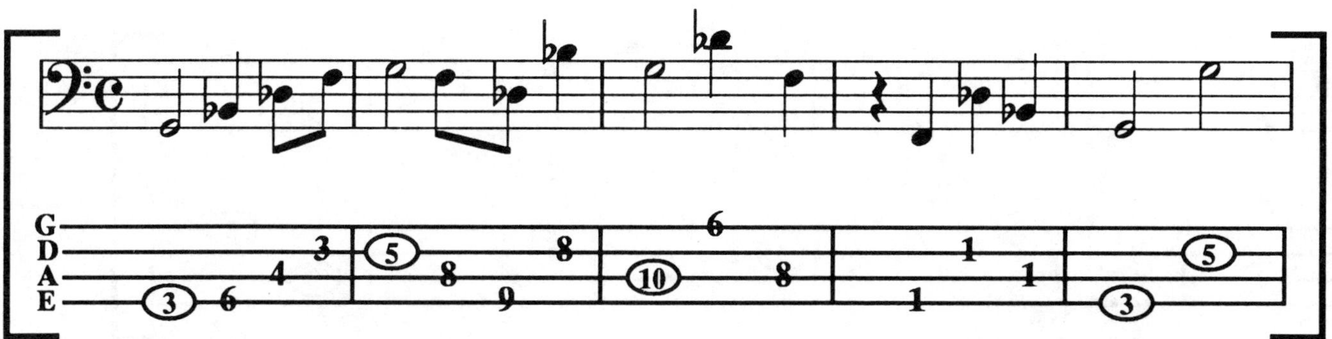

A HALF-DIMINISHED 7TH

FORMULA - (A) Root (C) ♭3rd (E♭) ♭5th (G) ♭7th

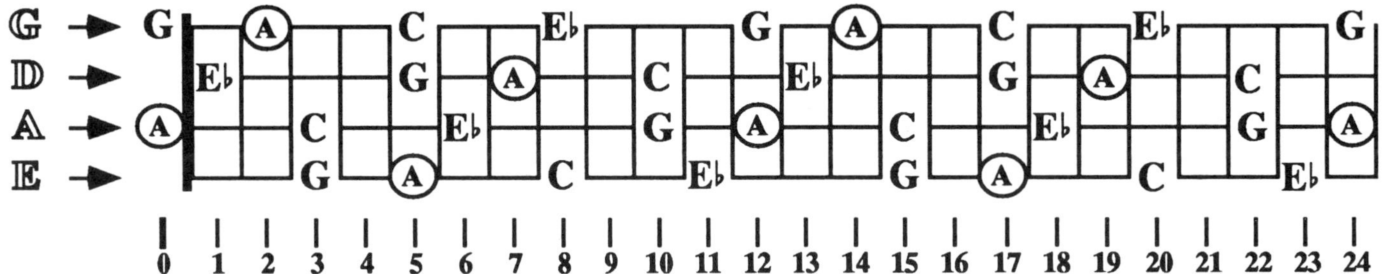

Positions

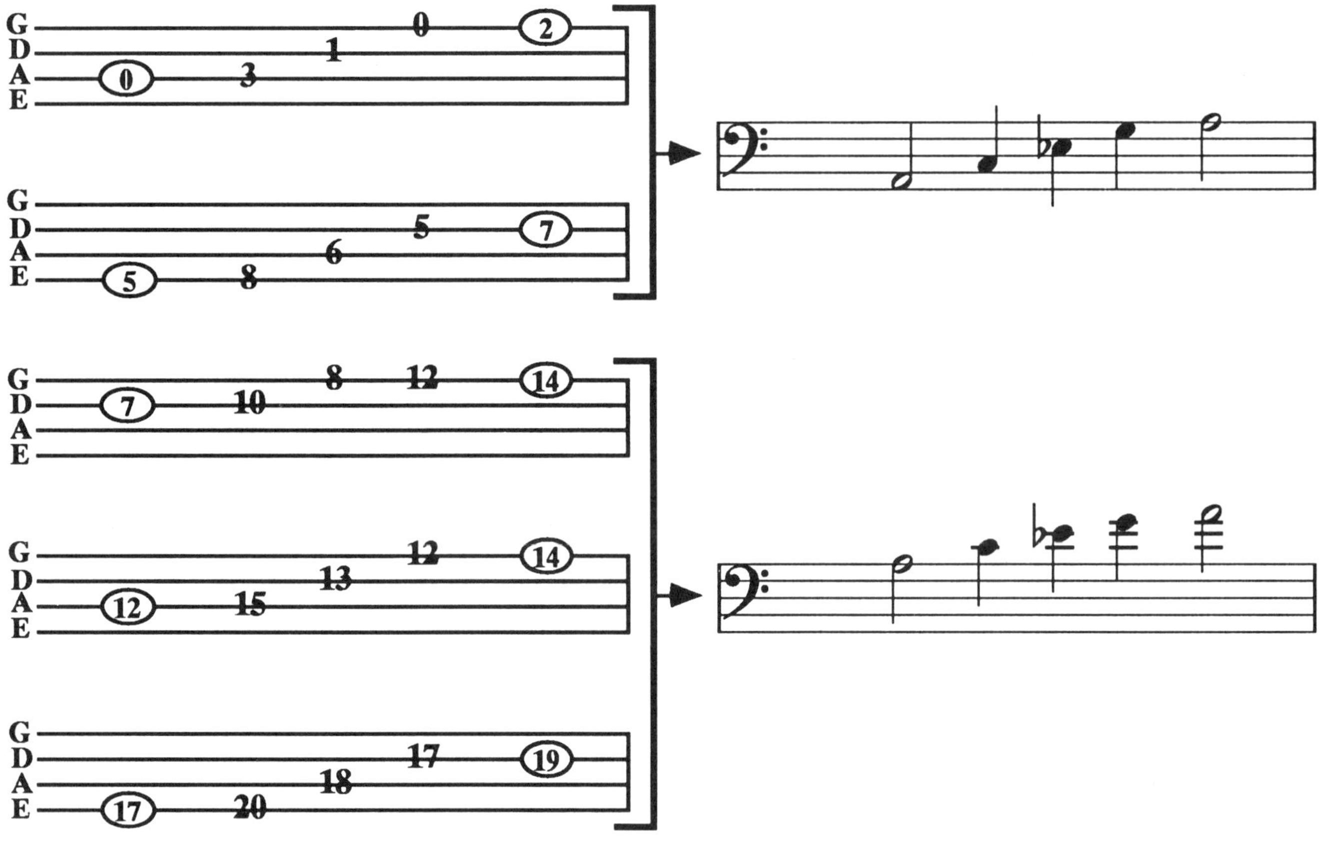

Riff

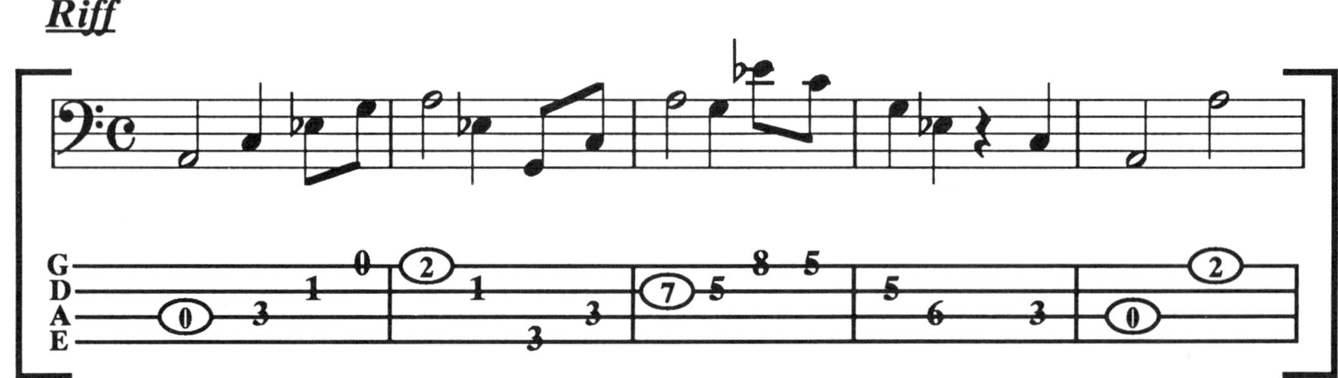

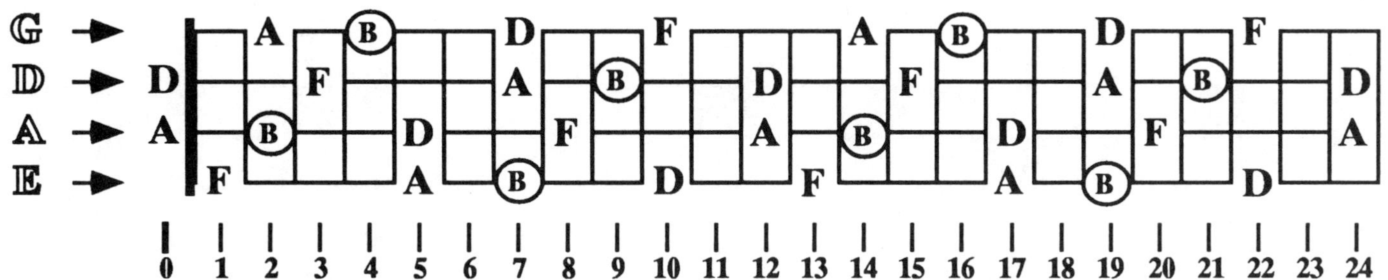

B   HALF-DIMINISHED 7TH
FORMULA - (B) Root (D) ♭3rd (F) ♭5th (A) ♭7th
B∅7

Positions

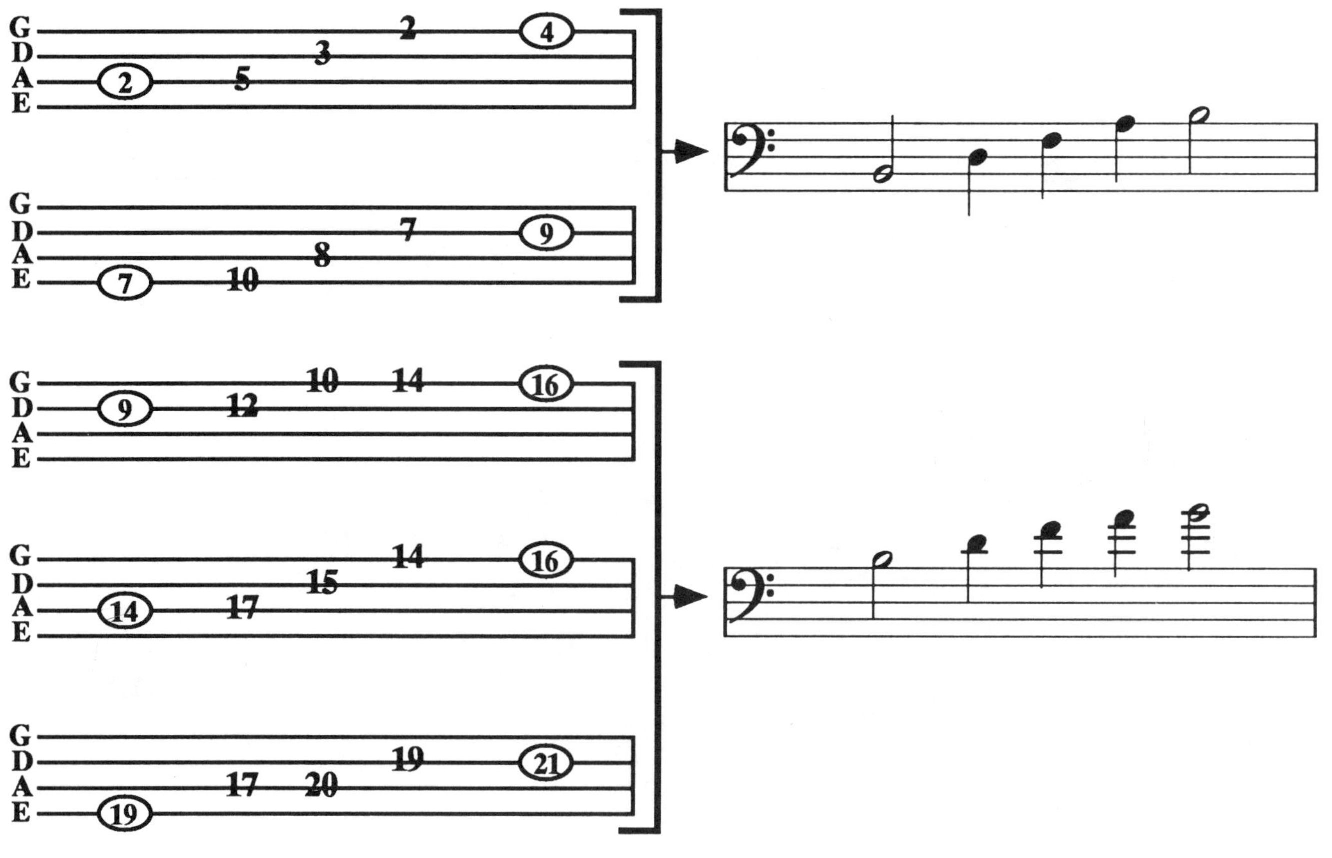

Riff

C AUGMENTED

FORMULA - (C) Root (E) 3rd (G♯) ♯5th

C+

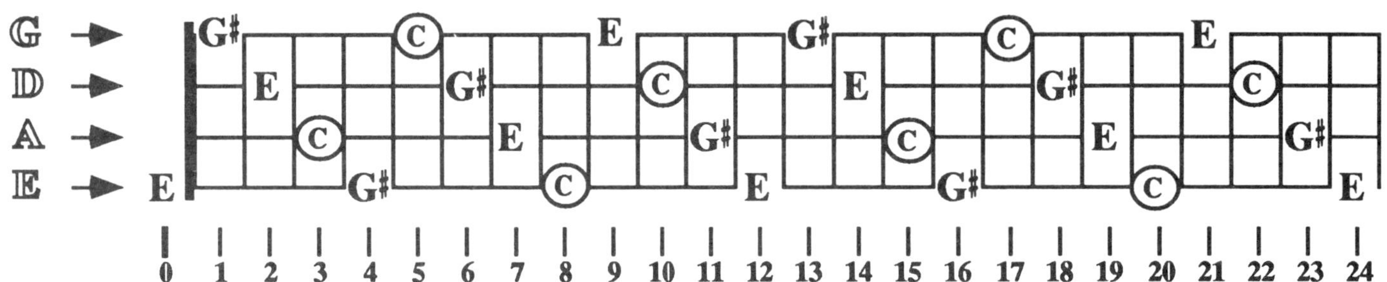

Positions

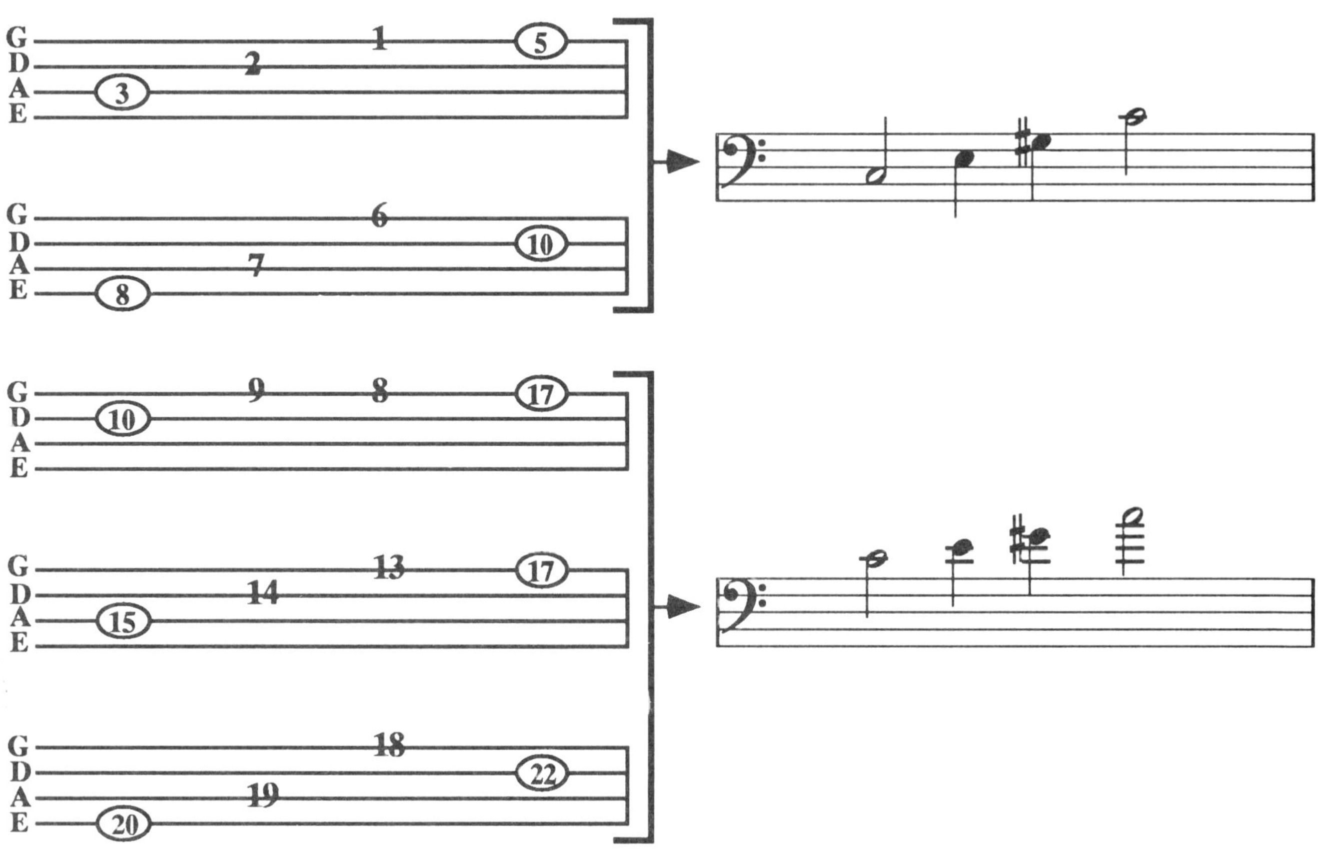

Riff

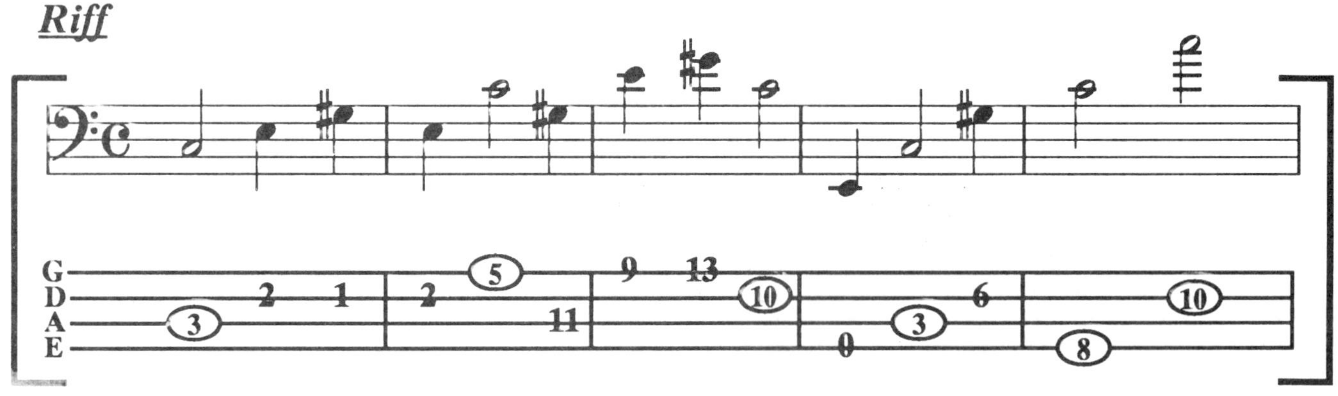

D AUGMENTED
FORMULA - (D) Root (F#) 3rd (A#) #5th

D+

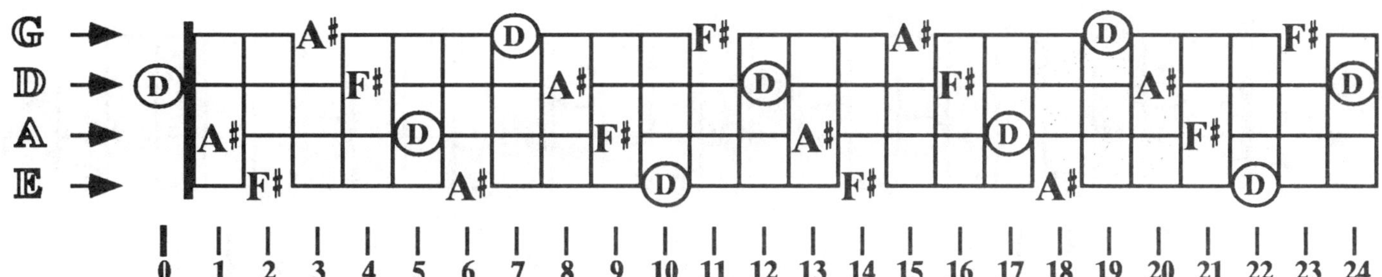

Positions

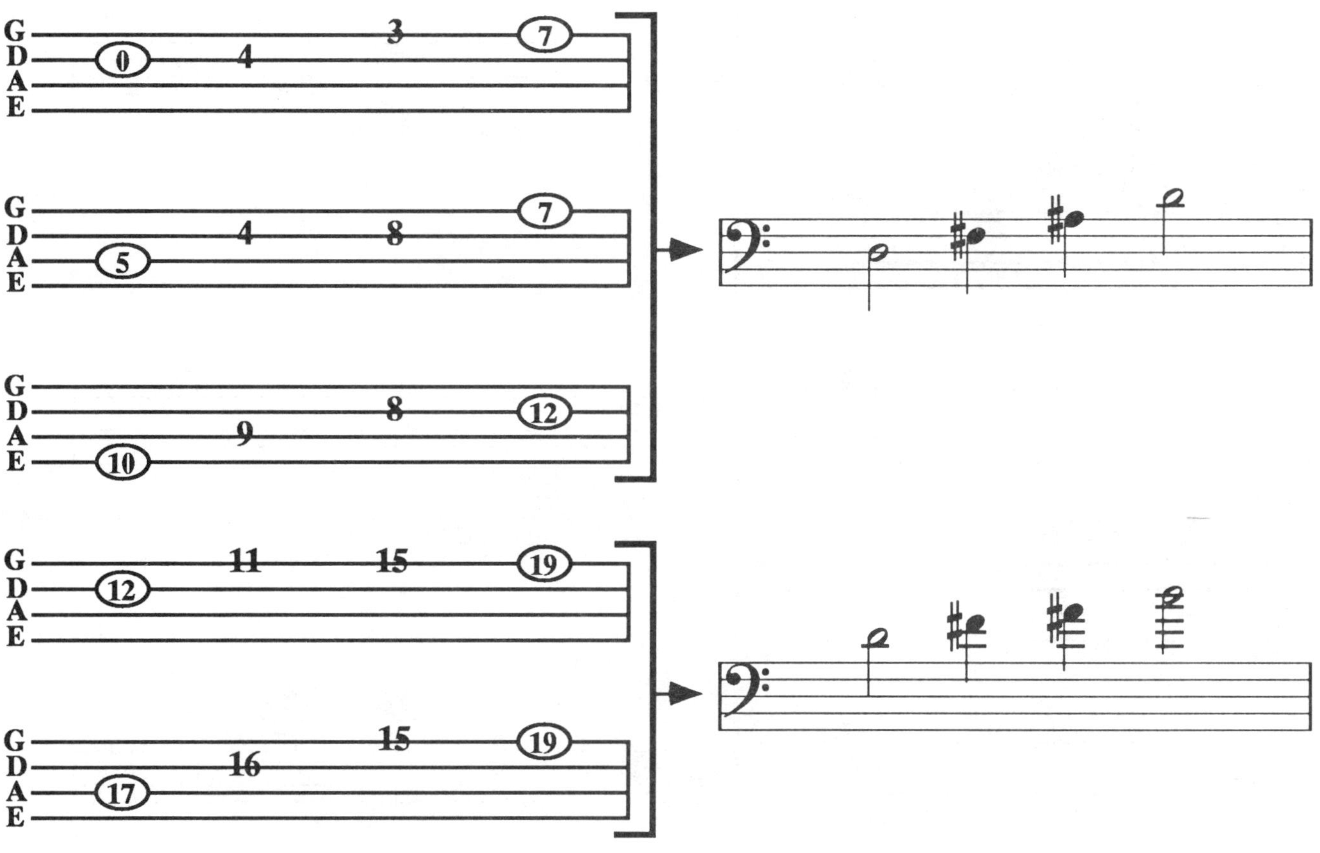

Riff

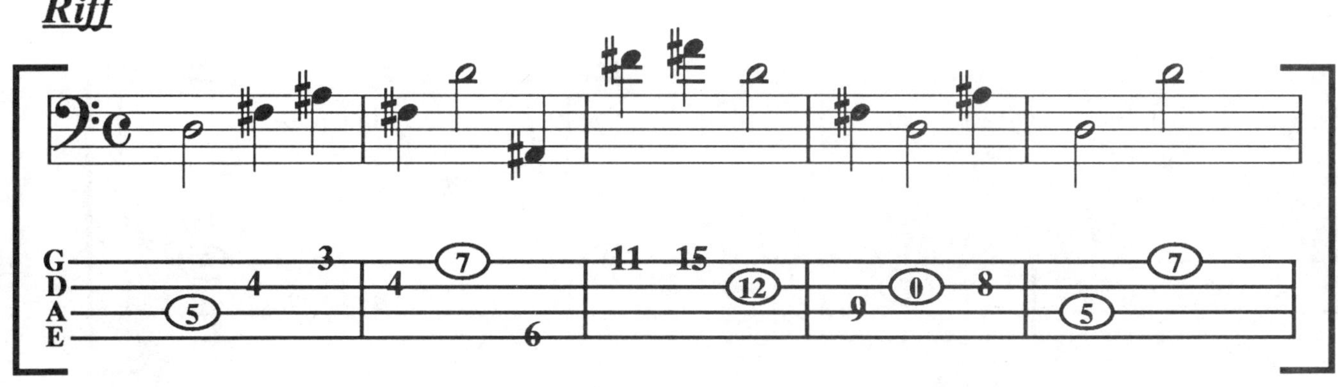

E AUGMENTED

FORMULA - (E) Root (G♯) 3rd (B♯) ♯5th

E+

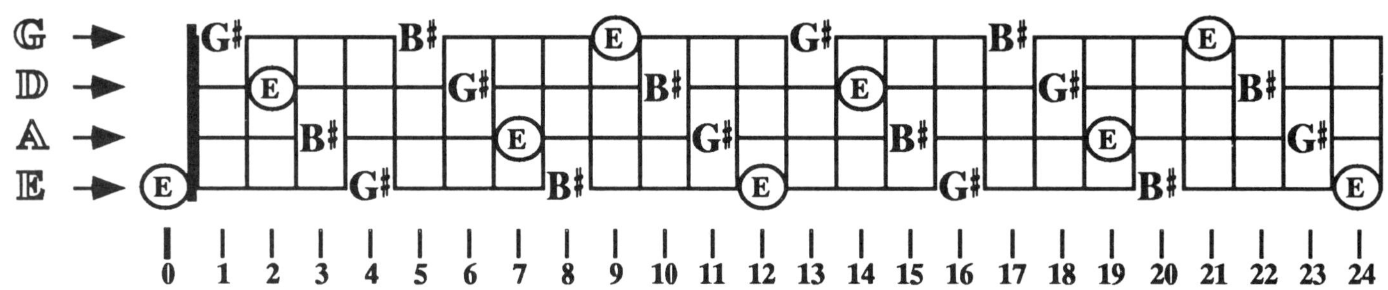

Positions

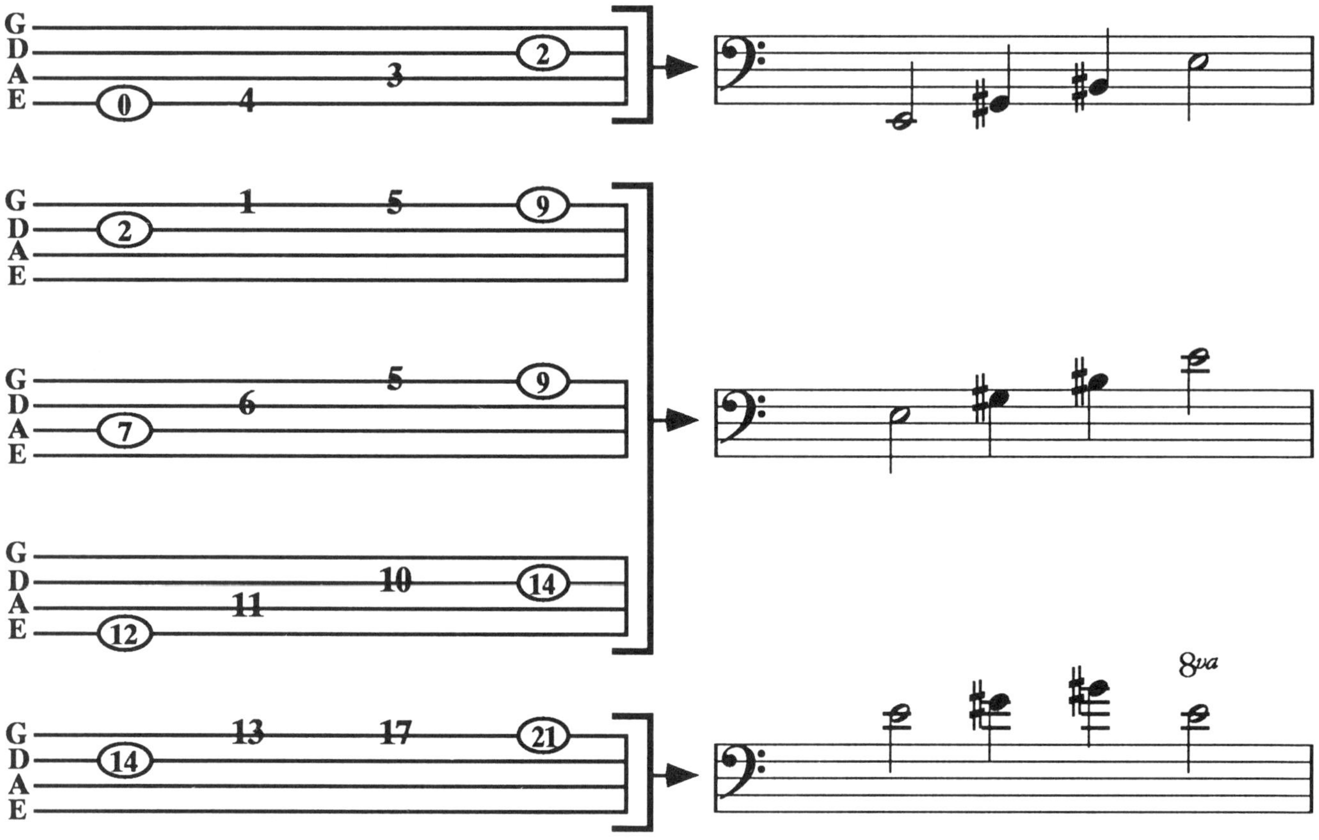

Riff

F AUGMENTED

FORMULA - (F) Root (A) 3rd (C♯) ♯5th

F +

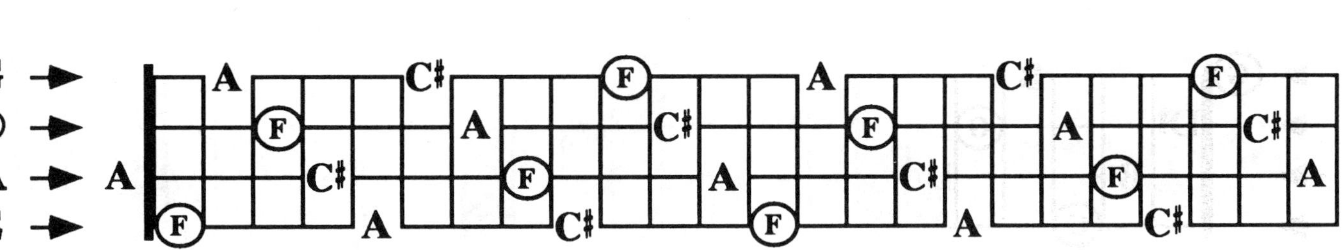

Positions

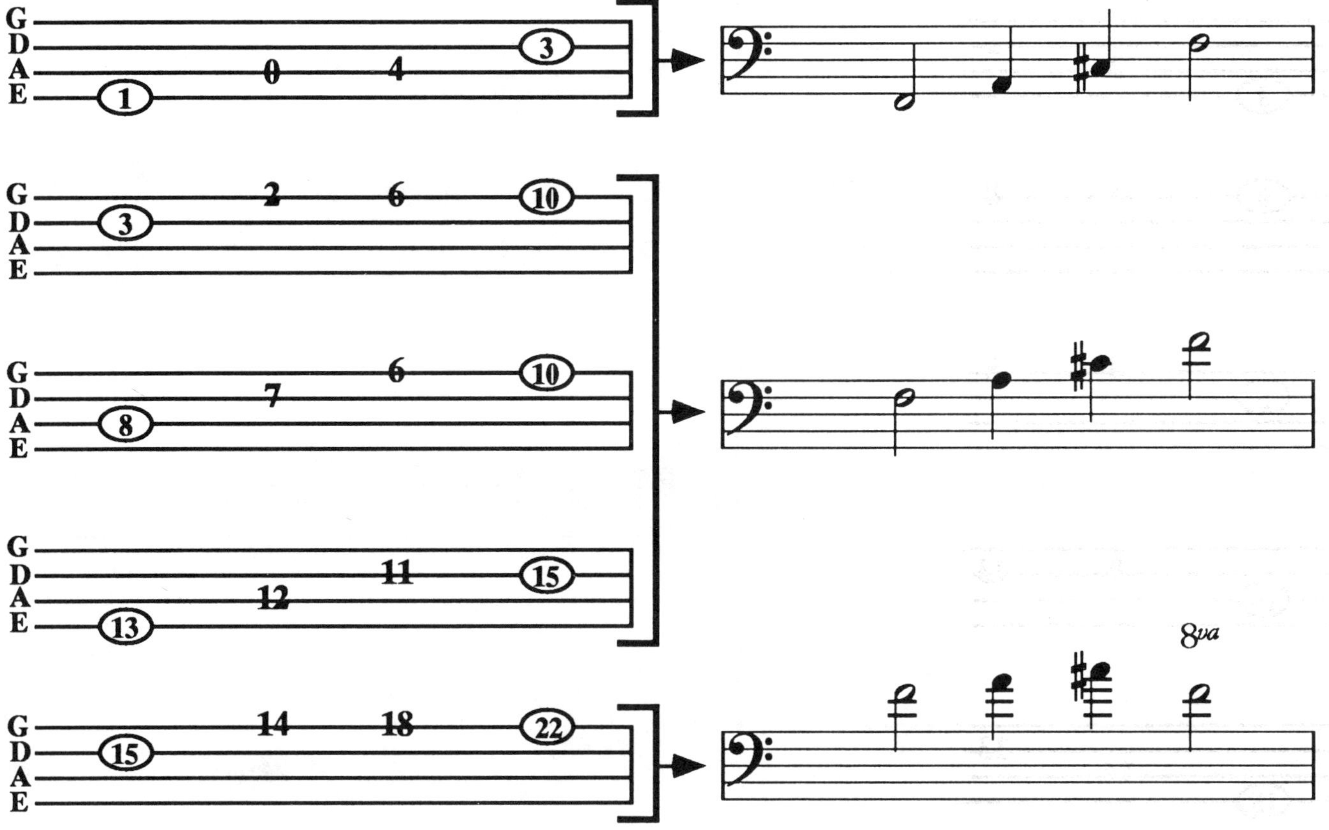

Riff

G AUGMENTED

FORMULA - (G) Root (B) 3rd (D#) #5th

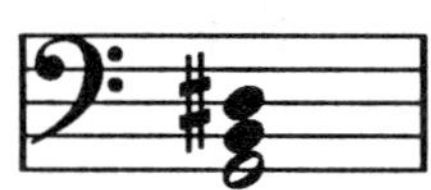

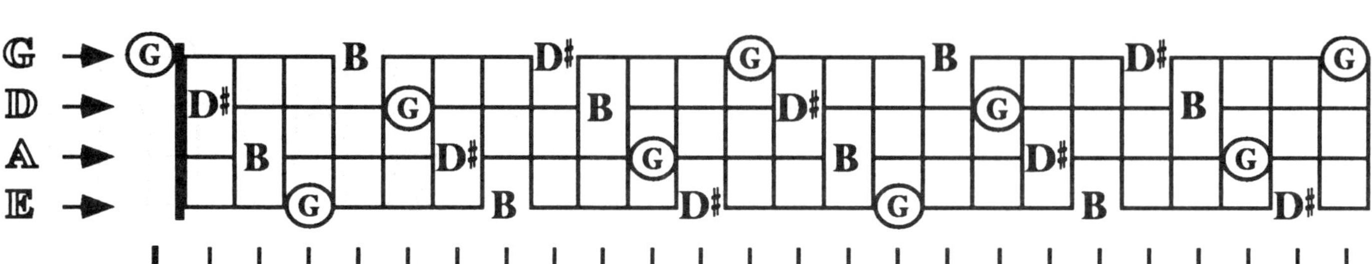

Positions

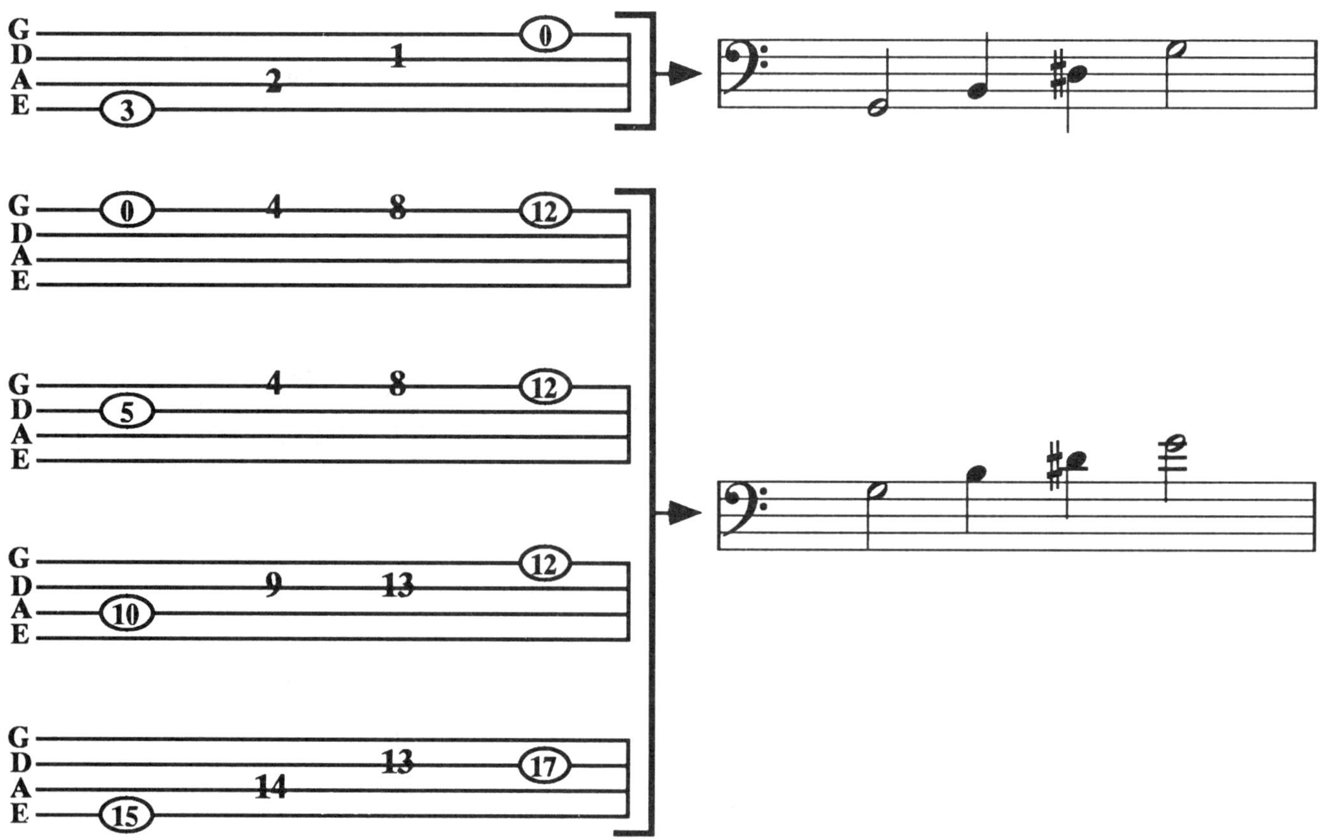

Riff

A AUGMENTED

FORMULA - (A) Root (C♯) 3rd (E♯) ♯5th

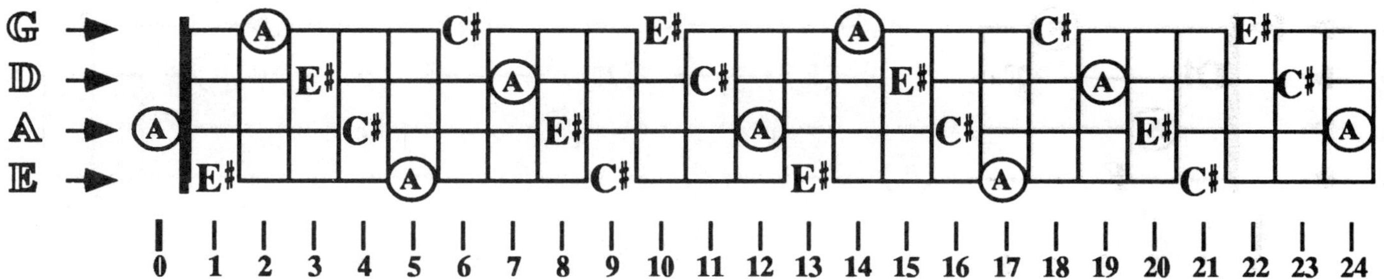

Positions

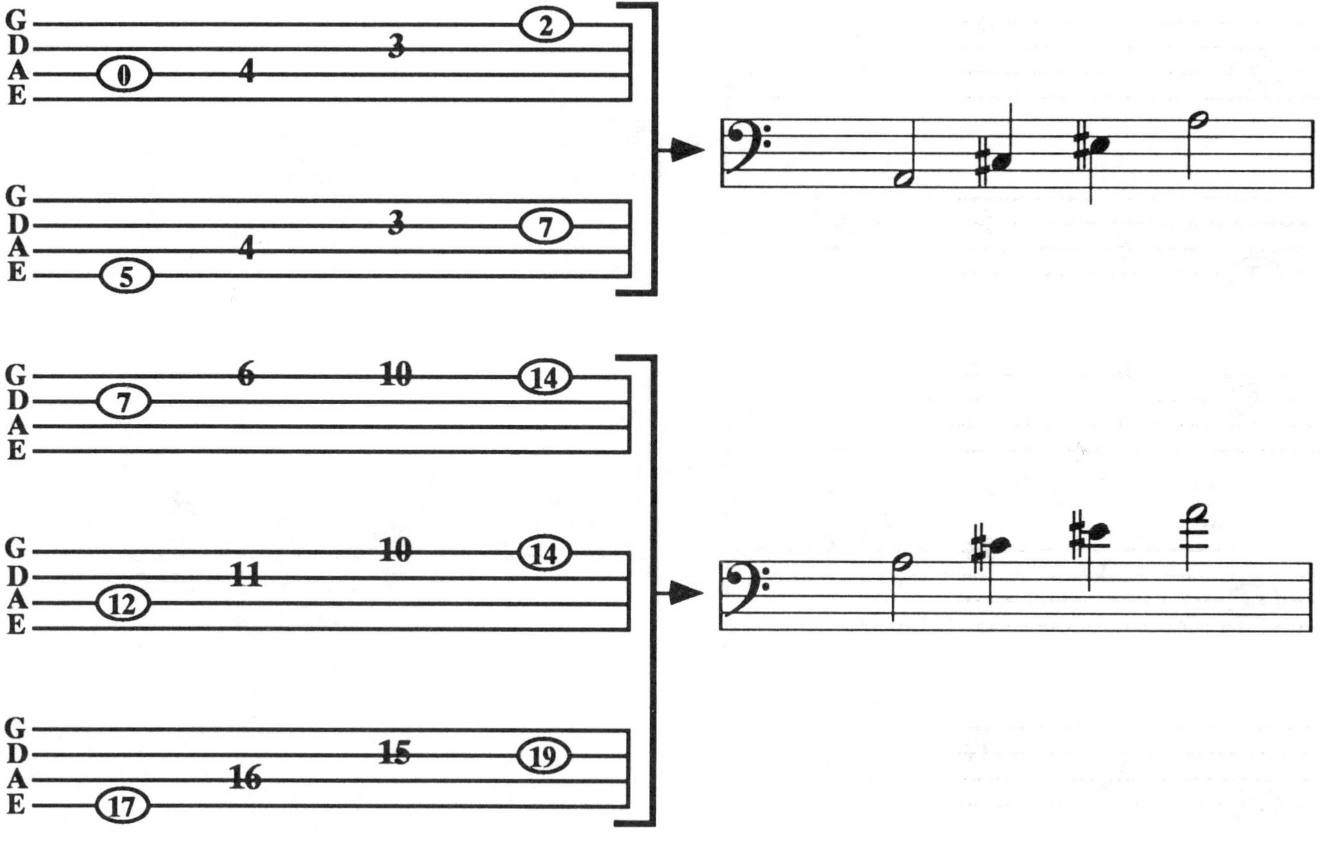

Riff

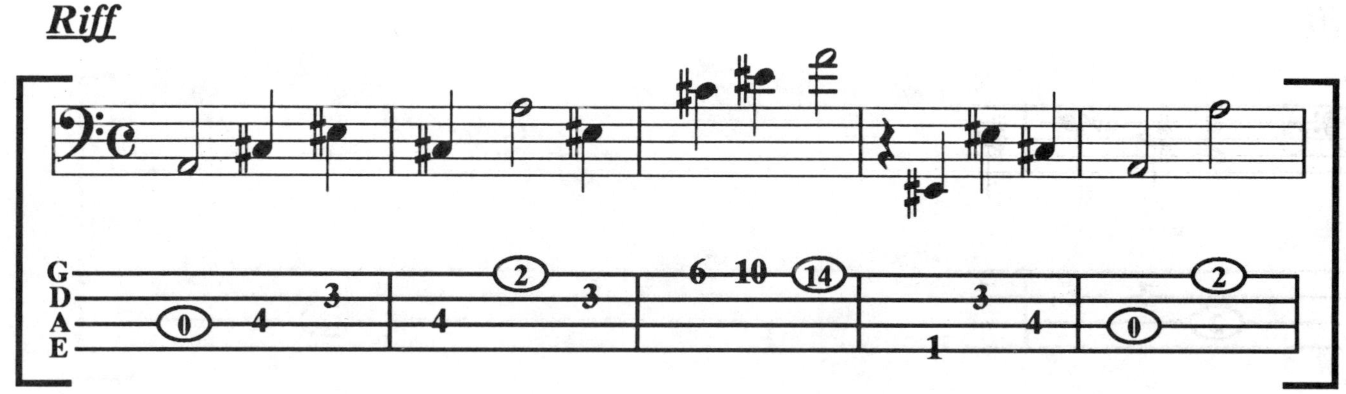

B AUGMENTED

FORMULA - (B) Root (D♯) 3rd (F×) ♯5th

B+

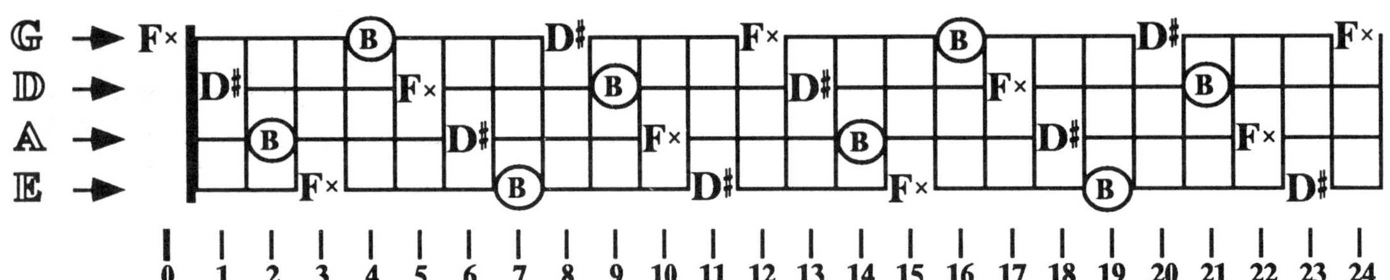

Positions

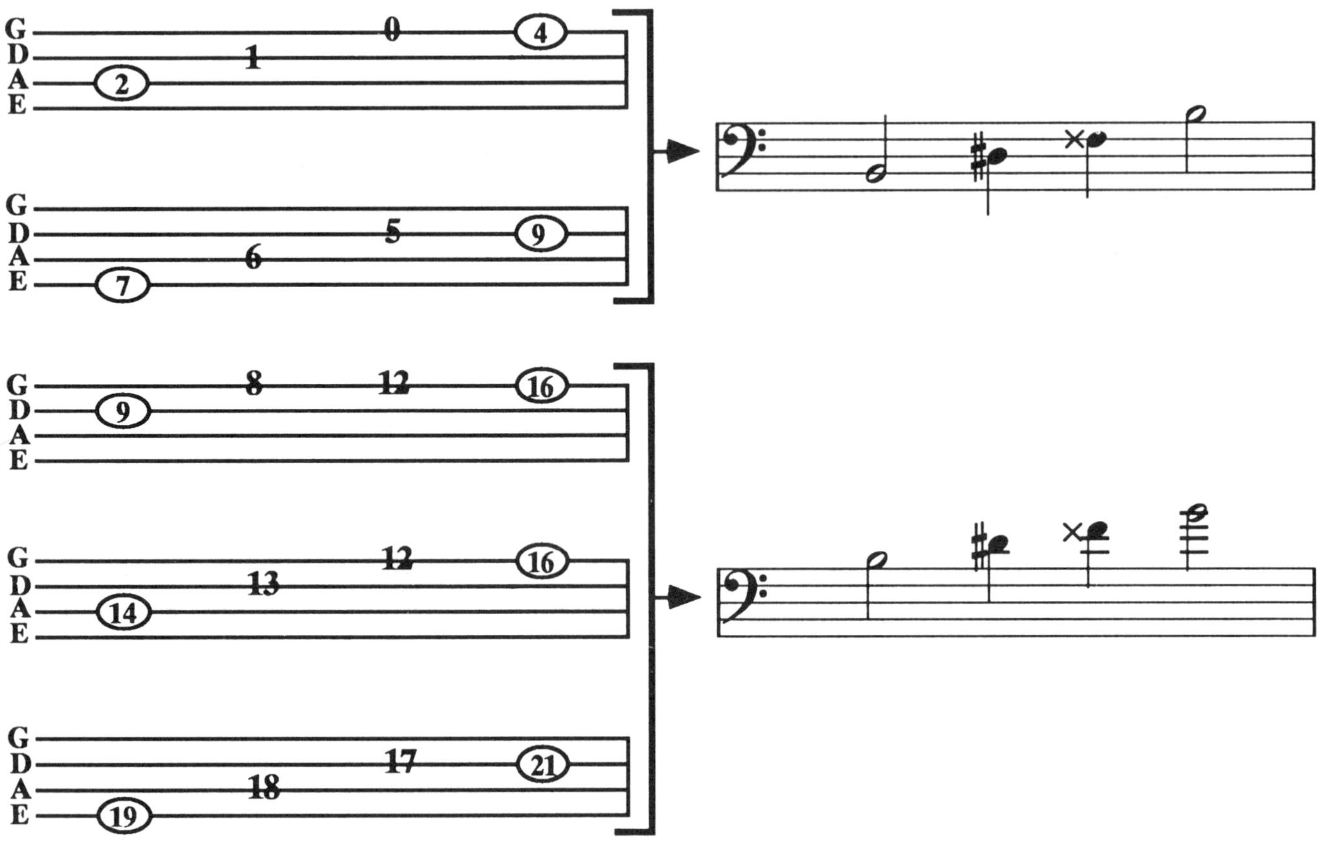

Riff

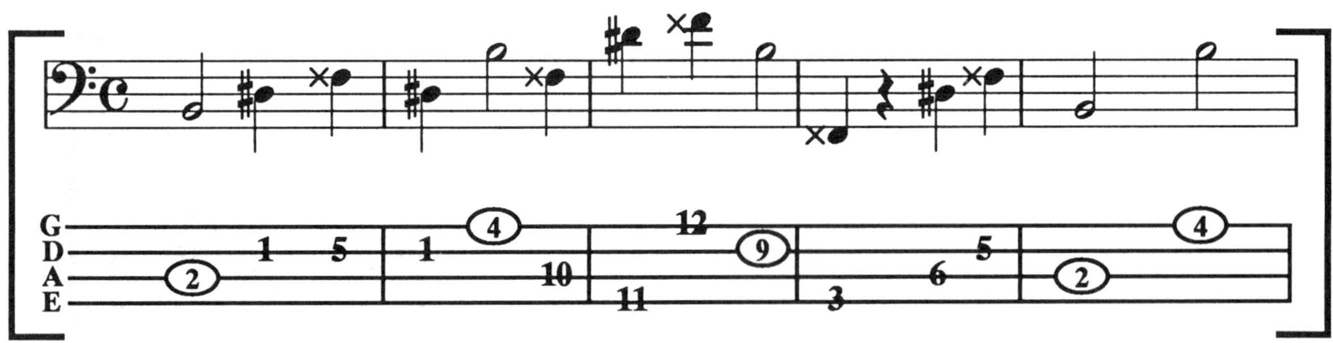

Examples Of Chords In Any Key

■ = Key Note

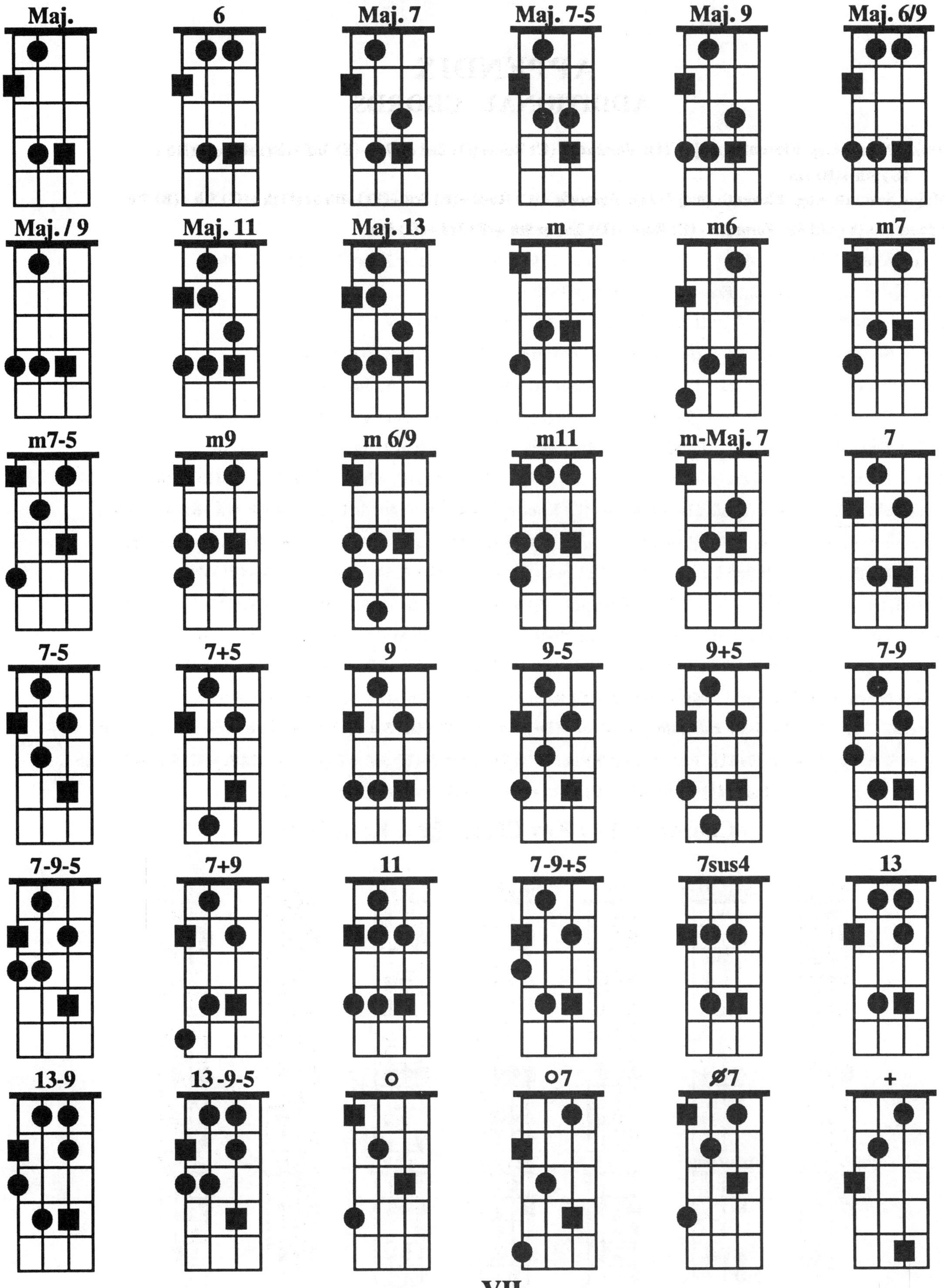

APPENDIX
ADDITIONAL CHORDS

Major Ninth Aug. Eleventh (maj 9+11): *Formula* - (C) Root+(D) 2nd or 9th+(E) 3rd +(F♯) ♯4th or ♯11th + (G) 5th +(B) 7th

Major Seventh Aug. Eleventh (maj 7+11): *Formula* - (C) Root +(E) 3rd +(F♯) ♯4th or ♯11th +(G) 5th +(B) 7th

Added Ninth (add 9): *Formula* - (C) Root +(D) 2nd or 9th +(E) 3rd +(G) 5th

Minor Added Ninth (m add 9) or (m/9): *Formula* - (C) Root +(D) 2nd or 9th +(E♭) ♭3rd +(G) 5th

Suspended Fourth (sus 4): *Formula* - (C) Root +(F) 4th +(G) 5th

Six Seven (6/7): *Formula* - (C) Root +(E) 3rd +(G) 5th +(A) 6th +(B♭) ♭7th

Minor Six Seven (m 6/7): *Formula* - (C) Root +(E♭) ♭3rd +(G) 5th +(A) 6th +(B♭) ♭7th

Six Seven Suspended (6/7 sus): *Formula* - (C) Root +(F) 4th +(G) 5th +(A) 6th +(B♭) ♭7th

Seven Eleven (7/11): *Formula* - (C) Root +(E) 3rd +(F) 4th or 11th +(G) 5th +(B♭) ♭7th

Minor Seven Eleven (m 7/11): *Formula* - (C) Root +(E♭) ♭3rd +(F) 4th or 11th +(G) 5th +(B♭) ♭7th

Minor Eleven (m11): *Formula* - (C) Root +(D) 2nd or 9th +(E♭) ♭3rd +(F) 4th or 11th +(G) 5th +(B♭) ♭7th

Minor Six Seven Eleven (m 6/7/11): *Formula* - (C) Root +(E♭) ♭3rd +(F) 4th or 11th +(G) 5th +(A) 6th +(B♭) ♭7th

Seventh Aug. Ninth Dim. Fifth (7+9-5): *Formula* - (C) Root +(D♯) ♯2nd or ♯9th +(E) 3rd +(G♭) ♭5th +(B♭) ♭7th

Minor Ninth Dim. Fifth (m9-5): *Formula* - (C) Root +(D) 2nd or 9th +(E♭) ♭3rd +(G♭) ♭5th +(B♭) ♭7th

Seventh Aug. Ninth Aug. Fifth (7+9+5): *Formula* - (C) Root +(D♯) ♯2nd or ♯9th +(E) 3rd +(G♯) ♯5th +(B♭) ♭7th

Minor / Major Ninth (min/maj 9): *Formula* - (C) Root +(D) 2nd or 9th +(E♭) ♭3rd +(G) 5th +(B) 7th

Minor Seventh Flat Nine (m7-9): *Formula* - (C) Root +(D♭) ♭2nd or ♭9th +(E♭) ♭3rd +(G) 5th +(B♭) ♭7th

Major Ninth Aug. Fifth (maj 9+5): *Formula* - (C) Root +(D) 2nd or 9th +(E) 3rd + (G♯) ♯5th +(B) 7th

Eleventh Dim. Ninth (11-9): *Formula* - (C) Root +(D♭) ♭2nd or ♭9th +(E) 3rd +(F) 4th or 11th +(G) 5th +(B♭) ♭7th

Seventh Aug. Eleventh (7+11): *Formula* - (C) Root +(D) 2nd or 9th +(E) 3rd +(F♯) ♯4th or ♯11th +(G) 5th +(B♭) ♭7th

Added Aug. Eleventh (add+11): *Formula* - (C) Root +(E) 3rd +(F♯) ♯4th or ♯11th +(G) 5th

Chords In Any Key Chart ■ = Root Note

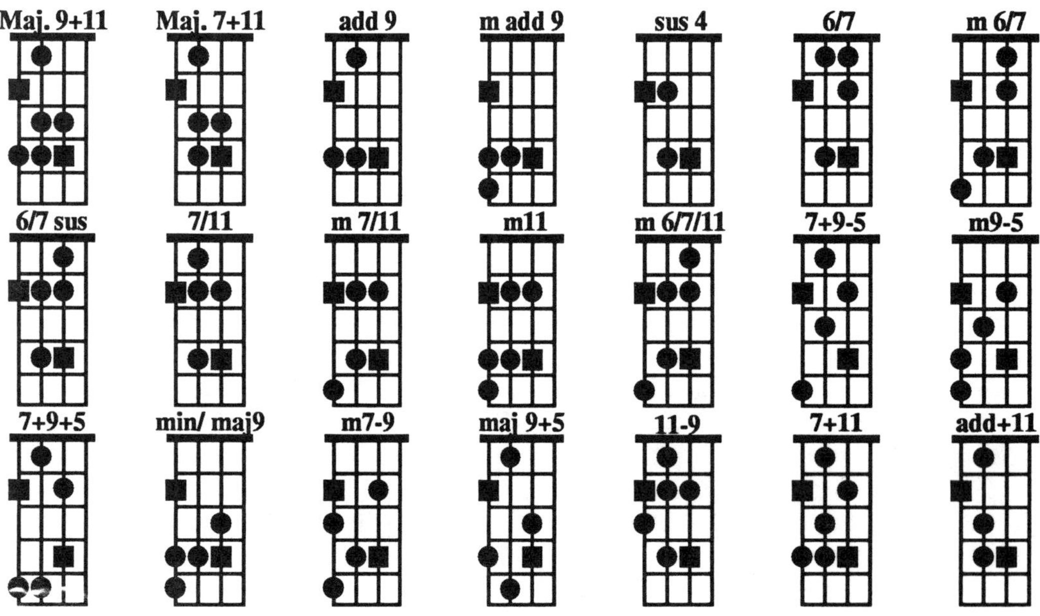